THE ANNOTATED

ANNE OF

GREEN GABLES

THE ANNOTATED ANNE OF GREEN GABLES

BY L.M. MONTGOMERY

Edited by

WENDY E. BARRY

MARGARET ANNE DOODY

MARY E. DOODY JONES

New York Oxford
Oxford University Press
1997

Oxford University Press

Oxford   New York
Athens Aukland Bangkok Bogotá Bombay
Buenos Aires Calcutta Cape Town Dar es Salaam
Delhi Florence Hong Kong Istanbul Karachi
Kuala Lumpur Madras Madrid Melbourne
Mexico City Nairobi Paris Singapore
Taipei Tokyo Toronto Warsaw

and associated companies in
Berlin   Ibadan

Published by Oxford University Press
198 Madison Avenue, New York, New York 10016

Library of Congress Cataloging-in-Publication Data

Montgomery, L. M. (Lucy Maud), 1874–1942.
The annotated Anne of Green Gables / L. M. Montgomery;
edited by Wendy E. Barry, Margaret Anne Doody, and Mary E. Doody Jones.
p. cm.
Summary: This edition of the classic novel about the Prince
Edward Island orphan contains critical material on the work
itself and its author, as well as essays, poems, and songs.
ISBN 0-19-510428-5
[1. Orphans—Fiction. 2. Friendship—Fiction.
3. Country life—Prince Edward Island—Fiction.
4. Prince Edward Island—Fiction
5. Montgomery, L. M. (Lucy Maud), 1874-1942. Anne of Green Gables.]
I. Barry, Wendy E.   II. Doody, Margaret Anne.   III. Jones, Mary E. Doody
IV. Montgomery, L. M. (Lucy Maud), 1874-1942. Anne of Green Gables.
V. Title
PZ7.M768At   1997   [Fic]—dc21   96-45018

3 5 7 9 8 6 4
Printed in the United States of America
on acid-free paper

CONTENTS

═══════ ❧ ═══════

PREFACE

We take great pleasure in presenting the *Annotated Anne of Green Gables.* L. M. Montgomery's ninety-year-old novel has continued to have wide and enduring appeal ever since its first publication. Moreover, scholarly interest in *Anne* has grown considerably in the last two decades. This book offers a new text based upon the manuscript. It also supplies complete explanatory notes. It provides informative short essays on subjects like "Education," "Elocution," "Orphans," "Handicrafts," and "Gardens," and of course the geography of Anne. We also present early reviews and copies of the hard-to-find recitation pieces mentioned in the novel. This edition also offers lyrics and music Anne and her friends sang, knit lace patterns, and illustrations of people, places, and objects that were part of Anne's world. Many aspects of the culture in which the heroine (and the author) grew and developed are recorded here. Our edition will give modern day readers a better understanding of references to material and popular culture.

We hope that the reader will get a good idea of the world that Anne lived in, as well as a greater understanding of the book's nature and meaning. Though *Anne* was once classified only as a children's book, it can now come into its own as a book for all ages, and all kinds of readers. Above all, we want the reader to enjoy the encounter with Anne herself, and to feel the realities of Montgomery's imagined Avonlea.

THE ANNOTATED
ANNE OF
GREEN GABLES

CHRONOLOGY OF THE LIFE OF LUCY MAUD MONTGOMERY

1874 **November 30:** Lucy Maud Montgomery ("Maud") born at Clifton, Prince Edward Island, to parents Clara (née Macneill) and Hugh John Montgomery.

1876 **September 14:** Maud's mother dies at the age of twenty-three. Maud goes to live with grandparents Alexander and Lucy Woolner Macneill.

1881 Maud starts school in a one-room schoolhouse in Cavendish. Her father visits the West.

1882 Hugh Montgomery begins to work for a Saskatchewan company, spending part of his time as that company's agent in P.E.I. Maud remains with her grandparents. Strong associations are built with Montgomery relations and Campbell cousins at Park Corner, Clifton. **Summer:** Maud acquires playmates in Wellington and David Nelson, boarding with the Macneills while attending school.

1883 The *Marco Polo,* a fast packet ship, is wrecked off Cavendish. The captain and crew board with the Macneills while awaiting insurance payments.

1884 Hugh John Montgomery settles permanently in Prince Albert, Saskatchewan.

1887 **April:** Montgomery marries his second wife, Mary Ann McRae, age twenty-four, in Ontario. The new couple live first in Battleford, Saskatchewan.

1888 Kate Montgomery, Maud's half-sister, is born (date uncertain). **Late summer:** Hattie Gordon comes to teach at the Cavendish school, remaining as schoolmistress until 1892.

1890 Maud's father sends for her from Prince Albert. She travels across the continent with her paternal grandfather, Senator Donald Montgomery.

August 16: She arrives in Prince Albert. **November 26:** Maud's first publication, a poem, "On Cape Le Force," based on a local P.E.I. story, is published in the Charlottetown *Daily Patriot.* **Winter 1890–91:** Maud attends high school in Prince Albert; her teacher, John Mustard, flirts with her.

1891 **January 31:** Maud's half-brother David Bruce is born. Maud is expected to look after him and is kept from school by domestic chores for nearly two months. **February:** Maud publishes an article, "The Wreck of the Marco Polo," in the Montreal *Witness.* **June:** She publishes an article on Saskatchewan, "A Western Eden," in the Prince Albert *Times,* and a poem, "June," in the Charlottetown *Daily Patriot.* Hugh John Montgomery runs for a seat in the national Parliament as a Liberal but is defeated. **August 25:** Maud leaves Prince Albert to return to P.E.I. **September 2:** Her poem, "Farewell," is published in *The Saskatchewan.*

1891–92 **Winter–spring:** Maud spends the winter in Park Corner, giving music lessons to cousins. A friendship develops with her cousin "Frede" (Frederica Campbell).

1892 **August:** Maud publishes a poem, "The Wreck of the Marcopolo," in the Charlottetown *Daily Patriot.* She enrolls in the Cavendish School to study for her entrance examinations for Prince of Wales College.

1893 **July:** Maud takes her entrance examinations in Charlottetown, ranking fifth in a list of 264 candidates. **September:** Her poem "A Violet's Spell" is accepted by *The Ladies' World* of New York, "paid" by two subscriptions to the magazine. Another half-brother, Hugh Carlyle (Carl), is born in this year.

Maud's poem "The Violet's Spell," from her journal, March 1901 (SJ I [March 21, 1901]: 261).

1893–94 Maud enters the second-year program at Prince of Wales College, taking two years of work in one year and studying for her teacher's license.

1894 Maud completes her examinations, with an honor certificate, and leads her year in English drama, English literature, agriculture, and school management. *June 9:* She delivers a graduate essay, "Portia— A Study," at the commencement exercises in the Charlottetown Opera House. She receives a second-class certificate as a teacher and takes a post at a one-room school in Bideford, P.E.I.

1895 *July 23:* Maud receives a first-class license for teaching. *September:* She enters Dalhousie College in Halifax, Nova Scotia, for a self-designed course in English literature under Dr. Archibald MacMechan. She boards at Halifax Ladies' College.

1896 *February:* Montgomery receives her first payment for fiction, $5 for the story "Our Charivari," by "Maud Cavendish," in *Golden Days.* **March:** She is paid $12 for the poem "Fisher Lassies," published in *Youth's Companion.* **April:** Her article on women's education, "A Girl's Place at Dalhousie College," is published in the Halifax *Herald.*

1896–97 Montgomery teaches school at Belmont, Lot 16, P.E.I.

1897 *June 8:* Montgomery becomes engaged to Edwin Simpson of Belmont, a second cousin studying for the Baptist ministry.

1897–98 "The year of mad passion": Montgomery teaches at Lower Bedeque, boarding with the Leard family. She falls in love with Herman Leard but thinks him "unworthy." She publishes nineteen short stories and fourteen poems in 1897–98.

1898 *March:* Montgomery breaks off her engagement with Edwin Simpson. *March 5:* Her grandfather Alexander Macneill dies. Montgomery gives up teaching and lives with her grandmother Macneill at Cavendish, assisting her in her capacity as postmistress (1898–1901).

1899 *June 30:* Herman Leard dies.

1899–1900 The first version of *A Golden Carol* is written. Unpublished, this book was repeatedly rejected and later burned.

1900 *January 16:* Montgomery's father, Hugh John Montgomery, dies in Prince Albert, at the age of fifty-eight.

1901–1902 *Fall–June:* Montgomery works as a newspaperwoman in Halifax, proofreader for the Halifax *Daily Echo* and editor of its society page. As "Cynthia" she writes a column, "Around the Tea Table." *March 1902:* Through Miriam Zieber's informal pen friends' club, Montgomery enters into correspondence with Ephraim Weber of Alberta and begins exchanging journal letters with him.

1903 Montgomery enters into correspondence with George Boyd Macmillan of Alloa, Scotland.

Ewan Macdonald is inducted as minister of the Presbyterian Church in Cavendish and lives in Stanley.

1905 *June: Anne of Green Gables* is begun. Ewan Macdonald comes to live in Cavendish.

1906 *Anne of Green Gables* is rejected by four publishers. Montgomery puts the manuscript away in a hatbox. *October 12:* Montgomery becomes engaged to the Rev. Ewan Macdonald. He departs to attend United Free Church College in Glasgow, 1906–1907.

1907 *February:* Montgomery sends a revised version of *Anne of Green Gables* to the L. C. Page Co. of Boston. *April 15:* She receives a letter of acceptance from Page, suggesting at the same time "a second story dealing with the same character." The royalties offer is only nine cents a copy. No provision is made in the contract for drama or film rights, which becomes an important consideration later.

1907–1908 Montgomery is busy writing *Anne of Avonlea,* dedicated to Hattie Gordon (now Smith).

1908 *June: Anne of Green Gables* is published. It goes through six editions and sells 19,000 copies in its first six months. *Winter:* "Una of the Garden" is published serially in a Minneapolis-based magazine, *The Housewife.*

1909 *February:* Montgomery receives her first royalty check, for $1,730. The first of many translations of *Anne* is made, into Swedish. *September: Anne of Avonlea* is published. About fifty of her short stories and poems are published during the year. *November 1909–January 1910:* Montgomery expands "Una of the Garden" to become *Kilmeny of the Orchard.*

1910 *Kilmeny of the Orchard* is published. The governor-general, Earl Grey, on a visit to Charlottetown, asks to meet "the author of *Anne.*" Montgomery dines with the viceregal party and presents signed copies of her books to Earl Grey. *November:* Montgomery is invited to Boston by her publisher and attends a reception given in her honor by the Boston Authors Club. She is interviewed by the Boston *Republic.* Ewan Macdonald accepts the ministry of a Presbyterian church with two congregations, in Leaskdale and Zephyr, Ontario.

1911 *March 10:* Grandmother Lucy Woolner Macneill dies. *May: The Story Girl,* the author's favorite among her own works, is published. *July 5:* Montgomery and Ewan Macdonald marry. *Summer:* They honeymoon in Scotland and England. *September:* They return to Canada. *October:* They settle in the manse at Leaskdale.

1912 *June: Chronicles of Avonlea* is published. *July 7:* The birth of Ewan and Maud Macdonald's first son, Chester Cameron.

1913 Montgomery begins work on her third *Anne* book. *Summer:* She makes a visit to P.E.I. *September: The Golden Road* is published. *November:* She finishes *Anne of Redmond,* which the publisher entitles *Anne of the Island.*

1914 *August 13:* A baby, named Hugh Alexander, is born dead, occasioning sorrow mixed with acute anxiety over the beginning of World War I.

1915 *April:* Montgomery nurses "Frede" Campbell through typhoid. *July:* Holiday at Park Corner, P.E.I. *Anne of the Island* is published. Her original contract with the L.C. Page Co. expires, and she signs a separate one with the company for a collection of short stories only. *October 7:* Ewan and Maud's second son, Ewan Stuart, is born.

1916 *The Watchman and Other Poems* is published, but sales are sluggish. Montgomery leaves Page for Stokes and the Toronto firm of McClelland & Stewart.

1917 *June–November:* A series of six autobiographical sketches runs in the Toronto magazine *Everywoman's World* and is published in book form as *The Alpine Path.* *August: Anne's House of Dreams* is published. **December 19:** Montgomery votes for the first time, as the sister of a serviceman, Carl. Despite Liberal sympathies she votes for Robert Borden's Conservatives and thus for conscription and the prosecution of the war. **December 19:** Uncle John Campbell dies, and Park Corner goes to his son George.

1918 **May 7:** Montgomery and Ewan buy their first automobile. **June–July:** They visit P.E.I. **October:** Montgomery is very ill with "Spanish flu." Her cousin George dies of it. **November:** She goes to Park Corner to nurse the Campbell family.

1919 **January:** Montgomery is in Boston for her first lawsuit with Page & Co., over reprint rights and their withholding of royalties on the *Anne* books. They settle, and Montgomery receives a check for $20,000. This marks the end of claims to royalties on the early *Anne* books, up to and including *Anne's House of Dreams.* "Frede" Campbell MacFarlane, ill with flu and pneumonia, sends for Montgomery, who arrives in St. Anne's, Quebec, just before "Frede" dies (January 25). *Rainbow Valley* is published. Ewan's melancholia intensifies. **June:** A consultation occurs with a "nerve specialist" in Boston about his condition. The film of *Anne of Green Gables,* with Mary Miles Minter as Anne, is made. L.C. Page & Co. receive $40,000 for the film rights, Montgomery nothing. She begins work on *Rilla of Ingleside.*

1920 **March:** Page brings out *Further Chronicles of Avonlea* from manuscripts in their vault, against the author's express command. **April:** Uncle John Franklin Macneill pulls down the house in Cavendish where Maud had lived with her grandparents. **May–July:** The Page case is heard in Boston; Montgomery testifies for three weeks. **September:** Page countersues, for libel. The original Page case is thrown out of court in August, and the company appeals to the Massachusetts Supreme Court and ultimately to the U.S. Supreme Court. The entire lawsuit is to last nine

years. **December:** Montgomery begins *Emily of New Moon.*

1921 *Rilla of Ingleside* is published. **June 12:** The Macdonald car, with Ewan driving, collides with a car driven by Marshall Pickering of Zephyr.

1922 **February:** Montgomery finishes *Emily of New Moon,* "the best book I have ever written." **March–April:** Marshall Pickering initiates a lawsuit, claiming compensation for injuries allegedly suffered in the June 12, 1921, car accident. **May:** Montgomery begins "Emily II." **November 23–24:** The Pickering suit comes to trial and the judge finds against Ewan, awarding damages of some $3,000. The Macdonalds decide to appeal. Pickering's lawyer endeavors to attach Ewan's salary.

1923 **January:** Montgomery is invited to become a Fellow of the Royal Society of Arts. **April:** A judge finds in her favor over the 1920 *Further Chronicles* case. The Page suit is thrown out by the Massachusetts Supreme Court. The Page Company files an appeal and institutes a new libel suit. **August:** *Emily of New Moon* is published.

1924 **Early June:** The Page libel suit is dismissed. **June 23:** Montgomery agrees to write four stories for *The Delineator* for $1,600.

1925 A controversy over a proposed union of the Presbyterians with the Methodists (voted for by the Presbyterian General Assembly of 1923 and now to be implemented) divides the Presbyterian church in Canada; Ewan and Montgomery are against the union. **March 5:** The U.S. Supreme Court decides against Page. **March:** Ewan has a bad mental relapse; Montgomery completes *Emily Climbs.* **April:** She begins *The Blue Castle,* set in the Muskoka, Ont., area. **June 20:** Members of the church at Zephyr vote to leave the Presbyterians for the United Church. **Summer:** *Emily Climbs* is published. **September 24:** Montgomery finishes her stories for *The Delineator.* **October:** The Supreme Court of New York dismisses the complaint of the Page Company.

December: Ewan accepts a call to the Presbyterian churches of Norval and Union, Ont.

1926 February: The Macdonalds move to the manse in Norval. *April:* Montgomery is at work on the third Emily book and hears that her playfellow Wellington Nelson recently died. *Spring:* Ewan has a bad attack of melancholia. *June:* Montgomery attends a Canadian Women's Press Club meeting in Toronto and has a visit from her half-sister Ila May ("one of the race of Joseph") and her three children. *August:* *The Blue Castle* is published. *November:* Montgomery finishes *Emily's Quest.*

1927 *The Delineator* offers $2,000 for a new series of four stories. *May:* A Mrs. Carroll of *The Delineator* calls and takes the Marigold stories back with her. *June:* Montgomery begins a book about Marigold. She undertakes the support of a female orphan, Flossie Roberts, at St. Anthony's Orphanage, Newfoundland, having earlier supported a male orphan up to working age. *Summer:* Talk of a play based on *The Blue Castle* comes to nothing. She makes a visit to P.E.I. and receives a letter of praise from Stanley Baldwin, the prime minister of Great Britain. *August:* The lieutenant-governor of Canada invites her to a garden party to meet the Prince of Wales (later King Edward VIII) and Prince George (later King George VI) as well as Mr. and Mrs. Stanley Baldwin. *October:* A new editor of *The Delineator* decides the Marigold stories are not to be printed, as not sophisticated enough.

1928 Spring: The beginnings of serious conflicts between Montgomery and her son Chester. *July:* She meets Ephraim Weber, her long-time correspondent, for the first time. *October 17:* She finishes *Magic for Marigold.* *October 20:* Montgomery receives a letter from her lawyer saying Page has lost its last plea and will settle. *November 6:* Montgomery opens Canadian Book Week in Toronto, speaking to an audience of 2,000 at Convention Hall. *November 7:* Montgomery receives a check for $15,000 of the $18,000 ultimately paid by Page in its settlement.

1929 April: One chapter of *Marigold* is published, in *Chatelaine* magazine. *May:* Montgomery begins work on *A Tangled Web. Magic for Marigold* is published.

1930 The author begins copying and editing her own journals, with photographs.

1931 February: Montgomery finishes *A Tangled Web,* published later in the year (in England it appears under the title *Aunt Becky Began It*). *Spring:* Montgomery begins *Pat of Silver Bush.* She makes her first radio broadcast, reading her poems, and publishes her "Open Letter from a Minister's Wife."

1932 *Pat of Silver Bush* is finished and published.

1933 September: Montgomery's second son, Stuart, enters the University of Toronto as a medical student. *December:* Chester reveals his secret marriage to Luella Reid.

1934 January 15: Montgomery begins a *Pat* sequel, called *The Chatelaine of Silver Bush,* later entitled by its publisher *Mistress Pat. May 17:* The birth of Montgomery's first grandchild, Luella. Ewan has a total breakdown and spends from June to August in Homewood Sanatorium, a mental hospital in Guelph, Ont. Montgomery herself is in bad health. She publishes *Courageous Women,* in collaboration with Marian Keith and Mabel Burns McKinley. *November 30:* On her sixtieth birthday she finishes *Mistress Pat.*

1935 Ewan, forced to leave Norval, retires from the ministry. *March:* The Macdonalds buy their own home in Toronto, with her money. *March 9:* Montgomery "unwillingly" begins a new *Anne* book and is elected to the Literary and Artistic Institute of France. *Mistress Pat* is published. The English publishers Hodder & Stoughton turn it down, but it is picked up by Harrap's. *August–November:* Montgomery is writing *Anne of Windy Poplars,* which is finished November 25. She is invested as a Companion of the Order of the British Empire (C.B.O.E.) in Ottawa, an award given by King George V on his Silver Jubilee.

1936   The Macdonalds move into their new home, "Journey's End," on Riverside Drive in Toronto. *Anne of Windy Poplars* is published. (The author preferred the title *Anne of Windy Willows,* used in the English edition.) *May:* The birth of a second grandchild, Cameron Stuart; Chester's marriage is foundering and there is talk of divorce. *August 21:* Montgomery begins writing *Jane of Lantern Hill.* A new film (a "talkie") is made of *Anne of Green Gables,* with the actress Dawn Paris (a.k.a. Dawn O'Day) in the title role. Dawn adopts the name "Anne Shirley" as her film name thereafter. *October:* Montgomery visits P.E.I. and discusses plans to turn the Cavendish area into a national park, with Green Gables as the central attraction.

1937   *The Reader's Digest* pays Montgomery $3 for one sentence from *Anne of Windy Poplars. Jane of Lantern Hill* is published. The author sees two different staged versions of *Anne of Green Gables.* Breakdown of Chester's marriage is clear. Montgomery tries to begin a new *Anne* book but is interrupted by a serious attack of madness in Ewan, who suffers badly from influenza over the winter.

1938   Urged by her publisher to produce another *Anne* book, Montgomery begins one on September 12. Chester joins the 48th Highlanders Reserve. *December 28:* Montgomery finishes *Anne of Ingleside.* Severe illness ensues.

1939   Twentieth Century-Fox pays $150 for the use of a story title. Montgomery signs a film contract with RKO for the rights to *Anne of Windy Poplars. Anne of Ingleside* is published. There is acute anxiety over the onset of war. *June 30:* The last entry in Montgomery's continuous journal. Chester finishes a law course, but eventually fails in practice. Stuart graduates from medical school. *Summer:* Montgomery's last visit to P.E.I.

1940   *January:* Ewan goes alone to Florida for his health for some months. Perhaps at this period Montgomery attempts to weave a collection of stories surrounding Anne, tentatively called *The Blythes Are Quoted* (published posthumously as edited by her son Stuart under the title *The Road to Yesterday,* 1974). The author has a physical breakdown. She fears her sons will join the armed forces, but Chester is rejected because of poor eyesight and Stuart, as a medical student, is not yet allowed to enlist. She tries to work on a sequel to *Jane of Lantern Hill,* but it is never completed.

1942   Montgomery writes to the Ryerson Press in an ultimately unsuccessful negotiation about a Canadian edition of her works. *April 24:* Lucy Maud Montgomery dies. Her funeral is held from Green Gables, with burial in the Cavendish graveyard near the site of her former home.

INTRODUCTION

LUCY MAUD MONTGOMERY left several detailed accounts of her writing of *Anne of Green Gables*. The most reliable is probably the succinct narrative in her journal for August 16, 1907:

> I have always kept a notebook in which I jotted down, as they occurred to me, ideas for plots, incidents, characters and descriptions. Two years ago in the spring of 1905 I was looking over this notebook in search of some suitable idea for a short serial I wanted to write for a certain Sunday School paper and I found a faded entry, written ten years before: — "Elderly couple apply to orphan asylum for a boy. By mistake, a girl is sent them." I thought this would do. I began to block out chapters, devise incidents and "brood up" my heroine. Somehow or other she seemed very real to me and took possession of me to an unusual extent. Her personality appealed to me and I thought it rather a shame to waste her on an ephemeral little serial. Then the thought came, "Write a book about her. You have the central idea and character...." The result of this was "Anne of Green Gables." (*Selected Journals* I: 330–31)

When Montgomery wrote this entry, *Anne* had already been accepted by the publishers, in April 1907, and was to appear in print in 1908.

In *The Alpine Path: The Story of My Career* (1917), the author gives a similar account of the genesis of *Anne*, but there she says that she began the novel in

Lucy Maud Montgomery on her departure for Halifax, 1901.

the spring of 1904 and finished it in 1905. Similarly, in a journal entry for April 1914 Montgomery says she clearly remembers writing the opening paragraph on a "sweet-scented evening in June ten years ago," when the writing was interrupted by the call of Ewan Macdonald, who "had just moved to Cavendish from Stanley" (*SJ* II: 147). But in 1906 she says that Ewan "was a practical outsider ... until the spring of 1905, when he came to live at Cavendish" (*SJ* I: 321), while in the journal for 1907 she says the novel was begun in May 1905 and finished "sometime in January 1906." Evidently the beginning of *Anne* was associated with a June evening and with the advent in the author's life of Ewan Macdonald (to whom she would become engaged in 1906); in any case, the correct date seems to be June 1905. The spring setting of the novel's opening chapters reflect the spring tide of its beginning.

Montgomery copied the handwritten novel in a typescript, on her "old second-hand typewriter that never makes the capitals plain and won't print 'w' at all" (*SJ* I: 331). The typescript was sent to Bobbs-Merrill, then to Macmillan and two other publishers; it was sent back each time, until its dispirited author "put 'Anne' away in an old hat box in the clothes room" (*ibid.*), intending someday to cannibalize the narrative for a magazine story. But she reread it in the winter of 1906–1907, decided it was not bad, and sent it off to L. C. Page & Co. of Boston, who accepted it. The manuscript of *Anne of Green Gables* thus went through some of the vicissitudes of its orphan heroine — it was rejected, sent from pillar to post, spurned — and then emerged, triumphant and beloved.

This book about a redheaded orphan was an immediate success. In its first five years of publication, *Anne of Green Gables* went into thirty-two printings, and it has never gone out of print. Moreover, it was to become a steady best-seller throughout the world. It has been translated into the major European languages, including Polish and Finnish, and has long been a leading book for girls in Japan. Two film versions were produced in Montgomery's lifetime, and there have been several stage versions and television productions. The *Avonlea* television series of the 1980s and '90s has been viewed around the world. Anne is indeed beloved, and her Avonlea has become one of the magic kingdoms of the world, more "real" than Camelot and Narnia and just as beautiful.

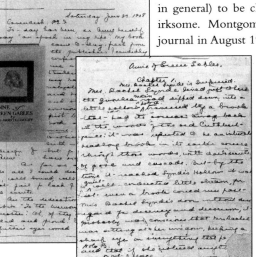

The success of *Anne of Green Gables*, as instantaneous as it was to be enduring, was a great surprise to its author. In her journal Montgomery expresses amazement at her own capacity to represent happiness at a time she did not think of as happy:

> One of the reviews says "the book radiates happiness and optimism." When I think of the conditions of worry and gloom and care under which it was written I wonder at this. Thank God, I can keep the shadows of my life out of my work. I would not wish to darken any other life—I want instead to be a messenger of optimism and sunshine. (*SJ* I: 339)

Undoubtedly, Montgomery in other moods would have disassociated herself from too much "optimism and sunshine." The duty of the writer for children (and of the female writer in general) to be cheerful and moral can be irksome. Montgomery complained to her journal in August 1901 about editors:

> I write a lot of juvenile yarns. I like doing these but would like it better if I didn't have to lug a moral into most of them. They won't sell without it. The kind of juvenile story I like to write—and read too, for the matter of that—is a rattling good jolly one —"art for art's sake"— or rather "fun for fun's sake"—with no insidious moral hidden away in it like a spoonful of jam. But the editors who cater to the "young person" take themselves too seriously for that and so in the moral must go. (*SJ* I: 263)

Anne of Green Gables came after the writing of such a moral work "intended . . . for a 'Sunday School Library book.'" That book was "modelled after the fashion of the 'Pansy' books of my childhood"—books that Anne also reads (see pp. 172–73 and Note). It was entitled *A Golden Carol;* its heroine, Carol Golden, summoned home from boarding school at the death of her mother, performs the usual Victorian self-sacrificing duties of keeping house for her father and brother. At first rebellious,

---

Bottom Right: Montgomery's handwritten first page of **Anne of Green Gables.**

Top Left: A page from Lucy Maud Montgomery's journals, with the cover from the first edition.

Carol comes graciously to accept her lot: "struggles and trials . . . culminating in a victory over self and a determination to . . . make life 'a golden Carol.'" Montgomery finally burned the manuscript of this book, which had failed to find a publisher, "vowing that never again would I try to create a Sunday School heroine." Looking back in 1925, Montgomery was thankful that *A Golden Carol* had not been published: "To have had that book accepted would have been the greatest misfortune. . . . I could never have risen above it" (*SJ* III: 240).

Anne of Green Gables succeeds partly because it is not a work of shallow optimism or conventional piety. The "shadows of life" are not kept out of the book. Redheaded Anne emerged from the literal ashes of the sleekly golden conformist Carol. As Montgomery says, "It was the re-action [*sic*] drove me to 'Anne' and probably kept me from making a dum-my of her" (*SJ* III: 240). Anne is certainly not "a dummy" and does not ventriloquize the prevailing Sunday school attitudes. Far from being a Sunday School heroine, she questions the values that Sunday School represents. *Anne* would not be what it is without the qualities of sorrow, even bitterness— but bitterness transformed.

The story (arising as it did from a reported incident in real life) of the orphan girl who should have been a boy strikes a universal chord in women. Not being a boy is a defect as culturally perceived. To be a girl is to be imperfect, a poor substitute for the real thing and thus in some sense unwanted. The central personage is an orphan found living in a dreary asylum without family. Orphans do not have a proper social identity, for this is supplied by family, especially the presence and name of the father. Orphans are not wanted, are superfluous, exciting and dangerous extras, "free radicals" in the social body. Characters in well-known Victorian novels that Montgomery loved—David Copperfield, Jane Eyre—are orphans.

In writing a book instead of merely a Sunday School–paper serial, Montgomery was entering the arena with authors like Dickens and Brontë. Many

novels were read together by or in families, and the division that we now find so strict between children's books and books for adults was not a rigid demarcation in the late nineteenth and early twentieth centuries. Grown-ups read the books of Edith Nesbit, Kenneth Grahame, Mark Twain. Montgomery's books have been kept pent up within categories marked Children's Books and Female Books and Canadian Literature. Insights from the study of all these areas have much to offer, but too severe an adherence to such categories is unfair to Montgomery's work—and certainly to its intention.

When she wrote her full-length book and sent it to American publishers of hardback novels, Montgomery was aware that her potential audience was a large one, both within and beyond the boundaries of Canada. She made the Maritime Provinces real to readers in other countries, but her own range of literary reference shows an unparochial cast that is not narrowly nationalist. Neither does such a range of literary allusion fit in with our view of what to expect in "books for children." Montgomery's novel, with its fine vocabulary and delicately interwoven quotations and allusions, is not "written down" to a child reader—unlike the Sunday School–paper stories. Once *Anne of Green Gables* found its way into print, it was not so very surprising that a fellow author like Mark Twain should read it or that a London literary magazine like *The Spectator* would review it (see Appendix, "Book Reviews").

The tale of what might be called "the Case of the Orphan" persisted in children's literature of the late nineteenth and early twentieth centuries, with wide appeal on both sides of the Atlantic. Tom Sawyer, another imaginist, is an orphan. The poor little drudge in James Whitcomb Riley's "Little Orphant [*sic*] Annie" (1883) is a teller of ghostly tales. Sara Crewe, in Frances Hodgson Burnett's 1888 work, reissued in 1905 as *A Little Princess,* is orphaned early in life and plunged into a dreary life like that of Anne before the time in which the novel opens. And Kate Douglas Wiggin in 1903 had already produced one of literature's most successful orphans in the heroine of *Rebecca of Sunnybrook Farm.* The resemblances between this book and *Anne* are quite striking and have been remarked upon by critics. In both novels, an imaginative heroine entertains an adult male with her chatter upon her entry to the village, where she lives with a stern older lady and makes a loyal if less intelligent friend, while her talents are elicited by a sympathetic female teacher. The resemblances between Anne and Rebecca indicate that the popular American tale had a profound effect on Montgomery, although the import of the two books remains quite different. Perry Nodelman points out a similar structure in a number of tales involving the female displaced child, starting with Johanna Spyri's *Heidi:* "The young girl, an orphan, arrives at her new home.... Her ... clothing does not suit her character; she is a spontaneous and ebullient child." The new home's inhabitants are unhappy, the home "bleak and sterile," yet the people are not bad but merely soured: "they only need the presence of our remarkable heroine" ("Progressive Utopias," 30–31). Anne does in part fit the model offered by the earlier Heidi and Rebecca and by the later Pollyanna, who may be taken as an effort to make an Anne-figure into a declared Christian of an evangelical kind and to remold her into a cheerful Griselda of virtuous patience. Mary in *The Secret Garden* broadly fits the pattern of the "remarkable heroine." She too is a life-bringer, if notably lacking a sunny disposition.

What to Nodelman seems an inadequate basis for narrative, conspicuous by its "lack of conflict" (*ibid.,* 34), seems rather the expression of a powerful myth in a world where myths of benign female power are not easy to come by. Andromedas have to wait chained to their rocks and be rescued. Anne is an anti-Andromeda, a rescuer. The myth arranged in these narrative forms endorses female storytelling and permits the fresh articulation of normally unperceived conflicts. Anne Shirley ought to be seen in connection with other fictional orphans both male

and female, light-bearers who are also bringers of conflict, for by their very presence they shrewdly interrogate the values of society and awaken their culture to possibilities previously discarded. The orphan children of Victorian and Edwardian literature remind us of what is abused by too strict an adherence to "family values" narrowly interpreted. Anne is saliently one of the most orphaned of her peers —unlike Heidi or Rebecca or Tom Sawyer, she possesses no remaining relative, no aunts or grandfather. She is truly alone in the world, has been already cast out.

The stories of Burnett and Wiggin, of Dickens and Twain, while certainly literary influences on the literary product that is *Anne,* are therefore best seen as only part of the story of its creation. Lucy Maud Montgomery was an orphan of a kind, as she reminds us in her dedication of this book to the memory of dead parents.

THE ORPHAN MAUD

Lucy Maud Montgomery, always called "Maud," was born November 30, 1874, in Clifton (now New London), Prince Edward Island. She was the only child of Clara Woolner Macneill and Hugh John Montgomery. When she was twenty-one months old, her mother died; Maud insisted that she could remember seeing her mother in her coffin. The father gave his child over to the care of her maternal grandparents while he tried a variety of occupations involving sales or shipping. In 1881 he went to Saskatchewan and, after spending a couple of summers in the Prince Albert area, emigrated altogether to the West. In *Pat of Silver Bush* (1932), the heroine's father, Alec Gardiner, thinks of going West, which sends his little daughter Pat into an agony of fear, as she cannot bear to leave Silver Bush or Prince Edward Island. Pat's father, happily, does not go, but Maud's father did. He worked as a real estate agent and in various other occupations at a time when land deals were booming and the town of Prince Albert was growing. Hugh John Montgomery, called

"Monty" by his peers, seems to have been something between a ne'er-do-well and a wheeler-dealer who had political ambitions (his own father was a senator), but he was doomed to perpetual mild failure. Hugh John seems, in short, a character typical of the Gilded Age.

In effect, Maud was orphaned by a father who insisted on being absent and invisible. Desertion by her father was a deep wound in young Maud's life, and she had no wish to probe it too hard. At Hugh John's death in January 1900 Maud was greatly shocked. In May of that year she registers the death and reconfigures her relationship to her father:

> I have nobody except poor old grandmother. And father and I have always been so much to each other. He was so good and kind and tender. . . . Even when he went so far away and for so many years we never grew apart, as some might have done. We always remained near and dear in spirit. . . . Have you left your "little Maudie" all alone? That was not like you. (*SJ* I: 249)

Maud was now truly an orphan, bereft of the dream of future union with the absent father. But Hugh John had really left his "little Maudie" all alone many years before, and they had been "apart" in more than distance. Maud has to reinvent the relationship, turning her father into a spiritual intimate. This imaginary "near and dear" spirit becomes satisfactorily embodied at last in Anne's Matthew: "Matthew and I are such kindred spirits I can read his thoughts without words at all" (p. 203).

Maud's father had in fact not altogether abandoned her in 1883 by settling in the West. In 1887 he married again and had a home to which to invite his girl. When he sent for her in 1890, she joyfully

"My mother" (Clara Woolner Macneill Montgomery).

traveled by rail across the country toward reunion. In *Jane of Lantern Hill* (1937), the heroine's deepest wishes are wonderfully fulfilled when, at last united after separation, father and daughter can be almost all in all to each other. No such thing happened, however, in the case of Lucy Maud and Hugh John Montgomery. Maud had to accept that there was a stepmother and a half- sister, with another child on the way.

Maud heartily disliked the life her father and stepmother forced her to live in Prince Albert. Letters to her cousin Penzie Macneill complain of homesickness and of the amount of baby tending demanded of her. Her reactions are here voiced in language more colloquial than the more highly styled writing practiced in her journals (see Bolger, *The Years Before "Anne"*). Maud was taken out of school for months at a time to assist with domestic chores and feared she would never succeed in getting a proper education. Even the poor high school at Prince Albert was much better than no school at all. In the summer of 1891 Maud returned to Prince Edward Island and remained there, obviously by her own choice.

Maud must have known upon her return that life with her grandparents would not be easy, for it never had been. Her mother's parents were already well advanced in middle age when they first took on the task of raising half-orphaned Maud. The elder Macneills were old-fashioned, strict, and narrow. However difficult they were, they did offer Maud a home and support for her education through high school, something not all girls received or even expected. If she had been a boy, Monty would not have had his oldest child—and such a bright child—leave school for months of baby care and housework. The dignified Calvinist Macneills at least appreciated Maud's diligence and intelligence.

Anne Shirley's education faithfully replicates that

of her author, as Montgomery makes Marilla and Matthew Cuthbert likewise willing to support the girl's schooling. Despite various legislative education acts (see Appendix, "Education"), children of both sexes were often withdrawn from school at the age of twelve or so, or at least removed from school for long periods of the year. Familial support for education could not be taken for granted. Anne and Maud each attended a one-room schoolhouse, at the mercy of young and often inadequate teachers. Maud was very fond of her teacher, Hattie Gordon, who served as a partial model for Miss Stacy, but Miss Stacy is really a dream teacher. Selena Robinson, who taught school at Cavendish in 1892–1893, "though a jolly girl and good friend, isn't any kind of a teacher," according to Maud (*SJ* I: 90). And the character Teddy Phillips, the bad teacher in *Anne* who is always flirting with Prissy Andrews, is drawn from life, but the model is Mr. John Mustard, the teacher in the Prince Albert school, and the girl he flirted with was Maud Montgomery.

Anne's education in most important respects duplicates Montgomery's own, although the author makes Anne a shade more successful than she was herself (see Appendices, "The Exceptional Orphan Anne" and "Education"). Maud Montgomery attended Prince of Wales College in Charlottetown,

Hugh John Montgomery's (Maud's father) home, called "Eglintoune Villa," in Prince Albert.

an academy which in *Anne* is called Queen's. It has been noted that this is a decided feminizing of the name, changing it to a place name that is empowering to women, "suggesting female glory and power" (Waterston, *Kindling Spirit*, 33). There may be an echo here of Ruskin's "Queen's Gardens" in his *Sesame and Lilies* (1865–1871), but ironically transformed. For Ruskin, the "Queen's Garden" is the sacred place of home, her proper sphere; for Montgomery, the Queen's realm also includes the lecture hall.

With a First Class License to teach (see Appendix, "Education") acquired at the end of her high-school training, Maud Montgomery was equipped to earn a living as a teacher. Her maternal grandparents presumably subsidized her schooling largely because they thought the orphan girl ought to have the means of earning a living, but Maud's grandmother assisted her financially in a much more unusual venture. In 1895 Maud used the one hundred dollars she had saved out of a salary of one hundred seventy-five dollars for teaching in Bideford and combined it with her grandmother's donation of eighty dollars to take one year of literary study at Dalhousie University. This was to be a combination of courses largely self-designed, not the freshman year of a university program. Unlike Anne, who goes to "Redmond," a fictional Dalhousie, in the ordinary way and takes the four-year course leading to the B.A., Montgomery could never afford a university degree, undoubtedly a subject of regret for her. Montgomery appreciated the fact that Dalhousie was co-educational (see her "A Girl's Place at Dalhousie College" in the Halifax *Herald*, 1896; reprinted by Bolger, *The Years Before "Anne,"* 161–68).

Maud was not financially able to take advantage of the women's new opportunities arising for higher education. Her one year of university-level work in French, Latin, and English, however, not only raised her teaching qualifications but, more important, gave her deeper confidence in her own abilities, broader knowledge, contact with other minds—and the welcome experience of a city larger than Charlottetown. Maud studied under the already famous and admired Dr. Archibald MacMechan and fortunately was not to know that he would take a very condescending view of her own writings in the first major critical work on Anglo-Canadian literature, *Headwaters of Canadian Literature* (1924). Fortunately for MacMechan's own self-esteem, he did not know in the autumn of 1895 that this student of his had written down her first impression of him in her journal for September 25: "Our English professor, Dr. MacMechan, seems very nice, but is, I think, rather a weak man" (*SJ* I: 145).

Maud's year at Dalhousie was a valuable experience, and her grandmother had shown unusual vision in helping her granddaughter fulfill such an atypical dream. In the *Anne* series, Anne's eventual pursuit of a university degree is enabled by the joint efforts of the scholarship-winning Anne as well as Marilla Cuthbert and Rachel Lynde and the powerful assistance of a thousand-dollar bequest from another strong woman, Miss Barry (*Anne of the Island*, ch. 18). Josephine Barry, a "kindred spirit," is, in the phrase so important to Maud and the mature Anne, "one of the race that knows Joseph." Anne has to put up with some negative remarks in her pursuit of education, as did Maud. Neighbors could see little sense in her Dalhousie project. As one woman sneered, "Do you want to be a preacher?" And Maud's own grandfather showed "no interest of any kind" (*SJ* I: 143).

Lucy Woolner Macneill deserves special commendation for her support of her granddaughter's ambition, because in realizing it she would lose the girl's companionship and help. This sort of loss is recognized in *Anne* when Marilla is afflicted with "the bitterest kind of a heart-ache" upon Anne's departure for Queen's, a pain which she bears without complaint (p. 360). This incident in *Anne* utilizes elements very like those in the 1906 Montgomery story "Jane Lavinia," although in that short narrative the heroine, returning for her forgotten watch shortly after her official departure for New York, hears her

stern Aunt Rebecca's grief and knows then that she is loved (in *Akin to Anne*, ed. Wilmshurst, 93–103).

Maud's relationship with her grandmother Lucy Macneill was always complex and strenuous, and the strain did not ease when Grandfather Macneill died in 1898. He left nothing to Maud, and to his wife bequeathed only the farmhouse for her lifetime. By staying with her grandmother, Maud enabled Lucy to finish her days in her own home. She did make another expedition, to Halifax in 1901, to work on the Halifax *Echo*, but had to return to Cavendish in 1902, as she felt her grandmother was being persecuted by Maud's uncle John and cousin Prescott, who were bent on denying Lucy her home. Had Lucy lacked in her old age the assistance Maud was able to give, the prospective male inheritors would have obtained the house much more rapidly.

Maud felt great resentment at her own lack of

Hugh John Montgomery and his second wife, Mary Ann McRae Montgomery.

inheritance, referring with asperity to her grandfather's "absurd will" (*SJ* I: 295, 310). But her grandfather had done only the normal thing in leaving the farm and farmhouse to male heirs, just as Monty and his second wife had done only the normal thing in taking a teenaged girl out of school to help with baby care and housework. Maud feared homelessness to come. She could see herself when her grandmother had gone, being forced to "migrate to Ch'Town . . . get a cheap boarding place, and write pot-boilers for a living. A pleasant outlook, truly!" (*SJ* I [Nov. 1905]: 311).

The only alternative to this disagreeable fate was marriage. Maud was evidently moved to think once more of marriage. In 1897–1898 she had had an unfortunate engagement to Edwin Simpson, which she had broken off. She had been startled by her own strong sexual attraction to a young farmer, Herman Leard, whom she met in Bedeque while teaching there in 1897–1898, but she felt that Herman was "not worthy" of her love. By the time she began writing *Anne of Green Gables* she had already made the acquaintance of the young minister Ewan Macdonald, to whom she was to become engaged in the summer of 1906, just before he went off to Glasgow to study. In a memorable passage in her journal for 1914 she associates Ewan with the writing of *Anne*:

I remember well the very evening I wrote the opening paragraph of *Green Gables*. It was a moist, showery, sweet-scented evening in June ten years ago. I was sitting *on the end of the table*, in the old kitchen, my feet on the sofa, beside the west window, because I wanted to get the last gleams of daylight on my portfolio. I did not for a moment dream that the book I had just begun was to bring me the fame and success I had long dreamed of. So I wrote the opening paragraphs quite easily, not feeling obliged to "write up" to any particular reputation or style. Just as I had finished my description of *Mrs. Lynde* and her home *Ewan* walked in. . . . He stayed and chatted most of the evening,

so no more of *Green Gables* was written that night. (*SJ* II: 147)

This passage indicates an association between the moist, sweet evening, the fecundity that gives birth to *Anne*, and the sexual hope and reawakening afforded by Ewan's presence. (Yet, on the other hand, his arrival breaks the spell and puts a stop to the flow of writing.) Ewan's courtship partly coincided with the writing of *Anne*; confusion over this sequence may contribute to Montgomery's perpetual uncertainty about the actual year in which she began to write the novel. The association with Ewan offered a new chance in life, and her engagement to him in the summer of 1906 relieved her anxieties about a future as a penniless old maid. The relief from these concerns, creating a renewed sense of future hope, may well have stimulated the production of *Anne of Green Gables*.

Yet Ewan Macdonald must not be seen as playing Gilbert Blythe to Maud Montgomery's Anne Shirley. In her journals of the time Maud's private discussions of Ewan's qualities are uncompromisingly cool. She felt some physical attraction to Ewan, but not too much. Although she found him suitable, she was very critical of him, her first impression of him being that, despite his Dalhousie B.A., he had "no culture" (*SJ* I: 321). She foresaw certain difficulties in living as a minister's wife, given her own doubts about the Presbyterian creed and her great dislike of the life of fearsome propriety that would be thrust upon her. But the suitable marriage offered respectability and, apparently, safety. It seemed so sensible! Maud could not know then that her husband-to-be was afflicted with religious melancholia and was to spend large parts of many years under the intermittent belief that he was one of the damned. Ewan kept his bouts of melancholia a secret during their engagement, and she later believed that had she known of them she would not have married him. Ewan's madness was to render her marriage a nightmare for much of the time after 1919.

Maud had foreseen potential conflicts between the role of writer and that of wife. By the time she and Ewan did marry, her writing had become so lucrative that her husband would never have urged her to give it up. We may wonder how Ewan could reconcile Maud's position as the wife of a Calvinist minister with the views expressed in her writings, but he appears never to have read her novels or stories.

In many of Montgomery's stories a heroine rejects a tempting opportunity to leave Prince Edward Island, as perhaps Montgomery at her marriage wished she could have rejected her banishment from Cavendish. In "Jane Lavinia," published in the year of Maud's engagement, the heroine chooses not to make her journey to New York but prefers instead to stay at home with the older woman who, she has discovered, loves and admires her. In response to a man who says, "You have exceptional talent, and I think you ought to cultivate it," Jane replies, "I am going to cultivate Aunt Rebecca." This relationship, of a talented girl with an apparently emotionless or stern older woman, forms a staple of Montgomery's fiction. She did indeed "cultivate" Lucy Woolner Macneill for her art, and her relationship with that difficult but important older woman was perhaps the major love of Maud's whole life.

The death of Maud's grandmother meant not just the young woman's freedom to marry but—as the *Journals* make clear—a loss of home, permanent exile. Montgomery seems never to have thought of buying a house of her own on the island, even though her first check from her publishers in February 1909 was for $1,730, easily enough for the purchase of a small farm or two, or several houses. A real home, in the life of P.E.I., was a matter of inheritance, and Maud was denied her inheritance—as she had known since 1898 she would be, because she wasn't a boy.

THE ORPHAN ANNE

In *Anne of Green Gables* an orphan adopted by a childless couple turns what is a house with land into a home, a homestead, an inheritance. This child is at first an outcast, with no home except an asylum, by definition not a true home. She has suffered from deprivation. In the anxieties and changes in her own life of 1905, the author looked over her personal history of loss and deprivation, examining her own loneliness from the time of early childhood:

The older I grow the more I realize what a starved childhood mine was *emotionally*. I was brought up by two old people, neither of whom at their best were ever very sympathetic and who had already grown into set, intolerant ways. They seemed to cherish and act upon the contradictory opinions that a child of ten or a girl of fifteen was as old as themselves and as young as a baby— that is, she should have no wish or taste that they did not have, and yet she should have no more right to an independent existence than an infant. Grandfather Macneill, in all the years I knew him, was a stern, domineering, irritable man. I was always afraid of him. . . .

As for grandmother, she was very kind to me in a material way. I was well-cared for, well-fed, and well-dressed—and I may also add that these benefits were unfailingly cast up to me whenever I showed any rebellion. But nature never made two people more dissimilar in every respect essential to mutual comfort. I was impulsive, warm-hearted, emotional; grandmother was cold and reserved, narrow in her affections and sensibilities. (*SJ* I: 300–301)

Montgomery sets down this firm but passionate statement in January 1905, probably just at the time *Anne* was beginning to take shape in her own mind. Evidently she was rereading her own girlhood journals, echoes of which are to be heard in *Anne of Green Gables*.

Anne and her creator are one in experiencing a "starved childhood *emotionally*." But Marilla Cuthbert, who is in some respects a reflection of Grand-

Hattie Gordon, an inspiring teacher for young Maud.

mother Macneill, has the rudiments of emotional wisdom and a latent capacity for love. Feeling begins to stir in Marilla for Anne after she hears the girl's account of the loss of her parents and her life of drudgery and baby care with Mrs. Thomas and Mrs. Hammond (ch. 5). Marilla registers her own capacity for both pity and sympathy in the very terms Montgomery uses in contemplating herself: "What a starved, unloved life she had had—a life of drudgery and poverty and neglect" (pp. 88–89). Marilla recognizes deprivation because of her own, suppressed, knowledge of her personal deprivation. But this doesn't detract from Marilla's moral heroism, because not everyone who has suffered the hunger of the heart feels, as both Marilla and Anne do, sympathy for the hunger of others. Anne herself at this point is

a long way from recognizing any heart hunger in older people. Like most children, she finds it hard to imagine any older persons (Marilla, Mrs. Lynde, Superintendent Bell) as ever having been children themselves.

"Anne's History" (ch. 5) is partly derived from the author's personal recollection of baby care, not for unfeeling strangers but for her uncomprehending father's second wife in Prince Albert. Maud Montgomery could never have admitted it, but there may be some psychological revenge taking place on Monty in the description of the drunken Mr. Thomas who was "killed falling under a train" (p. 87). Largely deprived of schooling and friends, and familyless, Anne was a kind of maid-of-all-work to poor families living precariously on the edge of the economy. These people also lack a community to belong to; their families break up and Mrs. Hammond even has to go to "the States." Avonlea, in contrast, supplies an almost ideal community that doesn't let people fall out like that. The threat of passing Anne on to somebody who could use "a girl" is averted. Marilla does not hand the child over to Mrs. Blewett, "a terrible worker and driver," for more drudgery and child care: "The baby's awful fractious, and I'm clean worn out attending to him. If you like I can take her right home now" (p. 94). A "girl" is not a child, only a machine for child care.

It is notable that Anne is spared, whereas other female characters are not. Drudgery is the normal lot of woman, or at least of lower-class woman. Sara Crewe ought not to drudge, only because she is well born; her devoted friend, the poor little maid-servant Becky, has to work. It is worth comparing this phenomenon with a treatment of the female drudge in another contemporary work. Nellie McClung's *Sowing Seeds in Danny* was Canada's best-seller of 1908—at one million copies it far outsold *Anne* (see the headnote by Sandra Campbell and Lorraine McMullen to McClung's "The Live Wire" in *New Women*, 243–44). McClung's novel has a lively bright girl-heroine gifted with imagination and considerable power of speech, like Anne. But little Pearl Watson is, most unlike Anne, truly a wonderful worker, a staunch performer at physical tasks, including washing dishes, scrubbing and sewing. Pearl keeps her large family going and is even hired out to pay off the debt for the family's living quarters—a castoff caboose—by her hard service. It has been argued that "McClung conveyed more frankly [than Montgomery] the traumas of a small girl in a harsh world" (Waterston, *Kindling Spirit*, 77). McClung approves her Pearl's efforts to keep smiling under the pressure of unsympathetic labor, whereas Montgomery questions the labor itself. Anne, unlike "Pearlie," is definitely not a master performer of housework: she neglects to scald the dishcloth, lets a mouse drown in a sauce, and flavors a cake with liniment. She is good at child care only *in extremis* and, unlike Rebecca, Pearlie, or Pollyanna, after her experience with three sets of twins betrays no longing to be around babies. According to certain standards of the day, Anne is too much the lily of the field that toils not.

Marilla Cuthbert seems at first to believe that she is entitled to a hard-working child like Pearl Watson and that an orphan child's worth lies only in the value of the work he or she can perform. At the beginning of her relationship with Anne, Marilla seems to be about to continue a general pattern of cold neglect. The first description of Marilla (see n. 15, ch. 1), like the entire narrative of the first phase in the relationship between Marilla and Anne, bears a resemblance to Harriet Beecher Stowe's description in *Oldtown Folks* (1869) of the harsh old maid Asphyxia Smith and her attempts to adopt and discipline newly

orphaned little Eglantine Percival, an experiment that is an uncompromising failure. We can see signs of future success, however, in the hints of Marilla's sense of humor. Unlike Asphyxia, she has an innate capacity to pass beyond harsh Calvinist doctrine and a strictly utilitarian view of things and persons.

The room Marilla gives Anne to sleep in seems indicative of neglect, for it is loveless, bare, and cold; even the muslin frill on the washstand is called "icy," and "the whole apartment was of a rigidity not to be described in words" (p. 72). The narrator's voice tells us that Anne weeps at her first experience under Marilla's roof: "a lonely, heart-hungry, friendless child cried herself to sleep" (p. 74).

At this point, only the narrator seems to see Anne as a *child*. It is evident from the manuscript that Montgomery takes particular care with the use of the word "child" in these early sections of the novel (see Textual Notes). Matthew, inadequately, calls Anne a "nice little thing," and Marilla thinks of her as the "odd little figure," "a girl," "a stray waif." But after hearing Anne's history, Marilla's view, as presented through the device known as *style indirect libre*, in which the narrator's voice takes on the color of a character's mind, seems closer to that of the general narrator and the reader. Marilla now sees Anne as a child; first "the child seemed a nice, teachable little thing" (p. 89); then, confronting Mrs. Blewett, Marilla "softened at the sight of the child's pale face" (p. 94).

Anne becomes a figure of need to which Marilla

Top: Maud's grandfather, Alexander Marquis Macneill.
Bottom: Maud's grandmother, Lucy Woolner Macneill.

can at last respond. "The child" is not, however, just a creature of humble needs but of ardent desires and creativity, and for these Marilla is not yet ready. The development of the story really follows the education of Marilla. The relation between Anne and Marilla is the central, most complex relation in the novel, to which even Anne's relations with Matthew and Diana (and with Gilbert, which follows behind all of these) must yield. This relationship draws upon the author's own association with her grandmother.

There is no character in *Anne* who so directly reflects Maud's relation with her grandfather. She was still full of irritation and anger at her grandfather's will, which had left both herself and her grandmother at the mercy of greedy uncles, with herself completely disinherited. Alexander Macneill in his will (like Hugh John more hurtfully in his careless absence) had implicitly expressed an opinion that girls were useless. Had Maud been a boy, she would almost certainly have been the chosen inheritor of the place she loved so much. Anne Shirley, like her author, also commits the sin of not being a boy —the boy who was sent for—but she is nevertheless instated and becomes the chosen one, the inheritor.

The sting of Maud's loss, her knowledge that she was in her earthly paradise on sufferance only and not by entitlement, played a large part in the hidden story of the author's creation of *Anne of Green Gables*. All Montgomery's characters are "of" somewhere. The essential place name is not that of a town or a region but of a small estate or homestead, a farm and its house: Green Gables, New Moon, Silver Bush. Only in Montgomery's later books do we find the names of houses alone—Ingleside, Windy Poplars, Lantern Hill—not true family estates. But one must be "of" a house and grounds in the Montgomery world. The need to be so grounded arose within the author's imagination once she knew she had lost her place and become but a pilgrim and sojourner.

Matthew is not the expression of Grandfather Macneill but his opposite. He is shy where Grand-father was imposing and self-willed, kind where Grandfather was peremptory. Moreover, he comes to value his girl more than any boy, and he tells her so. After doing that, Matthew has nothing left to do but to die, which he does—leaving Anne in effect his inheritor. She saves Green Gables for herself and Marilla, and, whatever difficulties they undergo, financial and otherwise, she always has a permanent home. No male interloper is created to demand it from her. She and Marilla eventually hand the farming of it over to Davy, but he is an orphan they have voluntarily taken in, an heir they have chosen for themselves.

Meanwhile, in *Anne of Green Gables,* Anne as magic heir or princess comes into her rightful place, with both Matthew and Marilla to herself. As this pair are not married, they do not have to pose as orthodox parents or an orthodox couple, nor do they distribute authority in the orthodox way. They are brother and sister, unawakened libido saved in both for concentration on Anne.

In the first serious full-length academic literary study of Montgomery, *The Fragrance of Sweet-Grass: L. M. Montgomery's Heroines and the Pursuit of Romance* (1992), Elizabeth R. Epperly discusses "romance" in Montgomery's novels chiefly as a matter of representing heterosexual love as it leads to marriage. This is certainly a large subject in Montgomery's oeuvre, and the recent publication of her short fiction reminds us of how the magazines of the era and their editors desired that "love stories" be represented. But in *Anne*, "romance" in that sense is clearly subordinate to the larger romance themes of quest, of search for identity, of imaginative reconciliation. From Heliodorus' *Aithiopika* to *A Winter's Tale, The Heart of Midlothian,* and *Jane Eyre,* fiction is rarely concerned only with finding the true lover; it instead reconstitutes the family, reorganizes the relations of the generations, and radically changes their prospects. *Anne of Green Gables* deals with the larger romance themes of the search for identity, quest, and the reconciliation of opposites. *Anne* is also "romantic" in the sense that the Romantic poets (which the novel quotes) are "romantic," validating the imagination as a mode of true perception.

As far as the novel's "love story" is concerned, Gilbert is an excellent figure for the masculine Other that the girl must both combat and recognize. But the real "love story" of the novel as a whole remains the difficult, evolving love between Anne and Marilla. Montgomery did not merely stumble onto this motif in writing *Anne*. As Rea Wilmshurst has shown in her collection of early Montgomery stories about orphans and strangers, *Akin to Anne* (1988), such tales of orphans and girls living with difficult elder guardians are common in Montgomery's early works. In the full-length novels, Anne Shirley's relationship with Marilla Cuthbert, Emily Starr's with her stern Aunt Elizabeth, and Marigold Lesley's relationship with frightening but exciting Old Grandmother are variations on this constant theme. But Anne and Marilla's relationship is the most liberating and experimental one, as these two females are not bound by any blood tie.

THE BOOK OF ANNE

In composing *Anne of Green Gables*, Lucy Maud Montgomery put to good use the skills she had acquired in turning out magazine stories, but she evidently treated the writing of her "first" (actually second) full-length book with especial care. The language of *Anne* is much richer and more complex than that of the Montgomery short stories of the same period, although there are many resemblances. Revisions made while writing indicate a constant desire to avoid sounding either too "high" or too "rural"; at the same time, there is more liberty of register than short stories usually allow. Yet Montgomery changes "chicken coop" to "chicken house," as perhaps she thought the former phrase too "low," and she saves Matthew from sounding too ignorantly rustic (see Textual Notes).

The handwritten manuscript now in the Confederation Art Gallery and Museum in Charlottetown

shows the thought that went into the writing of *Anne of Green Gables*. As Elizabeth R. Epperly says in her essay "Approaching the Montgomery Manuscripts," the holographic text of *Anne* is the "most clearly written, and most obviously inspired of the manuscripts. . . . The handwriting is rapid but easy to read, the revisions are made in order, and the scenes and dialogues are completely formed" (*Harvesting Thistles*, 75; see also Textual Notes). It is easy to believe that Montgomery had partly composed the story in her head before she took up her pen, but there are important changes made in the course of the writing. We can see in the early chapters, especially in Matthew's first encounter with Anne, that the voice of Anne is not yet fully developed in the very first writing. The material Montgomery adds expands our impression of Anne's imaginative life and extends the range of literary allusion, the scale of registers, and the comic effects.

We find in the important second chapter, for instance, that some of Anne's more significant and allusive remarks are added in Montgomery's revision notes. For example: "You could imagine you were dwelling in marble halls, couldn't you?" (MS Note C1); "I've got all my worldly goods in it, but it isn't heavy" (MS Note D1); and "It wouldn't be half so interesting . . . there'd be no scope for imagination then, would there?" (MS Note J1). Such additions show Montgomery's growing recognition that it is a characteristic of Anne-speech to draw the interlocutor in with interrogatives asking for agreement at the ends of sentences. The description of Anne's activity on the ferryboat and her account of the poor trees on the grounds of the orphan asylum are likewise additions, in these cases giving a greater sense of Anne's vitality and unconscious need.

In a different vein, the comedy of the chapter is heightened by the new touch describing Matthew's reaction to Anne's whirl of talk: "He felt as he had felt in his rash youth when another boy had enticed him on the merry-go-round at a picnic" (MS Note

O1). Matthew's entire timid and unadventurous life, from childhood until this point in time always the reverse of "rash," is elicited in that one sentence. His explanation of how Diana got her name from a schoolmaster is, however, an addition with a different function (MS Note W1). Montgomery needed some time in which to get used to the typical voices and thoughts of her new characters. We can see this in the first chapter where, for instance, Mrs. Lynde's statement "I'd rather look at people" is an addition (MS Note K), as is her reference to "another case where an adopted boy used to suck the eggs" (MS Note T). The authorial commentary also becomes less straightforward, more ironic, in the additions, as when Mrs. Lynde offers the scary tales of orphan girls poisoning benefactors—and even wells—and Marilla retorts that they're not getting a girl, "as if poisoning wells were a purely feminine accomplishment and not to be dreaded in the case of a boy" (MS Note V).

Here the dread of having one's well poisoned by a woman-child sets the atmosphere of the *dread* of the feminine. Two episodes in this novel in fact deal with forms of "poisoning": Anne inadvertently intoxicates Diana by plying her with wine instead of cordial, and she "poisons" her cake by flavoring it

*Left: **Lucy Maud Montgomery in her wedding trousseau dress.***
*Right: **The Rev. Ewan Macdonald.***

with liniment instead of vanilla. This disgusting dainty is then served to the minister and his wife. Anne as "poisoner'" is a dramatic figure to others and to herself—she is, after all, not only an orphan but also an immigrant and an alien. Avonlea initially suffers from fear of poisoning by an outsider, a fear that the inmost self may be broken in upon by alien forces, the life-supply drained by the vampirish or witchlike girl. The fears thus voiced by Mrs. Lynde in the first chapter add to our sense of the impact Anne makes, with her "feminine accomplishment" of poisoning the well of Avonlea's settled truths with her imagination. But the "freckled witch" ultimately redeems herself by being medicinal in a white-witch fashion. She saves Diana's sister, a personage who otherwise never directly appears, by pouring ipecac down her throat.

Anne comes to Avonlea in a reversal of the role of the Prince in *Sleeping Beauty*. Avonlea is the Beauty, sleeping in the rigid lethargy (imposed by patriarchal regulation) which the kiss of Anne, the Princess and Queen as well, must awaken. "Very green and neat and precise was that yard, set about on one side with great patriarchal willows, and on the other with prim Lombardies. Not a stray stick nor stone was to be seen" (p. 42). Yet Avonlea itself is full of richness and glory, hidden as it may be from the eyes of those who do not see. Once Anne is permitted to stay at Green Gables, she kisses the apple blossom (p. 105), an apparently casual, foolish, and lighthearted gesture, but not an insignificant one. The awakening is not Anne's but Avonlea's.

Anne comes to Prince Edward Island and Avonlea in the late June spring of a northern climate playing itself out in a fertile land. She is a Persephone returned from the Underworld. Anne is at one with the lush vegetation. She disgraces—or more truly declares—herself by weaving wild roses and buttercups about her hat and appearing thus garlanded at her Presbyterian Sunday School. One of the most subtle and serious games Montgomery is playing has to do with religion. On the surface Anne is, as

Marilla sees her, a young "heathen," who must be converted. And, on the surface Marilla succeeds. But Anne is never content with the Presbyterianism of Avonlea and is continually working out her own religion. Indeed, Montgomery herself had become what her clergy would have termed "heretical" in her opinions. She once commented sarcastically that even though she had given up belief in predestination and the Virgin Birth, she still had to believe in spring housecleaning—a significant connection of cultural beliefs and rituals. But had the author wished to confront her own immediate society directly on these issues, she could have created a little scandal and mortified various relatives. Had she written an "adult" novel about someone losing or severely modifying her Presbyterian and Calvinist faith, such a work might have shocked some and attracted others, but the issues it would have raised could have seemed already antique to many readers. When Montgomery gives direct expression to religious doubt or belief, as in her letters to Ephraim Weber, however daring these expressions may have seemed to her, she is merely adopting the most fashionable forms of unbelief of the late Victorian Age. The exploration of such matters had been the business of an earlier generation of writers in Europe and the United States like Mark Twain and Harriet Beecher Stowe. When she writes like an essayist on religion and the unorthodox, Montgomery has nothing new to say; in her fiction she does something more interesting.

In *Anne*, Montgomery is moving the reader, with some subtlety, toward what might be called for want of a better term a "feminine religion." Christianity in *Anne* is not abandoned, as Montgomery herself never entirely abandoned it. But it is reinterpreted, as Anne, surprisingly gifted in the rhetorical art of ecphrasis (voicing a description and analysis), in reading the picture of Christ (p. 104) reinterprets for the reader a religion rendered loveless in Marilla's past. The religion of this novel is not precisely a goddess religion, but Nature is customarily "she," a fact of which the author takes advantage. Entities in nature are consistently personified in the novel by feminine names. Montgomery uses the term "dryad" and later has Anne comment on what the word might mean (p. 141). The terms of ordinary things are subtly marked by a certain femininity. In the very first sentence of the manuscript, Montgomery changes "jewelweed" to "ladies' eardrops" (see n. 2, ch. 1 and Textual Note). Elizabeth Waterston comments that this added detail "suggests that female fashion and elegance also grow in the garden at the crossroads" (*Kindling Spirit*, 52). As soon as she arrives at Green Gables, Anne starts giving plants female names: "Snow Queen" and "Bonny" (p. 81; see also Appendix, "Gardens and Plants").

The material world is full of power—of feminine power—and creativity. The power and beauty of the fertile earth are not disconnected from the majesty and space of the sky. Elizabeth Epperly has observed that Montgomery refers to skies more than anything else. The ditch, the pool, the pond, the dog-rose are related to the purple and rose skies, to the flickering stars. Epperly also notes that Montgomery conversely describes the sky in terms of flowers and gems (*The Fragrance of Sweet-Grass*, 28). In the manuscript we can watch the process as the more conventional adjective "saffron" for a sunset sky is replaced with "marigold" (see Textual Note to p. 62). As above, so below; as in heaven, so on earth.

There is in Montgomery's books no division between Sky God and Earth Mother but one whole. Neither is woman cut off from the transcendent, for the transcendent is *within* Nature, not apart from it. Imagination for the Romantic poets ultimately means the disconnection of the (masculine) mighty spirit from its mere token Platonic emblems in the earth. It is hard for a woman writer to confront this inherent cultural transcendentalism. The traditional view has it that to love Earth means to reject Spirit. Woman is of the Earth, earthy. She is all dull, dead matter. Man is of the Spirit, spiritual, his body a mere unfortunate material accident, his sexuality the result of the lamentable attraction of the wily in-

Alexander Macneill's home, view from the orchard at the back.

ferior female. So runs our cultural story. It would be too much to expect any one woman writer to succeed in changing our collective mind, yet some have made decided inroads, Montgomery among them. All women who read *Anne* at a young age have within themselves a reassurance that they are spiritual and imaginative beings—but also that they do not have to achieve spirit and imagination by foregoing the dear Earth or their femaleness.

Anne is highly spiritual; her eyes are "full of spirit and vivacity" (p. 51) from the moment we first see her. It is curious and disconcerting to find, then, as Wendy Barry has discovered, that the magazine picture of the big-eyed girl with the large flower in her hair, the picture that inspired Montgomery in her

portrayal of Anne, is actually (unknown to Montgomery) a photograph of Evelyn Nesbit, later to figure notoriously in the story of Stanford White's murder (n. 6, ch. 2). Nesbit in soulful pose is herself a reflection of the same elements in the culture as those that affected Montgomery in her production of Anne. The connection of Anne with Evelyn suggests a certain degree of sexuality in Montgomery's heroine and further identifies her as a young woman of the early twentieth century, of a new era of female liberation and idealism. It likewise associates her with an idea of the natural and the service of Nature, an attachment not posed and coy like Nesbit's to her improbable flower.

Anne is the lover and mistress of the earth, reflected in its flush of luxuriant blossom. It used to be fashionable to make fun of Montgomery's descriptions of natural things, a tendency that is lessening now with every passing year. Soon she will be freshly discovered as a "Green" writer. The imaginative recuperation of "greenness" is only one aspect of Montgomery's recapturing of the material cosmos as a space for female spirituality. (Sylvie DuVernet's wild tract, *Theosophical Thoughts,* is the only study thus far to have glimpsed this, however one may assess its readability.) What Montgomery had to say —which is actually quite complex—about the web of phenomena, feelings, and visions we customarily lump under the term "religion" could not have been said in any other kind of novel. In its review of *Anne* the *Toronto Globe* complains about "the craze for problem novels," from which we might calculate the amount of resistance to certain kinds of discussion (see Appendix, "Book Reviews"). Any "problem novel" meant for adults only that tried overtly to deal with the re-creation of a religion hospitable to the feminine, a religion which did not sever material and spiritual life, would no doubt either have been dismissed as a cranky work (sinking without trace) or have drawn angry derision upon itself. What to the Victorians and Edwardians appeared to be a novel fit for the whole family to read actually offered a writer a certain scope. What we now term "children's literature" in fact allows authors to do things they are not allowed to do in adult fiction.

NAMES AND NAMING

One of the touches giving away the religious motif in *Anne of Green Gables* is the name of the girl who is to be the heroine's best friend. We know from the manuscript that Montgomery thought of calling this personage "Laura" and even "Gertrude" before she hit on "Diana." Having struck on that perfect name, Montgomery then immediately proceeded to make the characters comment on it, in a conversation between Anne and Matthew (p. 62):

"Oh!" [said Anne] with a long indrawing of breath. "What a perfectly lovely name!"

"Well now, I dunno. There's something dreadful heathenish about it, seems to me."

The name is "dreadful heathenish." "Great is Diana of the Ephesians!" cry the pagans of Ephesus against Paul (Acts 19:28). Here we find a quiet, comic sign that the author's ideas (particularly regarding women) are going to diverge somewhat from orthodoxy. The character Diana is both a comically realistic and a richly symbolic invention. Waterston points out the Dionysian nature of this Diana and her tea party, showing us that throughout the novel "the richest of reds cluster round Diana" (*Kindling Spirit,* 53). The echo of Anne's name in Diana's suggests that the friend is "a second anima," another aspect of Anne (*Kindling Spirit,* 43). Her red accompaniment expresses the unruly blood and fire found also in Anne's red hair. Diana (so much more generously imagined than the dull Emma Jane, the loyal friend of Rebecca Randall) is an embodiment of female body and female desire. But, like Diana, fierce goddess of chastity and the hunt, of the wild woods and shadowy groves, Anne-Diana will have neither sexuality nor friendship that is not on her own terms. The presence of the divinely named Diana suggests that the female libido is sacred.

Montgomery draws even more powerfully and freely on the names and traditions of Christianity. The first three words of the novel are "Mrs. Rachel Lynde," and we are much taken up with the realistic comedy of the inquisitive married lady of Avonlea who spends her time knitting and peering into her neighbor's activities. She cannot monitor everything; as Elizabeth Epperly comments (*The Fragrance of Sweet Grass,* 19), the brook described in that first paragraph has "dark secrets of pool and cascade" (p. 39) unknown to Mrs. Lynde.

But Mrs. Lynde is not just a figure of conformity. She is commonly seen as the comic obstruction or antagonist to Anne. Indeed that is one of her major functions in the novel, one she fulfills most satisfactorily. So, too, Marilla when we first meet her seems perfectly to fulfill the role of the rural spinster, repressed, soured, and confined. But each of these characters has other levels of significance. Montgomery's experience, starved childhood and all, did not alone make *Anne*. The strength of *Anne of Green Gables* comes partly from what might be called its multilayeredness. Rachel Lynde is the stout neighbor, the realistic country woman, talkative and limited. One of her closest literary relatives is Mrs. Poyser of George Eliot's *Adam Bede*, a novel of which Montgomery was fond. George Eliot's Mrs. Poyser informed Montgomery that country women and their style of speech could be interesting in fiction. But Rachel Lynde is no mere copy, nor is she devoid of larger life.

Mrs. Lynde's name, after all, is *Rachel*, evocative of the beloved of Jacob, who served twice seven years for her. She is *the* mother in Israel, the mother of Joseph. Rachel is an emblem of motherhood and female power, of femininity under the old law. Mrs. Lynde's obesity (at one level merely a comic defect) is a symptom of her power, a sign of her fertile beneficence as the Earth Mother, the great Woman from whom we all come. Patricia Parker has shown in *Literary Fat Ladies* (1987) how such ladies generate stories and stand for the generation of story. Mrs. Lynde broods over the beginning of the story, an immense comic female presence. Her knitting with the "cotton warp" (a thread designed for weaving) identifies her as one of the Fates—the most agreeable one, Clotho, who presides over birth and new beginnings. Mrs. Rachel Lynde, named thus even though she is not a widow, is a womb of beginning; she holds the promise of story and unstoppable flow, multiple pattern, as she knits her endless stream of patterned quilts. Her observation of what *is* in the world turns phenomenon into narrative, and thus into story. Fat ladies like Mrs. Lynde love words and are not easily repressed by the words of others. Anne, after all, finds it easy to make up with Mrs. Lynde after they have thoroughly offended each other through words, but the girl finds it impossible to make up through words with acerbic, thin, nonverbal Mrs. Barry. This character is the repository of the negative traits of grandmother Macneill. Like Maud's

grandmother (see, e.g., *SJ* I: 301–302), Mrs. Barry disapproves of a girl's reading (pp. 137–38) and is inimical to the flow of language and indeed to all story.

Like Anne and like Nature, Mrs. Lynde exhibits the female power to create design. Rachel has (even in a kind of parody) some of Anne's own qualities of quick temper, sensitivity to insult, curiosity, and artistic sense. It is she who comes to the rescue of both Anne and Matthew in making Anne's first pretty dress for her. Rachel's advice is sometimes based on views that are harsh or passé, as in her recommendation of "a fair-sized birch switch" (p. 116), but she demonstrates good common sense when she advises Marilla to yield to Anne on the point of staying away from school.

If Rachel is a powerful figure of motherhood, so too, paradoxically, is Marilla the spinster. For her name is a variant of Mary, and she is a Virgin Mary who does indeed become blessed in her (adoptive) progeny, the prodigious Anne. And Anne herself is also named after a mother. In Christian tradition, the mother of the Virgin Mary is St. Anne, a figure of whom Montgomery must surely have been aware, as French-Canadian Roman Catholics in the Maritime Provinces were and are much devoted to St. Anne. Anne, the grandmother of Christ, has in effect the same name as the mother of the prophet Samuel, the barren Hannah who gives birth to the miraculous prophesied child. It is of course Marilla, apparently doomed to a barren life, who gives metaphorical birth to a miraculous prophetic *female* child. Anne and Marilla keep switching natures as mother and child, mother and daughter, Demeter and Koré. It is a significant sign of their equality that Marilla refuses to have Anne call her either "Miss Cuthbert" or "Aunt Marilla." Unconsciously farsighted, Marilla repudiates social formality and class distinctions (including those between married and unmarried, and between generations) while also fending off fake family ties—as an aunt she would not be as close to Anne as she actually becomes. They call each other

"Marilla" and "Anne," with a freedom not allowed in that era to children with legitimate parents or guardians. The Child is Mother to the Woman. Anne the child is not only the mother of her more mature self but also the mother of Marilla. And Marilla becomes the mother under the New Law, the law of love rather than of authority.

At the center of the novel, then, there is a trilogy of three powerful women, three fates, three mothers: Rachel, Mary/Marilla, and Anne. These three Biblical Mothers are joined in a quaternity by the fourth important female we encounter: the comic, dark-haired embodiment of the goddess Diana. The friendship between Anne and Diana is genuine, deep, lasting. It will survive their marriages. Long before Virginia Woolf suggested that "Chloe liked Olivia," women writers had depicted female friendship in fiction: Anne Shirley and Diana Barry complement each other very well indeed.

Anne herself is, however, both Venus (under whose great "crystal-white star" she comes to Avonlea) and Diana of the grove, who sings to herself "with a wreath of rice lilies in her hair as if she were some wild divinity of the shadowy places" (p. 170). (These phrases were added by Montgomery in her first revision of the manuscript.) Anne forgets to return to school on time while she is acting like a votary of Diana or as Diana herself. That Anne could "run like a deer" (a Diana-characteristic defined in terms of an animal sacred to that goddess's hunting) only adds to her trouble. When her crude teacher makes her sit with a boy, he is insulting her with a joke against her sexual nature, an affront that would be most offensive to a true Diana. Anne's fierce, cool chastity, suited to a Diana votary, is related to her self-respect and is gradually tempered. We may notice with a start, near the end of the book, that Anne's cool and maidenly eastern chamber has been invaded by Cupidons. When she is sixteen she owns a "gilt-framed mirror with chubby pink cupids and purple grapes painted over its arched top" (p. 346).

At the core of the novel, then, we have the power-ful trinity Rachel-Marilla/Mary-Anne, balanced by the powerful pagan female presence Diana to make a quaternity. Beyond these stands the iron-willed, peppery, slightly glamorous, prophetic *Joseph*ine Barry. Named after the Old Testament hero, Aunt Josephine is a Joseph figure of wealth, status, and practical judgment, an unclaimed relative who at last claims kindship with the "Anne-girl." This Josephine is caricatured in the coarsely practical and malicious Josie Pye, the heroine's antagonist. Matthew, who bears the name of the first Evangelist, ironically has to communicate to all the primary four women, tongue-tied and shy as he is. It is Matthew, as Wendy Barry reminds us, who does not go upstairs even in his own house, thus living literally on another level from the women, but functioning as their medium of connection. Matthew helps bring them together and make an harmonious narrative where there might otherwise be only friction and separation. Matthew modulates individuality so that it is not utter separateness. He joins the quaternity, making of it a pentagon, a magical pentangle that cannot be broken into. Only after Matthew's death can Gilbert enter the pentangle, and it is then that he is accepted as the lover.

Gilbert's name is not a sacred one, being neither biblical nor mythological, though it is the name of a saint. His name speaks of masculinity and chivalry and could even evoke danger if we were to think of the aggressive and sophisticated Knight Templar, Sir Brian de Bois-Guilbert, of *Ivanhoe*. But his last name makes him a pure figure of happiness. In the manuscript, Montgomery wrote the name as "Blithe" and veiled its meaning only lightly by substitution of the "y." Gilbert as love object, the heterosexual Other, functions in Anne much as many female characters have in men's novels, as a figure of the desired named after some lovely quality. But he is also the challenger of Anne. Part of his chivalrous burden is to fight her so that she proves her own intellectual and moral strength. Anne accordingly contests with Gilbert and is therefore stimulated to achievement in school and examinations. Far from drawing back behind a boy in maidenly modesty, she is challenged to prove herself and succeed. Gilbert generously makes of her in effect a woman warrior.

This novel alerts us throughout to the meaning of names, for Anne is so conscious of them. Discontented (unwisely) with her own powerful name, she wishes to be called Cordelia, Elaine, Rosamond, or Geraldine. She is unknowingly fortunate in not being called any of these, for they are on the whole bad-luck names. Cordelia, King Lear's youngest daughter, is a girl-child thoroughly disinherited by the patriarchal system of her time, and then murdered as a result of her father's sins and follies. Elaine, the Lily Maid of Astolat in the Arthurian story, fell hopelessly in love with Launcelot and died of thwarted passion. Fair Rosamond, daughter of Walter [Anne's father's name] de Clifford, became mistress to King Henry II and was famously murdered by her jealous rival, queen Elinor. And Geraldine is the name of the mysterious witch woman, or lamia, in Samuel Taylor Coleridge's "Christabel": "My sire is of a noble line/And my name is Geraldine" ("Christabel" II: ll. 79–80). Anne likes names such as Fitz-Gerald, which speak of a "noble line" (i.e., a noble Irish-Norman line). She yearns after Norman names that bespeak aristocracy. The author herself was happy that her own father's name was aristocratic: "Montgomery" is a noble, Norman-derived name. Anne has something of her wish granted in that her parents' first names, Bertha and Walter, are European, noble, medieval, aristocratic. Yet "Walter Shirley," if indeed an aristocratic name, is a puzzling choice. This name belonged to an eighteenth-century hymn-writer, and Montgomery may have picked it up from a hymn book, but this hymn-writer was a brother of Laurence Shirley, Earl of Ferrars, a "belted earl" (see p. 53) who made history in being the only aristocrat hanged for murder; thus, the name Shirley has unconventional if not wild associations.

Anne herself is a wild aristocrat, one who eludes the decorous, passive misery of an Elaine or a Cor-

delia. If she is a noble Shirley, she is also Anne Surely, mothering her own confidence. Unlike Montgomery's golden good girl "Carol Golden," who had to die so that Anne could be born, Anne does not choose self-sacrifice. She is truly a twentieth-century and not a nineteenth-century heroine in her consistent preference for self-nurture and suspicion of self-sacrifice. Anne may do good—even noble—things, but she is not given to martyring herself. When she acts like a martyr in her forced confession (p. 153) she is really trying to find her way to the picnic and the ice cream. Likewise, when she decides to give up temporarily the dream of college in favor of looking after Marilla and Green Gables, she is doing what she most profoundly wants to do. And, as is not the case with the domestic Carol Golden, Anne's caretaking takes the form of getting a job. She always values her own self-esteem and dignity and, as moral agent, always chooses what deeply pleases her. Anne respects pleasure (including ice-cream). The road she treads is not the *via negativa* but the White Way of Delight, the road of joy. Anne is a provocative anomaly, a heavenly aristocrat in a cheap, tight dress, a virgin mother in an infant state, a Persephone with red hair.

RED HAIR

Anne's notorious red hair is one of the novel's most important emblems. This red hair singles her out. Her red hair is the more innocent equivalent of Hester Prynne's red "A" in Hawthorne's *The Scarlet Letter* (a novel Montgomery admired; see *SJ* I: 133). It is a sign of a superabundance treated as a defect, the proclamation of her difference. The red hair, Mrs. Lynde says, bespeaks a fiery temper, and Anne is indeed passionate—she does not give up her right to anger. Over the centuries, red hair has been used to indicate a bad, reprehensible, or at least unconforming character. (Judas, according to legend, had red hair.) In women particularly, red hair like red clothing, is emblematic of sexual passion.

Anne's hair shows that she is not going to be

"ladylike" as Avonlea understands the term. There is this intractable difference, a fiery core. Who can doubt that she is rebellious and will become sexually passionate when passion is finally aroused? Her red hair is a reclamation of her womanliness, defiant and unmutilated. It proves rather dreadful when she tries to tame her hair by dying it "raven black" (p. 290), to match Diana's. She succeeds only in turning it green, a color that seems appropriate for an earth maiden and vegetation deity living in *Green* Gables. But when her hair is chopped off, we lose a little of the Anne we knew. The sympathetic child reader may hope that Anne will be able to lose her red hair, but the adult reader can never really want her fiery hair to turn into the vague "auburn" she yearns for.

Anne's red hair is certainly a sign of her difference from others, yet this is paradoxical, for in some respects her hair is a sign that she belongs to her tribe—she just bears its standard more vividly than others do. For who has red hair but the descendants of the red-haired Franks? The Norseman (and the Normans) once conquered the British Isles, and their medieval depredations along the coast of Scotland and Ireland left red-haired progeny in their wake. Historically, the prejudice against red hair in the latter part of the nineteenth century has a class bias. Red-haired Irish immigrants in the streets of Boston and New York, London and Toronto, were visible signs of an immigrant minority despised as "low." Closer to home, even at Prince of Wales College, Maud Montgomery herself had teased a classmate, Austin Laird, about his red hair (Rubio and Waterston, *Writing a Life*, 26). And Montgomery's other works exhibit a variety of attitudes to red hair. *In Magic for Marigold* (1929), Marigold's Uncle Klondike has "his mane of tawny hair and the red-gold beard which had caused a sentimental . . . lady . . . to say that he made her think of those splendid old Vikings" (ch. 1). But in *Pat of Silver Bush*, red hair is associated with Irishness and is "low;" in that novel the Irish dognapper is a vulgar drunkard "with a

bushy red head and a week's growth of red whisker" (ch. 12).

Anne Shirley has not only telling red hair but gray-green eyes that look green in some lights. She is thus doubly witchlike, a fairy or changeling, as fairy-folk have green eyes rather than an honest blue or brown. Her coloring, form, and eyes thus bring Anne close to another orphan character, Thackeray's Becky Sharp in *Vanity Fair* (1847–1848). Becky has "sandy" (i.e., reddish) hair (which she is careful to lighten toward blond during her social climb) and green eyes that are "large, odd and attractive" (*Vanity Fair*, ch. 2). Becky's hair and eyes signal that she is the odd one out, the witch-woman who acts on her own and knows too much. She too has pretensions to Norman grandeur: "'I'm a Montmorency' . . . she spoke with ever so slight a foreign accent" (ch. 145). In *Anne of Windy Poplars* (1936) Anne calls her student Jen Pringle "a green-eyed bantling who looks as *Becky Sharp* must have looked

The Old Presbyterian Church, Cavendish.

at fourteen" (ch. 2). Evidently, by the 1930s L. M. Montgomery has in some sense made herself "forget" Anne's own disconcerting resemblance to Becky Sharp.

Both Becky and Anne trouble their society, for they know too much, though Anne's knowledge is imaginative and spiritual. Anne brings to Avonlea a revivifying reminder of its Celtic identity in her red hair. Avonlea has partly lost sight of its own identity and inheritance, and thus some of its vision. The name itself is important and asks to be considered. "Avonlea" as a name sounds English, to be sure; it sounds like the "lea" (meadow) on the "lee" (sheltered side) of the Avon, the river associated with Shakespeare's birthplace pointed out by Elizabeth Waterston in *Kindling Spirit* (48). There is also a Canadian Avon, a beautiful tidal river in the heart of Nova Scotia, the neighboring province that is Anne's birthplace. But Montgomery's "Avonlea" is almost an anagram for "Avalon," a Celtic place name sometimes said to mean "land of apples." In the story of Arthur, as told by both Malory and Tennyson, the wounded Arthur after his crushing defeat in battle is taken away by three queens on a barge. In his last speech to Sir Bedivere, in "The Passing of Arthur" (ll. 424–33), Tennyson has the king say that he is going

> . . . to the island-valley of Avilion;
> Where falls not hail, or rain, nor any snow,
> Nor ever wind blows loudly; but it lies
> Deep-meadow'd, happy, fair with orchard lawns
> And bowery hollows crown'd with summer sea,
> Where I will heal me of my grievous wound.
> ("The Passing of Arthur," ll.424–432)

Avonlea (and the Island of Prince Edward) certainly has hail, rain, snow, and wind. Montgomery loves all these phenomena and would deprive no good land of them. But "Avonlea," which certainly is a land of apples, is a vision of "Avalon," the mystic Celtic valley where one can be healed of a grievous

wound. The first descriptions of it, in the springtime flush of June, show it in its Tennysonian beauty. The Island that Anne first sees, the "bloomiest place," is indeed "deep-meadow'd, happy, fair with orchard lawns/And bowery hallows crown'd with summer sea." Anne and her author thus give back to Victoria's stolid Island of Prince Edward its Celtic undersong.

IMAGINATION

Lucy Maud Montgomery seems to endorse Anne's verbal and visionary quality as restoring an imaginative freedom to Avonlea. Yet, if Montgomery has little trouble in representing Anne's possession of the power of the word, she is less certain when it comes to dealing with Anne's imagination. How powerful ought a female imagination to be?

In Chapter 20, entitled "A Good Imagination Gone Wrong," Anne's *good* imagination has apparently "gone wrong." Here Anne and Diana, in conjuring up the specters of the Haunted Wood, have evidently merely gone in for the staple materials of lurid magazine stories derived from the "Gothic" tradition: "There's a white lady walks along the brook . . . and wrings her hands and utters wailing cries. . . . And the ghost of a little murdered child haunts the corner up by Idlewild. . . . And there's a headless man stalks up and down the path" (p. 230).

This is the stuff of legend as well as of magazine serials. The episode of the Haunted Wood in *Anne* is based on Montgomery's own experience, but in recounting it in *The Alpine Path* she blames the manufacture of ghosts on the *male* imagination. When Maud was eight, two boys her age had come to board at her grandparents' home. It was these male playmates, Wellington and David, who supplied the fictional material, according to the adult Montgomery:

> Well and Dave had a firm and rooted belief in ghosts. I used to argue with them over it with the depressing result that I became infected myself. . . .

The Haunted Wood was a harmless, pretty spruce grove.... None of us really believed at first that the grove was haunted, or that the mysterious "white things" ... were ought but the creations of our own fancy. But our minds were weak and our imaginations strong. (*Alpine Path*, 30)

The work of composing ghosts is, however, attributed in *Anne of Green Gables* entirely to females, Anne and Diana. The background of cultural belief is also silenced; for instance, Marilla interrupts Anne's tale of Avonlea people who have experienced ghosts. Such material is not to be investigated or even talked of, apparently. In other works, like *The Story Girl* (1901), Montgomery treats legend, popular belief and folktale with more respect. In *Emily of New Moon* (1923) she admits "supernatural" material into the main narrative and lets the heroine be gifted with "second sight." But in *Anne* such material is invoked only to be banned.

Psychology might urge that Anne's own unhappy early experiences must have a vent somewhere, some sort of representation. The soul shut within itself, as in Tennyson's "The Palace of Art" (see Appendix, "Literary Allusion"), will stumble on phantasms and murdered thoughts, and Anne's ghosts (the wailing white lady, the murdered child) are convincingly appropriate to a girl-child who lost her mother at birth and whose own identity has been hard-pressed. We may simply find Anne's imaginings totally funny and wildly unreal, but if we do not have such a simple reaction, we may well feel that the ending of the chapter is unsatisfactory, with no place left for Anne's perturbed spirits.

Anne's source of illumination is her imagination, so we are given to understand, and Montgomery urges us to prize the female imagination. Yet, as Patricia Spacks has pointed out in *The Female Imagination* (1975), imagination in women is perpetually represented as a problem. If woman is allowed an imagination, it must be a nice one. We remember how Louisa May Alcott's Jo March is reproved and

reformed by Professor Bhaer, who objects strongly to her writing the kind of popular Gothic tales Alcott also wrote (see Madeleine Stern's collection of Alcott's stories, *Behind a Mask*). Montgomery herself wrote for magazine publication some eerie tales of the supernatural (see the stories collected by Rea Wilmshurst in *Among the Shadows: Tales from the Darker Side,* 1990). To imagine ghosts is one thing; to show a girl in the process of such wild and forbidden imagining seems to be another, more culturally perplexing thing. We never know what Anne is to *do* with her imagination. Manifestation of that imagination consists of the employment of comically second-hand literary finery, the sort of stuff any young mind must seize upon, but we are persuaded that Anne has a real and creative imagination beyond what both the author and reader diagnose as borrowed stuff. Yet Anne is not to be an artist or an author. The point of her story is the success with which she rises within her own normal culture, without doing anything so outré and abnormal as being a writer. In the Emily Byrd Starr books, which are post–World War I productions, Montgomery in a challenging way portrays the girl as developing writer. Emily as a child is deep and determined. Unlike Anne, she is not sweet. As Montgomery knew, a writer is ever something of an alien, and Anne's story must be her accommodation to her new home. She must come to belong to her community of Avonlea as Emily never belongs to Blair Water.

Anne's citizenship in Avonlea depends on her negotiating successfully with reality, but without losing her individual insight. Some important sections of *Anne* are concerned with the boundary line between truth and fiction—a line notoriously hard to draw in itself but comically so in novels that are themselves fictions. Anne luxuriates in fantasy, expressing wishes for pleasure and power, to comic effect: "There is a couch all heaped with gorgeous silken cushions ... and I am reclining gracefully on it.... I am tall and regal" (p. 108). A tendency toward the grandiose was something Maud Montgomery had encountered within herself and certainly seems exhibited in her father, the "Monty" who called his plain little Prince Albert house "Eglintoune Villa," as the credulous Maud explained to Penzie Macneill, "after our ancestors the earls of Eglintoune" (Bolger, *The Years Before "Anne,"* 92). The older Montgomery channeled her matured sense of the ridiculousness of such pretension into the comedy of *Anne.* Yet there is a positive side to Anne's power of imagining she is the Lady Cordelia Fitzgerald, for such amplifications of her being have prevented her being crushed. Writers were typically apt to attribute such imaginings to servant girls and to mock them for such nonsense and getting "above their station." Montgomery makes us feel the value of such exalting fantasy. Anne is a kind of "female Quixote" to whom the fictional offers, in one of her favorite phrases, "scope for imagination," a phrase in which perhaps the emphasis should go on "scope" even more than "imagination."

The most satisfactory image for resolving the tension between reality and fiction, leaving the boundary between them still mysterious, is the central prize and object of quest in Chapter 14, "Anne's Confession." Observe the language in which the amethyst is spoken of in Anne's delusive "confession," her fiction:

> Oh, how it did shine in the sunlight! And then, when I was leaning over the bridge, it just slipped through my fingers—so—and went down—down—down, all purply-sparkling, and sank forevermore beneath the Lake of Shining Waters (p. 153).

Montgomery's fondness for and use of colors has been dealt with by Epperly and Waterston, who note her fondness for purple and for purple flowers like violets. But the purple amethyst is also a shining, glittering spectacle that mingles pure color with movement and scintillation, "all purply-sparkling." This is the stone it is ultimately impossible to re-capture, the precious life that slips through one's fingers and disappears. Yet it is never really lost but is, like Anne-Persephone herself, restored. In its purple sparkle the amethyst seems the image of enduring and unquenchable imagination itself. Marilla has linked the amethyst with the dead, and her worship of the dead needs to be broken into, the gem rebaptized in the water of life. But that Marilla possesses the amethyst at all marks her as possessing, if only potentially, the saving quality of true vision, spiritual insight.

The amethyst is one of the favorite precious stones of fiction. It is found in one of the earliest surviving Western novels, Heliodorus' *Aithiopika* (c. A.D. 300), where it is among the valuable gems that are the inheritance of the heroine and is traded off for her release from enslavement. This heroine's gem is set in a royal ring mounted with an Ethiopian amethyst of purest water—deep, sparkling fresh as springtime, with a pastoral scene carved upon it (*Aithiopika,* Book V, ch. 14). The amethyst was supposed to have been thus named because it keeps its wearer *amethysos,* neither drunken nor hallucinating. As it prevents intoxication, Diana should have been wearing it when she drank the currant wine. Anne should have carried the amethyst into the Haunted Wood. The amethyst wards off illusion. The amethyst's owner is not deceived and keeps a clear head and spirit, but the amethyst itself may be the bearer of fictional imagery. When she has "lost" the amethyst, Marilla loses her sense of reality in accusing Anne, then regains her senses when it is restored. Similarly, in George Eliot's *Middlemarch,* Dorothea rejects amethysts in favor of the more valuable emeralds, which represent chastity and aspiration. She gives the amethysts to her practical sister Celia, but the deluded Dorothea ("Dodo") should have kept the amethysts, for she is soon self-deluded into a bad marriage. The amethyst—sparkling purple, alive, promising, deep, radiant—represents the possibility of a radiant imagination that does not degenerate into the misty delusions that drag women down.

The purple sparkle of imagination counteracts the dangerous allurements of death. Part of the comic depth of *Anne* lies in its exhibiting the self-satisfactions of a culture over-responsive to death. If Anne is given to fantasy, so is her world. But Anne's imaginings are largely of life, while the world manufactures fantasies of the moribund. The poems in the children's school readers are almost unrelievedly dismal, teaching lists of melancholy vocabulary words such as "anguish" and "mortal." Anne revealingly offers to recite "The Dog at his Master's Grave" at Sunday School: "It isn't a really truly religious piece of poetry, but it's so sad and melancholy that it might as well be" (p. 132)—in a telling recognition of a connection in gloom between the approved literature and approved religion. The same lust after deathliness is found in the popular songs of the era (see various Notes and Appendix, "Music and Elocution.").

Contemplating graves, singing sadly of all earthly hope departed—these are the recreations of a late-Victorian world that is, at least in theory, more than half in love with easeful death. Anne borrows that culture's language temporarily when she is separated from Diana: "In school I can look at her and muse over days departed" (p. 193). But Anne with her Persephone-life perpetually rises up from death and refuses to give it overlordship. She learns "Nelly of the Hazel Dell" from Diana but sings it, paradoxically, "with a vigour and expression" while at her green work of shelling peas in the kitchen (p. 149). The vigorous, food-involved contemplation of Nelly's grave is a deeply comic oxymoron. Marilla's brooch is a more subtle one, with lively amethysts surrounded by the dead hair of a departed loved one. Anne praises the stones, wisely saying nothing about the hair (p. 148), nor does the hair figure in her fiction about the brooch. Why seek ye the living among the dead? or hold the dead among the living? By the time she has found the brooch again, Marilla has begun to learn detachment from the way of death, a detachment inculcated by the author.

The comic idyll does not endorse all the qualities of Avonlea, for Avonlea itself must change, and not only Avonlea but the greater world around it. Anne's world at large—including even the nineteenth century's version of Tin Pan Alley—has adored the melancholy. Schoolbooks, popular songs, and even a poet laureate collude in asking Anne—and us—to admire the entrancements of death and to be ourselves entranced. But Nelly of the Hazel Dell and the unfortunate Lily Maid and the grave among the "Snowy snowy daisies" must yield their power. Lilies, daisies, and hazels survive, as do the Lake of Shining Waters and the White Way of Delight. The Book of Anne tells us that the divine is ever-present. The spiritual moping that passes for religion and love must be abjured. There is no lost good time, no grave at which one must mourn forever, like the sadly faithful dog. The good time is now. Persephone returns.

FURTHER READING

All works by or about Lucy Maud Montgomery are listed in the main Bibliography at the end of the book.

Louisa May Alcott. *Behind a Mask: The Unknown Thrillers of Louisa May Alcott.* Ed. by Madeleine B. Stern. New York: Morrow, 1975.

Sandra Campbell and Lorraine McMullen, eds. *New Women: Short Stories by Canadian Women, 1900–1920.* Canadian Short Story Library, Series 2, no. 14. Ottawa: University of Ottawa, 1991.

George Eliot. *Middlemarch.* Ed. and with introduction by David Carroll. Oxford: Oxford Univ. Press, 1988.

Nathaniel Hawthorne. *The Scarlet Letter: A Romance.* Ed. by Seymour Gross. New York: Norton, 1988.

Heliodorus of Emesa. *Aithiopika. (Les Ethiopiques).* Ed. by R.M. Rattenbury, T.W. Lumb, and J. Maillon. 2nd ed. 3 vols. Paris: Belles Lettres, 1960.

Archibald MacMechan. *Headwaters of Canadian Literature.* Toronto: McClelland & Stewart, 1924.

Nellie McClung. *Sowing Seeds in Danny*. Toronto: Ryerson, 1908; Reprinted 1926.

Patricia Parker. *Literary Fat Ladies: Rhetoric, Gender Property*. London: Methuen, 1987.

Patricia Meyer Spacks. *The Female Imagination*. New York: Knopf, 1975.

Harriet Beecher Stowe. *Oldtown Folks*, in *Harriet Beecher Stowe: Three Novels*. Ed. by Kathryn Kish Sklar. New York: Library of America, 1982.

Alfred, Lord Tennyson. *Poems and Plays*. New York: Oxford Univ. Press, 1967.

William Makepeace Thackeray. *Vanity Fair*. Ed. and with introduction by J.I.M. Stewart. London: Penguin, 1985.

THE ANNOTATED
ANNE OF
GREEN GABLES

"There's no scope for imagination in patchwork." Illustration by Sybil Tawse, from the 1933 edition of Anne of Green Gables.

"The good stars met in your horoscope,
Made you of spirit and fire and dew."
— *Browning*★

To the Memory of My Father and Mother★★

★This epigraph to *Anne of Green Gables* is from Robert Browning's "Evelyn Hope," ll. 19-20. First published in *Men and Women,* 1855.

★★Montgomery's dedication for the original edition refers to John Hugh Montgomery (1841–1900) and Clara Woolner Macneill (1853–1876). See Introduction. The author here reminds us of her own orphan state.

EXPLANATORY NOTES
AND KEY TO ABBREVIATIONS

All Bible quotations are taken from the King James Version, the edition that the author and her characters knew.

All definitions are taken from the *Oxford English Dictionary,* unless otherwise stated.

All Canadian information comes from the *Canadian Encyclopedia.*

AP. The Alpine Path: The Story of My Career. L. M. Montgomery. Don Mills, Ont.: Fitzhenry and Whiteside, 1975.

CCL. Canadian Children's Literature / Littérature canadienne pour la jeunesse: A Journal of Criticism and Review. Department of English, University of Guelph, Guelph, Ontario.

OED. Oxford English Dictionary. 2nd Ed. Oxford: Oxford University Press, 1989.

SJ. The Selected Journals of L. M. Montgomery, Volumes I (1899–1910), II (1910–1921), and III (1921–1929). Toronto, Ont.: Oxford University Press Canada, 1985, 1987, 1992.

CHAPTER 1

MRS. RACHEL LYNDE
IS SURPRISED

MRS. RACHEL LYNDE lived just where the Avonlea[1] main road dipped down into a little hollow, fringed with alders and ladies' eardrops[2] and traversed by a brook that had its source away back in the woods of the old Cuthbert place; it was reputed to be an intricate, headlong brook in its earlier course through those woods, with dark secrets of pool and cascade. But by the time it reached Lynde's Hollow[3] it was a quiet well-conducted little stream,[4] for not even a brook could run past Mrs. Rachel Lynde's door without due regard for decency and decorum; it probably was conscious that Mrs. Rachel was sitting at her window, keeping a sharp eye on everything that passed, from brooks and children up, and that if she noticed anything odd or out of place she would never rest until she had ferreted out the whys and wherefores thereof.

There are plenty of people in Avonlea and out of it who can attend closely to their neighbours' business by dint of neglecting their own; but Mrs. Rachel Lynde was one of those capable creatures who can manage their own concerns and those of other folks into the bargain. She was a notable[5] housewife; her work was always done and well done; she "ran" the Sewing Circle, helped run the Sunday School, and

1. The town of Avonlea is based on the author's childhood home: Cavendish (*SJ* II [Jan. 27, 1911]: 38). See also Introduction.

2. *Impatiens capensis*, Balsaminaceae. Also called jewelweed or wild touch-me-not. Of the balsam family, bearing yellow or orange-yellow flowers with short spurs and seed pods that split at the touch when ripe. See Textual Note.

3. "Mrs. Rachel Lynde's house, with the brook below, was drawn from Pierce Macneill's house" (SJ II [Jan. 27, 1911]: 38). See Appendix, "Geography."

4. The image in this passage seems influenced by Alfred, Lord Tennyson's poem "The Brook"

(1855) with its inset quatrains beginning "I come from haunts of coot and hern, / I make a sudden sally, / And sparkle out among the fern, / To bicker down a valley" (ll. 24–27). See also quotations p. 327, n. 1; p. 370, n.2. "The Brook" was in the *Fifth Royal Reader* (21–22).

5. Managing, bustling, active in housekeeping.

6. The chief organizations for women in the Presbyterian church. After her marriage, Montgomery found one of the great sources of tedium in her existence as a minister's wife to be the necessity of attending meetings of the Foreign Missions Auxiliary: "We meet — the President . . . opens with a hymn and follows it with a stereotyped prayer. After a little business someone reads a dull chapter out of some book on missions, we sing another hymn, take up a collection and go home. The only part I enjoy is the collection. I like to give the money—and it comes near the last!" (*SJ* II [Oct. 24, 1911]: 91). The Foreign Missions Auxiliaries sometimes engaged in sewing for the "heathen," but the Church Aid Society was even more practical, as its contributions went to charity recipients closer to home.

7. A particular kind of yarn sold in stores and identified as such on the label. When it first came in, in the 1820s, this very soft yarn was used principally for weaving. What Mrs. Lynde makes is, strictly speaking, not a quilt but a bedspread. The common way of making such spreads with cotton or other

was the strongest prop of the Church Aid Society and Foreign Missions Auxiliary.[6] Yet with all this Mrs. Rachel found abundant time to sit for hours at her kitchen window, knitting "cotton warp" quilts[7]—she had knitted sixteen of them, as Avonlea housekeepers were wont to tell in awed voices—and keeping a sharp eye on the main road that crossed the hollow and wound up the steep red hill beyond. Since Avonlea occupied a little triangular peninsula jutting out into the Gulf of St. Lawrence,[8] with water on two sides of it, anybody who went out of it or into it had to pass over that hill road and so run the unseen gauntlet of Mrs. Rachel's all-seeing eye.

She was sitting there one afternoon in early June. The sun was coming in at the window warm and bright; the orchard on the slope below the house was in a bridal flush of pinky-white bloom, hummed over by a myriad of bees. Thomas Lynde—a meek little man whom Avonlea people called "Rachel Lynde's husband"—was sowing his late turnip seed on the hill field beyond the barn; and Matthew Cuthbert ought to have been sowing his on the big red brook field away over by Green Gables. Mrs. Rachel knew that he ought because she had heard him tell Peter Morrison the evening before in William J. Blair's store over at Carmody[9] that he meant to sow his turnip seed the next afternoon. Peter had asked him, of course, for Matthew Cuthbert had never been known to volunteer information about anything in his whole life.

And yet here was Matthew Cuthbert, at half-past three on the afternoon of a busy day, placidly driving over the hollow and up the hill; moreover, he wore a white collar and his best suit of clothes, which was plain proof that he was going out of Avonlea; and he had the buggy and the sorrel mare,[10] which betokened that he was going a considerable distance. Now, where was Matthew Cuthbert going and why was he going there?

Had it been any other man in Avonlea Mrs. Rachel, deftly putting this and that together, might have given a pretty good guess as to both questions. But Matthew so rarely went from home that it must be something pressing and unusual which was taking him; he was the shyest man alive and hated to have to go among strangers or to any place where he might have to talk. Matthew dressed up with a white collar and driving in a buggy was something that didn't happen often. Mrs. Rachel, ponder as she might, could make nothing of it, and her afternoon's enjoyment was spoiled.

"I'll just step over to Green Gables after tea and find out from Marilla where he's gone and why," the worthy woman finally concluded. "He doesn't generally go to town this time of year and he *never* visits; if he'd run out of turnip seed he wouldn't dress up and take the buggy to go for more; he wasn't driving fast enough to be going for a doctor. Yet something must have happened since last night to start him off. I'm clean puzzled, that's what, and I won't know a minute's peace of mind or conscience until I know what has taken Matthew Cuthbert out of Avonlea to-day."

Accordingly after tea Mrs. Rachel set out; she had not far to go; the big, rambling, orchard-embowered house where the Cuthberts lived was a scant quarter of a mile up the road from Lynde's Hollow. To be sure, the long lane made it a good deal further. Matthew Cuthbert's father, as shy and silent as his son after him, had got as far away as he possibly could from his fellow men without actually retreating into the woods when he founded his homestead. Green Gables was built at the furthest edge of his cleared land, and there it was to this day, barely visible from the main road along which all the other Avonlea houses were so sociably situated. Mrs. Rachel Lynde did not call living in such a place *living* at all.

"It's just *staying*, that's what," she said as she stepped along the deep-rutted, grassy lane bordered with wild rose bushes.

thread is to knit squares on the bias and stitch them together, but Mrs. Lynde's quilt knitting involves elaborate lacy patterns. Montgomery herself knitted three such patterned quilts (see Appendix, "Homemade Artifacts").

Rachel Lynde is an expert in making patchwork quilts which are made up of three layers: the top, the batting, and the back. All are quilted, or stitched together. The top can be either patchwork or appliqué. She gives Anne a patchwork quilt and lends her five more during her college days. Diana on the occasion of her wedding is given "one of her beloved knitted quilts of the 'tobacco stripe' pattern" (*Anne of the Island*, chs. 16, 29). And Mrs. Lynde more than lives up to her promise of giving Anne a quilt when she marries (*Island*, ch. 29): "I'm going to give Anne two of my cotton warp spreads . . . a tobacco-stripe one and an apple-leaf one. . . . I don't believe there's anything prettier for a spare-room bed than a nice apple-leaf spread, that's what" (*Anne's House of Dreams*, ch. 2).

8. See Appendix, "Geography."

9. An imaginary name for a place based on the real Stanley. See Appendix, "Geography."

Cotton knit quilt, Anne's Room, P.E.I. National Park.

10. The North American buggy is a light one-horse vehicle with four wheels. Matthew's buggy is drawn by a mare (a female horse) of a red or bright chestnut color. The sorrel mare would have presented a smarter appearance than the heavier horses used for farmwork. People on P.E.I., like those in many rural farming communities, considered their horses important, like part of the family. It is odd, therefore, that in a novel in which even the geraniums have names the sorrel mare does not. (John Robert Cousins, "Horses in the Folklife of Western Prince Edward Island").

11. The source of this particular proverb is not known, but it bears relation to many proverbial statements about immunity to pain being based upon proximity to it. Rachel Lynde's statement here depends on a familiar prejudicial belief that the Irish are particularly prone to criminal activity, hence immune to the pain of being

"It's no wonder Matthew and Marilla are both a little odd, living away back here by themselves. Trees aren't much company, though dear knows if they were there'd be enough of them. I'd ruther look at people. To be sure, they seem contented enough; but then, I suppose, they're used to it. A body can get used to anything, even to being hanged, as the Irishman said."[11]

With this Mrs. Rachel stepped out of the lane into the backyard of Green Gables. Very green and neat and precise was that yard, set about on one side with great patriarchal willows and on the other with prim Lombardies.[12] Not a stray stick nor stone was to be seen, for Mrs. Rachel would have seen it if there had been. Privately she was of the opinion that Marilla Cuthbert swept that yard over as often as she swept her house. One could have eaten a meal off the ground without overbrimming the proverbial peck of dirt.[13]

Mrs. Rachel rapped smartly at the kitchen door and stepped in when bidden to do so. The kitchen at Green Gables was a cheerful apartment—or would have been cheerful if it had not been so painfully clean as to give it something of the

appearance of an unused parlour. Its windows looked east and west; through the west one, looking out on the back yard, came a flood of mellow June sunlight; but the east one, whence you got a glimpse of the bloom-white cherry-trees in the left orchard and nodding, slender birches down in the hollow by the brook, was greened over by a tangle of vines. Here sat Marilla Cuthbert, when she sat at all, always slightly distrustful of sunshine, which seemed to her too dancing and irresponsible a thing for a world which was meant to be taken seriously; and here she sat now, knitting, and the table behind her was laid for supper.

Mrs. Rachel, before she had fairly closed the door, had taken mental note of everything that was on that table. There were three plates laid, so that Marilla must be expecting some one home with Matthew to tea;[14] but the dishes were every-day dishes and there was only crab-apple preserves and one kind of cake, so that the expected company could not be any particular company. Yet what of Matthew's white collar and the sorrel mare? Mrs. Rachel was getting fairly dizzy with this unusual mystery about quiet, unmysterious Green Gables.

"Good evening, Rachel," Marilla said briskly. "This is a real fine evening, isn't it? Won't you sit down? How are all your folks?"

Something that for lack of any other name might be called friendship existed and always had existed between Marilla Cuthbert and Mrs. Rachel, in spite of—or perhaps because of—their dissimilarity.

Marilla was a tall thin woman, with angles and without curves; her dark hair showed some gray streaks and was always twisted up in a hard little knot behind with two wire hairpins stuck aggressively through it. She looked like a woman of narrow experience and rigid conscience,[15] which she was; but there was a saving something about her mouth which, if it had been ever so slightly developed, might have been considered indicative of a sense of humour.

hanged, as it has happened to them so often. There are further examples of the xenophobia of the Avonlea's attitude to other racial and ethnic groups, as for instance Marilla's view of the pedlar who sells Anne hair dye.

12. The Lombardies, or Lombardy poplars, are Montgomery's own innovation. They were scarcely common on the Prince Edward Island of her time, but she inserts them in most of her P. E. I. novels and stories, perhaps because they invoke the Mediterranean. See Appendix, "Geography."

13. There is a proverb that states, with variants, that "you must [or will] eat a peck of dirt before you die," but that saying refers to the peck measure (one-quarter bushel) or merely uses *peck* to mean a large amount. Montgomery, however, seems to have in mind the other meaning of *peck* as a dainty nibble, or a small amount.

14. Not the polite "afternoon tea" but the last meal of the day, as in the North of England today.

15. Marilla belongs to the type that Kate Douglas Wiggins calls "thin, spare, New England spinsters" and in attitude resembles Aunt Miranda in *Rebecca of Sunnybrook Farm*, but the details of the description resemble the old maid Miss Asphyxia Smith in *Oldtown Folks* (1869), by Harriet Beecher Stowe: "Miss Asphyxia was tall and spare. . . . She had

Opposite: Mr. Crew, Old Cavendish mailman, riding in a buggy similar to the one Matthew Cuthbert would have used.

allowed her muscles no cushioned repose of fat, no redundant smoothness of outline. There was nothing to her but good, strong solid bone, and tough, wiry, well-strung muscle. She was past fifty, and her hair was already well streaked with gray . . . tied . . . in a very tight knot, and then secured by a horn comb on the top of her head." Montgomery's early stories (see *Akin to Anne*) contain a number of such characters who are brought into contact with orphans. See Introduction.

16. "Bright River Is Hunter River" (*SJ* II [Jan. 27, 1911]: 40). See Appendix, "Geography."

17. Montgomery got the idea from a news story (see Introduction). But she also said that "the idea of getting a child from an orphan asylum was suggested to me years ago as a possible germ for a story by the fact that Pierce Macneill got a little girl from one, and I jot-

"We're all pretty well," said Mrs. Rachel. "I was kind of afraid *you* weren't, though, when I saw Matthew starting off to-day. I thought maybe he was going to the doctor's."

Marilla's lips twitched understandingly. She had expected Mrs. Rachel up; she had known that the sight of Matthew jaunting off so unaccountably would be too much for her neighbor's curiosity.

"Oh, no, I'm quite well although I had a bad headache yesterday," she said. "Matthew went to Bright River.[16] We're getting a little boy from an orphan asylum[17] in Nova Scotia[18] and he's coming on the train to-night."

If Marilla had said that Matthew had gone to Bright River to meet a kangaroo from Australia Mrs. Rachel could not have been more astonished. She was actually stricken dumb for five seconds. It was unsupposable that Marilla was making fun of her, but Mrs. Rachel was almost forced to suppose it.

"Are you in earnest, Marilla?" she demanded when voice returned to her.

"Yes, of course," said Marilla, as if getting boys from orphan asylums in Nova Scotia were part of the usual spring work on

any well-regulated Avonlea farm instead of being an unheard-of innovation.

Mrs. Rachel felt that she had received a severe mental jolt. She thought in exclamation points. A boy! Marilla and Matthew Cuthbert of all people adopting a boy! From an orphan asylum! Well, the world was certainly turning upside down! She would be surprised at nothing after this! Nothing!

"What on earth put such a notion into your head?" she demanded disapprovingly.

This had been done without her advice being asked, and must perforce be disapproved.

"Well, we've been thinking about it for some time—all winter in fact," returned Marilla. "Mrs. Alexander Spencer was up here one day before Christmas and she said she was going to get a little girl from the asylum over in Hopetown[19] in the spring. Her cousin lives there and Mrs. Spencer has visited her and knows all about it. So Matthew and I have talked it over off and on ever since. We thought we'd get a boy. Matthew is getting up in years, you know—he's sixty—and he isn't so spry as he once was. His heart troubles him a good deal. And you know how desperate hard it's got to be to get hired help. There's never anybody to be had but those stupid half-grown little French boys;[20] and as soon as you do get one broke into your ways and taught something he's up and off to the lobster canneries[21] or the States. At first Matthew suggested getting a Barnardo boy.[22] But I said 'no' flat to that. 'They may be all right—I'm not saying they're not—but no London street-Arabs[23] for me,' I said. 'Give me a native born at least. There'll be a risk, no matter who we get. But I'll feel easier in my mind and sleep sounder at nights if we get a born Canadian.' So in the end we decided to ask Mrs. Spencer to pick us out one when she went over to get her little girl. We heard last week she was going, so we sent her word by Richard Spencer's folks at Carmody to bring us a smart, likely boy of about ten or eleven. We decided that would be the best age—

ted it down in my notebook" (*SJ* II [Jan. 27, 1911]: 40).

18. The nearby province of mainland Canada, separated from Prince Edward Island by the narrow Northumberland Strait. It is much larger (and more populous then and now) than P.E.I. Its name, meaning "New Scotland," signals its Scottish heritage.

19. The real orphan asylum in Nova Scotia was in the Halifax-Dartmouth area. Hopetown is a made-up name. See Textual Note.

20. There is a long history of conflict between the French and Scottish settlers of Prince Edward Island. The majority of the French, or Acadian, population of the island live in the eastern part. French and English boys were often hired to do the larger part of a man's work on a farm, as Perry Miller is hired by the Murrays of New Moon in *Emily of New Moon*. In *Anne of Avonlea* (ch. 2) there are complaints about Martin, a French "hired man" first heard of in *Anne of Green Gables* (ch. 37), where his French identity is not so apparent. See Gavin White, "L. M. Montgomery and the French," *CCL* 78 (1995): 65, for a more detailed discussion of the attitude to the French in *Anne*.

21. The lobster cannery nearest Cavendish was at French River. Maud at Park Corner in May 1892 refers to "the crowd of factory boys on the road" (*SJ* I [May 7, 1892]: 79). Lobster and fish canneries were providing employment

Opposite: Protestant Orphan's Home, Halifax, Nova Scotia, 1874.

throughout the Maritime Provinces as the Canadians realized they could profit by completing the manufacturing process instead of engaging only in the fishing or trapping.

22. An orphan boy from one of Doctor Barnardo's Homes in England, first opened in 1870. In 1876 Barnardo reported that "some 30,000 children under sixteen years of age slept out in the streets, under the arches . . . in empty barrels . . . anywhere" (Frances Sheppard, *London, 1808–1870: The Infernal Wen* [1971], 367). The objective of the Barnardo homes was to rescue homeless children from a life of crime; every boy was to be taught to work and put out to some worthwhile occupation. The colonies seemed a desirable destination for the young men thus trained. See Appendix, "Orphans and Orphanages." The 1908 edition of *Anne* has "a 'Home' boy" (see Textual Note).

23. Homeless children of the London streets. See illustration.

old enough to be of some use in doing chores right off and young enough to be trained up proper. We mean to give him a good home and schooling. We had a telegram from Mrs. Alexander Spencer today—the mail-man brought it from the station—saying they were coming on the five-thirty train to-night. So Matthew went to Bright River to meet him. Mrs. Spencer will drop him off there. Of course she goes on to White Sands[24] station herself."

Mrs. Rachel prided herself on always speaking her mind; she proceeded to speak it now, having adjusted her mental attitude to this amazing piece of news.

"Well, Marilla, I'll just tell you plain that I think you're doing a mighty foolish thing—a risky thing, that's what. You don't know what you're getting. You're bringing a strange child into your house and home, and you don't know a single thing about him nor what his disposition is nor what sort of parents he had nor how he's likely to turn out. Why, it was only last week I read in the paper how a man and his wife up west of the Island took a boy out of an orphan asylum and he set fire to the house at night—set fire to it *on purpose*, Marilla—and nearly burnt them to a crisp in their beds. And I know another case where an adopted boy used to suck the eggs—they couldn't break him of it. If you had asked my advice in the matter—which you didn't do, Marilla—I'd have said for mercy's sake not to think of such a thing, that's what."

This Job's comforting[25] seemed neither to offend nor alarm Marilla. She knitted steadily on.

"I don't deny there's something in what you say, Rachel. I've had some qualms myself. But Matthew was terrible set on it. I could see that, so I gave in. It's so seldom Matthew sets his mind on anything; that when he does I always feel it my duty to give in. And as for the risks, there's risks in pretty near everything a body does in this world. There's risk in people having children of their own if it comes to that—they don't always turn out well. And then Nova Scotia is right close to the Island. It isn't as if we were getting him from England or the States. He can't be much different from ourselves."

"Well, I hope it will turn out all right,'" said Mrs. Lynde, in a tone that plainly indicated her painful doubts. "Only don't say I didn't warn you if he burns Green Gables down or puts strychnine[26] in the well—I heard of a case over in New Brunswick[27] where an orphan asylum child did that, and the whole family died in fearful agonies. Only, it was a girl in that instance."

"Well, we're not getting a girl," said Marilla, as if poisoning wells were a purely feminine accomplishment and not to be dreaded in the case of a boy. "I'd never dream of taking a girl to bring up. I wonder at Mrs. Alexander Spencer for doing it. But there, *she* wouldn't shrink from adopting a whole orphan asylum if she took it into her head."

Mrs. Rachel would have liked to stay until Matthew came home with his imported orphan. But reflecting that it would be a good two hours at least before his arrival she concluded to go up the road to Robert Bell's and tell them the news. It would certainly make a sensation second to none and Mrs. Rachel dearly loved to make a sensation. So she took herself away, somewhat to Marilla's relief, for the latter felt her doubts and fears reviving under the influence of Mrs. Rachel's pessimism.

"Well, of all things that ever were or will be!" ejaculated Mrs. Rachel, when she was safely out in the lane. "It does really seem as if I must be dreaming. Well, I'm sorry for that poor young one and no mistake. Matthew and Marilla don't know anything about children and they'll expect him to be wiser and steadier than his own grandfather, if so be's as he ever had a grandfather, which is doubtful. It seems uncanny to think of a child at Green Gables somehow; there's never been one there, for Matthew and Marilla were grown up when the

24. Cf. "White Sands Was Rustico" (*SJ* II [Jan. 27, 1911]: 40). See Appendix, "Geography."

25. The usual phrase is "Job's comforters," referring to the three friends of Job who come to him in his tribulations and only make matters worse by trying to point out that he was to blame for his troubles (Job 4–31).

26. "A highly poisonous vegetable alkaloid ($C_{21} H_{22} N_2 O_2$), obtained chiefly from *Strychnos Nux vomica* and other plants of the same genus." Sometimes used as a stimulant.

27. The other mainland province near P.E.I., also accessible by ferry, larger than Nova Scotia and at the time less prosperous and less well settled. The three provinces of Nova Scotia, P.E.I., and New Brunswick then constituted the Maritime Provinces, or "the Maritimes" (now with the addition of Newfoundland). They were then largely settled by fishermen and farmers, although Nova Scotia and New Brunswick had mines and some industry.

new house was built—if they ever *were* children, which is
hard to believe when one looks at them. I wouldn't be in that
orphan's shoes for anything. My, but I pity him, that's what."

So said Mrs. Rachel to the wild rose bushes out of the
fullness of her heart; but if she could have seen the child who
was waiting patiently at the Bright River station at that very
moment her pity would have been still deeper and more
profound.

CHAPTER II

MATTHEW CUTHBERT
IS SURPRISED

MATTHEW CUTHBERT and the sorrel mare jogged comfortably over the eight miles to Bright River. It was a pretty road, running along between snug farmsteads, with now and again a bit of balsamy fir wood to drive through, or a hollow where wild plums hung out their filmy bloom. The air was sweet with the breath of many apple orchards, and the meadows sloped away in the distance to horizon mists of pearl and purple; while

> The little birds sang as if it were
> The one day of summer in all the year.[1]

Matthew enjoyed the drive after his own fashion, except during the moments when he met women and had to nod to them—for in Prince Edward Island you are supposed to nod to all and sundry you meet on the road whether you know them or not.

Matthew dreaded all women except Marilla and Mrs. Rachel; he had an uncomfortable feeling that the mysterious creatures were secretly laughing at him. He may have been quite right in thinking so for he was an odd-looking person-

1. James Russell Lowell, "The Vision of Sir Launfal" (I.ii. ll. 3–4), a verse parable in which the plot is derived from legends of the Holy Grail in Malory. The poem, first published in 1848, may have influenced Tennyson's *Idylls*. "Sir Launfal" begins, "And what is so rare as a day in June?" See Textual Note and Appendix, "Literary Allusion."

2. A stack of wooden roof tiles, small pieces of wood cut each with one end thinner than the other for a roof covering.

3. Free rein for the activity of the imagination. The phrase ultimately comes from a statement by Lawrence Sterne's character Parson Yorick, "I gave full scope to my imagination," in *Sentimental Journey* (1768).

age, with an ungainly figure and long iron-gray hair that touched his stooping shoulders, and a full, soft brown beard which he had worn ever since he was twenty. In fact, he had looked at twenty very much as he looked at sixty, lacking a little of the grayness.

When he reached Bright River there was no sign of any train; he thought he was too early, so he tied his horse in the yard of the small Bright River hotel and went over to the station-house. The long platform was almost deserted; the only living creature in sight being a girl who was sitting on a pile of shingles[2] at the extreme end. Matthew, barely noting that it *was* a girl, sidled past her as quickly as possible without looking at her. Had he looked he could hardly have failed to notice the tense rigidity and expectation of her attitude and expression. She was sitting there waiting for something or somebody, and, since sitting and waiting was the only thing to do just then, she sat and waited with all her might and main.

Matthew encountered the station-master locking up the ticket-office preparatory to going home for supper, and asked him if the five-thirty train would soon be along.

"The five-thirty train has been in and gone half an hour ago," answered that brisk official. "But there was a passenger dropped off for you—a little girl. She's sitting out there on the shingles. I asked her to go into the ladies' waiting-room, but she informed me gravely that she preferred to stay outside. 'There was more scope for imagination,'[3] she said. She's a case, I should say."

"I'm not expecting a girl," said Matthew blankly. "It's a boy I've come for. He should be here. Mrs. Alexander Spencer was to bring him over from Nova Scotia for me."

The station-master whistled.

"Guess there's some mistake," he said. "Mrs. Spencer came off the train with that girl and gave her into my charge. Said you and your sister were adopting her from an orphan asylum and that you would be along for her presently. That's all *I* know about it—and I haven't got any more orphans concealed hereabouts."

"I don't understand," said Matthew helplessly, wishing that Marilla were at hand to cope with the situation.

"Well, you'd better question the girl," said the station-master carelessly. "I dare say she'll be able to explain—she's got a tongue of her own, that's certain. Maybe they were out of boys of the brand you wanted."

He walked jauntily away, being hungry, and the unfortunate Matthew was left to do that which was harder for him than bearding a lion in its den[4]—walk up to a girl—a strange girl—an orphan girl—and demand of her why she wasn't a boy. Matthew groaned in spirit as he turned about and shuffled gently down the platform towards her.

She had been watching him ever since he had passed her and she had her eyes on him now. Matthew was not looking at her and would not have seen what she was really like if he had been, but an ordinary observer would have seen this:

A child of about eleven, garbed in a very short, very tight, very ugly dress of yellowish-gray wincey.[5] She wore a faded brown sailor hat and beneath the hat, extending down her back, were two braids of very thick, decidedly red hair. Her face was small, white and thin, also much freckled; her mouth was large and so were her eyes, that looked green in some lights and moods and gray in others.

So far, the ordinary observer; an extraordinary observer might have seen that the chin was pointed and pronounced; that the big eyes were full of spirit and vivacity; that the mouth was sweet-lipped and expressive; that the forehead was broad and full; in short, our discerning extraordinary observer might have concluded that no commonplace soul inhabited the body of this stray woman-child of whom shy Matthew Cuthbert was so ludicrously afraid.[6]

4. "And dar'st thou, then, / To beard the lion in his den, / The Douglas in his hall?" (Sir Walter Scott, *Marmion, A Tale of Flodden Field* [1808], "The Battle," Canto 6, ll. 22–25). *Marmion*, a narrative in tetrameter couplets by Sir Walter Scott, is set in 1513, the year of the decisive defeat of James IV of Scotland by the English. A section of *Marmion* under the title "The Parting of Marmion and Douglas" appears in the *Fifth Royal Reader*. See n. 15, ch. 5; n. 9, ch. 27.

5. Alteration of linsey-woolsey, a durable cloth having a linen warp and a woolen weft. This cloth is not particularly ugly or cheap, but the author may have chosen it for the connotation of "wince." Nellie McClung's poverty-stricken heroine, Pearlie Watson, also wears wincey. "Maudie Ducker had on a new plaid dress with velvet trimming, and Maudie knew it. 'Is that your Sunday dress,' she asked Pearl, looking critically at Pearlie's faded little brown winsey. 'My, no!' Pearlie answered cheerfully. 'This is just my morning dress. I wear my blue satting [satin] in the afternoon, and on Sundays, my purple velvet with the watter-plait, and basque-yoke of tartaric plaid, garnished with lace.'" (Nellie McClung, *Sowing Seeds in Danny*, 1908 ed., 90–91).

6. Compare this description of Anne with the photograph of a young girl from an American magazine which Montgomery says she used as her model for Anne (Rubio, *Harvesting Thistles,* 3). She

had no idea who the girl was and wondered what she would think if she knew her face was the model for Anne. We have identified the photograph as that of Evelyn Nesbit, an artist's model and chorus girl who was the focus of a scandalous murder trial in 1906 that was the subject of intense media attention. Nesbit's husband, Harry K. Thaw, shot and killed Stanford White, the well-known New York architect. Thaw alleged that he was defending his wife's honor.

7. A traveling bag, properly one made of carpet. An advertisement in the *Boston Directory* in 1830 is the first recorded reference to this kind of bag.

8. Cf. "I dreamt that I dwelt in marble halls, / With vassals and serfs at my side." Song by Alfred Bunn (1796–1860) in his 1843 opera *The Bohemian Girl* (Act 2). It was probably influenced by Henry Wadsworth Longfellow's "Hymn to the Night" (1839): "I heard the trailing garments of the Night / Sweep through her marble halls!" (ll. 1–2).

9. Cf. "With all my worldly goods I thee endow," from the "Solemni-

Matthew, however, was spared the ordeal of speaking first, for as soon as she concluded that he was coming to her she stood up, grasping with one thin brown hand the handle of a shabby, old-fashioned carpet-bag;[7] the other she held out to him.

"I suppose you are Mr. Matthew Cuthbert of Green Gables?" she said in a peculiarly clear, sweet voice. "I'm very glad to see you. I was beginning to be afraid you weren't coming for me and I was imagining all the things that might have happened to prevent you. I had made up my mind that if you didn't come for me to-night I'd go down the track to that big wild cherry-tree at the bend, and climb up into it to stay all night. I wouldn't be a bit afraid, and it would be lovely to sleep in a wild cherry-tree all white with bloom in the moonshine, don't you think? You could imagine you were dwelling in marble halls,[8] couldn't you? And I was quite sure you would come for me in the morning, if you didn't to-night."

Matthew had taken the scrawny little hand awkwardly in his; then and there he decided what to do. He could not tell this child with the glowing eyes that there had been a mistake; he would take her home and let Marilla do that. She couldn't be left at Bright River anyhow, no matter what mistake had been made, so all questions and explanations might as well be deferred until he was safely back at Green Gables.

"I'm sorry I was late," he said shyly. "Come along. The horse is over in the yard. Give me your bag."

"Oh, I can carry it," the child responded cheerfully. "It isn't heavy. I've got all my worldly goods[9] in it but it isn't heavy. And if it isn't carried in just a certain way the handle pulls out—so I'd better keep it because I know the exact knack of it.[10] It's an extremely old carpet-bag. Oh, I'm very glad you've come, even if it would have been nice to sleep in a wild cherry-tree. We've got to drive a long piece,[11] haven't we? Mrs. Spencer said it was eight miles. I'm glad because I love driving. Oh, it seems so wonderful that I'm going to live with you and belong to you. I've never belonged to anybody—not really. But the asylum was the worst. I've only been in it four months but that was enough. I don't suppose you ever were an orphan in an asylum so you can't possibly understand what it is like. It's worse than anything you could imagine. Mrs. Spencer said it was wicked of me to talk like that but I didn't mean to be wicked. It's so easy to be wicked without knowing it, isn't it ? They were good, you know—the asylum people. But there is so little scope for imagination in an asylum—only just in the other orphans. It *was* pretty interesting to imagine things about them—to imagine that perhaps the girl who sat next to you was really the daughter of a belted earl,[12] who had been stolen away from her parents in her infancy by a cruel nurse who died before she could confess. I used to lie awake at night and imagine things like that, because I didn't have time in the day. I guess that's why I'm so thin—I *am* dreadfully thin, ain't I ? There isn't a pick on my bones.[13] I do love to imagine I'm nice and plump with dimples in my elbows."

With this Matthew's companion stopped talking, partly because she was out of breath and partly because they had reached the buggy. Not another word did she say until they had left the village and were driving down a steep little hill, the road part of which had been cut so deeply into the soft soil that the banks, fringed with blooming wild-cherry trees and slim white birches, were several feet above their heads.

The child put out her hand and broke off a branch of wild plum that brushed against the side of the buggy.

"Isn't that beautiful? What did that tree, leaning out from the bank, all white and lacy, make you think of ?" she asked.

"Well now, I dunno," said Matthew.

"Why, a bride, of course—a bride all in white with a lovely misty veil. I've never seen one, but I can imagine what she

zation of Matrimony" in *The Book of Common Prayer*. Although this is the Anglican prayer book, the formula was well known and often repeated. Anne's phrase may also be an echo of "The Courtship of the Yonghy Bonghy Bò" in *Laughable Lyrics*, 1877, by Edward Lear: "These were all his worldly goods: / In the middle of the woods, / These were all the worldly goods, / Of the Yonghy Bonghy Bò" (ll. 7–11).

10. The trick of dexterous performance; an acquired facility of doing something cleverly, adroitly, and successfully.

11. Colloquial term for a fairly long distance.

12. An earl is distinguished by a belt or cincture worn as a mark of rank.

13. The word "pick" is used colloquially here as a term for a scrap or morsel, either of food or human flesh. A "significantly rural, especially less educated, expression" probably acquired by Anne from her keepers (Pratt, *Dictionary of Prince Edward Island*).

14. A person sent out by a religious community into foreign lands for the conversion of the heathen. Women could be missionaries, and indeed such work was often the only opportunity for travel and adventure open to them.

15. Anne probably got this set of ideas from fashion magazines. Large hats with feathers (the "nodding plumes") were popular at the end of the nineteenth century, and this outfit seems in the style of the 1890s. No person of taste—of any rank—would have dressed a child in this fashion. In *Anne of Avonlea*, one of Anne's students is a severely overdressed little girl: "Anne wondered what sort of mother the child had, to send her to school dressed as she was. She wore a faded pink silk dress, trimmed

An outfit similar to the one Anne would have imagined (from **Godey's Magazine**, *Vol. CXXXII, 1896).*

would look like. I don't ever expect to be a bride myself. I'm so homely nobody will ever want to marry me—unless it might be a foreign missionary.[14] I suppose a foreign missionary mightn't be very particular. But I do hope that some day I shall have a white dress. That is my highest ideal of earthly bliss. I just love pretty clothes. And I've never had a pretty dress in my life that I can remember—but of course it's all the more to look forward to, isn't it? And then I can imagine that I'm dressed gorgeously. This morning when I left the asylum I felt so ashamed because I had to wear this horrid old wincey dress. All the orphans had to wear them, you know. A merchant in Hopetown last winter donated three hundred yards of wincey to the asylum. Some people said it was because he couldn't sell it but I'd rather believe that it was out of the kindness of his heart, wouldn't you? When we got on the train I felt as if everybody must be looking at me and pitying me. But I just went to work and imagined that I had on the most beautiful pale blue silk dress—because when you *are* imagining you might as well imagine something worth while—and a big hat all flowers and nodding plumes, and a gold watch and kid gloves and boots.[15] I felt cheered up right away and I enjoyed my trip to the Island with all my might. I wasn't a bit sick coming over in the boat.[16] Neither was Mrs. Spencer, although she generally is. She said she hadn't time to get sick, watching to see that I didn't fall overboard. She said she never saw the beat of me[17] for prowling about. But if it kept her from being seasick it's a mercy I did prowl, isn't it? And I wanted to see everything that was to be seen on that boat, because I didn't know whether I'd ever have another opportunity. Oh, there are a lot more cherry-trees all in bloom! This Island is the bloomiest place. I just love it already and I'm glad I'm going to live here. I've always heard that Prince Edward Island is the prettiest place in the world, and I used to imagine I was living here but I never really expected I would. It's delightful when your imaginations come true, isn't it? But those red roads are so funny. When we got into the train at Charlottetown and the red roads began to flash past I asked Mrs. Spencer what made them red and she said she didn't know and for pity's sake not to ask her any more questions. She said I must have asked her a thousand already. I suppose I had, too, but how are you going to find out about things if you don't ask questions? And what *does* make the roads red?"[18]

"Well now, I dunno," said Matthew.

"Well, that is one of the things to find out sometime. Isn't it splendid to think of all the things there are to find out about? It just makes me feel glad to be alive — it's such an interesting world. It wouldn't be half so interesting if we knew all about everything, would it? There'd be no scope for imagination then, would there? But am I talking too much? People are always telling me I do. Would you rather I didn't talk? If you say so I'll stop. I *can* stop when I make up my mind to it, although it's difficult."

Matthew, much to his own surprise, was enjoying himself. Like most quiet folks he liked talkative people when they were willing to do the talking themselves and did not expect him to keep up his end of it. But he had never expected to enjoy the society of a little girl. Women were bad enough in all conscience but little girls were worse. He detested the way they had of sidling past him timidly, with sidewise glances, as if they expected him to gobble them up at a mouthful if they ventured to say a word. This was the Avonlea type of well-bred little girl. But this freckled witch was very different, and although he found it rather difficult for his slower intelligence to keep up with her brisk mental processes he thought that he "kind of liked her chatter." So he said as shyly as usual:

"Oh, you can talk as much as you like. I don't mind."

"Oh, I'm so glad. I know you and I are going to get along

with a great deal of cotton lace, soiled white kid slippers, and silk stockings." When Clarice Almira's mother turns up dressed in "a pale blue summer silk, puffed, frilled, and shirred" and wearing "a white chiffon hat, bedecked with three long but rather stringy ostrich feathers," Anne thinks she looks like "a collision between a fashion plate and a nightmare" *(Avonlea,* ch. 5).

Mrs. Donnell is a parody of Anne's earlier version of herself in the pale blue silk dress. Magazines and newspapers would show the latest fashions even in an exaggerated manner.

16. Montgomery gives this account of her own first journey on the ferry (going in the opposite direction from Anne): "I crossed in the St. Lawrence, a wobbling old tub of a boat. It was quite rough but at first it was pleasant enough. The sun, pouring through ragged, sullen clouds changed the water to burnished copper and land came out from between its misty curtains. Later on, I was a little seasick and had to lie down until we got to Pictou Harbor" *(SJ* I [Sept. 17, 1895]: 143).

17. A North American colloquial phrase dating from the 1830s. Its usage occurs predominantly in New England and means something surpassing. In other words, Mrs. Spencer has never seen anyone who could surpass Anne at prowling around. (Frederic G. Cassidy, ed. *Dictionary of American Regional English*).

18. The red color of the roads is caused by a high concentration of iron in the soil. Anne eventually learns the cause herself (see n. 6, ch. 18).

19. Mrs. Spencer's mock explanation for Anne's extreme talkativeness. If Anne's tongue were attached in the middle she would be able to move it twice as much as a person whose tongue was "firmly fastened at one end."

20. The *Linnea Borealis* or *americana*, Caprofoliaceae, also known as twinflowers. Pink or white bell-shaped flowers of the honeysuckle family, which grow in terminal pairs. They bloom from late June to early August. See Appendix, "Gardens and Plants," and illustration.

Opposite: The ferry S. S. Stanley, on the St. Lawrence in the 1890s.

together fine. It's such a relief to talk when one wants to and not be told that children should be seen and not heard. I've had that said to me a million times if I have once. And people laugh at me because I use big words. But if you have big ideas you have to use big words to express them, haven't you?"

"Well now, that seems reasonable," said Matthew.

"Mrs. Spencer said my tongue must be hung in the middle.[19] But it isn't—it's firmly fastened at one end. Mrs. Spencer said your place was named Green Gables. I asked her all about it. And she said there were trees all around it. I was gladder than ever. I just love trees. And there weren't any at all about the asylum, only a few poor weeny-teeny things out in front with little whitewashed cagey things about them. They just looked like orphans themselves, those trees did. It used to make me want to cry to look at them. I used to say to them, 'Oh, you *poor* little things! If you were out in a great big woods with other trees all around you and little mosses and Junebells[20] growing over your roots and a brook not far away and birds singing in your branches, you could grow, couldn't you? But you can't where you are. I know just exactly how you feel, little trees.' I felt sorry to leave them behind this morning. You do get so attached to things like that, don't you? Is there a brook anywhere near Green Gables? I forgot to ask Mrs. Spencer that."

"Well now, yes, there's one just below the house."

"Fancy! It's always been one of my dreams to live near a brook. I never expected I would, though. Dreams don't often come true, do they? Wouldn't it be nice if they did? But just now I feel pretty nearly perfectly happy. I can't feel perfectly happy because—well, what colour would you call this?"

She twitched one of her long glossy braids over her thin shoulder and held it up before Matthew's eyes. Matthew was not used to deciding on the tints of ladies' tresses, but in this case there couldn't be much doubt.

"It's red, ain't it?" he said.

The girl let the braid drop back with a sigh that seemed to come from her very toes and to exhale forth all the sorrows of the ages.

"Yes, it's red," she said resignedly. "Now you see why I can't be perfectly happy. Nobody could who had red hair. I don't mind the other things so much—the freckles and the green eyes and my skinniness. I can imagine them away. I can imagine that I have a beautiful rose-leaf complexion and lovely starry violet eyes. But I *cannot* imagine that red hair away. I do my best. I think to myself, 'Now my hair is a glorious black, black as the raven's wing.' But all the time I *know* it is just plain red, and it breaks my heart. It will be my lifelong sorrow. I read of a girl once in a novel who had a lifelong sorrow but it wasn't red hair. Her hair was pure gold, rippling back from her alabaster brow. What is an alabaster brow?[21] I never could find out. Can you tell me?"

"Well now, I'm afraid I can't," said Matthew, who was getting a little dizzy. He felt as he had once felt in his rash youth

21. A literary cliché ultimately from *Othello:* "Yet I'll not shed her blood, / Nor scar that whiter skin of hers than snow, / And smooth as monumental alabaster" (V.ii. ll. 3–5). Alabaster is a translucent, whitish, fine-grained variety of gypsum used for statues, vases, etc.

22. A fictional name. See
Appendix, "Geography."

when another boy had enticed him on the merry-go-round at a picnic.

"Well, whatever it was it must have been something nice because she was divinely beautiful. Have you ever imagined what it must feel like to be divinely beautiful?"

"Well now, no, I haven't," confessed Matthew ingenuously.

"I have, often. Which would you rather be if you had the choice — divinely beautiful or dazzlingly clever or angelically good?"

"Well now, I — I don't know exactly."

"Neither do I. I can never decide. But it doesn't make much real difference for it isn't likely I'll ever be either. It's certain I'll never be angelically good. Mrs. Spencer says — oh, Mr. Cuthbert! Oh, Mr. Cuthbert!! Oh, Mr. Cuthbert!!!"

That was not what Mrs. Spencer had said; neither had the child tumbled out of the buggy nor had Matthew done anything astonishing. They had simply rounded a curve in the road and found themselves in the "Avenue."

The "Avenue," so called by the Newbridge[22] people, was a stretch of road four or five hundred yards long, completely arched over by huge wide-spreading apple-trees, planted years ago by an eccentric old farmer. Overhead was one long canopy of snowy fragrant bloom. Below the boughs the air was full of a purple twilight and far ahead a glimpse of painted sunset sky shone like a great rose window at the end of a cathedral aisle.

Its beauty seemed to strike the child dumb. She leaned back in the buggy, her thin hands clasped before her, her face lifted rapturously to the white splendour above. Even when they had passed out and were driving down the long slope to Newbridge she never moved or spoke. Still with rapt face she gazed afar into the sunset west, with eyes that saw visions trooping splendidly across that glowing background. Through Newbridge, a bustling little village where dogs barked at them and small boys hooted and curious faces peered from the windows, they drove, still in silence. When three more miles had dropped away behind them the child had not spoken. She could keep silence, it was evident, as energetically as she could talk.

"I guess you're feeling pretty tired and hungry," Matthew ventured at last, accounting for her long visitation of dumbness[23] with the only reason he could think of. "But we haven't very far to go now—only another mile."

She came out of her reverie with a deep sigh and looked at him with the dreamy gaze of a soul that had been wondering afar, star-led.

"Oh, Mr. Cuthbert," she whispered, "that place we came through—that white place—what was it?"

"Well now, you must mean the Avenue," said Matthew after a few moments' profound reflection. "It is kind of a pretty place."

"Pretty? Oh, *pretty* doesn't seem the right word to use. Nor beautiful, either. They don't go far enough. Oh, it was wonderful—wonderful. It's the first thing I ever saw that couldn't be improved upon by imagination. It just satisfied me here" —she put one hand on her breast—"it made a queer funny ache and yet it was a pleasant ache. Did you ever have an ache like that, Mr. Cuthbert?"

"Well now, I just can't recollect that I ever had."

"I have it lots of times—whenever I see anything royally beautiful. But they shouldn't call that lovely place the Avenue. There is no meaning in a name like that. They should call it —let me see—the White Way of Delight.[24] Isn't that a nice imaginative name? When I don't like the name of a place or a person I always imagine a new one and always think of them so. There was a girl at the asylum whose name was Hepzibah[25] Jenkins, but I always imagined her as Rosalia DeVere. Other people may call that place the Avenue, but I shall al-

23. The author is humorously likening Anne's temporary silence to that of biblical figures who cannot speak for a period of time. For instance, Zacharias, the father of John the Baptist, is struck dumb by the angel Gabriel (Luke 1:20). The implication is that it would take a miracle to quiet Anne.

24. See Appendix, "Geography."

25. A name meaning "my delight is in her." In 2 Kings 21:1 she is the mother of Manasseh, king of Judah; in Isaiah 62:4 the name is used as a symbolic one for Jerusalem.

*Anne's "Lake of Shining Waters":
Campbell's Pond at Park Corner.*

ways call it the White Way of Delight. Have we really only
another mile to go before we get home? I'm glad and I'm
sorry. I'm sorry because this drive has been so pleasant and
I'm always sorry when pleasant things end. Something still
pleasanter may come after, but you can never be sure. And it's
so often the case that it isn't pleasanter. That has been my
experience anyhow. But I'm glad to think of getting home.
You see, I've never had a real home since I can remember. It
gives me that pleasant ache again just to think of coming to a
really truly home. Oh, isn't that pretty!"

They had driven over the crest of a hill. Below them was a
pond, looking almost like a river so long and winding was it.
A bridge spanned it midway and from there to its lower end,
where an amber-hued belt of sand-hills shut it from the dark-

blue gulf [26]beyond, the water was a glory of many shifting hues—the most spiritual shadings of crocus and rose and ethereal green, with other elusive tintings for which no name has ever been found. Above the bridge the pond ran up into fringing groves of fir and maple and lay all darkly translucent in their wavering shadows. Here and there a wild plum leaned out from the bank like a white-clad girl tiptoeing to her own reflection. From the marsh at the head of the pond came the clear, mournfully sweet chorus of the frogs.[27] There was a little gray house peering around a white apple orchard on a slope beyond and, although it was not yet quite dark, a light was shining from one of its windows.

"That's Barry's pond," said Matthew.

"Oh, I don't like that name, either. I shall call it—let me see—the Lake of Shining Waters.[28] Yes, that is the right name for it. I know because of the thrill. When I hit on a name that suits exactly it gives me a thrill. Do things ever give you a thrill?"

Matthew ruminated.

"Well now, yes. It always kind of gives me a thrill to see them ugly white grubs that spade up[29] in the cucumber beds. I hate the look of them."

"Oh, I don't think that can be exactly the same kind of a thrill. Do you think it can? There doesn't seem to be much connection between grubs and lakes of shining waters, does there? But why do other people call it Barry's Pond?"

"I reckon because Mr. Barry lives up there in that house. Orchard Slope's the name of his place. If it wasn't for that big bush[30] behind it you could see Green Gables from here. But we have to go over the bridge and round by the road, so it's near half a mile further."

"Has Mr. Barry any little girls? Well, not so very little either—about my size."

"He's got one about eleven. Her name is Diana."

26. The Gulf of Saint Lawrence.

27. The frog's song functions to bring the sexes together for breeding. Each species has its own characteristic call; males have resonating pouches in their throats that amplify the sound. The singing frogs of Avonlea belong to a species of small tree frog called spring peepers, or *Hyla crucifer*.

28. This was "Campbell's Pond at Park Corner" (*AP*, 14). See Appendix, "Geography."

29. Ugly white wormlike larvae, such as of a beetle, that appear in soil dug up with a spade.

30. Uncleared natural woodland; we are told later that this bush is of "spruce and fir" (p. 76).

31. Diana was the Roman goddess of virginity, the hunt, and the moon. She was closely associated with the Greek goddess Artemis. See Introduction.

32. Montgomery had a lifelong fear of drawbridges. "I was always horribly frightened of draw-bridges, and am to this day. Do what I will, I cringe secretly from the time the horse steps on the bridge until I am safely over the draw" (*AP*, 43).

Diana, bronze sculpture by Augustus Saint-Gaudens, 1893.

"Oh!" with a long indrawing of breath. "What a perfectly lovely name!"

"Well now, I dunno. There's something dreadful heathen-ish[31] about it, seems to me. I'd ruther Jane or Mary or some sensible name like that. But when Diana was born there was a schoolmaster boarding there and they gave him the naming of her and he called her Diana."

"I wish there had been a schoolmaster like that around when *I* was born, then. Oh, here we are at the bridge. I'm going to shut my eyes tight. I'm always afraid going over bridges. I can't help imagining that perhaps, just as we get to the middle they'll crumple up like a jack-knife and nip us. So I shut my eyes. But I always have to open them for all when I think we're getting near the middle. Because, you see, if the bridge *did* crumple up[32] I'd want to *see* it crumple. What a jolly rumble it makes! I always like the rumble part of it. Isn't it splendid there are so many things to like in this world ? There, we're over. Now I'll look back. Good night, dear Lake of Shining Waters. I always say good night to the things I love just as I would to people. I think they like it. That water looks as if it was smiling at me."

When they had driven up the further hill and around a corner Matthew said:

"We're pretty near home now. That's Green Gables over—"

"Oh, don't tell me," she interrupted breathlessly, catching at his partially raised arm and shutting her eyes that she might not see his gesture. "Let me guess—I'm sure I'll guess right."

She opened her eyes and looked about her. They were on the crest of a hill. The sun had set some time since, but the landscape was still clear in the mellow afterlight. To the west a dark church spire rose up against a marigold sky. Below was a little valley, and beyond a long gently-rising slope with snug farmsteads scattered along it. From one to another the child's eyes darted, eager and wistful. At last they lingered on one away to the left, far back from the road, dimly white with blossoming trees in the twilight of the surrounding woods. Over it, in the stainless south-west sky, a great crystal-white star was shining like a lamp of guidance and promise.[33]

"That's it, isn't it?" she said, pointing.

Matthew slapped the reins on the sorrel's back delightedly.

"Well now, you've guessed it! But I reckon Mrs. Spencer described it so's you could tell."

"No, she didn't—really she didn't. All she said might just as well have been about most of those other places. I hadn't any real idea what it looked like. But just as soon as I saw it I felt it was home. Oh, it seems as if I must be in a dream. Do you know, my arm must be black and blue from the elbow up, for I've pinched myself so many times to-day. Every little while a horrible sickening feeling would come over me and I'd be so afraid it was all a dream. Then I'd pinch myself[34] to see if it was real—until suddenly I remembered that even supposing it was only a dream I'd better go on dreaming as long as I could; so I stopped pinching. But it *is* real and we're nearly home."

With a sigh of rapture she relapsed into silence. Matthew stirred uneasily. He felt glad that it would be Marilla and not he who would have to tell this waif of the world that the home she longed for was not to be hers after all. They drove over Lynde's Hollow, where it was already quite dark, but not so dark that Mrs. Rachel could not see them from her window vantage, and up the hill and into the long lane of Green Gables. By the time they arrived at the house Matthew was shrinking from the approaching revelation with an energy he did not understand. It was not of Marilla or himself he was thinking or of the trouble this mistake was probably going to make for them but of the child's disappointment. When he thought of that rapt light being quenched in her eyes he had an uncomfortable feeling that he was going to assist at murdering something—much the same feeling that came over

33. The "evening star," really the planet Venus.

34. It is a commonly held belief that one can distinguish between a dream and the waking state by pinching oneself. Anne has been trying all day to determine by this means if she is dreaming.

him when he had to kill a lamb or calf or any other innocent little creature.

The yard was quite dark as they turned into it, and the poplar leaves were rustling silkily all round it.

"Listen to the trees talking in their sleep," she whispered, as he lifted her to the ground. "What nice dreams they must have!"

Then, holding tightly to the carpet-bag which contained "all her worldly goods," she followed him into the house.

CHAPTER III

MARILLA CUTHBERT
IS SURPRISED

MARILLA CAME briskly forward as Matthew opened the door. But when her eyes fell on the odd little figure in the stiff ugly dress, with the long braids of red hair and the eager, luminous eyes, she stopped short in amazement.

"Matthew Cuthbert, who's that?" she ejaculated. "Where is the boy?"

"There wasn't any boy," said Matthew wretchedly. "There was only *her*."

He nodded at the child, remembering that he had never even asked her name.

"No boy! But there *must* have been a boy," insisted Marilla. "We sent word to Mrs. Spencer to bring a boy."

"Well, she didn't. She brought *her*. I asked the station-master. And I had to bring her home. She couldn't be left there, no matter where the mistake had come in."

"Well, this is a pretty piece of business!" ejaculated Marilla.

During this dialogue the child had remained silent, her eyes roving from one to the other, all the animation fading out of her face. Suddenly she seemed to grasp the full meaning of what had been said. Dropping her precious carpet-bag she sprang forward a step and clasped her hands.

"You don't want me!" she cried. "You don't want me because I'm not a boy! I might have expected it! Nobody ever did want me. I might have known it was all too beautiful to last. I might have known nobody really did want me. Oh, what shall I do? I'm going to burst into tears!"

Burst into tears she did. Sitting down on a chair by the

table, flinging her arms out upon it, and burying her face in them, she proceeded to cry stormily. Marilla and Matthew looked at each other deprecatingly across the stove. Neither of them knew what to say or do. Finally Marilla stepped lamely into the breach.

"Well, well, there's no need to cry so about it."

"Yes, there *is* need!" The child raised her head quickly, revealing a tear-stained face and trembling lips. "*You* would cry, too, if you were an orphan and had come to a place you thought was going to be home and found that they didn't want you because you weren't a boy. Oh, this is the most *tragical* thing that ever happened to me!"

Something like a reluctant smile, rather rusty from long disuse, mellowed Marilla's grim expression.

"Well, don't cry any more. We're not going to turn you out-of-doors to-night. You'll have to stay here until we investigate this affair. What's your name?"

The child hesitated for a moment.

"Will you please call me Cordelia[1]?" she said eagerly.

"*Call* you Cordelia? Is that your name?"

"No-o-o, it's not exactly my name, but I would love to be called Cordelia. It's such a perfectly elegant name."

"I don't know what on earth you mean. If Cordelia isn't your name, what is?"

"Anne Shirley," reluctantly faltered forth the owner of that name. "But—oh, please do call me Cordelia. It can't matter much to you what you call me if I'm only going to be here a little while, can it? And Anne is such an unromantic name."

"Unromantic fiddlesticks!" said the unsympathetic Marilla. "Anne is a real good plain sensible name. You've no need to be ashamed of it."

"Oh, I'm not ashamed of it," explained Anne, "only I like Cordelia better. I've always imagined that my name was Cordelia—at least, I have of late years. When I was young I used

1. A name from Middle Welsh meaning "jewel of the sea." The most famous character of this name is Shakespeare's Cordelia, King Lear's daughter, an example of true filial devotion and an interesting choice for the orphaned Anne. See Introduction.

"Marilla set the candle on the three-legged table." Illustration by Sybil Tawse, from the 1933 edition.

to imagine it was Geraldine, but I like Cordelia better now. But if you call me Anne please call me Anne spelled with an *e*."

"What difference does it make how it's spelled?" asked Marilla with another rusty smile as she picked up the teapot.

"Oh, it makes *such* a difference. It *looks* so much nicer. When you hear a name pronounced can't you always see it in your mind just as if it was printed out? I can; and A-n-n looks dreadful, but A-n-n-e looks so much more distinguished.[2] If you'll only call me Anne spelled with an *e* I shall try to reconcile myself to not being called Cordelia."

"Very well, then, Anne spelled with an *e*, can you tell us how this mistake came to be made? We sent word to Mrs. Spencer to bring us a boy. Were there no boys at the asylum?"

"Oh, yes, there was an abundance of them. But Mrs. Spencer said *distinctly* you wanted a girl about eleven years old. And the matron said she thought I would do. You don't know how delighted I was. I couldn't sleep all last night for joy. Oh," she added reproachfully, turning to Matthew, "why didn't you tell me at the station that you didn't want me and leave me there? If I hadn't seen the White Way of Delight and the Lake of Shining Waters it wouldn't be so hard."

"What on earth does she mean?" demanded Marilla, staring at Matthew.

"She—she's just referring to some conversation we had on the road," said Matthew hastily. "I'm going out to put the mare in, Marilla. Have tea ready when I come back."

"Did Mrs. Spencer bring anybody over besides you?" continued Marilla when Matthew had gone out.

"She brought Lily Jones for herself. Lily is only five years old and she is very beautiful. She has nut-brown hair.[3] If I was very beautiful and had nut-brown hair would you keep me?"

"No. We want a boy to help Matthew on the farm. A girl would be of no use to us. Take off your hat. I'll lay it and your bag on the hall table."

2. Lucy Maud Montgomery preferred to be called Maud rather than Lucy, and she decidedly did not spell her name with an *e,* becoming annoyed with those who added one to her name.

3. In "The Nut-Brown Maid," a fifteenth-century ballad, when the lover tells the maid that he has been banished to the greenwood, she responds by declaring that she will accompany him. At this evidence of her fidelity he reveals that he is really an earl's son and is not banished at all. This ballad was the basis of Matthew Prior's "Henry and Emma" (1709). The phrases "nut-brown hair" and "nut-brown maid" recur in such traditional songs as "The Star of the County Down" as recorded, for instance, by Van Morrison and the Chieftains on *Irish Heartbeat* (1988).

4. The spare room of a farmhouse was typically one of its grandest apartments, with expensive and gloomy furnishings. In other novels, Montgomery points out that dying relatives are put in the spare room so they can receive last visits on their death-bed in state. The spare room was seldom in use. "Today I cleaned the parlor and 'spare room'—those solemn rooms of state which seemed such princely apartments to my childish eyes. . . . The spare room was quite frequently used however. I remember when I was a child I had an avid desire to sleep in it—just because it *was* the spare room and such a wonderful-seeming place. My desire was never given me" (*SJ* II [May 2, 1910]: 7).

5. A gable is a triangular section of wall at the end of a ridged roof, from the level of the eaves to the ridge peak. Anne's room has a sloping ceiling and her window faces the dawn.

Anne took off her hat meekly. Matthew came back presently and they sat down to supper. But Anne could not eat. In vain she nibbled at the bread and butter and pecked at the crab-apple preserve out of the little scalloped dish by her plate. She did not really make any headway at all.

"You're not eating anything," said Marilla sharply, eyeing her as if it were a serious shortcoming

Anne sighed.

"I can't. I'm in the depths of despair. Can you eat when you are in the depths of despair?"

"I've never been in the depths of despair, so I can't say," responded Marilla.

"Weren't you? Well, did you ever try to *imagine* you were in the depths of despair?"

"No, I didn't."

"Then I don't think you can understand what it's like. It's a very uncomfortable feeling indeed. When you try to eat a lump comes right up in your throat and you can't swallow anything, not even if it was a chocolate caramel. I had one chocolate caramel once two years ago and it was simply delicious. I've often dreamed since then that I had a lot of chocolate caramels but I always wake up just when I'm going to eat them. I do hope you won't be offended because I can't eat. Everything is extremely nice, but still I cannot eat."

"I guess she's tired," said Matthew, who hadn't spoken since his return from the barn. "Best put her to bed, Marilla."

Marilla had been wondering where Anne should be put to bed. She had prepared a couch in the kitchen chamber for the desired and expected boy. But, although it was neat and clean, it did not seem quite the thing to put a girl there somehow. But the spare room[4] was out of the question for such a stray waif, so there remained only the east gable room.[5] Marilla lighted a candle and told Anne to follow her, which Anne spiritlessly did, taking her hat and carpet-bag from the hall

table as she passed. The hall was fearsomely clean; the little
gable chamber in which she presently found herself seemed
still cleaner.

Marilla set the candle on a three-legged, three-cornered
table and turned down the bed-clothes.

"I suppose you have a nightgown?" she questioned.

Anne nodded.

"Yes, I have two. The matron of the asylum made them for
me. They're fearfully skimpy. There is never enough to go
around in an asylum, so things are always skimpy—at least in
a poor asylum like ours. I hate skimpy night-dresses. But one
can dream just as well in them as in lovely trailing ones, with
frills around the neck, that is one consolation."

"Well, undress as quick as you can and go to bed. I'll come

*Nine-patch quilt in a gable room.
P.E.I. National Park.*

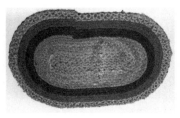

6. Wool or cotton rags often were and are braided, with the braids then sewn together to make rugs. Traditionally, these rugs were a way of using up old scraps of material, but nowadays new material is used in "rag" rugs sold to tourists. See Appendix, "Homemade Artifacts."

7. From "wash-hand stand." The washstand customarily included a jug of water, a basin, and a roller or peg at the side for towels. Underneath would have been the cupboard for the chamberpot.

back in a few minutes for the candle. I daren't trust you to put it out yourself. You'd likely set the place on fire."

When Marilla had gone Anne looked around her wistfully. The whitewashed walls were so painfully bare and staring that she thought they must ache over their own bareness. The floor was bare, too, except for a round braided mat[6] in the middle such as Anne had never seen before. In one corner was the bed, a high, old-fashioned one, with four dark, low, turned posts. In the other corner was the aforesaid three-cornered table adorned with a fat red velvet pincushion hard enough to turn the point of the most adventurous pin. Above it hung a little six-by-eight mirror. Midway between table and bed was the window, with an icy white muslin frill over it, and opposite it was the wash-stand.[7] The whole apartment was of a rigidity not to be described in words, but which sent a shiver to the very marrow of Anne's bones. With a sob she hastily discarded her garments, put on the skimpy nightgown and sprang into bed, where she burrowed face downward into the pillow and pulled the clothes over her head. When Marilla came up for the light, various skimpy articles of raiment scattered most untidily over the floor and a certain tempestuous appearance of the bed were the only indications of any presence save her own.

She deliberately picked up Anne's clothes, placed them neatly on a prim yellow chair, and then, taking up the candle, went over to the bed.

"Good night," she said, a little awkwardly, but not unkindly.

Anne's white face and big eyes appeared over the bedclothes with a startling suddenness.

"How can you call it a *good* night when you know it must be the very worst night I've ever had?" she said reproachfully.

Then she dived down into invisibility again.

Marilla went slowly down to the kitchen and proceeded to wash the supper dishes. Matthew was smoking—a sure sign of perturbation of mind. He seldom smoked, for Marilla set her face against it[8] as a filthy habit; but at certain times and seasons he felt driven to it and then Marilla winked at the practice, realizing that a mere man must have some vent for his emotions.

"Well, this is a pretty kettle of fish,"[9] she said wrathfully. "This is what comes of sending word instead of going ourselves. Robert Spencer's folks have twisted that message somehow. One of us will have to drive over and see Mrs. Spencer to-morrow, that's certain. This girl will have to be sent back to the asylum."

"Yes, I suppose so," said Matthew reluctantly.

"You *suppose* so! Don't you know it?"

"Well now, she's a real nice little thing, Marilla. It's kind of a pity to send her back when she's so set on staying here."

"Matthew Cuthbert, you don't mean to say you think we ought to keep her!"

Marilla's astonishment could not have been greater if Matthew had expressed a predilection for standing on his head.

"Well now, no, I suppose not—not exactly," stammered Matthew, uncomfortably driven into a corner for his precise meaning. "I suppose—we could hardly be expected to keep her."

"I should say not. What good would she be to us?"

"We might be some good to her," said Matthew suddenly and unexpectedly.

"Matthew Cuthbert, I believe that child has bewitched you! I can see as plain as plain that you want to keep her."

"Well now, she's a real interesting little thing," persisted Matthew. "You should have heard her talk coming from the station."

"Oh, she can talk fast enough. I saw that at once. It's nothing in her favour, either. I don't like children who have so much to say. I don't want an orphan girl and if I did she isn't the style I'd pick out. There's something I don't understand

8. Marilla does not want her sanctuary profaned by tobacco: "And I will set my face against that man, and will cut him off from among his people; because he hath given of his seed unto Molech, to defile my sanctuary, and to profane my holy name" (Leviticus 20:3).

9. This expression comes from an old custom of the gentry residing along the river Tweed who entertained their neighbors and friends with a Fête Champetre, which they called giving "a kettle of fish." Scott mentions such a picnic in *St. Ronan's Well.* Since the eighteenth century this phrase has been used figuratively for a mess, muddle, disagreeable, or awkward state of things. See Charles Funk, *Heavens to Betsy! And Other Curious Sayings* (New York, 1955).

about her. No, she's got to be despatched straightway back to where she came from."

"I could hire a French boy to help me," said Matthew, "and she'd be company for you."

"I'm not suffering for company," said Marilla shortly. "And I'm not going to keep her."

"Well now, it's just as you say, of course, Marilla," said Matthew, rising and putting his pipe away. "I'm going to bed."

To bed went Matthew. And to bed, when she had put her dishes away, went Marilla, frowning most resolutely. And upstairs, in the east gable, a lonely, heart-hungry, friendless child cried herself to sleep.

CHAPTER IV

MORNING AT GREEN GABLES

 IT WAS BROAD daylight when Anne awoke and sat up in bed, staring confusedly at the window through which a flood of cheery sunshine was pouring and outside of which something white and feathery waved across glimpses of blue sky.

For a moment she could not remember where she was. First came a delightful thrill, as of something very pleasant; then a horrible remembrance. This was Green Gables and they didn't want her because she wasn't a boy!

But it was morning and, yes, it was a cherry-tree in full bloom outside of her window. With a bound she was out of bed and across the floor. She pushed up the sash—it went up stiffly and creakily, as if it hadn't been opened for a long time, which was the case; and it stuck so tight that nothing was needed to hold it up.

Anne dropped on her knees and gazed out into the June morning, her eyes glistening with delight. Oh, wasn't it beautiful! Wasn't it a lovely place! Suppose she wasn't really going to stay here! She would imagine she was. There was scope for imagination here.

A huge cherry-tree grew outside, so close that its boughs tapped against the house, and it was so thick-set with blos-

1. A self-quotation from the author's journal (*SJ* I [Sept. 21, 1899]: 1). See n. 8. Montgomery may have been rereading her own early journals for hints as to the character of the youthful Anne.

soms that hardly a leaf was to be seen. On both sides of the house was a big orchard, one of apple-trees and one of cherry-trees, also showered over with blossoms; and their grass was all sprinkled with dandelions. In the garden below were lilac-trees purple with flowers and their dizzily sweet fragrance drifted up to the window on the morning wind.

Below the garden a green field lush with clover sloped down to the hollow where the brook ran and where scores of white birches grew, upspringing airily out of an undergrowth suggestive of delightful possibilities in ferns and mosses and woodsy things generally. Beyond it was a hill, green and feathery with spruce and fir; there was a gap in it where the gray gable end of the little house she had seen from the other side of the Lake of Shining Waters was visible.

Off to the left were the big barns and beyond them, away down over green low-sloping fields, was a sparkling blue glimpse of sea.

Anne's beauty-loving eyes lingered on it all, taking everything greedily in; she had looked on so many unlovely places in her life, poor child; but this was as lovely as anything she had ever dreamed.

She knelt there, lost to everything but the loveliness around her, until she was startled by a hand on her shoulder. Marilla had come in unheard by the small dreamer.

"It's time you were dressed," she said curtly.

Marilla really did not know how to talk to the child, and her uncomfortable ignorance made her crisp and curt when she did not mean to be.

Anne stood up and drew a long breath.

"Oh, isn't it wonderful?" she said, waving her hand comprehensively at the good world outside.

"It's a big tree," said Marilla, "and it blooms great but the fruit don't amount to much never — small and wormy."

"Oh, I don't mean just the tree; of course it's lovely — yes, it's *radiantly* lovely — it blooms as if it meant it[1] — but I meant

everything, the garden and the orchard and the brook and the woods, the whole big dear world. Don't you feel as if you just loved the world on a morning like this? And I can hear the brook laughing all the way up here. Have you ever noticed what cheerful things brooks are? They're always laughing. Even in winter-time I've heard them under the ice. I'm so glad there's a brook near Green Gables. Perhaps you think it doesn't make any difference to me when you're not going to keep me but it does. I shall always like to remember that there is a brook at Green Gables even if I never see it again. If there wasn't a brook I'd be *haunted* by the uncomfortable feeling that there ought to be one. I'm not in the depths of despair this morning. I never can be in the morning. Isn't it a splen-did thing that there are mornings? But I feel very sad. I've just

"A view from my window."
Cavendish, in the 1890s.

2. Cf. "He found him in a desert
land, and in the waste howling
wilderness; he led him about, he
instructed him, he kept him as the
apple of his eye" (Deuteronomy
32:10).

*Opposite: The kitchen at Green
Gables, set for the 1880s–90s,
P.E.I. National Park.*

been imagining that it was really me you wanted after all and
that I was to stay here for ever and ever. It was a great comfort while it lasted. But the worst of imagining things is that
the time comes when you have to stop and that hurts."

"You'd better get dressed and come down-stairs and never
mind your imaginings," said Marilla as soon as she could get a
word in edgewise. "Breakfast is waiting. Wash your face and
comb your hair. Leave the window up and turn your bed-
clothes back over the foot of the bed. Be as smart as you can."

Anne could evidently be smart to some purpose for she was
downstairs in ten minutes' time, with her clothes neatly on,
her hair brushed and braided, her face washed, and a comfortable consciousness pervading her soul that she had fulfilled all
Marilla's requirements. As a matter of fact, however, she had
forgotten to turn back the bedclothes.

"I'm pretty hungry this morning," she announced, as she
slipped into the chair Marilla placed for her. "The world
doesn't seem such a howling wilderness[2] as it did last night.
I'm so glad it's a sunshiny morning. But I like rainy mornings
real well, too. All sorts of mornings are interesting, don't you
think? You don't know what's going to happen through the
day, and there's so much scope for imagination. But I'm glad
it's not rainy to-day because it's easier to be cheerful and bear
up under affliction on a sunshiny day. I feel that I have a good
deal to bear up under. It's all very well to read about sorrows
and imagine yourself living through them heroically, but it's
not so nice when you really come to have them, is it?"

"For pity's sake hold your tongue," said Marilla. "You talk
entirely too much for a little girl."

Thereupon Anne held her tongue so obediently and thoroughly that her continued silence made Marilla rather nervous, as if in the presence of something not exactly natural.
Matthew also held his tongue—but this at least was natural
—so that the meal was a very silent one.

As it progressed Anne became more and more abstracted, eating mechanically, with her big eyes fixed unswervingly and unseeingly on the sky outside the window. This made Marilla more nervous than ever; she had an uncomfortable feeling that while this odd child's body might be there at the table her spirit was far away in some remote airy cloudland, borne aloft on the wings of imagination. Who would want such a child about the place?

Yet Matthew wished to keep her, of all unaccountable things! Marilla felt that he wanted it just as much this morning as he had the night before, and that he would go on wanting it. That was Matthew's way—take a whim into his head and cling to it with the most amazing silent persistency —a persistency ten times more potent and effectual in its very silence than if he had talked it out.

3. From the well-known poem (found in the *Fifth Royal Reader*, pages 184–88) by Thomas Gray: "Elegy in a Country Churchyard": "For thee, who mindful of the unhonored dead / Dost in these lines their artless tale relate, / If chance, by lonely contemplation led, / Some kindred spirit shall inquire thy fate" (Stanza 24, ll. 93–96). Elizabeth Epperly in *The Fragrance of Sweet Grass* (5) points out that this phrase is also used in Olive Schreiner's *The Story of An African Farm* and in Elizabeth Von Arnim's *Elizabeth and Her German Garden*.

4. A case or cover containing feathers, flock, or the like, forming a mattress or pillow. "Ticking" is the term for the strong hard linen or cotton material used to make such cases. In *Anne of Avonlea*, when Anne undertakes a difficult and feathery job—"I'm going to shift the feathers from my old bedtick to the new one" (ch. 19) —she is discovered covered in feathers (ch. 20).

5. Dinner was the chief meal of the day, eaten about mid-day.

6. A hollow, conical cap for extinguishing the light of a candle or lamp. Montgomery may be recalling Charles Dickens's *A Christmas Carol* (1843) in which the Spirit of Christmas Past is thus described: "But the strangest thing about it was, that from the crown of its head there sprung a bright clear jet of light . . . which was doubtless the occasion of its using, in its duller moments, a great extinguisher for a cap, which it held

When the meal ended Anne came out of her reverie and offered to wash the dishes.

"Can you wash dishes right?" asked Marilla distrustfully.

"Pretty well. I'm better at looking after children, though. I've had so much experience at that. It's such a pity you haven't any here for me to look after."

"I don't feel as if I wanted any more children to look after than I've got at present. *You're* problem enough in all conscience. What's to be done with you I don't know. Matthew is a most ridiculous man."

"I think he's lovely," said Anne reproachfully. "He is so very sympathetic. He didn't mind how much I talked—he seemed to like it. I felt that he was a kindred spirit[3] as soon as ever I saw him."

"You're both queer enough, if that's what you mean by kindred spirits," said Marilla with a sniff. "Yes, you may wash the dishes. Take plenty of hot water, and be sure you dry them well. I've got enough to attend to this morning for I'll have to drive over to White Sands in the afternoon and see Mrs. Spencer. You'll come with me and we'll settle what's to be done with you. After you've finished the dishes go upstairs and make your bed."

Anne washed the dishes deftly enough, as Marilla, who kept a sharp eye on the process, discerned. Later on she made her bed less successfully, for she had never learned the art of wrestling with a feather tick.[4] But it was done somehow and smoothed down; and then Marilla, to get rid of her, told her she might go out-of-doors and amuse herself until dinner-time.[5]

Anne flew to the door, face alight, eyes glowing. On the very threshold she stopped short, wheeled about, came back and sat down by the table, light and glow as effectually blotted out as if some one had clapped an extinguisher[6] on her.

"What's the matter now?" demanded Marilla.

"I don't dare go out," said Anne, in the tone of a martyr

relinquishing all earthly joys. "If I can't stay here there is no use in my loving Green Gables. And if I go out there and get acquainted with all those trees and flowers and the orchard and the brook I'll not be able to help loving it. It's hard enough now, so I won't make it any harder. I want to go out so much—everything seems to be calling to me, 'Anne, Anne, come out to us. Anne, Anne, we want a playmate'—but it's better not. There is no use in loving things if you have to be torn from them, is there? And it's *so* hard to keep from loving things, isn't it? That was why I was so glad when I thought I was going to live here. I thought I'd have so many things to love and nothing to hinder me. But that brief dream is over. I am resigned to my fate now, so I don't think I'll go out for fear I'll get unresigned again. What is the name of that geranium on the window-sill, please?"

"That's the apple-scented geranium."[7]

"Oh, I don't mean that sort of a name. I mean just a name you gave it yourself. Didn't you give it a name? May I give it one then? May I call it—let me see—Bonny would do— may I call it Bonny while I'm here? Oh, do let me!"

"Goodness, I don't care. But where on earth is the sense of naming a geranium?"

"Oh, I like things to have handles even if they are only geraniums.[8] It makes them seem more like people. How do you know but that it hurts a geranium's feelings just to be called a geranium and nothing else? You wouldn't like to be called nothing but a woman all the time. Yes, I shall call it Bonny. I named that cherry-tree outside my bedroom window this morning. I called it Snow Queen because it was so white.[9] Of course, it won't always be in blossom, but one can imagine that it is, can't one?"

"I never in all my life saw or heard anything to equal her," muttered Marilla, beating a retreat down cellar after potatoes. "She *is* kind of interesting, as Matthew says. I can feel already that I'm wondering what on earth she'll say next. She'll be

under its arm. . . . Perhaps, Scrooge could not have told anybody why . . . but he had a special desire to see the Spirit in his cap; and begged him to be covered. 'What!' exclaimed the Ghost, 'Would you so soon put out, with worldly hands, the light I give?' (Stave II, "The First of the Three Spirits").

7. A geranium, or pelargonium, with soft leaves and a sweet scent. A kitchen herb, its leaves were used sometimes in flavourings.

8. That is, to have names. "There wasn't any school, so I amused myself repotting all my geraniums. Dear things, how I love them! The 'mother' of them all is a matronly old geranium called 'Bonny.' I got Bonny ages ago—it must be as much as two or three years. . . . I called it Bonny—I like things to have handles even if they are only geraniums. . . . And it blooms as if it *meant* it. I believe that old geranium has a soul!" (*SJ* I [Sept. 21, 1889]: 1). See Appendix, "Gardens and Plants."

9. "The Snow Queen" is the title of a story by Hans Christian Andersen, the Danish author who

also wrote "The Princess and the Pea," "The Emperor's New Clothes," and "The Ugly Duckling." His fairy tales were first translated into English in 1846. Montgomery tells us that for her "Hans Andersen's Tales were a perennial joy" (*AP*, 49). Montgomery, like Anne, also named the individual trees around her home. "Behind the barn grew a pair of trees I always called 'The Lovers,' a spruce and a maple, and so closely intertwined that the boughs of the spruce were literally woven into the boughs of the maple. . . . In a corner of the front orchard grew a beautiful young birch tree. I named it 'The White Lady,' and had a fancy about it to the effect that it was the beloved of all the dark spruces near, and that they were rivals for her love" (*AP*, 33).

10. Jerry's last name would have been pronounced "Boot" by English speakers. It is not clear what Creek is meant, but the author may have been thinking of the "French River" near Clifton. Jerry is evidently young, a schoolchild who can hire out his services for the summer when much of the heavy work of mowing, crop gathering, and so on is to be done. See n. 20, ch. 1. If the Cuthberts keep Anne, they will nevertheless still have to pay for a hired hand to help Matthew.

casting a spell over me, too. She's cast it over Matthew. That look he gave me when he went out said everything he said or hinted last night over again. I wish he was like other men and would talk things out. A body could answer back then and argue him into reason. But what's to be done with a man who just *looks*?"

Anne had relapsed into reverie, with her chin in her hands and her eyes on the sky, when Marilla returned from her cellar pilgrimage. There Marilla left her until the early dinner was on the table.

"I suppose I can have the mare and buggy this afternoon, Matthew?" said Marilla.

Matthew nodded and looked wistfully at Anne. Marilla intercepted the look and said grimly:

"I'm going to drive over to White Sands and settle this thing. I'll take Anne with me and Mrs. Spencer will probably make arrangements to send her back to Nova Scotia at once. I'll set your tea out for you and I'll be home in time to milk the cows."

Still Matthew said nothing and Marilla had a sense of having wasted words and breath. There is nothing more aggravating than a man who won't talk back—unless it is a woman who won't.

Matthew hitched the sorrel into the buggy in due time and Marilla and Anne set off. Matthew opened the yard gate for them and as they drove slowly through, he said, to nobody in particular, as it seemed:

"Little Jerry Buote from the Creek was here this morning, and I told him I guessed I'd hire him for the summer."[10]

Marilla made no reply, but she hit the unlucky sorrel such a vicious clip with the whip that the fat mare, unused to such treatment, whizzed indignantly down the lane at an alarming pace. Marilla looked back once as the buggy bounced along and saw that aggravating Matthew leaning over the gate, looking wistfully after them.

CHAPTER V

ANNE'S HISTORY

"DO YOU KNOW," said Anne confidentially, "I've made up my mind to enjoy this drive. It's been my experience that you can nearly always enjoy things if you make your mind up firmly that you will. Of course, you must make it up *firmly*. I am not going to think about going back to the asylum while we're having our drive. I'm just going to think about the drive. Oh, look, there's one little early wild rose out! Isn't it lovely? Don't you think it must be glad to be a rose? Wouldn't it be nice if roses could talk? I'm sure they could tell us such lovely things. And isn't pink the most bewitching colour in the world? I love it but I can't wear it. Red-headed people can't wear pink, not even in imagination. Did you ever know of anybody whose hair was red when she was young but got to be another colour when she grew up?"

"No, I don't know as I ever did," said Marilla mercilessly, "and I shouldn't think it likely to happen in your case, either."

Anne sighed.

"Well, that is another hope gone. My life is a perfect graveyard of buried hopes.[1] That's a sentence I read in a book once, and I say it over to comfort myself whenever I'm disappointed in anything."

1. The source of Anne's allusion is unknown.

2. According to the author, "The 'shore road' has a real existence, and is a very beautiful drive" (*SJ* II [Jan. 27, 1911]: 40). See Appendix, "Geography," and Textual Note.

"I don't see where the comforting comes in myself," said Marilla.

"Why, because it sounds so nice and romantic, just as if I was a heroine in a book, you know. I am so fond of romantic things, and a graveyard full of buried hopes is about as romantic a thing as one can imagine, isn't it? I'm rather glad I have one. Are we going across the Lake of Shining Waters today?"

"We're not going over Barry's Pond, if that's what you mean by your Lake of Shining Waters. We're going by the Shore Road."[2]

"Shore Road sounds nice," said Anne dreamily. "Is it as nice as it sounds? Just when you said 'Shore Road' I saw it in a picture in my mind, as quick as that! And White Sands is a pretty name, too, but I don't like it as well as Avonlea. Avonlea is a lovely name. It just sounds like music. How far is it to White Sands?"

"It's five miles; and as you're evidently bent on talking you

Park Corner shore, 1890s.

might as well talk to some purpose by telling me what you know about yourself."

"Oh, what I *know* about myself isn't really worth telling," said Anne eagerly. "If you'll only let me tell you what *I imagine* about myself you'll think it ever so much more interesting."

"No, I don't want any of your imaginings. Just you stick to bald facts. Begin at the beginning. Where were you born and how old are you?"

"I was eleven last March," said Anne, resigning herself to bald facts with a little sigh. "And I was born in Bolingbroke, Nova Scotia.[3] My father's name was Walter Shirley[4] and he was a teacher in the Bolingbroke High School. My mother's name was Bertha Shirley.[5] Aren't Walter and Bertha lovely names? I'm so glad my parents had nice names. It would be a real disgrace to have a father named—well, say Jedediah,[6] wouldn't it?"

"I guess it doesn't matter what a person's name is as long as he behaves himself," said Marilla, feeling herself called upon to inculcate a good and useful moral.

"Well, I don't know." Anne looked thoughtful. "I read in a book once that a rose by any other name would smell as sweet,[7] but I've never been able to believe it. I don't believe a rose *would* be as nice if it was called a thistle or a skunk-cabbage.[8] I suppose my father could have been a good man even if he had been called Jedediah; but I'm sure it would have been a cross.[9] Well, my mother was a teacher in the High School, too, but when she married father she gave up teaching, of course. A husband was enough responsibility. Mrs. Thomas said that they were a pair of babies and as poor as church mice. They went to live in a weeny-teeny little yellow house in Bolingbroke. I've never seen that house, but I've imagined it thousands of times.[10] I think it must have had honeysuckle over the parlour window and lilacs in the

3. A fictional name, alluding to the first Viscount Bolingbroke, Henry St. John (1678–1751), English statesman and Tory political writer. The name presumably comes by process of analogy from the nominal connection between Oxford, Nova Scotia, and Robert Harley, first Earl of Oxford (1661–1724), Bolingbroke's close associate in Queen Anne's Tory administration.

4. Walter comes from the Old Norman French term meaning "to rule." Anne later names her second son Walter and her youngest son Shirley. See *Rainbow Valley* and *Anne of Ingleside.*

5. Bertha comes from an Old High German term meaning "bright one." Anne's youngest daughter is named Bertha Marilla Blythe (*Anne of Ingleside,* ch. 11).

6. Another name for Solomon. A short story by Montgomery, "The Romance of Jedediah" (1912), collected in *After Many Days,* begins, "Jedediah was not a name that savoured of romance. His last name was Crane, which is little better."

7. From "What's in a name? That which we call a rose / By any other word would smell as sweet" (*Romeo and Juliet,* II.ii. ll. 43–44).

8. A North American weed, a "perennial stemless plant of the arum family (*Symplocarpus foetidus*) giving out an offensive odour."

9. A cross to bear, a particular affliction trying a Christian's patience.

10. In Chapter 21 of *Anne of the Island*, "Roses of Yesterday," Anne does go to see her parents' house: "But the sweetest incident of Anne's sojourn in Bolingbroke was the visit to her birthplace—the little shabby yellow house in an out-of-the-way street she had so often dreamed about." Montgomery says that "the house in which Anne was born was drawn from my own little birthplace at Clifton" (*SJ* II [Jan. 27, 1911]: 41). See Appendix, "Geography."

front yard, and lilies of the valley just inside the gate. Yes, and muslin curtains in all the windows. Muslin curtains give a house such an air. I was born in that house. Mrs. Thomas said I was the homeliest baby she ever saw, I was so scrawny and tiny and nothing but eyes, but that mother thought I was perfectly beautiful. I should think a mother would be a better judge than a poor woman who came in to scrub, wouldn't you? I'm glad she was satisfied with me anyhow. I would feel so sad if I thought I was a disappointment to her—because she didn't live very long after that, you see. She died of fever when I was just three months old. I do wish she'd lived long enough for me to remember calling her mother. I think it would be so sweet to say 'mother,' don't you? And father died four days afterwards from fever, too. That left me an orphan and folks were at their wits' end, so Mrs. Thomas said, what to do with me. You see, nobody wanted me even then. It seems to be my fate. Father and mother had both come from places far away and it was well known they hadn't any relatives living. Finally Mrs. Thomas said she'd take me, though

she was poor and had a drunken husband. She brought me up by hand.[11] Do you know if there is anything in being brought up by hand that ought to make people who are brought up that way better than other people? Because whenever I was naughty Mrs. Thomas would ask me how I could be such a bad girl when she had brought me up by hand — reproachful-like.

"Mr. and Mrs. Thomas moved away from Bolingbroke to Marysville,[12] and I lived with them until I was eight years old. I helped look after the Thomas children — there were four of them younger than me — and I can tell you they took a lot of looking after. Then Mr. Thomas was killed falling under a train, and his mother offered to take Mrs. Thomas and the children but she didn't want me. Mrs. Thomas was at *her* wits' end, so she said, what to do with me. Then Mrs. Hammond from up the river came down and said she'd take me, seeing I was handy with children, and I went up the river to live with her in a little clearing among the stumps.[13] It was a very lonesome place. I'm sure I could never have lived there if I hadn't an imagination. Mr. Hammond worked a little saw-mill up there, and Mrs. Hammond had eight children. She had twins three times. I like babies in moderation, but twins three times in succession is *too much*. I told Mrs. Hammond so firmly, when the last pair came. I used to get so dreadfully tired carrying them about.

"I lived up river with Mrs. Hammond over two years, and then Mr. Hammond died and Mrs. Hammond broke up housekeeping. She divided her children among her relatives and went to the States. I had to go to the asylum at Hopetown, because nobody would take me. They didn't want me at the asylum, either; they said they were overcrowded as it was. But they had to take me and I was there four months until Mrs. Spencer came."

Anne finished up with another sigh, of relief this time.

11. This phrase can be understood in two ways, first in the sense that Anne's foster mother was personally and intimately involved in Anne's rearing. "By hand" in this sense is used to mean that she did it herself, the way a person would say she sewed something by hand, as opposed to using a machine. The phrase also carries the implication, however, that she disciplined Anne with corporal punishment.

12. A fictional name, possibly with Roman Catholic associations.

13. Recently cleared land, still dotted with stumps of trees, the roots not yet removed to enable planting; indicates a remote semisettlement and poor way of life.

Opposite: Lucy Maud Montgomery's birthplace in Clifton, 1880s.

14. See Appendices, "The Settlers of P.E.I.," "Literary Allusion," and "Recitation Pieces."

15. See Appendices, "The Settlers of P.E.I.," "Literary Allusion," and "Recitation Pieces." See also n. 4, ch. 2 on *"Marmion: A Tale of Flodden Field."*

16. See Appendices, "Literary Allusion" and "Recitation Pieces."

17. A narrative poem in six cantos by Sir Walter Scott, first published in 1810. The story is set in the Trossachs around Loch Katrine in the Scotland of James V (1513–1542). It was regarded in its day as the most successful of Scott's ballad epics. The publication of *The Lady of the Lake* did much to make the Highlands popular with nineteenth-century tourists. An abridged version appears in the *Sixth Royal Reader* (149–67).

18. A set of poems in blank verse by James Thomson first published in four books between 1726 and 1730. *The Seasons* is sometimes held to be the first considerable treatment of nature in the manner of the Romantic school. "I had been reading Thomson's *Seasons*, of which a little, black, curly-covered atrociously printed copy had fallen into my hands. So I composed a 'poem' called 'Autumn' in blank verse in imitation thereof" (*AP*, 53). *The Seasons* has a similar effect on Emily Starr's writing in *Emily of New Moon* (ch. 9). *The Seasons* was acceptable reading matter to the descendants of the Puritans because it was religious, scientific, and nonfictional.

Evidently she did not like talking about her experiences in a world that had not wanted her.

"Did you ever go to school?" demanded Marilla, turning the sorrel mare down the Shore Road.

"Not a great deal. I went a little the last year I stayed with Mrs. Thomas. When I went up river we were so far from a school that I couldn't walk it in winter and there was vacation in summer, so I could only go in the spring and fall. But of course I went while I was at the asylum. I can read pretty well and I know ever so many pieces of poetry off by heart—'The Battle of Hohenlinden'[14] and 'Edinburgh after Flodden,'[15] and 'Bingen on The Rhine,'[16] and lots of the 'Lady of the Lake'[17] and most of 'The Seasons,'[18] by James Thomson.[19] Don't you just love poetry that gives you a crinkly feeling up and down your back? There is a piece in the Fifth Reader[20]—'The Downfall of Poland'[21]—that is just full of thrills. Of course, I wasn't in the Fifth Reader—I was only in the Fourth—but the big girls used to lend me theirs to read."

"Were those women—Mrs. Thomas and Mrs. Hammond —good to you?" asked Marilla, looking at Anne out of the corner of her eye.

"O-o-o-h," faltered Anne. Her sensitive little face suddenly flushed scarlet and embarrassment sat on her brow. "Oh, they *meant* to be—I know they meant to be just as good and kind as possible. And when people mean to be good to you, you don't mind very much when they're not quite—always. They had a good deal to worry them, you know. It's very trying to have a drunken husband, you see; and it must be very trying to have twins three times in succession, don't you think? But I feel sure they meant to be good to me."

Marilla asked no more questions. Anne gave herself up to a silent rapture over the Shore Road and Marilla guided the sorrel abstractedly while she pondered deeply. Pity was suddenly stirring in her heart for the child. What a starved, un-loved life she had had—a life of drudgery and poverty and neglect; for Marilla was shrewd enough to read between the lines of Anne's history and divine the truth. No wonder she had been so delighted at the prospect of a real home. It was a pity she had to be sent back. What if she, Marilla, should indulge Matthew's unaccountable whim and let her stay? He was set on it; and the child seemed a nice teachable little thing.

"She's got too much to say," thought Marilla, "but she might be trained out of that. And there's nothing rude or slangy in what she does say. She's ladylike. It's likely her people were nice folks."

The Shore Road was "woodsy and wild and lonesome."[22] On the right hand, scrub firs,[23] their spirits quite unbroken by long years of tussle with the gulf winds, grew thickly. On the left were the steep red sandstone cliffs, so near the track in places that a mare of less steadiness than the sorrel might have tried the nerves of the people behind her. Down at the base of the cliffs were heaps of surf-worn rocks or little sandy coves inlaid with pebbles as with ocean jewels; beyond lay the sea, shimmering and blue, and over it soared the gulls, their pinions flashing silvery in the sunlight.

"Isn't the sea wonderful?" said Anne, rousing from a long, wide-eyed silence. "Once, when I lived in Marysville, Mr. Thomas hired an express-wagon[24] and took us all to spend the day at the shore ten miles away. I enjoyed every moment of that day, even if I had to look after the children all the time. I lived it over in happy dreams for years. But this shore is nicer than the Marysville shore. Aren't those gulls splendid? Would you like to be a gull? I think I would—that is, if I couldn't be a human girl. Don't you think it would be nice to wake up at sunrise and swoop down over the water and away out over that lovely blue all day; and then at night to fly back

19. James Thomson (1700–1748), a poet born in the Scottish border country, became lionized in London after the publication of "Winter." As well as *The Seasons*, Thomson also wrote *The Castle of Indolence* (1748), *Ode to the Memory of Sir Isaac Newton* (1727), and *Liberty* (1734–1736), as well as plays, including the masque *Alfred*, which contains the song "Rule, Britannia." See Textual Note.

20. *The Royal Reader* series published by Nelson for the use of schools. P.E.I. schools probably used the same series as "prescribed by the Council of Public Instruction for use in the Public Schools in Nova Scotia" (Halifax: A. & W. MacKinlay, 1875), as Anne makes no mention of any transition to an unfamiliar Reader in her new school. When her author started school, "I was in the second book of the old Royal Reader series . . . thus skipping the First Reader. When I went to school and found that there was a First Reader, I felt greatly aggrieved to think that I had never gone through it" (*AP*, 27–28). See Appendices, "Education" and "Music and Elocution."

21. See Appendices, "Literary Allusion" and "Recitation Pieces."

22. From "Cobbler Keezar's Vision," by the American poet John Greenleaf Whittier: "woodsy and wild and lonesome, / The swift stream wound away, / Through birches and scarlet maples / Flashing in foam and spray" (Stanza 6).

23. Short, underdeveloped trees that grow where the land is too sandy and windy for them to grow to full height.

24. Perhaps the wagon was hired from the post office. Montgomery's grandparents kept the post office in Cavendish.

25. American tourists were drawn to the Maritimes by an interest in Longfellow's *Evangeline* (1849) and the attractions of pleasantly cool summer nights and sunny days, shore views and sandy beaches, good food, clean lodging, and cheap accommodations. See Appendix, "Geography."

to one's nest. Oh, I can just imagine myself doing it. What big house is that just ahead, please?"

"That's the White Sands Hotel. Mr. Kirk runs it, but the season hasn't begun yet. There are heaps of Americans come there for the summer.[25] They think this shore is just about right."

"I was afraid it might be Mrs. Spencer's place," said Anne mournfully. "I don't want to get there. Somehow, it will seem like the end of everything."

CHAPTER VI

MARILLA MAKES
UP HER MIND

 GET THERE they did, however, in due season. Mrs. Spencer lived in a big yellow house at White Sands Cove, and she came to the door with surprise and welcome mingled on her benevolent face.

"Dear, dear," she exclaimed, "you're the last folks I was looking for to-day, but I'm real glad to see you. You'll put your horse in? And how are you, Anne?"

"I'm as well as can be expected, thank you," said Anne smilelessly. A blight seemed to have descended on her.

"I suppose we'll stay a little while to rest the mare," said Marilla, "but I promised Matthew I'd be home early. The fact is, Mrs. Spencer, there's been a queer mistake somewhere, and I've come over to see where it is. We sent word, Matthew and I, for you to bring us a boy from the asylum. We told your brother Robert to tell you we wanted a boy ten or eleven years old."

"Marilla Cuthbert, you don't say so!" said Mrs. Spencer in distress. "Why, Robert sent the word down by his daughter Nancy and she said you wanted a girl—didn't she, Flora Jane?" appealing to her daughter who had come out to the steps.

1. The Deity: "The foreknowing and beneficent care and government of God . . . hence applied to the Deity as exercising prescient power and direction."

2. As Proverbs 12:10 has it, "A righteous man regardeth the life of his beast: but the tender mercies of the wicked are cruel."

"She certainly did, Miss Cuthbert," corroborated Flora Jane earnestly.

"I'm dreadfully sorry," said Mrs. Spencer. "It is too bad; but it certainly wasn't my fault, you see, Miss Cuthbert. I did the best I could and I thought I was following your instructions. Nancy is a terrible flighty thing. I've often had to scold her well for her heedlessness."

"It was our own fault," said Marilla, resignedly. "We should have come to you ourselves and not left an important message to be passed along by word of mouth in that fashion. Anyhow, the mistake has been made and the only thing to do now is to set it right. Can we send the child back to the asylum? I suppose they'll take her back, won't they?"

"I suppose so," said Mrs. Spencer thoughtfully, "but I don't think it will be necessary to send her back. Mrs. Peter Blewett was up here yesterday and she was saying to me how much she wished she'd sent by me for a little girl to help her. Mrs. Peter has a large family, you know, and she finds it hard to get help. Anne will be the very girl for her. I call it positively Providential."

Marilla did not look as if she thought Providence[1] had much to do with the matter. Here was an unexpectedly good chance to get this unwelcome orphan off her hands, and she did not even feel grateful for it.

She knew Mrs. Peter Blewett only by sight as a small, shrewish-faced woman without an ounce of superfluous flesh on her bones. But she had heard of her. "A terrible worker and driver," Mrs. Peter was said to be; and discharged servant girls told fearsome tales of her temper and stinginess and her family of pert, quarrelsome children. Marilla felt a qualm of conscience at the thought of handing Anne over to her tender mercies.[2]

"Well, I'll go in and we'll talk the matter over," she said.

"And if there isn't Mrs. Peter coming up the lane this blessed minute!" exclaimed Mrs. Spencer, bustling her guests through the hall into the parlour, where a deadly chill struck on them as if the air had been strained so long through dark green, closely-drawn blinds that it had lost every particle of warmth it had ever possessed. "That is real lucky for we can settle the matter right away. Take the arm-chair, Miss Cuthbert. Anne, you sit here on the ottoman and don't wriggle. Let me take your hats. Flora Jane, go out and put the kettle on. Good afternoon, Mrs. Blewett. We were just saying how fortunate it was you happened along. Let me introduce you two ladies. Mrs. Blewett, Miss Cuthbert. Please excuse me for just a moment. I forgot to tell Flora Jane to take the buns out of the oven."

Mrs. Spencer whisked away after pulling up the blinds. Anne, sitting mutely on the ottoman, with her hands clasped tightly in her lap, stared at Mrs. Blewett as one fascinated. Was she to be given into the keeping of this sharp-faced, sharp-eyed woman? She felt a lump coming up in her throat, and her eyes smarted painfully. She was beginning to be afraid she couldn't keep the tears back when Mrs. Spencer returned, flushed and beaming, quite capable of taking any and every difficulty, physical, mental or spiritual, into consideration and settling it out of hand.

"It seems there's been a mistake about this little girl, Mrs. Blewett," she said. "I was under the impression that Mr. and Miss Cuthbert wanted a little girl to adopt. I was certainly told so. But it seems it was a boy they wanted. So, if you're still of the same mind you were yesterday, I think she'll be just the thing for you."

Mrs. Blewett darted her eyes over Anne from head to foot.

"How old are you and what's your name?" she demanded.

"Anne Shirley," faltered the shrinking child, not daring to make any stipulations regarding the spelling thereof, "and I'm eleven years old."

"Humph! You don't look as if there was much to you. But you're wiry. I don't know but the wiry ones are the best after

3. From the Latin *frangere, fractum*, to break. A word used especially of children considered hard to manage, refractory, or peevish.

all. Well, if I take you you'll have to be a good girl, you know —good and smart and respectful. I'll expect you to earn your keep, and no mistake about that. Yes, I suppose I might as well take her off your hands, Miss Cuthbert. The baby's awful fractious,[3] and I'm clean worn out attending to him. If you like I can take her right home now."

Marilla looked at Anne and softened at the sight of the child's pale face with its look of mute misery—the misery of a helpless little creature who finds itself once more caught in the trap from which it had escaped. Marilla felt an uncomfortable conviction that, if she denied the appeal of that look, it would haunt her to her dying day. Moreover, she did not fancy Mrs. Blewett. To hand a sensitive, "high-strung" child over to such a woman! No, she could not take the responsibility of doing that!

"Well, I don't know," she said slowly. "I didn't say that Matthew and I had absolutely decided that we wouldn't keep her. In fact, I may say that Matthew is disposed to keep her. I just came over to find out how the mistake had occurred. I think I'd better take her home again and talk it over with Matthew. I feel that I oughtn't to decide on anything without consulting him. If we make up our mind not to keep her we'll bring or send her over to you to-morrow night. If we don't you may know that she is going to stay with us. Will that suit you, Mrs. Blewett?"

"I suppose it'll have to," said Mrs. Blewett ungraciously.

During Marilla's speech a sunrise had been dawning on Anne's face. First the look of despair faded out; then came a faint flush of hope; her eyes grew deep and bright as morning stars. The child was quite transfigured; and a moment later, when Mr. Spencer and Mrs. Blewett went out in quest of a recipe the latter had come to borrow, she sprang up and flew across the room to Marilla.

"Oh, Miss Cuthbert, did you really say that perhaps you would let me stay at Green Gables?" she said, in a breathless whisper, as if speaking aloud might shatter the glorious possibility. "Did you really say it? Or did I only imagine that you did?"

"I think you'd better learn to control that imagination of yours, Anne, if you can't distinguish between what is real and what isn't," said Marilla crossly. "Yes, you did hear me say just that and no more. It isn't decided yet and perhaps we will conclude to let Mrs. Blewett take you after all. She certainly needs you much more than I do."

"I'd rather go back to the asylum than go to live with her," said Anne passionately. "She looks exactly like a—like a gimlet."[4]

Marilla smothered a smile under the conviction that Anne must be reproved for such a speech.

"A little girl like you should be ashamed of talking so about a lady and a stranger," she said severely. "Go back and sit down quietly and hold your tongue, and behave as a good girl should."

"I'll try to do and be anything you want me, if you'll only keep me," said Anne, returning meekly to her ottoman.

When they arrived back at Green Gables that evening Matthew met them in the lane. Marilla from afar had noted him prowling along it and guessed his motive. She was prepared for the relief she read in his face when he saw that she had at least brought Anne back with her. But she said nothing to him, relative to the affair, until they were both out in the yard behind the barn milking the cows. Then she briefly told him Anne's history and the result of the interview with Mrs. Spencer.

"I wouldn't give a dog I liked to that Blewett woman," said Matthew with unusual vim.

"I don't fancy her style myself," admitted Marilla, "but it's that or keeping her ourselves, Matthew. And, since you seem to want her, I suppose I'm willing—or have to be. I've been thinking over the idea until I've got kind of used to it. It seems a sort of duty. I've never brought up a child, especially a

4. A gimlet is a kind of boring tool with "a grooved steel body and a cross handle at one end." A "gimlet eye" is a piercing eye.

5. To interfere or meddle. The image comes from rowing a boat: only one person must row at a time or there is a risk of changing the boat's direction. The first recorded appearance in English of this phrase is in the *Apophthegmes, That is to Saie, Prompte Saiyings*, or Latin adages garnered by Erasmus, published in 1500 and translated by Nicolas Udall in 1542. This phrase becomes a recurrent metaphor for Matthew's relation to Marilla's bringing up of Anne.

girl, and I dare say I'll make a terrible mess of it. But I'll do my best. So far as I'm concerned, Matthew, she may stay."

Matthew's shy face was a glow of delight.

"Well now, I reckoned you'd come to see it in that light, Marilla," he said. "She's such an interesting little thing."

"It'd be more to the point if you could say she was a useful little thing," retorted Marilla, "but I'll make it my business to see she's trained to be that. And mind, Matthew, you're not to go interfering with my methods. Perhaps an old maid doesn't know much about bringing up a child, but I guess she knows more than an old bachelor. So you just leave me to manage her. When I fail it'll be time enough to put your oar in."[5]

"There, there Marilla, you can have your own way," said Matthew reassuringly. "Only be as good and kind to her as you can be without spoiling her. I kind of think she's one of the sort you can do anything with if you only get her to love you."

Marilla sniffed, to express her contempt for Matthew's opinions concerning anything feminine, and walked off to the dairy with the pails.

"I won't tell her to-night that she can stay," she reflected, as she strained the milk into the creamers. "She'd be so excited that she wouldn't sleep a wink. Marilla Cuthbert, you're fairly in for it. Did you ever suppose you'd see the day when you'd be adopting an orphan girl? It's surprising enough; but not so surprising as that Matthew should be at the bottom of it, him that always seemed to have such a mortal dread of little girls. Anyhow, we've decided on the experiment and goodness only knows what will come of it."

CHAPTER VII

ANNE SAYS HER PRAYERS[1]

WHEN MARILLA took Anne up to bed that night she said stiffly:

"Now, Anne, I noticed last night that you threw your clothes all about the floor when you took them off. That is a very untidy habit, and I can't allow it at all. As soon as you take off any article of clothing fold it neatly and place it on the chair. I haven't any use at all for little girls who aren't neat."

"I was so harrowed up in my mind last night at I didn't think about my clothes at all," said Anne. "I'll fold them nicely to-night. They always made us do that at the asylum. Half the time, though, I'd forget, I'd be in such a hurry to get into bed, nice and quiet, and imagine things."

"You'll have to remember a little better if you stay here," admonished Marilla. "There, that looks something like. Say your prayers now and get into bed."

"I never say any prayers," announced Anne.

Marilla looked horrified astonishment.

"Why, Anne, what do you mean? Were you never taught to say your prayers? God always wants little girls to say their prayers. Don't you know who God is, Anne?"

"'God is a spirit, infinite, eternal and unchangeable, in His

1. The story of an orphan girl being taught to pray had an immediate appeal for a Victorian audience, as is seen in the phenomenal and continuous popularity of *Jessica's First Prayer* (1867), a serious evangelical work by "Hesba Stretton" (pen-name of Sarah Smith, 1832–1911). Jessica is a true "street-Arab," and her awkward first prayer affects the reader with both its comedy and its pathos. Montgomery, however, is offering a subtle critique of this kind of pious narrative.

2. This definition of God comes from the Presbyterian *Shorter Catechism* (Question 1, 4–12). *The Shorter Catechism* was written by the Westminster Assembly of Divines between 1643 and 1652 and approved by the General Assembly of the Kirk of Scotland.

being, wisdom, power, holiness, justice, goodness and truth,'"[2] responded Anne promptly and glibly.

Marilla looked rather relieved.

"So you do know something then, thank goodness! You're not quite a heathen. Where did you learn that?"

"Oh, at the asylum Sunday School. They made us learn the whole catechism. I liked it pretty well. There's something splendid about some of the words. 'Infinite, eternal and unchangeable.' Isn't that grand? It has such a roll to it—just like a big organ playing. You couldn't quite call it poetry, I suppose, but it sounds a lot like it, doesn't it?"

"We're not talking about poetry, Anne—we are talking about saying your prayers. Don't you know it's a terrible wicked thing not to say your prayers every night? I'm afraid you are a very bad little girl."

"You'd find it easier to be bad than good if you had red hair," said Anne reproachfully. "People who haven't red hair don't know what trouble is. Mrs. Thomas told me that God made my hair red *on purpose*, and I've never cared about Him since. And anyhow, I'd always be too tired at night to bother saying prayers. People who have to look after twins can't be expected to say their prayers. Now, do you honestly think they can?"

Marilla decided that Anne's religious training must begun at once. Plainly there was no time to be lost.

"You must say your prayers while you are under my roof, Anne."

"Why, of course, if you want me to," assented Anne cheerfully. "I'd do anything to oblige you. But you'll have to tell me what to say for this once. After I get into bed I'll imagine out a real nice prayer to say always. I believe that it will be quite interesting, now that I come to think of it."

"You must kneel down," said Marilla in embarrassment.

Anne knelt at Marilla's knee and looked up gravely.

"Why must people kneel down to pray? If I really wanted to pray I'll tell you what I'd do. I'd go out into a great big field all alone or into the deep, deep woods, and I'd look up into the sky—up—up—up—into that lovely blue sky that looks as if there was no end to its blueness. And then I'd just feel a prayer. Well, I'm ready. What am I to say?"

Marilla felt more embarrassed than ever. She had intended to teach Anne the childish classic, "Now I lay me down to sleep."[3] But she had, as I have told you, the glimmerings of a sense of humour—which is simply another name for a sense of the fitness of things; and it suddenly occurred to her that that simple little prayer, sacred to white-robed childhood lisping at motherly knees, was entirely unsuited to this freckled witch of a girl who knew and cared nothing about God's love since she had never had it translated to her through the medium of human love.

"You're old enough to pray for yourself, Anne," she said finally. "Just thank God for your blessings and ask Him humbly for the things you want."

"Well, I'll do my best," promised Anne, burying her face in Marilla's lap. "Gracious Heavenly Father—that's the way the ministers say it in church, so I suppose it's all right in a private prayer, isn't it?" she interjected, lifting her head for a moment. "Gracious Heavenly Father, I thank Thee for the White Way of Delight and the Lake of Shining Waters and Bonny and the Snow Queen. I'm really extremely grateful for them. And that's all the blessings I can think of just now to thank Thee for. As for the things I want, they're so numerous that it would take a great deal of time to name them all, so I will only mention the two most important. Please let me stay at Green Gables; and please let me be good-looking when I grow up. I remain,

Yours respectfully,
ANNE SHIRLEY"

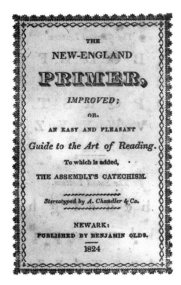

3. This well-known child's prayer was originally published in *The New England Primer*, a Calvinist schoolbook compiled and published by Benjamin Harris. The first edition probably appeared in 1683. Harris's primer, frequently revised, is estimated to have sold more than 5 million copies. It contained the letters of the alphabet, illustrated by rhymed couplets and woodcuts, and simple moral texts based on Old Testament history and wisdom, as well as this prayer: "Now I lay me down to sleep / I pray the Lord my soul to keep / If I should die before I wake / I pray the Lord my soul to take" (James D. Hart, ed. *The Oxford Companion to American Literature*, 5th ed., 530).

4. The minister's house. In England originally, a manse was a measure of land regarded as sufficient for the support of a family. It was used specifically of ecclesiastical endowments and came to refer particularly to the house and property set aside for the use of a Protestant minister.

THE

PEEP OF DAY;

OR,

A SERIES

OF

THE EARLIEST RELIGIOUS INSTRUCTION

THE INFANT MIND

IS C.   ...CEIVING;

THE

PEEP OF DAY.

VERSE

LESSON I.

OF THE BODY.

MY DEAR LITTLE CHILDREN—You have seen the sun in the sky. Who put the sun in the sky? God.

Can you reach up so high? No.

Who holds up the sun, that it does not fall? It is God.

God lives in heaven; heaven is much higher than the sun.

Can you see God? No.

Yet he can see you, for God sees every thing.

God made every thing at first, and God takes care of every thing. God made the sun, and God makes it shine every day. God made the rain. God pours it down. God made the wind, and he makes it blow. God made you, my little child, and God keeps you alive.

5. These were Methodist Sunday school tracts by Mrs. Favell Lee (Bevan) Mortimer, published from the 1830s on by the American Tract Society of Boston. Montgomery observed, "I was always nagged about 'reading too much' and scolded because I preferred stories to the 'Peep of Day' series" (*SJ* I [Jan. 2, 1905]: 302).

"There, did I do it all right?" she asked eagerly getting up. "I could have made it much more flowery if I'd had a little more time to think it over."

Poor Marilla was only preserved from complete collapse by remembering that it was not irreverence, but simply spiritual ignorance on the part of Anne that was responsible for this extraordinary petition. She tucked the child up in bed, mentally vowing that she should be taught a prayer the very next day, and was leaving the room with the light when Anne called her back.

"I've just thought of it now. I should have said 'Amen' in place of 'Yours respectfully,' shouldn't I?—the way the ministers do. I'd forgotten it, but I felt a prayer should be finished off in some way, so I put in the other. Do you suppose it will make any difference?"

"I—I don't suppose it will," said Marilla. "Go sleep now like a good child. Good-night."

"I can say good-night to-night with a clear conscience," said Anne, luxuriously cuddling down among her pillows.

Marilla retreated to the kitchen, set the candle firmly on the table and glared at Matthew.

"Matthew Cuthbert, it's about time somebody adopted that child and taught her something. She's next door to a perfect heathen. Will you believe that she never said a prayer in her life until to-night? I'll send to the manse[4] to-morrow and borrow the Peep of Day[5] series, that's what I'll do. And she shall go to Sunday School just as soon as I can get some suitable clothes made for her. I foresee that I shall have my hands full. Well, well, we can't get through this world without our share of trouble. I've had a pretty easy life of it so far but my time has come at last and I suppose I'll just have to make the best of it."

CHAPTER VIII

ANNE'S BRINGING-UP IS BEGUN

FOR REASONS best known to herself, Marilla did not tell Anne that she was to stay at Green Gables until the next afternoon. During the forenoon she kept the child busy with various tasks and watched over her with a keen eye while she did them. By noon she had concluded that Anne was smart and obedient, willing to work and quick to learn; her most serious shortcoming seemed to be a tendency to fall into day-dreams in the middle of a task and forget all about it until such time as she was sharply recalled to earth by a reprimand or a catastrophe.

When Anne had finished washing the dinner dishes she suddenly confronted Marilla with the air and expression of one desperately determined to learn the worst. Her thin little body trembled from head to foot; her face flushed and her eyes dilated until they were almost black; she clasped her hands tightly and said in an imploring voice:

"Oh, please, Miss Cuthbert, won't you tell me if you are going to send me away or not? I've tried to be patient all the morning, but I really feel that I cannot bear not knowing any longer. It's a dreadful feeling. Please tell me."

"You haven't scalded the dish-cloth[1] in clean hot water as I

1. Without washing machines, doing laundry by hand was a hard job, not for every day. Daily cleaning of the dishcloth was ensured by boiling it. The detail shows Marilla's high standards.

2. Cf. "The heart is deceitful above all things, and desperately wicked: who can know it?" (Jeremiah 17:9). 2.

told you to do," said Marilla immovably. "Just go and do it before you ask any more questions, Anne."

Anne went and attended to the dish-cloth. Then she returned to Marilla and fastened imploring eyes on the latter's face.

"Well," said Marilla, unable to find any excuse for deferring her explanation longer, "I suppose I might as well tell you. Matthew and I have decided to keep you—that is, if you will try to be a good little girl and show yourself grateful. Why, child, whatever is the matter?"

"I'm crying," said Anne in a tone of bewilderment. "I can't think why. I'm glad as glad can be. Oh, *glad* doesn't seem the right word at all. I was glad about the White Way and the cherry blossoms—but this! Oh, it's something more than glad. I'm so happy. I'll try to be so good. It will be uphill work, I expect, for Mrs. Thomas often told me I was desperately wicked.[2] However, I'll do my very best. But can you tell me why I'm crying?"

"I suppose it's because you're all excited and worked up," said Marilla disapprovingly. "Sit down on that chair and try to calm yourself. I'm afraid you both cry and laugh far too easily. Yes, you can stay here and we will try to do right by you. You must go to school; but it's only a fortnight till vacation so it isn't worth while for you to start before it opens again in September."

"What am I to call you?" asked Anne. "Shall I always say Miss Cuthbert? Can I call you Aunt Marilla?"

"No; you'll call me just plain Marilla. I'm not used to being called Miss Cuthbert and it would make me nervous."

"It sounds awfully disrespectful to say just Marilla," protested Anne.

"I guess there'll be nothing disrespectful in it if you're careful to speak respectfully. Everybody, young and old, in Avonlea calls me Marilla except the minister. He says Miss Cuthbert—when he thinks of it."

"I'd love to call you Aunt Marilla," said Anne wistfully. "I've never had an aunt or any relation at all—not even a grand-mother. It would make me feel as if I really belonged to you. Can't I call you Aunt Marilla?"

"No. I'm not your aunt and I don't believe in calling people names that don't belong to them."

"But we could imagine you were my aunt."

"I couldn't," said Marilla grimly.

"Do you never imagine things different from what they really are?" asked Anne wide-eyed.

"No."

"Oh!" Anne drew a long breath. "Oh, Miss—Marilla, how much you miss!"

"I don't believe in imagining things different from what they really are," retorted Marilla. "When the Lord puts us in certain circumstances He doesn't mean for us to imagine them away. And that reminds me. Go into the sitting-room, Anne—be sure your feet are clean and don't let any flies in —and bring me out the illustrated card that's on the mantel-piece. The Lord's Prayer[3] is on it and you'll devote your spare time this afternoon to learning it off by heart. There's to be no more of such praying as I heard last night."

"I suppose I was very awkward," said Anne apologetically, "but then, you see, I'd never had any practice. You couldn't really expect a person to pray very well the first time she tried, could you? I thought out a splendid prayer after I went to bed, just as I promised you I would. It was nearly as long as a minister's and so poetical. But would you be-lieve it? I couldn't remember one word when I woke up this morning. And I'm afraid I'll never be able to think out another one as good. Somehow, things never are so good when they're thought out a second time. Have you ever noticed that?"

"Here is something for you to notice, Anne. When I tell you to do a thing I want you to obey me at once and not

3. See n. 6.

4. A photo lithograph in color. Photography had made possible the art of producing designs upon lithographic stone from which color prints could be made.

5. An illustration based on an incident in the life of Jesus: "And they brought young children to him, that he should touch them: and his disciples rebuked those that brought them. But when Jesus saw it, he was much displeased, and said unto them, 'Suffer the little children to come unto me, and forbid them not: for of such is the kingdom of God. Verily I say unto you, Whosoever shall not receive the kingdom of God as a little child, he shall not enter therein.' And he took them up in his arms, put his hands upon them, and blessed them" (Mark 10:13–16; see also Matthew 19:13–15).

Painting of Christ blessing little children, by Gar Van Vogelstein. From the 1890s.

stand stock-still and discourse about it. Just you go and do as I bid you."

Anne promptly departed for the sitting-room across the hall; she failed to return; after waiting ten minutes Marilla laid down her knitting and marched after her with a grim expression. She found Anne standing motionless before a picture hanging on the wall between the two windows, with her hands clasped behind her, her face uplifted, and her eyes astar with dreams. The white and green light strained through apple-trees and clustering vines outside fell over the rapt little figure with a half-unearthly radiance.

"Anne, whatever are you thinking of ?" demanded Marilla sharply.

Anne came back to earth with a start.

"That," she said, pointing to the picture—a rather vivid chromo[4] entitled "Christ Blessing Little Children"[5]—"and I was just imagining I was one of them—that I was the little girl in the blue dress, standing off by herself in the corner as if she didn't belong to anybody, like me. She looks lonely and sad, don't you think? I guess she hadn't any father or mother of her own. But she wanted to be blessed, too, so she just crept shyly up on the outside of the crowd, hoping nobody would notice her except—Him. I'm sure I know just how she felt. Her heart must have beat and her hands must have got cold, like mine did when I asked you if I could stay. She was afraid He mightn't notice her. But it's likely He did, don't you think? I've been trying to imagine it all out—her edging a little nearer all the time until she was quite close to Him; and then He would look at her and put His hand on her hair and oh, such a thrill of joy as would run over her! But I wish the artist hadn't painted Him so sorrowful-looking. All His pictures are like that, if you've noticed. But I don't believe He could really have looked so sad or the children would have been afraid of Him."

"Anne," said Marilla, wondering why she had not broken

into this speech long before, "you shouldn't talk that way. It's irreverent—positively irreverent."

Anne's eyes marvelled.

"Why, I felt just as reverent as could be. I'm sure I didn't mean to be irreverent."

"Well, I don't suppose you did—but it doesn't sound right to talk so familiarly about such things. And another thing, Anne, when I send you after something you're to bring it at once and not fall into mooning and imagining before pictures. Remember that. Take that card and come right to the kitchen. Now, sit down in the corner and learn that prayer off by heart."

Anne set the card up against the jugful of apple blossoms she had brought in to decorate the dinner-table—Marilla had eyed that decoration askance, but had said nothing—propped her chin on her hands, and fell to studying it intently for several silent minutes.

"I like this," she announced at length. "It's beautiful. I've heard it before—I heard the superintendent of the asylum Sunday School say it over once. But I didn't like it then. He had such a cracked voice and he prayed it so mournfully. I really felt sure he thought praying was a disagreeable duty. This isn't poetry, but it makes me feel just the same way poetry does. 'Our Father which art in heaven hallowed be Thy name.'[6] That is just like line of music. Oh, I'm so glad you thought of asking me learn this, Miss—Marilla."

"Well, learn it and hold your tongue," said Marilla shortly.

Anne tipped the vase of apple blossoms near enough to bestow a soft kiss on a pink-cupped bud, and then studied diligently for some moments longer.

"Marilla," she demanded presently, "do you think that I shall ever have a bosom friend[7] in Avonlea?"

"A—a what kind of a friend?"

"A bosom friend—an intimate friend, you know—a really kindred spirit to whom I can confide my inmost soul. I've

6. The beginning of "The Lord"s Prayer" (Matthew 6: 9–13): "After this manner therefore pray ye: 'Our Father which art in heaven, Hallowed be thy name. Thy kingdom come. Thy will be done in earth, as it is in heaven. Give us this day our daily bread. And forgive us our debts, as we forgive our debtors. And lead us not into temptation, but deliver us from evil.' (The Roman Catholic prayer ends here, but the Protestant one usually continues: "For thine is the kingdom, and the power, and the glory, forever and ever. Amen.")

7. First use dates from 1590. Montgomery's use is probably partly inspired by John Keats's "To Autumn" (1820): "Season of mist and mellow fruitfulness, / Close bosom-friend of the maturing sun" (ll. 1–2).

8. A character in Lewis Carroll's *Alice's Adventures in Wonderland* (1865) who points out morals in everything, *e.g.*, "flamingoes and mustard both bite. And the moral of that is— "Birds of a feather flock together" (Oxford World's Classics, 80).

9. Montgomery records that "Anne's Katie Maurice was mine. In our sitting room there had always stood a big book-case used as a china cabinet. In each door was a large oval glass, dimly reflecting the room. When I was very small each of my reflections in these glass doors were 'real folk' to my imagination. The one in the left–hand door was Katie Maurice . . . a little girl like myself, and I loved her dearly. I would stand before that door and prattle to Katie for hours, giving and receiving confidences. In especial, I liked to do this at twilight, when the fire had been lit and the room and its reflections were a glamour of light and shadow" (*AP*, 74).

dreamed of meeting her all my life. I never really supposed I would, but so many of my loveliest dreams have come true all at once that perhaps this one will, too. Do you think it's possible?"

"Diana Barry lives over at Orchard Slope and she's about your age. She's a very nice little girl, and perhaps she will be a playmate for you when she comes home. She's visiting her aunt over at Carmody just now. You'll have to be careful how you behave yourself, though. Mrs. Barry is a very particular woman. She won't let Diana play with any little girl who isn't nice and good."

Anne looked at Marilla through the apple blossoms, her eyes aglow with interest.

"What is Diana like? Her hair isn't red, is it? Oh, I hope not. It's bad enough to have red hair myself, but I positively couldn't endure it in a bosom friend."

"Diana is a very pretty little girl. She has black eyes and hair and rosy cheeks. And she is good and smart, which is better than being pretty."

Marilla was as fond of morals as the Duchess in Wonderland,[8] and was firmly convinced that one should be tacked on to every remark made to a child who was being brought up.

But Anne waved the moral inconsequently aside and seized only on the delightful possibilities before it.

"Oh, I'm so glad she's pretty. Next to being beautiful one-self—and that's impossible in my case—it would be best to have a beautiful bosom friend. When I lived with Mrs. Thom-as she had a bookcase in her sitting-room with glass doors. There weren't any books in it; Mrs. Thomas kept her best china and her preserves there—when she had any preserves to keep. One of the doors was broken. Mr. Thomas smashed it one night when he was slightly intoxicated. But the other was whole and I used to pretend that my reflection in it was another little girl who lived in it. I called her Katie Maurice,[9] and we were very intimate. I used to talk to her by the hour, especially on Sunday, and tell her everything. Katie was the comfort and consolation of my life. We used to pretend that the bookcase was enchanted and that if I only knew the spell I could open the door and step right into the room where Katie Maurice lived, instead of into Mrs. Thomas' shelves of preserves and china. And then Katie Maurice would have taken me by the hand and led me out into a wonderful place, all flowers and sunshine and fairies, and we would have lived there happy for ever after. When I went to live with Mrs. Hammond it just broke my heart to leave Katie Maurice. She felt it dreadfully, too, I know she did, for she was crying when she kissed me good-bye through the bookcase door. There was no bookcase at Mrs. Hammond's. But just up the river a little way from the house there was a long green valley, and the loveliest echo lived there. It echoed back every word you said, even if you didn't talk a bit loud. So I imagined that it was a little girl called Violetta[10] and we were great friends and I loved her almost as well as I loved Katie Maurice—not quite, but almost, you know. The night before I went to the asylum I said good-bye to Violetta, and oh, her good-bye came back to me in such sad, sad tones. I had become so attached to her that I hadn't the heart to imagine a bosom friend at the asylum, even if there had been any scope for imagination."

"I think it's just as well there wasn't," said Marilla drily. "I don't approve of such goings-on. You seem to half believe your own imaginations. It will be well for you to have a real live friend to put such nonsense out of your head. But don't let Mrs. Barry hear you talking about your Katie Maurices and your Violettas or she'll think you tell stories."

"Oh, I won't. I couldn't talk of them to everybody—their memories are too sacred for that. But I thought I'd like to have you know about them. Oh, look, here's a big bee just tumbled out of an apple blossom. Just think what a lovely

10. The personification of the echo is Ovidian (*Meta* III, ll. 352–400). The name "Violetta" is yet another reflection of the author's fondness for violets, cf. "Violet Vale" (n. 6, ch. 8). She had already published a poem called "The Violet's Spell," which was accepted by *The Ladies' World* in 1893. "Only a Violet" was also accepted by that publication in 1901 (*SJ* I [Mar. 21, 1901]: 261). In Montgomery's own childhood her other imaginary friend in the bookcase was "Lucy Gray."

11. Passages such as this one are reminiscent of Emily Brontë in *Wuthering Heights* (ch. 24):

> He said the pleasantest manner of spending a hot July day was lying . . . in the middle of the moors, with the bees humming dreamily about among the bloom . . . and the blue sky and bright sun shining steadily and cloudlessly. That was his most perfect idea of heaven's happiness—mine was rocking in a rustling green tree, with a west wind blowing, and bright, white clouds flitting rapidly above . . . and not only larks, but throstles, and blackbirds . . . pouring out music on every side . . . and the whole world awake and wild with joy. He wanted all to lie in an ecstacy [*sic*] of peace; I wanted all to sparkle, and dance in glorious jubilee.

So says Cathy the younger about herself and young Linton. Anne combines both forms of imagined ecstatic being, as she wishes to be not only the bee but also the sea-gull and the wind (pp. 89, 126).

12. This is "the wood of *Swietenia Mahagoni*, a tree indigenous to the tropical parts of America. . . . It is very hard and fine grained and takes a high polish" (*OED*). Its rarity makes it expensive. Much of the upper-class Victorian furniture, especially dining-room tables, was made of solid mahogany. But Anne would not have seen any, because of its expense. She certainly will not see any at Green Gables or perhaps anywhere in Avonlea.

place to live—in an apple blossom! Fancy going to sleep in it when the wind was rocking it! If I wasn't a human girl I think I'd like to be a bee and live among the flowers."[11]

"Yesterday you wanted to be a sea-gull," sniffed Marilla. "I think you are very fickle-minded. I told you to learn that prayer and not talk But it seems impossible for you to stop talking if you've got anybody that will listen to you. So go up to your room and learn it."

"Oh, I know it pretty nearly all now—all but just the last line."

"Well, never mind, do as I tell you. Go to your room and finish learning it well, and stay there until I call you down to help me get tea."

"Can I take the apple blossoms with me for company?" pleaded Anne.

"No; you don't want your room cluttered up with flowers. You should have left them on the tree in the first place."

"I did feel a little that way, too," said Anne. "I kind of felt I shouldn't shorten their lovely lives by picking them—I wouldn't want to be picked if I were an apple blossom. But the temptation was *irresistible*. What do you do when you meet with an irresistible temptation?"

"Anne, did you hear me tell you to go to your room?"

Anne sighed, retreated to the east gable, and sat down in a chair by the window.

"There—I know this prayer. I learned that last sentence coming upstairs. Now I'm going to imagine things into this room so that they'll always stay imagined. The floor is covered with a white velvet carpet with pink roses all over it and there are pink silk curtains at the windows. The walls are hung with gold and silver brocade tapestry. The furniture is mahogany.[12] I never saw any mahogany, but it does sound *so* luxurious. This is a couch all heaped with gorgeous silken cushions, pink and blue and crimson and gold, and I am reclining gracefully on it. I can see my reflection in that splendid big mirror hanging on the wall. I am tall and regal, clad in a gown of trailing white lace, with a pearl cross on my breast and pearls in my hair. My hair is of midnight darkness, and my skin is a clear ivory pallor. My name is the Lady Cordelia Fitzgerald. No, it isn't—I can't make *that* seem real."

She danced up to the little looking-glass and peered into it. Her pointed freckled face and solemn gray eyes peered back at her.

"You're only Anne of Green Gables," she said earnestly, "and I see you, just as you are looking now, whenever I try to imagine I'm the Lady Cordelia. But it's a million times nicer to be Anne of Green Gables than Anne of nowhere in particular, isn't it?"

She bent forward, kissed her reflection affectionately, and betook herself to the open window.

"Dear Snow Queen, good afternoon. And good afternoon, dear birches down in the hollow. And good afternoon, dear gray house up on the hill. I wonder if Diana is to be my bosom friend. I hope she will and I shall love her very much. But I must never quite forget Katie Maurice and Violetta. They would feel so hurt if I did and I'd hate to hurt anybody's feelings, even a little bookcase-girl's or a little echo-girl's. I must be careful to remember them and send them a kiss every day."

Anne blew a couple of airy kisses from her fingertips past the cherry blossoms and then, with her chin in her hands, drifted luxuriously out on a sea of day-dreams.

"I hate you," she cried in a choked voice, stamping her foot on the floor. Illustration by Elizabeth R. Withington, from the 1931 edition.

CHAPTER IX

MRS. RACHEL LYNDE IS PROPERLY HORRIFIED

ANNE HAD been a fortnight at Green Gables before Mrs. Lynde arrived to inspect her. Mrs. Rachel, to do her justice, was not to blame for this. A severe and unseasonable attack of grippe[1] had confined that good lady to her house ever since the occasion of her last visit to Green Gables. Mrs. Rachel was not often sick and had a well-defined contempt for people who were; but grippe, she asserted, was like no other illness on earth and could only be interpreted as one of the special visitations of Providence. As soon as her doctor allowed her to put her foot out-of-doors she hurried up to Green Gables, bursting with curiosity to see Matthew's and Marilla's orphan, concerning whom all sorts of stories and suppositions had gone abroad in Avonlea.

Anne had made good use of every waking moment of that fortnight. Already she was acquainted with every tree and shrub about the place. She had discovered that a lane opened out below the apple orchard and ran up through a belt of woodland; and she had explored it to its farthest end in all its delicious vagaries of brook and bridge, fir coppice[2] and wild cherry arch, corners thick with fern, and branching byways of maple and mountain ash.

1. Influenza. A French word from 1776; anglicized, pronounced as in *grip*, it means a seizure or twinge of pain.

2. A small wood or thicket consisting of the underwood and small trees grown for periodic cutting.

3. Small woodland plants *(Trientalis borealis, Primulaceae)* of the primrose family, with white or pink, five-petaled star-shaped flowers. See illustration.

4. A fine filmy substance consisting of cobwebs, spun by small spiders; it is seen floating in the air in calm weather, especially in autumn, or spread over a grassy surface: a thread or web of gossamer.

5. New growth on fir or spruce, or catkins on the underbrush.

She had made friends with the spring down in the hollow — that wonderful deep, clear icy-cold spring; it was set about with smooth red sandstones and rimmed in by great, palm-like clumps of water fern; and beyond it was a log bridge over the brook.

That bridge led Anne's dancing feet up over a wooded hill beyond, where perpetual twilight reigned under the straight, thick-growing firs and spruces; the only flowers there were myriads of delicate "June bells," those shyest and sweetest of woodland blooms, and a few pale, aerial starflowers,[3] like the spirits of last year's blossoms. Gossamers[4] glimmered like threads of silver among the trees and the fir boughs and tassels[5] seemed to utter friendly speech.

All these raptured voyages of exploration were made in the odd half-hours which she was allowed for play, and Anne talked Matthew and Marilla half-deaf over her discoveries. Not that Matthew complained, to be sure; he listened to it all with a wordless smile of enjoyment on his face; Marilla permitted the "chatter" until she found herself becoming too interested in it, whereupon she always promptly quenched Anne by a curt command to hold her tongue.

Anne was out in the orchard when Mrs. Rachel came, wandering at her own sweet will through the lush, tremulous grasses splashed with ruddy evening sunshine; so that good lady had an excellent chance to talk her illness fully over, describing every ache and pulse-beat with such evident enjoyment that Marilla thought even grippe must bring its compensations. When details were exhausted Mrs. Rachel introduced the real reason of her call.

"I've been hearing some surprising things about you and Matthew."

"I don't suppose you are any more surprised than I am myself," said Marilla. "I'm getting over my surprise now."

"It was too bad there was such a mistake," said Mrs. Rachel sympathetically. "Couldn't you have sent her back?"

"I suppose we could, but we decided not to. Matthew took a fancy to her. And I must say I like her myself—although I admit she has her faults. The house seems a different place already. She's a real bright little thing."

Marilla said more than she had intended to say when she began, for she read disapproval in Mrs. Rachel's expression.

"It's a great responsibility you've taken on yourself," said that lady gloomily, "especially when you've never had any experience with children. You don't know much about her or her real disposition, I suppose, and there's no guessing how a child like that will turn out. But I don't want to discourage you I'm sure, Marilla."

"I'm not feeling discouraged," was Marilla's dry response.

Back of the orchard at the old home, 1890s.

6. Without bias either for or against, impervious to blackmail, harassment, or prejudice.

"When I make up my mind to do a thing it stays made up. I suppose you'd like to see Anne. I'll call her in."

Anne came running in presently, her face sparkling with the delight of her orchard rovings; but, abashed at finding herself in the unexpected presence of a stranger, she halted confusedly inside the door. She certainly was an odd-looking little creature in the short, tight wincey dress she had worn from the asylum, below which her thin legs seemed ungracefully long. Her freckles were more numerous and obtrusive than ever; the wind had ruffled her hatless hair into over-brilliant disorder; it had never looked redder than at that moment.

"Well, they didn't pick you for your looks, that's sure and certain," was Mrs. Rachel Lynde's emphatic comment. Mrs. Rachel was one of those delightful and popular people who pride themselves on speaking their mind without fear or favour.[6] "She's terrible skinny and homely, Marilla. Come here, child, and let me have a look at you. Lawful heart, did any one ever see such freckles? And hair as red as carrots! Come here, child, I say."

Anne "came there," but not exactly as Mrs. Rachel expected. With one bound she crossed the kitchen floor and stood before Mrs. Rachel, her face scarlet with anger, her lips quivering, and her whole slender form trembling from head to foot.

"I hate you," she cried in a choked voice, stamping her foot on the floor. "I hate you—I hate you—I hate you!"—a louder stamp with each assertion of hatred. "How dare you call me skinny and ugly? How dare you say I'm freckled and red-headed? You are a rude, impolite, unfeeling woman!"

"Anne!" exclaimed Marilla in consternation.

But Anne continued to face Mrs. Rachel undauntedly, head up, eyes blazing, hands clenched, passionate indignation exhaling from her like an atmosphere.

"How dare you say such things about me?" she repeated vehemently. "How would you like to have such things said about you? How would you like to be told that you are fat and clumsy and probably hadn't a spark of imagination in you? I don't care if I do hurt your feelings by saying so! I hope I hurt them. You have hurt mine worse than they were ever hurt before even by Mrs. Thomas' intoxicated husband. And I'll *never* forgive you for it, never, never!"

Stamp! Stamp!

"Did anybody ever see such a temper!" exclaimed the horrified Mrs. Rachel.

"Anne, go to your room and stay there until I come up," said Marilla, recovering her powers of speech with difficulty.

Anne, bursting into tears, rushed to the hall door, slammed it until the tins on the porch wall outside rattled in sympathy, and fled through the hall and up the stairs like a whirlwind. A subdued slam above told that the door of the east gable had been shut with equal vehemence.

"Well, I don't envy you your job bringing *that* up, Marilla," said Mrs. Rachel with unspeakable solemnity.

Marilla opened her lips to say she knew not what of apology or deprecation. What she did say was a surprise to herself then and ever afterwards.

"You shouldn't have twitted[7] her about her looks, Rachel."

"Marilla Cuthbert, you don't mean to say that you are upholding her in such a terrible display of temper as we've just seen?" demanded Mrs. Rachel indignantly.

"No," said Marilla slowly, "I'm not trying to excuse her. She's been very naughty and I'll have to give her a talking to about it. But we must make allowances for her. She's never been taught what is right. And you *were* too hard on her, Rachel."

Marilla could not help tacking on that last sentence, although she was again surprised at herself for doing it. Mrs. Rachel got up with an air of offended dignity.

"Well, I see that I'll have to be very careful what I say after this, Marilla, since the fine feelings of orphans, brought from goodness knows where, have to be considered before any-

7. To twit, from *atwite* or *twite*, dating from the early sixteenth century and meaning to reproach, blame, or taunt.

thing else. Oh, no, I'm not vexed—don't worry yourself. I'm too sorry for you to leave any room for anger in my mind. You'll have your own troubles with that child. But if you'll take my advice—which I suppose you won't do, although I've brought up ten children and buried two—you'll do that 'talking to' you mention with a fair-sized birch switch. I should think *that* would be the most effective language for that kind of a child. Her temper matches her hair I guess. Well, good evening, Marilla. I hope you'll come down to see me often as usual. But you can't expect me to visit here again in a hurry if I'm liable to be flown at and insulted in such a fashion. It's something new in *my* experience."

Whereat Mrs. Rachel swept out and away—if a fat woman who always waddled *could* be said to sweep away—and Marilla with a very solemn face betook herself to the east gable.

On the way upstairs she pondered uneasily as to what she ought to do. She felt no little dismay over the scene that had just been enacted. How unfortunate that Anne should have displayed such temper before Mrs. Rachel Lynde, of all people! Then Marilla suddenly became aware of an uncomfortable and rebuking consciousness that she felt more humiliation over this than sorrow over the discovery of such a serious defect in Anne's disposition. And how was she to punish her? The amiable suggestion of the birch switch—to the efficiency of which all of Mrs. Rachel's own children could have borne smarting testimony—did not appeal to Marilla. She did not believe she could whip a child. No, some other method of punishment must be found to bring Anne to a proper realization of the enormity of her offense.

Marilla found Anne face downward on her bed, crying bitterly, quite oblivious of muddy boots on a clean counterpane.

"Anne," she said, not ungently.

No answer.

"Anne," with greater severity, "get off that bed this minute and listen to what I have to say to you."

Anne squirmed off the bed and sat rigidly on a chair beside it, her face swollen and tear-stained, and her eyes fixed stubbornly on the floor.

"This is a nice way for you to behave, Anne! Aren't you ashamed of yourself?"

"She hadn't any right to call me ugly and red-headed," retorted Anne, evasive and defiant.

"You hadn't any right to fly into such a fury and talk the way you did to her, Anne. I was ashamed of you—thoroughly ashamed of you. I wanted you to behave nicely to Mrs. Lynde, and instead of that you have disgraced me. I'm sure I don't know why you should lose your temper like that just because Mrs. Lynde said you were red-haired and homely. You say it yourself often enough."

"Oh, but there's such a difference between saying a thing yourself and hearing other people say it," wailed Anne. "You may know a thing is so, but you can't help hoping other people don't quite think it is. I suppose you think I have an awful temper, but I couldn't help it. When she said those things something just rose right up in me and choked me. I *had* to fly out at her."

"Well, you made a fine exhibition of yourself I must say. Mrs. Lynde will have a nice story to tell about you everywhere—and she'll tell it, too. It was a dreadful thing for you to lose your temper like that, Anne."

"Just imagine how you would feel if somebody told you to your face that you were skinny and ugly," pleaded Anne tearfully.

An old remembrance suddenly rose up before Marilla. She had been a very small child when she had heard one aunt say of her to another, "What a pity she is such a dark homely little thing." Marilla was every day of forty before the sting had gone out of that memory.

"I don't say that I think Mrs. Lynde was exactly right in saying what she did to you, Anne," she admitted in a softer

8. The horsemen of Parthia, an ancient kingdom of western Asia, were known for discharging their missiles backward while in real or pretended flight.

tone. "Rachel is too outspoken. But that is no excuse for such behavior on your part. She was a stranger and an elderly person and my visitor—all three very good reasons why you should have been respectful to her. You were rude and saucy and"—Marilla had a saving inspiration of punishment—"you must go to her and tell her you are very sorry for your bad temper and ask her forgive you."

"I can never do that," said Anne determinedly and darkly. "You can punish me in any way you like, Marilla. You can shut me up in a dark damp dungeon inhabited by snakes and toads and feed me only on bread and water and I shall not complain. But I cannot ask Mrs. Lynde to forgive me."

"We're not in the habit of shutting people up in dark, damp dungeons," said Marilla drily, "especially as they're rather scarce in Avonlea. But apologize to Mrs. Lynde you must and shall and you'll stay here in your room until you can tell me you're willing to do it."

"I shall have to stay here forever then," said Anne mournfully, "because I can't tell Mrs. Lynde I'm sorry I said those things to her. How can I? I'm *not* sorry. I'm sorry I've vexed you; but I'm *glad* I told her just what I did. It was a great satisfaction. I can't say I'm sorry when I'm not, can I? I can't even *imagine* I'm sorry."

"Perhaps your imagination will be in better working order by the morning," said Marilla, rising to depart. "You'll have the night to think over your conduct in and come to a better frame of mind. You said you would try to be a very good girl if we kept you at Green Gables but I must say it hasn't seemed very much like it this evening."

Leaving this Parthian shaft[8] to rankle in Anne's stormy bosom Marilla descended to the kitchen, grievously troubled in mind and vexed in soul. She was as angry with herself as with Anne, because, whenever she recalled Mrs. Rachel's dumbfounded countenance her lips twitched with amusement and she felt a most reprehensible desire to laugh.

CHAPTER X

ANNE'S APOLOGY

MARILLA SAID nothing to Matthew about the affair that evening; but when Anne proved still refractory the next morning an explanation had to be made to account for her absence from the breakfast-table. Marilla told Matthew the whole story, taking pains to impress him with a due sense of the enormity of Anne's behaviour.

"It's a good thing Rachel Lynde got a calling down; she's a meddlesome old gossip," was Matthew's consolatory rejoinder.

"Matthew Cuthbert, I'm astonished at you. You know that Anne's behaviour was dreadful, and yet you take her part! I suppose you'll be saying next thing that she oughtn't to be punished at all."

"Well now—no—not exactly," said Matthew uneasily. "I reckon she ought to be punished a little. But don't be too hard on her, Marilla. Recollect she hasn't ever had any one to teach her right. You're—you're going to give her something to eat, aren't you?"

"When did you ever hear of me starving people into good behaviour?" demanded Marilla indignantly. "She'll have her meals regular, and I'll carry them up to her myself. But she'll stay up there until she's willing to apologize to Mrs. Lynde, and that's final, Matthew."

Breakfast, dinner, and supper were very silent meals—for Anne still remained obdurate. After each meal Marilla carried a well-filled tray to the east gable and brought it down later on not noticeably depleted. Matthew eyed its last descent with a troubled eye. Had Anne eaten anything at all?

When Marilla went out that evening to bring the cows from the back pasture, Matthew, who had been hanging about the barns and watching, slipped into the house with the air of a burglar and crept upstairs. As a general thing Matthew gravitated between the kitchen and the little bedroom off the hall where he slept; once in a while he ventured uncomfortably into the parlour or sitting-room when the minister came to tea. But he had never been upstairs in his own house since the spring he helped Marilla paper the spare bedroom, and that was four years ago.

He tiptoed along the hall and stood for several minutes outside the door of the east gable before he summoned courage to tap on it with his fingers and then open the door to peep in.

Anne was sitting on the yellow chair by the window, gazing mournfully out into the garden. Very small and unhappy she looked, and Matthew's heart smote him. He softly closed the door and tiptoed over to her.

"Anne," he whispered, as if afraid of being overheard, "how are you making it, Anne?"

Anne smiled wanly.

"Pretty well. I imagine a good deal, and that helps to pass the time. Of course, it's rather lonesome. But then, I may as well get used to that."

Anne smiled again, bravely facing the long years of solitary imprisonment before her.

Matthew recollected that he must say what he had come to say without loss of time lest Marilla return prematurely.

"Well now, Anne, don't you think you'd better do it and

have it over with?" he whispered. "It'll have to be done sooner or later, you know, for Marilla's a dreadful determined woman —dreadful determined, Anne. Do it right off, I say, and have it over."

"Do you mean apologize to Mrs. Lynde?"

"Yes—apologize—that's the very word," said Matthew eagerly. "Just smooth it over so to speak. That's what I was trying to get at."

"I suppose I could do it to oblige you," said Anne thoughtfully. "It would be true enough to say I'm sorry, because I *am* sorry now. I wasn't a bit sorry last night. I was mad clear through, and I stayed mad all night. I know I did because I woke up three times and I was just furious every time. But this morning it was all over. I wasn't in a temper any more— and it left a dreadful sort of gone-ness, too. I felt so ashamed of myself. But I just couldn't think of going and telling Mrs. Lynde so. It would be so humiliating. I made up my mind I'd stay shut up here for ever rather than do that. But still—I'd do anything for you—if you really want me to—"

"Well now, of course I do. It's terrible lonesome downstairs without you. Just go and smooth it over—that's a good girl."

"Very well," said Anne resignedly. "I'll tell Marilla as soon as she comes in that I've repented."

"That's right—that's right, Anne. But don't tell Marilla I said anything about it. She might think I was putting my oar in and I promised not to do that."

"Wild horses won't drag the secret from me,"[1] promised Anne solemnly. "How would wild horses drag a secret from a person anyhow?"

But Matthew was gone, scared at his own success. He fled hastily to the remotest corner of the horse pasture lest Marilla should suspect what he had been up to. Marilla herself, upon her return to the house, was agreeably surprised to hear a plaintive voice calling, "Marilla," over the banisters.

1. One old form of punishment and execution was to tie the victim's limbs to four wild horses, which would then proceed to tear the victim apart when they ran away. This practice was one method of "quartering." Anne's question regarding the extraction of secrets is a good one, for this form of torture was not very efficient in extracting information, since the victim invariably died.

2. Under the sky, *i.e.*, in the world.

"Well?" she said, going into the hall.

"I'm sorry I lost my temper and said rude things and I'm willing to go and tell Mrs. Lynde so."

"Very well." Marilla's crispness gave no sign of her relief. She had been wondering what under the canopy[2] she should do if Anne did not give in. "I'll take you down after milking."

Accordingly, after milking, behold Marilla and Anne walking down the lane, the former erect and triumphant, the latter drooping and dejected. But half-way down Anne's dejection vanished as if by enchantment. She lifted her head and stepped lightly along, her eyes fixed on the sunset sky and an air of subdued exhilaration about her. Marilla beheld the change disapprovingly. This was no meek penitent such as it behoved her to take into the presence of the offended Mrs. Lynde.

"What are you thinking of, Anne?" she asked sharply.

"I'm imagining out what I must say to Mrs. Lynde," answered Anne dreamily.

This was satisfactory—or should have been so. But Marilla could not rid herself of the notion that something in her scheme of punishment was going askew. Anne had no business to look so rapt and radiant.

Rapt and radiant Anne continued until they were in the very presence of Mrs. Lynde, who was sitting knitting by her kitchen window. Then the radiance vanished. Mournful penitence appeared on every feature. Before a word was spoken Anne suddenly went down on her knees before the astonished Mrs. Rachel and held out her hands beseechingly.

"Oh, Mrs. Lynde, I am so extremely sorry," she said with a quiver in her voice. "I could never express all my sorrow, no, not if I used up a whole dictionary. You must just imagine it. I behaved terribly to you—and I've disgraced the dear friends, Matthew and Marilla, who have let me stay at Green Gables although I'm not a boy. I'm a dreadfully wicked and ungrateful girl and I deserve to be punished and cast out by respectable people for ever. It was very wicked of me to fly into a temper because you told me the truth. It *was* the truth; every word you said was true. My hair is red and I'm freckled and skinny and ugly. What I said to you was true, too, but I shouldn't have said it. Oh, Mrs. Lynde, please, please, forgive me. If you refuse it will be a lifelong sorrow to me. You wouldn't like to inflict a lifelong sorrow on a poor little orphan girl, would you, even if she had a dreadful temper? Oh, I am sure you wouldn't. Please say you forgive me, Mrs. Lynde."

Anne clasped her hands together, bowed her head, and waited for the word of judgment.

There was no mistaking her sincerity—it breathed in every tone of her voice. Both Marilla and Mrs. Lynde recognized its unmistakable ring. But the former understood in dismay that Anne was actually enjoying her valley of humiliation— was revelling in the thoroughness of her abasement. Where was the wholesome punishment upon which she, Marilla, had plumed herself?[3] Anne had turned it into a species of positive pleasure.

Good Mrs. Lynde, not being overburdened with perception, did not see this. She only perceived that Anne had made a very thorough apology and all resentment vanished from her kindly, if somewhat officious, heart.

"There, there, get up, child," she said heartily. "Of course I forgive you. I guess I was a little too hard on you, anyway. But I'm such an outspoken person. You just mustn't mind me, that's what. It can't be denied your hair is terrible red; but I knew a girl once—went to school with her, in fact—whose hair was every mite as red as yours when she was young, but when she grew up it darkened to a real handsome auburn.[4] I wouldn't be a mite surprised if yours did, too—not a mite."

"Oh, Mrs. Lynde!" Anne drew a long breath as she rose to her feet. "You have given me a hope. I shall always feel that you are a benefactor. Oh, I could endure anything if I only thought my hair would be a handsome auburn when I grew up. It would be so much easier to be good if one's hair was a

3. Prided herself, "especially regarding something trivial" with allusion to an Aesopic dressing in borrowed plumes or feathers (Aesop, *Tales,* "The Jay in Peacock's Feathers").

4. From Old French *alborne,* meaning whitish. In Renaissance English, an aural association with the word *brown* changed the meaning and it came to refer to a golden brown or ruddy brown.

5. The narcissus *(Narcissus,* Amaryllidaceae), a variety of daffodil, is a bulbous plant flowering in spring with a single white flower having an undivided corona sometimes edged with crimson and yellow. Mrs. Lynde refers to these flowers as "June lilies," Anne, like her author, as "narcissi." See illustration.

handsome auburn, don't you think? And now may I go out into your garden and sit on that bench under the apple-trees while you and Marilla are talking? There is so much more scope for imagination out there."

"Laws, yes, run along, child. And you can pick a bouquet of them white June lilies[5] over in the corner if you like."

As the door closed behind Anne Mrs. Lynde got briskly up to light a lamp.[6]

"She's a real odd little thing. Take this chair, Marilla; it's easier than the one you've got; I just keep that for the hired boy to sit on. Yes, she certainly is an odd child, but there is something kind of taking about her after all. I don't feel so surprised at you and Matthew keeping her as I did—nor so sorry for you, either. She may turn out all right. Of course, she has a queer way of expressing herself—a little too—well, too kind of forcible, you know; but she'll likely get over that now that she's come to live among civilized folks. And then, her temper's pretty quick, I guess; but there's one comfort, a child that has a quick temper, just blaze up and cool down, ain't never likely to be sly or deceitful. Preserve me from a sly child, that's what. On the whole, Marilla, I kind of like her."

When Marilla went home Anne came out of the fragrant twilight of the orchard with a sheaf of white narcissi in her hands.

"I apologized pretty well, didn't I?" she said proudly as they went down the lane. "I thought since I had to do it I might as well do it thoroughly."

"You did it thoroughly, all right enough," was Marilla's comment. Marilla was dismayed at finding herself inclined to laugh over the recollection. She had also an uneasy feeling that she ought to scold Anne for apologizing so well; but then, that was ridiculous! She compromised with her conscience by saying severely:

"I hope you won't have occasion to make many more such apologies. I hope you'll try to control your temper now, Anne."

"That wouldn't be so hard if people wouldn't twit me about my looks," said Anne with a sigh. "I don't get cross about other things; but I'm *so* tired of being twitted about my hair and it just makes me boil right over. Do you suppose my hair will really be a handsome auburn when I grow up?"

"You shouldn't think so much about your looks, Anne. I'm afraid you are a very vain little girl."

"How can I be vain when I know I'm homely?" protested Anne. "I love pretty things; and I hate to look in the glass and see something that isn't pretty. It makes me feel so sorrowful —just as I feel when I look at any ugly thing. I pity it because it isn't beautiful."

"Handsome is as handsome does,"[7] quoted Marilla.

"I've had that said to me before, but I have my doubts about it," remarked sceptical Anne, sniffing at her narcissi. "Oh, aren't these flowers sweet! It was lovely of Mrs. Lynde to give them to me. I have no hard feelings against Mrs. Lynde now. It gives you a lovely comfortable feeling to apologize and be forgiven, doesn't it? Aren't the stars bright tonight? If you could live in a star, which one would you pick?

6. A kerosene lamp with a base as a container for combustible oil, with a wick emerging from the top, and a tall glass chimney to contain the flame, sometimes with a colored shade. See illustration of 1880s lamp.

7. Cf. "Handsome is that handsome does," *The Vicar of Wakefield* (1766), by Oliver Goldsmith.

I'd like that lovely clear big one away over there above that dark hill."

"Anne, do hold your tongue," said Marilla, thoroughly worn out trying to follow the gyrations of Anne's thoughts.

Anne said no more until they turned into their own lane. A little gipsy wind came down it to meet them, laden with the spicy perfume of young dew-wet ferns. Far up in the shadows a cheerful light gleamed out through the trees from the kitchen at Green Gables. Anne suddenly came close to Marilla and slipped her hand into the older woman's hard palm.

"It's lovely to be going home and know it's home," she said. "I love Green Gables already and I never loved any place before. No place ever seemed like home. Oh, Marilla, I'm so happy. I could pray right now and not find it a bit hard."

Something warm and pleasant welled up in Marilla's heart at the touch of that thin little hand in her own—a throb of the maternity she had missed, perhaps. Its very unaccustomedness and sweetness disturbed her. She hastened to restore her sensations to their normal calm by inculcating a moral.

"If you'll be a good girl you'll always be happy, Anne. And you should never find it hard to say your prayers."

"Saying one's prayers isn't exactly the same thing as praying," said Anne meditatively. "But I'm going to imagine that I'm the wind that is blowing up there in those tree-tops. When I get tired of the trees I'll imagine I'm gently waving down here in the ferns—and then I'll fly over to Mrs. Lynde's garden and set the flowers dancing—and then I'll go with one great swoop over the clover field—and then I'll blow over the Lake of Shining Waters and ripple it all up into little sparkling waves. Oh, there's so much scope for imagination in a wind! So I'll not talk any more just now, Marilla."

"Thanks be to goodness for that," breathed Marilla in devout relief.

CHAPTER XI

ANNE'S IMPRESSIONS OF SUNDAY SCHOOL

"WELL, HOW do you like them?" said Marilla. Anne was standing in the gable-room, looking solemnly at three new dresses spread out on the bed. One was of snuffy-coloured gingham[1] which Marilla had been tempted to buy from a peddler the preceding summer because it looked so serviceable; one was of black-and-white checked sateen[2] which she had picked up at a bargain counter in the winter; and one was a stiff print of an ugly blue shade which she had purchased that week at a Carmody store.

She had made them up herself, and they were all made alike —plain skirts fulled tightly to plain waists, with sleeves as plain as waist and skirt and tight as sleeves could be.

"I'll imagine that I like them," said Anne soberly.

"I don't want you to imagine it," said Marilla, offended. "Oh, I can see you don't like the dresses! What is the matter with them? Aren't they neat and clean and new?"

"Yes."

"Then why don't you like them?"

"They're — they're not — pretty," said Anne reluctantly.

"Pretty!" Marilla sniffed. "I didn't trouble my head about getting pretty dresses for you. I don't believe in pampering vanity, Anne, I'll tell you that right off. Those dresses are good,

1. A kind of cotton or linen cloth woven of dyed yarn, often in stripes, checks, and other patterns. "Snuffy-coloured" refers to its resemblance to snuff or powdered tobacco in being yellowish or brown.

2. Cotton or woolen fabric with a glossy surface like that of satin. The word is derived from *satin* by analogy with *velveteen*.

3. As the author noted in her 1905 journal, "An old-time fashion plate with big sleeves! The puffed sleeves are in again now. When I put on a new dress the other day with big sleeves it gave me the oddest sense of being a Dalhousie girl again— for that was the year they came to their fullest balloon-like inflation, stiffened out with 'fibre-chamois' etc. 'Stuff me in' was an inelegant phrase constantly heard when one girl wanted another to poke the huge sleeves of her dress into the sleeves of her coat" (*SJ* I [July 30, 1905]: 309). See illustration (1896). Montgomery became a "Dalhousie girl" in 1895. "Anne's tribulations over puffed sleeves were an echo of my old childish longing after 'bangs.' 'Bangs' came in when I was about ten. . . . Well, bangs were 'all the rage.' All the girls in school had them. I wanted a 'bang' terribly. But grandfather and grandmother would never hear of it" (*SJ* II [Jan. 27, 1911]: 41).

4. Lesson notes for Sunday Schools, issued every three months.

5. Very angry, offended, or resentful, from *dudgeon*, the handle of a

sensible, serviceable dresses, without any frills and furbelows about them, and they're all you'll get this summer. The brown gingham and the blue print will do you for school when you begin to go. The sateen is for church and Sunday School. I'll expect you to keep them neat and clean and not tear them. I should think you'd be grateful to get most anything after those skimpy wincey things you've been wearing."

"Oh, I *am* grateful," protested Anne. "But I'd be ever so much gratefuller if—if you'd made just one of them with puffed sleeves.[3] Puffed sleeves are so fashionable now. It would give me such a thrill, Marilla, just to wear a dress with puffed sleeves."

"Well, you'll have to do without your thrill. I hadn't any material to waste on puffed sleeves. I think they are ridiculous-looking things anyhow. I prefer the plain, sensible ones."

"But I'd rather look ridiculous when everybody else does than plain and sensible all by myself," persisted Anne mournfully.

'Trust you for that! Well, hang those dresses carefully up in your closet. and then sit down and learn the Sunday School lesson. I got a quarterly[4] from Mr. Bell for you and you'll go to Sunday School to-morrow," said Marilla, disappearing downstairs in high dudgeon.[5]

Anne clasped her hands and looked at the dresses.

"I did hope there would be a white one with puffed sleeves," she whispered disconsolately. "I prayed for one, but I didn't much expect it on that account. I didn't suppose God would have time to bother about a little orphan girl's dress. I knew I'd just have to depend on Marilla for it. Well, fortunately I can imagine that one of them is of snow-white muslin with lovely lace frills and three-puffed sleeves."

The next morning warnings of a sick headache prevented Marilla from going to Sunday School with Anne.

"You'll have to go down and call for Mrs. Lynde, Anne," she said. "She'll see that you get into the right class. Now, mind you behave yourself properly. Stay to preaching afterwards and ask Mrs. Lynde to show you our pew. Here's a cent for collection. Don't stare at people and don't fidget. I shall expect you to tell me the text when you come home."

Anne started off irreproachably, arrayed in the stiff black-and-white sateen, which, while decent as regards length and certainly not open to the charge of skimpiness, contrived to emphasize every corner and angle of her thin figure. Her hat was a little, flat, glossy, new sailor,[6] the extreme plainness of which had likewise much disappointed Anne, who had permitted herself secret visions of ribbon and flowers. The latter, however, were supplied before Anne reached the main road, for, being confronted half-way down the lane with a golden frenzy of wind-stirred buttercups[7] and a glory of wild roses, Anne promptly and liberally garlanded her hat with a heavy wreath of them. Whatever other people might have thought of the result it satisfied Anne, and she tripped gaily down the road, holding her ruddy head with its decoration of pink and yellow very proudly.

When she reached Mrs. Lynde's house she found that lady gone. Nothing daunted Anne proceeded onward to the church alone. In the porch she found a crowd of little girls, all more or less gaily attired in whites and blues and pinks, and all staring with curious eyes at this stranger in their midst, with her extraordinary head adornment. Avonlea little girls had already heard queer stories about Anne; Mrs. Lynde said she had an awful temper; Jerry Buote, the hired boy at Green Gables, said she talked all the time to herself or to the trees and flowers like a crazy girl. They looked at her and whispered to each other behind their quarterlies. Nobody made any friendly advances, then or later on when the opening exercises were over and Anne found herself in Miss Rogerson's class.

Miss Rogerson was a middle-aged lady who had taught a Sunday School class for twenty years. Her method of teaching was to ask the printed questions from the quarterly and look

knife or dagger; thus, to be "in high dudgeon" is to be ready to draw your dagger.

6. A hat with a flat brim of even breadth all around, of the type once worn by sailors.

7. Apparently composed during the writing of *Anne* (see Textual Note) but perhaps mined from an earlier poem, this phrase emerges only slightly changed as a line in one of Emily's poems read by her teacher Mr. Carpenter, who approves it: "Buttercups in a golden frenzy" — 'a golden frenzy' — girl, I *see* the wind shaking the buttercups" (*Emily of New Moon*, ch. 31).

sternly over its edge at the particular little girl she thought ought to answer the question. She looked very often at Anne, and Anne, thanks to Marilla's drilling, answered promptly; but it may be questioned if she understood very much about either question or answer.

She did not think she liked Miss Rogerson, and she felt very miserable; every other little girl in the class had puffed sleeves. Anne felt that life was really not worth living without puffed sleeves.

"Well, how did you like Sunday School?" Marilla wanted to know when Anne came home. Her wreath having faded, Anne had discarded it in the lane, so Marilla was spared the knowledge of that for a time.

"I didn't like it a bit. It was horrid."

"Anne Shirley!" said Marilla rebukingly.

Anne sat down on the rocker with a long sigh, kissed one of Bonny's leaves, and waved her hand to a blossoming fuchsia.[8]

"They might have been lonesome while I was away," she explained. "And now about the Sunday School. I behaved well, just as you told me. Mrs. Lynde was gone, but I went right on myself. I went into the church, with a lot of other little girls, and I sat in the corner of a pew by the window while the opening exercises went on. Mr. Bell made an aw-fully long prayer. I would have been dreadfully tired before he got through if I hadn't been sitting by that window. But it looked right out on the Lake of Shining Waters, so I just gazed at that and imagined all sorts of splendid things."

"You shouldn't have done anything of the sort. You should have listened to Mr. Bell."

"But he wasn't talking to me," protested Anne. "He was talking to God and he didn't seem to be very much interested in it, either. I think he thought God was too far off to make it worth while. I said a little prayer myself, though. There was a long row of white birches hanging over the lake and the sunshine fell down through them, 'way, 'way down, deep into the water. Oh, Marilla, it was like a beautiful dream! It gave me a thrill and I just said, 'Thank you for it, God,' two or three times."

"Not out loud, I hope," said Marilla anxiously.

"Oh, no, just under my breath. Well, Mr. Bell did get through at last and they told me to go into the classroom with Miss Rogerson's class. There were nine other girls in it.

8. Shrubby plants of the evening primrose family, with pink, red or purple flowers hanging from the ends of the branches. Fuchsia was brought to England from South America in the nineteenth century.

"A pensive Sunday school scholar." Lucy Maud Montgomery, age ten.

9. A rhymed version of a psalm or other scripture passages. In the Church of Scotland and other Presbyterian churches the paraphrases are the hymns contained in the *Translations and Paraphrases, in verse, of several passages of sacred scripture: collected . . . in order to be sung in Churches*. These passages are usually appended to the Metrical Psalter in Scottish editions of the Bible or New Testament. The first edition, entitled *Translations and Paraphrases of several passages of Sacred Scripture, collected and prepared by a Committee appointed by the General Assembly of the Church of Scotland*, was printed and issued for consideration in 1745; the version finally adopted was published in 1781.

10. A poem by Mrs. Lydia Howard Huntly Sigourney (1791–1865), of Norwich, Conn., the author of some sixty books including *Moral Pieces in Prose and Verse* (1815) and an autobiography, *Letters of Life* (1866). Anne's suggestion that the poem is a dismal one is borne out by its last two stanzas. See Appendix, "Recitation Pieces," where the *Royal Reader* version is reproduced with illustration and vocabulary.

11. These lines are from a hymn based on Judges 8 and Isaiah 9 that begins, "The race that long in darkness pin'd." It is by John Morison of Aberdeen, a member of the committee appointed by the General Assembly of the Church of Scotland to revise the *Translations and Paraphrases* of 1745. Published as Number 19 in the *Translations and Paraphrases* in 1781,

They all had puffed sleeves. I tried to imagine mine were puffed, too, but I couldn't. Why couldn't I? It was as easy as could be to imagine they were puffed when I was alone in the east gable, but it was awfully hard there among the others who had really truly puffs."

"You shouldn't have been thinking about your sleeves in Sunday School. You should have been attending to the lesson. I hope you knew it."

"Oh, yes, and I answered a lot of questions. Miss Rogerson asked ever so many. I don't think it was fair for her to do all the asking. There were lots I wanted to ask her, but I didn't like to because I didn't think she was a kindred spirit. Then all the other little girls recited a paraphrase.[9] She asked me if I knew any. I told her I didn't, but I could recite, 'The Dog at his Master's Grave'[10] if she liked. That's in the Third Royal Reader. It isn't a really truly religious piece of poetry but it's so sad and melancholy that it might as well be. She said it wouldn't do and she told me to learn the nineteenth paraphrase for next Sunday. I read it over in church afterwards and it's splendid. There are two lines in particular that just thrill me.

> Quick as the slaughtered squadrons fell
> In Midian's evil day.[11]

"I don't know what 'squadrons' means nor ' Midian' either, but it sounds so tragical. I can hardly wait until next Sunday to recite it. I'll practise it all the week. After Sunday School I asked Miss Rogerson—because Mrs. Lynde was too far away—to show me your pew. I sat just as still as I could and the text was Revelations, third chapter, second and third verses.[12] It was a very long text. If I was a minister I'd pick the short, snappy ones. The sermon was awfully long, too. I suppose the minister had to match it to the text. I didn't think he was a bit interesting. The trouble with him seems to be that he hasn't enough imagination. I didn't listen to him very much. I just let my thoughts run and I thought of the most surprising things."

Marilla felt helplessly that all this should be sternly reproved, but she was hampered by the undeniable fact that some of the things Anne had said, especially about the minister's sermons and Mr. Bell's prayers, were what she herself had really thought deep down in her heart for years but had never given expression to. It almost seemed to her that those secret, unuttered, critical thoughts had suddenly taken visible and accusing shape and form in the person of this outspoken morsel of neglected humanity.

it was still in Presbyterian hymnals in 1911. Montgomery writes in her journal that "The *Spectator*, in reviewing *Green Gables*—*very favorably*, I might say—said that possibly *Anne's* precocity was slightly overdrawn in the statement that a child of eleven would appreciate the dramatic effect of the lines, 'Quick as the slaughtered squadrons fell / In Midian's evil day.' But I was only nine years old when those lines thrilled my very soul as I recited them in Sunday School. All through the following sermon I kept repeating them to myself. To this day they give me a mysterious pleasure" (*SJ* II [Jan. 27, 1911]: 42). See Appendix, "Book Reviews."

12. The Revelation of St. John the Divine is the last book of the New Testament. The verses referred to are "Be watchful, and strengthen the things which remain, that are ready to die: for I have not found thy works perfect before God," and "Remember therefore how thou hast received and heard, and hold fast, and repent. If therefore thou shalt not watch, I will come on thee as a thief, and thou shalt not know what hour I will come upon thee."

Illustration by Elizabeth R. Withington, from the 1931 edition.

CHAPTER XII

A SOLEMN VOW
AND PROMISE

IT WAS NOT until the next Friday that Marilla heard the story of the flower-wreathed hat. She came home from Mrs. Lynde's and called Anne to account.

"Anne, Mrs. Rachel says you went to church last Sunday with your hat rigged out ridiculous with roses and buttercups. What on earth put you up to such a caper? A pretty-looking object you must have been!"

"Oh, I know pink and yellow aren't becoming to me," began Anne.

"Becoming fiddlesticks! It was putting flowers on your hat at all, no matter what colour they were, that was ridiculous. You are the most aggravating child!"

"I don't see why it's any more ridiculous to wear flowers on your hat than on your dress," protested Anne. "Lots of little girls there had bouquets pinned on their dresses. What was the difference?"

Marilla was not to be drawn from the safe concrete into dubious paths of the abstract.

"Don't answer me back like that, Anne. It was very silly of you to do such a thing. Never let me catch you at such a trick again. Mrs. Rachel says she thought she would sink through the floor when she saw you come in all rigged out like that.

1. A general term applied to a wasting of the body by disease; specifically tuberculosis. Young Helen Burns, in *Jane Eyre*, is one of the best-known literary characters to suffer from consumption.

She couldn't get near enough to tell you to take them off till it was too late. She says people talked about it something dreadful. Of course they would think I had no better sense than to let you go decked out like that."

"Oh, I'm so sorry," said Anne, tears welling into her eyes. "I never thought you'd mind. The roses and buttercups were so sweet and pretty I thought they'd look lovely on my hat. Lots of the little girls had artificial flowers on their hats. I'm afraid I'm going to be a dreadful trial to you. Maybe you'd better send me back to the asylum. That would be terrible; I don't think I could endure it; most likely I would go into consumption;[1] I'm so thin as it is, you see. But that would be better than being a trial to you."

"Nonsense," said Marilla, vexed at herself for having made the child cry. "I don't want to send you back to the asylum, I'm sure. All I want is that you should behave like other little girls and not make yourself ridiculous. Don't cry any more. I've got some news for you. Diana Barry came home this afternoon. I'm going up to see if I can borrow a skirt-pattern from Mrs. Barry, and if you like you can come with me and get acquainted with Diana."

Anne rose to her feet, with clasped hands, the tears still glistening on her cheeks; the dish-towel she had been hemming slipped unheeded to the floor.

"Oh, Marilla, I'm frightened—now that it has come I'm actually frightened. What if she shouldn't like me! It would be the most tragical disappointment of my life."

"Now, don't get into a fluster. And I do wish you wouldn't use such long words. It sounds so funny in a little girl. I guess Diana'll like you well enough. It's her mother you've got to reckon with. If she doesn't like you it won't matter how much Diana does. If she has heard about your outburst to Mrs. Lynde and going to church with buttercups round your hat I don't know what she'll think of you. You must be polite and

well-behaved, and don't make any of your startling speeches.
For pity's sake, if the child isn't actually trembling!"

Anne *was* trembling. Her face was pale and tense.

"Oh, Marilla, you'd be excited, too, if you were going to
meet a little girl you hoped to be your bosom friend and
whose mother mightn't like you," she said as she hastened to
get her hat.

They went over to Orchard Slope by the short cut across
the brook and up the firry hill grove. Mrs. Barry came to the
kitchen door in answer to Marilla's knock. She was a tall,
black-eyed, black-haired woman, with a very resolute mouth.
She had the reputation of being very strict with her children.

"How do you do, Marilla?" she said cordially. "Come in.
And this is the little girl you have adopted, I suppose?"

"Yes, this is Anne Shirley," said Marilla.

"Spelled with an *e*," gasped Anne, who, tremulous and excited as she was, was determined there should be no misun-
derstanding on that important point.

Mrs. Barry, not hearing or not comprehending, merely
shook hands and said kindly:

"How are you?"

"I am well in body although considerably rumpled up in
spirit, thank you, ma'am," said Anne gravely. Then aside to
Marilla in an audible whisper, "There wasn't anything startling
in that, was there, Marilla?"

Diana was sitting on the sofa, reading a book which she
dropped when the callers entered. She was a very pretty little
girl, with her mother's black eyes and hair, and rosy cheeks,
and the merry expression which was her inheritance from
her father.

"This is my little girl, Diana," said Mrs. Barry. "Diana, you
might take Anne out into the garden and show her your
flowers. It will be better for you than straining your eyes over
that book. She reads entirely too much —" this to Marilla as

it's not a clever one ! Still, you're the righ colour, and that goe a long way."

2. A lily *(Lilium tigrinum*, Liliaceae), having orange flowers with purplish black spots. In *Through the Looking-Glass* (World's Classics, ch. 2, p. 138) Alice meets a talking Tiger-lily. " 'O Tiger-lily!' said Alice, addressing herself to one that was waving gracefully about in the wind, 'I *wish* you could talk!' 'We *can* talk,' said the Tiger-lily, 'when there's anybody worth talking to.' " See Textual Note.

3. The Barry garden is a garden of delight based on the author's vision of the perfect garden. See Appendix, "Gardens and Plants."

4. *Dicentra spectabilis*, Papaveraceae or Fumariaceae. Plants with fern-like leaves and drooping clusters of pink or reddish heart-shaped flowers; akin to Dutchman's-breeches.

5. *Paeonia officinalis*. These Ranunculaceae have large handsome globular flowers of red and white.

6. The Burnet rose or "Scots briar" *(Rosa spinosissima)* of English authors. These pale creamy yellow flowers bloom in early summer. W. R. Robinson in *The English Flower Garden and Home Grounds*

the little girls went out—"and I can't prevent her, for her father aids and abets her. She's always poring over a book. I'm glad she has the prospect of a playmate—perhaps it will take her more out-of-doors."

Outside in the garden, which was full of mellow sunset light streaming through the dark old firs to the west of it, stood Anne and Diana, gazing bashfully at one another over a gorgeous clump of tiger lilies.[2]

The Barry garden[3] was a bowery wilderness of flowers which would have delighted Anne's heart at any time less fraught with destiny. It was encircled by huge old willows and tall firs, beneath which flourished flowers that loved the shade. Prim, right-angled paths, neatly bordered with clam-shells, intersected it like moist red ribbons and in the beds between old-fashioned flowers ran riot. There were rosy bleeding-hearts[4] and great splendid crimson peonies;[5] white, fragrant narcissi and thorny, sweet Scotch roses;[6] pink and blue and white columbines[7] and lilac-tinted Bouncing Bets;[8] clumps of southernwood[9] and ribbon grass[10] and mint;[11] purple Adam-and-Eve,[12] daffodils, and masses of sweet clover white with its delicate, fragrant, feathery sprays; scarlet-lightning[13] that shot its fiery lances over prim white musk-flowers;[14] a garden it was where sunshine lingered and bees hummed, and winds beguiled into loitering purred and rustled.

"Oh, Diana," said Anne at last, clasping her hands and speaking almost in a whisper, "do you think—oh, do you think you can like me a little—enough to be my bosom friend?"

Diana laughed. Diana always laughed before she spoke.

"Why, I guess so," she said frankly. "I'm awfully glad you've come to live at Green Gables. It will be jolly to have somebody to play with. There isn't any other girl who lives near enough to play with, and I've no sisters big enough."

"Will you swear to be my friend for ever and ever?" demanded Anne eagerly.

Diana looked shocked.

(777) says of the Scotch rose, "They are as callous to frost and snow, wind and storm, as the proverbial Highlander in his plaid." See illustration, bottom.

7. *Aquilegia vulgaris*, Ranunculaceae, plants of the buttercup family with showy, spurred flowers of various colors, blooming in early summer. The inverted flower resembles five pigeons clustered together; hence the name, from *columbinus*, "dovelike." See illustration, top.

8. Soapwort *(Saponaria officinalis, Caryophyllaceae)* a perennial plant of the pink family, with clusters of pinkish flowers; its sap forms a lather with water. See illustration, center.

9. A hardy deciduous shrub or plant *(Artemisia abrotanum)*, also known as Lad's Love, with a fragrant aromatic smell and sour taste, formerly cultivated for medicinal purposes.

10. The *Phalarus arundinacea*, Gramineae, also known as *Picta*, or *Gardener's Garters*, is distinguished by its longitudinal white stripes on narrow green leaves.

11. Garden mint or spearmint (genus *Menthus*, esp. *Mentha veridis*), well known in cookery.

12. An American orchid *(Aplectrum hyemale)* with clusters of yellowish-brown flowers, one leaf at the base of the stem, and a sticky substance in its bulbs. Also known as putty-root.

13. *Lychnis chalcedonica*, a plant with bright red flowers introduced into North America in the seventeenth

century. It is also known as "Maltese cross" or "Jerusalem cross" because of the way the flowers are formed and is typical of the gardens of the period. This perennial produces flowers that are extremely bright, but not fragrant (Joanne Gardiner, Heritage Garden expert, Nova Scotia).

14. Probably white musk-mallow (*Melva moschata alba*), which is a variant—the regular musk flower is pink. Introduced into North American gardens in the eighteenth century, the musk mallow has some valued qualities as a healing herb. The flower is velvety with a musk scent. A perennial, it goes well with the "scarlet-lightning" (see n. 13), and the two are often said to be found together in gardens of the period. Montgomery may also have been influenced by the Keatsian garden and the association of "the coming musk-rose full of dewy wine" ("Ode to a Nightingale," l. 49).

15. These may be wild lilies-of-the-valley, also known as "Canadian mayflower" (*Maianthemum canadense*), which grow on the floor of spruce woods, where Anne is wandering when she makes and wears the wreath and gets into trouble with Mr. Phillips (see p. 170).

"Why, it's dreadfully wicked to swear," she said rebukingly.

"Oh no, not my kind of swearing. There are two kinds, you know."

"I never heard of but one kind," said Diana doubtfully.

"There really is another. Oh, it isn't wicked at all. It just means vowing and promising solemnly."

"Well, I don't mind doing that," agreed Diana, relieved. "How do you do it?"

"We must join hands—so," said Anne gravely. "It ought to be over running water. We'll just imagine this path is running water. I'll repeat the oath first. I solemnly swear to be faithful to my bosom friend, Diana Barry, as long as the sun and moon shall endure. Now you say it and put my name in."

Diana repeated the "oath" with a laugh fore and aft. Then she said:

"You're a queer girl, Anne. I heard before that you were queer. But I believe I'm going to like you real well."

When Marilla and Anne went home Diana went with them as far as the log bridge. The two little girls walked with their arms about each other. At the brook they parted with many promises to spend the next afternoon together.

"Well, did you find Diana a kindred spirit?" asked Marilla as they went up through the garden of Green Gables.

"Oh, yes," sighed Anne, blissfully unconscious of any sarcasm on Marilla's part. "Oh, Marilla, I'm the happiest girl on Prince Edward Island this very moment. I assure you I'll say my prayers with a right good will to-night. Diana and I are going to build a playhouse in Mr. William Bell's birch grove to-morrow. Can I have those broken pieces of china that are out in the wood-shed? Diana's birthday is in February and mine is in March. Don't you think that is a very strange coincidence? Diana is going to lend me a book to read. She says it's perfectly splendid and tremenjusly exciting. She's going to show me a place back in the woods where rice lilies[15] grow. Don't you think Diana has got very soulful eyes? I wish I had soulful eyes. Diana is going to teach me to sing a song called 'Nelly in the Hazel Dell.'[16] She's going to give me a picture to put up in my room; it's a perfectly beautiful picture, she says— a lovely lady in a pale blue silk dress. A sewing-machine agent[17] gave it to her. I wish I had something to give Diana. I'm an inch taller than Diana, but she is ever so much fatter; she says she'd like to be thin because it's so much more graceful, but I'm afraid she only said it to soothe my feelings. We're going to the shore some day to gather shells. We have agreed to call the spring down by the log bridge the Dryad's Bubble. Isn't that a perfectly elegant name? I read a story once about a spring called that. A dryad is a sort of grown-up fairy[18] I think."

"Well, all I hope is you won't talk Diana to death," said Marilla. "But remember this in all your planning, Anne. You're not going to play all your time nor most of it. You'll have your work to do and it'll have to be done first."

Anne's cup of happiness was full, and Matthew caused it to overflow. He had just got home from a trip to the store at Carmody, and he sheepishly produced a small parcel from his pocket and handed it to Anne, with a deprecatory look at Marilla.

"I heard you say you liked chocolate sweeties, so I got you some," he said.

"Humph," sniffed Marilla. "It'll ruin her teeth and stomach. There, there, child, don't look so dismal. You can eat those, since Matthew has gone and got them. He'd better have brought you peppermints. They're wholesomer. Don't sicken yourself eating them all at once now."

"Oh, no, indeed, I won't," said Anne eagerly. "I'll just eat one to-night, Marilla. And I can give Diana half of them, can't I? The other half will taste twice as sweet to me if I give some to her. It's delightful to think I have something to give her."

"I will say it for the child," said Marilla when Anne had gone to her gable, "she isn't stingy. I'm glad, for of all faults I

16. More properly, "Nelly of the Hazel Dell" or "The Hazel Dell," a song by George Frederick Root (1820–1895), first published under the name of Würzel. It was Root's first big hit, vying with Stephen Foster's "My Old Kentucky Home" as the most popular song of 1853, surviving to be included in *Heart Songs Dear to the American People* (1909). Root, who wrote over 200 pieces, became even more famous for Civil War songs, including "Just Before the Battle, Mother" (1863). "The Hazel Dell" is a lugubrious song. See Introduction and Appendix, "Songs."

17. A traveling salesman of sewing machines. The picture Diana was given was presumably some kind of advertisement. Pictures drawing female attention to the sewing machine were widely disseminated (see illustration). Isaac Merritt Singer (1811–1875), a U.S. inventor, improved the sewing machine in 1840, although it did not become widely available until the 1860s.

I. M. Singer & Company, along with other early sewing machine companies, established several innovative sales tactics. As Ruth Brandon says in *A Capitalist Romance*, "Although the Yankee peddler with his smart tricks and wooden nutmegs was an established part of American tradition, the country had never seen a concerted attack on the domestic market to compare with that of the sewing machine salesman, and it aroused considerable public comment and opposition."

18. In classical mythology a nymph who lives in a tree, particularly an oak. Her life is dependent on that of her tree. Although *dryad* specifically refers to classical mythology, Celtic folklore is also peopled by tree spirits.

detest stinginess in a child. Dear me, it's only three weeks since she came, and it seems as if she'd been here always. I can't imagine the place without her. Now, don't be looking I-told-you-so, Matthew. That's bad enough in a woman, but it isn't to be endured in a man. I'm perfectly willing to own up that I'm glad I consented to keep the child and that I'm getting fond of her, but don't you rub it in, Matthew Cuthbert."

CHAPTER XIII

THE DELIGHTS
OF ANTICIPATION

"IT'S TIME Anne was in to do her sewing," said Marilla, glancing at the clock and then out into the yellow August afternoon where everything drowsed in the heat. "She stayed playing with Diana more than half an hour more'n I gave her leave to; and now she's perched out there on the woodpile[1] talking to Matthew, nineteen to the dozen;[2] when she knows perfectly well that she ought to be at her work. And of course he's listening to her like a perfect ninny. I never saw such an infatuated man. The more she talks and the odder the things she says, the more he's delighted evidently. Anne Shirley, you come right in here this minute, do you hear me!"

A series of staccato taps on the west window brought Anne flying in from the yard, eyes shining, cheeks faintly flushed with pink, unbraided hair streaming behind her in a torrent of brightness.

"Oh, Marilla," she exclaimed breathlessly, "there's going to be a Sunday-school picnic next week—in Mr. Harmon Andrews' field, right near the Lake of Shining Waters. And Mrs. Superintendent Bell and Mrs. Rachel Lynde are going to make ice-cream[3]—think of it, Marilla—*ice-cream!* And oh, Marilla, can I go to it?"

1. A stack of deciduous cut wood used in stoves and fireplaces for heat and cooking.

2. For every dozen words a normal person can speak, Anne can cram in nineteen.

3. Made using a hand-cranked machine, ice cream would have required time, effort, and real cream. The cream, sugar, and other flavorings are placed in a cylindrical container around which is packed ice and salt. As the crank is turned and the contents of the container stirred, more ice and salt must be continuously added until the ice cream hardens to the point where the crank is impossible to turn.

4. Anne tells us that this name is her own invention (see p. 145). Montgomery may have heard of the part of Jamaica Bay, New York, called Idlewild (later Idlewild Airport, the New York International Airport).

"Just look at the clock, if you please, Anne. What time did I tell you to come in?"

"Two o'clock—but isn't it splendid about the picnic, Marilla? Please can I go? Oh, I've never been to a picnic—I've dreamed of picnics, but I've never—"

"Yes, I told you to come at two o'clock. And it's a quarter to three. I'd like to know why you didn't obey me, Anne."

"Why, I meant to, Marilla, as much as could be. But you have no idea how fascinating Idlewild[4] is. And then, of course, I had to tell Matthew about the picnic. Matthew is such a sympathetic listener. Please can I go?"

"You'll have to learn to resist the fascination of Idle-what-ever-you-call-it. When I tell you to come in at a certain time I mean that time and not half an hour later. And you needn't stop to discourse with sympathetic listeners on your way, either. As for the picnic, of course you can go. You're a Sunday-school scholar, and it's not likely I'd refuse to let you go when all the other little girls are going."

"But—but," faltered Anne, "Diana says that everybody must take a basket of things to eat. I can't cook, as you know, Marilla, and—and—I don't mind going to a picnic without puffed sleeves so much, but I'd feel terribly humiliated if I had to go without a basket. It's been preying on my mind ever since Diana told me."

"Well, it needn't prey any longer. I'll bake you a basket."

"Oh, you dear good Marilla. Oh, you are so kind to me. Oh, I'm so much obliged to you."

Getting through with her "ohs" Anne cast herself into Marilla's arms and rapturously kissed her sallow cheek. It was the first time in her whole life that childish lips had voluntarily touched Marilla's face. Again that sudden sensation of startling sweetness thrilled her. She was secretly vastly pleased at Anne's impulsive caress, which was probably the reason she said brusquely:

"There, there, never mind your kissing nonsense. I'd sooner see you doing strictly as you're told. As for cooking, I mean to begin giving you lessons in that some of these days. But you're so feather-brained, Anne, I've been waiting to see if you'd sober down a little and learn to be steady before I begin. You've got to keep your wits about you in cooking and not stop in the middle of things to let your thoughts rove over all creation. Now, get out your patchwork[5] and have your square done before tea-time."

"I do *not* like patchwork," said Anne dolefully, hunting out her workbasket and sitting down before little heap of red and white diamonds with a sigh. "I think some kinds of sewing would be nice; but there's no scope for imagination in patchwork. It's just one little seam after another and you never seem to be getting anywhere. But of course I'd rather be Anne of Green Gables sewing patchwork than Anne of any other place with nothing to do but play. I wish time went as quick sewing patches as it does when I'm playing with Diana, though. Oh, we do have such elegant times, Marilla. I have to furnish most of the imagination, but I'm well able to do that. Diana is simply perfect in every other way. You know that little piece of land across the brook that runs up between our farm and Mr. Barry's. It belongs to Mr. William Bell, and right in the corner there is a little ring of white birch-trees — the most romantic spot, Marilla. Diana and I have our playhouse there. We call it Idlewild. Isn't that a poetical name? I assure you it took me some time to think it out. I stayed awake nearly a whole night before I invented it. Then, just as I was dropping off to sleep, it came like an inspiration. Diana was *enraptured* when she heard it. We have got our house fixed up elegantly. You must come and see it, Marilla, won't you? We have great big stones, all covered with moss, for seats, and boards from tree to tree for shelves. And we have all our dishes on them. Of course, they're all broken but it's the easi-

5. A needlework art consisting of sewing small scrap pieces of various patterns of cloth together to form one article, especially a quilt, cushion cover, and so on. North American women have found an outlet for their creativity in patchwork for generations, but according to Sherry Davidson, a collector of antique quilts, almost all of those made on P.E.I. during the 1880s and 1890s were alike: diamonds and triangles of red and white. See Appendix, "Homemade Artifacts."

6. Literally "lake of Willows". Montgomery says, "*Willowmere* and *Violet Vale* were compact of imagination" (*SJ* II [Jan. 27, 1911]: 42).

est thing in the world to imagine that they are whole. There's a piece of a plate with a spray of red and yellow ivy on it that is especially beautiful. We keep it in the parlour and we have the fairy glass there, too. The fairy glass is as lovely as a dream. Diana found it out in the woods behind their chicken house. It's all full of rainbows—just little young rainbows that haven't grown big yet—and Diana's mother told her it was broken off a hanging lamp they once had. But it's nicer to imagine the fairies lost it one night when they had a ball, so we call it the fairy glass. Matthew is going to make us a table. Oh, we have named that little round pool over in Mr. Barry's field Willowmere.[6] I got that name out of the book Diana lent me. That was a thrilling book, Marilla. The heroine had five lovers. I'd be satisfied with one, wouldn't you? She was very handsome and she went through great tribulations. She could faint as easy as anything. I'd love to be able to faint, wouldn't you, Marilla? It's so romantic. But I'm really very healthy for all I'm so thin. I believe I'm getting fatter though. Don't you think I am? I look at my elbows every morning when I get up to see if any dimples are coming. Diana is having a new dress made with elbow sleeves. She is going to wear it to the picnic. Oh, I do hope it will be fine next Wednesday. I don't feel that I could endure the disappointment if anything happened to prevent me from getting to the picnic. I suppose I'd live through it but I'm certain it would be a life-long sorrow. It wouldn't matter if I got to a hundred picnics in after years; they wouldn't make up for missing this one. They're going to have boats on the Lake of Shining Waters—and ice-cream as I told you. I have never tasted ice-cream. Diana tried to explain what it was like but I guess ice-cream is one of those things that are beyond imagination."

"Anne, you have talked even on for ten minutes by the clock," said Marilla. "Now, just for curiosity's sake, see if you can hold your tongue for the same length of time."

Anne held her tongue as desired. But for the rest of the week she talked picnic and thought picnic and dreamed picnic. On Saturday it rained and she worked herself up into such a frantic state lest it should keep on raining until and over Wednesday that Marilla made her sew an extra patchwork square by way of steadying her nerves.

On Sunday Anne confided to Marilla on the way home from church that she grew actually cold all over with excitement when the minister announced the picnic from the pulpit.

"Such a thrill as went up and down my back, Marilla! I don't think I've ever really believed until then that there was honestly going to be a picnic. I couldn't help fearing I'd only imagined it. But when a minister says a thing in the pulpit you just have to believe it."

"You set your heart too much on things, Anne," said Marilla with a sigh. "I'm afraid there'll be a great many disappointments in store for you through life."

"Oh, Marilla, looking forward to things is half the pleasure of them," exclaimed Anne. "You mayn't get the things themselves; but nothing can prevent you from having the fun of looking forward to them. Mrs. Lynde says, 'Blessed are they who expect nothing for they shall not be disappointed.'[7] But I think it would be worse to expect nothing than to be disappointed."

Marilla wore her amethyst brooch to church that day as usual. Marilla always wore her amethyst brooch to church. She would have thought it rather sacrilegious to leave it off— as bad as forgetting her Bible or her collection dime.[8] That amethyst brooch was Marilla's most treasured possession.[9] A sea-faring uncle had given it to her mother who in turn had bequeathed it to Marilla. It was an old-fashioned oval, containing a braid of her mother's hair, surrounded by a border of very fine amethysts. Marilla knew too little about precious

7. Cf. "Blessed is the man who expects nothing, for he shall never be disappointed was the ninth beatitude" (Alexander Pope to William Fortescue, 1725).

8. Ten cents to put in the collection plate or bag passed around at church for offerings from the congregation.

9. The amethyst, a semiprecious stone consisting of quartz colored by manganese or a combination of iron and soda, is a purple or blue-violet clear stone. It is found in Nova Scotia and is thus relatively inexpensive in the Maritimes. Marilla's brooch is mid-Victorian in shape and design. It was fashionable in Victoria's reign to wear the hair of dead relatives made up into shapes or acting as settings for precious objects. Anne cuts a lock of Diana's hair as a keepsake later when Mrs. Barry forbids Diana to associate with Anne (p. 192). See illustration of a hair brooch from 1870s. See also Introduction, p. 32.

10. As Montgomery admitted in her journal, "Anne's idea that diamonds looked like amethysts was once mine" (*SJ* II (Jan. 27, 1911]: 42).

stones to realize how fine the amethysts actually were; but she thought them very beautiful and was always pleasantly conscious of their violet shimmer at her throat, above her good brown satin dress, even although she could not see it.

Anne had been smitten with delighted admiration when she first saw that brooch.

"Oh, Marilla, it's a perfectly elegant brooch. I don't know how you can pay attention to the sermon or the prayers when you have it on. *I* couldn't, I know. I think amethysts are just sweet. They are what I used to think diamonds were like. Long ago, before I had ever seen a diamond, I read about them, and I tried to imagine what they would be like. I thought they would be lovely glimmering purple stones.[10] When I saw a real diamond in a lady's ring one day I was so disappointed I cried. Of course, it was very lovely but it wasn't my idea of a diamond. Will you let me hold the brooch for one minute, Marilla? Do you think amethysts can be the souls of good violets?"

CHAPTER XIV

ANNE'S CONFESSION

ON THE MONDAY evening before the picnic Marilla came down from her room with a troubled face.

"Anne," she said to that small personage who was shelling peas by the spotless table and singing "Nelly of the Hazel Dell" with a vigour and expression that did credit to Diana's teaching, "did you see anything of my amethyst brooch? I thought I stuck it in my pincushion when I came home from church yesterday evening, but I can't find it anywhere."

"I—I saw it this afternoon when you were away at the Aid Society," said Anne, a little slowly. "I was passing your door when I saw it on the cushion so I went in to look at it."

"Did you touch it?" said Marilla sternly.

"Y-e-e-s," admitted Anne, "I took it up and pinned it on my breast just to see how it would look."

"You had no business to do anything of the sort. It's very wrong in a little girl to meddle. You shouldn't have gone into my room in the first place and you shouldn't have touched a brooch that didn't belong to you in the second. Where did you put it?"

"Oh, I put it back on the bureau. I hadn't it on a minute. Truly I didn't mean to meddle, Marilla. I didn't think about

1. Royal or noble persons going to be executed, especially in the sixteenth century, were "led to the block," or chopping block, to have the head struck off by the executioner's axe, whereas common people were usually hanged. Anne Boleyn, Mary Queen of Scots, and Charles I all met this end. After Simon Fraser, the twelfth Baron Lovat, was beheaded for high treason in 1747, this form of execution ceased.

its being wrong to go in and try on the brooch; but I see now that it was and I'll never do it again. That's one good thing about me. I never do the same naughty thing twice."

"You didn't put it back," said Marilla. "That brooch isn't anywhere on the bureau. You've taken it out or something, Anne."

"I *did* put it back," said Anne quickly—pertly, Marilla thought. "I don't just remember whether I stuck it on the pincushion or laid it in the china tray. But I'm perfectly certain I put it back."

"I'll go and have another look," said Marilla, determining to be just. "If you put that brooch back it's there still. If it isn't I'll know you didn't, that's all!"

Marilla went to her room and made a thorough search, not only over the bureau but in every other place she thought the brooch might possibly be. It was not to be found and she returned to the kitchen.

"Anne, the brooch is gone. By your own admission you were the last person to handle it. Now, what have you done with it? Tell me the truth at once. Did you take it out and lose it?"

"No, I didn't," said Anne solemnly, meeting Marilla's angry gaze squarely. "I never took the brooch out of your room and that is the truth, if I was to be led to the block[1] for it although I'm not very certain what a block is. So there, Marilla."

Anne's "so there" was only intended to emphasize her assertion, but Marilla took it as a display of defiance.

"I believe you are telling me a falsehood, Anne," she said sharply. "I know you are. There, now, don't say anything more unless you are prepared to tell the whole truth. Go to your room and stay there until you are ready to confess."

"Will I take the peas with me?" said Anne meekly.

"No, I'll finish shelling them myself. Do as I bid you."

When Anne had gone, Marilla went about her evening tasks in a very disturbed state of mind. She was worried about her valuable brooch. What if Anne had lost it? And how wicked of the child to deny having taken it, when anybody could see she must have! With such an innocent face, too!

"I don't know what I wouldn't sooner have had happen," thought Marilla, as she nervously shelled the peas. "Of course, I don't suppose she meant to steal it or anything like that. She's just taken it to play with, or help along that imagination of hers. She must have taken it, that's clear, for there hasn't been a soul in that room since she was in it, by her own story, until I went up to-night. And the brooch is gone, there's nothing surer. I suppose she has lost it and is afraid to own up for fear she'll be punished. It's a dreadful thing to think she tells falsehoods. It's a far worse thing than her fit of temper. It's a fearful responsibility to have a child in your house you can't trust. Slyness and untruthfulness—that's what she has displayed. I declare I feel worse about that than the brooch. If she'd only have told the truth about it I wouldn't mind so much."

Marilla went to her room at intervals all through the evening and searched for the brooch, without finding it. A bedtime visit to the east gable produced no result. Anne persisted in denying that she knew anything about the brooch but Marilla was only the more firmly convinced that she did.

She told Matthew the story the next morning. Matthew was confounded and puzzled; he could not so quickly lose faith in Anne but he had to admit that circumstances were against her.

"You're sure it hasn't fell down behind the bureau?" was the only suggestion he could offer.

"I've moved the bureau and I've taken out the drawers and I've looked in every crack and cranny," was Marilla's positive answer. "The brooch is gone and that child has taken it and

2. The white lily *(Lilium candidum,* Liliaceae), often represented with the Madonna in paintings. A very fragrant flower, in religious iconography it is a symbol of charity or purity. See Introduction. In *Kilmeny of the Orchard* (1910), ch. 13: "those Mary-lilies up in the orchard" are also "long stemmed, white Madonna lilies." See illustration.

3. Invisible winds, from *Measure for Measure:* "To be imprisoned in the viewless winds" (III.i. l. 124).

lied about it. That is the plain, ugly truth, Matthew Cuthbert, and we might as well look it in the face."

"Well now, what are you going to do about it?" Matthew asked forlornly, feeling secretly thankful that Marilla and not he had to deal with the situation. He felt no desire to put his oar in this time.

"She'll stay in her room until she confesses," said Marilla grimly, remembering the success of this method in the former case. "Then we'll see. Perhaps we'll be able to find the brooch if she'll only tell where she took it; but in any case she'll have to be severely punished, Matthew."

"Well now, you'll have to punish her," said Matthew, reaching for his hat. "I've nothing to do with it, remember. You warned me off yourself."

Marilla felt deserted by everyone. She could not even go to Mrs. Lynde for advice. She went up to the east gable with a very serious face and left it with a face more serious still. Anne steadfastly refused to confess. She persisted in asserting that she had not taken the brooch. The child had evidently been crying and Marilla felt a pang of pity which she sternly repressed. By night she was, as she expressed it, "beat out."

"You'll stay in this room until you confess, Anne. You can make up your mind to that," she said firmly.

"But the picnic is to-morrow, Marilla," cried Anne. "You won't keep me from going to that, will you? You'll just let me out for the afternoon, won't you? Then I'll stay here as long as you like afterwards *cheerfully.* But I *must* go to the picnic."

"You'll not go to picnics nor anywhere else until you've confessed, Anne."

"Oh, Marilla," gasped Anne.

But Marilla had gone out and shut the door.

Wednesday morning dawned as bright and fair as if expressly made to order for the picnic. Birds sang around Green Gables; the Madonna lilies[2] in the garden sent out whiffs of perfume that entered in on viewless winds[3] at every door and window, and wandered through halls and rooms like spirits of benediction. The birches in the hollow waved joyful hands as if watching for Anne's usual morning greeting from the east gable. But Anne was not at her window. When Marilla took her breakfast up to her she found the child sitting primly on her bed, pale and resolute, with tight-shut lips and gleaming eyes.

"Marilla, I'm ready to confess."

"Ah!" Marilla laid down her tray. Once again her method had succeeded, but her success was very bitter to her. "Let me hear what you have to say then, Anne."

ROSA BLANDA

4. Hips, the fruit of the wild rose or of roses in general.

"I took the amethyst brooch," said Anne, as if repeating a lesson she had learned. "I took it just as you said. I didn't mean to take it when I went in. But it did look so beautiful, Marilla, when I pinned it on my breast that I was overcome by an irresistible temptation. I imagined how perfectly thrilling it would be to take it to Idlewild and play I was the Lady Cordelia Fitzgerald. It would be so much easier to imagine I was the Lady Cordelia if I had a real amethyst brooch on. Diana and I made necklaces of roseberries[4] but what are roseberries compared to amethysts? So I took the brooch. I thought I could put it back before you came home. I went all the way around by the road to lengthen out the time. When I was going over the bridge across the Lake of Shining Waters I took the brooch off to have another look at it. Oh, how it did shine in the sunlight! And then, when I was leaning over the bridge, it just slipped through my fingers — so — and went down — down — down, all purply-sparkling, and sank forevermore beneath the Lake of Shining Waters. And that's the best I can do at confessing, Marilla."

Marilla felt hot anger surge up into her heart again. This child had taken and lost her treasured amethyst brooch and now sat there calmly reciting the details thereof without the least apparent compunction or repentance.

5. A biblical abjuration against second thoughts or delay: "And Jesus said unto him, 'No man, having put his hand to the plough, and looking back, is fit for the kingdom of God'" (Luke 9:62).

"Anne, this is terrible," she said, trying to speak calmly. "You are the very wickedest girl I ever heard of."

"Yes, I suppose I am," agreed Anne tranquilly. "And I know I'll have to be punished. It'll be your duty to punish me, Marilla. Won't you please get it over right off because I'd like to go to the picnic with nothing on my mind."

"Picnic, indeed! You'll go to no picnic to-day, Anne Shirley. That shall be your punishment. And it isn't half severe enough either for what you've done!"

"Not go to the picnic!" Anne sprang to her feet and clutched Marilla's hand. "But you *promised* me I might! Oh, Marilla, I must go to the picnic. That was why I confessed. Punish me any way you like but that. Oh, Marilla, please, please, let me go to the picnic. Think of the ice-cream! For anything you know I may never have a chance to taste ice-cream again."

Marilla disengaged Anne's clinging hands stonily.

"You needn't plead, Anne. You are not going to the picnic and that's final. No, not a word."

Anne realized that Marilla was not to be moved. She clasped her hands together, gave a piercing shriek, and then flung herself face downwards on the bed, crying and writhing in an utter abandonment of disappointment and despair.

"For the land's sake!" gasped Marilla, hastening from the room. "I believe the child is crazy. No child in her senses would behave as she does. If she isn't she's utterly bad. Oh dear, I'm afraid Rachel was right from the first. But I've put my hand to the plough and I won't look back."[5]

That was a dismal morning. Marilla worked fiercely and scrubbed the porch floor and the dairy shelves when she could find nothing else to do. Neither the shelves nor the porch needed it—but Marilla did. Then she went out and raked the yard.

When dinner was ready she went to the stairs and called

Anne. A tear-stained face appeared, looking tragically over the banisters.

"Come down to your dinner, Anne."

"I don't want any dinner, Marilla," said Anne sobbingly. "I couldn't eat anything. My heart is broken. You'll feel remorse of conscience some day, I expect, for breaking it, Marilla, but I forgive you. Remember when the time comes that I forgive you. But please don't ask me to eat anything, especially boiled pork and greens. Boiled pork and greens are so unromantic when one is in affliction."

Exasperated Marilla returned to the kitchen and poured out her tale of woe to Matthew who, between his sense of justice and his unlawful sympathy with Anne, was a miserable man.

"Well now, she shouldn't have taken the brooch, Marilla, or told stories about it," he admitted, mournfully surveying his plateful of unromantic pork and greens as if he, like Anne, thought it a food unsuited to crises of feeling, "but she's such a little thing—such an interesting little thing. Don't you think it's pretty rough not to let her go to the picnic when she's so set on it?"

"Matthew Cuthbert, I'm amazed at you. I think I've let her off entirely too easy. And she doesn't appear to realize how wicked she's been at all—that's what worries me most. If she'd really felt sorry it wouldn't be so bad. And you don't seem to realize it neither; you're making excuses all the time for her to yourself—I can see that."

"Well now, she's such a little thing," feebly reiterated Matthew. "And there should be allowances made, Marilla. You know she's never had any bringing up."

"Well, she's having it now," retorted Marilla.

The retort silenced Matthew, if it did not convince him. That dinner was a very dismal meal. The only cheerful thing about it was Jerry Buote, the hired boy, and Marilla resented his cheerfulness as a personal insult.

6. The soft fermenting dough of which bread is made.

7. Supposedly from "Ragman roll," a "succession of incoherent statements, an unconnected or rambling discourse, a long-winded harangue of little meaning or importance."

When her dishes were washed and her bread sponge[6] set and her hens fed Marilla remembered that she had noticed a small rent in her best black lace shawl when she had taken it off on Monday afternoon on returning from the Ladies' Aid. She would go and mend it.

The shawl was in a box in her trunk. As Marilla lifted it out, the sunlight, falling through the vines that clustered thickly about the window, struck upon something caught in the shawl — something that glittered and sparkled in facets of violet light. Marilla snatched at it with a gasp. It was the amethyst brooch, hanging to a thread of the lace by its catch.

"Dear life and heart," said Marilla blankly, "what does this mean? Here's my brooch safe and sound that I thought was at the bottom of Barry's pond. Whatever did that girl mean by saying she took it and lost it? I declare I believe Green Gables is bewitched. I remember now that when I took off my shawl Monday afternoon I laid it on the bureau for a minute. I suppose the brooch got caught in it somehow. Well!"

Marilla betook herself to the east gable, brooch in hand. Anne had cried herself out and was sitting dejectedly by the window.

"Anne Shirley," said Marilla solemnly, "I've just found my brooch hanging to my black lace shawl. Now I want to know what that rigmarole[7] you told me this morning meant."

"Why, you said you'd keep me here until I confessed," returned Anne wearily, "and so I decided to confess because I was bound to get to the picnic. I thought out a confession last night after I went to bed and made it as interesting as I could. And I said it over and over so that I wouldn't forget it. But you wouldn't let me go to the picnic after all, so all my trouble was wasted."

Marilla had to laugh in spite of herself. But her conscience pricked her.

"Anne, you do beat all! But I was wrong — I see that now. I shouldn't have doubted your word when I'd never known you to tell a story. Of course, it wasn't right for you to confess to a thing you hadn't done—it was very wrong to do so. But I drove you to it. So if you'll forgive me, Anne, I'll forgive you and we'll start square again. And now get yourself ready for the picnic."

Anne flew up like a rocket.

"Oh, Marilla, isn't it too late?"

"No, it's only two o'clock. They won't be more than well gathered yet and it'll be an hour before they have tea. Wash your face and comb your hair and put on your gingham. I'll fill a basket for you. There's plenty of stuff baked in the house. And I'll get Jerry to hitch up the sorrel and drive you down to the picnic ground."

"Oh, Marilla," exclaimed Anne, flying to the wash-stand. "Five minutes ago I was so miserable I was wishing I'd never been born and now I wouldn't change places with an angel!"

That night a thoroughly happy, completely tired-out Anne returned to Green Gables in a state of beatification impossible to describe.

"Oh, Marilla, I've had a perfectly scrumptious[8] time. Scrumptious is a new word I learned to-day. I heard Mary Alice Bell use it. Isn't it very expressive? Everything was lovely. We had a splendid tea and then Mr. Harmon Andrews took us all for a row on the Lake of Shining Waters—six of us at a time. And Jane Andrews nearly fell overboard. She was leaning out to pick water lilies and if Mr. Andrews hadn't caught her by her sash just in the nick of time she'd have fallen in and prob'ly been drowned. I wish it had been me. It would be such a romantic experience to have been nearly drowned. It would be such a thrilling tale to tell. And we had ice-cream. Words fail me to describe that ice-cream. Marilla, I assure you it was sublime."

That evening Marilla told the whole story to Matthew over her stocking basket.[9]

"I'm willing to own up that I made a mistake," she con-

8. "First rate," "glorious" (1836). Always a colloquial or vulgar expression, belonging to the schoolgirl slang of the period.

9. A basket of stockings that have to be mended.

cluded candidly, "but I've learned a lesson. I have to laugh when I think of Anne's 'confession,' although I suppose I shouldn't for it really was a falsehood. But it doesn't seem as bad as the other would have been, somehow, and anyhow I'm responsible for it. That child is hard to understand in some respects. But I believe she'll turn out all right yet. And there's one thing certain, no house will ever be dull that she's in."

CHAPTER XV

A TEMPEST IN THE SCHOOL TEAPOT[1]

"WHAT a splendid day!" said Anne, drawing a long breath. "Isn't it good just to be alive on a day like this? I pity the people who aren't born yet for missing it. They may have good days, of course, but they can never have this one. And it's splendider still to have such a lovely way to go to school by, isn't it?"

"It's a lot nicer than going round by the road; that is so dusty and hot," said Diana practically, peeping into her dinner basket and mentally calculating if the three juicy, toothsome raspberry tarts reposing there were divided among ten girls how many bites each girl would have.

The little girls of Avonlea school always pooled their lunches and to eat three raspberry tarts all alone or even to share them only with one's best chum would have forever and ever branded as "awful mean" the girl who did it. And yet, when the tarts were divided among ten girls you just got enough to tantalize you.

The way Anne and Diana went to school *was* a pretty one. Anne thought those walks to and from school with Diana couldn't be improved upon even by imagination. Going around by the main road would have been so unromantic; but

1. From expression commonly "storm in a teapot," derived ultimately from Cicero, *"Excitabat enim fluctus in simpulo"* (*De Legibus* III, 16).

2. The author noted that "Lover's Lane was of course *my* Lover's Lane" (*SJ* II [Jan. 27, 1911]: 42). See Appendix, "Geography."

3. See n. 10, ch. 8; see also Textual Note.

4. A fictional invention. See Appendix, "Geography."

Birch trees, Park Corner.

to go by Lover's Lane[2] and Willowmere and Violet Vale[3] and the Birch Path[4] was romantic, if ever anything was.

Lover's Lane opened out below the orchard at Green Gables and stretched far up into the woods to the end of the Cuthbert farm. It was the way by which the cows were taken to the back pasture and the wood hauled home in winter. Anne had named Lover's Lane before she had been a month at Green Gables.

"Not that lovers ever really walk there," she explained to Marilla, "but Diana and I are reading a perfectly magnificent book and there's a Lover's Lane in it. So we want to have one, too. And it's a very pretty name, don't you think? So romantic! We can imagine the lovers into it, you know. I like that lane because you can think out loud there without people calling you crazy."

Anne, starting out alone in the morning, went down Lover's Lane as far as the brook. Here Diana met her, and the two little girls went on up the lane under the leafy arch of maples—"maples are such sociable trees," said Anne, "they're always rustling and whispering to you,"—until they came to a rustic bridge. Then they left the lane and walked through Mr. Barry's back field and past Willowmere. Beyond Willowmere came Violet Vale—a little green dimple in the shadow of Mr. Andrew Bell's big woods. "Of course there are no violets there now," Anne told Marilla, "but Diana says there are millions of them in spring. Oh, Marilla, can't you just imagine you see them? It actually takes away my breath. I named it Violet Vale. Diana says she never saw the beat of me for hitting on fancy names for places. It's nice to be clever at something, isn't it? But Diana named the Birch Path. She wanted to, so I let her; but I'm sure I could have found something more poetical than plain Birch Path. Anybody can think of a name like that. But the Birch Path is one of the prettiest places in the world, Marilla."

It was. Other people besides Anne thought so when they stumbled on it. It was a little narrow, twisting path, winding down over a long hill straight through Mr. Bell's woods, where the light came down sifted through so many emerald screens that it was as flawless as the heart of a diamond. It was fringed in all its length with slim young birches, white-stemmed and lissom-boughed;[5] ferns and starflowers and wild lilies-of-the-valley and scarlet tufts of pigeon-berries[6] grew thickly along it. And always there was a delightful spiciness in the air and music of bird calls and the murmur and laugh of wood winds in the trees overhead. Now and then you might see a rabbit skipping across the road if you were quiet—which, with Anne and Diana, happened about once in a blue moon.[7] Down in the valley the path came out to the main road and then it was just up the spruce hill to the school.

The Avonlea school was a white-washed building low in the eaves and wide in the windows, furnished inside with comfortable, substantial, old-fashioned desks that opened and shut, and were carved all over their lids with the initials and hieroglyphics of three generations of school-children. The schoolhouse was set back from the road and behind it was a dusky fir wood and a brook where all the children put their bottles of milk in the morning to keep cool and sweet until dinner hour.[8]

Marilla had seen Anne start off to school on the first day of September with many secret misgivings. Anne was such an odd girl. How would she get on with the other children? And how on earth would she ever manage to hold her tongue during school hours?

Things went better than Marilla feared, however. Anne came home that evening in high spirits.

"I think I'm going to like school here," she announced. "I don't think much of the master, though. He's all the time curling his mustache and making eyes at Prissy Andrews.

5. With supple, limber boughs.

Fruit

6. The berries of pokeweed (*Phylotacca americana*), a coarse American perennial herb with dark purple juicy berries. See illustration.

7. A new moon appearing a second time in a month, used proverbially for something that hardly ever happens.

8. Based on Montgomery's own schooldays: "And there was a brook in it too—a delightful brook . . . and no end of pools and nooks where the pupils put their bottles of milk to keep sweet and cold until dinner hour" (*AP*, 25).

9. Based on Prince of Wales College in Charlottetown. As the statement suggests, it could be entered only by taking a public examination. Anne later attends Queen's herself, as Montgomery did Prince of Wales: "In the fall of 1893 I went to Charlottetown, and attended the Prince of Wales College that winter studying for a teacher's license" (*AP*, 59). See also Introduction, p. 14, and Appendix, "Education."

10. A colloquial expression meaning infatuated. See Textual Note. On the schoolmaster's flirtation see Introduction.

11. A tablet of slate, set in a frame of wood, used for writing. Children used slates, which could be easily erased, instead of paper, which was scarce and expensive. Exercises were rarely set out on paper until the higher classes of composition. See also nn. 3 and 6, ch. 17.

12. Another reference to the *Royal Readers*. Anne's contemporaries have finished the *Fourth Reader* and advanced to the *Fifth*, while Anne,

Cavendish school children, c. 1890s.

Prissy is grown-up, you know. She's sixteen and she's studying for the entrance examination into Queen's Academy[9] at Charlottetown next year. Tillie Boulter says the master is *dead gone*[10] on her. She's got a beautiful complexion and curly brown hair and she does it up so elegantly. She sits in the long seat at the back and he sits there too, most of the time — to explain her lessons, he says. But Ruby Gillis says she saw him writing something on her slate[11] and when Prissy read it she blushed as red as a beet and giggled; and Ruby Gillis says she doesn't believe it had anything to do with the lesson."

"Anne Shirley, don't let me hear you talking about your teacher it that way again," said Marilla sharply. "You don't go to school to criticize the master. I guess he can teach *you* something and it's your business to learn. And I want you to understand right off that you are not to come home telling tales about him. That is something I won't encourage. I hope you were a good girl."

"Indeed I was," said Anne comfortably. "It wasn't so hard as you might imagine, either. I sit with Diana. Our seat is right by the window and we can look down to the Lake of Shining Waters. There are a lot of nice girls in school and we had scrumptious fun playing at dinner time. It's so nice to have a lot of little girls to play with. But of course I like Diana best and always will. I *adore* Diana. I'm dreadfully far behind the others. They're all in the fifth book and I'm only in the fourth.[12] I feel that it's a kind of disgrace. But there's not one of them has such an imagination as I have and I soon found that out. We had reading and geography and Canadian History and dictation to-day. Mr. Phillips said my spelling was disgraceful and he held up my slate so that everybody could see it, marked all over. I felt so mortified, Marilla; he might have been politer to a stranger, I think. Ruby Gillis gave me an apple and Sophia Sloane lent me a lovely pink card with 'May I see you home?' on it. I'm to give it back to her to-morrow. And Tillie Boulter let me wear her bead ring all the afternoon. Can I have some of those pearl beads off the old pincushion in the garret to make myself a ring? And oh, Marilla, Jane Andrews told me that Minnie MacPherson told her that she heard Prissy Andrews tell Sara Gillis that I had a very pretty nose. Marilla, that is the first compliment I have ever had in my life and you can't imagine what a strange feeling it gave me. Marilla, have I really a pretty nose? I know you'll tell me the truth."

"Your nose is well enough," said Marilla shortly. Secretly she thought Anne's nose was a remarkably pretty one; but she had no intention of telling her so.

That was three weeks ago and all had gone smoothly so far. And now this crisp September morning, Anne and Diana were tripping blithely down the Birch Path, two of the happiest little girls in Avonlea.

"I guess Gilbert Blythe will be in school to-day," said Diana. "He's been visiting his cousins over in New Brunswick all summer and he only came home Saturday night. He's *aw'fly* handsome, Anne. And he teases the girls something terrible. He just torments our lives out."

Diana's voice indicated that she rather liked having her life tormented out than not.

"Gilbert Blythe?" said Anne. "Isn't it his name that's written up on the porch wall with Julia Bell's and a big 'Take Notice'[13] over them?"

"Yes," said Diana tossing her head, "but I'm sure he doesn't like Julia Bell so very much. I've heard him say he studied the multiplication table by her freckles."

"Oh, don't speak about freckles to me," implored Anne. "It isn't delicate when I've got so many. But I do think that writing take-notices up on the wall about the boys and girls is the silliest ever. I should just like to see anybody dare to write my name up with a boy's. Not, of course," she hastened to add, "that anybody would."

Anne sighed. She didn't want her name written up. But it

who earlier said she had only got to the *Fourth Reader* (p. 88) is made to pursue the material in that text. This small school is divided not into grades but according to levels of ability.

13. This schoolyard expression may be a way of pronouncing the intentions signified by the two letters N.B. from the Latin *nota bene*, note well. Schoolyard graffiti, especially the incised sort, are unlikely to require many letters to achieve a message.

14. Like Maud Montgomery in her visit to Prince Albert, Gilbert has been impeded in his progress in school because of a trip West for the sake of a father. See Introduction, p. 13.

15. Cf. "I alas, had no rights in the brook" (*AP*, 26). See also n. 8.

was a little humiliating to know that there was no danger of it.

"Nonsense," said Diana, whose black eyes and glossy tresses had played such havoc with the hearts of Avonlea schoolboys that her name figured on the porch walls in half a dozen take-notices. "It's only meant as a joke. And don't you be too sure your name won't ever be written up. Charlie Sloane is *dead gone* on you. He told his mother—his *mother*, mind you —that you were the smartest girl in school. That's better than being good-looking."

"No, it isn't," said Anne, feminine to the core. "I'd rather be pretty than clever. And I hate Charlie Sloane. I can't bear a boy with goggle eyes. If any one wrote my name up with his I'd *never* get over it, Diana Barry. But it *is* nice to keep head of your class."

"You'll have Gilbert in your class after this," said Diana, "and he's used to being head of his class, I can tell you. He's only in the fourth book although he's nearly fourteen. Four years ago his father was sick and had to go out to Alberta for his health and Gilbert went with him. They were there three years and Gil didn't go to school hardly any until they came back.[14] You won't find it so easy to keep head after this, Anne."

"I'm glad," said Anne quickly. "I couldn't really feel proud of keeping head of little boys and girls of just nine or ten. I got up yesterday spelling 'ebullition.' Josie Pye was head and mind you, she peeped in her book. Mr. Phillips didn't see her —he was looking at Prissy Andrews—but I did. I just swept her a look of freezing scorn and she got as red as a beet and spelled it wrong after all."

"Those Pye girls are cheats all round," said Diana indignantly, as they climbed the fence of the main road. "Gertie Pye actually went and put her milk bottle in my place in the brook[15] yesterday. Did you ever? I don't speak to her now."

When Mr. Phillips was in the back of the room hearing Prissy Andrews' Latin Diana whispered to Anne:

"That's Gilbert Blythe sitting right across the aisle from you, Anne. Just look at him and see if you don't think he's handsome."

Anne looked accordingly. She had a good chance to do so, for the said Gilbert Blythe was absorbed in stealthily pinning the long yellow braid of Ruby Gillis, who sat in front of him, to the back of her seat. He was a tall boy with curly brown hair, roguish hazel eyes and a mouth twisted into a teasing smile. Presently Ruby Gillis started up to take a sum to the master; she fell back into her seat with a little shriek, believing that her hair was pulled out by the roots. Everybody looked at her and Mr. Phillips glared so sternly that Ruby began to cry. Gilbert had whisked the pin out of sight and was studying his history with the soberest face in the world; but when the commotion subsided he looked at Anne and winked with inexpressible drollery.

"I think your Gilbert Blythe *is* handsome," confided Anne to Diana, "but I think he's very bold. It isn't good manners to wink at a strange girl."

But it was not until the afternoon that things really began to happen.

Mr. Phillips was back in the corner explaining a problem in algebra to Prissy Andrews and the rest of the scholars were doing pretty much as they pleased, eating green apples, whispering, drawing pictures on their slates, and driving crickets, harnessed to strings,[16] up and down the aisle. Gilbert Blythe was trying to make Anne Shirley look at him and failing utterly because Anne was at that moment totally oblivious, not only of the very existence of Gilbert Blythe, but of every other scholar in Avonlea school and of Avonlea school itself. With her chin propped on her hands and her eyes fixed on the blue glimpse of the Lake of Shining Waters that the west window afforded, she was far away in a gorgeous dreamland, hearing and seeing nothing save her own wonderful visions.

16. An amusement of late summer and early autumn. Lacking mechanical toys, boys would catch crickets, tie strings to them, and race them. On Anne's first day of teaching, "Morley Andrews was caught driving a pair of trained crickets in the aisle. Anne stood Morley on the platform for an hour and . . . which Morley felt more keenly . . . confiscated his crickets. She set them free . . . but Morley believed . . . that she took them home and kept them for her own private amusement" (*Anne of Avonlea*, ch. 5).

"'You mean, hateful boy!' she exclaimed passionately." Illustration by Sybil Tawse,
from the 1933 edition.

Gilbert Blythe wasn't used to putting himself out to make a girl look at him and meeting with failure. She *should* look at him, that red-haired Shirley girl with the little pointed chin and the big eyes that weren't like the eyes of any other girl in Avonlea school.

Gilbert reached across the aisle, picked up the end of Anne's long red braid, held it out at arm's length and said in a piercing whisper:

"Carrots! Carrots!"

Then Anne looked at him with a vengeance. She did more than look. She sprang to her feet, her bright fancies fallen into cureless ruin. She flashed one indignant glance at Gilbert from eyes whose angry sparkle was swiftly quenched in equally angry tears.

"You mean, hateful boy!" she exclaimed passionately. "How dare you!"

And then—Thwack! Anne had brought her slate down on Gilbert's head and cracked it—slate, not head—clear across.

Avonlea school always enjoyed a scene. This was an especially enjoyable one. Everybody said, "Oh" in horrified delight. Diana gasped. Ruby Gillis, who was inclined to be hysterical, began to cry. Tommy Sloane let his team of crickets escape him altogether while he stared open-mouthed at the tableau.

Mr. Phillips stalked down the aisle and laid his hand heavily on Anne's shoulder.

"Anne Shirley, what does this mean?" he said angrily.

Anne returned no answer. It was asking too much of flesh and blood to expect her to tell before the whole school that she had been called "Carrots." Gilbert it was who spoke up stoutly.

"It was my fault, Mr. Phillips. I teased her."

Mr. Phillips paid no heed to Gilbert.

"I am sorry to see a pupil of mine displaying such a temper and such a vindictive spirit," he said in a solemn tone, as if the mere fact of being a pupil of his ought to root out all evil

17. From the Common Psaltery of the sixteenth century, which was used by the Puritans before and after the publication of the King James Version. In Cranmer's translation (1552), Psalm 105 verse 18 reads, "Whose feet they hurt in the stocks: the iron entered into his soul."

passions from the hearts of small, imperfect mortals. "Anne, go and stand on the platform in front of the blackboard for the rest of the afternoon."

Anne would have infinitely preferred a whipping to this punishment under which her sensitive spirit quivered as from a whiplash. With a white, set face she obeyed. Mr. Phillips took a chalk crayon and wrote on the blackboard above her head:

"Ann Shirley has a very bad temper. Ann Shirley must learn to control her temper," and then read it out loud so that even the primer class, who couldn't read writing, should understand it.

Anne stood there the rest of the afternoon with that legend above her. She did not cry or hang her head. Anger was still too hot in her heart for that and it sustained her amid all her agony of humiliation. With resentful eyes and passion-red cheeks she confronted alike Diana's sympathetic gaze and Charlie Sloane's indignant nods and Josie Pye's malicious smiles. As for Gilbert Blythe, she would not even look at him. She would *never* look at him again! She would never speak to him!!

When school was dismissed Anne marched out with her red head held high. Gilbert Blythe tried to intercept her at the porch door.

"I'm awful sorry I made fun of your hair, Anne," he whispered contritely. "Honest I am. Don't be mad for keeps now."

Anne swept by disdainfully, without look or sign of hearing. "Oh, how could you, Anne?" breathed Diana as they went down the road, half reproachfully, half admiringly. Diana felt that *she* could never have resisted Gilbert's plea.

"I shall never forgive Gilbert Blythe," said Anne firmly. "And Mr. Phillips spelled my name without an *e*, too. The iron has entered into my soul,[17] Diana."

Diana hadn't the least idea what Anne meant but she understood it was something terrible.

"You mustn't mind Gilbert making fun of your hair," she said soothingly. "Why, he makes fun of all the girls. He laughs at mine because it's so black. He's called me a crow a dozen times; and I never heard him apologize for anything before, either."

"There's a great deal of difference between being called a crow and being called carrots," said Anne with dignity. "Gilbert Blythe has hurt my feelings *excruciatingly*, Diana."

It is possible the matter might have blown over without more excruciation if nothing else had happened. But when things begin to happen they are apt to keep on.

Avonlea scholars often spent noon hour picking gum in Mr. Bell's spruce grove[18] over the hill and across his big pasture field. From there they could keep an eye on Eben Wright's house, where the master boarded. When they saw Mr. Phillips emerging therefrom they ran for the schoolhouse; but the distance being about three times longer than Mr. Wright's lane they were very apt to arrive there, breathless and gasping, some three minutes too late.

On the following day Mr. Phillips was seized with one of his spasmodic fits of reform and announced before going home to dinner that he should expect to find all the scholars in their seats when he returned. Any one who came in late would be punished.

All the boys and some of the girls went to Mr. Bell's spruce grove as usual, fully intending to stay only long enough to "pick a chew."[19] But spruce groves are seductive and yellow nuts of gum beguiling; they picked and loitered and strayed; and, as usual, the first thing that recalled them to a sense of the flight of time was Jimmy Glover shouting from the top of a patriarchal old spruce, "Master's coming."

The girls, who were on the ground, started first and managed to reach the schoolhouse in time but without a second to spare. The boys, who had to wriggle hastily down from the trees, were later; and Anne, who had not been picking gum at

18. A grove of the common spruce *(Picea abies)* of the Pinaceae family. Spruce are evergreen trees rather conical in shape, with pendulous cones.

19. Spruce gum is formed by the congealed sap of the spruce tree. When in Prince Albert, Montgomery was grateful to her cousin Penzie for sending her some Cavendish spruce gum: "First I must thank you heartily for that gum. It was just delicious and it did so put me in mind of the piles of fun you and I used to have gum-picking in the dear old days" (Oct. 18, 1890; *The Years Before "Anne,"* 94).

all but was wandering happily in the far end of the grove, waist deep among the bracken, singing softly to herself, with a wreath of rice lilies on her hair as if she were some wild divinity of the shadowy places, was latest of all. Anne could run like a deer, however; run she did with the impish result that she overtook the boys at the door and was swept into the schoolhouse among them just as Mr. Phillips was in the act of hanging up his hat.

Mr. Phillips' brief reforming energy was over; he didn't want the bother of punishing a dozen pupils; but it was necessary to do something to save his word, so he looked about for a scapegoat and found it in Anne, who had dropped into her seat, gasping for breath, with her forgotten lily wreath hanging askew over one ear and giving her a particularly rakish and dishevelled appearance.

"Anne Shirley, since you seem to be so fond of the boys' company we shall indulge your taste for it this afternoon," he said sarcastically. "Take those flowers out of your hair and sit with Gilbert Blythe."

The other boys snickered. Diana, turning pale with pity, plucked the wreath from Anne's hair and squeezed her hand. Anne stared at the master as if turned to stone.

"Did you hear what I said, Anne?" queried Mr. Phillips sternly.

"Yes, sir," said Anne slowly, "but I didn't suppose you really meant it."

"I assure you I did"—still with the sarcastic inflection which all the children, and Anne especially, hated. It flicked on the raw. "Obey me at once."

For a moment Anne looked as if she meant to disobey. Then, realizing that there was no help for it, she rose haughtily, stepped across the aisle, sat down beside Gilbert Blythe, and buried her face in her arms on the desk. Ruby Gillis, who got a glimpse of it as it went down, told the others going home from school that she'd "ackshually never seen anything like it—it was so white, with awful little red spots on it."

To Anne, this was the end of all things. It was bad enough to be singled out for punishment from among a dozen equally guilty ones; it was worse still to be sent to sit with a boy; but that that boy should be Gilbert Blythe was heaping insult on injury to a degree utterly unbearable. Anne felt that she could *not* bear it and it would be of no use to try. Her whole being seethed with shame and anger and humiliation.

At first the other scholars looked and whispered and giggled and nudged. But as Anne never lifted her head and as Gilbert worked fractions as if his whole soul was absorbed in them and them only, they soon returned to their own tasks and Anne was forgotten. When Mr. Phillips called the history class out Anne should have gone; but Anne did not move and Mr. Phillips, who had been writing some verses, "To Priscilla," before he called the class, was thinking about an obstinate rhyme still and never missed her. Once when nobody was looking Gilbert took from his desk a little pink candy heart with a gold motto on it, "You are Sweet," and slipped it under the curve of Anne's arm. Whereupon Anne arose, took the pink heart gingerly between the tips of her fingers, dropped it on the floor, ground it to powder beneath her heel, and resumed her position without deigning to bestow a glance on Gilbert.

When school went out Anne marched to her desk, ostentatiously took out everything therein, books and writing tablet, pen and ink, testament and arithmetic, and piled them neatly on her cracked slate.

"What are you taking all those things home for, Anne?" Diana wanted to know, as soon as they were out on the road. She had not dared to ask the question before.

"I am not coming back to school any more," said Anne.

20. Probably some form of softball.

21. Isabella Alden, née Macdonald (1841–1930), published her first novel in 1866 under the nickname "Pansy" and kept writing under this name after her marriage to a Presbyterian minister. She edited a Presbyterian Sunday School magazine, also called *Pansy*, and the *Presbyterian Primary Quarterly*. She wrote some 120 books for children, largely for girls. As she was a founder of the Chautauqua movement, which stressed religion in action, some of her novels deal with girls' experiences at this religious retreat in Chautauqua, New York. Alden admires energy and self-reliance in her heroines (see the entry in *The Feminist Companion to Literature in English*). Alden's books of course found their way into Presbyterian (and other) Sunday School libraries and were given to girls as suitable gifts. New "Pansy" books were appearing frequently during the period of Anne's childhood. These books

Diana gasped and stared at Anne to see if she meant it.

"Will Marilla let you stay home?" she asked.

"She'll have to," said Anne. "I'll *never* go to school to that man again."

"Oh, Anne!" Diana looked as if she were ready to cry. "I do think you're mean. What shall I do? Mr. Phillips will make me sit with that horrid Gertie Pye—I know he will, because she is sitting alone. Do come back, Anne."

"I'd do almost anything in the world for you, Diana," said Anne sadly. "I'd let myself be torn limb from limb if it would do you any good. But I can't do this, so please don't ask it. You harrow up my very soul."

"Just think of all the fun you will miss," mourned Diana. "We are going to build the loveliest new house down by the brook; and we'll be playing ball[20] next week, and you've never played ball, Anne. It's tremenjusly exciting. And we're going to learn a new song—Jane Andrews is practising it up now; and Alice Andrews is going to bring a new Pansy[21] book next week and we're all going to read it out loud, chapter about, down by the brook. And you know you are so fond of reading out loud, Anne."

Nothing moved Anne in the least. Her mind was made up. She would not go to school to Mr. Phillips again; she told Marilla so when she got home.

"Nonsense," said Marilla.

"It isn't nonsense at all," said Anne, gazing at Marilla with solemn reproachful eyes. "Don't you understand, Marilla? I've been insulted."

"Insulted fiddlesticks! You'll go to school to-morrow as usual."

"Oh, no." Anne shook her head gently. "I'm not going back, Marilla. I'll learn my lessons at home and I'll be as good as I can be and hold my tongue all the time if it's possible at all. But I will not go back to school I assure you."

Marilla saw something remarkably like unyielding stubbornness looking out of Anne's small face. She understood that she would have trouble in overcoming it; but she resolved wisely to say nothing more just then.

"I'll run down and see Rachel about it this evening," she thought. "There's no use reasoning with Anne now. She's too worked up and I've an idea she can be awful stubborn when she takes the notion. Far as I can make out from her story, Mr. Phillips has been carrying matters with a rather high hand. But it would never do to say so to her. I'll just talk it over with Rachel. She's sent ten children to school so she ought to know something about it. She'll have heard the whole story, too, by this time."

Marilla found Mrs. Lynde knitting quilts as industriously and cheerfully as usual.

"I suppose you know what I've come about," she said, a little shamefacedly.

Mrs. Rachel nodded.

"About Anne's fuss in school, I reckon," she said. "Tillie Boulter was in on her way home from school and told me about it."

"I don't know what to do with her," said Marilla "She declares she won't go back to school. I never saw a child so worked up. I've been expecting trouble ever since she started to school. I knew things were going too smooth to last. She's so high-strung. What would you advise, Rachel?"

"Well, since you've asked my advice, Marilla," said Mrs. Lynde amiably—Mrs. Lynde dearly loved to be asked for advice—"I'd just humour her a little at first, that's what I'd do. It's my belief that Mr. Phillips was in the wrong. Of course, it doesn't do to say so to the children, you know. And of course he did right to punish her yesterday for giving way to temper. But to-day it was different. The others who were late should have been punished as well as Anne, that's what. And I don't believe in making the girls sit with the boys for punishment. It isn't modest. Tillie Boulter was real indignant. She took Anne's

were probably formative influences on the young Lucy Maud in her early reading years, but in *Anne* she makes it quite clear that she does not share the pious views of such writers for girls. Stylistically, the Pansy books would be easier for Anne's schoolmates to follow than some of the works Anne evidently loves, such as poetry, but Anne is not critical of her classmates' reading level. Montgomery writes in her journal that "my class was of little girls and not one of them knew a single thing about the lesson, not even its name, but they had a fearful knack of asking awkward and irrelevant questions. It all seemed like a chapter out of a 'Pansy' book—but I did not feel at all like a 'Pansy' heroine" (*SJ* I [Dec. 14, 1890]: 37).

22. The noun *fry* means "off-spring," "progeny," in the plural, especially the roe of a fish. The term *young fry* is derived from *Macbeth:* "What, you egg! / Young fry of treachery!" (IV.ii. ll. 84–85).

part right through and said all the scholars did, too. Anne seems real popular among them, somehow. I never thought she'd take with them so well."

"Then you really think I'd better let her stay home," said Marilla in amazement.

"Yes. That is, I wouldn't say school to her again until she said it herself. Depend upon it, Marilla, she'll cool off in a week or so and be ready enough to go back of her own accord, that's what, while, if you were to make her go back right off, dear knows what freak or tantrum she'd take next and make more trouble than ever. The less fuss made the better in my opinion. She won't miss much by not going to school, as far as *that* goes. Mr. Phillips isn't any good at all as a teacher. The order he keeps is scandalous, that's what and he neglects the young fry[22] and puts all his time on those big scholars he's getting ready for Queen's. He'd never have got the school for another year if his uncle hadn't been a trustee — *the* trustee, for he just leads the other two around by the nose, that's what. I declare, I don't know what education in this Island is coming to."

Mrs. Rachel shook her head, as much as to say if she were only at the head of the educational system of the Province things would be much better managed.

Marilla took Mrs. Rachel's advice and not another word was said to Anne about going back to school. She learned her lessons at home, did her chores, and played with Diana in the chilly purple autumn twilights; but when she met Gilbert Blythe on the road or encountered him in Sunday School she passed him by with an icy contempt that was no whit thawed by his evident desire to appease her. Even Diana's efforts as peacemaker were of no avail. Anne had evidently made up her mind to hate Gilbert Blythe to the end of life.

As much as she hated Gilbert, however, did she love Diana, with all the love of her passionate little heart, equally intense in its likes and dislikes. One evening Marilla, coming in from the orchard with a basket of apples, found Anne sitting alone by the east window in the twilight, crying bitterly.

"Whatever's the matter now, Anne?" she asked.

"It's about Diana," sobbed Anne luxuriously. "I love Diana so, Marilla. I cannot ever live without her. But I know very well when we grow up that Diana will get married and go away and leave me. And oh, what shall I do? I hate her husband—I just hate him furiously. I've been imagining it all out —the wedding and everything—Diana dressed in snowy garments, with a veil, and looking as beautiful and regal as a queen; and me the bridesmaid, with a lovely dress, too, and puffed sleeves, but with a breaking heart hid beneath my smiling face. And then bidding Diana good-bye-e-e—" Here Anne broke down entirely and wept with increasing bitterness.

Marilla turned quickly away to hide her twitching face; but it was no use; she collapsed on the nearest chair and burst into such a hearty and unusual peal of laughter that Matthew, crossing the yard outside, halted in amazement. When had he heard Marilla laugh like that before?

"Well, Anne Shirley," said Marilla as soon as she could speak, "if you must borrow trouble, for pity's sake borrow it handier home. I should think you had an imagination, sure enough."

Illustration by Barbara DiLella from The Anne of Green Gables Cookbook *by Kate Macdonald.*

CHAPTER XVI

DIANA IS INVITED TO TEA
WITH TRAGIC RESULTS

OCTOBER WAS a beautiful month at Green Gables when the birches in the hollow turned as golden as sunshine and the maples behind the orchard were royal crimson and the wild cherry-trees along the lane put on the loveliest shades of dark red and bronzy green, while the fields sunned themselves in aftermaths.

Anne revelled in the world of colour about her.

"Oh, Marilla," she exclaimed one Saturday morning, coming dancing in with her arms full of gorgeous boughs, "I'm so glad I live in a world where there are Octobers. It would be terrible if we just skipped from September to November, wouldn't it? Look at these maple branches. Don't they give you a thrill—several thrills? I'm going to decorate my room with them."

"Messy things," said Marilla, whose aesthetic sense was not noticeably developed. "You clutter your room up entirely too much with out-of-doors stuff, Anne. Bedrooms were made to sleep in."

"Oh, and dream in, too, Marilla. And you know one can dream so much better in a room where there are pretty things. I'm going to put these boughs in the old blue jug and set them on my table."

1. Pour hot water on the tea and allow it to steep. Tea is "drawn" as the virtue is drawn out of the leaves of the plant. The emphasis here on long steeping suggests that the people of Avonlea like their tea strong, perhaps even stewed on the stove.

"Mind you don't drop leaves all over the stairs then. I'm going to a meeting of the Aid Society at Carmody this afternoon, Anne, and I won't likely be home before dark. You'll have to get Matthew and Jerry their supper, so mind you don't forget to put the tea to draw[1] until you sit down at the table as you did last time."

"It was dreadful of me to forget," said Anne apologetically, "but that was the afternoon I was trying to think of a name for Violet Vale and it crowded other things out. Matthew was so good. He never scolded a bit. He put the tea down himself and said we could wait awhile as well as not. And I told him a lovely fairy story while we were waiting, so he didn't find the time long at all. It was a beautiful fairy story, Marilla. I forgot the end of it, so I made up an end for it myself and Matthew said he couldn't tell where the join came in."

"Matthew would think it all right, Anne, if you took a notion to get up and have dinner in the middle of the night. But you keep your wits about you this time. And—I don't really know if I'm doing right—it may make you more addle-pated than ever—but you can ask Diana to come over and spend the afternoon with you and have tea here."

"Oh, Marilla!" Anne clasped her hands. "How perfectly lovely! You *are* able to imagine things after all or else you'd never have understood how I've longed for that very thing. It will seem nice and grown-uppish. No fear of my forgetting to put the tea to draw when I have company. Oh, Marilla, can I use the rosebud tea-set?"

"No, indeed! The rosebud tea-set! Well, what next? You know I never use that except for the minister or the Aids. You'll put down the old brown tea-set. But you can open the little yellow crock of cherry preserves. It's time it was being used anyhow—I believe it's beginning to go. And you can cut some fruit-cake and have some of the cookies and snaps."

"I can just imagine sitting down at the head of the table and pouring out the tea," said Anne, shutting her eyes ecstat-

ically. "And asking Diana if she takes sugar! I know she doesn't, but of course I'll ask her just as if I didn't know. And then pressing her to take another piece of fruit-cake and another helping of preserves. Oh, Marilla, it's a wonderful sensation just to think of it. Can I take her into the spare room to lay off her hat when she comes? And then into the parlour to sit?"

"No. The sitting-room will do for you and your company. But there's a bottle half full of raspberry cordial[2] that was left over from the church social the other night. It's on the second shelf of the sitting-room closet and you and Diana can have it if you like, and a cooky to eat along with it in the afternoon, for I daresay Matthew'll be late coming in to tea since he's hauling potatoes to the vessel."[3]

Anne flew down to the hollow, past the Dryad's Bubble and up the Spruce Path to Orchard Slope, to ask Diana to tea. As

2. The original meaning of the word *cordial* implies a spiritous drink good for the heart, but here it is used for a cooling non-alcoholic drink rather like a "shrub," concocted from fresh raspberries simmered in water and sugar to make a light syrup, perhaps with lemon juice added. See a recipe for "Diana Barry's Favorite Raspberry Cordial" in *The Anne of Green Gables Cookbook* (Toronto: Oxford Univ. Press, 1985) by Kate Macdonald, granddaughter of the author.

3. Matthew Cuthbert is transporting his own freshly dug potatoes to a ship, having sold them,

Loading farm produce near Montague, P.E.I. (date unknown).

perhaps ultimately for export. The potato is still one of the major export crops in the Maritimes.

4. A sweet-flavored variety of apple from the sixteenth century; any antique variety.

a result, just after Marilla had driven off to Carmody, Diana came over, dressed in her second best dress and looking exactly as it is proper to look when asked out to tea. At other times she was wont to run into the kitchen without knocking, but now she knocked primly at the front door. And when Anne, dressed in *her* second best, as primly opened it, both little girls shook hands gravely as if they had never met before. This unnatural solemnity lasted until after Diana had been taken to the east gable to lay off her hat and then had sat for ten minutes in the sitting-room, toes in position.

"How is your mother?" inquired Anne politely just as if she had not seen Mrs. Barry picking apples that morning in excellent health and spirits.

"She is very well, thank you. I suppose Mr. Cuthbert is hauling potatoes to the *Lily Sands* this afternoon, is he?" said Diana, who had ridden down to Mr. Harmon Andrews' that morning in Matthew's cart.

"Yes. Our potato crop is very good this year. I hope your father's potato crop is good, too."

"It is fairly good, thank you. Have you picked many of your apples yet?"

"Oh, ever so many," said Anne, forgetting to be dignified and jumping up quickly. "Let's go out to the orchard and get some of the Red Sweetings,[4] Diana. Marilla says we can have all that are left on the tree. Marilla is a very generous woman. She said we could have fruit-cake and cherry preserves for tea. But it isn't good manners to tell your company what you are going to give them to eat, so I won't tell you what she said we could have to drink. Only it begins with an *r* and a *c* and it's a bright red colour. I love bright red drinks, don't you? They taste twice as good as any other colour."

The orchard, with its great sweeping boughs that bent to the ground with fruit, proved so delightful that the little girls spent most of the afternoon in it, sitting in a grassy corner where the frost had spared the green and the mellow autumn sunshine lingered warmly, eating apples and talking as hard as they could. Diana had much to tell Anne of what went on in school. She had to sit with Gertie Pye and she hated it. Gertie squeaked her pencil all the time and it just made her —Diana's—blood run cold; Ruby Gillis had charmed all her warts away, true's you live, with a magic pebble that old Mary Joe from the Creek gave her. You had to rub the warts with the pebble and then throw it away over your left shoulder at the time of the new moon and the warts would all go. Charlie Sloane's name was written up with Em White's on the porch wall and Em White was *awful mad* about it; Sam Boulter had "sassed" Mr. Phillips in class and Mr. Phillips whipped him and Sam's father came down to the school and dared Mr. Phillips to lay a hand on one of his children again; and Mattie Andrews had a new red hood and blue crossover with tassels on it[5] and the airs she put on about it were perfectly sickening; and Lizzie Wright didn't speak to Mamie Wilson because Mamie Wilson's grown-up sister had cut out Lizzie Wright's grown-up sister with her beau; and everybody missed Anne so and wished she'd come to school again; and Gilbert Blythe —

But Anne didn't want to hear about Gilbert Blythe. She jumped up hurriedly and said suppose they go in and have some raspberry cordial.

Anne looked on the second shelf of the sitting-room pantry but there was no bottle of raspberry cordial there. Search revealed it away back on the top shelf. Anne put it on a tray and set it on the table with a tumbler.

"Now, please help yourself, Diana," she said politely. "I don't believe I'll have any just now. I don't feel as if I wanted any after all those apples."

Diana poured herself out a tumblerful, looked at its bright-red hue admiringly, and then sipped it daintily.

"That's awfully nice raspberry cordial, Anne," she said. "I didn't know raspberry cordial was so nice."

5. A red woolen hood and a knitted shawl, evidently fringed with tassels, wrapped around the body and tied in the back. (Virginia Careless, Curator of History, Royal British Columbia Museum.) As Montgomery recalled, "Those old hoods were cosy things. Mine, I remember, were generally crocheted out of 'cardinal' wool, with cardinal satin ribbon run through the holes, and [a] perky bow of ribbon just over the forehead, and ties of ribbon. The last hood I ever wore was when I was twelve" (*SJ* III [Sept. 18, 1922]: 71).

"I'm real glad you like it. Take as much as you want. I'm going to run out and stir the fire up. There are so many responsibilities on a person's mind when they're keeping house, isn't there?"

When Anne came back from the kitchen Diana was drinking her second glassful of cordial; and, being entreated thereto by Anne, she offered no particular objection to the drinking of a third. The tumblerfuls were generous ones and the raspberry cordial was certainly very nice.

"The nicest I ever drank," said Diana. "It's ever so much nicer than Mrs. Lynde's although she brags of hers so much. It doesn't taste a bit like hers."

"I should think Marilla's raspberry cordial would prob'ly be much nicer than Mrs. Lynde's," said Anne loyally. "Marilla is a famous cook. She is trying teach me to cook but I assure you, Diana, it is uphill work. There's so little scope for imagination in cookery. You just have to go by rules. The last time I made a cake I forgot to put the flour in. I was thinking the loveliest story about you and me, Diana. I thought you were desperately ill with smallpox and everybody deserted you, but I went boldly to your bedside and nursed you back to life; and then I took the smallpox and died and I was buried under those poplar-trees in the graveyard and you planted a rose-bush by my grave and watered it with your tears; and you never, never forgot the friend of your youth who sacrificed her life for you. Oh, it was such a pathetic little tale, Diana. The tears just rained down over my cheeks while I mixed the cake. But I forgot the flour and the cake was a dismal failure. Flour is so essential to cakes, you know. Marilla was very cross and I don't wonder. I'm a great trial to her. She was terribly mortified about the pudding sauce last week. We had a plum pudding for dinner on Tuesday and there was half the pudding and a pitcherful of sauce left over. Marilla said there was enough for another dinner and told me to set it on the pantry shelf and cover it. I meant to cover it just as much

*Park Corner pantry, c. 1890s. Montgomery loved visiting her cousins in Park
Corner and fondly recalled "Best of all, that famous old pantry, stored with
good things, into which it was our habit to crowd at bedtime and gnaw bones,
crunch fruitcake, and scream with laughter. That pantry is historical." (SJ I
[Mar. 2, 1901]: 247).*

6. Anne's story here is reminiscent of the story by the eleven-year-old Helen Keller, "The Frost King" who, "lest we should mourn for the bright faces of the flowers . . . paints the leaves with gold and crimson and emerald." Keller's story, which first met great approbation at the Perkins Institute for the Blind, was later discovered to be closely derived from the published story "The Frost Fairies" in *Birdie and His Fairy Friends*, by Margaret T. Canby, read to Keller in 1888. "The Frost King" came to her mind like an original idea in 1891. In these stories, both of which are reproduced in Keller's biography, *The Story of My Life* (1903, 406–13), careless fairies let the treasure with which they are entrusted melt away so that the trees are covered with melted gold and gems: "The oaks and maples were arrayed in gorgeous dresses of gold and crimson and emerald" (Keller's "The Frost King," *ibid.*, 411). The king thus gets the idea of having his fairies purposely paint the leaves with treasure. Anne's addition to this motif is the idea of will; for her, the trees are turned whatever color they *want* to be.

as could be, Diana, but when I carried it in I was imagining I was a nun—of course I'm a Protestant but I imagined I was a Catholic—taking the veil to bury a broken heart in cloistered seclusion, and I forgot all about covering the pudding sauce. I thought of it next morning and ran to the pantry. Diana, fancy if you can my extreme horror at finding a mouse drowned in that pudding sauce! I lifted the mouse out with a spoon and threw it out in the yard and then I washed the spoon in three waters. Marilla was out milking and I fully intended to ask her when she came in if I'd give the sauce to the pigs; but when she did come in I was imagining that I was a frost-fairy going through the woods turning the trees red and yellow, whichever they wanted to be,[6] so I never thought about the pudding sauce again and Marilla sent me out to pick apples. Well, Mr. and Mrs. Chester Ross from Spencervale came here that morning. You know they are very stylish people, especially Mrs. Chester Ross. When Marilla called me in dinner was all ready and everybody was at the table. I tried to be as polite and dignified as I could be, for I wanted Mrs. Chester Ross to think I was a ladylike little girl even if I wasn't pretty. Everything went right until I saw Marilla coming with the plum pudding in one hand and the pitcher of pudding sauce, *warmed up* in the other. Diana, that was a terrible moment. I remembered everything and I just stood up in my place and shrieked out, 'Marilla, you mustn't use that pudding sauce. There was a mouse drowned in it. I forgot to tell you before.' Oh, Diana, I shall never forget that awful moment if I live to be a hundred. Mrs. Chester Ross just *looked* at me and I thought I would sink through the floor with mortification. She is such a perfect housekeeper and fancy what she must have thought of us. Marilla turned red as fire but she never said a word—then. She just carried that sauce and pudding out and brought in some strawberry preserves. She even offered me some, but I couldn't swallow a mouthful. It was like heaping coals of fire on my head.[7] After Mrs. Chester Ross went away Marilla gave me a dreadful scolding. Why, Diana, what is the matter?"

Diana had stood up very unsteadily; then she sat down again, putting her hands to her head.

"I'm—I'm awful sick," she said, a little thickly. "I—I—must go right home."

"Oh, you mustn't dream of going home without your tea," cried Anne in distress. "I'll get it right off—I'll go and put the tea down this very minute."

"I must go home," repeated Diana, stupidly but determinedly.

"Let me get you a lunch anyhow," implored Anne. "Let me give you a bit of fruit-cake and some of the cherry preserves. Lie down on the sofa for a little while and you'll be better. Where do you feel bad?"

"I must go home," said Diana, and that was all she would say. In vain Anne pleaded.

"I never heard of company going home without tea," she mourned. "Oh, Diana, do you suppose that it's possible you're really taking the smallpox? If you are I'll go and nurse you, you can depend on that. I'll never forsake you. But I do wish you'd stay till after tea. Where do you feel bad?"

"I'm awful dizzy," said Diana.

And, indeed, she walked very dizzily. Anne, with tears of disappointment in her eyes, got Diana's hat and went with her as far as the Barry yard fence. Then she wept all the way back to Green Gables, where she sorrowfully put the remainder of the raspberry cordial back into the pantry and got tea ready for Matthew and Jerry, with all the zest gone out of the performance.

The next day was Sunday and as the rain poured down in torrents from dawn till dusk Anne did not stir abroad from Green Gables. Monday afternoon Marilla sent her down to

7. Cf. "If thine enemy be hungry, give him bread to eat; and if he be thirsty, give him water to drink: / For thou shalt heap coals of fire upon his head, and the LORD shall reward thee." (Proverbs 25:21–22).

8. Wine made from currants, the small, sour, red, white, or black berry of several species of hardy shrubs (genus *Ribes)* of the saxifrage family used for jellies and jam as well as wine. Marilla in her talent for winemaking resembles Montgomery's grandmother:

I have been busy lately decanting "home brew." Last summer I made some red currant wine and some raspberry wine, from my recollection of Grandmother's method. Grandmother was famed for her currant wine. It *was* delicious — even Chateau Yquem was not much its superior. I was doubtful of my success . . . my "brew" is delicious — clear, ruby, sparkling, with a quite sufficient "bite" (*SJ* III [Dec. 16, 1922]: 105–106).

9. Many Presbyterians of P. E. I. were staunch believers in total abstention, and the temperance campaign was designed to influence people to pledge never to take alcohol in any form. Many of Marilla's neighbors would disapprove of her winemaking, and it hints at a certain richness, sensuousness, and rebellion in her own makeup. In 1901, P. E. I. voted for Prohibition and became totally dry, so Marilla's wine would have been illegal at the time the novel was written.

Mrs. Lynde's on an errand. In a very short space of time Anne came flying back up the lane, with tears rolling down her cheeks. Into the kitchen she dashed and flung herself face downwards on the sofa in an agony.

"Whatever has gone wrong now, Anne?" queried Marilla in doubt and dismay. "I do hope you haven't gone and been saucy to Mrs. Lynde again."

No answer from Anne save more tears and stormier sobs!

"Anne Shirley, when I ask you a question I want to be answered. Sit right up this very minute and tell me what you are crying about."

Anne sat up, tragedy personified.

"Mrs. Lynde was up to see Mrs. Barry to-day and Mrs. Barry was in an awful state," she wailed. "She says that I set Diana *drunk* Saturday and sent her home in a disgraceful condition. And she says I must be a thoroughly bad, wicked little girl and she's never, never going to let Diana play with me again. Oh, Marilla, I'm just overcome with woe."

Marilla stared in blank amazement.

"Set Diana drunk!" she said when she found her voice. "Anne, are you or Mrs. Barry crazy? What on earth did you give her?"

"Not a thing but raspberry cordial," sobbed Anne. "I never thought raspberry cordial would set people drunk, Marilla — not even if they drank three big tumblerfuls as Diana did. Oh, it sounds so — so — like Mrs. Thomas' husband! But I didn't mean to set her drunk."

"Drunk fiddlesticks!" said Marilla, marching to the sitting-room pantry. There on the shelf was a bottle which she at once recognized as one containing some of her three year old home-made currant-wine[8] for which she was celebrated in Avonlea, although certain of the stricter sort, Mrs. Barry among them, disapproved strongly of it.[9] And at the same time Marilla recollected that she had put the bottle of raspberry cordial down in the cellar instead of in the pantry as she had told Anne.

She went back to the kitchen with the wine bottle in her hand. Her face was twitching in spite of herself.

"Anne, you certainly have a genius for getting into trouble. You went and gave Diana currant-wine instead of raspberry cordial. Didn't you know the difference yourself?"

"I never tasted it," said Anne. "I thought it was the cordial. I meant to be so — so — hospitable. Diana got awfully sick and had to go home. Mrs. Barry told Mrs. Lynde she was simply dead drunk. She just laughed silly-like when her mother asked her what was the matter and went to sleep and slept for hours. Her mother smelled her breath and knew she was drunk. She had a fearful headache all day yesterday. Mrs. Barry is so indignant. She will never believe but what I did it on purpose."

"I should think she would better punish Diana for being so greedy as to drink three glassfuls of anything," said Marilla shortly. "Why, three of those big glasses would have made her sick even if it had only been cordial. Well, this story will be a nice handle for those folks who are so down on me for making currant-wine, although I haven't made any for three years ever since I found out that the minister didn't approve. I just kept that bottle for sickness. There, there, child, don't cry. I can't see as you were to blame although I'm sorry it happened so."

"I must cry," said Anne. "My heart is broken. The stars in their courses fight against me,[10] Marilla. Diana and I are parted forever. Oh, Marilla, I little dreamed of this when first we swore our vows of friendship."

"Don't be foolish, Anne. Mrs. Barry will think better of it when she finds you're not really to blame. I suppose she thinks you've done it for a silly joke or something of that sort. You'd best go up this evening and tell her how it was."

10. Cf. "They fought from heaven; The stars in their courses fought against Sisera" ("The Song of Deborah"; Judges 5:20).

11. A phrase from medieval legal French describing a wrong or injury purposely done, with malice aforethought.

"My courage fails me at the thought of facing Diana's injured mother," sighed Anne. "I wish you'd go, Marilla. You're so much more dignified than I am. Likely she'd listen to you quicker than to me."

"Well, I will," said Marilla, reflecting that it would probably be the wiser course. "Don't cry any more, Anne. It will be all right."

Marilla had changed her mind about its being all right by the time she got back from Orchard Slope. Anne was watching for her coming and flew to the porch door to meet her.

"Oh, Marilla, I know by your face that it's been no use," she said sorrowfully. "Mrs. Barry won't forgive me?"

"Mrs. Barry, indeed!" snapped Marilla. "Of all the unreasonable women I ever saw she's the worst. I told her it was all a mistake and you weren't to blame, but she just simply didn't believe me. And she rubbed it well in about my currant-wine and how I'd always said it couldn't have the least effect on anybody. I just told her plainly that currant-wine wasn't meant to be drunk three tumblerfuls at a time and that if a child I had to do with was so greedy I'd sober her up with a right good spanking."

Marilla whisked into the kitchen, grievously disturbed, leaving a very much distracted little soul in the porch behind her. Presently Anne stepped out bare-headed into the chill autumn dusk; very determinedly and steadily she took her way down through the sere clover field over the log bridge and up through the spruce grove, lighted by a pale little moon hanging low over the western woods. Mrs. Barry, coming to the door in answer to a timid knock, found a white-lipped, eager-eyed suppliant on the doorstep.

Her face hardened. Mrs. Barry was a woman of strong prejudices and dislikes and her anger was of the cold sullen sort which is always hardest to overcome. To do her justice, she really believed Anne had made Diana drunk out of sheer malice prepense,[11] and she was honestly anxious to preserve her little daughter from the contamination of further intimacy with such a child.

"What do you want?" she said stiffly.

Anne clasped her hands.

"Oh, Mrs. Barry, please forgive me. I did not mean to—to —intoxicate Diana. How could I? Just imagine if you were a poor little orphan girl that kind people had adopted and you had just one bosom friend in all the world. Do you think you would intoxicate her on purpose? I thought it was only raspberry cordial. I was firmly convinced it was raspberry cordial. Oh, please don't say that you won't let Diana play with me anymore. If you do you will cover my life with a dark cloud of woe."

This speech, which would have softened good Mrs. Lynde's heart in a twinkling, had no effect on Mrs. Barry except to irritate her still more. She was suspicious of Anne's big words and dramatic gestures and imagined that the child was making fun of her. So she said coldly and cruelly:

"I don't think you are a fit little girl for Diana to associate with. You'd better go home and behave yourself."

Anne's lip quivered.

"Won't you let me see Diana just once to say farewell?" she implored.

"Diana has gone over to Carmody with her father," said Mrs. Barry, going in and shutting the door.

Anne went back to Green Gables calm with despair.

"My last hope is gone," she told Marilla. "I went up and saw Mrs. Barry myself and she treated me very insultingly. Marilla, I do *not* think she is a well-bred woman. There is nothing more to do except to pray and I haven't much hope that that'll do much good because, Marilla, I do not believe that God Himself can do very much with such an obstinate woman as Mrs. Barry."

"Anne, you shouldn't say such things," rebuked Marilla, striving to overcome that unholy tendency to laughter which she was dismayed to find growing upon her. And, indeed, when she told the whole story to Matthew that night, she did laugh heartily over Anne's tribulations.

But when she slipped into the east gable before going to bed and found that Anne had cried herself to sleep an unaccustomed softness crept into her face.

"Poor little soul," she murmured, lifting a loose curl of hair from the child's tear-stained face. Then she bent down and kissed the flushed cheek on the pillow.

CHAPTER XVII

A NEW INTEREST IN LIFE

 THE NEXT afternoon Anne, bending over her patchwork at the kitchen window, happened to glance out and beheld Diana down by the Dryad's Bubble beckoning mysteriously. In a trice Anne was out of the house and flying down to the hollow, astonishment and hope struggling in her expressive eyes. But the hope faded when she saw Diana's dejected countenance.

"Your mother hasn't relented?" she gasped.

Diana shook her head mournfully.

"No; and oh, Anne, she says I'm never to play with you again. I've cried and cried and I told her it wasn't your fault, but it wasn't any use. I had ever such a time coaxing her to let me come down and say good-bye to you. She said I was only to stay ten minutes and she's timing me by the clock."

"Ten minutes isn't very long to say an eternal farewell in," said Anne tearfully. "Oh, Diana, will you promise faithfully never to forget me, the friend of your youth, no matter what dearer friends may caress thee?"

"Indeed I will," sobbed Diana, "and I'll never have another bosom friend—I don't want to have. I couldn't love anybody as I love you."

"Oh, Diana," cried Anne, clasping her hands, "do you *love* me?"

"Why, of course I do. Didn't you know that?"

"No." Anne drew a long breath. "I thought you *liked* me of course, but I never hoped you *loved* me. Why, Diana, I didn't think anybody could love me. Nobody ever loved me since I can remember. Oh, this is wonderful! It's a ray of light which will forever shine on the darkness of a path severed from thee, Diana. Oh, just say it once again."

"I love you devotedly, Anne," said Diana stanchly, "and I always will, you may be sure of that."

"And I will always love thee, Diana," said Anne, solemnly extending her hand. "In the years to come thy memory will shine like a star over my lonely life, as that last story we read together says. Diana, wilt thou give me a lock of thy jet-black tresses in parting to treasure forever more?"

"Have you got anything to cut it with?" queried Diana, wiping away the tears which Anne's affecting accents had caused to flow afresh, and returning to practicalities.

"Yes. I've got my patchwork scissors in my apron pocket fortunately," said Anne. She solemnly clipped one of Diana's curls. "Fare thee well, my beloved friend. Henceforth we must be as strangers though living side by side. But my heart will ever be faithful to thee."

Anne stood and watched Diana out of sight, mournfully waving her hand to the latter whenever she turned to look back. Then she returned to the house, not a little consoled for the time being by this romantic parting.

"It is all over," she informed Marilla. "I shall never have another friend. I'm really worse off than ever before, for I haven't Katie Maurice and Violetta now. And even if I had it wouldn't be the same. Somehow, little dream girls are not satisfying after a real friend. Diana and I had such an affecting farewell down by the spring. It will be sacred in my memory forever. I used the most pathetic language[1] I could think of and said 'thou' and thee.' 'Thou' and 'thee' seem so much more romantic than 'you.' Diana gave me a lock of her hair and I'm going to sew it up in a little bag and wear it around my neck all my life. Please see that it is buried with me, for I don't believe I'll live very long. Perhaps when she sees me lying cold and dead before her Mrs. Barry may feel remorse for what she has done and will let Diana come to my funeral."

"I don't think there is much fear of your dying of grief as long as you can talk, Anne," said Marilla unsympathetically.

The following Monday Anne surprised Marilla by coming down from her room with her basket of books on her arm and her lips primmed up into a line of determination.

"I'm going back to school," she announced. "That is all there is left in life for me, now that my friend has been ruthlessly torn from me. In school I can look at her and muse over days departed."

"You'd better muse over your lessons and sums," said Marilla, concealing her delight at this development of the situation. "If you're going back to school I hope we'll hear no more of breaking slates over people's heads and such carryings-on. Behave yourself and do just what your teacher tells you."

"I'll try to be a model pupil," agreed Anne dolefully. "There won't be much fun in it, I expect. Mr. Phillips said Minnie Andrews was a model pupil and there isn't a spark of imagination or life in her. She is just dull and poky and never seems to have a good time. But I feel so depressed that perhaps it will come easy to me now. I'm going round by the road. I couldn't bear to go by the Birch Path all alone. I should weep bitter tears if I did."

Anne was welcomed back to school with open arms. Her imagination had been sorely missed in games, her voice in the singing, and her dramatic ability in the perusal aloud of books at dinner hour. Ruby Gillis smuggled three blue plums over

2. Edgings of knit lace were used on household textiles and under-clothing as well as simple garments. See Appendix, "Homemade Artifacts." See also illustration.

3. To erase a slate efficiently, a sponge and some water were required, so it was useful to have some water in a little bottle in one's desk.

4. Probably a keepsake album verse of the kind commonly used in autograph albums and homemade greeting cards.

5. At least seven varieties of apple are so described, and the name also varied with its local application. The strawberry apple may be one of the older sweet apples such as the Strawberry Pippin, which originated in England in the early nineteenth century: a flat, pale yellow apple with bright red stripes (see *Apple Varieties Descriptions*, comp. Daryl Hunter). Betty Howatt, P.E.I. heritage orchardist, suggests it refers to Duchess of Oldenburg, a Russian import to England in 1824, the Crimson Beauty, or a Fameuse (Snow Apple) variant.

6. A stick of soft slate to be used for writing on a slate. These very

to her during testament reading; Ella May Macpherson gave her an enormous yellow pansy cut from the covers of a floral catalogue—a species of desk decoration much prized in Avonlea school. Sophia Sloane offered to teach her a perfectly elegant new pattern of knit lace,[2] *so* nice for trimming aprons. Katie Boulter gave her a perfume bottle to keep slate-water[3] in and Julia Bell copied carefully on a piece of pale pink paper scalloped on the edges, the following effusion:

To Anne

When twilight drops her curtain down
And pins it with a star
Remember that you have a friend
Though she may wander far.[4]

"It's so nice to be appreciated," sighed Anne rapturously to Marilla that night.

The girls were not the only scholars who "appreciated" her. When Anne went to her seat after dinner hour—she had been told by Mr. Phillips to sit with the model Minnie Andrews—she found on her desk a big luscious "strawberry apple."[5] Anne caught it up all ready to take a bite, when she remembered that the only place in Avonlea where strawberry apples grew was in the old Blythe orchard on the other side of the Lake of Shining Waters. Anne dropped the apple as if it were a red-hot coal and ostentatiously wiped her fingers on her handkerchief. The apple lay untouched on her desk until the next morning, when little Timothy Andrews, who swept the school and kindled the fire, annexed it as one of his perquisites. Charlie Sloane's slate pencil,[6] gorgeously bedizened with striped red and yellow paper, costing two cents where ordinary pencils cost only one, which he sent up to her after dinner hour, met with a more favourable reception. Anne was graciously pleased to accept it and rewarded the donor with a smile which exalted that infatuated youth straightway into the seventh heaven of delight and caused him to make such fearful errors in his dictation that Mr. Phillips kept him in after school to rewrite it.

But as

> The Caesar's pageant shorn of Brutus' bust
> Did but of Rome's best son remind her more,[7]

so the marked absence of any tribute or recognition from Diana Barry, who was sitting with Gertie Pye, embittered Anne's little triumph.

"Diana might have smiled at me just once, I think," she mourned to Marilla that night. But the next morning a note, most fearfully and wonderfully[8] twisted and folded, and a small parcel, were passed across to Anne.

> DEAR ANNE (ran the former),
>
> Mother says I'm not to play with you or talk to you even in school. It isn't my fault and don't be cross at me, because I love you as much as ever. I miss you awfully to tell all my secrets to and I don't like Gertie Pye one bit. I made you one of the new bookmarkers out of red tissue paper. They are awfully fashionable now and only three girls in school know how to make them. When you look at it remember
>
> > Your true friend,
> > DIANA BARRY

Anne read the note, kissed the bookmark, and despatched a prompt reply back to the other side of the school.

thin pencils make a bluish-gray mark.

7. From *Childe Harolde's Pilgrimage* by George Gordon, Lord Byron, (Canto 4, Stanza 59).

8. Cf. "I will praise thee; for I am fearfully and wonderfully made" (Psalm 139:14).

MY OWN DARLING DIANA,

Of course I am not cross at you because you have to obey your mother. Our spirits can commune. I shall keep your lovely present forever. Minnie Andrews is a very nice little girl—although she has no imagination—but after having been Diana's busum friend I cannot be Minnie's. Please excuse mistakes because my spelling isn't very good yet, although much improoved.

Yours until death us do part,

ANNE or CORDELIA SHIRLEY.

P. S. I shall sleep with your letter under my pillow to-night.

A. or C.S.

Marilla pessimistically expected more trouble since Anne had again begun to go to school, but none developed. Perhaps Anne caught something of the "model" spirit from Minnie Andrews; at least she got on very well with Mr. Phillips thenceforth. She flung herself into her studies heart and soul, determined not to be outdone in any class by Gilbert Blythe. The rivalry between them was soon apparent; it was entirely good-natured on Gilbert's side; but it is much to be feared that the same thing cannot be said of Anne, who had certainly an unpraiseworthy tenacity for holding grudges. She was as intense in her hatreds as in her loves. She would not stoop to admit that she meant to rival Gilbert in school work, because that would have been to acknowledge his existence which Anne persistently ignored; but the rivalry was there and honours fluctuated between them. Now Gilbert was head of the spelling class; now Anne, with a toss of her long red braids, spelled him down. One morning Gilbert had all his sums done correctly and had his name written on the blackboard on the roll of honour; the next morning Anne, having wrestled wildly with decimals the entire evening before, would be first. One awful day they were ties and their names were written up together. It was almost as bad as a "take-notice" and Anne's mortification was as evident as Gilbert's satisfaction. When the written examinations at the end of each month were held the suspense was terrible. The first month Gilbert came out three marks ahead. The second Anne beat him by five. But her triumph was marred by the fact that Gilbert congratulated her heartily before the whole school. It would have been ever so much sweeter to her if he had felt the sting of his defeat.

Mr. Phillips might not be a very good teacher; but a pupil so inflexibly determined on learning as Anne was could hardly escape making progress under any kind of a teacher. By the end of the term Anne and Gilbert were both promoted into the fifth class and allowed to begin studying the elements of "the branches" — by which Latin, geometry, French, and algebra were meant. In geometry Anne met her Waterloo.[9]

"It's perfectly awful stuff, Marilla," she groaned. "I'm sure I'll never be able to make head or tail of it. There is no scope for imagination in it at all. Mr. Phillips says I'm the worst dunce he ever saw at it. And Gil — I mean some of the others are so smart at it. It is extremely mortifying, Marilla. Even Diana gets along better than I do. But I don't mind being beaten by Diana. Even although we meet as strangers now I still love her with an *inextinguishable* love. It makes me very sad at times to think about her. But really, Marilla, one can't stay sad very long in such an interesting world, can one?"

9. The popular name given to the battle fought outside the village of Waterloo, near Brussels, Belgium, on June 18, 1815, in which Napoleon was decisively and finally defeated. Hence, a decisive and final defeat.

"The two little girls worked patiently over the suffering Minnie May." Illustration by Sybil Tawse, from the 1933 edition.

CHAPTER XVIII

ANNE TO THE RESCUE

ALL THINGS great are wound up with all things little. At first glance it might not seem that the decision of a certain Canadian Premier[1] to include Prince Edward Island in a political tour could have much or anything to do with the fortunes of little Anne Shirley at Green Gables. But it had.

It was in January the Premier came, to address his loyal supporters and such of his non-supporters as chose to be present at the monster mass meeting[2] held in Charlottetown. Most of the Avonlea people were on the Premier's side of politics; hence, on the night of the meeting nearly all the men and a goodly proportion of the women had gone to town, thirty miles away. Mrs. Rachel Lynde had gone too. Mrs. Rachel Lynde was a red-hot politician and couldn't have believed that the political rally could be carried through without her, although she was on the opposite side of politics.[3] So she went to town and took her husband—Thomas would be useful in looking after the horse—and Marilla Cuthbert with her. Marilla had a sneaking interest in politics herself and as she thought it might be her only chance to see a real live Premier, she promptly took it, leaving Anne and Matthew to keep house until her return the following day.

1. The first minister of the crown, a term still used for the head of the Canadian government. The prime minister Montgomery here refers to is evidently Sir John A. MacDonald (1815–1891), who twice served as Conservative Prime Minister (1867–1873, 1878–1891). "MacDonald visited P. E. I. in 1890," according to Virginia Careless. No prime minister would choose to visit Charlottetown in the dead of winter, because of the danger of having the Strait freeze over and not being able to get out. Most of the English-speaking people of P.E.I. would have been on the premier's side in political matters.

2. A nineteenth-century term used for a political gathering once the railways made meetings of many thousands of people possible. This English phrase is particularly associated with rallies in favor of women's suffrage in London and Manchester.

3. John A. MacDonald is a Conservative, or Tory, prime minister, while Mrs. Lynde considers herself a Liberal (Grit), although

1879 cartoon from **Grip** *illustrating the Canadian Premier presiding over the Provinces, depicted as little girls.*

she cannot vote while her husband can. (For "Grit," see pp. 201–202, and n.9.) Thomas Lynde, however, unlike Rachel, appears to take no interest in politics.

4. A distinctive style of a wood or coal-burning stove, popular in the Maritimes. "Old-fashioned," probably dating from the 1860s or 1870s, it was all black without chrome or white enamel trim. Montgomery wrote of her cousin's house at Park Corner: "Each room has its memories—the kitchen where we toasted our toes at the glowing old 'Waterloo,' the

Hence, while Marilla and Mrs. Rachel were enjoying themselves hugely at the mass meeting Anne and Matthew had the cheerful kitchen at Green Gables all to themselves. A bright fire was glowing in the old-fashioned Waterloo stove[4] and blue-white frost crystals were shining on the window-panes. Matthew nodded over a *Farmers' Advocate*[5] on the sofa and Anne at the table studied her lessons with grim determination, despite sundry wistful glances at the clock shelf, where lay a new book that Jane Andrews had lent her that day. Jane had assured her that it was warranted to produce any number of thrills, or words to that effect, and Anne's fingers tingled to reach out for it. But that would mean Gilbert Blythe's triumph on the morrow. Anne turned her back on the clock shelf and tried to imagine it wasn't there.

"Matthew, did you ever study geometry when you went to school?"

"Well now, no, I didn't," said Matthew, coming out of his doze with a start.

"I wish you had," sighed Anne, "because then you'd be able to sympathize with me. You can't sympathize properly if you've never studied it. It is casting a cloud over my whole life. I'm such a dunce at it, Matthew."

"Well now, I dunno," said Matthew soothingly. "I guess you're all right at anything. Mr. Phillips told me last week in Blair's store at Carmody that you was the smartest scholar in school and was making rapid progress. 'Rapid progress' was his very words. There's them as runs down Teddy Phillips and says he ain't much of a teacher; but I guess he's all right."

Matthew would have thought anyone who praised Anne was "all right."

"I'm sure I'd get on better with geometry if only he wouldn't change the letters," complained Anne. "I learn the proposition off by heart and then he draws it on the blackboard and puts different letters from what are in the book and I get all mixed up. I don't think a teacher should take such a mean advantage, do you? We're studying agriculture now and I've found out at last what makes the roads red.[6] It's a great comfort. I wonder how Marilla and Mrs. Lynde are enjoying themselves. Mrs. Lynde says Canada is going to the dogs the way things are being run at Ottawa, and that it's an awful warning to the electors. She says if women were allowed to vote we would soon see a blessed change.[7] What way do you vote, Matthew?"

"Conservative,"[8] said Matthew promptly. To vote Conservative was part of Matthew's religion.

"Then I'm Conservative too," said Anne decidedly. "I'm glad, because Gil—because some of the boys in school are Grits.[9] I guess Mr. Phillips is a Grit, too, because Prissy Andrews' father is one, and Ruby Gillis says that when a man is courting he always has to agree with the girl's mother in religion and her father in politics. Is that true, Matthew?"

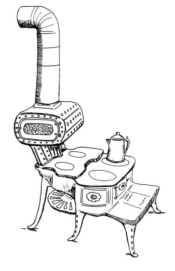

front room where we spent so many jolly evenings, the big bedrooms upstairs where we slept and talked" (*SJ* I [Mar. 2, 1901]: 257).

5. Published in London, Ont., from 1866 to 1951, the periodical was also known as the *Farmer's Advocate and Home Magazine*, and included advertisements and advice for farmers on all aspects of agriculture.

6. Anne says that she now knows, but she does not tell us. See also n. 18, ch. 2.

7. Women had never been allowed to vote in the Canada of this period. Not until the Wartime Elections Act of 1917 did Canada give the vote to any women, and then only to mothers, wives, or sisters of men on active service. The advent of this form of the vote is dealt with in Montgomery's *Rilla of Ingleside* (ch. 27). As she commented to her journal in 1917, "The Ontario government has given the suffrage to women. So I

may vote yet ere I die! Certainly I shall never vote along merely party lines. But I am glad it has come. Soon, I think, all the provinces will fall into line and then we will have Dominion suffrage. But I truly doubt whether it will make as much change in things as its advocates hope or its opponents fear" (*SJ* II [Mar. 4, 1917]: 211). In fact the suffrage soon was extended to all women.

8. The official name of the Conservative, or Tory, party, one of the two major political parties in Canada.

9. The nickname for the Liberal party in Canada from 1884 on; a slang term originally from the phrase "clear grit." The sense of "grit" meaning minute pieces of stone or sand indicates toughness and resistance.

10. This name for a variety of eating apple comes from the color russet, a reddish brown. Russet apples are reddish-brown with a rough skin. They go back to the eighteenth century, but the Cuthbert russets are probably more recent, like the St. Edmunds Pippins: "Originated at Bury, St. Edmunds in 1870. One of the prettiest of russets, being entirely covered with a flawless velvety fawn coloured russet. The flesh is juicy, crisp with a strong pear flavour. A good bearer . . . Ripens in mid-September" (*Apple Varieties Descriptions*, comp. Daryl Hunter). Apples are stored in a cool, dark place to keep over the winter, which is why Anne has to go to the cellar for them.

"Well now, I dunno," said Matthew.

"Did you ever go courting, Matthew?"

"Well now, no, I dunno's I ever did," said Matthew, who had certainly never thought of such a thing in his whole existence.

Anne reflected with her chin in her hands.

"It must be rather interesting, don't you think, Matthew? Ruby Gillis says when she grows up she's going to have ever so many beaus on the string and have them all crazy about her; but I think that would be too exciting. I'd rather have just one in his right mind. But Ruby Gillis knows a great deal about such matters because she has so many big sisters and Mrs. Lynde says the Gillis girls have gone off like hot cakes. Mr. Phillips goes up to see Prissy Andrews nearly every evening. He says it is to help her with her lessons but Miranda Sloane is studying for Queen's, too, and I should think she needed help a lot more than Prissy because she's ever so much stupider but he never goes to help her in the evenings at all. There are a great many things in this world that I can't understand very well, Matthew."

"Well now, I dunno as I comprehend them all myself," acknowledged Matthew.

"Well, I suppose I must finish up my lessons. I won't allow myself to open that new book Jane lent me until I'm through. But it's a terrible temptation, Matthew. Even when I turn my back on it I can see it there just as plain. Jane said she cried herself sick over it. I love a book that makes me cry. But I think I'll carry that book into the sitting-room and lock it in the jam closet and give you the key. And you must *not* give it to me, Matthew, until my lessons are done, not even if I implore you on my bended knees. It's all very well to say resist temptation but it's ever so much easier to resist it if you can't get the key. And then shall I run down the cellar and get some russets,[10] Matthew? Wouldn't you like some russets?"

"Well now, I dunno but what I would," said Matthew, who never ate russets but knew Anne's weakness for them.

Just as Anne emerged triumphantly from the cellar with her plateful of russets came the sound of flying footsteps on the icy board walk outside and the next moment the kitchen door was flung open and in rushed Diana Barry, white-faced and breathless, with a shawl wrapped hastily around her head. Anne promptly let go of her candle[11] and plate in her surprise, and plate, candle, and apples crashed together down the cellar ladder and were found at the bottom embedded in melted grease the next day by Marilla, who gathered them up and thanked mercy the house hadn't been set on fire.

"Whatever is the matter, Diana?" cried Anne. "Has your mother relented at last?"

"Oh, Anne, do come quick," implored Diana nervously. "Minnie May is awful sick—she's got croup,[12] Young Mary Joe says—and father and mother are away to town and there's nobody to go for the doctor. Minnie May is awful bad and Young Mary Joe doesn't know what to do—and oh, Anne, I'm so scared!"

Matthew, without a word, reached out for cap and coat, slipped past Diana and away into the darkness of the yard.

"He's gone to harness the sorrel mare to go to Carmody for the doctor," said Anne, who was hurrying on hood and jacket. "I know it as well as if he'd said so. Matthew and I are such kindred spirits I can read his thoughts without words at all."

"I don't believe he'll find the doctor at Carmody," sobbed Diana. "I know that Doctor Blair went to town and I guess Doctor Spencer would go too. Young Mary Joe never saw anybody with croup and Mrs. Lynde is away. Oh, Anne!"

"Don't cry, Di," said Anne cheerily. "I know exactly what to do for croup. You forget that Mrs. Hammond had twins three times. When you look after three pairs of twins you naturally get a lot of experience. They all had croup regularly. Just wait

11. Although the Green Gables inhabitants use kerosene lamps (see n. 6, ch. 10), candles are also used, especially when movement from place to place is required. They are slightly safer than the lamps, and common candlesticks are less breakable. In *Emily of New Moon* and *Emily Climbs*, Montgomery makes clear that the use of candles is regarded as old-fashioned. See n. 5, ch. 19.

12. An inflammatory disease of the throat, trachea, and larynx in children. Marked by a peculiar sharp cough, it often proves quickly fatal, as the child chokes on phlegm. The word *croup*, from the southeast of Scotland, was introduced into medical use by Professor Francis Home of Edinburgh in 1765.

13. "*Ipecac*" is a shortened form of *ipecacuanha*, the root of *Cephailis ipecacuanha* N.O. Cinchonaceae, a small South American shrubby plant that possesses emetic, diaphoretic, and purgative properties. In solution, ipecac helps a croupy child vomit phlegm.

till I get the ipecac[13] bottle—you mayn't have any at your house. Come on now."

The two little girls hastened out hand in hand and hurried through Lover's Lane and across the crusted field beyond, for the snow was too deep to go by the shorter wood way. Anne, although sincerely sorry for Minnie May, was far from being insensible to the romance of the situation and to the sweetness of once more sharing that romance with a kindred spirit.

The night was clear and frosty, all ebony of shadow and silver of snowy slope; big stars were shining over the silent fields; here and there the dark pointed firs stood up with snow powdering their branches and the wind whistling through them. Anne thought it was truly delightful to go skimming through all this mystery and loveliness with your bosom friend who had been so long estranged.

Minnie May, aged three, was really very sick. She lay on the kitchen sofa, feverish and restless, while her hoarse breathing could be heard all over the house. Young Mary Joe, a buxom, broad-faced French girl from the Creek, whom Mrs. Barry had engaged to stay with the children during her absence, was

helpless and bewildered, quite incapable of thinking what to do, or doing it if she thought of it.

Anne went to work with skill and promptness.

"Minnie May has croup all right; she's pretty bad, but I've seen them worse. First we must have lots of hot water. I declare, Diana, there isn't more than a cupful in the kettle! There, I've filled it up, and, Mary Joe, you may put some wood in the stove. I don't want to hurt your feelings, but it seems to me you might have thought of this before, if you'd any imagination. Now, I'll undress Minnie May and put her to bed, and you try to find some soft flannel cloths, Diana. I'm going to give her a dose of ipecac first of all."

Minnie May did not take kindly to the ipecac, but Anne had not brought up three pairs of twins for nothing. Down that ipecac went, not only once, but many times during the long, anxious night when the two little girls worked patiently over the suffering Minnie May, and Young Mary Joe, honestly anxious to do all she could, kept on a roaring fire and heated more water than would have been needed for a hospital of croupy babies.

It was three o'clock when Matthew came with the doctor, for he had been obliged to go all the way to Spencervale for one. But the pressing need for assistance was past. Minnie May was much better and was sleeping soundly.

"I was awfully near giving up in despair," explained Anne. "She got worse and worse until she was sicker than ever the Hammond twins were, even the last pair. I actually thought she was going to choke to death. I gave her every drop of ipecac in that bottle, and when the last dose went down I said to myself—not to Diana or Young Mary Joe, because I didn't want to worry them any more than they were worried, but I had to say it to myself just to relieve my feelings—'This is the last lingering hope and I fear 'tis a vain one.'[14] But in about three minutes she coughed up the phlegm and began

14. An echo of Felicia Dorothea Hemans's "The Siege of Valencia": "And my last lingering hope, that thou / shouldst win" (l. 185.) The speaker is Emilia, the mother of two sons whose lives must be sacrificed for the sake of the city. Like Emilia, Anne uses the phrase to express fear for a child's life.

Opposite: Winter in Cavendish.

to get better right away. You must just imagine my relief, doctor, because I can't express it in words. You know there are some things that cannot be expressed in words."

"Yes, I know," nodded the doctor. He looked at Anne as if he were thinking some things about her that couldn't be expressed in words. Later on, however, he expressed them to Mr. and Mrs. Barry.

"That little red-headed girl they have over at Cuthbert's is as smart as they make 'em. I tell you she saved that baby's life, for it would have been too late by the time I got here. She seems to have a skill and presence of mind perfectly wonderful in a child of her age. I never saw anything like the eyes of her when she was explaining the case out to me."

Anne had gone home in the wonderful, white-frosted winter morning, heavy-eyed from loss of sleep, but still talking unweariedly to Matthew as they crossed the long white field and walked under the glittering fairy arch of the Lover's Lane maples.

"Oh, Matthew, isn't it a wonderful morning? The world looks like something God had just imagined for His own pleasure, doesn't it? The trees look as if I could blow them away with a breath—pouf! I'm so glad I live in a world where there are white frosts, aren't you? And I'm so glad Mrs. Hammond had three pairs of twins after all. If she hadn't I mightn't have known what to do for Minnie May. I'm real sorry I was ever cross with Mrs. Hammond for having twins. But, oh, Matthew, I'm so sleepy. I can't go to school. I just know I couldn't keep my eyes open and I'd be so stupid. But I hate to stay home for Gil—some of the others will get head of the class, and it's so hard to get up again—although of course the harder it is the more satisfaction you have when you do get up, haven't you?"

"Well now, I guess you'll manage all right," said Matthew, looking at Anne's white little face and the dark shadows under her eyes. "You just go right to bed and have a good sleep. I'll do all the chores."

Anne accordingly went to bed and slept so long and soundly that it was well on in the white and rosy winter afternoon when she awoke and descended to the kitchen where Marilla, who had arrived home in the meantime, was sitting knitting.

"Oh, did you see the Premier?" exclaimed Anne at once. "What did he look like, Marilla?"

"Well, he never got to be Premier on account of his looks," said Marilla. " Such a nose as that man had![15] But he can speak. I was proud of being a Conservative. Rachel Lynde, of course, being a Liberal, had no use for him. Your dinner is in the oven, Anne; and you can get yourself some blue-plum preserve out of the pantry. I guess you're hungry. Matthew has been telling me about last night. I must say it was fortunate you knew what to do. I wouldn't have had any idea myself, for I never saw a case of croup. There now, never mind talking till you've had your dinner. I can tell by the look of you that you're just full up with speeches, but they'll keep."

Marilla had something to tell Anne, but she did not tell it just then, for she knew if she did Anne's consequent excitement would lift her clear out of the region of such material matters as appetite or dinner. Not until Anne had finished her saucer of blue plums did Marilla say:

"Mrs. Barry was here this afternoon, Anne. She wanted to see you, but I wouldn't wake you up. She says you saved Minnie May's life, and she is very sorry she acted as she did in that affair of the currant-wine. She says she knows now you didn't mean to set Diana drunk, and she hopes you'll forgive her and be good friends with Diana again. You're to go over this evening if you like, for Diana can't stir outside the door on account of a bad cold she caught last night.

15. Marilla's reference to the premier's nose makes it clear that Sir John A. MacDonald is the one referred to, for his nose was famous and appeared prominently in caricatures (see Virginia Careless, "The Highjacking of 'Anne'").

16. Evidently Anne has been reading Mrs. Hemans recently; cf. "Night Scene in Genoa": "Oblivion's mantle o'er the past" (l. 83).

Now, Anne Shirley, for pity's sake don't fly clean up into the air."

The warning seemed not unnecessary, so uplifted and aerial was Anne's expression and attitude as she sprang to her feet, her face irradiated with the flame of her spirit.

"Oh, Marilla, can I go right now—without washing my dishes? I'll wash them when I come back, but I cannot tie myself down to anything so unromantic as dish-washing at this thrilling moment."

"Yes, yes, run along," said Marilla indulgently. "Anne Shirley—are you crazy? Come back this instant and put something on you. I might as well call to the wind. She's gone without a cap or wrap. Look at her tearing through the orchard with her hair streaming. It'll be a mercy if she doesn't catch her death of cold."

Anne came dancing home in the purple winter twilight across the snowy places. Afar in the southwest was the great shimmering pearl-like sparkle of an evening star in a sky that was pale golden and ethereal rose over gleaming white spaces and dark glens of spruce. The tinkles of sleigh-bells among the snowy hills came like elfin chimes through the frosty air, but their music was not sweeter than the song in Anne's heart and on her lips.

"You see before you a perfectly happy person, Marilla," she announced. "I'm perfectly happy—in spite of my red hair. Just at present I have a soul above red hair. Mrs. Barry kissed me and cried and said she was so sorry and she could never repay me. I felt fearfully embarrassed, Marilla, but I just said as politely as I could, 'I have no hard feelings for you, Mrs. Barry. I assure you once for all that I did not mean to intoxicate Diana and henceforth I shall cover the past with the mantle of oblivion.'[16] That was a pretty dignified way of speaking, wasn't it, Marilla? I felt that I was heaping coals of fire on Mrs. Barry's head. And Diana and I had a lovely afternoon.

Diana showed me a new fancy crochet stitch[17] her aunt over at Carmody taught her. Not a soul in Avonlea knows it but us, and we pledged a solemn vow never to reveal it to any one else. Diana gave me a beautiful card with a wreath of roses on it and a verse of poetry:

> If you love me as I love you
> Nothing but death can part us two.[18]

And that is true, Marilla. We're going to ask Mr. Phillips to let us sit together in school again, and Gertie Pye can go with Minnie Andrews. We had an elegant tea. Mrs. Barry had the very best china set out, Marilla, just as if I was real company. I can't tell you what a thrill it gave me. Nobody ever used their very best china on my account before. And we had fruit-cake and pound-cake and dough-nuts and two kinds of preserves, Marilla. And Mrs. Barry asked me if I took tea and said, 'Pa, why don't you pass the biscuits to Anne?' It must be lovely to be grown-up, Marilla, when just being treated as if you were is so nice."

"I don't know about that," said Marilla with a brief sigh.

"Well, anyway, when I am grown up," said Anne decidedly, "I'm always going to talk to little girls as if they were, too, and I'll never laugh when they use big words. I know from sorrowful experience how that hurts one's feelings. After tea Diana and I made taffy.[19] The taffy wasn't very good, I suppose because neither Diana nor I had ever made any before. Diana left me to stir it while she buttered the plates and I forgot and let it burn; and then when we set it out on the platform to cool the cat walked over one plate and that had to be thrown away. But the making of it was splendid fun. Then when I came home Mrs. Barry asked me to come over as often as I could and Diana stood at the window and threw kisses to me all the way down to Lover's Lane. I

17. Crocheting is a type of needlework done with one long hooked needle, making a chain of stitches, forming patterns and shapes. Crochet is used almost solely for fancy work. See Appendix, "Homemade Artifacts."

18. Rea Wilmshurst *(CCL* 56: 1989) notes that this is a keepsake album verse.

19. A candy or sweet similar to what in England is called toffee. *The Fanny Farmer Cookbook*, in print since 1896, offers a recipe for taffy as "Velvet Molasses Candy":

Put in a heavy pan 1/2 cup molasses, 1 cup sugar, 1/2 cup water and 1 tablespoon vinegar. Cook, stirring constantly, to the boiling point. Add 1/4 teaspoon cream of tartar. Boil to 256°, stirring constantly during the last part of the cooking. When nearly done, add 1/4 cup melted butter and 1/8 teaspoon baking soda. Pour into a buttered pan. As the candy cools around the sides, fold towards the center. When it is cool enough to handle, butter your hands and pull it, using your fingertips and thumb, until it is porous and light-colored. Shape into a rope and cut in small pieces with scissors or a sharp knife. Put on wax paper to harden. Makes about 1 pound.

It is more entertaining to have two or more persons involved in "taffy pulling." Boys and girls could make taffy together, so it offered an entertainment for those who, for religious or other reasons, did

not dance. In a Montgomery short story "The Pursuit of the Ideal" (1904), the hero has "an inner vision of Freda making taffy with Tim and he did not approve of it" *(At the Altar: Matrimonial Tales*, 70). See also *Rilla of Ingleside* (ch. 3). Candy was usually homemade in the Maritimes of Anne's day, although Matthew did once extravagantly buy chocolate caramels for Anne (see p. 141).

assure you, Marilla, that I feel like praying to-night and I'm going to think out a special brand-new prayer in honour of the occasion."

"Pulling candy." Illustration for **Harper's Young People,** *October 12, 1886.*

CHAPTER XIX

A CONCERT, A CATASTROPHE,
AND A CONFESSION

"MARILLA, CAN I go over to see Diana just for a minute?" asked Anne, running breathlessly down from the east gable one February evening.

"I don't see what you want to be trapesing about after dark for," said Marilla shortly. "You and Diana walked home from school together and then stood down there in the snow for half an hour more, your tongues going the whole blessed time, clickety-clack. So I don't think you're very badly off to see her again."

"But she wants to see me," pleaded Anne. "She has something very important to tell me."

"How do you know she has?"

"Because she just signalled to me from her window. We have arranged a way to signal with our candles and cardboard. We set the candle on the window-sill and make flashes by passing the cardboard back and forth. So many flashes mean a certain thing. It was my idea, Marilla."

"I'll warrant you it was," said Marilla emphatically. "And the next thing you'll be setting fire to the curtains with your signalling nonsense."

"Oh, we're very careful, Marilla. And it's so interesting. Two flashes mean, 'Are you there?' Three mean 'yes' and four 'no.'

1. A one-horse sleigh or sledge
used in New England; a toboggan,
from a Chippewa word meaning
"instrument for drawing" or "that
on which something is drawn."

Five mean, 'Come over as soon as possible, because I have something important to reveal.' Diana has just signalled five flashes, and I'm really suffering to know what it is."

"Well, you needn't suffer any longer," said Marilla sarcastically. "You can go, but you're to be back here in just ten minutes, remember that."

Anne did remember it and was back in the stipulated time, although probably no mortal will ever know just what it cost her to confine the discussion of Diana's important communication within the limits of ten minutes. But at least she had made good use of them.

"Oh, Marilla, what do you think? You know to-morrow is Diana's birthday. Well, her mother told her she could ask me to go home with her from school and stay all night with her. And her cousins are coming over from Newbridge in a big pung sleigh[1] to go to the Debating Club concert at the hall to-morrow night. And they are going to take Diana and me to the concert—if you'll let me go, that is. You will, won't you, Marilla? Oh, I feel so excited."

"You can calm down then, because you're not going. You're better at home in your own bed, and as for that Club concert, it's all nonsense, and little girls should not be allowed to go out to such places at all."

"I'm sure the Debating Club is a most respectable affair," pleaded Anne.

"I'm not saying it isn't. But you're not going to begin gadding about to concerts and staying out all hours of the night. Pretty doings for children. I'm surprised at Mrs. Barry's letting Diana go."

"But it's such a very special occasion," mourned Anne, on the verge of tears. "Diana has only one birthday in a year. It isn't as if birthdays were common things, Marilla. Prissy Andrews is going to recite 'Curfew Must Not Ring To-night.'[2] That is such a good moral piece, Marilla, I'm sure it would do me lots of good to hear it. And the choir are going to sing four lovely pathetic songs that are pretty near as good as hymns. And oh, Marilla, the minister is going to take part; yes, indeed, he is; he's going to give an address. That will be just about the same thing as a sermon. Please, mayn't I go, Marilla?"

"You heard what I said, Anne, didn't you? Take off your boots now and go to bed. It's past eight."

"There's just one more thing, Marilla," said Anne, with the air of producing the last shot in her locker.[3] "Mrs. Barry told Diana that we might sleep in the spare-room bed. Think of the honour of your little Anne being put in the spare-room bed."

"It's an honour you'll have to get along without. Go to bed, Anne, and don't let me hear another word out of you."

When Anne, with tears rolling over her cheeks, had gone sorrowfully upstairs, Matthew, who had been apparently sound asleep on the lounge[4] during the whole dialogue, opened his eyes and said decidedly:

2. A popular ballad by Rose Hartwick Thorpe (1850–1939), first published in a Detroit newspaper in 1867. See Appendix, "Recitation Pieces."

3. A chest or compartment to hold ammunition, especially on board a warship.

4. The meaning is the same as "on the sofa" in the previous chapter (p. 200). *Lounge* as a term for "sofa or easy chair on which one can lie at length" came into general use in the mid-nineteenth century.

Opposite: Although not a pung sleigh, this is a typical nineteenth-century sleigh.

"Well now, Marilla, I think you ought to let Anne go."

"I don't then," retorted Marilla. "Who's bringing this child up, Matthew, you or me?"

"Well now, you," admitted Matthew.

"Don't interfere then."

"Well now, I ain't interfering. It ain't interfering to have your own opinion. And my opinion is that you ought to let Anne go."

"You'd think I ought to let Anne go to the moon if she took the notion, I've no doubt," was Marilla's amiable rejoinder. "I might have let her spend the night with Diana, if that was all. But I don't approve of this concert plan. She'd go there and catch cold like as not, and have her head filled up with nonsense and excitement. It would unsettle her for a week. I understand that child's disposition and what's good for it better than you, Matthew."

"I think you ought to let Anne go," repeated Matthew firmly. Argument was not his strong point, but holding fast to his opinion certainly was. Marilla gave a gasp of helplessness and took refuge in silence. The next morning, when Anne was washing the breakfast dishes in the pantry, Matthew paused on his way out to the barn to say to Marilla again:

"I think you ought to let Anne go, Marilla."

For a moment Marilla looked things not lawful to be uttered. Then she yielded to the inevitable and said tartly:

"Very well, she can go, since nothing else'll please you."

Anne flew out of the pantry, dripping dish-cloth in hand.

"Oh, Marilla, Marilla, say those blessed words again."

"I guess once is enough to say them. This is Matthew's doings and I wash my hands of it. If you catch pneumonia sleeping in a strange bed or coming out of that hot hall in the middle of the night, don't blame me, blame Matthew. Anne Shirley, you're dripping greasy water all over the floor. I never saw such a careless child."

"Oh, I know I'm a great trial to you, Marilla," said Anne

repentantly. "I make so many mistakes. But then just think of all the mistakes I don't make although I might. I'll get some sand[5] and scrub up the spots before I go to school. Oh, Marilla, my heart was just set on going to that concert. I never was to a concert in my life and when the other girls talk about them in school I feel so out of it. You didn't know just how I felt about it but you see Matthew did. Matthew understands me, and it's so nice to be understood, Marilla."

Anne was too excited to do herself justice as to lessons that morning in school. Gilbert Blythe spelled her down in class and left her clear out of sight in mental arithmetic. Anne's consequent humiliation was less than it might have been, however, in view of the concert and the spare-room bed. She and Diana talked so constantly about it all day that with a stricter teacher than Mr. Phillips dire disgrace must inevitably have been their portion.

Anne felt that she could not have borne it if she had not been going to the concert, for nothing else was discussed that day in school. The Avonlea Debating Club,[6] which met fortnightly all winter, had had several smaller free entertainments; but this was to be a big affair, admission ten cents, in aid of the library. The Avonlea young people had been practising for weeks, and all the scholars were especially interested in it by reason of older brothers and sisters who were going to take part. Everybody in school over nine years of age expected to go, except Carrie Sloane, whose father shared Marilla's opinions about small girls going out to night concerts. Carrie Sloane cried into her grammar all the afternoon and felt that life was not worth living.

For Anne the real excitement began with the dismissal of school and increased therefrom in crescendo until it reached to a crash of positive ecstasy in the concert itself. They had a "perfectly elegant" tea; and then came the delicious occupation of dressing in Diana's little room upstairs. Diana did

5. The sand the author and Anne would have used is white sand from the Cavendish beach, cleaned but not refined. Maritime housekeepers used a British Navy technique for scrubbing pine decks. Common flooring consisted of six-by-ten-foot pine planks that, sanded down, looked almost white, according to Boyd Beck of the Charlottetown Museum. There is a detailed description of sanding a floor in *Emily Climbs* (ch. 4) in which Emily sands the kitchen floor "in the beautiful and complicated 'herring-bone pattern' which was one of the New Moon traditions . . . other housewives had long ago begun to use 'new-fangled' devices and patent cleaners for making their floors white. But Dame Elizabeth Murray would have none of such; as long as she reigned at New Moon so long should candles burn and sanded floors gleam whitely."

6. Evidently a society for young people in their late teens and twenties, rather like the Avonlea Village Improvement Society instituted by Anne, Diana, Gilbert, and others in *Anne of Avonlea*. Such clubs allowed their members to practice public speaking, although the actual team debating was commonly left to the males of the group. Small clubs like these proliferated in North America in the nineteenth century, enabling rural areas to keep pace with new developments.

7. The pompadour, after the Marquise de Pompadour, sometime mistress of Louis XV, is both the style of arranging the hair rolled back from the forehead (sometimes over a pad) to make it stand high on the head, and the high front roll of hair so produced. It is a style associated with the 1890s to 1908 (Virginia Careless, "The Highjacking of 'Anne,'" *CCL* 67 [1992]:54). Putting one's hair up is a sign of adulthood. Diana dresses only Anne's front hair in the pompadour style because they are not quite old enough to put it all up. See illustration.

8. Either a blouse or a simple dress. The word *dress* is used for clothes suitable for evening wear (see ch. 34).

9. In "Curfew Must Not Ring Tonight" the line reads: "climbed the *dusty* ladder, *on which fell* no ray of light." The misquotation might be Montgomery's or might otherwise be ascribed to Prissy Andrews. See Appendix, "Recitation Pieces."

Anne's front hair in the new pompadour[7] style and Anne tied Diana's bows with the especial knack she possessed; and they experimented with at least half a dozen different ways of arranging their back hair. At last they were ready, cheeks scarlet and eyes glowing with excitement.

True, Anne could not help a little pang when she contrasted her plain black tam and shapeless, tight-sleeved, home-made gray cloth coat with Diana's jaunty fur cap and smart little jacket. But she remembered in time that she had an imagination and could use it.

Then Diana's cousins, the Murrays from Newbridge, came; they all crowded into the big pung sleigh, among straw and furry robes. Anne revelled in the drive to the hall, slipping along over satin-smooth roads with the snow crisping under the runners. There was a magnificent sunset, and the snowy hills and deep blue water of the St. Lawrence Gulf seemed to rim in the splendour like a huge bowl of pearl and sapphire brimmed with wine and fire. Tinkles of sleigh-bells and distant laughter that seemed like the mirth of wood elves, came from every quarter.

"Oh, Diana," breathed Anne, squeezing Diana's mittened hand under the fur robe, "isn't it all like a beautiful dream? Do I really look the same as usual? I feel so different that it seems to me it must show in my looks."

"You look awfully nice," said Diana, who, having just received a compliment from one of her cousins, felt that she ought to pass it on. "You've got the loveliest colour."

The programme that night was a series of "thrills" for at least one listener in the audience, and, as Anne assured Diana, every succeeding thrill was thrillier than the last. When Prissy Andrews, attired in a new pink silk waist[8] with a string of pearls about her smooth white throat and real carnations in her hair—rumour whispered that the master had sent all the way to town for them for her—"climbed the slimy ladder, dark without one ray of light,"[9] Anne shivered in luxurious

10. The song's title is properly "Far above the Daisies" (lyrics by George Cooper, music by Harrison Millard; copyright 1869). Like other songs and poems in *Anne*, this song, which is advertised as companion to a song called "Under the Daisies," cultivates a pleasing melancholy. Anne's gaze upward as if the ceiling were "frescoed with angels" is best explained by the third and last stanza. See Appendix, "Songs."

11. A piece of comic dialect writing supposedly written by a Germanic immigrant named Sockery, describing his misadventures in the barn when, trying to place eggs under a high-roosting hen, he slipped and fell into a barrel. See Appendix, "Recitation Pieces." Montgomery seems to have drawn on the action of this comic piece in *Anne of Avonlea*, when Anne falls through a henhouse and is stuck, like "Sockery" in his "parrel," until someone can cut her out. *Burdett's Dutch Dialect Recitations and Humorous Readings* (1884) includes "Sockery Kadahkut's Kat," in which Sockery mistakes a skunk under his house for a cat, an incident imported into the first movie version of *Anne*.

12. See *Julius Caesar* (III.ii. ll. 73–230).

13. Mr. Phillips's speech included the following lines of Mark Antony's peroration (*Julius Caesar*, III.ii. ll. 221–25):

But were I Brutus
And Brutus Antony, there were
    an Antony
Would ruffle up your spirits,

sympathy; when the choir sang "Far above the Gentle Daisies,"[10] Anne gazed at the ceiling as if it were frescoed with angels; when Sam Sloane proceeded to explain and illustrate "How Sockery Set a Hen,"[11] Anne laughed until people sitting near her laughed too, more out of sympathy with her than with amusement at a selection that was rather threadbare even in Avonlea; and when Mr. Phillips gave Mark Antony's oration over the dead body of Caesar[12] in the most heart-stirring tones—looking at Prissy Andrews at the end of every sentence—Anne felt that she could rise and mutiny[13] on the spot if but one Roman citizen led the way.

Only one number on the programme failed to interest her. When Gilbert Blythe recited "Bingen on the Rhine,"[14] Anne picked up Rhoda Murray's library book and read it until he

and put a tongue
    In every wound of Caesar that
        should move
    The stones of Rome to rise
        and mutiny.

14. See n. 16, ch. 5 and Appendix, "Recitation Pieces."

15. Gilbert, in impersonating the dying soldier, creates his own emphasis; compare "Bingen on the Rhine," Stanza 5. This is a prophetic moment. Later in her life Anne realizes she loves Gilbert, when she hears that he is dying: "If Gilbert went away from her without one word or sign or message, she could not live" (*Anne of the Island*, ch. 40). Diana refers to this incident of Gilbert's recitation in *Anne's House of Dreams* (ch. 1).

had finished, when she sat rigidly stiff and motionless while Diana clapped her hands until they tingled.

It was eleven when they got home, sated with dissipation, but with the exceeding sweet pleasure of talking it all over still to come. Everybody seemed asleep and the house was dark and silent. Anne and Diana tiptoed into the parlour, a long narrow room out of which the spare room opened. It was pleasantly warm and dimly lighted by the embers of a fire in the grate.

"Let's undress here," said Diana. "It's so nice and warm."

"Hasn't it been a delightful time?" sighed Anne rapturously. "It must be splendid to get up and recite there. Do you suppose we will ever be asked to do it, Diana?"

"Yes, of course, some day. They're always wanting the big scholars to recite. Gilbert Blythe does often and he's only two years older than us. Oh, Anne, how could you pretend not to listen to him? When he came to the line,

There's another, *not* a sister, [15]

he looked right down at you."

"Diana," said Anne with dignity, "you are my bosom friend but I cannot allow even you to speak to me of that person. Are you ready for bed? Let's run a race and see who'll get to the bed first."

The suggestion appealed to Diana. The two little white-clad figures flew down the long room, through the spare-room door, and bounded on the bed at the same moment. And then —something—moved beneath them, there was a gasp and a cry—and somebody said in muffled accents:

"Merciful goodness!"

Anne and Diana were never able to tell just how they got off that bed and out of the room. They only knew that after one frantic rush they found themselves tiptoeing shiveringly upstairs.

"Oh, who was it—*what* was it?" whispered Anne, her teeth chattering with cold and fright.

"It was Aunt Josephine," said Diana, gasping with laughter. "Oh, Anne, it was Aunt Josephine, however she came to be there. Oh, and I know she will be furious. It's dreadful—it's really dreadful—but did you ever know anything so funny, Anne?"

"Who is your Aunt Josephine?"

"She's father's aunt and she lives in Charlottetown. She's awfully old—seventy anyhow—and I don't believe she was *ever* a little girl. We were expecting her out for a visit, but not so soon. She's awfully prim and proper and she'll scold dreadfully about this, I know. Well, we'll have to sleep with Minnie May—and you can't think how she kicks."

Miss Josephine Barry did not appear at the early breakfast the next morning. Mrs. Barry smiled kindly at the two little girls.

"Did you have a good time last night? I tried to stay awake until you came home, for I wanted to tell you Aunt Josephine had come and that you would have to go upstairs after all, but I was so tired I fell asleep. I hope you didn't disturb your aunt, Diana."

Diana preserved a discreet silence, but she and Anne exchanged furtive smiles of guilty amusement across the table. Anne hurried home after breakfast and so remained in blissful ignorance of the disturbance which presently resulted in the Barry household until the late afternoon, when she went down to Mrs. Lynde's on an errand for Marilla.

"So you and Diana nearly frightened poor old Miss Barry to death last night?" said Mrs. Lynde severely, but with a twinkle in her eye. "Mrs. Barry was here a few minutes ago on her way to Carmody. She's feeling real worried over it. Old Miss Barry was in a terrible temper when she got up this morning—and Josephine Barry's temper is no joke, I can tell you that. She wouldn't speak to Diana at all."

16. Cf. "Look ere you leap" (John Haywood, *Proverbs* [1546], Pt. I, Ch. 2); "Thou should have looked before thou hadst leapt" (Jonson, Chapman, and Marston, *Eastward Ho* [1605], V.i.); and "And look before you ere you leap; / For as you sow, ye are like to reap" (Samuel Butler, *Hudibras* [1663], Pt. II).

"It wasn't Diana's fault," said Anne contritely. "It was mine. I suggested racing to see who would get into bed first."

"I knew it!" said Mrs. Lynde with the exultation of a correct guesser. "I knew that idea came out of your head. Well, it's made a nice lot of trouble, that's what. Old Miss Barry came out to stay for a month, but she declares she won't stay another day and is going right back to town to-morrow, Sunday and all as it is. She'd have gone to-day if they could have taken her. She had promised to pay for a quarter's music lessons for Diana, but now she is determined to do nothing at all for such a tomboy. Oh, I guess they had a lively time of it there this morning. The Barrys must feel cut up. Old Miss Barry is rich and they'd like to keep on the good side of her. Of course, Mrs. Barry didn't say just that to me, but I'm a pretty good judge of human nature, that's what."

"I'm such an unlucky girl," mourned Anne. "I'm always getting into scrapes myself and getting my best friends—people I'd shed my heart's blood for—into them, too. Can you tell me why it is so, Mrs. Lynde?"

"It's because you're too heedless and impulsive, child, that's what. You never stop to think—whatever comes into your head to say or do you say or do it without a moment's reflection."

"Oh, but that's just the best of it," protested Anne. "Something just flashes into your mind, so exciting, and you must out with it. If you stop to think it over you spoil it all. Haven't you ever felt that yourself, Mrs. Lynde?"

No, Mrs. Lynde had not. She shook her head sagely.

"You must learn to think a little, Anne, that's what. The proverb you need to go by is 'Look before you leap'[16]—especially into spare-room beds."

Mrs. Lynde laughed comfortably over her mild joke, but Anne remained pensive. She saw nothing to laugh at in the situation, which to her eyes appeared very serious. When she left Mrs. Lynde's she took her way across the crusted fields to Orchard Slope. Diana met her at the kitchen door.

"Your Aunt Josephine was very cross about it, wasn't she?" whispered Anne.

"Yes," answered Diana, stifling a giggle with an apprehensive glance over her shoulder at the closed sitting-room door. "She was fairly dancing with rage, Anne. Oh, how she scolded. She said I was the worst-behaved girl she ever saw and that my parents ought to be ashamed of the way they had brought me up. She says she won't stay and I'm sure I don't care. But father and mother do."

"Why didn't you tell them it was my fault?" demanded Anne.

"It's likely I'd do such a thing, isn't it?" said Diana with just scorn. "I'm no tell-tale, Anne Shirley, and anyhow I was just as much to blame as you."

"Well, I'm going in to tell her myself," said Anne resolutely. Diana stared.

"Anne Shirley, you'd never! why—she'll eat you alive!"

"Don't frighten me any more than I am frightened," implored Anne. "I'd rather walk up to a cannon's mouth. But I've got to do it, Diana. It was my fault and I've got to confess. I've had practice in confessing fortunately."

"Well, she's in the room," said Diana. "You can go in if you want to. I wouldn't dare. And I don't believe you'll do a bit of good."

With this encouragement Anne bearded the lion in its den —that is to say, walked resolutely up to the sitting-room door and knocked faintly. A sharp "Come in" followed.

Miss Josephine Barry, thin, prim and rigid, was knitting fiercely by the fire, her wrath quite unappeased and her eyes snapping through her gold-rimmed glasses. She wheeled around in her chair, expecting to see Diana, and beheld a white-faced girl whose great eyes were brimmed up with a mixture of desperate courage and shrinking terror.

"Who are you?" demanded Miss Josephine Barry without ceremony.

"I'm Anne of Green Gables," said the small visitor tremulously, clasping her hands with her characteristic gesture, "and I've come to confess, if you please."

"Confess what?"

"That it was all my fault about jumping into bed on you last night. I suggested it. Diana would never have thought of such a thing, I am sure. Diana is a very lady-like girl, Miss Barry. So you must see how unjust it is to blame her."

"Oh, I must, hey? I rather think Diana did her share in the jumping at least. Such carryings-on in a respectable house!"

"But we were only in fun," persisted Anne. "I think you ought to forgive us, Miss Barry, now that we've apologized. And anyhow, please forgive Diana and let her have her music lessons. Diana's heart is set on her music lessons, Miss Barry, and I know too well what it is to set your heart on a thing and not get it. If you must be cross with any one, be cross with me. I've been so used in my early days to having people cross at me that I can endure it much better than Diana can."

Much of the snap had gone out of the old lady's eyes by this time and was replaced by a twinkle of amused interest. But she still said severely:

"I don't think it is any excuse for you that you were only in fun. Little girls never indulged in that kind of fun when I was young. You don't know what it is to be awakened out of a sound sleep, after a long and arduous journey, by two great girls coming bounce down on you."

"I don't *know*, but I can *imagine*," said Anne eagerly. "I'm sure it must have been very disturbing. But then, there is our side of it too. Have you any imagination, Miss Barry? If you have, just put yourself in our place. We didn't know there was anybody in that bed and you nearly scared us to death. It was simply awful, the way we felt. And then we couldn't sleep in the spare room after being promised. I suppose you are used to sleeping in spare rooms. But just imagine what you would feel like if you were a little orphan girl who had never had such an honour."

All the snap had gone by this time. Miss Barry actually laughed—a sound which caused Diana, waiting in speechless anxiety in the kitchen outside, to give a great gasp of relief.

"I'm afraid my imagination is a little rusty—it's so long since I used it," she said. "I dare say your claim to sympathy is just as strong as mine. It all depends on the way we look at it. Sit down here and tell me about yourself."

"I am very sorry I can't," said Anne firmly. "I would like to, because you seem like an interesting lady, and you might even be a kindred spirit, although you don't look very much like it. But it is my duty go home to Miss Marilla Cuthbert. Miss Marilla Cuthbert is a very kind lady who has taken me to bring up properly. She is doing her best but it is very discouraging work. You must not blame her because I jumped on the bed. But before I go I do wish you would tell me if you will forgive Diana and stay just as long as you meant to in Avonlea."

"I think perhaps I will if you will come over and talk to me occasionally," said Miss Barry.

That evening Miss Barry gave Diana a silver bangle bracelet[17] and told the senior members of the household that she had unpacked her valise.

"I've made up my mind to stay simply for the sake of getting better acquainted with that Anne-girl," she said frankly. "She amuses me and at my time of life an amusing person is a rarity."

Marilla's only comment when she heard the story was, "I told you so." This was for Matthew's benefit.

17. An individual silver bracelet might be worn upon almost any occasion in the nineteenth century but, as Virginia Careless points out ("The Highjacking of 'Anne'"), bangles (emphasized also in ch. 25) are characteristic of the dress of the 1890s to the early 1900s.

Miss Barry stayed her month out and over. She was a more agreeable guest than usual, for Anne kept her in good humour. They became firm friends.

When Miss Barry went away she said:

"Remember, you Anne-girl, when you come to town you're to visit me and I'll put you in my very sparest spare-room bed to sleep."

"Miss Barry was a kindred spirit after all," Anne confided to Marilla. "You wouldn't think so to look at her, but she is. You don't find it right out at first, as in Matthew's case, but after awhile you come to see it. Kindred spirits are not so scarce as I used to think. It's splendid to find out there are so many of them in the world."

CHAPTER XX

A GOOD IMAGINATION GONE WRONG

SPRING HAD COME once more to Green Gables—the beautiful, capricious, reluctant Canadian spring, lingering along through April and May in a succession of sweet, fresh, chilly days, with pink sunsets and miracles of resurrection and growth. The maples in Lover's Lane were red-budded and little curly ferns pushed up around the Dryad's Bubble. Away up in the barrens,[1] behind Mr. Silas Sloane's place, the Mayflowers[2] blossomed out, pink and white stars of sweetness under their brown leaves. All the school girls and boys had one golden afternoon gathering them, coming home in the clear, echoing twilight with arms and baskets full of flowery spoil.

"I'm so sorry for people who live in lands where there are no Mayflowers," said Anne. "Diana says perhaps they have something better, but there couldn't be anything better than Mayflowers, could there, Marilla? And Diana says if they don't know what they are like they don't miss them. But I think that it is the saddest thing of all. I think it would be *tragic*, Marilla, not to know what Mayflowers are like and *not* to miss them. Do you know what I think Mayflowers are, Marilla? I think they must be the souls of the flowers that died last summer and this is their heaven. But we had a splendid time to-

1. Sandy or marshy spaces unsuitable for agriculture and not bearing large trees. Maritime people speak of "blueberry barrens" where wild blueberries grow.

2. Trailing arbutus or ground laurel *(Epigaea repens*, the heath family). The mayflower, akin to rhododendron and mountain laurel, is the emblem of Nova Scotia, with the motto "We bloom amid the snow." As Montgomery described them in her journal of April 27, 1910), "This evening I walked up to the barrens and picked an armful of Mayflowers. They are even more beautiful than usual this year. I never saw such large pink and white clusters. As somebody said of strawberries so say I of Mayflowers, "God might have made a sweeter blossom but God never did.' (*SJ* II: 7). See illustration.

3. The issuing of and responding to dares constitutes an unofficial children's game that revolves around challenging each other to foolhardy deeds to prove one's skill or nerve. Here Arty Gillis cannot endure to be dared and not respond. In this sense, "to take a dare" is to put up with it without making a courageous response.

4. *Hamlet* (V.i. l. 237). Gertrude is speaking of flowers for the dead Ophelia.

5. Lyrics and music by W. C. Baker (New York: Charles W. Harris, 1866). This is the only cheerful song in all of *Anne*. See Appendix, "Songs."

day, Marilla. We had our lunch down in a big mossy hollow by an old well—such a *romantic* spot. Charlie Sloane dared Arty Gillis to jump over it, and Arty did because he wouldn't take a dare.[3] Nobody would in school. It is very *fashionable* to dare. Mr. Phillips gave all the Mayflowers he found to Prissy Andrews and I heard him say 'sweets to the sweet.'[4] He got that out of a book, I know; but it shows he has some imagination. I was offered some Mayflowers too, but I rejected them with scorn. I can't tell you the person's name because I have vowed never to let it cross my lips. We made wreaths of the Mayflowers and put them on our hats; and when the time came to go home we marched in procession down the road, two by two, with our bouquets and wreaths, singing 'My Home on the Hill.'[5] Oh, it was so thrilling, Marilla. All Mr. Silas Sloane's folks rushed out to see us and everybody we met on the road stopped and stared after us. We made a real sensation."

"Not much wonder! Such silly doings!" was Marilla's response.

After the Mayflowers came the violets and Violet Vale was empurpled with them. Anne walked through it on her way to school with reverent steps and worshipping eyes, as if she trod on holy ground.

"Somehow," she told Diana, "when I'm going through here I don't really care whether Gil—whether anybody gets ahead of me in class or not. But when I'm up in school it's all different and I care as much as ever. There's such a lot of different Annes in me. I sometimes think that is why I'm such a troublesome person. If I was just the one Anne it would be ever so much more comfortable, but then it wouldn't be half so interesting."

One June evening, when the orchards were pink-blossomed again, when the frogs were singing silvery-sweet in the marshes about the head of the Lake of Shining Waters, and the air was full of the savour of clover fields and balsamic fir woods, Anne was sitting by her gable window. She had been studying her lessons, but it had grown too dark to see the book, so she had fallen into wide-eyed reverie, looking out past the boughs of the Snow Queen, once more bestarred with its tufts of blossom.

In all essential respects the little gable chamber was unchanged. The walls were as white, the pincushion as hard, the chairs as stiffly and yellowly upright as ever. Yet the whole character of the room was altered. It was full of a new vital, pulsing personality that seemed to pervade it and to be quite independent of schoolgirl books and dresses and ribbons, and even of the cracked blue jug full of apple blossoms on the table. It was as if all the dreams, sleeping and waking, of its vivid occupant had taken a visible although immaterial form and had tapestried the bare room with splendid filmy tissues of rainbow and moonshine. Presently Marilla came briskly in with some of Anne's freshly ironed school aprons.[6]

She hung them over a chair and sat down with a short sigh. She had had one of her headaches that afternoon, and although the pain had gone she felt weak and "tuckered out," as she expressed it. Anne looked at her with eyes limpid with sympathy.

"I do truly wish I could have had the headache in your place, Marilla. I would have endured it joyfully for your sake."

"I guess you did your part in attending to the work and letting me rest," said Marilla. "You seem to have got on fairly well and made fewer mistakes than usual. Of course it wasn't exactly necessary to starch Matthew's handkerchiefs! And most people when they put a pie in the oven to warm up for dinner take it out and eat it when it gets hot instead of leaving it to be burned to a crisp. But that doesn't seem to be your way evidently."

Headaches always left Marilla somewhat sarcastic.

"Oh, I'm so sorry," said Anne penitently. "I never thought about that pie from the moment I put it in the oven till now,

6. Young girls wore full—and even elaborate—aprons complete with a yoke and a skirt covering most of the body, tying or fastening with buttons in the back. Some styles even provided full sleeves. They were thought simpler and more readily washable than dresses and could be worn over a plain dress to provide color or pattern in checks and embroidery. See Appendix, "Homemade Artifacts."

7. May 24th, Queen Victoria's birthday, also known as Empire Day. See illustration.

Above: Queen Victoria pictured at her Diamond Jubilee, 1897.

Opposite: The "haunted woods" of Cavendish, c. 1890s.

although I felt *instinctively* that there was something missing on the dinner table. I was firmly resolved, when you left me in charge this morning, not to imagine anything, but keep my thoughts on facts. I did pretty well until I put the pie in, and then an irresistible temptation came to me to imagine I was an enchanted princess shut up in a lonely tower with a handsome knight riding to my rescue on a coal-black steed. So that is how I came to forget the pie. I didn't know I starched the handkerchiefs. All the time I was ironing I was trying to think of a name for a new island Diana and I have discovered up the brook. It's the most ravishing spot, Marilla. There are two maple-trees on it and the brook flows right round it. At last it struck me that it would be splendid to call it Victoria Island because we found it on the Queen's birthday.[7] Both Diana and I are very loyal. But I'm sorry about that pie and the handkerchiefs. I wanted to be extra good to-day because it's an anniversary. Do you remember what happened this day last year, Marilla?"

"No, I can't think of anything special."

"Oh, Marilla, it was the day I came to Green Gables. I shall never forget it. It was the turning-point in my life. Of course it wouldn't seem so important to you. I've been here for a year and I've been so happy. Of course, I've had my troubles but one can live down troubles. Are you sorry you kept me, Marilla?"

"No, I can't say I'm sorry," said Marilla, who sometimes wondered how she could have lived before Anne came to Green Gables, "no, not exactly sorry. If you've finished your lessons, Anne, I want you to run over and ask Mrs. Barry if she'll lend me Diana's apron pattern."

"Oh—it's—it's too dark," cried Anne.

"Too dark? Why, it's only twilight. And goodness knows you've gone over often enough after dark."

"I'll go over early in the morning," said Anne eagerly. "I'll get up at sunrise and go over, Marilla."

"What has got into your head now, Anne Shirley? I want that pattern to cut out your new apron this evening. Go at once and be smart, too."

"I'll have to go around by the road, then," said Anne, taking up her hat reluctantly.

"Go by the road and waste half an hour! I'd like to catch you."

"I can't go through the Haunted Wood,[8] Marilla," cried Anne desperately.

Marilla stared.

"The Haunted Wood! Are you crazy? What under the canopy is the Haunted Wood?"

"The spruce wood over the brook," said Anne in a whisper.

"Fiddlesticks! There is no such thing as a haunted wood anywhere. Who has been telling you such stuff?"

"Nobody," confessed Anne. "Diana and I just imagined the wood was haunted. All the places around here are so — so —

8. In her journals Montgomery says, "The idea of the *Haunted Wood* was of course taken from the old Haunted Wood of the Nelson boys and myself" (*SJ* II: 41). See Appendix, "Geography," and Introduction.

commonplace. We just got this up for our own amusement. We began it in April. A haunted wood is so very romantic, Marilla. We chose the spruce grove because it's so gloomy. Oh, we have imagined the most harrowing things. There's a white lady walks along the brook just about this time of the night and wrings her hands and utters wailing cries. She appears when there is to be a death in the family. And the ghost of a little murdered child haunts the corner up by Idlewild; it creeps up behind you and lays its cold fingers on your hand —so. Oh, Marilla, it gives me a shudder to think of it. And there's a headless man stalks up and down the path and skeletons glower at you between the boughs. Oh, Marilla, I wouldn't go through the Haunted Wood after dark now for anything. I'd be sure that white things would reach out from behind the trees and grab me."

"Did ever anyone hear the like!" ejaculated Marilla, who had listened in dumb amazement. "Anne Shirley, do you mean to tell me you believe all that wicked nonsense of your own imagination?"

"Not believe *exactly*," faltered Anne. "At least, I don't believe it in daylight. But after dark, Marilla, it's different. That is when ghosts walk."

"There are no such things as ghosts, Anne."

"Oh, but there are, Marilla," cried Anne eagerly. "I know people who have seen them. And they are respectable people. Charlie Sloane says that his grandmother saw his grandfather driving home the cows one night after he'd been buried for a year. You know Charlie Sloane's grandmother wouldn't tell a story for anything. She's a very religious woman. And Mrs. Thomas' father was pursued home one night by a lamb of fire with its head cut off hanging by a strip of skin. He said he knew it was the spirit of his brother and that it was a warning he would die within nine days. He didn't, but he died two years after, so you see it was really true. And Ruby Gillis says—"

"Anne Shirley," interrupted Marilla firmly, "I never want to hear you talking in this fashion again. I've had my doubts about that imagination of yours right along, and if this is going to be the outcome of it, I won't countenance any such doings. You'll go right over to Barry's, and you'll go through that spruce grove, just for a lesson and a warning to you. And never let me hear a word out of your head about haunted woods again."

Anne might plead and cry as she liked—and did, for her terror was very real. Her imagination had run away with her and she held the spruce grove in mortal dread after nightfall. But Marilla was inexorable. She marched the shrinking ghost-seer down to the spring and ordered her to proceed straight-way over the bridge and into the dusky retreats of wailing ladies and headless spectres beyond.

"Oh, Marilla, how can you be so cruel?" sobbed Anne. "What would you feel like if a white thing did snatch me up and carry me off?"

"I'll risk it," said Marilla unfeelingly. "You know I always mean what I say. I'll cure you of imagining ghosts into places. March, now."

Anne marched. That is, she stumbled over the bridge and went shuddering up the horrible dim path beyond. Anne never forgot that walk. Bitterly did she repent the license she had given to her imagination. The goblins of her fancy lurked in every shadow about her, reaching out their cold fleshless hands to grasp the terrified small girl who had called them into being. A white strip of birch bark blowing up from the hollow over the brown floor of the grove made her heart stand still. The long drawn wail of two old boughs rubbing against each other brought out the perspiration in beads on her forehead. The swoop of bats in the darkness over her was as the wings of unearthly creatures. When she reached Mr. William Bell's field she fled across it as if pursued by an army of white things, and arrived at the Barry kitchen door so out of breath that she could hardly gasp out her request for the apron pattern. Diana was away so that she had no excuse to linger. The dreadful return journey had to be faced. Anne went back over it with shut eyes, preferring to take the risk of dashing her brains out among the boughs to that of seeing a white thing. When she finally stumbled over the log bridge she drew one long shivering breath of relief.

"Well, so nothing caught you?" said Marilla unsympathetically.

"Oh, Mar—Marilla," chattered Anne, "I'll b-b-be cont-t-tented with c-c-commonplace places after this."

CHAPTER XXI

A NEW DEPARTURE IN FLAVOURINGS

"DEAR ME, there is nothing but meetings and partings in this world, as Mrs. Lynde says," remarked Anne plaintively, putting her slate and books down on the kitchen table on the last day of June and wiping her red eyes with a very damp handkerchief. "Wasn't it fortunate, Marilla, that I took an extra handkerchief to school to-day? I had a presentiment that it would be needed."

"I never thought you were so fond of Mr. Phillips that you'd require two handkerchiefs to dry your tears just because he was going away," said Marilla.

"I don't think I was crying because I was really so very fond of him," reflected Anne. "I just cried because all the others did. It was Ruby Gillis started it. Ruby Gillis has always declared she hated Mr. Phillips but just as soon as he got up to make his farewell speech she burst into tears. Then all the girls began to cry, one after the other. I tried to hold out, Marilla. I tried to remember the time Mr. Phillips made me sit with Gil —with a boy; and the time he spelled my name without an *e* on the blackboard; and how he said I was the worst dunce he ever saw at geometry and laughed at my spelling; and all the times he had been so horrid and sarcastic; but somehow I couldn't, Marilla, and I just had to cry, too. Jane Andrews has been talking for a month about how glad she'd be when Mr. Phillips went away and she declared she'd never shed a tear. Well, she was worse than any of us and had to borrow a handkerchief from her brother—of course the boys didn't cry—because she hadn't brought one of her own, not expecting to need it. Oh, Marilla, it was heartrending. Mr. Phillips made such a beautiful farewell speech beginning, 'The time has come for us to part.' It was very affecting. And he had tears in his eyes, too, Marilla. Oh, I felt dreadfully sorry and remorseful for all the times I'd talked in school and drawn pictures of him on my slate and made fun of him and Prissy. I can tell you I wished I'd been a model pupil like Minnie Andrews. *She* hadn't anything on her conscience. The girls cried all the way home from school. Carrie Sloane kept saying every few minutes 'The time has come for us to part' and that would start us off again whenever we were in any danger of cheering up. I do feel dreadfully sad, Marilla. But one can't feel quite in the depths of despair with two months vacation before them, can they, Marilla? And besides, we met the new minister and his wife coming from the station. For all I was feeling so bad about Mr. Phillips going away I couldn't help taking a little interest in a new minister, could I? His wife is very pretty. Not exactly regally lovely, of course— it wouldn't do, I suppose, for a minister to have a regally lovely wife, because it might set a bad example. Mrs. Lynde says the minister's wife over at Newbridge sets a very bad example because she dresses so fashionably. Our new minister's wife was dressed in blue muslin with lovely puffed sleeves and a hat trimmed with roses. Jane Andrews said she thought puffed sleeves were too worldly for a minister's wife, but I didn't make any such uncharitable remark, Marilla, because I know what it is to long for puffed sleeves. Besides, she's only been a minister's wife for a little while, so one should make allowances, shouldn't they? They are going to board with Mrs. Lynde until the manse is ready."

If Marilla, in going down to Mrs. Lynde's that evening, was actuated by any motive save her avowed one of returning the quilting frames[1] she had borrowed the preceding winter, it was an amiable weakness[2] shared by most of the Avonlea people. Many a thing Mrs. Lynde had lent, sometimes never expecting to see it again, came home that night in charge of the borrowers thereof. A new minister, and moreover a minister with a wife, was a lawful object of curiosity in a quiet little country settlement where sensations were few and far between.

Old Mr. Bentley, the minister whom Anne had found lacking in imagination, had been pastor of Avonlea for eighteen years. He was a widower when he came, and a widower he remained, despite the fact that gossip regularly married him to this, that, or the other one, every year of his sojourn. In the preceding February he had resigned his charge and departed amid the regrets of his people, most of whom had the affection born of long intercourse for their good old minister in spite of his shortcomings as an orator. Since then the Avonlea church had enjoyed a variety of religious dissipation in listening to the many and various candidates and "supplies" who came Sunday after Sunday to preach on trial. These stood or fell by the judgment of the fathers and mothers in Israel;[3] but a certain small red-headed girl who sat meekly in the corner of the old Cuthbert pew also had her opinions about them and discussed the same in full with Matthew, Marilla always declining from principle to criticize ministers in any shape or form.

"I don't think Mr. Smith would have done, Matthew," was Anne's final summing up. "Mrs. Lynde says his delivery was so poor, but I think his worst fault was just like Mr. Bentley's— he had no imagination. And Mr. Terry had too much; he let it run away with him just as I did mine in the matter of the Haunted Wood. Besides, Mrs. Lynde says his theology wasn't sound. Mr. Gresham was a very good man and a very religious man, but he told too many funny stories, and made the

1. Pieces of wood clamped together that hold the layers of a patchwork quilt, stretched out at their full extent while it is being stitched, usually by a number of people at the same time. Such a wood-and-clamp arrangement frames the quilt and holds it in place, keeping it even.

2. Phrase from Henry Fielding's *The History of Tom Jones, A Foundling* (1749), Bk. 10, Ch. 8.

3. Cf. "I Deborah arose, that I arose a mother in Israel" (Song of Deborah, Judges 5:7).

4. By 1908, Montgomery herself was making more than $500 a year by writing, but she had made only $180 a year when she had begun teaching (Rubio and Waterston, *SJ* I: 403, n.). If we imagine the time of *Anne* as being the 1890s, $750 a year would not be a bad salary, but it would be less attractive in 1908.

people laugh in church; he was undignified, and you must have some dignity about a minister, mustn't you, Matthew? I thought Mr. Marshall decidedly attractive; but Mrs. Lynde says he isn't married, or even engaged, because she made special inquiries about him, and she says it would never do to have a young unmarried minister in Avonlea, because he might marry in the congregation and that would make trouble. Mrs. Lynde is a very far-seeing woman, isn't she, Matthew? I'm very glad they've called Mr. Allan. I liked him because his sermon was interesting and he prayed as if he meant it and not just as if he did it because he was in the habit of it. Mrs. Lynde says he isn't perfect but she says she supposes we couldn't expect a perfect minister for seven hundred and fifty dollars a year,[4] and anyhow his theology is sound because she questioned him thoroughly on all the points of doctrine. And she knows his wife's people and they are most respectable and the women are all good housekeepers. Mrs. Lynde says that sound doctrine in the man and good house-keeping in the woman make an ideal combination for a minister's family."

The new minister and his wife were a young pleasant-faced couple, still in their honeymoon, and full of all good and beautiful enthusiasms for their chosen life work. Avonlea opened its heart to them from the start. Old and young liked the frank, cheerful young man with his high ideals, and the bright, gentle little lady who assumed the mistress-ship of the manse. With Mrs. Allan Anne fell promptly and whole-heartedly in love. She had discovered another kindred spirit.

"Mrs. Allan is perfectly lovely," she announced one Sunday afternoon. "She's taken our class and she's a splendid teacher. She said right away she didn't think it was fair for the teacher to ask all the questions, and you know, Marilla, that is exactly what I've always thought. She said we could ask her any question we liked, and I asked ever so many. I'm good at asking questions, Marilla."

"I believe you," was Marilla's emphatic comment.

"Nobody else asked any except Ruby Gillis, and she asked if there was to be a Sunday-school picnic this summer. I didn't think that was a very proper question to ask because it hadn't any connection with the lesson—the lesson was about Daniel in the lions' den[5]—but Mrs. Allan just smiled and said she thought there would be. Mrs. Allan has a lovely smile; she has such *exquisite* dimples in her cheeks. I wish I had dimples in my cheeks, Marilla. I'm not half so skinny as I was when I came here, but I have no dimples yet. If I had perhaps I could influence people for good. Mrs. Allan said we ought always to try to influence other people for good. She talked so nice about everything. I never knew before that religion was such a cheerful thing. I always thought it was kind of melancholy, but Mrs. Allan's isn't, and I'd like to be a Christian if I could be one like her. I wouldn't want to be one like Mr. Superintendent Bell."

"It's very naughty of you to speak so about Mr. Bell," said Marilla severely. "Mr. Bell is a real good man."

"Oh, of course he's good," agreed Anne, "but he doesn't seem to get any comfort out of it. If I could be good I'd dance and sing all day because I was glad of it. I suppose Mrs. Allan is too old to dance and sing and of course it wouldn't be dignified in a minister's wife. But I can just feel she's glad she's a Christian and that she'd be one even if she could get to heaven without it."

"I suppose we must have Mr. and Mrs. Allan up to tea some day soon," said Marilla reflectively. "They've been most everywhere but here. Let me see. Next Wednesday would be a good time to have them. But don't say a word to Matthew about it, for if he knew they were coming he'd find some excuse to be away that day. He's got so used to Mr. Bentley he didn't mind him, but he's going to find it hard to get acquainted with a new minister, and a new minister's wife will frighten him to death."

5. Daniel 6:16–23. The Lord saved Daniel in the midst of roaring lions because he was faithful.

6. The traditional phrase is "secret as the grave."

7. The oily resin of the fir trees makes an iridescent slick on water.

8. Marilla is giving a bravura exhibition of her resources as a cook; see Appendix, "Food Preparation."

9. "dyspeptic." Suffering from dyspepsia, a difficulty in digestion; given to indigestion. New bread is freshly baked, while old has aged several days. New bread might still have too much active yeast in it, which could lead to a digestive upset in those with sensitive stomachs.

"I'll be as secret as the dead,"[6] assured Anne. "But oh, Marilla, will you let me make a cake for the occasion? I'd love to do something for Mrs. Allan, and you know I can make a pretty good cake by this time."

"You can make a layer cake," promised Marilla.

Monday and Tuesday great preparations went on at Green Gables. Having the minister and his wife to tea was a serious and important undertaking, and Marilla was determined not to be eclipsed by any of the Avonlea housekeepers. Anne was wild with excitement and delight. She talked it all over with Diana on Tuesday night in the twilight, as they sat on the big red stones by the Dryad's Bubble and made rainbows in the water with little twigs dipped in fir balsam.[7]

"Everything is ready, Diana, except my cake, which I'm to make in the morning, and the baking-powder biscuits which Marilla will make just before tea-time. I assure you, Diana, that Marilla and I have had a busy two days of it. It's such a responsibility having a minister's wife to tea. I never went through such an experience before. You should just see our pantry. It's a sight to behold. We're going to have jellied chicken and cold tongue. We're to have two kinds of jelly, red and yellow, and whipped cream and lemon pie and cherry pie, and three kinds of cookies and fruit-cake, and Marilla's famous yellow-plum preserves that she keeps especially for ministers, and pound cake and layer cake, and biscuits, as aforesaid[8]; and new bread and old both, in case the minister is dyspeptic[9] and can't eat new. Mrs. Lynde says ministers mostly are dyspeptic, but I don't think Mr. Allan has been a minister long enough for it to have had a bad effect on him. I just grow cold when I think of my layer cake. Oh, Diana, what if it shouldn't be good! I dreamed last night that I was chased all round by a fearful goblin with a big layer cake for a head."

"It'll be good, all right," assured Diana, who was a very comfortable sort of friend. "I'm sure that piece of the one

you made that we had for lunch in Idlewild two weeks ago
was perfectly elegant."

"Yes; but cakes have such a terrible habit of turning out bad
just when you especially want them to be good," sighed
Anne, setting a particularly well-balsamed twig afloat. "However, I suppose I shall just have to trust to Providence and be
careful to put in the flour. Oh, look, Diana, what a lovely
rainbow! Do you suppose the dryad will come out after we
go away and take it for a scarf?"

"You know there is no such thing as a dryad," said Diana.
Diana's mother had found out about the Haunted Wood and

*Illustration by Barbara DiLella
from* **The Anne of Green
Gables Cookbook** *by Kate
Macdonald.*

10. See Appendix, "Food Preparation."

had been decidedly angry over it. As a result Diana had abstained from any further imitative flights of imagination and did not think it prudent to cultivate a spirit of belief even in harmless dryads.

"But it's so easy to imagine there is," said Anne. "Every night, before I go to bed, I look out of my window and wonder if the dryad is really sitting here combing her locks with the spring for a mirror. Sometimes I look for her footprints in the dew in the morning. Oh, Diana, don't give up your faith in the dryad!"

Wednesday morning came. Anne got up at sunrise because she was too excited to sleep. She had caught a severe cold in the head by reason of her dabbling in the spring on the preceding evening; but nothing short of absolute pneumonia could have quenched her interest in culinary matters that morning. After breakfast she proceeded to make her cake. When she finally shut the oven door upon it she drew a long breath.

"I'm sure I haven't forgotten anything this time, Marilla. But do you think it will rise? Just suppose perhaps the baking powder isn't good? I used it out of the new can. And Mrs. Lynde says you can never be sure of getting good baking powder nowadays when everything is so adulterated.[10] Mrs. Lynde says the Government ought to take the matter up but she says we'll never see the day when a Tory Government will do it. Marilla, what if that cake doesn't rise?"

"We'll have plenty without it," was Marilla's unimpassioned way of looking at the subject.

The cake did rise, however, and came out of the oven as light and feathery as golden foam. Anne, flushed with delight, clapped it together with layers of ruby jelly and, in imagination, saw Mrs. Allan eating it and possibly asking for another piece.

"You'll be using the best tea-set, of course, Marilla," she said. "Can I fix up the table with ferns and wild roses?"

"I think that's all nonsense," sniffed Marilla. "In my opinion it's the eatables that matter and not flummery decorations."

"Mrs. Barry had *her* table decorated," said Anne, who was not entirely guiltless of the wisdom of the serpent,[11] "and the minister paid her an elegant compliment. He said it was a feast for the eye as well as the palate."[12]

"Well, do as you like," said Marilla, who was quite determined not to be surpassed by Mrs. Barry or anybody else. "Only mind you leave enough room for the dishes and the food."

Anne laid herself out to decorate in a manner and after a fashion that should leave Mrs. Barry's nowhere. Having abundance of roses and ferns and a very artistic taste of her own, she made that tea-table such a thing of beauty that when the minister and his wife sat down to it they exclaimed in chorus over its loveliness.

"It's Anne's doings," said Marilla, grimly just; and Anne felt that Mrs. Allan's approving smile was almost too much happiness for this world.

Matthew was there, having been inveigled into the party only goodness and Anne knew how. He had been in such a state of shyness and nervousness that Marilla had given him up in despair, but Anne took him in hand so successfully that he now sat at the table in his best clothes and white collar and talked to the minister not uninterestingly. He never said a word to Mrs. Allan but that perhaps was not to be expected.

All went merry as a marriage bell[13] until Anne's layer cake was passed. Mrs. Allan, having already been helped to a bewildering variety, declined it. But Marilla, seeing the disappointment on Anne's face, said smilingly:

"Oh, you must take a piece of this, Mrs. Allan. Anne made it on purpose for you."

"In that case I must sample it," laughed Mrs. Allan, helping herself to a plump triangle, as did also the minister and Marilla.

11. Cf. "Be ye therefore wise as serpents, and harmless as doves" (Matthew 10:16). Anne is here appealing to Marilla's pride and competitiveness to manipulate her. The serpent is also associated with the idea of envy and subtlety: "The serpent was more subtil than any beast of the field" (Genesis 3:1).

12. Elegant, even fussy, floral decorations for the home were becoming fashionable. See Appendix, "Food Preparation."

13. Cf. George Gordon, Lord Byron: "There was a sound of revelry by night, / . . . And all went merry as a marriage bell, / But hush! hark! a deep sound strikes like a rising knell!" *(Childe Harold's Pilgrimage* III. Stanza 21).

14. A remedy for assuaging pain, probably the pungent Minard's Liniment popular in the Maritimes, which advertised itself on the label as "good for Man and Beast." The events in the author's life leading up to this incident are described by her as follows (*AP*, 74–75):

The notable incident of the liniment cake happened when I was teaching school in Bideford and boarding at the Methodist parsonage there. Its charming mistress flavoured a layer cake with anodyne liniment one day. Never shall I forget the taste of that cake and the fun we had over it, for the mistake was not discovered until tea-time. A strange minister was there to tea that night. He ate every crumb of his piece of cake. What he thought of it we never discovered. Possibly he imagined it was simply some new-fangled flavouring.

The unfortunate cook of this incident was Mrs. Estey, wife of the Reverend J. F. Estey, the Methodist minister at Bideford from 1892 to 1895 (Bolger, *The Years Before "Anne,"* 145).

Mrs. Allan took a mouthful of hers and a most peculiar expression crossed her face; not a word did she say, however, but ate steadily away at it. Marilla saw the expression and hastened to taste the cake.

"Anne Shirley!" she exclaimed, "what on earth did you put into that cake?"

"Nothing but what the recipe said, Marilla," cried Anne with a look of anguish. "Oh, isn't it all right?"

"All right! It's simply horrible. Mrs. Allan, don't try to eat it. Anne, taste it yourself. What flavouring did you use?"

"Vanilla," said Anne, her face scarlet with mortification after tasting the cake. "Only vanilla. Oh, Marilla, it must have been the baking-powder. I had my suspicions of that bak—"

"Baking-powder fiddlesticks! Go and bring me the bottle of vanilla you used."

Anne fled to the pantry and returned with a small bottle partially filled with a brown liquid and labelled yellowly, "Best Vanilla."

Marilla took it, uncorked it, smelled it.

"Mercy on us, Anne, you've flavoured that cake with *anodyne liniment*.[14] I broke the liniment bottle last week and poured what was left into an old empty vanilla bottle. I suppose it's partly my fault—I should have warned you—but for pity's sake why couldn't you have smelled it?"

Anne dissolved into tears under this double disgrace.

"I couldn't—I had such a cold!" and with this she fairly fled to the gable chamber, where she cast herself on the bed and wept as one who refuses to be comforted.

Presently a light step sounded on the stairs and somebody entered the room.

"Oh, Marilla," sobbed Anne without looking up, "I'm disgraced for ever. I shall never be able to live this down. It will get out—things always do get out in Avonlea. Diana will ask me how my cake turned out and I shall have to tell her the truth. I shall always be pointed at as the girl who flavoured a cake with anodyne liniment. Gil—the boys in school will never get over laughing at it. Oh, Marilla, if you have a spark of Christian pity don't tell me that I must go down and wash the dishes after this. I'll wash them when the minister and his wife are gone, but I cannot ever look Mrs. Allan in the face again. Perhaps she'll think I tried to poison her. Mrs. Lynde says she knows an orphan girl who tried to poison her benefactor.[15] But the liniment isn't poisonous. It's meant to be taken internally—but not in cakes. Won't you tell Mrs. Allan so, Marilla?"

"Suppose you jump up and tell her so yourself," said a merry voice.

Anne flew up to find Mrs. Allan standing by her bed, surveying her with laughing eyes.

"My dear little girl, you mustn't cry like this," she said, genuinely disturbed by Anne's tragic face. "Why, it's all just a funny mistake that anybody might make."

"Oh, no, it takes me to make such a mistake," said Anne forlornly. "And I wanted to have that cake so nice for you, Mrs. Allan."

"Yes, I know, dear. And I assure you I appreciate your kindness and thoughtfulness just as much as if it had turned out all right. Now, you mustn't cry any more, but come down with me and show me your flower garden. Miss Cuthbert tells me you have a little plot all your own. I want to see it, for I'm very much interested in flowers."

Anne permitted herself to be led down and comforted, reflecting that it was really Providential that Mrs. Allan was a kindred spirit. Nothing more was said about the liniment cake, and when the guests went away Anne found that she had enjoyed the evening more than could have been expected, considering that terrible incident. Nevertheless she sighed deeply.

"Marilla, isn't it nice to think that to-morrow is a new day with no mistakes in it yet?"

15. The tale Mrs. Lynde told Marilla in Chapter 1 involved not just an attempt but the success of an orphan girl in poisoning a whole family. Has Anne heard this story, or has Mrs. Lynde softened it, or even told a different tale to the girl?

16. Another indication that "the French" were considered lower on the human scale than Scottish Presbyterians. See n. 20, ch. 1; n. 10, ch. 4

"I'll warrant you'll make plenty in it," said Marilla. "I never saw your beat for making mistakes, Anne."

"Yes, and well I know it," admitted Anne mournfully. "But have you ever noticed one encouraging thing about me, Marilla? I never make the same mistake twice."

"I don't know as that's much benefit when you're always making new ones."

"Oh, don't you see, Marilla? There *must* be a limit to the mistakes one person can make, and when I get to the end of them, then I'll be through with them. That's a very comforting thought."

"Well, you'd better go and give that cake to the pigs," said Marilla. "It isn't fit for any human to eat, not even Jerry Buote."[16]

CHAPTER XXII

ANNE IS INVITED
OUT TO TEA

"AND WHAT are your eyes popping out of your head about now?" asked Marilla, when Anne had just come in from a run to the post-office. "Have you discovered another kindred spirit?"

Excitement hung around Anne like a garment, shone in her eyes, kindled in every feature. She had come dancing up the lane, like a wind-blown sprite, through the mellow sunshine and lazy shadows of the August evening.

"No, Marilla, but oh, what do you think? I am invited to tea at the manse to-morrow afternoon! Mrs. Allan left the letter for me at the post-office. Just look at it, Marilla. 'Miss Anne Shirley, Green Gables.' That is the first time I was ever called 'Miss.' Such a thrill as it gave me! I shall cherish it for ever among my choicest treasures."

"Mrs. Allan told me she meant to have all the members of her Sunday-achool class to tea in turn," said Marilla, regarding the wonderful event very coolly. "You needn't get in such a fever over it. Do learn to take things calmly, child."

For Anne to take things calmly would have been to change her nature. All "spirit and fire and dew,"[1] as she was, the pleasures and pains of life came to her with trebled intensity. Marilla felt this and was vaguely troubled over it, realizing that

1. See epigraph, p. 37. In a 1904 story by Montgomery, "The Pursuit of the Ideal," the phrase "spirit and fire and dew" is used to describe the heroine, Freda. It means "vivid, and unconventional, and lovable" (*At the Altar,* 71).

the ups and downs of existence would probably bear hardly on this impulsive soul and not sufficiently understanding that the equally great capacity for delight might more than compensate. Therefore Marilla conceived it to be her duty to drill Anne into a tranquil uniformity of disposition as impossible and alien to her as to a dancing sunbeam in one of the brook shallows. She did not make much headway, as she sorrowfully admitted to herself. The downfall of some dear hope or plan plunged Anne into "deeps of affliction." The fulfilment thereof exalted her to dizzy realms of delight. Marilla had almost begun to despair of ever fashioning this waif of the world into her model little girl of demure manners and prim deportment. Neither would she have believed that she really liked Anne much better as she was.

Anne went to bed that night speechless with misery because Matthew had said the wind was round north-east and he feared it would be a rainy day to-morrow. The rustle of the poplar leaves about the house worried her, it sounded so like pattering raindrops, and the dull, far-away roar of the gulf, to which she listened delightedly at other times, loving its strange, sonorous, haunting rhythm, now seemed like a prophecy of storm and disaster to a small maiden who particularly wanted a fine day. Anne thought that the morning would never come.

But all things have an end, even nights before the day on which you are invited to take tea at the manse. The morning, in spite of Matthew's predictions, was fine and Anne's spirits soared to their highest.

"Oh, Marilla, there is something in me to-day that makes me just love everybody I see," she exclaimed as she washed the breakfast dishes. "You don't know how good I feel! Wouldn't it be nice if it could last? I believe I could be a model child if I were just invited out to tea every day. But oh, Marilla, it's a solemn occasion, too. I feel so anxious. What if I shouldn't behave properly? You know I never had tea at a manse before, and I'm not sure that I know all the rules of etiquette, although I've been studying the rules given in the Etiquette Department of the *Family Herald*[2] ever since I came here. I'm so afraid I'll do something silly or forget to do something I should do. Would it be good manners to take a second helping of anything if you wanted to *very* much?"

"The trouble with you, Anne, is that you're thinking too much about yourself. You should just think of Mrs. Allan and what would be nicest and most agreeable for her," said Marilla, hitting for once in her life on a very sound and pithy piece of advice. Anne instantly realized this.

"You are right, Marilla. I'll try not to think about myself at all."

Anne evidently got through her visit without any serious breach of "etiquette" for she came home through the twilight, under a great, high-sprung sky gloried over with trails of saffron and rosy cloud, in a beatified state of mind and told Marilla all about it happily, sitting on the big red sandstone slab at the kitchen door, with her tired curly head in Marilla's gingham lap.

A cool wind was blowing down over the long harvest fields from the rims of firry western hills and whistling through the poplars. One clear star hung above the orchard and the fireflies were flitting over in Lover's Lane, in and out among the ferns and rustling boughs. Anne watched them as she talked and somehow felt that wind and stars and fireflies were all tangled up together into something unutterably sweet and enchanting.

"Oh, Marilla, I've had a most *fascinating* time. I feel that I have not lived in vain, and I shall always feel like that even if I should never be invited to tea at a manse again. When I got there Mrs. Allan met me at the door. She was dressed in the sweetest dress of pale pink organdy,[3] with dozens of frills and elbow sleeves, and she looked just like a seraph.[4] I really think I'd like to be a minister's wife when I grow up, Marilla. A

2. *The Family Herald and Weekly Star*, a weekly newspaper addressed to farming families. It contained serial fiction as well as advice on animal husbandry, veterinary procedures, etiquette, and so on.

3. A very sheer, crisp cotton fabric used for dresses, curtains, and the like. The dress pictured above is made out of this material (advertisement from *Godey's Magazine*, Vol. CXXXII, 1896).

4. One of the seraphim, the highest order of angels; a seraphic person, an angel.

5. The doctrine of original sin holds that humankind is innately depraved as a direct result of Adam's fall. Original sin is thus theologically the condition of common human depravity as distinct from "actual sin," sins committed by the individual.

minister mightn't mind my red hair because he wouldn't be thinking of such worldly things. But then of course one would have to be naturally good and I'll never be that, so I suppose there's no use in thinking about it. Some people are naturally good, you know, and others are not. I'm one of the others. Mrs. Lynde says I'm full of original sin.[5] No matter how hard I try to be good I can never make such a success of it as those who are naturally good. It's a good deal like geometry, I expect. But don't you think the trying so hard ought to count for something? Mrs. Allan is one of the naturally good people. I love her passionately. You know there are some people, like Matthew and Mrs. Allan, that you can love right off without any trouble. And there are others, like Mrs. Lynde, that you have to try very hard to love. You know you *ought* to love them because they know so much and are such active workers in the church, but you have to keep reminding yourself of it all the time or else you forget. There was another little girl at the manse to tea, from the White Sands Sunday School. Her name was Lauretta Bradley, and she was a very nice little girl. Not exactly a kindred spirit, you know, but still very nice. We had an elegant tea, and I think I kept all the rules of etiquette pretty well. After tea Mrs. Allan played and sang and she got Lauretta and me to sing, too. Mrs. Allan says I have a good voice and she says I must sing in the Sunday-school choir after this. You can't think how I was thrilled at the mere thought. I've longed so to sing in the Sunday-school choir, as Diana does, but I feared it was an honour I could never aspire to. Lauretta had to go home early because there is a big concert in the White Sands hotel to-night and her sister is to recite at it. Lauretta says that the Americans at the hotel give a concert every fortnight in aid of the Charlottetown hospital and they ask lots of the White Sands people to recite. Lauretta said she expected to be asked herself some day. I just gazed at her in awe. After she had gone Mrs. Allan and I had a heart-to-heart talk. I told her everything—about Mrs.

Thomas and the twins and Katie Maurice and Violetta and coming to Green Gables and my troubles over geometry. And would you believe it, Marilla? Mrs. Allan told me she was a dunce at geometry, too. You don't know how that encouraged me. Mrs. Lynde came to the manse just before I left and what do you think, Marilla? The trustees have hired a new teacher and it's a lady. Her name is Miss Muriel Stacy. Isn't that a romantic name? Mrs. Lynde says they've never had a female teacher in Avonlea before and she thinks it is a dangerous innovation.[6] But I think it will be splendid to have a lady teacher and I really don't see how I'm going to live through the two weeks before school begins, I'm so impatient to see her."

6. A female teacher might have been taken as an indication of Avonlea's relative unimportance. Larger or more important schools would have had a male head. See Appendix, "Education."

"Balanced herself uprightly on that precarious footing." Illustration by M.A. and
W.A.J. Claus. From the first edition of Anne of Green Gables, *published in*
1908.

CHAPTER XXIII

ANNE COMES TO GRIEF IN AN AFFAIR OF HONOUR

ANNE HAD to live through more than two weeks, as it happened. Almost a month having elapsed since the liniment-cake episode, it was high time for her to get into fresh trouble of some sort, little mistakes, such as absent-mindedly emptying a pan of skim milk[1] into a basket of yarn balls in the pantry instead of into the pigs' bucket,[2] and walking clean over the edge of the log bridge into the brook while wrapped in imaginative reverie, not really being worth counting.

A week after the tea at the manse, Diana Barry gave a party.

"Small and select," Anne assured Marilla. "Just the girls in our class."

They had a very good time and nothing untoward happened until after tea, when they found themselves in the Barry garden, a little tired of all their games and ripe for any enticing form of mischief which might present itself. This presently took the form of "daring."[3]

Daring was the fashionable amusement among the Avonlea small fry just then. It had begun among the boys, but soon spread to the girls, and all the silly things that were done in Avonlea that summer because the doers thereof were "dared" to do them would fill a book by themselves.

1. The nonfat milk left over after cream is skimmed or butter is made; not highly regarded at that time and thought unsuited to human consumption.

2. The bucket of slops used to feed the pigs.

3. See n. 3, ch. 20.

4. A parody of an old form of legal indictment for serious crimes, in which it is charged that a person "did willfully and not having the fear of God before his eyes" do such and such (see *The Old Bailey Sessions Papers).*

5. The horizontal timber or beam at the ridge of a roof to which the upper ends of the rafters are attached. See illustration, p. 250.

First of all Carrie Sloane dared Ruby Gillis to climb to a certain point in the huge old willow-tree before the front door; which Ruby Gillis, albeit in mortal dread of the fat green caterpillars with which said tree was infested and with the fear of her mother before her eyes[4] if she should tear her new muslin dress, nimbly did, to the discomfiture of the aforesaid Carrie Sloane.

Then Josie Pye dared Jane Andrews to hop on her left leg around the garden without stopping once or putting her right foot to the ground; which Jane Andrews gamely tried to do, but gave out at the third corner and had to confess herself defeated.

Josie's triumph being rather more pronounced than good taste permitted, Anne Shirley dared her to walk along the top of the board fence which bounded the garden to the east. Now, to "walk" board fences requires more skill and steadiness of head and heel than one might suppose who has never tried it. Josie Pye, if deficient in some qualities that make for popularity, had at least a natural and inborn gift, duly cultivated, for walking board fences. Josie walked the Barry fence with an airy unconcern which seemed to imply that a little thing like that wasn't worth a "dare." Reluctant admiration greeted her exploit, for most of the other girls could appreciate it, having suffered many things themselves in their efforts to walk fences. Josie descended from her perch, flushed with victory, and darted a defiant glance at Anne.

Anne tossed her red braids.

"I don't think it's such a very wonderful thing to walk a little, low board fence," she said. "I knew a girl in Marysville who could walk the ridge-pole[5] of a roof."

"I don't believe it," said Josie flatly. "I don't believe anybody could walk a ridge-pole. *You* couldn't anyhow."

"Couldn't I?" cried Anne rashly.

"Then I dare you to do it," said Josie defiantly. "I dare you to climb up there and walk the ridge-pole of Mr. Barry's kitchen roof."

Anne turned pale but there was clearly only one thing to be done. She walked towards the house, where a ladder was leaning against the kitchen roof. All the fifth-class girls said "Oh!" partly in excitement, partly in dismay.

"Don't you do it, Anne," entreated Diana. "You'll fall off and be killed. Never mind Josie Pye. It isn't fair to dare anybody to do anything so dangerous."

"I must do it. My honour is at stake," said Anne solemnly. "I shall walk that ridge-pole, Diana, or perish in the attempt. If I am killed you are to have my pearl-bead ring."

Anne climbed the ladder amid breathless silence, gained the ridge-pole, balanced herself uprightly on that precarious footing and started to walk along it, dizzily conscious that she was uncomfortably high up in the world and that walking ridge-poles was not a thing in which your imagination helped you out much. Nevertheless, she managed to take several steps before the catastrophe came. Then she swayed, lost her balance, stumbled, staggered and fell, sliding down over the sun-baked roof and crashing off it through the tangle of Virginia creeper[6] beneath—all before the dismayed circle below could give a simultaneous, terrified shriek.

If Anne had tumbled off the roof on the side up which she ascended Diana would probably have fallen heir to the pearl-bead ring then and there. Fortunately she fell on the other side, where the roof extended down over the porch so nearly to the ground that a fall therefrom was a much less serious thing. Nevertheless, when Diana and the other girls had rushed frantically around the house—except Ruby Gillis, who remained as if rooted to the ground and went into hysterics—they found Anne lying all white and limp among the wreck and ruin of the Virginia creeper.

"Anne, are you killed?" shrieked Diana, throwing herself on

6. *Vitis quinquefolia* or *Ampelopsis quinquefolia*, an ornamental climbing plant of the vine family with foliage that changes in the fall of the year to various shades of crimson, scarlet, and purple; a popular decorative cover for walls in the Victorian period (W. R. Robinson, *The English Flower Garden and Home Grounds*, 866). See Appendix, "Gardens and Plants."

her knees beside her friend. "Oh, Anne, dear Anne, speak just one word to me and tell me if you're killed."

To the immense relief of all the girls, and especially of Josie Pye, who, in spite of lack of imagination, had been seized with horrible visions of a future branded as the girl who was the cause of Anne Shirley's early and tragic death, Anne sat dizzily up and answered uncertainly:

"No, Diana, I am not killed, but I think I am rendered unconscious."

"Where?" sobbed Carrie Sloane. "Oh, where, Anne?"

Before Anne could answer Mrs. Barry appeared on the scene. At sight of her Anne tried to scramble to her feet, but sank back again with a sharp little cry of pain.

"What's the matter? Where have you hurt yourself?" demanded Mrs. Barry.

"My ankle," gasped Anne. "Oh, Diana, please find your father and ask him to take me home. I know I can never walk there. And I'm sure I couldn't hop so far on one foot when Jane couldn't even hop around the garden."

Marilla was out in the orchard picking a panful of summer apples when she saw Mr. Barry coming over the log bridge and up the slope, with Mrs. Barry beside him and a whole procession of little girls trailing after him. In his arms he carried Anne, whose head lay limply against his shoulder.

At that moment Marilla had a revelation. In the sudden stab of fear that pierced to her very heart she realized what Anne had come to mean to her. She would have admitted that she liked Anne—nay, that she was very fond of Anne. But now she knew as she hurried wildly down the slope that Anne was dearer to her than anything on earth.

"Mr. Barry, what has happened to her?" she gasped, more white and shaken than the self-contained, sensible Marilla had been for many years.

Anne herself answered, lifting her head.

"Don't be frightened, Marilla. I was walking the ridge-pole and I fell off. I expect I have sprained my ankle. But, Marilla, I might have broken my neck. Let us look on the bright side of things."

"I might have known you'd go and do something of the sort when I let you go to that party," said Marilla, sharp and shrewish in her very relief. "Bring her in here, Mr. Barry, and lay her on the sofa. Mercy me, the child has gone and fainted!"

It was quite true. Overcome by the pain of her injury, Anne had one more of her wishes granted to her. She had fainted dead away.

Matthew, hastily summoned from the harvest-field, was straightway despatched for the doctor, who in due time came, to discover that the injury was more serious than they had supposed. Anne's ankle was broken.

That night, when Marilla went up to the east gable, where a white-faced girl was lying, a plaintive voice greeted her from the bed.

"Aren't you very sorry for me, Marilla?"

"It was your own fault," said Marilla, twitching down the blind and lighting a lamp.

"And that is just why you should be sorry for me," said Anne, "because the thought that it *is* all my own fault is what makes it so hard. If I could blame it on anybody else I would feel so much better. But what would you have done, Marilla, if you had been dared to walk a ridge-pole?"

"I'd have stayed on good firm ground and let them dare away. Such absurdity!" said Marilla.

Anne sighed.

"But you have such strength of mind, Marilla. I haven't. I just felt that I couldn't bear Josie Pye's scorn. She would have crowed over me all my life. And I think I have been punished so much that you needn't be very cross with me, Marilla. It's not a bit nice to faint, after all. And the doctor hurt me dreadfully when he was setting my ankle. I won't be able to go around for six or seven weeks and I'll miss the new lady teacher. She won't be new any more by the time I'm able to go to school. And Gil—everybody will get ahead of me in class. Oh, I am an afflicted mortal. But I'll try to bear it all bravely if only you won't be cross with me, Marilla."

"There, there, I'm not cross," said Marilla. "You're an unlucky child, there's no doubt about that; but, as you say, you'll have the suffering of it. Here, now, try and eat some supper."

"Isn't it fortunate I've got such an imagination?" said Anne. "It will help me through splendidly, I expect. What do people who haven't any imagination do when they break their bones, do you suppose, Marilla?"

Anne had good reason to bless her imagination many a time and oft during the tedious seven weeks that followed. But she was not solely dependent on it. She had many visitors and not a day passed without one or more of the schoolgirls dropping in to bring her flowers and books and tell her all the happenings in the juvenile world of Avonlea.

"Everybody has been so good and kind, Marilla," sighed Anne happily, on the day when she could first limp across the floor. "It isn't very pleasant to be laid up; but there *is* a bright side to it, Marilla. You find out how many friends you have. Why, even Superintendent Bell came to see me, and he's really a very fine man. Not a kindred spirit, of course; but still I like him and I'm awfully sorry I ever criticized his prayers. I believe now he really does mean them only he has got into the habit of saying them as if he didn't. He could get over that if he'd take a little trouble. I gave him a good broad hint. I told him how hard I tried to make my own little private prayers interesting. He told me all about the time he broke his ankle when he was a boy. It does seem so strange to think of Superintendent Bell ever being a boy. Even my imagination has its limits for I can't imagine *that*. When I try to imagine him as a boy I see him with gray whiskers and spectacles, just as he looks in Sunday School, only small. Now, it's so easy to imagine Mrs. Allan as a little girl. Mrs. Allan has been to see me fourteen times. Isn't that something to be proud of, Marilla? When a minister's wife has so many claims on her time! She is such a cheerful person to have visit you, too. She never tells you it's your own fault and she hopes you'll be a better girl on account of it. Mrs. Lynde always told me that when she came to see me, and she said it in a kind of way that made me feel she might hope I'd be a better girl but didn't really believe I would. Even Josie Pye came to see me. I received her as politely as I could, because I think she was sorry she dared me to walk a ridge-pole. If I had been killed she would have had to carry a dark burden of remorse all her life. Diana has been a faithful friend. She's been over every day to cheer my lonely pillow. But oh, I shall be so glad when I can go to school for I've heard such exciting things about the new teacher. The girls all think she is perfectly sweet. Diana says she has the loveliest fair curly hair and such fascinating eyes. She dresses beautifully, and her sleeve puffs are bigger than anybody else's in Avonlea. Every other Friday afternoon she has recitations and everybody has to say a piece or take part in a dialogue. Oh, it's just glorious to think of it. Josie Pye says she hates it, but that is just because Josie has so little imagination. Diana and Ruby Gillis and Jane Andrews are preparing a dialogue called 'A Morning Visit,'[7] for next Friday. And the Friday afternoons they don't have recitations Miss Stacy takes them all to the woods for a 'field' day and they study ferns and flowers and birds. And they have physical culture exercises morning and evening.[8] Mrs. Lynde says she never heard of such goings-on and it all comes of having a lady teacher. But

7. Anne seems to be referring to a dialogue much like "The Society for the Suppression of Gossip" mentioned on p. 262 (see Appendix, "Recitation Pieces") and included in *Friday Afternoon Dialogues*. There is a poem by Oliver Wendell Holmes called "The Morning Visit," which humorously describes the bad behavior of doctors to patients and the benefits of friendly visits. It includes advice on how to visit a sick person, all of which would be relevant to Anne's situation.

8. These are new subjects whose introduction signals that Miss Stacy is a modern woman and a modern educator. See Introduction and Appendix, "Education."

I think it must be splendid and I believe I shall find that Miss Stacy is a kindred spirit."

"There's one thing plain to be seen, Anne," said Marilla, "and that is that your fall off the Barry roof hasn't injured your tongue at all."

CHAPTER XXIV

MISS STACY AND HER PUPILS GET UP A CONCERT

IT WAS October again when Anne was ready to go back to school—a glorious October, all red and gold, with mellow mornings when the valleys were filled with delicate mists as if the spirit of autumn had poured them in for the sun to drain—amethyst, pearl, silver, rose, and smoke-blue. The dews were so heavy that the fields glistened like cloth of silver and there were such heaps of rustling leaves in the hollows of many-stemmed woods to run crisply through. The Birch Path was a canopy of yellow and the ferns were sear and brown all along it. There was a tang in the very air that inspired the hearts of small maidens tripping, unlike snails, swiftly and willingly to school;[1] and it *was* jolly to be back again at the little brown desk beside Diana, with Ruby Gillis nodding across the aisle and Carrie Sloane sending up notes and Julia Bell passing a "chew" of gum down from the back seat. Anne drew a long breath of happiness as she sharpened her pencil and arranged her picture cards in her desk. Life was certainly very interesting.

In the new teacher she found another true and helpful friend. Miss Stacy was a bright, sympathetic young woman with the happy gift of winning and holding the affections of her pupils and bringing out the best that was in them men-

1. *As You Like It:* "And then the whining school-boy, with his satchel / And shining morning face, creeping like snail / Unwillingly to school" (II.vii. ll. 145–46).

2. See Appendix, "Recitation Pieces."

3. Upon the murder of her favorite, Rizzio, Mary invokes her father's courage, for which his arm is a metaphor, and dismisses her "woman's heart," because it represents weakness and cowardice.

A portrait of Mary Queen of Scots during her late teens.

tally and morally. Anne expanded like a flower under this wholesome influence and carried home to the admiring Matthew and the critical Marilla glowing accounts of school work and aims.

"I love Miss Stacy with my whole heart, Marilla. She is so ladylike and she has such a sweet voice. When she pronounces my name I feel *instinctively* that she's spelling it with an *e*. We had recitations this afternoon. I just wish you could have been there to hear me recite 'Mary Queen of Scots.'[2] I just put my whole soul into it. Ruby Gillis told me coming home that the way I said the line,

> 'Now for my father's arm, she said, my
> woman's heart farewell,'[3]

just made her blood run cold."

"Well now, you might recite it for me some of these days, out in the barn," suggested Matthew.

"Of course I will," said Anne meditatively, "but I won't be able to do it so well, I know. It won't be so exciting as it is when you have a whole schoolful before you hanging breathlessly on your words. I know I won't be able to make your blood run cold."

"Mrs. Lynde says it made *her* blood run cold to see the boys climbing to the very tops of those big trees on Bell's hill after crows' nests last Friday," said Marilla. "I wonder at Miss Stacy for encouraging it."

"But we wanted a crow's nest for nature study," explained Anne. "That was on our field afternoon. Field afternoons are splendid, Marilla. And Miss Stacy explains everything so beautifully. We have to write compositions on our field afternoons and I write the best ones."

"It's very vain of you to say so then. You'd better let your teacher say it."

"But she *did* say it, Marilla. And indeed I'm not vain about it. How can I be, when I'm such a dunce at geometry? Although I'm really beginning to see through it a little, too. Miss Stacy makes it so clear. Still, I'll never be good at it and I assure you it is a humbling reflection. But I love writing compositions. Mostly Miss Stacy lets us choose our own subjects; but next week we are to write a composition on some remarkable person. It's hard to choose among so many remarkable people who have lived. Mustn't it be splendid to be remarkable and have compositions written about you after you're dead? Oh, I would dearly love to be remarkable. I think when I grow up I'll be a trained nurse and go with the Red Crosses[4] to the field of battle as a messenger of mercy. That is, if I don't go out as a foreign missionary. That would be very romantic, but one would have to be very good to be a missionary, and that would be a stumbling-block. We have physical culture exercises every day, too. They make you graceful and promote digestion."

"Promote fiddlesticks!" said Marilla, who honestly thought it was all nonsense.

But all the field afternoons and recitation Fridays and physical culture contortions paled before a project which Miss Stacy brought forward in November. This was that the scholars of Avonlea school should get up a concert and hold it in the hall on Christmas night, for the laudable purpose of helping to pay for a schoolhouse flag.[5] The pupils one and all taking graciously to this plan, the preparations for a programme were begun at once. And of all the excited performers-elect none was so excited as Anne Shirley, who threw herself into the undertaking heart and soul, hampered as she was by Marilla's disapproval. Marilla thought it all rank foolishness.

"It's just filling your heads up with nonsense and taking time that ought to be put on your lessons," she grumbled. "I don't approve of children's getting up concerts and racing about to practices. It makes them vain and forward and fond of gadding."

4. The members of the Red Cross, an international organization with national affiliates whose main purpose is to prevent and alleviate human suffering. Henri Dunant, a young Swiss, witnessed the Battle of Solferino in Italy on June, 24, 1859, and urged relief volunteers to organize. The result was a meeting in Geneva on August 8–22, 1864, which gave rise to the first in a series of treaties now known as the Geneva Conventions. Clara (Clarissa) Barton (1821–1912) was the founder of the American Red Cross. After the Civil War she traveled to Europe and worked for the International Committee of the Red Cross during 1870–1871. Montgomery may have been influenced by Barton's *A Story of the Red Cross* (1904).

5. Perhaps Miss Stacy is raising money for a Canadian flag for the school. Early in this century, the official flag of Canada was the red ensign adapted from the flag of the British merchant marine. After Confederation, in 1867, Canadians became more conscious of a need for a flag specifically their own.

From 1874, a red ensign with a four-province badge on it was used as an official flag flown over the Parliament buildings in Ottawa. Not until 1924 did the Canadian government approve its use as the official flag on government buildings abroad, but at home the Red Ensign had been flown on official sites, and schools had long used it. Is Miss Stacy's interest in a flag a hidden reference to the new Canadian patriotism that is now expected to flourish alongside loyalty to the Queen and the Union Jack? See Appendix, "Education."

6. As Montgomery notes in her journal, " 'The Society for the Suppression of Gossip' and 'The Fairy Queen' were old stand-bys of schooldays. We had the former at our first school concert in which I personated the amiable 'Miss Wise,' and the latter at a school examination. I was the *Fairy Queen*, being thought fitted for the part by reason of my long hair which I wore crimped and floating over my shoulder from a wreath of pink tissue roses" (*SJ* II [Jan. 27, 1911]: 43). A ballad, "The Fairy Queen," appears in the third volume of *Reliques of Ancient English Poetry*, by Bishop Thomas Percy, who attributes the song to

Opposite: The Red Ensign with the British Flag and provincial coats of arms had many variants until 1921. This version, between 1875 and 1903, shows seven coats of arms. These are encircled by a wreath with one branch of maple leaves, the other oak, joined at the bottom by a beaver and on top by a Victorian crown.

"But think of the worthy object," pleaded Anne. "A flag will cultivate a spirit of patriotism, Marilla."

"Fudge! There's precious little patriotism in the thoughts of any of you. All you want is a good time."

"Well, when you can combine patriotism and fun, isn't it all right? Of course it's real nice to be getting up a concert. We're going to have six choruses and Diana is to sing a solo. I'm in two dialogues — *The Society for the Suppression of Gossip* and *The Fairy Queen*.[6] The boys are going to have a dialogue, too. And I'm to have two recitations, Marilla. I just tremble when I think of it, but it's a nice thrilly kind of tremble. And we're to have a tableau[7] at the last — *Faith, Hope* and *Charity*. Diana and Ruby and I are to be in it, all draped in white with flowing hair. I'm to be Hope, with my hands clasped — so — and my eyes uplifted. I'm going to practise my recitations in the garret. Don't be alarmed if you hear me groaning. I have to groan heartrendingly in one of them, and it's really hard to get up a good artistic groan, Marilla. Josie Pye is sulky because she didn't get the part she wanted in the dialogue. She wanted to be the fairy queen. That would have been ridiculous, for who ever heard of a fairy queen as fat as Josie? Fairy queens must be slender. Jane Andrews is to be the queen and I am to be one of her maids of honour. Josie says she thinks a red-haired fairy is just as ridiculous as a fat one but I do not let myself mind what Josie says. I'm to have a wreath of white roses on my hair and Ruby Gillis is going to lend me her slippers[8] because I haven't any of my own. It's necessary for fairies to have slippers, you know. You couldn't imagine a fairy wearing boots, could you? Especially with copper toes?[9] We are going to decorate the hall with creeping spruce[10] and fir mottoes with pink tissue-paper roses in them. And we are all to march in two by two after the audience is seated, while Emma White plays a march on the organ.[11] Oh, Marilla, I know you are not so enthusiastic about it as I am, but don't you hope your little Anne will distinguish herself?"

"All I hope is that you'll behave yourself. I'll be heartily glad when all this fuss is over and you'll be able to settle down. You are simply good for nothing just now with your head stuffed full of dialogues and groans and tableaus. As for your tongue, it's a marvel it's not clean worn out."

Anne sighed and betook herself to the back yard, over which a young new moon was shining through the leafless poplar boughs from an apple-green western sky, and where Matthew was splitting wood. Anne perched herself on a block and talked the concert over with him, sure of an appreciative and sympathetic listener in this instance at least.

"Well now, I reckon it's going to be a pretty good concert. And I expect you'll do your part fine," he said, smiling down into her eager, vivacious little face. Anne smiled back at him. Those two were the best of friends and Matthew thanked his stars many a time and oft that he had nothing to do with bringing her up. That was Marilla's exclusive duty; if it had been his he would have been worried over frequent conflicts between inclination and said duty. As it was, he was free to "spoil Anne" — Marilla's phrasing — as much as he liked. But it was not such a bad arrangement after all; a little "appreciation" sometimes does quite as much good as all the conscientious "bringing up" in the world.

an anonymous seventeenth-century work called "The Mysteries of Love and Eloquence." See Appendix, "Recitation Pieces."

7. A short form of *tableau vivant*, literally "living picture." A tableau is a representation of a personage, character, scene, incident, or such, or of a well-known painting or statue, by one person or group of people in suitable costumes and attitudes, who remain silent and motionless. Faith, hope, and charity are the traditional Christian virtues: "And now abideth faith, hope, charity, these three; but the greatest of these is charity" (Corinthians I 13:13).

8. Light indoor shoes, as opposed to boots. The dressy slippers sent by Josephine Barry are of expensive kid (leather from the hide of a young goat) and elaborately adorned. See p. 274.

9. Boys and girls of the period, especially in rural areas, wore thick, serviceable boots, ankle high and tipped with metal, usually copper, to prevent wear and tear.

10. The creeping spruce *(Picea, Pinaceae)* and fir evergreens were made into flexible garlands used to form letters and words.

11. Not the grand style of organ found in city churches and theatres, but the humble harmonium, a small reed organ operated by a bellows, usually kept going by the furious pedaling of the keyboard artist's feet.

Lucy Maud Montgomery, age fourteen.

CHAPTER XXV

MATTHEW INSISTS ON PUFFED SLEEVES

MATTHEW WAS having a bad ten minutes of it. He had come into the kitchen, in the twilight of a cold, gray December evening, and had sat down in the wood-box corner[1] to take off his heavy boots, unconscious of the fact that Anne and a bevy of her schoolmates were having a practice of *The Fairy Queen* in the sitting-room. Presently they came trooping through the hall and out into the kitchen, laughing and chattering gaily. They did not see Matthew, who shrank bashfully back into the shadows beyond the wood-box with a boot in one hand and a boot-jack[2] in the other, and he watched them shyly for the aforesaid ten minutes as they put on caps and jackets and talked about the dialogue and the concert. Anne stood among them, bright-eyed and animated as they; but Matthew suddenly became conscious that there was something about her different from her mates. And what worried Matthew was that the difference impressed him as being something that should not exist. Anne had a brighter face, and bigger, starrier eyes, and more delicate features than the others; even shy, unobservant Matthew had learned to take note of these things; but the difference that disturbed him did not consist in any of these respects. Then in what did it consist?

1. The part of the room where the wood for the fire and stove were kept.

2. An instrument that provides leverage to assist in taking off one's boots.

Matthew was haunted by this question long after the girls had gone, arm in arm, down the long, hard-frozen lane and Anne had betaken herself to her books. He could not refer it to Marilla, who, he felt, would be quite sure to sniff scornfully and remark that the only difference she saw between Anne and the other girls was that they sometimes kept their tongues quiet while Anne never did. This, Matthew felt, would be no great help.

He had recourse to his pipe that evening to help him study it out, much to Marilla's disgust. After two hours of smoking and hard reflection Matthew arrived at the solution of his problem. Anne was not dressed like the other girls!

The more Matthew thought about the matter the more he was convinced that Anne never had been dressed like the other girls—never since she had come to Green Gables. Marilla kept her clothed in plain, dark dresses, all made after the same unvarying pattern. If Matthew knew there was such a thing as fashion in dress it is as much as he did; but he was quite sure that Anne's sleeves did not look at all like the sleeves the other girls wore. He recalled the cluster of little girls he had seen around her that evening—all gay in waists of red and blue and pink and white—and he wondered why Marilla always kept her so plainly and soberly gowned.

Of course, it must be all right. Marilla knew best and Marilla was bringing her up. Probably some wise inscrutable motive was to be served thereby. But surely it would do no harm to let the child have one pretty dress—something like Diana Barry always wore. Matthew decided that he would give her one; that surely could not be objected to as an unwarranted putting in of his oar. Christmas was only a fortnight off. A nice new dress would be the very thing for a present. Matthew, with a sigh of satisfaction, put away his pipe and went to bed, while Marilla opened all the doors and aired the house.

The very next evening Matthew betook himself to Carmody to buy the dress, determined to get the worst over and

Opposite: The inside of S. A. MacDonald's general store, c. 1900, P.E.I.

have done with it. It would be, he felt assured, no trifling
ordeal. There were some things Matthew could buy and prove
himself no mean bargainer; but he knew he would be at the
mercy of shop-keepers when it came to buying a girl's dress.

After much cogitation Matthew resolved to go to Samuel
Lawson's store instead of William Blair's. To be sure, the Cuthberts always had gone to William Blair's; it was almost as much
a matter of conscience with them as to attend the Presbyterian church and vote Conservative. But William Blair's
two daughters frequently waited on customers there and
Matthew held them in absolute dread. He could contrive to
deal with them when he knew exactly what he wanted and
could point it out; but in such a matter as this, requiring
explanation and consultation, Matthew felt that he must be
sure of a man behind the counter. So he would go to
Lawson's, where Samuel or his son would wait on him.

3. See n. 17, ch. 19.

Alas! Matthew did not know that Samuel, in the recent expansion of his business, had set up a lady clerk also; she was a niece of his wife's and a very dashing young person indeed, with a huge, drooping pompadour, big, rolling brown eyes, and a most extensive and bewildering smile. She was dressed with exceeding smartness and wore several bangle bracelets that glittered and rattled and tinkled with every movement of her hands.[3] Matthew was covered with confusion at finding her there at all; and those bangles completely wrecked his wits at one fell swoop.

"What can I do for you this evening, Mr. Cuthbert?" Miss Lucilla Harris inquired, briskly and ingratiatingly, tapping the counter with both hands.

"Have you any—any—any well now, say any garden rakes?" stammered Matthew.

Miss Harris looked somewhat surprised, as well she might, to hear a man inquiring for garden rakes in the middle of December.

"I believe we have one or two left over," she said, "but they're upstairs in the lumber-room. I'll go and see."

During her absence Matthew collected his scattered senses for another effort.

When Miss Harris returned with the rake and cheerfully inquired: "Anything else to-night, Mr. Cuthbert?" Matthew took his courage in both hands and replied: "Well now, since you suggest it, I might as well—take—that is—look at—buy some—some hayseed."

Miss Harris had heard Matthew Cuthbert called odd. She now concluded he was entirely crazy.

"We only keep hayseed in the spring," she explained loftily. "We've none on hand just now."

"Oh, certainly—certainly—just as you say," stammered unhappy Matthew, seizing the rake and making for the door. At the threshold he recollected that he had not paid for it and he turned miserably back. While Miss Harris was counting out his change he rallied his powers for a final desperate attempt.

"Well now—if it isn't too much trouble—I might as well—that is—I'd like to look at—at—some sugar."

"White or brown?" queried Miss Harris patiently.

"Oh—well now—brown," said Matthew feebly.

"There's a barrel of it over there," said Miss Harris, shaking her bangles at it. "It's the only kind we have."

"I'll—I'll take twenty pounds of it," said Matthew, with beads of perspiration standing on his forehead.

Matthew had driven half-way home before he was his own man again. It had been a gruesome experience, but it served him right, he thought, for committing the heresy of going to a strange store. When he reached home he hid the rake in the tool-house, but the sugar he carried in to Marilla.

"Brown sugar!" exclaimed Marilla. "Whatever possessed you to get so much? You know I never use it except for the hired man's porridge or black fruit-cake. Jerry's gone and I made my cake long ago. It's not good sugar, either—it's coarse and dark—William Blair doesn't usually keep sugar like that."

"I—thought it might come in handy sometime," said Matthew, making good his escape.

When Matthew came to think the matter over he decided that a woman was required to cope with the situation. Marilla was out of the question. Matthew felt sure she would throw cold water on his project at once. Remained only Mrs. Lynde; for of no other woman in Avonlea would Matthew have dared to ask advice. To Mrs. Lynde he went accordingly, and that good lady promptly took the matter out of the harassed man's hands.

"Pick out a dress[4] for you to give Anne? To be sure I will. I'm going to Carmody to-morrow and I'll attend to it. Have you anything in particular in mind? No? Well, I'll just go by my own judgment then. I believe a nice rich brown would just suit Anne, and William Blair has some new gloria[5] in

4. Part of Matthew's trouble lies in the fact that one does not in the rural Avonlea of the late nineteenth century buy a ready-made dress. Mrs. Lynde is offering not only to choose and buy the material but also to go to the trouble of making the garment. See Appendix, "Homemade Artifacts."

5. A closely woven fabric of silk and wool or cotton, used for dresses, umbrella coverings, and so on.

6. A method of finding a fourth number from three other given numbers when the first is in the same proportion to the second as the third is to the unknown: *e.g.*, if 12 / X = 3/4, then X = 16. Also called "the golden rule of proportion."

that's real pretty. Perhaps you'd like me to make it up for her, too, seeing that if Marilla was to make it Anne would probably get wind of it before the time and spoil the surprise? Well, I'll do it. No, it isn't a mite of trouble. I like sewing. I'll make it to fit my niece, Jenny Gillis, for she and Anne are as like as two peas as far as figure goes."

"Well now, I'm much obliged," said Matthew, "and — and — I dunno — but I'd like — I think they make the sleeves different nowadays to what they used to be. If it wouldn't be asking too much I — I'd like them made the new way."

"Puffs? Of course. You needn't worry a speck more about it, Matthew. I'll make it up in the very latest fashion," said Mrs. Lynde. To herself she added when Matthew had gone:

"It'll be a real satisfaction to see that poor child wearing something decent for once. The way Marilla dresses her is positively ridiculous, that's what, and I've ached to tell her so plainly a dozen times. I've held my tongue though, for I can see Marilla doesn't want advice and she thinks she knows more about bringing children up than I do for all she's an old maid. But that's always the way. Folks that has brought up children know that there's no hard and fast method in the world that'll suit every child. But them as never have think it's all as plain and easy as Rule of Three[6] — just set your three terms down so-fashion, and the sum'll work out correct. But flesh and blood don't come under the head of arithmetic and that's where Marilla Cuthbert makes her mistake. I suppose she's trying to cultivate a spirit of humility in Anne by dressing her as she does; but it's more likely to cultivate envy and discontent. I'm sure the child must feel the difference between her clothes and the other girls'. But to think of Matthew taking notice of it! That man is waking up after being asleep for over sixty years."

Marilla knew all the following fortnight that Matthew had something on his mind, but what it was she could not guess, until Christmas Eve, when Mrs. Lynde brought up the new dress. Marilla behaved pretty well on the whole, although it is very likely she distrusted Mrs. Lynde's diplomatic explanation that she had made the dress because Matthew was afraid Anne would find out about it too soon if Marilla made it.

"So this is what Matthew has been looking so mysterious over and grinning about to himself for two weeks, is it?" she said, a little stiffly but tolerantly. "I knew he was up to some foolishness. Well, I must say I don't think Anne needed any more dresses. I made her three good, warm, serviceable ones this fall, and anything more is sheer extravagance. There's enough material in those sleeves alone to make a waist, I declare there is. You'll just pamper Anne's vanity, Matthew, and she's as vain as a peacock now. Well, I hope she'll be satisfied at last, for I know she's been hankering after those silly sleeves ever since they came in, although she never said a word after the first. The puffs have been getting bigger and more ridiculous right along; they're as big as balloons now. Next year anybody who wears them will have to go through a door sideways."

Christmas morning broke on a beautiful white world. It had been a very mild December and people had looked forward to a green Christmas; but just enough snow fell softly in the night to transfigure Avonlea. Anne peeped out from her frosted gable window with delighted eyes. The firs in the Haunted Wood were all feathery and wonderful; the birches and wild cherry-trees were outlined in pearl; the ploughed fields were stretches of snowy dimples; and there was a crisp tang in the air that was glorious. Anne ran downstairs singing until her voice re-echoed through Green Gables.

"Merry Christmas, Marilla! Merry Christmas, Matthew! Isn't it a lovely Christmas? I'm so glad it's white. Any other kind of Christmas doesn't seem real, does it? I don't like green Christmases. They're *not* green—they're just nasty faded browns and grays. What makes people call them green? Why —why—Matthew, is that for me? Oh, Matthew!"

Matthew had sheepishly unfolded the dress from its paper swathings and held it out with a deprecatory glance at Marilla, who feigned to be contemptuously filling the teapot, but nevertheless watched the scene out of the corner of her eye with a rather interested air.

Anne took the dress and looked at it in reverent silence. Oh, how pretty it was—a lovely soft brown gloria with all the gloss of silk; a skirt with dainty frills and shirrings; a waist elaborately pin-tucked in the most fashionable way, with a little ruffle of filmy lace at the neck. But the sleeves—they were the crowning glory! Long elbow cuffs and above them two beautiful puffs divided by rows of shirring and bows of brown silk ribbon.

"That's a Christmas present for you, Anne," said Matthew shyly. "Why—why—Anne, don't you like it? Well now—well now."

For Anne's eyes had suddenly filled with tears.

"*Like* it! Oh, Matthew!" Anne laid the dress over a chair and clasped her hands. "Matthew, it's perfectly exquisite. Oh, I can never thank you enough. Look at those sleeves! Oh, it seems to me this must be a happy dream."

"Well, well, let us have breakfast," interrupted Marilla. "I must say, Anne, I don't think you needed the dress; but since Matthew has got it for you, see that you take good care of it. There's a hair ribbon Mrs. Lynde left for you. It's brown, to match the dress. Come now, sit in."

"I don't see how I'm going to eat breakfast," said Anne rapturously. "Breakfast seems so commonplace at such an exciting moment. I'd rather feast my eyes on that dress. I'm so glad that puffed sleeves are still fashionable. It did seem to me that I'd never get over it if they went out before I had a dress with them. I'd never have felt quite satisfied, you see. It was lovely of Mrs. Lynde to give me the ribbon, too. I feel that I ought to be a very good girl indeed. It's at times like this I'm sorry I'm not a model little girl; and I always resolve that I will be

"But the sleeves—they were the crowning glory!" Illustration by Sybil Tawse, from the 1933 edition.

7. A long, loose heavy overcoat, especially one with a belt; originally made of Irish frieze, hence associated with Ulster, a province of Ireland.

8. From *All's Well That Ends Well*: "It were all one / That I should love a bright particular star" (I.i. l. 97).

in future. But somehow it's hard to carry out your resolutions when irresistible temptations come. Still, I really will make an extra effort after this."

When the commonplace breakfast was over Diana appeared, crossing the white log bridge in the hollow, a gay little figure in her crimson ulster.[7] Anne flew down the slope to meet her.

"Merry Christmas, Diana! And oh, it's a wonderful Christmas. I've something splendid to show you. Matthew has given me the loveliest dress, with *such* sleeves. I couldn't even imagine any nicer."

"I've got something more for you," said Diana breathlessly. "Here — this box. Aunt Josephine sent us out a big box with ever so many things in it — and this is for you. I'd have brought it over last night, but it didn't come until after dark and I never feel very comfortable coming through the Haunted Wood in the dark now."

Anne opened the box and peeped in. First a card with "For the Anne-girl and Merry Christmas," written on it; and then, a pair of the daintiest little kid slippers, with beaded toes and satin bows and glistening buckles.

"Oh," said Anne, "Diana, this is too much. I must be dreaming."

"*I* call it providential," said Diana. "You won't have to borrow Ruby's slippers now, and that's a blessing, for they're two sizes too big for you, and it would be awful to hear a fairy shuffling. Josie Pye would be delighted. Mind you, Rob Wright went home with Gertie Pye from the practice night before last. Did you ever hear anything equal to that?"

All the Avonlea scholars were in a fever of excitement that day, for the hall had to be decorated and a last grand rehearsal held.

The concert came off in the evening and was a pronounced success. The little hall was crowded; all the performers did excellently well, but Anne was the bright particular star[8] of the occasion, as even envy, in the shape of Josie Pye, dared not deny.

"Oh, hasn't it been a brilliant evening?" sighed Anne, when it was all over and she and Diana were walking home together under a dark, starry sky.

"Everything went off very well," said Diana practically. "I guess we must have made as much as ten dollars. Mind you, Mr. Allan is going to send an account of it to the Charlottetown papers."

"Oh, Diana, will we really see our names in print? It makes me thrill to think of it. Your solo was perfectly elegant, Diana. I felt prouder than you did when it was encored. I just said to myself, 'It is my dear bosom friend who is so honoured.'"

"Well, your recitations just brought down the house, Anne. That sad one was simply splendid."

"Oh, I was so nervous, Diana. When Mr. Allan called out my name I really cannot tell how I ever got up on that platform. I felt as if a million eyes were looking at me and through me, and for one dreadful moment I was sure I couldn't begin at all. Then I thought of my lovely puffed sleeves and took courage. I knew that I must live up to those sleeves, Diana. So I started in, and my voice seemed to be coming from ever so far away. I just felt like a parrot. It's providential that I practised those recitations so often up in the garret, or I'd never have been able to get through. Did I groan all right?"

"Yes, indeed, you groaned lovely," assured Diana.

"I saw old Mrs. Sloane wiping away tears when I sat down. It was splendid to think I had touched somebody's heart. It's so romantic to take part in a concert, isn't it? Oh, it's been a very memorable occasion indeed."

"Wasn't the boys' dialogue fine?" said Diana. "Gilbert Blythe was just splendid. Anne, I do think it's awful mean the way you treat Gil. Wait till I tell you. When you ran off the platform after the fairy dialogue one of your roses fell out of your hair. I saw Gil pick it up and put it in his breast-pocket.[9]

9. In *Anne's House of Dreams* (ch. 1), Anne remembers "the first pretty dress I ever had—the brown gloria Matthew gave me for our school concert." Diana in reply conflates the two concerts, the one in which Gilbert recited "Bingen on the Rhine" and the later one in which Anne as a fairy wore the tissue rose he picked up. Diana also thinks the rose was pink, whereas the Anne of *Green Gables* is very clear that she cannot wear pink because of her red hair, and thus wears white roses at the concert. Either Diana forgets, or her author does.

There now. You're so romantic that I'm sure you ought to be pleased at that."

"It's nothing to me what that person does," said Anne loftily. "I simply never waste a thought on him, Diana."

That night Marilla and Matthew, who had been out to a concert for the first time in twenty years, sat for awhile by the kitchen fire after Anne had gone to bed.

"Well now, I guess our Anne did as well as any of them," said Matthew proudly.

"Yes, she did," admitted Marilla. "She's a bright child, Matthew. And she looked real nice, too. I've been kind of opposed to this concert scheme, but I suppose there's no real harm in it after all. Anyhow, I was proud of Anne to-night, although I'm not going to tell her so."

"Well now, I was proud of her and I did tell her so 'fore she went upstairs," said Matthew. "We must see what we can do for her some of these days, Marilla. I guess she'll need something more than Avonlea school by and by."

"There's time enough to think of that," said Marilla. "She's only thirteen in March. Though to-night it struck me she was growing quite a big girl. Mrs. Lynde made that dress a mite too long, and it makes Anne look so tall. She's quick to learn and I guess the best thing we can do for her will be to send her to Queen's after a spell. But nothing need be said about that for a year or two yet."

"Well now, it'll do no harm to be thinking it over off and on," said Matthew. "Things like that are all the better for lots of thinking over."

CHAPTER XXVI

THE STORY CLUB
IS FORMED

JUNIOR AVONLEA found it hard to settle down to humdrum existence again. To Anne in particular things seemed fearfully flat, stale, and unprofitable[1] after the goblet of excitement she had been sipping for weeks. Could she go back to the former quiet pleasures of those faraway days before the concert? At first, as she told Diana, she did not really think she could.

"I'm positively certain, Diana, that life can never be quite the same again as it was in those olden days," she said mournfully, as if referring to a period of at least fifty years back. "Perhaps after awhile I'll get used to it, but I'm afraid concerts spoil people for every-day life. I suppose that is why Marilla disapproves of them. Marilla is such a sensible woman. It must be a great deal better to be sensible; but still, I don't believe I'd really want to be a sensible person, because they are so unromantic. Mrs. Lynde says there is no danger of my ever being one, but you can never tell. I feel just now that I may grow up to be sensible yet. But perhaps that is only because I'm tired. I simply couldn't sleep last night for ever so long. I just lay awake and imagined the concert over and over again. That's one splendid thing about such affairs—it's so lovely to look back to them."

1. Cf. *Hamlet* (I.ii. ll. 129–34):

O that this too too solid flesh
    would melt,
Thaw, and resolve itself into a
    dew!
Or that the Everlasting had not
    fix'd
His canon 'gainst self slaughter!
    O God, O God,
How weary, stale, flat, and
    unprofitable
Seem to me all the uses of this
    world!

2. This quarrel is not made up for many years. In *Anne of the Island*, Ruby remembers how "they quarrelled at the time of the school concert" and tells Anne they have made it up: "She said she'd have spoken years ago, only she thought I wouldn't. And I never spoke to her because I was sure she wouldn't speak to me" (ch. 14).

3. This unfortunate lad has been named after two prominent revivalist preachers, Dwight Lyman Moody (1837–1899) and Charles Haddon Spurgeon (1834–1892). Moody, an evangelist of Massachusetts, started as a shoe salesman, became a preacher, and in 1889 founded the Chicago Bible Institute, later the Moody Bible Institute. He founded religious schools and wrote hymns of widespread popularity, some of which can be found in *Gospel Hymns and Sacred Songs*, edited by Bliss and Sankey. Spurgeon, an English Baptist, was minister of New Park Street Chapel and then the Metropolitan Tabernacle, London, which was built for him. A major force in revived Calvinist thought, Spurgeon published talks and lectures, preached and traveled. Moody Spurgeon is obviously destined by his parents for a career in religious work.

Eventually, however, Avonlea school slipped back into its old groove and took up its old interests. To be sure, the concert left traces. Ruby Gillis and Emma White, who had quarrelled over a point of precedence in their platform seats, no longer sat at the same desk, and a promising friendship of three years was broken up.[2] Josie Pye and Julia Bell did not "speak" for three months, because Josie Pye had told Bessie Wright that Julia Bell's bow when she got up to recite made her think of a chicken jerking its head, and Bessie told Julia. None of the Sloanes would have any dealings with the Bells, because the Bells had declared that the Sloanes had too much to do in the programme, and the Sloanes had retorted that the Bells were not capable of doing the little they had to do properly. Finally, Charlie Sloane fought Moody Spurgeon MacPherson,[3] because Moody Spurgeon had said that Anne Shirley put on airs about her recitations, and Moody Spurgeon was "licked"; consequently, Moody Spurgeon's sister, Ella May, would not "speak" to Anne Shirley all the rest of the winter. With the exception of these trifling frictions, work in Miss Stacy's little kingdom went on with regularity and smoothness.

The winter weeks slipped by. It was an unusually mild winter, with so little snow that Anne and Diana could go to school nearly every day by way of the Birch Path. On Anne's

D. L. Moody's first Sunday-school class in Chicago.

birthday they were tripping lightly down it, keeping eyes and ears alert amid all their chatter, for Miss Stacy had told them that they must soon write a composition on "A Winter's Walk in the Woods," and it behoved them to be observant.

"Just think, Diana, I'm thirteen years old to-day,"[4] remarked Anne in an awed voice. "I can scarcely realize that I'm in my teens. When I woke this morning it seemed to me that everything must be different. You've been thirteen for a month, so I suppose it doesn't seem such a novelty to you as it does to me. It makes life seem so much more interesting. In two more years I'll be really grown up. It's a great comfort to think that I'll be able to use big words then without being laughed at."

"Ruby Gillis says she means to have a beau as soon as she's fifteen," said Diana.

"Ruby Gillis thinks of nothing but beaus," said Anne disdainfully. "She's actually delighted when any one writes her name up in a take-notice for all she pretends to be so mad. But I'm afraid that is an uncharitable speech. Mrs. Allan says we should never make uncharitable speeches; but they do slip out so often before you think, don't they? I simply can't talk about Josie Pye without making an uncharitable speech, so I never mention her at all. You may have noticed that. I'm trying to be as much like Mrs. Allan as I possibly can, for I think she's perfect. Mr. Allan thinks so too. Mrs. Lynde says he just worships the ground she treads on and she doesn't really think it right for a minister to set his affections so much on a mortal being. But then, Diana, even ministers are human and have their besetting sins just like everybody else. I had such an interesting talk with Mrs. Allan about besetting sins[5] last Sunday afternoon. There are just a few things it's proper to talk about on Sundays and that is one of them. My besetting sin is imagining too much and forgetting my duties. I'm striving very hard to overcome it and now that I'm really thirteen perhaps I'll get on better."

4. The date of Anne's birthday is never actually given, but we are repeatedly told it is in March. It would be appropriate for her to have her birthday on March 25, the date celebrated in the Catholic calendar (and formerly in the English legal calendar) as the date of the Annunciation to the Blessed Virgin Mary, or "Lady Day."

5. The sins that beset or surround one with hostile intent and press upon one; thus the sins or faults one is prone to. From the Epistle to the Hebrews: "let us lay aside every weight, and the sin which doth so easily beset us, and let us run with patience the race that is set before us" (Hebrews 12:1).

6. Anne's inspiration for this story is almost certainly "Lady Geraldine's Courtship" by Elizabeth Barrett Browning. Not only is the heroine's name the same — so is the hero's. Anne has added her alter ego, Cordelia, for her own story. Browning's heroine requires only two eight-line stanzas to accept Bertram, whereas Anne's heroine takes an entire page. The story also seems to recall the ending of Eliot's *The Mill on the Floss*, where Tom and Maggie are drowned together in the flood and buried in one grave with a tombstone reading "In Death They Were Not Divided." The phrase ultimately comes from David's lament: "Saul and Jonathan were lovely and pleasant in their lives and in their death they were not divided: they were swifter than eagles, they were stronger than lions" (II Samuel 2:23).

7. An echo of Alfred, Lord Tennyson's *Maude:* "He sets the jewel print of your feet / In violets blue as your eyes" (Part I, XXII, VII, ll. 890–891).

"In four more years we'll be able to put our hair up," said Diana. "Alice Bell is only sixteen and she is wearing hers up, but I think that's ridiculous. I shall wait until I'm seventeen."

"If I had Alice Bell's crooked nose," said Anne decidedly, "I wouldn't — but there! I won't say what I was going to because it was extremely uncharitable. Besides, I was comparing it with my own nose and that's vanity. I'm afraid I think too much about my nose ever since I heard that compliment about it long ago. It really is a great comfort to me. Oh, Diana, look, there's a rabbit. That's something to remember for our woods composition. I really think the woods are just as lovely in winter as in summer. They're so white and still, as if they were asleep and dreaming pretty dreams."

"I won't mind writing that composition when its time comes," sighed Diana. "I can manage to write about the woods, but the one we're to hand in Monday is terrible. The idea of Miss Stacy telling us to write a story out of our own heads!"

"Why, it's as easy as wink," said Anne.

"It's easy for you because you have an imagination," retorted Diana, "but what would you do if you had been born without one? I suppose you have your composition all done?"

Anne nodded, trying hard not to look virtuously complacent and failing miserably.

"I wrote it last Monday evening. It's called 'The Jealous Rival, or In Death Not Divided.'[6] I read it to Marilla and she said it was stuff and nonsense. Then I read it to Matthew and he said it was fine. That is the kind of critic I like. It's a sad, sweet story. I just cried like a child while I was writing it. It's about two beautiful maidens called Cordelia Montmorency and Geraldine Seymour who lived in the same village and were devotedly attached to each other. Cordelia was a regal brunette with a coronet of midnight hair and duskly flashing eyes. Geraldine was a queenly blonde with hair like spun gold and velvety purple eyes."[7]

"I never saw anybody with purple eyes," said Diana dubiously.

"Neither did I. I just imagined them. I wanted something out of the common. Geraldine had an alabaster brow, too. I've found out what an alabaster brow is. That is one of the advantages of being thirteen. You know so much more than you did when you were only twelve."

"Well, what became of Cordelia and Geraldine?" asked Diana, who was beginning to feel rather interested in their fate.

"They grew in beauty side by side until they were sixteen. Then Bertram De Vere came to their native village and fell in love with the fair Geraldine. He saved her life when her horse ran away with her in a carriage, and she fainted in his arms and he carried her home three miles; because, you understand, the carriage was all smashed up. I found it rather hard to imagine the proposal because I had no experience to go by. I asked Ruby Gillis if she knew anything about how men proposed because I thought she'd likely be an authority on the subject, having so many sisters married. Ruby told me she was hid in the hall pantry when Malcolm Andrews proposed to her sister Susan. She said Malcolm told Susan that his dad had given him the farm in his own name and then said, 'What do you say, darling pet, if we get hitched this fall?' And Susan said, 'Yes—no—I don't know—let me see'— and there they were, engaged as quick as that. But I didn't think that sort of a proposal was a very romantic one, so in the end I had to imagine it out as well as I could. I made it very flowery and poetical and Bertram went on his knees although Ruby Gillis says it isn't done nowadays. Geraldine accepted him in a speech a page long. I can tell you I took a lot of trouble with that speech. I rewrote it five times and I look upon it as my masterpiece. Bertram gave her a diamond ring and a ruby necklace and told her they would go to Europe for a wedding tour, for he was immensely wealthy. But then, alas, shadows began to darken over their path. Cordelia

8. "The Story Club was suggested by a little incident of one summer long ago when Jamie Simpson, Amanda Macneill, and I all wrote a story on the same plot. I furnished the plot and I remembered only that it was a very tragic one and the heroine was drowned" (*SJ* II [Jan. 27, 1911]: 43).

was secretly in love with Bertram herself and when Geraldine told her about the engagement she was simply furious, especially when she saw the necklace and the diamond ring. All her affection for Geraldine turned to bitter hate and she vowed that she should never marry Bertram. But she pretended to be Geraldine's friend the same as ever. One evening they were standing on the bridge over a rushing turbulent stream and Cordelia, thinking they were alone, pushed Geraldine over the brink with a wild, mocking, 'Ha, ha, ha.' But Bertram saw it all and he at once plunged into the current, exclaiming, 'I will save thee, my peerless Geraldine.' But alas, he had forgotten he couldn't swim and they were both drowned, clasped in each other's arms. Their bodies were washed ashore soon afterwards. They were buried in the one grave and their funeral was most imposing, Diana. It's so much more romantic to end a story up with a funeral than a wedding. As for Cordelia, she went insane with remorse and was shut up in a lunatic asylum. I thought that was a poetical retribution for her crime."

"How perfectly lovely!" sighed Diana, who belonged to Matthew's school of critics. "I don't see how you can make up such thrilling things out of your own head, Anne. I wish my imagination was as good as yours."

"It would be if you'd only cultivate it," said Anne cheeringly. "I've just thought of a plan, Diana. Let you and I have a story club[8] all our own and write stories for practice. I'll help you along until you can do them by yourself. You ought to cultivate your imagination, you know. Miss Stacy says so. Only we must take the right way. I told her about the Haunted Wood, but she said we went the wrong way about it in that."

This was how the story club came into existence. It was limited to Diana and Anne at first, but soon it was extended to include Jane Andrews and Ruby Gillis and one or two others who felt that their imaginations needed cultivating. No boys were allowed in it—although Ruby Gillis opined that their admission would make it more exciting—and each member had to produce one story a week.

"It's extremely interesting," Anne told Marilla. "Each girl has to read her story out loud and then we talk it over. We are going to keep them all sacredly and have them to read to our descendants. We each write under a nom-de-plume.[9] Mine is Rosamond Montmorency. All the girls do pretty well. Ruby Gillis is rather sentimental. She puts too much love-making into her stories and you know too much is worse than too little. Jane never puts any because she says it makes her feel so silly when she has to read it out aloud. Jane's stories are extremely sensible. Then Diana puts too many murders into hers. She says most of the time she doesn't know what to do with the people so she kills them off to get rid of them. I mostly always have to tell them what to write about, but that isn't hard for I've millions of ideas."

"I think this story-writing business is the foolishest yet," scoffed Marilla. "You'll get a pack of nonsense into your heads and waste time that should be put on your lessons. Reading stories is bad enough but writing them is worse."

"But we're so careful to put a moral into them all, Marilla," explained Anne. "I insist upon that. All the good people are rewarded and all the bad ones are suitably punished. I'm sure that must have a wholesome effect. The moral is the great thing. Mr. Allan says so. I read one of my stories to him and Mrs. Allan and they both agreed that the moral was excellent. Only they laughed in the wrong places. I like it better when people cry. Jane and Ruby almost always cry when I come to the pathetic parts. Diana wrote her Aunt Josephine about our club and her Aunt Josephine wrote back that we were to send her some of our stories. So we copied out four of our very best and sent them. Miss Josephine Barry wrote back that she had never read anything so amusing in her life. That kind of puzzled us because the stories were all very pathetic and almost everybody died. But I'm glad Miss Barry liked

9. Pen name, pseudonym.

them. It shows our club is doing some good in the world. Mrs. Allan says that ought to be our object in everything. I do really try to make it my object but I forget so often when I'm having fun. I hope I shall be a little like Mrs. Allan when I grow up. Do you think there is any prospect of it, Marilla?"

"I shouldn't say there was a great deal," was Marilla's encouraging answer. "I'm sure Mrs. Allan was never such a silly forgetful little girl as you are."

"No; but she wasn't always so good as she is now either," said Anne seriously. "She told me so herself—that is, she said she was a dreadful mischief when she was a girl and was always getting into scrapes. I felt so encouraged when I heard that. Is it very wicked of me, Marilla, to feel encouraged when I hear that other people have been bad and mischievous? Mrs. Lynde says it is. Mrs. Lynde says she always feels shocked when she hears of any one ever having been naughty, no matter how small they were. Mrs. Lynde says she once heard a minister confess that when he was a boy he stole a strawberry tart out of his aunt's pantry and she never had any respect for that minister again. Now, I wouldn't have felt that way. I'd have thought that it was real noble of him to confess it, and I'd have thought what an encouraging thing it would be for small boys nowadays who do naughty things and are sorry for them to know that perhaps they may grow up to be ministers in spite of it. That's how I'd feel, Marilla."

"The way I feel at present, Anne," said Marilla, "is that it's high time you had those dishes washed. You've taken half an hour longer than you should with all your chattering. Learn to work first and talk afterwards."

VANITY AND
VEXATION OF SPIRIT[1]

MARILLA, WALKING home one late April evening from an Aid meeting, realized that the winter was over and gone with the thrill of delight that spring never fails to bring to the oldest and saddest as well as to the youngest and merriest. Marilla was not given to subjective analysis of her thoughts and feelings. She probably imagined that she was thinking about the Aids and their missionary box and the new carpet for the vestry room, but under these reflections was a harmonious consciousness of red fields smoking into pale-purply mists in the declining sun, of long, sharp-pointed fir shadows falling over the meadow beyond the brook, of still, crimson-budded maples around a mirror-like wood-pool, of a wakening in the world and a stir of hidden pulses under the gray sod. The spring was abroad in the land[2] and Marilla's sober, middle-aged step was lighter and swifter because of its deep, primal gladness.

Her eyes dwelt affectionately on Green Gables, peering through its network of trees and reflecting the sunlight back from its windows in several little coruscations of glory. Marilla, as she picked her steps along the damp lane, thought that it was really a satisfaction to know that she was going home to a briskly snapping wood fire and a table nicely spread for

1. "I have seen all the works that are done under the sun; and, behold, all is vanity and vexation of spirit" (Ecclesiastes 1:14).

2. This whole paragraph has subtle echoes of the Song of Solomon: "For lo, the winter is past, the rain is over and gone, and the voice of the turtle [dove] is heard in the land" (Song of Solomon 2:11–12).

3. The archangel especially associated in the Christian tradition with the Annunciation to Mary. See Daniel 9:21, Luke 1:19–20, Luke 1:26–38.

tea, instead of to the cold comfort of old Aid meetings before Anne had come to Green Gables.

Consequently, when Marilla entered her kitchen and found the fire black out, with no sign of Anne anywhere, she felt justly disappointed and irritated. She had told Anne to be sure and have tea ready at five o'clock, but now she must hurry to take off her second-best dress and prepare the meal herself against Matthew's return from ploughing.

"I'll settle Miss Anne when she comes home," said Marilla grimly, as she shaved up kindlings with a carving knife and more vim than was strictly necessary. Matthew had come in and was waiting patiently for his tea in his corner. "She's gadding off somewhere with Diana, writing stories or practising dialogues or some such tomfoolery, and never thinking once about the time or her duties. She's just got to be pulled up short and sudden on this sort of thing. I don't care if Mrs. Allan does say she's the brightest and sweetest child she ever knew. She may be bright and sweet enough, but her head is full of nonsense and there's never any knowing what shape it'll break out in next. Just as soon as she grows out of one freak she takes up with another. But there! Here I am saying the very thing I was so riled with Rachel Lynde for saying at the Aid to-day. I was real glad when Mrs. Allan spoke up for Anne for if she hadn't I know I'd have said something too sharp to Rachel before everybody. Anne's got plenty of faults, goodness knows, and far be it from me to deny it. But I'm bringing her up and not Rachel Lynde, who'd pick faults in the Angel Gabriel[3] himself if he lived in Avonlea. Just the same, Anne has no business to leave the house like this when I told her she was to stay home this afternoon and look after things. I must say, with all her faults, I never found her disobedient or untrustworthy before and I'm real sorry to find her so now."

"Well now, I dunno," said Matthew, who, being patient and

wise and, above all, hungry, had deemed it best to let Marilla talk her wrath out unhindered, having learned by experience that she got through with whatever work was on hand much quicker if not delayed by untimely argument. "Perhaps you're judging her too hasty, Marilla. Don't call her untrustworthy until you're sure she has disobeyed you. Mebbe it can all be explained—Anne's a great hand at explaining."

"She's not here when I told her to stay," retorted Marilla. "I reckon she'll find it hard to explain *that* to my satisfaction. Of course I knew you'd take her part, Matthew. But I'm bringing her up, not you."

It was dark when supper was ready, and still no sign of Anne, coming hurriedly over the log bridge or up Lover's Lane, breathless and repentant with a sense of neglected duties. Marilla washed and put away the dishes grimly. Then, wanting a candle to light her down cellar, she went up to the east gable for the one that generally stood on Anne's table. Lighting it, she turned around to see Anne herself lying on the bed, face downward among the pillows.

"Mercy on us," said astonished Marilla, "have you been asleep, Anne?"

"No," was the muffled reply.

"Are you sick then?" demanded Marilla anxiously, going over to the bed.

Anne cowered deeper into her pillows as if desirous of hiding herself forever from mortal eyes.

"No. But please, Marilla, go away and don't look at me. I'm in the depths of despair and I don't care who gets head in class or writes the best composition or sings in the Sunday-school choir any more. Little things like that are of no importance now because I don't suppose I'll ever be able to go anywhere again. My career is closed. Please, Marilla, go away and don't look at me."

"Did any one ever hear the like?" the mystified Marilla

wanted to know. "Anne Shirley, whatever is the matter with you? What have you done? Get right up this minute and tell me. This minute, I say. There now, what is it?"

Anne had slid to the floor in despairing obedience.

"Look at my hair, Marilla," she whispered.

Accordingly, Marilla lifted her candle and looked scrutinizingly at Anne's hair, flowing in heavy masses down her back. It certainly had a very strange appearance.

"Anne Shirley, what have you done to your hair? Why, it's *green!*"

Green it might be called, if it were any earthly colour—a queer, dull, bronzy green, with streaks here and there of the original red to heighten the ghastly effect. Never in all her life had Marilla seen anything so grotesque as Anne's hair at that moment.

"Yes, it's green," moaned Anne. "I thought nothing could be as bad as red hair. But now I know it's ten times worse to have green hair. Oh, Marilla, you little know how utterly wretched I am."

"I little know how you got into this fix but I mean to find out," said Marilla. "Come right down to the kitchen—it's too cold up here—and tell me just what you've done. I've been expecting something queer for some time. You haven't got into any scrape for over two months and I was sure another one was due. Now, then, what did you do to your hair?"

"I dyed it."

"Dyed it! Dyed your hair! Anne Shirley, didn't you know it was a wicked thing to do?"

"Yes, I knew it was a little wicked," admitted Anne. "But I thought it was worth while to be a little wicked to get rid of red hair. I counted the cost, Marilla. Besides, I meant to be extra good in other ways to make up for it."

"Well," said Marilla sarcastically, "if I'd decided it was worth while to dye my hair I'd have dyed it a decent colour at least. I wouldn't have dyed it green."

"But I didn't mean to dye it green, Marilla," protested Anne dejectedly. "If I was wicked I meant to be wicked to some purpose. He said it would turn my hair a beautiful raven black —he positively assured me that it would. How could I doubt his word, Marilla? I know what it feels like to have your word doubted. And Mrs. Allan says we should never suspect anyone of not telling us the truth unless we have proof that they're not. I have proof now—green hair is proof enough for anybody. But I hadn't then and I believed every word he said *implicitly*."

"Who said? Who are you talking about?"

"The pedlar[4] that was here this afternoon. I bought the dye from him."

"Anne Shirley, how often have I told you never to let one of those Italians[5] in the house! I don't believe in encouraging them to come around at all."

4. A person who goes about carrying small goods for sale, usually in a bundle or pack; a traveling chapman or vendor of small wares.

5. Marilla's prejudices require no exactness; all foreigners look alike to her. There were, however Italian pedlars (or peddlers) and itinerant entertainers in North America, as in England. The villain of *Kilmeny of the Orchard* is the son of "a couple of Italian pack peddlers" (ch. 4).

"Old Pedlar," oil on canvas by William Raphael, 1859.

6. Jews had many reasons—principally the pogroms in Russia, which sent many into Germany and Austro-Hungary and thence abroad—to travel.

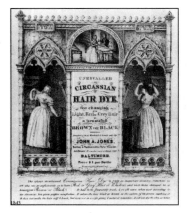

7. The dye is cheap, but the peddler is probably ignorant of the bad effects it could have. The reaction in Anne's case, apparently the effect of the presence of copper oxide, could be the result of chemicals in the dye reacting with elements in local water. Anne's hair probably turned green as copper roofs turn green, with the brightness of her own red hair merely intensifying the effect.

8. Anne is apparently given some portion of the hen-house produce for herself, either eggs or small chickens, which she can then sell.

Advertisement (1843) for Circassian Hair Dye, named after the Circassian women of the Black Sea area.

"Oh, I didn't let him in the house. I remembered what you told me, and I went out, carefully shut the door, and looked at his things on the step. Besides, he wasn't an Italian—he was a German Jew.[6] He had a big box full of very interesting things and he told me he was working hard to make enough money to bring his wife and children out from Germany. He spoke so feelingly about them that it touched my heart. I wanted to buy something from him to help him in such a worthy object. Then all at once I saw the bottle of hair dye. The pedlar said it was warranted to dye any hair a beautiful raven black and wouldn't wash off. In a trice I saw myself with beautiful raven black hair and the temptation was irresistible. But the price of the bottle was seventy-five cents[7] and I had only fifty cents left out of my chicken money.[8] I think the pedlar had a very kind heart, for he said that, seeing it was me, he'd sell it for fifty cents and that was just giving it away. So I bought it, and as soon as he had gone I came up here and applied it with an old hair-brush as the directions said. I used up the whole bottle, and oh, Marilla, when I saw the dreadful colour it turned my hair I repented of being wicked, I can tell you. And I've been repenting ever since."

"Well, I hope you'll repent to good purpose," said Marilla severely, "and that you've got your eyes opened to where your vanity has led you, Anne. Goodness knows what's to be done. I suppose the first thing is to give your hair a good washing and see if that will do any good."

Accordingly, Anne washed her hair, scrubbing it vigorously with soap and water, but for all the difference it made she might as well have been scouring its original red. The pedlar had certainly spoken the truth when he declared that the dye wouldn't wash off, however his veracity might be impeached in other respects.

"Oh, Marilla, what shall I do?" questioned Anne in tears. "I can never live this down. People have pretty well forgotten my other mistakes—the liniment cake and setting Diana drunk and flying into a temper with Mrs. Lynde. But they'll never forget this. They will think I am not respectable. Oh, Marilla, 'what a tangled web we weave when first we practise to deceive!'[9] That is poetry, but it is true. And oh, how Josie Pye will laugh! Marilla, I *cannot* face Josie Pye. I am the unhappiest girl in Prince Edward Island."

Anne's unhappiness continued for a week. During that time she went nowhere and shampooed her hair every day. Diana alone of outsiders knew the fatal secret, but she promised solemnly never to tell and it may be stated here and now that she kept her word. At the end of the week Marilla said decidedly:

"It's no use, Anne. That is fast dye if ever there was any. Your hair must be cut off; there is no other way. You can't go out with it looking like that."

Anne's lips quivered, but she realized the bitter truth of Marilla's remarks. With a dismal sigh she went for the scissors.

"Please cut it off at once, Marilla, and have it over. Oh, I feel that my heart is broken. This is such an unromantic affliction. The girls in books lose their hair in fevers or sell it to get money for some good deed,[10] and I'm sure I wouldn't mind losing my hair in some such fashion half so much. But there is nothing comforting in having your hair cut off because you've dyed it a dreadful colour, is there? I'm going to weep all the time you're cutting it off, if it won't interfere. It seems such a tragic thing."

Anne wept then, but later on, when she went upstairs and looked in the glass, she was calm with despair. Marilla had done her work thoroughly and it had been necessary to shingle the hair as closely as possible. The result was not becoming, to state the case as mildly as may be. Anne promptly turned her glass to the wall.

"I'll never, never look at myself again until my hair grows," she exclaimed passionately.

Then she suddenly righted the glass.

9. From Sir Walter Scott's *Marmion* (Canto 6, "The Battle," Stanza 17). A later book (1931) by Montgomery bears the title *A Tangled Web*.

10. The most famous case of a girl who sells her hair as a good deed is that of Jo March, in Alcott's *Little Women* (1868), who sells her hair so that her father can be helped in hospital and assisted on his journey home: "It will do my brains good to have that mop taken off; my head feels deliciously light and cool, and the barber said I could soon have a curly crop, which will be boyish, becoming, and easy to keep in order" (ch. 15). In 1900 Montgomery wrote in her journal, "The Alcott stories . . . I read in my teens and have a liking for yet" (*SJ* I: 252). The O. Henry story, "The Gift of the Magi," in which the heroine sells her hair to buy a watch fob for her husband, was published in 1904. Among the girls losing their hair from fever is Pat Gardiner, who loses hers to scarlet fever (*Pat of Silver Bush*, ch. 26).

11. In Scottish use, a distinguishing hairband worn by unmarried women. In the medieval fashion, a hairnet or fabric bag holding the hair.

"Yes, I will, too. I'll do penance for being wicked that way. I'll look at myself every time I come to my room and see how ugly I am. And I won't try to imagine it away, either. I never thought I was vain about my hair, of all things, but now I know I was, in spite of its being red, because it was so long and thick and curly. I expect something will happen to my nose next."

Anne's clipped head made a sensation in school on the following Monday, but to her relief nobody guessed the real reason for it, not even Josie Pye, who, however, did not fail to inform Anne that she looked like a perfect scarecrow.

"I didn't say anything when Josie said that to me," Anne confided that evening to Marilla, who was lying on the sofa after one of her headaches, "because I thought it was part of my punishment and I ought to bear it patiently. It's hard to be told you look like a scarecrow and I wanted to say something back. But I didn't. I just swept her one scornful look and then I forgave her. It makes you feel very virtuous when you forgive people, doesn't it? I mean to devote all my energies to being good after this and I shall never try to be beautiful again. Of course it's better to be good. I know it is, but it's sometimes so hard to believe a thing even when you know it. I do really want to be good, Marilla, like you and Mrs. Allan and Miss Stacy, and grow up to be a credit to you. Diana says when my hair begins to grow to tie a black velvet ribbon around my head with a bow at one side. She says she thinks it will be very becoming. I will call it a snood[11]—that sounds so romantic. But am I talking too much, Marilla? Does it hurt your head?"

"My head is better now. It was terrible bad this afternoon, though. These headaches of mine are getting worse and worse. I'll have to see a doctor about them. As for your chatter, I don't know that I mind it—I've got so used to it."

Which was Marilla's way of saying that she liked to hear it.

CHAPTER XXVIII

AN UNFORTUNATE LILY MAID[1]

"OF COURSE YOU must be Elaine,[2] Anne," said Diana. "I could never have the courage to float down there."

"Nor I," said Ruby Gillis with a shiver. "I don't mind floating down when there's two or three of us in the flat and we can sit up. It's fun then. But to lie down and pretend I was dead—I just couldn't. I'd die really of fright."

"Of course it would be romantic," conceded Jane Andrews. "But I know I couldn't keep still. I'd be popping up every minute or so to see where I was and if I wasn't drifting too far out. And you know, Anne, that would spoil the effect."

"But it's so ridiculous to have a red-headed Elaine," mourned Anne. "I'm not afraid to float down and I'd *love* to be Elaine. But it's ridiculous just the same. Ruby ought to be Elaine because she is so fair and has such lovely long golden hair—Elaine had 'all her bright hair streaming down,' you know. And Elaine was the lily maid. Now, a red-haired person cannot be a lily maid."

"Your complexion is just as fair as Ruby's," said Diana earnestly, "and your hair is ever so much darker than it used to be before you cut it."

1. From Alfred, Lord Tennyson's, phrase "Elaine, the lily maid of Astolat" in "Lancelot and Elaine," (*Idylls of the King*, 1859, l. 2).

2. In Tennyson's *Idylls of the King*, based on Malory's *Morte d'Arthur*, Elaine dies of hopeless love for Lancelot, who is attached to Queen Guinevere, the wife of King Arthur. Montgomery writes in her journal: "I detest Tennyson's *Arthur*! If I'd been Guinevere I'd have been unfaithful to him too. But not for *Lancelot*—he is just as unbearable in another way. As for Geraint, if I'd been Enid I'd have *bitten* him" (*SJ* I [Sept. 1909]: 358). Anne and her friends are basing their game upon the following passage in the *Idylls* (ll. 1130–1154):

> But when the next sun brake
> from underground,
> Then those two brethren slowly
> with bent brows
> Accompanying, the sad chariot-
> bier
> Past like a shadow thro' the
> field, that shone

Full-summer, to that stream
  whereon the barge,
Pall'd all its length in blackest
  samite, lay.
There sat the lifelong creature
  of the house,
Loyal, the dumb old servitor, on
  deck
Winking his eyes, and twisted all
  his face.
So those two brethren from the
  chariot took
And on the black decks laid her
  in the bed,
Set in her hand a lily, o'er her
  hung
The silken case with braided
  blazonings,
And kiss'd her quiet brows, and
  saying to her
"Sister, farewell for ever," and
  again
"Farewell, sweet sister," parted
  all in tears.
Then rose the old dumb servitor, and the dead,
Oar'd by the dumb, went
  upward with the flood—
In her right hand the lily, in her
  left
The letter—all her bright hair
  streaming down—

"Oh, do you really think so?" exclaimed Anne, flushing sensitively with delight. "I've sometimes thought it was myself—but I never dared to ask any one for fear she would tell me it wasn't. Do you think it could be called auburn now, Diana?"

"Yes, and I think it is real pretty," said Diana, looking admiringly at the short silky curls that clustered over Anne's head and were held in place by a very jaunty black velvet ribbon and bow.

They were standing on the bank of the pond, below Orchard Slope, where a little headland fringed with birches ran out from the bank; at its tip was a small wooden platform built out into the water for the convenience of fishermen and duck hunters. Ruby and Jane were spending the midsummer afternoon with Diana, and Anne had come over to play with them.

Anne and Diana had spent most of their playtime that summer on and about the pond. Idlewild was a thing of the past, Mr. Bell having ruthlessly cut down the little circle of trees in his back pasture in the spring. Anne had sat among the stumps and wept, not without an eye to the romance of it; but she was speedily consoled, for, after all, as she and Diana said, big girls of thirteen, going on fourteen, were too old for such childish amusements as play-houses, and there were more fascinating sports to be found about the pond. It was

splendid to fish for trout over the bridge and the two girls learned to row themselves about in the little flat-bottomed dory[3] Mr. Barry kept for duck shooting.

It was Anne's idea that they dramatize Elaine. They had studied Tennyson's poem in school the previous winter, the Superintendent of Education having prescribed it in the English course for the Prince Edward Island Schools. They had analyzed it and parsed it and torn it to pieces in general until it was a wonder there was any meaning at all left in it for them, but at least the fair lily maid and Lancelot and Guinevere and King Arthur had become very real people to them, and Anne was devoured by secret regret that she had not been born in Camelot.[4] Those days, she said, were so much more romantic than the present.

Anne's plan was hailed with enthusiasm. The girls had discovered that if the flat[5] were pushed off from the landing-place it would drift down with the current under the bridge and finally strand itself on another headland lower down which ran out at a curve in the pond. They had often gone down like this and nothing could be more convenient for playing Elaine.

"Well, I'll be Elaine," said Anne, yielding reluctantly, for, although she would have been delighted to play the principal character, yet her artistic sense demanded fitness for it and this, she felt, her limitations made impossible. "Ruby, you must be King Arthur and Jane will be Guinevere and Diana must be Lancelot. But first you must be the brothers and the father. We can't have the old dumb servitor[6] because there isn't room for two in the flat when one is lying down. We must pall[7] the barge all its length in blackest samite.[8] That old black shawl of your mother's will be just the thing, Diana."

The black shawl having been procured, Anne spread it over the flat and then lay down on the bottom, with closed eyes and hands folded over her breast.

And all the coverlid was cloth of
  gold
Drawn to her waist, and she
  herself in white
All but her face, and that clear-
  featured face
Was lovely, for she did not seem
  as dead,
But fast asleep, and lay as tho'
  she smiled.

This erotic scene was a favorite subject of artists of the Pre-Raphaelite Brotherhood such as Ernest Normand and Briton Riviere.

3. A small flat-bottomed rowboat used in sea fishing to go out from a larger vessel or alongshore, or in lakes and ponds.

4. The legendary home of King Arthur and his court, associated with an actual site near Glastonbury, England, and with Winchester.

5. Short for flat-bottomed dory. See n. 3.

6. "Dumb" in the sense of mute, not stupid. *Servitor* is an archaic term for manservant. See the Tennyson quotation in n. 2.

7. To cover with a cloak, especially a heavy cloth of mourning.

8. See the Tennyson quotation in n. 2. Samite is a rich silk fabric sometimes interwoven with gold.

Opposite: Park Corner Bridge.

9. An oblong piece of imported silk to drape over a piano. The vogue for Japanese styles in objects was increasing in the 1880s and 1890s; witness Gilbert and Sullivan's *The Mikado* (1885).

10. A sharp-pointed stick, presumably manmade, set into the earth or mud.

11. Also "batten," "a bar or strip nailed or glued across parallel boards to hold them together, or prevent warping."

"Oh, she does look really dead," whispered Ruby Gillis nervously, watching the still, white little face under the flickering shadows of the birches. "It makes me feel frightened, girls. Do you suppose it's really right to act like this? Mrs. Lynde says that all play-acting is abominably wicked."

"Ruby, you shouldn't talk about Mrs. Lynde," said Anne severely. "It spoils the effect because this is hundreds of years before Mrs. Lynde was born. Jane, you arrange this. It's silly for Elaine to be talking when she's dead."

Jane rose to the occasion. Cloth of gold for coverlet there was none, but an old piano scarf[9] of yellow Japanese crape was an excellent substitute. A white lily was not obtainable just then, but the effect of a tall blue iris placed in one of Anne's folded hands was all that could be desired.

"Now, she's all ready," said Jane. "We must kiss her quiet brows and, Diana, you say, 'Sister, farewell for ever,' and Ruby, you say, 'Farewell, sweet sister,' both of you as sorrowfully as you possibly can. Anne, for goodness sake smile a little. You know Elaine 'lay as though she smiled.' That's better. Now push the flat off."

The flat was accordingly pushed off, scraping roughly over an old embedded stake[10] in the process. Diana and Jane and Ruby only waited long enough to see it caught in the current and headed for the bridge before scampering up through the woods, across the road, and down to the lower headland where, as Lancelot and Guinevere and the King, they were to be in readiness to receive the lily maid.

For a few minutes Anne, drifting slowly down, enjoyed the romance of her situation to the full. Then something happened not at all romantic. The flat began to leak. In a very few moments it was necessary for Elaine to scramble to her feet, pick up her cloth of gold coverlet and pall of blackest samite and gaze blankly at a big crack in the bottom of her barge through which the water was literally pouring. That sharp stake at the landing had torn off the strip of batting[11] nailed on the flat. Anne did not know this, but it did not take her long to realize that she was in a dangerous plight. At this rate the flat would fill and sink long before it could drift to the lower headland. Where were the oars? Left behind at the landing!

Anne gave one gasping little scream which nobody ever heard; she was white to the lips, but she did not lose her self-possession. There was one chance — just one.

"I was horribly frightened," she told Mrs. Allan the next day, "and it seemed like years while the flat was drifting down to the bridge and the water rising in it every moment. I prayed, Mrs. Allan, most earnestly, but I didn't shut my eyes to pray, for I knew the only way God could save me was to let the flat float close enough to one of the bridge piles[12] for me to climb up on it. You know the piles are just old tree trunks and there are lots of knots and old branch stubs[13] on them. It was proper to pray, but I had to do my part by watching out and right well I knew it. I just said, 'Dear God, please take the flat close to a pile and I'll do the rest,' over and over again. Under such circumstances you don't think much about making a flowery prayer. But mine was answered, for the flat bumped right into a pile for a minute and I flung the scarf and the shawl over my shoulder and scrambled up on a big Providential stub. And there I was, Mrs. Allan, clinging to that slippery old pile with no way of getting up or down. It was a very unromantic position, but I didn't think about that at the time. You don't think much about romance when you have just escaped from a watery grave. I said a grateful prayer at once and then I gave all my attention to holding on tight, for I knew I should probably have to depend on human aid to get back to dry land."

The flat drifted under the bridge and then promptly sank in midstream. Ruby, Jane, and Diana, already awaiting it on the lower headland, saw it disappear before their very eyes and had not a doubt but that Anne had gone down with it. For a

12. The piers or pillars of a bridge.

13. Stubs of branches left on a tree when the branches are cut off.

moment they stood still, white as sheets, frozen with horror at the tragedy; then, shrieking at the tops of their voices, they started on a frantic run up through the woods, never pausing as they crossed the main road to glance the way of the bridge. Anne, clinging desperately to her precarious foothold, saw their flying forms and heard their shrieks. Help would soon come, but meanwhile her position was a very uncomfortable one.

The minutes passed by, each seeming an hour to the unfortunate lily maid. Why didn't somebody come? Where had the girls gone? Suppose they had fainted, one and all! Suppose nobody ever came! Suppose she grew so tired and cramped that she could hold on no longer! Anne looked at the wicked green depths below her, wavering with long, oily shadows, and shivered. Her imagination began to suggest all manner of gruesome possibilities to her.

Then, just as she thought she really could not endure the ache in her arms and wrists another moment, Gilbert Blythe came rowing under the bridge in Harmon Andrews' dory!

Gilbert glanced up and, much to his amazement, beheld a little white scornful face looking down upon him with big, frightened but also scornful gray eyes.

"Anne Shirley! How on earth did you get there?" he exclaimed.

Without waiting for an answer he pulled close to the pile and extended his hand. There was no help for it; Anne, clinging to Gilbert Blythe's hand, scrambled down into the dory, where she sat, drabbled and furious, in the stern with her arms full of dripping shawl and wet crape. It was certainly extremely difficult to be dignified under the circumstances!

"What has happened, Anne?" asked Gilbert, taking up his oars.

"We were playing Elaine," explained Anne frigidly, without even looking at her rescuer, "and I had to drift down to Camelot in the barge—I mean the flat. The flat began to leak and

"He pulled close to the pile and extended his hand." Illustration by Elizabeth R. Withington, from the 1931 edition.

I climbed out on the pile. The girls went for help. Will you be kind enough to row me to the landing?"

Gilbert obligingly rowed to the landing and Anne, disdaining assistance, sprang nimbly on shore.

"I'm very much obliged to you," she said haughtily as she turned away. But Gilbert had also sprung from the boat and now laid a detaining hand on her arm.

"Anne," he said hurriedly, "look here. Can't we be good friends? I'm awfully sorry I made fun of your hair that time. I didn't mean to vex you and I only meant it for a joke. Besides, it's so long ago. I think your hair is awfully pretty now —honest I do. Let's be friends."

For a moment Anne hesitated. She had an odd, newly-awakened consciousness under all her outraged dignity that the half-shy, half-eager expression in Gilbert's hazel eyes was something that was very good to see. Her heart gave a quick, queer little beat. But the bitterness of her old grievance promptly stiffened up her wavering determination. That scene of two years before flashed back into her recollection as vividly as if it had taken place yesterday. Gilbert had called her "Carrots" and had brought about her disgrace before the whole school. Her resentment, which to other and older people might be as laughable as its cause, was in no whit allayed and softened by time seemingly. She hated Gilbert Blythe! She would never forgive him.

"No," she said coldly, "I shall never be friends with you, Gilbert Blythe; and I don't want to be!"

"All right!" Gilbert sprang into his skiff with an angry colour in his cheeks. "I'll never ask you to be friends again, Anne Shirley. And I don't care either!"

He pulled away with swift defiant strokes, and Anne went up the steep, ferny little path under the maples. She held her head very high, but she was conscious of an odd feeling of regret. She almost wished she had answered Gilbert differently. Of course, he had insulted her terribly, but still—! Altogether, Anne rather thought it would be a relief to sit down and have a good cry. She was really quite unstrung, for the reaction from her fright and cramped clinging was making itself felt.

Half-way up the path she met Jane and Diana rushing back to the pond in a state narrowly removed from positive frenzy. They had found nobody at Orchard Slope, both Mr. and Mrs. Barry being away. Here Ruby Gillis had succumbed to hysterics, and was left to recover from them as best she might, while Jane and Diana flew through the Haunted Wood and across the brook to Green Gables. There they had found nobody either, for Marilla had gone to Carmody and Matthew was making hay in the back field.

"Oh, Anne," gasped Diana, fairly falling on the former's neck and weeping with relief and delight, "Oh, Anne—we thought—you were—drowned—and we felt like murderers—because we had made—you be—Elaine. And Ruby is in hysterics—oh, Anne, how did you escape?"

"I climbed up on one of the piles," explained Anne wearily, "and Gilbert Blythe came along in Mr. Andrews' dory and brought me to land."

"Oh, Anne, how splendid of him! Why, it's so romantic!" said Jane, finding breath enough for utterance at last. "Of course you'll speak to him after this."

"Of course I won't," flashed Anne with a momentary return of her old spirit. "And I don't want ever to hear the word romantic again, Jane Andrews. I'm awfully sorry you were so frightened, girls. It is all my fault. I feel sure I was born under an unlucky star.[14] Everything I do gets me or my dearest friends into a scrape. We've gone and lost your father's flat, Diana, and I have a presentiment[15] that we'll not be allowed to row on the pond any more."

Anne's presentiment proved more trustworthy than presen-

14. Poetic use of the old astrological belief that the position of the stars at the moment of birth determines one's temperament and destiny; e.g., "My third comfort (starr'd) most unluckily" (The Winter's Tale; III.viii l. 98). Compare also the epigraph from Browning.

15. An intuitive feeling about something that will happen in the future; a foreboding or an anticipation.

16. From Tennyson's "The Lady of Shalott": "In the stormy east-wind straining, / The pale yellow woods were waning, / The broad stream in his banks complaining / Heavily the low sky raining / Over tower'd Camelot" (Pt. IV, ll. 118–22).

timents are apt to do. Great was the consternation in the Barry and Cuthbert households when the events of the afternoon became known.

"Will you *ever* have any sense, Anne?" groaned Marilla.

"Oh, yes, I think I will, Marilla," returned Anne optimistically. A good cry, indulged in the grateful solitude of the east gable, had soothed her nerves and restored her to her wonted cheerfulness. "I think my prospects of becoming sensible are brighter now than ever."

"I don't see how," said Marilla.

"Well," explained Anne, "I've learned a new and valuable lesson to-day. Ever since I came to Green Gables I've been making mistakes, and each mistake has helped to cure me of some great shortcoming. The affair of the amethyst brooch cured me of meddling with things that didn't belong to me. The Haunted Wood mistake cured me of letting my imagination run away with me. The liniment cake mistake cured me of carelessness in cooking. Dyeing my hair cured me of vanity. I never think about my hair and nose now—at least, very seldom. And today's mistake is going to cure me of being too romantic. I have come to the conclusion that it is no use trying to be romantic in Avonlea. It was probably easy enough in towered Camelot[16] hundreds of years ago, but romance is not appreciated now. I feel quite sure that you will soon see a great improvement in me in this respect, Marilla."

"I'm sure I hope so," said Marilla skeptically.

But Matthew, who had been sitting mutely in his corner, laid a hand on Anne's shoulder when Marilla had gone out.

"Don't give up all your romance, Anne," he whispered shyly. "A little of it is a good thing—not too much, of course—but keep a little of it, Anne, keep a little of it."

CHAPTER XXIX

AN EPOCH[1]
IN ANNE'S LIFE

 ANNE WAS bringing the cows home from the back pasture by way of Lover's Lane. It was a September evening and all the gaps and clearings in the woods were brimmed up with ruby sunset light. Here and there the lane was splashed with it, but for the most part it was already quite shadowy beneath the maples, and the spaces under the firs were filled with a clear violet dusk like airy wine. The winds were out in their tops, and there is no sweeter music on earth than that which the wind makes in the fir-trees at evening.

The cows swung placidly down the lane, and Anne followed them dreamily, repeating aloud the battle canto from *Marmion*[2]—which had also been part of their English course the preceding winter and which Miss Stacy had made them learn off by heart—and exulting in its rushing lines and the clash of spears in its imagery. When she came to the lines:

> The stubborn spearsmen still made good
> Their dark impenetrable wood,[3]

she stopped in ecstasy to shut her eyes that she might the better fancy herself one of that heroic ring.

1. "The beginning of a new era, or a distinctive period in the history of anything."

2. See n. 4, ch. 2.

3. From *Marmion* (Canto 6, Stanza 34, ll. 12–13).

4. Church weddings were insisted upon by Anglicans, but other English Protestant denominations preferred to conduct weddings at home. After the Restoration, English Protestants who wanted a church wedding would have been compelled to marry in Anglican churches. Church weddings became law in England, though not in Scotland, with Hardwick's Marriage Act of 1753. Home weddings were customary in middle-class North American Protestant families. Meg March, for instance, is married to John Brooks at home. See Montgomery's story "Aunt Philippa and the Men" (1915), in which the crotchety aunt insists, "You write to your young man to come here and be married respectable under my roof, same as a Goodwin ought to" (*At the Altar*, 13). Compare also Anne's wedding at Green Gables in *Anne's House of Dreams:* "They were married in the sunshine of the old orchard" (ch. 4). Maud Montgomery and Ewan MacDonald were married in the parlor at Park Corner, with about 20 guests present. See illustration.

5. The Charlottetown Exhibition, established in 1879, moved to grounds outside the city in 1890,

Parlour at Park Corner where Montgomery was married.

When she opened them again it was to behold Diana coming through the gate that led into the Barry field and looking so important that Anne instantly divined there was news to be told. But betray too eager curiosity she would not.

"Isn't this evening just like a purple dream, Diana? It makes me so glad to be alive. In the mornings I always think the mornings are best; but when evening comes I think it's lovelier still."

"It's a very fine evening," said Diana, "but oh, I have such news, Anne. Guess. You can have three guesses."

"Charlotte Gillis is going to be married in the church[4] after all and Mrs. Allan wants us to decorate it," cried Anne.

"No. Charlotte's beau won't agree to that, because nobody ever has been married in the church yet, and he thinks it would seem too much like a funeral. It's too mean, because it would be such fun. Guess again."

"Jane's mother is going to let her have a birthday party?"

Diana shook her head, her black eyes dancing with merriment.

"I can't think what it can be," said Anne in despair, "unless it's that Moody Spurgeon MacPherson saw you home from prayer-meeting last night. Did he?"

"I should think not," exclaimed Diana indignantly. "I wouldn't be likely to boast of it if he did, the horrid creature! I knew you couldn't guess it. Mother had a letter from Aunt Josephine to-day, and Aunt Josephine wants you and me to go to town next Tuesday and stop with her for the Exhibition.[5] There!"

"Oh, Diana," whispered Anne, finding it necessary to lean up against a maple-tree for support, "do you really mean it? But I'm afraid Marilla won't let me go. She will say that she can't encourage gadding about. That was what she said last week when Jane invited me to go with them in their double-seated buggy to the American concert at the White Sands Hotel. I wanted to go, but Marilla said I'd be better at home learning my lessons and so would Jane. I was bitterly disappointed, Diana. I felt so heart-broken that I wouldn't say my prayers when I went to bed. But I repented of that and got up in the middle of the night and said them."

"I'll tell you," said Diana, "we'll get mother to ask Marilla. She'll be more likely to let you go then; and if she does we'll have the time of our lives, Anne. I've never been to an Exhibition, and it's so aggravating to hear the other girls talking about their trips. Jane and Ruby have been twice, and they're going this year again."

"I'm not going to think about it at all until I know whether I can go or not," said Anne resolutely. "If I did and then was disappointed, it would be more than I could bear. But in case I do go I'm very glad my new coat will be ready by that time. Marilla didn't think I needed a new coat. She said my old one would do very well for another winter and that I ought to be satisfied with having a new dress. The dress is

but within the city, three blocks from Prince of Wales College, there were horse and cattle parades and Scottish dancing (*SJ* I: 401, note). Like the U.S. state fairs, Provincial exhibitions served—and continue to serve—agricultural communities, displaying new breeds of livestock, and new farm equipment, etc. Held after the main work of harvesting was done (in Charlottetown in the last week of September and the beginning of October), exhibitions attracted large crowds, and competitions drew aspirants provincewide. They also presented cultural events. As Montgomery writes (Oct. 7, 1900), "Last week I betook myself to Ch'Town to attend the Exhibition and get my gray matter stirred up a bit. We would get too mossy if we stayed always in the same place!" (*SJ* I: 253).

6. A fine grade of woolen cloth.

7. A typical head-covering for a child of either sex during the Victorian era.

very pretty, Diana—navy blue and made so fashionably. Marilla always makes my dresses fashionably now, because she says she doesn't intend to have Matthew going to Mrs. Lynde to make them. I'm so glad. It is ever so much easier to be good if your clothes are fashionable. At least, it is easier for me. I suppose it doesn't make such a difference to naturally good people. But Matthew said I must have a new coat, so Marilla bought a lovely piece of blue broadcloth,[6] and it's being made by a real dressmaker over at Carmody. It's to be done Saturday night, and I'm trying not to imagine myself walking up the church aisle on Sunday in my new suit and cap, because I'm afraid it isn't right to imagine such things. But it just slips into my mind in spite of me. My cap is so pretty. Matthew bought it for me the day we were over at Carmody. It is one of those little blue velvet ones that are all the rage, with gold cord and tassels.[7] Your new hat is elegant, Diana, and so becoming. When I saw you come into church last Sunday my heart swelled with pride to think you were my dearest friend. Do you suppose it's wrong for us to think so much about our clothes? Marilla says it is very sinful. But it *is* such an interesting subject, isn't it?"

Marilla agreed to let Anne go to town, and it was arranged that Mr. Barry should take the girls in on the following Tuesday. As Charlottetown was thirty miles away and Mr. Barry wished to go and return the same day, it was necessary to make a very early start. But Anne counted it all joy, and was up before sunrise on Tuesday morning. A glance from her window assured her that the day would be fine, for the eastern sky behind the firs of the Haunted Wood was all silvery and cloudless. Through the gap in the trees a light was shining in the western gable of Orchard Slope, a token that Diana was also up.

Anne was dressed by the time Matthew had the fire on, and had the breakfast ready when Marilla came down, but for her

own part was much too excited to eat. After breakfast the
jaunty new cap and jacket were donned, and Anne hastened
over the brook and up through the firs to Orchard Slope. Mr.
Barry and Diana were waiting for her, and they were soon on
the road.

It was a long drive, but Anne and Diana enjoyed every
minute of it. It was delightful to rattle along over the moist
roads in the early red sunlight that was creeping across the
shorn harvest fields. The air was fresh and crisp, and little
smoke-blue mists curled through the valleys and floated off
from the hills. Sometimes the road went through woods
where maples were beginning to hang out scarlet banners;
sometimes it crossed rivers on bridges that made Anne's flesh
cringe with the old, half-delightful fear; sometimes it wound
along a harbour shore and passed by a little cluster of weather-
gray fishing huts; again it mounted to hills whence a far sweep
of curving upland or misty blue sky could be seen; but wherever it went there was much of interest to discuss. It was
almost noon when they reached town and found their way to
Beechwood. It was quite a fine old mansion, set back from
the street in a seclusion of green elms and branching beeches.
Miss Barry met them at the door with a twinkle in her sharp
black eyes.

"So you've come to see me at last, you Anne-girl," she said.
"Mercy, child, how you have grown! You're taller than I am, I
declare. And you're ever so much better-looking than you
used to be, too. But I dare say you know that without being
told."

"Indeed I didn't," said Anne radiantly. "I know I'm not so
freckled as I used to be, so I've much to be thankful for, but I
really hadn't dared to hope there was any other improvement.
I'm so glad you think there is, Miss Barry."

Miss Barry's house was furnished with "great magnifi-
cence," as Anne told Marilla afterwards. The two little country

8. See n. 2, ch. 17; see also Appendix, "Homemade Artifacts."

9. A variety of dessert apple with large fruit and a yellow, red-streaked skin (see *Apple Varieties Descriptions,* comp. Daryl Hunter).

girls were rather abashed by the splendour of the parlour where Miss Barry left them when she went to see about dinner.

"Isn't it just like a palace?" whispered Diana. "I never was in Aunt Josephine's house before, and I'd no idea it was so grand. I just wish Julia Bell could see this—she puts on such airs about her mother's parlour."

"Velvet carpet," sighed Anne luxuriously, "*and* silk curtains! I've dreamed of such things, Diana. But do you know I don't believe I feel very comfortable with them after all. There are so many things in this room and all so splendid that there is no scope for imagination. That is one consolation when you are poor—there are so many more things you can imagine about."

Their sojourn in town was something that Anne and Diana dated from for years. From first to last it was crowded with delights.

On Wednesday Miss Barry took them to the Exhibition grounds and kept them there all day.

"It was splendid," Anne related to Marilla later on. "I never imagined anything so interesting. I don't really know which department was the most interesting. I think I liked the horses and the flowers and the fancy work best. Josie Pye took first prize for knitted lace.[8] I was real glad she did. And I was glad that I felt glad, for it shows I'm improving, don't you think, Marilla, when I can rejoice in Josie's success? Mr. Harmon Andrews took second prize for Gravenstein apples[9] and Mr. Bell took first prize for a pig. Diana said she thought it was ridiculous for a Sunday-school superintendent to take a prize in pigs, but I don't see why. Do you? She said she would always think of it after this when he was praying so solemnly. Clara Louise MacPherson took a prize for painting, and Mrs. Lynde got first prize for home-made butter and cheese. So Avonlea was pretty well represented, wasn't it? Mrs. Lynde was there that day, and I never knew how much I really liked her until I saw her familiar face among all those strangers. There were thousands of people there, Marilla. It made me feel dreadfully insignificant. And Miss Barry took us up to the grandstand to see the horse-races.[10] Mrs. Lynde wouldn't go; she said horse-racing was an abomination, and she, being a church member, thought it her bounden duty to set a good example by staying away. But there were so many there I don't believe Mrs. Lynde's absence would ever be noticed. I don't think, though, that I ought to go very often to horse-races, because they *are* awfully fascinating. Diana got so excited that she offered to bet me ten cents that the red horse would win. I didn't believe he would, but I refused to bet, because I wanted to tell Mrs. Allan all about everything, and I felt sure it wouldn't do to tell her that. It's always wrong to do anything you can't tell the minister's wife. It's as good as an extra conscience to have a minister's wife for your friend. And I was very glad I didn't bet, because the red horse *did* win, and I would have lost ten cents. So you see that virtue was its own reward.[11] We saw a man go up in a balloon. I'd love to go up in a balloon, Marilla; it would be simply thrilling; and we saw a man selling fortunes. You paid him ten cents and a little bird picked out your fortune for you. Miss Barry gave Diana and me ten cents each to have our fortunes told. Mine was that I would marry a dark-complected man who was very wealthy, and I would go across water to live. I looked carefully at all the dark men I saw after that, but I didn't care much for any of them, and anyhow I suppose it's too early to be looking out for him yet. Oh, it was a never-to-be-forgotten day, Marilla. I was so tired I couldn't sleep at night. Miss Barry put us in the spare room, according to promise. It was an elegant room, Marilla, but somehow sleeping in a spare room isn't what I used to think it was. That's the worst of growing up, and I'm beginning to realize it. The things you wanted so much when you were a child don't seem half so wonderful to you when you get them."

10. The Charlottetown Driving Park at the northeast side of the city opened with its first harness race in 1890. In harness racing the horse pulls a driver in a light vehicle called a sulky.

11. John Home, in his play *Douglas* (1756): "Virtue is its own reward" (II.i. l.).

12. A female star of operatic performances.

13. A made-up name, but Montgomery is probably recalling the only Canadian diva of the period, Emma Lajeunesse, who called herself "Madame Albani" in tribute to Albany, New York, where she studied music. Born in Chambly, Quebec, Lajeunesse became internationally famous; she sang for Queen Victoria and was to sing at the Queen's funeral. In her tours of the world Albani never forgot her native land and gave a number of recitals in Canada. She is recognized in *Courageous Women* (1934), the book for girls by Montgomery and two other women writers; she is called "Canada's Queen of Song." Madame Albani's public appearance is recollected in terms similar to those used here: " . . . when the vision in shining satin and blazing diamonds burst upon the stage" (*Courageous Women*, 146). See illustration.

14. Refers to Charlottetown's electric system. Montgomery did not have electric lights in her own

Thursday the girls had a drive in the park, and in the evening Miss Barry took them to a concert in the Academy of Music, where a noted prima donna[12] was to sing. To Anne the evening was a glittering vision of delight.

"Oh, Marilla, it was beyond description. I was so excited I couldn't even talk, so you may know what it was like. I just sat in enraptured silence. Madame Selitsky[13] was perfectly beautiful, and wore white satin and diamonds. But when she began to sing I never thought about anything else. Oh, I can't tell you how I felt. But it seemed to me that it could never be hard to be good any more. I felt like I do when I look up to the stars. Tears came into my eyes, but oh, they were such happy tears. I was so sorry when it was all over, and I told Miss Barry I didn't see how I was ever to return to common life again. She said she thought if we went over to the restaurant across the street and had an ice-cream it might help me. That sounded so prosaic; but to my surprise I found it true. The ice-cream was delicious, Marilla, and it was so lovely and dissipated to be sitting there eating it at eleven o'clock at night. Diana said she believed she was born for city life. Miss Barry asked me what my opinion was, but I said I would have to think it over very seriously before I could tell her what I really thought. So I thought it over after I went to bed. That is the best time to think things out. And I came to the conclusion, Marilla, that I wasn't born for city life and that I was glad of it. It's nice to be eating ice-cream at brilliant[14] restaurants at eleven o'clock at night once in awhile; but as a regular thing I'd rather be in the east gable at eleven, sound asleep, but kind of knowing even in my sleep that the stars were shining outside and that the wind was blowing in the firs across the brook. I told Miss Barry so at breakfast the next morning and she laughed. Miss Barry generally laughed at anything I said, even when I said the most solemn things. I don't think I liked it, Marilla, because I wasn't trying to be funny. But she is a most hospitable lady and treated us royally."

Friday brought going-home time, and Mr. Barry drove in for the girls.

"Well, I hope you've enjoyed yourselves," said Miss Barry, as she bade them good-bye.

"Indeed we have," said Diana.

"And you, Anne-girl?"

"I've enjoyed every minute of the time," said Anne, throwing her arms impulsively about the old woman's neck and kissing her wrinkled cheek. Diana would never have dared to do such a thing, and felt rather aghast at Anne's freedom. But Miss Barry was pleased, and she stood on her veranda and watched the buggy out of sight. Then she went back into her big house with a sigh. It seemed very lonely, lacking those fresh young lives. Miss Barry was a rather selfish old lady, if the truth must be told, and had never cared much for anybody but herself. She valued people only as they were of service to her or amused her. Anne had amused her, and consequently stood high in the old lady's good graces. But Miss Barry found herself thinking less about Anne's quaint speeches than of her fresh enthusiasms, her transparent emotions, her little winning ways, and the sweetness of her eyes and lips.

"I thought Marilla Cuthbert was an old fool when I heard she'd adopted a girl out of an orphan asylum," she said to herself, "but I guess she didn't make much of a mistake after all. If I'd a child like Anne in the house all the time I'd be a better and happier woman."

Anne and Diana found the drive home as pleasant as the drive in — pleasanter, indeed, since there was the delightful consciousness of home waiting at the end of it. It was sunset when they passed through White Sands and turned into the Shore Road. Beyond, the Avonlea hills came out darkly against the saffron sky. Behind them the moon was rising out of the sea that grew all radiant and transfigured in her light. Every little cove along the curving road was a marvel of dancing ripples. The waves broke with a soft swish on the

home until the Macdonalds moved to the manse at Norval in 1926. Charlottetown had gas lighting in 1854, one year before the town's incorporation. In 1884 a Montreal company submitted a bid for supplying electricity to light the city's streets, and the first electric lights went on in Charlottetown on December 15, 1885. The Prince Edward Island Electric Company, a subsidiary of the Montreal firm, was established in 1886. At first there were only arc lights, but soon the brighter incandescent lights were installed. In 1896 the last gas company wound up its affairs and in 1899 through a series of mergers the Charlottetown Light and Power Company incorporated the gas company with the electric suppliers (A. Kenneth Bell, *Getting Out the Lights,* 7–9).

rocks below them, and the tang of the sea was in the strong, fresh air.

"Oh, but it's good to be alive and to be going home," breathed Anne.

When she crossed the log bridge over the brook the kitchen light of Green Gables winked her a friendly welcome back, and through the open door shone the hearth fire, sending out its warm red glow athwart the chilly autumn night. Anne ran blithely up the hill and into the kitchen, where a hot supper was waiting on the table.

"So you've got back?" said Marilla, folding up her knitting.

"Yes, and, oh, it's so good to be back," said Anne joyously. "I could kiss everything, even to the clock. Marilla, a broiled chicken! You don't mean to say you cooked that for me!"

"Yes, I did," said Marilla. "I thought you'd be hungry after such a drive and need something real appetizing. Hurry and take off your things, and we'll have supper as soon as Matthew comes in. I'm glad you've got back, I must say. It's been fearful lonesome here without you, and I never put in four longer days."

After supper Anne sat before the fire between Matthew and Marilla, and gave them a full account of her visit.

"I've had a splendid time," she concluded happily, "and I feel that it marks an epoch in my life. But the best of it all was the coming home."

CHAPTER XXX

THE QUEEN'S CLASS
IS ORGANIZED

 MARILLA LAID her knitting on her lap and leaned back in her chair. Her eyes were tired, and she thought vaguely that she must see about having her glasses changed the next time she went to town, for her eyes had grown tired very often of late.

It was nearly dark, for the dull November twilight had fallen around Green Gables, and the only light in the kitchen came from the dancing red flames in the stove.

Anne was curled up Turk-fashion[1] on the hearth-rug, gazing into that joyous glow where the sunshine of a hundred summers was being distilled from the maple cord-wood.[2] She had been reading, but her book had slipped to the floor, and now she was dreaming, with a smile on her parted lips. Glittering castles in Spain[3] were shaping themselves out of the mists and rainbows of her lively fancy; adventures wonderful and enthralling were happening to her in cloudland—adventures that always turned out triumphantly and never involved her in scrapes like those of actual life.

Marilla looked at her with a tenderness that would never have been suffered to reveal itself in any clearer light than that soft mingling of fireshine and shadow. The lesson of a love that should display itself easily in spoken word and open look

1. To sit with crossed legs, in a lotus or modified lotus position.

2. Wood stacked in cords; "wood for fuel cut in lengths, usually of four feet."

3. Originally *châteaux en Espagne*, a medieval phrase that conjures up imaginary places of joy, dream worlds: "Thou shalt make castels thanne in Spayne, / And dreme of joy, all but in vayne" (Jean de Meun, *Roman de la Rose*, trans. Geoffrey Chaucer).

"Anne was curled up Turk-fashion on the hearth-rug." Illustration by Sybil Tawse, from the 1933 edition.

was one Marilla could never learn. But she had learned to love this slim, gray-eyed girl with an affection all the deeper and stronger from its very undemonstrativeness. Her love made her afraid of being unduly indulgent, indeed. She had an uneasy feeling that it was rather sinful to set one's heart so intensely on any human creature as she had set hers on Anne, and perhaps she performed a sort of unconscious penance for this by being stricter and more critical than if the girl had been less dear to her. Certainly Anne herself had no idea how Marilla loved her. She sometimes thought wistfully that Marilla was very hard to please and distinctly lacking in sympathy and understanding. But she always checked the thought reproachfully, remembering what she owed to Marilla.

"Anne," said Marilla abruptly, "Miss Stacy was here this afternoon when you were out with Diana."

Anne came back from her other world with a start and a sigh.

"Was she? Oh, I'm so sorry I wasn't in. Why didn't you call me, Marilla? Diana and I were only over in the Haunted Wood. It's lovely in the woods now. All the little wood things —the ferns and the satin leaves and the crackerberries[4]— have gone to sleep, just as if somebody had tucked them away until spring under a blanket of leaves. I think it was a little gray fairy with a rainbow scarf that came tiptoeing along the last moonlight night and did it. Diana wouldn't say much about that, though. Diana has never forgotten the scolding her mother gave her about imagining ghosts into the Haunted Wood. It had a very bad effect on Diana's imagination. It blighted it. Mrs. Lynde says Myrtle Bell is a blighted being. I asked Ruby Gillis why Myrtle was blighted, and Ruby said she guessed it was because her young man had gone back on her. Ruby Gillis thinks of nothing but young men, and the older she gets the worse she is. Young men are all very well in their place, but it doesn't do to drag them into everything, does it? Diana and I are thinking seriously of promising each

4. Probably the berries of the jewelweed or ladies' ear drops that burst with a loud pop or crack when you press them. See n. 2, ch. 1.

5. The novel *Ben Hur: A Tale of the Christ* (1880), by Lew Wallace (1827–1905), an American writer, soldier, and diplomat. The story concerns the conversion to Christianity of a Jewish patrician temporarily turned Roman officer. The most dramatic scene in the novel is a chariot race. There have been three different film versions. In 1926 Montgomery went to see the version starring Raymond Novarro. "About the only movie of a book I have not been disappointed in. The chariot race was amazing" (*SJ* III [Sept. 16, 1926]: 306).

other that we will never marry but be nice old maids and live together for ever. Diana hasn't quite made up her mind though, because she thinks perhaps it would be nobler to marry some wild, dashing, wicked young man and reform him. Diana and I talk a great deal about serious subjects now, you know. We feel that we are so much older than we used to be that it isn't becoming to talk of childish matters. It's such a solemn thing to be almost fourteen, Marilla. Miss Stacy took all us girls who are in our teens down to the brook last Wednesday, and talked to us about it. She said we couldn't be too careful what habits we formed and what ideals we acquired in our teens, because by the time we were twenty our characters would be developed and the foundation laid for our whole future life. And she said if the foundation was shaky we could never build anything really worth while on it. Diana and I talked the matter over coming home from school. We felt extremely solemn, Marilla. And we decided that we would try to be very careful indeed and form respectable habits and learn all we could and be as sensible as possible, so that by the time we were twenty our characters would be properly developed. It's perfectly appalling to think of being twenty, Marilla. It sounds so fearfully old and grown up. But why was Miss Stacy here this afternoon?"

"That is what I want to tell you, Anne, if you'll ever give me a chance to get a word in edgewise. She was talking about you."

"About me?" Anne looked rather scared. Then she flushed and exclaimed:

"Oh, I know what she was saying. I meant to tell you, Marilla, honestly I did, but I forgot. Miss Stacy caught me reading *Ben Hur*[5] in school yesterday afternoon when I should have been studying my Canadian history. Jane Andrews lent it to me. I was reading it at dinner-hour, and I had just got to the chariot-race when school went in. I was simply wild to know how it turned out—although I felt sure Ben Hur must win, because it wouldn't be poetical justice[6] if he didn't — so I spread the history open on my desk-lid and then tucked *Ben Hur* between the desk and my knee.[7] It just looked as if I were studying Canadian history, you know, while all the while I was revelling in *Ben Hur*. I was so interested in it that I never noticed Miss Stacy coming down the aisle until all at once I just looked up and there she was looking down at me, so reproachful like. I can't tell you how ashamed I felt, Marilla, especially when I heard Josie Pye giggling. Miss Stacy took *Ben Hur* away, but she never said a word then. She kept me in at recess and talked to me. She said I had done very wrong in two respects. First, I was wasting the time I ought to have put on my studies; and secondly I was deceiving my teacher in trying to make it appear I was reading a history when it was only a story-book instead. I had never realized until that moment, Marilla, that what I was doing was deceitful. I was shocked. I cried bitterly, and asked Miss Stacy to forgive me and I'd never do such a thing again; and I offered to do penance by never so much as looking at *Ben Hur* for a whole week, not even to see how the chariot-race turned out. But Miss Stacy said she wouldn't require that, and she forgave me freely. So I think it wasn't very kind of her to come up here to you about it after all."

"Miss Stacy never mentioned such a thing to me, Anne, and it's only your guilty conscience that's the matter with you. You have no business to be taking story-books to school. You read too many novels anyhow. When I was a girl I wasn't so much as allowed to look at a novel."

"Oh, how can you call *Ben Hur* a novel when it's really such a religious book?" protested Anne. "Of course it's a little too exciting to be proper reading for Sunday, and I only read it on week-days. And I never read *any* book now unless either Miss Stacy or Mrs. Allan thinks it is a proper book for a girl thirteen and three-quarters to read. Miss Stacy made me promise that. She found me reading a book one day called *The Lurid*

6. Or "poetic justice," the doctrine derived from Aristotle that in literary works the good characters should succeed and the bad be punished (*Poetics* III.A.1).

7. In October 1900, Montgomery describes in her journal how in her school days she indulged in pleasure reading by similar methods. One time a friend lent her de la Motte Fouqué's *Undine* (1811), a Romantic German novella about the love of a knight for a sylph: "I read . . . all behind my desk in that delightful, roomy old 'back-seat' which was so splendidly convenient for such doings. No doubt I should have been studying English History or geography at the time — but then I would soon have forgotten the history and I have never forgotten *Undine*." Unlike Anne, her author is uncaught and unrepentant (*SJ* I: 253).

8. A made-up title, as manuscript variations make clear.

9. The tuition costs at Prince of Wales College were nominal: five dollars for a student from the country, ten dollars for a city dweller (Rubio and Waterston, *SJ* I: 401, note). But for rural people the chief cost of high school consisted in the expense of boarding a teenager in Charlottetown, to which was added the cost of railway or other transport, books, and more presentable clothing than that needed on the farm.

Mystery of the Haunted Hall.[8] It was one Ruby Gillis had lent me, and, oh, Marilla, it was so fascinating and creepy. It just curdled the blood in my veins. But Miss Stacy said it was a very silly unwholesome book, and she asked me not to read any more of it or any like it. I didn't mind promising not to read any more like it, but it was *agonizing* to give back that book without knowing how it turned out. But my love for Miss Stacy stood the test and I did. It's really wonderful, Marilla, what you can do when you're truly anxious to please a certain person."

"Well, I guess I'll light the lamp and get to work," said Marilla. "I see plainly that you don't want to hear what Miss Stacy had to say. You're more interested in the sound of your own tongue than in anything else."

"Oh, indeed, Marilla, I do want to hear it," cried Anne contritely. "I won't say another word—not one. I know I talk too much, but I am really trying to overcome it, and although I say far too much, yet if you only knew how many things I want to say and don't, you'd give me some credit for it. Please tell me, Marilla."

"Well, Miss Stacy wants to organize a class among her advanced students who mean to study for the entrance examination into Queen's. She intends to give them extra lessons for an hour after school. And she came to ask Matthew and me if we would like to have you join it. What do you think about it yourself, Anne? Would you like to go to Queen's and pass for a teacher?"

"Oh, Marilla!" Anne straightened to her knees and clasped her hands. "It's been the dream of my life—that is, for the last six months, ever since Ruby and Jane began to talk of studying for the entrance. But I didn't say anything about it, because I supposed it would be perfectly useless. I'd love to be a teacher. But won't it be dreadfully expensive? Mr. Andrews says it cost him one hundred and fifty dollars[9] to put Prissy through, and Prissy wasn't a dunce in geometry."

"I guess you needn't worry about that part of it. When Matthew and I took you to bring up we resolved we would do the best we could for you and give you a good education. I believe in a girl being fitted to earn her own living whether she ever has to or not. You'll always have a home at Green Gables as long as Matthew and I are here, but nobody knows what is going to happen in this uncertain world, and it's just as well to be prepared. So you can join the Queen's class if you like, Anne."

"Oh, Marilla, thank you." Anne flung her arms about Marilla's waist and looked up earnestly into her face. "I'm extremely grateful to you and Matthew. And I'll study as hard as I can and do my very best to be a credit to you. I warn you not to expect much in geometry, but I think I can hold my own in anything else if I work hard."

"I dare say you'll get along well enough. Miss Stacy says you are bright and diligent." Not for worlds would Marilla have told Anne just what Miss Stacy had said about her; that would have been to pamper vanity. "You needn't rush to any extreme of killing yourself over your books. There is no hurry. You won't be ready to try the entrance for a year and a half yet. But it's well to begin in time and be thoroughly grounded, Miss Stacy says."

"I shall take more interest than ever in my studies now," said Anne blissfully, "because I have a purpose in life. Mr. Allan says everybody should have a purpose in life and pursue it faithfully. Only he says we must first make sure that it is a worthy purpose. I would call it a worthy purpose to want to be a teacher like Miss Stacy, wouldn't you, Marilla? I think it's a very noble profession."

The Queen's class was organized in due time. Gilbert Blythe, Anne Shirley, Ruby Gillis, Jane Andrews, Josie Pye, Charlie Sloane, and Moody Spurgeon MacPherson joined it. Diana Barry did not, as her parents did not intend to send her to Queen's. This seemed nothing short of a calamity to Anne.

10. Here the Old Testament "bitterness of death" of Samuel I 15:32 is combined with the New Testament "taste of death" from Matthew 16:28 and elsewhere.

11. There was no one less generous and more avaricious than a person who would skim milk twice and feed his family on the watery milk remaining. There is also the sense that nothing is less rich or less generous than that unappetizing product, skim milk being thought fit only for animal consumption.

Never, since the night on which Minnie May had had the croup, had she and Diana been separated in anything. On the evening when the Queen's class first remained in school for the extra lessons and Anne saw Diana go slowly out with the others, to walk home alone through the Birch Path and Violet Vale, it was all the former could do to keep her seat and refrain from rushing impulsively after her chum. A lump came into her throat, and she hastily retired behind the pages of her uplifted Latin grammar to hide the tears in her eyes. Not for worlds would Anne have had Gilbert Blythe or Josie Pye see those tears.

"But, oh, Marilla, I really felt that I had tasted the bitterness of death,[10] as Mr. Allan said in his sermon last Sunday, when I saw Diana go out alone," she said mournfully that night. "I thought how splendid it would have been if Diana had only been going to study for the Entrance, too. But we can't have things perfect in this imperfect world, as Mrs. Lynde says. Mrs. Lynde isn't exactly a comforting person sometimes, but there's no doubt she says a great many very true things. And I think the Queen's class is going to be extremely interesting. Jane and Ruby are just going to study to be teachers. That is the height of their ambition. Ruby says she will only teach for two years after she gets through, and then she intends to be married. Jane says she will devote her whole life to teaching, and never, never marry, because you are paid a salary for teaching, but a husband won't pay you anything, and growls if you ask for a share in the egg and butter money. I expect Jane speaks from mournful experience, for Mrs. Lynde says that her father is a perfect old crank, and meaner than second skimmings.[11] Josie Pye says she is just going to college for education's sake, because she won't have to earn her own living; she says of course it is different with orphans who are living on charity — *they* have to hustle. Moody Spurgeon is going to be a minister. Mrs. Lynde says he couldn't be anything else with a name like that to live up to. I hope it isn't wicked of me, Marilla, but really the thought of Moody Spurgeon being a minister makes me laugh. He's such a funny-looking boy with that big fat face, and his little blue eyes, and his ears sticking out like flaps. But perhaps he will be more intellectual-looking when he grows up. Charlie Sloane says he's going to go into politics and be a member of Parliament, but Mrs. Lynde says he'll never succeed at that, because the Sloanes are all honest people, and it's only rascals that get on in politics nowadays."

"What is Gilbert Blythe going to be?" queried Marilla, seeing that Anne was opening her Caesar.[12]

"I don't happen to know what Gilbert Blythe's ambition in life is—if he has any," said Anne scornfully.

There was open rivalry between Gilbert and Anne now. Previously the rivalry had been rather one-sided, but there was no longer any doubt that Gilbert was as determined to be first in class as Anne was. He was a foeman worthy of her steel.[13] The other members of the class tacitly acknowledged their superiority, and never dreamed of trying to compete with them.

Since the day by the pond when she had refused to listen to his plea for forgiveness, Gilbert, save for the aforesaid determined rivalry, had evinced no recognition whatever of the existence of Anne Shirley. He talked and jested with the other girls, exchanged books and puzzles with them, discussed lessons and plans, sometimes walked home with one or the other of them from prayer-meeting or Debating Club. But Anne Shirley he simply ignored, and Anne found out that it is not pleasant to be ignored. It was in vain that she told herself with a toss of her head that she did not care. Deep down in her wayward feminine little heart she knew that she did care, and that if she had that chance of the Lake of Shining Waters again she would answer very differently. All at once, as it seemed, and to her secret dismay, she found that the old resentment she had cherished against him was gone—gone

12. Julius Caesar's *Commentarii de bello Gallico (Commentaries on the Gallic Wars)* or excerpts from that work in a school text.

13. Cf. "Respect was mingled with surprise / And the stern joy which warriors feel / In foemen worthy of their steel" (Sir Walter Scott, *The Lady of the Lake*, Canto V, Stanza 10).

14. See n. 16, ch. 18.

just when she most needed its sustaining power. It was in vain that she recalled every incident and emotion of that memorable occasion and tried to feel the old satisfying anger. That day by the pond had witnessed its last spasmodic flicker. Anne realized that she had forgiven and forgotten without knowing it. But it was too late.

And at least neither Gilbert nor anybody else, not even Diana, should ever suspect how sorry she was and how much she wished she hadn't been so proud and horrid! She determined to "shroud her feelings in deepest oblivion,"[14] and it may be stated here and now that she did it, so successfully that Gilbert, who possibly was not quite so indifferent as he seemed, could not console himself with any belief that Anne felt his retaliatory scorn. The only poor comfort he had was that she snubbed Charlie Sloane, unmercifully, continually and undeservedly.

Otherwise the winter passed away in a round of pleasant duties and studies. For Anne the days slipped by like golden beads on the necklace of the year. She was happy, eager, interested; there were lessons to be learned and honours to be won; delightful books to read; new pieces to be practised for the Sunday-school choir; pleasant Saturday afternoons at the manse with Mrs. Allan; and then, almost before Anne realized it, spring had come again to Green Gables and all the world was abloom once more.

Studies palled just a wee bit then; the Queen's class, left behind in school while the others scattered to green lanes and leafy wood-cuts and meadow byways, looked wistfully out of the windows and discovered that Latin verbs and French exercises had somehow lost the tang and zest they had possessed in the crisp winter months. Even Anne and Gilbert lagged and grew indifferent. Teacher and taught were alike glad when the term was ended and the glad vacation days stretched rosily before them.

"But you've done good work this past year," Miss Stacy told them on the last evening, "and you deserve a good, jolly vacation. Have the best time you can in the out-of-door world and lay in a good stock of health and vitality and ambition to carry you through next year. It will be the tug of war, you know—the last year before the Entrance."

"Are you going to be back next year, Miss Stacy?" asked Josie Pye.

Josie Pye never scrupled to ask questions; in this instance the rest of the class felt grateful to her; none of them would have dared to ask it of Miss Stacy, but all wanted to, for there had been alarming rumours running at large through the school for some time that Miss Stacy was not coming back the next year—that she had been offered a position in the graded school[15] of her own home district and meant to accept. The Queen's class listened in breathless suspense for her answer.

"Yes, I think I will," said Miss Stacy. "I thought of taking another school, but I have decided to come back to Avonlea. To tell the truth, I've grown so interested in my pupils here that I found I couldn't leave them. So I'll stay and see you through."

"Hurrah!" said Moody Spurgeon. Moody Spurgeon had never been so carried away by his feelings before, and he blushed uncomfortably every time he thought about it for a week.

"Oh, I'm so glad," said Anne with shining eyes. "Dear Miss Stacy, it would be perfectly dreadful if you didn't come back. I don't believe I could have the heart to go on with my studies at all if another teacher came here."

When Anne got home that night she stacked all her textbooks away in an old trunk in the attic, locked it, and threw the key into the blanket box.

"I'm not even going to look at a school-book in vacation,"

15. A school divided into classes or grades according to students' ages and progress; thus, superior to the one-room school.

16. Ladies were expected to wear longer skirts and dresses, girls shorter ones.

17. Electricity came early to some rural sections due to the inhabitants' inventiveness. The major source of electric power was steam from burning coal, but throughout the island some creeks and dams were used for hydro power, customarily at the sites of gristmills. "From 1885 on there were as many as fifteen such plants on Prince Edward Island, incorporating themselves as small electric companies" (A. Kenneth Bell, *Getting the Lights*, 49). As Bell points out (7–8), the original electric company "was empowered to acquire, hold and effect an electric light station in several cities and towns and villages on this Island, 'for the purpose of generating electric power to supply electric energy to hotels, public buildings, stores, dwellings, streets, warehouses, wheresoever, for what purpose soever the same might be required.'" Montgomery presumably thinks of her White Sands Hotel as being lit by electricity, but Avonlea appears to have none. The rural electrification of P. E. I. continued, with some acceleration in the 1920s.

she told Marilla. "I've studied as hard all the term as I possibly could and I've pored over that geometry until I know every proposition in the first book off by heart, even when the letters *are* changed. I just feel tired of everything sensible and I'm going to let my imagination run riot for the summer. Oh, you needn't be alarmed, Marilla. I'll only let it run riot within reasonable limits. But I want to have a real good, jolly time this summer, for maybe it's the last summer I'll be a little girl. Mrs. Lynde says that if I keep stretching out next year as I've done this I'll have to put on longer skirts.[16] She says I'm all running to legs and eyes. And when I put on longer skirts I shall feel that I have to live up to them and be very dignified. It won't even do to believe in fairies then, I'm afraid; so I'm going to believe in them with all my whole heart this summer. I think we're going to have a very gay vacation. Ruby Gillis is going to have a birthday party soon and there's the Sunday-school picnic and the missionary concert next month. And Mr. Barry says that some evening he'll take Diana and me over to the White Sands Hotel and have dinner there. They have dinner there in the evening, you know. Jane Andrews was over once last summer and she says it was a dazzling sight to see the electric lights[17] and the flowers and all the lady guests in such beautiful dresses. Jane says it was her first glimpse into high life and she'll never forget it to her dying day."

Mrs. Lynde came up the next afternoon to find out why Marilla had not been at the Aid meeting on Thursday. When Marilla was not at Aid meeting people knew there was something wrong at Green Gables.

"Matthew had a bad spell with his heart on Thursday," Marilla explained, "and I didn't feel like leaving him. Oh, yes, he's all right again now, but he takes them spells oftener than he used to and I'm anxious about him. The doctor says he must be careful to avoid excitement. That's easy enough, for

Matthew doesn't go about looking for excitement by any means and never did, but he's not to do any very heavy work either and you might as well tell Matthew not to breathe as not to work. Come and lay off your things, Rachel. You'll stay to tea?"

"Well, seeing you're so pressing, perhaps I might as well stay," said Mrs. Rachel, who had not the slightest intention of doing anything else.

Mrs. Rachel and Marilla sat comfortably in the parlour while Anne got the tea and made hot biscuits[18] that were light and white enough to defy even Mrs. Rachel's criticism.

"I must say Anne has turned out a real smart girl," admitted Mrs. Rachel, as Marilla accompanied her to the end of the lane at sunset. "She must be a great help to you."

"She is," said Marilla, "and she's real steady and reliable now. I used to be afraid she'd never get over her feather-brained ways, but she has and I wouldn't be afraid to trust her in anything now."

"I never would have thought she'd have turned out so well that first day I was here three years ago," said Mrs. Rachel. "Lawful heart, shall I ever forget that tantrum of hers! When I went home that night I says to Thomas, says I, 'Mark my words, Thomas, Marilla Cuthbert'll live to rue the step she's took.' But I was mistaken and I'm real glad of it. I ain't one of those kind of people, Marilla, as can never be brought to own up that they've made a mistake. No, that never was my way, thank goodness. I did make a mistake in judging Anne, but it weren't no wonder for an odder, unexpecteder witch of a child there never was in this world, that's what. There was no ciphering her out by the rules that worked with other children. It's nothing short of wonderful how she's improved these three years, but especially in looks. She's a real pretty girl got to be,[19] though I can't say I'm overly partial to that pale, big-eyed style myself. I like more snap and colour, like Diana

18. Baking powder biscuits, a form of unsweetened scone.

19. See Textual Note.

Barry has or Ruby Gillis. Ruby Gillis' looks are real showy.
But somehow—I don't know how it is but when Anne and
them are together, though she ain't half as handsome, she
makes them look kind of common and overdone—something like them white June lilies she calls narcissus alongside
of the big, red peonies, that's what."

CHAPTER XXXI

WHERE THE BROOK AND RIVER MEET[1]

ANNE HAD her "good" summer and enjoyed it whole-heartedly. She and Diana fairly lived out of doors, revelling in all the delights that Lover's Lane and the Dryad's Bubble and Willowmere and Victoria Island afforded. Marilla offered no objections to Anne's gipsyings. The Spencervale doctor who had come the night Minnie May had the croup met Anne at the house of a patient one afternoon early in vacation, looked her over sharply, screwed up his mouth, shook his head, and sent a message to Marilla Cuthbert by another person. It was:

"Keep that red-headed girl of yours in the open air all summer and don't let her read books until she gets more spring into her step."

This message frightened Marilla wholesomely. She read Anne's death warrant by consumption in it unless it was scrupulously obeyed. As a result, Anne had the golden summer of her life as far as freedom and frolic went. She walked, rowed, berried and dreamed to her heart's content; and when September came she was bright-eyed and alert, with a step that would have satisfied the Spencervale doctor and a heart full of ambition and zest once more.

"I feel just like studying with might and main," she declared

1. From Henry Wadsworth Longfellow's "Maidenhood" (1842): "Standing with reluctant feet, / Where the brook and river meet, / Womanhood and childhood fleet!" (Stanza 3). While the reference is undoubtedly to Longfellow, the image picks up Tennyson's later poem "The Brook," itself influenced by Longfellow: "There the river; and there / Stands Philip's farm where brook and river meet" (l. 38). See n. 4, ch. 1; see also Appendix, "Literary Allusion."

2. Cf. "The heavens declare the glory of God; and the firmament sheweth his handywork. . . . In them hath he set a tabernacle for the sun, Which is as a bridegroom coming out of his chamber, and rejoiceth as a strong man to run a race" (Psalm 19:1, 5).

3. Although women could be lay preachers in many denominations as early as the eighteenth century, particularly in Methodist and other sects that emphasized the gifts of the Holy Spirit, the first fully ordained female minister was Antoinette Louisa Brown (above), in a South Butler, N.Y., Congregational church in 1853. By 1888 there were only an estimated twenty women in the United States serving as pastors, excluding the approximately 350 Quaker women who served as ministers. The Methodist, Congregational, Baptist, Universalist, and Unitarian denominations were among the first to ordain women. More traditional Christian sects, such as the Presbyterian and Anglican, took

as she brought her books down from the attic. "Oh, you good old friends, I'm glad to see your honest faces once more — yes, even you, geometry. I've had a perfectly beautiful summer, Marilla, and now I'm rejoicing as a strong man to run a race,[2] as Mr. Allan said last Sunday. Doesn't Mr. Allan preach magnificent sermons? Mrs. Lynde says he is improving every day and the first thing we know some city church will gobble him up and then we'll be left and have to turn to and break in another green preacher. But I don't see the use of meeting trouble half-way, do you, Marilla? I think it would be better just to enjoy Mr. Allan while we have him. If I was a man I think I'd be a minister. They can have such an influence for good if their theology is sound; and it must be thrilling to preach splendid sermons and stir your hearers' hearts. Why can't women be ministers, Marilla? I asked Mrs. Lynde that and she was shocked and said it would be a scandalous thing. She said there might be female ministers in the States and she believed there was, but thank goodness we hadn't got to that stage in Canada yet and she hoped we never would.[3] But I don't see why. I think women would make splendid ministers. When there is a social to be got up or a church tea or anything else to raise money the women have to turn to and do the work. I'm sure Mrs. Lynde can pray every bit as well as Superintendent Bell and I've no doubt she could preach too with a little practice."

"Yes, I believe she could," said Marilla dryly. "She does plenty of unofficial preaching as it is. Nobody has much of a chance to go wrong in Avonlea with Rachel to oversee them."

"Marilla," said Anne in a burst of confidence, "I want to tell you something and ask you what you think about it. It has worried me terribly — on Sunday afternoons, that is, when I think specially about such matters. I do really want to be good; and when I'm with you or Mrs. Allan or Miss Stacy I want it more than ever and I want to do just what would please you and what you would approve of. But mostly when I'm with Mrs. Lynde I feel desperately wicked and as if I wanted to go and do the very thing she tells me I oughtn't to do. I feel irresistibly tempted to do it. Now, what do you think is the reason I feel like that? Do you think it's because I'm really bad and unregenerate?"

Marilla looked dubious for a moment. Then she laughed.

"If you are I guess I am too, Anne, for Rachel often has that very effect on me. I sometimes think she'd have more of an influence for good, as you say yourself, if she didn't keep nagging people to do right. There should have been a special commandment against nagging. But there, I shouldn't talk so. Rachel is a good Christian woman and she means well. There isn't a kinder soul in Avonlea and she never shirks her share of work."

"I'm very glad you feel the same," said Anne decidedly. "It's so encouraging. I sha'n't worry so much over that after this. But I dare say there'll be other things to worry me. They keep coming up new all the time—things to perplex you, you know. You settle one question and there's another right after. There are so many things to be thought over and decided when you're beginning to grow up. It keeps me busy all the time thinking them over and deciding what is right. It's a serious thing to grow up, isn't it, Marilla? But when I have such good friends as you and Matthew and Mrs. Allan and Miss Stacy I ought to grow up successfully, and I'm sure it will be my own fault if I don't. I feel it's a great responsibility because I have only the one chance. If I don't grow up right I can't go back and begin over again. I've grown two inches this summer, Marilla. Mr. Gillis measured me at Ruby's party. I'm so glad you made my new dresses longer. That dark green one is so pretty and it was sweet of you to put on the flounce. Of course I know it wasn't really necessary, but flounces are so stylish this fall and Josie Pye has flounces on all

longer to implement the change. In Canada the first woman did not receive full ministerial ordination until 1936, in the United Church of Canada (Rosemary Radford Ruether and Rosemary Skinner Keller, eds., *Women and Religion in America*, 154).

4. Cf. "Gird up now thy loins like a man; for I will demand of thee, and answer thou me" (Job 38:3; see also Luke 12:35). The biblical phrase means to prepare for action by putting on a belt or sword belt.

5. Originally, "Hills peep o'er hills, and Alps on Alps arise!" (Alexander Pope, *An Essay on Criticism*, 1711, l. 232).

her dresses. I know I'll be able to study better because of mine. I shall have such a comfortable feeling deep down in my mind about that flounce."

"It's worth something to have that," admitted Marilla.

Miss Stacy came back to Avonlea school and found all her pupils eager for work once more. Especially did the Queen's class gird up their loins[4] for the fray, for at the end of the coming year, dimly foreshadowing their pathway already, loomed up that fateful thing known as "the Entrance," at the thought of which one and all felt their hearts sink into their very shoes. Suppose they did not pass! That thought was doomed to haunt Anne through the waking hours of that winter, Sunday afternoons inclusive, to the almost entire exclusion of moral and theological problems. When Anne had bad dreams she found herself staring miserably at pass lists of the Entrance exams, where Gilbert Blythe's name was blazoned at the top and in which hers did not appear at all.

But it was a jolly, busy, happy swift-flying winter. School work was as interesting, class rivalry as absorbing, as of yore. New worlds of thought, feeling, and ambition, fresh, fascinating fields of unexplored knowledge seemed to be opening out before Anne's eager eyes.

Hills peeped o'er hills and Alps on Alps arose.[5]

Much of all this was due to Miss Stacy's tactful, careful, broad-minded guidance. She led her class to think and explore and discover for themselves and encouraged straying from the old beaten paths to a degree that quite shocked Mrs. Lynde and the school trustees, who viewed all innovations on established methods rather dubiously.

Apart from her studies Anne expanded socially, for Marilla, mindful of the Spencervale doctor's dictum, no longer vetoed occasional outings. The Debating Club flourished and gave several concerts; there were one or two parties almost verging on grown-up affairs; there were sleigh drives and skating frolics galore.

Between times Anne grew, shooting up so rapidly that Marilla was astonished one day, when they were standing side by side, to find the girl was taller than herself.

"Why, Anne, how you've grown!" she said, almost unbelievingly. A sigh followed on the words. Marilla felt a queer regret over Anne's inches. The child she had learned to love had vanished somehow and here was this tall, serious-eyed girl of fifteen, with the thoughtful brows and the proudly poised little head, in her place. Marilla loved the girl as much as she had loved the child, but she was conscious of a queer, sorrowful sense of loss. And that night, when Anne had gone to prayer-meeting with Diana, Marilla sat alone in the wintry twilight and indulged in the weakness of a cry. Matthew, coming in with a lantern, caught her at it and gazed at her in such consternation that Marilla had to laugh through her tears.

"I was thinking about Anne," she explained. "She's got to be such a big girl—and she'll probably be away from us next winter. I'll miss her terrible."

"She'll be able to come home often," comforted Matthew, to whom Anne was as yet, and always would be the little eager girl he had brought home from Bright River on that June evening four years before. "The branch railroad[6] will be built to Carmody by that time."

"It won't be the same thing as having her here all the time," sighed Marilla gloomily, determined to enjoy her luxury of grief uncomforted. "But then—men can't understand these things!"

There were other changes in Anne no less real than the physical change. For one thing, she became much quieter. Perhaps she thought all the more and dreamed as much as ever, but she certainly talked less. Marilla noticed and commented on this also.

6. A short rail line joining a main one. Canada's rail mileage grew from twenty-two in 1848 to sixty-six in 1850 and 2,065 by 1860. Then, in 1873, P. E. I. with its 218 miles in the works was forced to join the federation formed six years earlier because of economic overextension resulting from the railroad's rapid growth. See Hubbard Freeman, *Encyclopedia of North American Railroading*. Montgomery records her first trip on the railroad in her journal during August 1890. She and her grandfather first had to drive in a horse-drawn vehicle to Kensington to take the train out west (*SJ* I: 25).

Kensington train station, 1895.
Both Anne and her creator used
this station.

"You don't chatter half as much as you used to, Anne, nor use half as many big words. What has come over you?"

Anne coloured and laughed a little, as she dropped her book and looked dreamily out of the window, where big fat red buds were bursting out on the creeper in response to the lure of spring sunshine.

"I don't know — I don't want to talk as much," she said, denting her chin thoughtfully with her forefinger. "It's nicer to think dear, pretty thoughts and keep them in one's heart, like treasures. I don't like to have them laughed at or wondered over. And somehow I don't want to use big words any more. It's almost a pity, isn't it, now that I'm really growing big enough to say them if I did want to. It's fun to be almost grown up in some ways, but it's not the kind of fun I expected, Marilla. There's so much to learn and do and think that there isn't time for big words. Besides, Miss Stacy says the short ones are much stronger and better. She makes us write all our essays as simply as possible. It was hard at first. I was so used to crowding in all the fine big words I could think of—and I thought of any number of them. But I've got used to it now and I see it's so much better."

"What has become of your story club? I haven't heard you speak of it for a long time."

"The story club isn't in existence any longer. We hadn't time for it—and anyhow I think we had got tired of it. It was silly to be writing about love and murder and elopements and mysteries. Miss Stacy sometimes has us write a story for training in composition but she won't let us write anything but what might happen in Avonlea in our own lives, and she criticizes it very sharply and makes us criticize our own too. I never thought my compositions had so many faults until I began to look for them myself. I felt so ashamed I wanted to give up altogether, but Miss Stacy said I could learn to write well if I only trained myself to be my own severest critic. And so I'm trying to."

"You've only two more months before the Entrance," said Marilla. "Do you think you'll be able to get through?"

Anne shivered.

"I don't know. Sometimes I think I'll be all right—and then I get horribly afraid. We've studied hard and Miss Stacy has drilled us thoroughly, but we mayn't get through for all that. We've each got a stumbling block.[7] Mine is geometry of course, and Jane's is Latin and Ruby's and Charlie's is algebra and Josie's is arithmetic. Moody Spurgeon says he feels it in his bones that he is going to fail in English history. Miss Stacy is going to give us examinations in June just as hard as we'll have at the Entrance[8] and mark us just as strictly, so we'll have some idea. I wish it was all over, Marilla. It haunts me. Sometimes I wake up in the night and wonder what I'll do if I don't pass."

"Why, go to school next year and try again," said Marilla unconcernedly.

7. A biblical phrase (see, *e.g.*, Leviticus 19:14 and I Corinthians 1:23) denoting something to stumble on or over, an impediment.

8. The examinations for entrance to high school were set and marked by a board established by the provincial government, and all students in the province had to take them on the same day. The results in one's own school tests did not count toward acceptance.

"Oh, I don't believe I'd have the heart for it. It would be such a disgrace to fail, especially if Gil—if the others passed. And I get so nervous in an examination that I'm likely to make a mess of it. I wish I had nerves like Jane Andrews. Nothing rattles her."

Anne sighed and, dragging her eyes from the witcheries of the spring world, the beckoning day of breeze and blue, and the green things upspringing in the garden, buried herself resolutely in her book. There would be other springs, but if she did not succeed in passing the Entrance Anne felt convinced that she would never recover sufficiently to enjoy them.

CHAPTER XXXII

THE PASS LIST IS OUT

WITH THE END of June came the close of the term and the close of Miss Stacy's rule in Avonlea school. Anne and Diana walked home that evening feeling very sober indeed. Red eyes and damp handkerchiefs bore convincing testimony to the fact that Miss Stacy's farewell words must have been quite as touching as Mr. Phillips' had been under similar circumstances three years before. Diana looked back at the school-house from the foot of the spruce hill and sighed deeply.

"It does seem as if it was the end of everything, doesn't it?" she said dismally.

"You oughtn't to feel half as badly as I do," said Anne, hunting vainly for a dry spot on her handkerchief. "You'll be back again next winter, but I suppose I've left the dear old school for ever—if I have good luck, that is."

"It won't be a bit the same. Miss Stacy won't be there, nor you nor Jane nor Ruby probably. I shall have to sit all alone, for I couldn't bear to have another deskmate after you. Oh, we have had jolly times, haven't we, Anne? It's dreadful to think they're all over."

Two big tears rolled down by Diana's nose.

1. Slang term meaning to stuff the memory with facts hastily for an occasion, such as an examination; first used in 1825.

"If you would stop crying I could," said Anne imploringly. "Just as soon as I put away my hanky I see you brimming up and that starts me off again. As Mrs. Lynde says, 'If you can't be cheerful be as cheerful as you can.' After all, I dare say I'll be back next year. This is one of the times I *know* I'm not going to pass. They're getting alarmingly frequent."

"Why, you came out splendidly in the exams Miss Stacy gave."

"Yes, but those exams didn't make me nervous. When I think of the real thing you can't imagine what a horrid, cold fluttery feeling comes round my heart. And then my number is thirteen and Josie Pye says it's so unlucky. I'm *not* superstitious and I know it can make no difference. But still I wish it wasn't thirteen."

"I do wish I were going in with you," said Diana. "Wouldn't we have a perfectly elegant time? But I suppose you'll have to cram[1] in the evenings."

"No; Miss Stacy has made us promise not to open a book at all. She says it would only tire and confuse us and we are to go out walking and not think about the exams at all and go to bed early. It's good advice, but I expect it will be hard to follow; good advice is apt to be, I think. Prissy Andrews told me that she sat up half the night every night of her Entrance week and crammed for dear life; and I had determined to sit up *at least* as long as she did. It was so kind of your Aunt Josephine to ask me to stay at Beechwood while I'm in town."

"You'll write to me while you're in, won't you?"

"I'll write Tuesday night and tell you how the first day goes," promised Anne.

"I'll be haunting the post office on Wednesday," vowed Diana.

Anne went to town the following Monday and on Wednesday Diana haunted the post office, as agreed, and got her letter.

Dearest Diana [wrote Anne],

Here it is Tuesday night and I'm writing this in the library at Beechwood. Last night I was horribly lonesome all alone in my room and wished so much you were with me. I couldn't cram because I'd promised Miss Stacy not to, but it was as hard to keep from opening my history as it used to be to keep from reading a story before my lessons were learned.

This morning Miss Stacy came for me and we went to the Academy, calling for Jane and Ruby and Josie on our way. Ruby asked me to feel her hands and they were as cold as ice. Josie said I looked as if I hadn't slept a wink and she didn't believe I was strong enough to stand the grind of the teacher's course even if I did get through. There are times and seasons even yet when I don't feel that I've made any great headway in learning to like Josie Pye!

When we reached the Academy there were scores of students there from all over the Island. The first person we saw was Moody Spurgeon sitting on the steps and muttering away to himself. Jane asked him what on earth he was doing and he said he was repeating the multiplication table over and over to steady his nerves and for pity's sake not to interrupt him, because if he stopped for a moment he got frightened and forgot everything he ever knew but the multiplication table kept all his facts firmly in their proper places!

When we were assigned to our rooms

2. Greek mathematician ca. 300 B.C. whose name became almost synonymous with geometry. Euclid's *Elements of Plane Geometry* was a standard school text.

Miss Stacy had to leave us. Jane and I sat together and Jane was so composed that I envied her. No need of the multiplication table for good steady sensible Jane! I wondered if I looked as I felt and if they could hear my heart thumping clear across the room. Then a man came in and began distributing the English examination sheets. My hands grew cold then and my head fairly whirled around as I picked it up. Just one awful moment—Diana, I felt exactly as I did four years ago when I asked Marilla if I might stay at Green Gables—and then everything cleared up in my mind and my heart began beating again—I forgot to say that it had stopped altogether!—for I knew I could do something with *that* paper anyhow.

At noon we went home for dinner and then back again for history in the afternoon. The history was a pretty hard paper and I got dreadfully mixed up in the dates. Still, I think I did fairly well to-day. But oh, Diana, to-morrow the geometry exam comes off and when I think of it it takes every bit of determination I possess to keep from opening my Euclid.[2] If I thought the multiplication table would help me any I would recite it from now till to-morrow morning.

I went down to see the other girls this evening. On my way I met Moody Spurgeon wandering distractedly around. He said he knew he had failed in history and he was born to be a disappointment to his parents and he was going home on the morning train; and it would be easier to be a carpenter than a minister anyhow. I cheered him up and persuaded him to stay to the end because it would be unfair to Miss Stacy if he didn't. Sometimes I've wished I was born a boy, but when I see Moody Spurgeon I'm always glad I'm a girl and not his sister.

Ruby was in hysterics when I reached their boarding-house; she had just discovered a fearful mistake she had made in her English paper. When she recovered we went up-town and had an ice-cream. How we wished you had been with us.

Oh, Diana, if only the geometry examination were over! But there, as Mrs. Lynde would say, the sun will go on rising and setting whether I fail in geometry or not. That is true but not especially comforting. I think I'd rather it *didn't* go on if I failed!

Yours devotedly,

ANNE

The geometry examination and all the others were over in due time and Anne arrived home on Friday evening, rather tired but with an air of chastened triumph about her. Diana was over at Green Gables when she arrived and they met as if they had been parted for years.

"You old darling, it's perfectly splendid to see you back again. It seems like an age since you went to town and oh, Anne, how did you get along?"

"Pretty well, I think, in everything but the geometry. I don't know whether I passed in it or not and I have a creepy, crawly presentiment that I didn't. Oh, how good it is to be back! Green Gables is the dearest, loveliest spot in the world."

"How did the others do?"

"The girls say they know they didn't pass, but I think they did pretty well. Josie says the geometry was so easy a child of ten could do it! Moody Spurgeon still thinks he failed in history and Charlie says he failed in algebra. But we don't really know anything about it and won't until the pass list is out. That won't be for a fortnight. Fancy living a fortnight in such suspense! I wish I could go to sleep and never wake up until it is over."

Diana knew it would be useless to ask how Gilbert Blythe had fared, so she merely said:

"Oh, you'll pass all right. Don't worry."

"I'd rather not pass at all than not come out pretty well up on the list," flashed Anne, by which she meant—and Diana knew she meant—that success would be incomplete and bitter if she did not come out ahead of Gilbert Blythe.

With this end in view Anne had strained every nerve during the examinations. So had Gilbert. They had met and passed each other on the street a dozen times without any sign of recognition and every time Anne had held her head a little higher and wished a little more earnestly that she had made friends with Gilbert when he asked her, and vowed a little more determinedly to surpass him in the examination. She knew that all Avonlea junior was wondering which would come out first; she even knew that Jimmy Glover and Ned Wright had a bet on the question and that Josie Pye had said there was no doubt in the world that Gilbert would be first; and she felt that her humiliation would be unbearable if she failed.

But she had another and nobler motive for wishing to do well. She wanted to "pass high" for the sake of Matthew and Marilla—especially Matthew. Matthew had declared to her his conviction that she would "beat the whole Island." That, Anne felt, was something it would be foolish to hope for even in the wildest dreams. But she did hope fervently that she would be among the first ten at least, so that she might see Matthew's kindly brown eyes gleam with pride in her achievement. That, she felt, would be a sweet reward indeed for all her hard work and patient grubbing among unimaginative equations and conjugations.

At the end of the fortnight Anne took to "haunting" the post office also, in the distracted company of Jane, Ruby and Josie, opening the Charlottetown dailies[3] with shaking hands and cold, sinkaway feelings, as bad as any experienced during the Entrance week. Charlie and Gilbert were not above doing this too, but Moody Spurgeon stayed resolutely away.

"I haven't got the grit to go there and look at a paper in cold blood," he told Anne. "I'm just going to wait until somebody comes and tells me suddenly whether I've passed or not."

When three weeks had gone by without the pass list appearing Anne began to feel that she really couldn't stand the strain much longer. Her appetite failed and her interest in Avonlea doings languished. Mrs. Lynde wanted to know what else you could expect with a Tory superintendent of education at the head of affairs, and Matthew, noting Anne's paleness and indifference and the lagging steps that bore her home from the post office every afternoon, began seriously to wonder if he hadn't better vote Grit at the next election.

But one evening the news came. Anne was sitting at her open window, for the time forgetful of the woes of examinations and the cares of the world, as she drank in the beauty of the summer dusk, sweet-scented with flower-breaths from the garden below and sibilant and rustling from the stir of poplars. The eastern sky above the firs was flushed faintly pink from the reflection of the west, and Anne was wondering dreamily if the spirit of colour looked like that, when she saw Diana come flying down through the firs, over the log bridge, and up the slope, with a fluttering newspaper in her hand.

Anne sprang to her feet, knowing at once what that paper

3. Newspapers published all the results of the public examinations, giving a clear indication of an individual's grade. Thus, the entire provincial public could know how any one individual candidate had fared. The results of Montgomery's own matriculation were published in the *Daily Patriot* for July 15, 1893 (Bolger, *The Years Before "Anne,"* 139 and n.). She attained 470 out of a possible 650 and came in fifth of all the Prince Edward Island candidates (*SJ* I: 91).

4. A container for matches, which kept them safe from being accidentally lit in the days before modern safety matches.

5. Awarded a pass on condition that more work be performed.

contained. The pass list was out! Her head whirled and her heart beat until it hurt her. She could not move a step. It seemed an hour to her before Diana came rushing along the hall and burst into the room without even knocking, so great was her excitement.

"Anne, you've passed," she cried, "passed the *very first*—you and Gilbert both—you're ties—but your name is first. Oh, I'm so proud!"

Diana flung the paper on the table and herself on Anne's bed, utterly breathless and incapable of further speech. Anne lighted the lamp, oversetting the match-safe[4] and using up half a dozen matches before her shaking hands could accomplish the task. Then she snatched up the paper. Yes, she had passed—there was her name at the very top of a list of two hundred! That moment was worth living for.

"You did just splendidly, Anne," puffed Diana, recovering sufficiently to sit up and speak, for Anne, starry-eyed and rapt, had not uttered a word. "Father brought the paper home from Bright River not ten minutes ago—it came out on the afternoon train, you know, and won't be here till to-morrow by mail—and when I saw the pass list I just rushed over like a wild thing. You've all passed, every one of you, Moody Spurgeon and all, although he's conditioned in history.[5] Jane and Ruby did pretty well—they're half-way up—and so did Charlie. Josie just scraped through with three marks to spare, but you'll see she'll put on as many airs as if she'd led. Won't Miss Stacy be delighted? Oh, Anne, what does it feel like to see your name at the head of a pass list like that? If it were me I know I'd go crazy with joy. I am pretty near crazy as it is, but you're as calm and cool as a spring evening."

"I'm just dazzled inside," said Anne. "I want to say a hundred things, and I can't find words to say them in. I never dreamed of this—yes, I did, too, just once! I let myself think *once*, 'What if I should come out first?' quakingly, you know, for it seemed so vain and presumptuous to think I could lead the Island. Excuse me a minute, Diana. I must run right out to the field to tell Matthew. Then we'll go up the road and tell the good news to the others."

They hurried to the hayfield below the barn where Matthew was coiling hay,[6] and, as luck would have it, Mrs. Lynde was talking to Marilla at the lane fence.

"Oh, Matthew," exclaimed Anne, "I've passed and I'm first—or one of the first! I'm not vain, but I'm thankful."

"Well now, I always said it," said Matthew, gazing at the pass list delightedly. "I knew you could beat them all easy."

"You've done pretty well, I must say, Anne," said Marilla, trying to hide her extreme pride in Anne from Mrs. Rachel's critical eye. But that good soul said heartily:

"I just guess she has done well, and far be it from me to be backward in saying it. You're a credit to your friends, Anne, that's what, and we're all proud of you."

That night Anne, who had wound up a delightful evening by a serious little talk with Mrs. Allan at the manse, knelt sweetly by her open window in a great sheen of moonshine and murmured a prayer of gratitude and aspiration that came straight from her heart. There was in it thankfulness for the past and reverent petition for the future; and when she slept on her white pillow her dreams were as fair and bright and beautiful as maidenhood might desire.

6. Local term for raking the hay into small haycocks, according to Montgomery's reminiscences:

I see the great hayfield—ruffling in the wind—lying in lustrous, fragrant swathes after mowing—covered with "coils" in the light of July sunsets. . . . "Down home" the real little cones into which the raked hay was hurriedly made up when rain threatened were always called "coils." Here in Ontario, that name is unknown. They are called "cocks." Many a time I have helped "coil" the hay, when a fine afternoon gave promise of a sudden shower and everybody was pressed into service to get the hay saved. It was not hard work —and the surroundings made it pleasant. I remember that Pensie and I coiled a whole field of hay one evening when the men were away, and a thunderstorm was brewing (MS Journals [1925], VI, 328–329).

"'There's something so stylish about you, Anne,' said Diana." Illustration by M. A. and W. A. J. Claus, from the first edition (1908).

CHAPTER XXXIII

THE HOTEL CONCERT

"PUT ON YOUR white organdy,[1] by all means, Anne," advised Diana decidedly.

They were together in the east gable chamber; outside it was only twilight—a lovely yellowish-green twilight with a clear blue cloudless sky. A big round moon, slowly deepening from her pallid lustre into burnished silver, hung over the Haunted Wood; the air was full of sweet summer sounds—sleepy birds twittering, freakish breezes, faraway voices and laughter. But in Anne's room the blind was drawn and the lamp lighted, for an important toilet[2] was being made.

The east gable was a very different place from what it had been on that night four years before, when Anne had felt its bareness penetrate to the marrow of her spirit with its inhospitable chill. Changes had crept in, Marilla conniving at them resignedly, until it was as sweet and dainty a nest as a young girl could desire.

The velvet carpet with the pink roses and the pink silk curtains of Anne's early visions had certainly never materialized; but her dreams had kept pace with her growth, and it is not probable she lamented them. The floor was covered with a pretty matting, and the curtains that softened the high win-

1. See n. 3, ch. 22.

2. *I.e.*, "toilette," the process of dressing.

3. The most delicately woven cotton fabric, a fashionable fabric for curtains and hangings.

4. See n.12, ch. 8.

Lucy Maud Montgomery's old room at Cavendish.

dow and fluttered in the vagrant breezes were of pale green art muslin.[3] The walls, hung not with gold and silver brocade tapestry, but with a dainty apple-blossom paper, were adorned with a few good pictures given Anne by Mrs. Allan. Miss Stacy's photograph occupied the place of honour, and Anne made a sentimental point of keeping fresh flowers on the bracket under it. To-night a spike of white lilies faintly perfumed the room like the dream of a fragrance. There was no "mahogany furniture"[4] but there was a white painted bookcase filled with books, a cushioned wicker rocker, a toilet-table befrilled with white muslin, a quaint, gilt-framed mirror with chubby pink cupids and purple grapes painted over its arched top, that used to hang in the spare room, and a low white bed.

Anne was dressing for a concert at the White Sands Hotel.

The guests had got it up in aid of the Charlottetown hospital and had hunted out all the available amateur talent in the surrounding districts to help it along. Bertha Sampson and Pearl Clay of the White Sands Baptist choir had been asked to sing a duet; Milton Clark of Newbridge was to give a violin solo; Winnie Adella Blair of Carmody was to sing a Scotch ballad; and Laura Spencer of Spencervale and Anne Shirley of Avonlea were to recite.

As Anne would have said at one time, it was "an epoch in her life,"[5] and she was deliciously athrill with the excitement of it. Matthew was in the seventh heaven of gratified pride over the honour conferred on his Anne and Marilla was not far behind, although she would have died rather than admit it, and said she didn't think it was very proper for a lot of young folks to be gadding over to the hotel without any responsible person with them.

Anne and Diana were to drive over with Jane Andrews and her brother Billy in their double seated buggy; and several other Avonlea girls and boys were going, too. There was a party of visitors expected out from town, and after the concert a supper was to be given to the performers.

"Do you really think the organdy will be best?" queried Anne anxiously. "I don't think it's as pretty as my blue-flowered muslin—and it certainly isn't so fashionable."

"But it suits you ever so much better," said Diana. "It's so soft and frilly and clinging. The muslin is stiff, and makes you look too dressed up. But the organdy seems as if it grew on you."

Anne sighed and yielded. Diana was beginning to have a reputation for notable taste in dressing and her advice on such subjects was much sought-after. She was looking very pretty herself on this particular night in a dress of the lovely wild-rose pink, from which Anne was for ever debarred; but she was not to take any part in the concert, so her appearance

5. See n. 1, ch. 29.

Illustration by Elizabeth R. Withington, from the 1931 edition.

was of minor importance. All her pains were bestowed upon Anne, who, she vowed, must, for the credit of Avonlea, be dressed and combed and adorned to the queen's taste.

"Pull out that frill a little more—so; here, let me tie your sash; now for your slippers. I'm going to braid your hair in two thick braids, and tie them half way up with big white bows—no, don't pull out a single curl over your forehead —just have the soft part. There is no way you do your hair suits you so well, Anne, and Mrs. Allan says you look like a Madonna[6] when you part it so. I shall fasten this little white house-rose[7] just behind your ear. There was just one on my bush and I saved it for you."

"Shall I put my pearl beads on?" asked Anne. "Matthew brought me a string from town last week and I know he'd like to see them on me."

Diana pursed up her lips, put her black head on one side critically, and finally pronounced in favour of the beads, which were thereupon tied around Anne's slim milk-white throat.

"There's something so stylish about you, Anne," said Diana, with unenvious admiration. "You hold your head with such an air. I suppose it's your figure. I am just a dumpling. I've always been afraid of it, and now I know it is so. Well, I suppose I shall just have to resign myself to it."

"But you have such dimples," said Anne, smiling affectionately into the pretty, vivacious face so near her own. "Lovely dimples, like little dents in cream. I have given up all hope of dimples. My dimple-dream will never come true; but so many of my dreams have that I mustn't complain. Am I all ready now?"

"All ready," assured Diana, as Marilla appeared in the doorway, a gaunt figure with grayer hair than of yore and no fewer angles, but with a much softer face. "Come right in and look at our elocutionist,[8] Marilla. Doesn't she look lovely?"

6. Presumably one of Raphael's Madonnas.

7. A potted plant for indoors as distinct from a garden rose.

8. An expert in elocution, or the art of public speaking. "Travelling performers of recitation pieces practiced a complex rhetorical art—a major theatrical form in the 1890s" (Rubio and Waterston, *SJ* I: 398, note). Emily's friend Ilse Burnley makes this her profession (see *Emily's Quest*). See Appendix, "Music and Elocution."

9. From Elizabeth Barrett
Browning's *Aurora Leigh* (Book 4,
l. 1013.

10. Echo of a hymn by John
Keble: "New every morning is the
love / Our wakening and uprising
prove," first published in *The
Christian Year* (1827).

Marilla emitted a sound between a sniff and a grunt.

"She looks neat and proper. I like that way of fixing her
hair. But I expect she'll ruin that dress driving over there in
the dust and dew with it, and it looks most too thin for these
damp nights. Organdy's the most unserviceable stuff in the
world anyhow, and I told Matthew so when he got it. But
there is no use in saying anything to Matthew nowadays.
Time was when he would take my advice, but now he just
buys things for Anne regardless, and the clerks at Carmody
know they can palm anything off on him. Just let them tell
him a thing is pretty and fashionable, and Matthew plunks
his money down for it. Mind you keep your skirt clear of the
wheel, Anne, and put your warm jacket on."

Then Marilla stalked down-stairs, thinking proudly how
sweet Anne looked, with that

One moonbeam from the forehead to the crown[9]

and regretting that she could not go to the concert herself to
hear her girl recite.

"I wonder if it *is* too damp for my dress," said Anne anxiously.

"Not a bit of it," said Diana, pulling up the window blind.
"It's a perfect night, and there won't be any dew. Look at the
moonlight."

"I'm so glad my window looks east into the sun-rising,"
said Anne, going over to Diana. "It's so splendid to see the
morning coming up over those long hills and glowing
through those sharp fir tops. It's new every morning,[10] and I
feel as if I washed my very soul in that bath of earliest sunshine. Oh, Diana, I love this little room so dearly. I don't
know how I'll get along without it when I go to town next
month."

"Don't speak of your going away to-night," begged Diana.

"I don't want to think of it, it makes me so miserable, and I do want to have a good time this evening. What are you going to recite, Anne? And are you nervous?"

"Not a bit. I've recited so often in public I don't mind at all now. I've decided to give 'The Maiden's Vow.'[11] It's so pathetic. Laura Spencer is going to give a comic recitation, but I'd rather make people cry than laugh."

"What will you recite if they encore you?"

"They won't dream of encoring me," scoffed Anne, who was not without her own secret hopes that they would, and already visioned herself telling Matthew all about it at the next morning's breakfast-table. "There are Billy and Jane now—I hear the wheels. Come on."

Billy Andrews insisted that Anne should ride on the front seat with him, so she unwillingly climbed up. She would have much preferred to sit back with the girls, where she could have laughed and chattered to her heart's content. There was not much of either laughter or chatter in Billy. He was a big fat stolid youth of twenty, with a round, expressionless face, and a painful lack of conversational gifts. But he admired Anne immensely, and was puffed up with pride over the prospect of driving to White Sands with that slim, upright figure beside him.

Anne, by dint of talking over her shoulder to the girls and occasionally passing a sop of civility to Billy—who grinned and chuckled and never could think of any reply until it was too late—contrived to enjoy the drive in spite of all. It was a night for enjoyment. The road was full of buggies, all bound for the hotel, and laughter, silver clear, echoed and re-echoed along it. When they reached the hotel it was a blaze of light from top to bottom. They were met by the ladies of the concert committee, one of whom took Anne off to the performers' dressing-room, which was filled with the members of a Charlottetown Symphony Club,[12] among whom Anne

11. There are at least two possible candidates for this poem referred to only by its title. One is "The Maiden's Vow" by Caroline Oliphant (later Baroness Nairne), found in *Life and Songs of the Baroness Nairne* (ed. Rev. Charles Rogers, 1869). It begins; "I've made a vow, I'll keep it true / I'll never married be." Although it has a somewhat sad ending, this poem seems too crisp and undramatic to be the piece given to such effect by Anne. The other candidate seems much more likely. This is "Mars La Tour, or, The Maiden's Vow," by Stafford MacGregor (see Appendix, "Recitation Pieces"). The imagery of the "white maid" and lines like "so a mystic white vision in the moon light did gleam" chime with images in *Anne*. In this poem the heroine, before the ill-fated battle, vows to marry her lover Maurice and no other; if he dies (as he does) she will be true to death. In *Anne of the Island*, Anne comes to realize that her feelings for Gilbert are like those of Reinette for her vanquished lover, although at the time of the concert she is still acting and feeling in opposition to him. He is really the member of the audience most affected by the poem and by the possibility for passion and fidelity within Anne that the concert episode illustrates.

12. An association formed by the people in the highest circles of the city to support a symphony orchestra and thus raise the general cultural level. Charlottetown, like other cities in the late nineteenth and early twentieth

centuries, felt the need of a symphony orchestra to ensure the status of the place. See Appendix, "Music and Elocution."

13. A bumpkin is by definition an awkward country fellow, a lout, so the adjective is superfluous; *belles* was once used seriously as a complimentary word for beautiful females, but *rustic (i.e., rural)* makes the phrase oxymoronic.

felt suddenly shy and frightened and countrified. Her dress which, in the east gable, had seemed so dainty and pretty, now seemed simple and plain—too simple and plain, she thought, among all the silks and laces that glistened and rustled around her. What were her pearl beads compared to the diamonds of the big, handsome lady near her? And how poor her one wee white rose must look beside all the hot-house flowers the others wore! Anne laid her hat and jacket away and shrank miserably into a corner. She wished herself back in the white room at Green Gables.

It was still worse on the platform of the big concert hall of the hotel, where she presently found herself. The electric lights dazzled her eyes, the perfume and hum bewildered her. She wished she were sitting down in the audience with Diana and Jane, who seemed to be having a splendid time away at the back. She was wedged in between a stout lady in pink silk and a tall, scornful-looking girl in a white lace dress. The stout lady occasionally turned her head squarely round and surveyed Anne through her eyeglasses until Anne, acutely sensitive of being so scrutinized, felt that she must scream aloud; and the white-lace girl kept talking audibly to her next neighbour about the "country bumpkins" and "rustic belles"[13] in the audience, languidly anticipating "such fun" from the displays of local talent on the programme. Anne believed that she would hate that white-lace girl to the end of life.

Unfortunately for Anne, a professional elocutionist was staying at the hotel and had consented to recite. She was a lithe, dark-eyed woman in a wonderful gown of shimmering gray stuff like woven moonbeams, with gems on her neck and in her dark hair. She had a marvellously flexible voice and wonderful power of expression; the audience went wild over her selection. Anne, forgetting all about herself and her troubles for the time, listened with rapt and shining eyes; but when the recitation ended she suddenly put her hands over her face.

She could never get up and recite after that—never. Had she ever thought she could recite? Oh, if she were only back at Green Gables!

At this unpropitious moment her name was called. Somehow, Anne—who did not notice the rather guilty little start of surprise the white-lace girl gave and would not have understood the subtle compliment implied therein if she had —got on her feet, and moved dizzily out to the front. She was so pale that Diana and Jane, down in the audience, clasped each other's hands in nervous sympathy.

Anne was the victim of an overwhelming attack of stage fright. Often as she had recited in public she had never before faced such an audience as this, and the sight of it paralyzed her energies completely. Everything was so strange, so brilliant, so bewildering—the rows of ladies in evening dress, the critical faces, the whole atmosphere of wealth and culture about her. Very different this from the plain benches at the Debating Club, filled with the homely, sympathetic faces of friends and neighbours. These people, she thought, would be merciless critics. Perhaps, like the white-lace girl, they anticipated amusement from her "rustic" efforts. She felt hopelessly, helplessly ashamed and miserable. Her knees trembled, her heart fluttered, a horrible faintness came over her; not a word could she utter, and the next moment she would have fled from the platform despite the humiliation which, she felt, must ever after be her portion if she did so.

But suddenly, as her dilated, frightened eyes gazed out over the audience, she saw Gilbert Blythe away at the back of the room, bending forward with a smile on his face—a smile which seemed to Anne at once triumphant and taunting. In reality it was nothing of the kind. Gilbert was merely smiling with appreciation of the whole affair in general and of the effect produced by Anne's slender white form and spiritual face against a background of palms in particular. Josie Pye, whom he had driven over, sat beside him, and her face certainly was triumphant and taunting. But Anne did not see Josie, and would not have cared if she had. She drew a long breath and flung her head up proudly, courage and determination tingling over her like an electric shock. She *would not* fail before Gilbert Blythe—he should never be able to laugh at her, never, never! Her fright and nervousness vanished; and she began her recitation, her clear, sweet voice reaching to the farthest corner of the room without a tremor or a break. Self-possession was fully restored to her, and in the reaction from that horrible moment of powerlessness she recited as she had never done before. When she finished there were bursts of honest applause. Anne, stepping back to her seat, blushing with shyness and delight, found her hand vigorously clasped and shaken by the stout lady in pink silk.

"My dear, you did splendidly," she puffed. I've been crying like a baby, actually I have. There, they're encoring you—they're bound to have you back!"

"Oh, I can't go," said Anne confusedly. "But yet—I must, or Matthew will be disappointed. He said they would encore me."

"Then don't disappoint Matthew," said the pink lady, laughing.

Smiling, blushing, limpid-eyed, Anne tripped back and gave a quaint, funny little selection that captivated her audience still further. The rest of the evening was quite a little triumph for her.

When the concert was over, the stout pink lady—who was the wife of an American millionaire—took her under her wing and introduced her to everybody, and everybody was very nice to her. The professional elocutionist, Mrs. Evans, came and chatted with her, telling her that she had a charming voice and "interpreted" her selections beautifully. Even the white-lace girl paid her a languid little compliment. They had supper in the big, beautifully decorated dining-room;

Diana and Jane were invited to partake of this also since they had come with Anne, but Billy was nowhere to be found, having decamped in mortal fear of some such invitation. He was in waiting for them, with the team, however, when it was all over, and the three girls came merrily out into the calm white moonshine radiance. Anne breathed deeply, and looked into the clear sky beyond the dark boughs of the firs.

Oh, it was good to be out again in the purity and silence of the night! How great and still and wonderful everything was, with the murmur of the sea sounding through it and the darkling cliffs beyond like grim giants guarding enchanted coasts.

"Hasn't it been a perfectly splendid time?" sighed Jane, as they drove away. "I just wish I was a rich American and could spend my summer at a hotel and wear jewels and low-necked dresses and have ice-cream and chicken salad every blessed day. I'm sure it would be ever so much more fun than teaching school. Anne, your recitation was simply great, although I thought at first you were never going to begin. I think it was better than Mrs. Evans'."

"Oh, no, don't say things like that, Jane," said Anne quickly, "because it sounds silly. It couldn't be better than Mrs. Evans', you know, for she is a professional, and I'm only a schoolgirl, with a little knack of reciting. I'm quite satisfied if the people just liked mine pretty well."

"I've a compliment for you, Anne," said Diana. "At least I think it must be a compliment because of the tone he said it in. Part of it was anyhow. There was an American sitting behind Jane and me—such a romantic-looking man, with coal-black hair and eyes. Josie Pye says he is a distinguished artist and that her mother's cousin in Boston is married to a man that used to go to school with him. Well, we heard him say—didn't we, Jane?—'Who is that girl on the platform with the splendid Titian hair? She has a face I should like to paint.' There now, Anne. But what does Titian hair[14] mean?"

14. Red-gold in color, like the hair on women in paintings by the Venetian painter Tiziano Vecellio (ca. 1487–1576).

15. Cf. "Now faith is the substance of things hoped for, the evidence of things not seen" (Hebrews 11:1). See Variants.

"Being interpreted it means plain red, I guess," laughed Anne. "Titian was a very famous artist, who liked to paint red-haired women."

"*Did* you see all the diamonds those ladies wore?" sighed Jane. "They were simply dazzling. Wouldn't you just love to be rich, girls?"

"We are rich," said Anne stanchly. "Why, we have sixteen years to our credit, and we're happy as queens, and we've all got imaginations more or less. Look at that sea, girls—all silver and shadow and vision of things not seen.[15] We couldn't enjoy its loveliness any more if we had millions of dollars and ropes of diamonds. You wouldn't change into any of those women if you could. Would you want to be that white-lace girl and wear a sour look all your life, as if you'd been born turning up your nose at the world? Or the pink lady, kind and nice as she is, so short and stout that you'd really no figure at all? Or even Mrs. Evans, with that sad, sad look in her eyes? She must have been dreadfully unhappy sometime to have such a look. You *know* you wouldn't, Jane Andrews!"

"I *don't* know—exactly," said Jane unconvinced. "I think diamonds would comfort a person for a good deal."

"Well, I don't want to be any one but myself, even if I go uncomforted by diamonds all my life," declared Anne. "I'm quite content to be Anne of Green Gables, with my string of pearl beads. I know Matthew gave me as much love with them as ever went with Madame the Pink Lady's jewels."

CHAPTER XXXIV

A QUEEN'S GIRL

THE NEXT three weeks were busy ones at Green Gables, for Anne was getting ready to go to Queen's, and there was much sewing to be done, and many things to be talked over and arranged. Anne's outfit was ample and pretty, for Matthew saw to that and Marilla for once made no objections whatever to anything he purchased or suggested. More—one evening she went up to the east gable with her arms full of a delicate pale green material.

"Anne, here's something for a nice light dress for you. I don't suppose you really need it; you've plenty of pretty waists; but I thought maybe you'd like something real dressy to wear if you were asked out anywhere of an evening in town, to a party or anything like that. I hear that Jane and Ruby and Josie have got 'evening dresses' as they call them, and I don't mean you shall be behind them. I got Mrs. Allan to help me pick it in town last week and we'll get Emily Gillis to make it for you. Emily has got taste and her fits aren't to be equalled."

"Oh, Marilla, it's just lovely," said Anne. "Thank you so much. I don't believe you ought to be so kind to me—it's making it harder every day for me to go away."

The green dress was made up with as many tucks and frills

and shirrings as Emily's taste permitted. Anne put it on one evening for Matthew's and Marilla's benefit, and recited "The Maiden's Vow" for them in the kitchen. As Marilla watched the bright, animated face and graceful motions her thoughts went back to the evening Anne had arrived at Green Gables, and memory recalled a vivid picture of the odd, frightened child in her preposterous yellowish-brown wincey dress, the heartbreak looking out of her tearful eyes. Something in the memory brought tears to Marilla's own eyes.

"I declare, my recitation has made you cry, Marilla," said Anne gaily, stooping over Marilla's chair to drop a butterfly kiss on that lady's cheek. "Now, I call that a positive triumph."

"No, I wasn't crying over your piece," said Marilla, who would have scorned to be betrayed into such weakness by any "poetry stuff." "I just couldn't help thinking of the little girl you used to be, Anne. And I was wishing you could have stayed a little girl, even with all your queer ways. You're grown up now and you're going away; and you look so tall and stylish and so — so — different altogether in that dress — as if you didn't belong in Avonlea at all — and I just got lonesome thinking it all over."

"Marilla!" Anne sat down on Marilla's gingham lap, took Marilla's lined face between her hands, and looked gravely and tenderly into Marilla's eyes. "I'm not a bit changed — not really. I'm only just pruned down and branched out. The real *me* — back here — is just the same. It won't make a bit of difference where I go or how much I change outwardly; at heart I shall always be your little Anne who will love you and Matthew and dear Green Gables more and better every day of her life."

Anne laid her fresh young cheek against Marilla's faded one, and reached out a hand to pat Matthew's shoulder. Marilla would have given much just then to have possessed Anne's power of putting her feelings into words; but nature and habit had willed it otherwise, and she could only put

"I'm not a bit changed—not really." Illustration by Sybil Tawse, from the 1933 edition.

her arms close about her girl and hold her tenderly to her heart, wishing that she need never let her go.

Matthew, with a suspicious moisture in his eyes, got up and went out of doors. Under the stars of the blue summer night he walked agitatedly across the yard to the gate under the poplars.

"Well now, I guess she ain't been much spoiled," he muttered proudly. "I guess my putting in my oar occasional never did much harm after all. She's smart and pretty, and loving, too, which is better than all the rest. She's been a blessing to us, and there never was a luckier mistake than what Mrs. Spencer made—if it *was* luck. I don't believe it was any such thing. It was Providence, because the Almighty saw we needed her, I reckon."

The day finally came when Anne must go to town. She and Matthew drove in one fine September morning, after a tearful parting with Diana and an untearful practical one—on Marilla's side at least—with Marilla. But when Anne had gone Diana dried her tears and went to a beach picnic at White Sands with some of her Carmody cousins, where she contrived to enjoy herself tolerably well; while Marilla plunged fiercely into unnecessary work and kept at it all day long with the bitterest kind of a heart-ache—the ache that burns and gnaws and cannot wash itself away in ready tears. But that night, when Marilla went to bed, acutely miserably conscious that the little gable room at the end of the hall was untenanted by any vivid young life and unstirred by any soft breathing, she buried her face in her pillow, and wept for her girl in a passion of sobs that appalled her when she grew calm enough to reflect how very wicked it must be to "take on" so about a sinful fellow creature.

Anne and the rest of the Avonlea scholars reached town just in time to hurry off to the Academy. That first day passed pleasantly enough in a whirl of excitement, meeting all the new students, learning to know the professors by sight and being assorted and organized into classes. Anne intended taking up the Second Year work,[1] being advised to do so by Miss Stacy; Gilbert Blythe elected to do the same. This meant getting a First Class teacher's license in one year instead of two, if they were successful; but it also meant much more and harder work. Jane, Ruby, Josie, Charlie, and Moody Spurgeon, not being troubled with the stirrings of ambition, were content to take up the Second Class work. Anne was conscious of a pang of loneliness when she found herself in a room with fifty other students, not one of whom she knew, except the tall brown-haired boy across the room; and knowing him in the fashion she did, did not help her much, as she reflected pessimistically. Yet she was undeniably glad that they were in the same class; the old rivalry could still be carried on, and Anne would hardly have known what to do if it had been lacking.

"I wouldn't feel comfortable without it," she thought. "Gilbert looks awfully determined. I suppose he's making up his mind, here and now, to win the medal. What a splendid chin he has! I never noticed it before. I do wish Jane and Ruby had gone in for First Class, too. I suppose I won't feel so much like a cat in a strange garret when I get acquainted, though. I wonder which of the girls here are going to be my friends. It's really an interesting speculation. Of course I promised Diana that no Queen's girl, no matter how much I liked her, should ever be as dear to me as she is; but I've lots of second-best affections to bestow. I like the look of that girl with the brown eyes and the crimson waist.[2] She looks vivid and red-rosy; then there's that pale fair one gazing out of the window. She has lovely hair, and looks as if she knew a thing or two about dreams. I'd like to know them both — know them well — well enough to walk with my arm about their waists, and call them nicknames. But just now I don't know them and they don't know me, and probably don't want to know me particularly. Oh, it's lonesome!"

1. See Introduction, pp. 13–14, and Appendix, "Education."

2. *I.e.*, a red dress. See n. 8, ch. 19.

Lucy Maud Montgomery with Prince of Wales College schoolmates, 1894.

3. A very English phrase describing a woman of gentle birth who is used to good society but is in "reduced circumstances" or under new financial constraints, thus being forced into a life not the equal of that to which she has been accustomed.

4. By 1885, "An Act to Incorporate the Telephone Company of Prince Edward Island" was passed. Margaret Lord Gray's 1890 diary (May 9 entry) shows that there was a working system by 1890 (*One Woman's Charlottetown*, 125). By 1894, "An Act Respecting Telephone Extension" encouraged the connection of Charlottetown with all other areas.

5. Cf. "To see her trampled under alien feet!" (L. Morris, "An Ode to Free Rome: September 1870," Stanza 8, l. 9).

It was lonesomer still when Anne found herself alone in her hall bedroom that night at twilight. She was not to board with the other girls, who all had relatives in town to take pity on them. Miss Josephine Barry would have liked to board her, but Beechwood was so far from the Academy that it was out of the question; so Miss Barry hunted up a boarding house, assuring Matthew and Marilla that it was the very place for Anne.

"The lady who keeps it is a reduced gentlewoman,"[3] explained Miss Barry. "Her husband was a British officer, and she is very careful what sort of boarders she takes. Anne will not meet with any objectionable persons under her roof. The table is good and the house is near the Academy in a quiet neighbourhood."

All this might be true and, indeed, proved to be so, but it did not materially help Anne in the first agony of homesickness that seized upon her. She looked dismally about her narrow little room, with its dull-papered, pictureless walls, its small iron bedstead and empty bookcase; and a horrible choke came into her throat as she thought of her own white room at Green Gables, where she would have the pleasant consciousness of a great, green, still outdoors, of sweet-peas growing in the garden, and moonlight falling on the orchard, of the brook below the slope and the spruce boughs tossing in the night wind beyond it, of a vast starry sky, and the light from Diana's window shining out through the gap in the trees. Here there was nothing of this. Anne knew that outside of her window was a hard street, with a network of telephone wires shutting out the sky,[4] the tramp of alien feet,[5] and a thousand lights gleaming on stranger faces. She knew that she was going to cry, and fought against it.

"I *won't* cry. It's silly—and weak—there's the third tear splashing down by my nose. There are more coming! I must think of something funny to stop them. But there's nothing funny except what is connected with Avonlea, and that only makes things worse—four—five—I'm going home next Friday, but that seems a hundred years away. Oh, Matthew is nearly home by now—and Marilla is at the gate, looking down the lane for him—six—seven—eight—oh, there's no use in counting them! They're coming in a flood presently. I can't cheer up—I don't *want* to cheer up. It's nicer to be miserable!"

The flood of tears would have come, no doubt, had not Josie Pye appeared at that moment. In the joy of seeing a familiar face Anne forgot that there had never been much love lost between her and Josie. As a part of Avonlea life even a Pye was welcome.

"I'm so glad you came up," Anne said sincerely.

"You've been crying," remarked Josie, with aggravating pity. "I suppose you're homesick—some people have so little self-control in that respect. I've no intention of being homesick, I can tell you. Town's too jolly after that poky old Avonlea. I wonder how I ever existed there so long. You shouldn't cry, Anne; it isn't becoming for your nose and eyes get red, and then you seem all red. I'd a perfectly scrumptious time in the Academy today. Our French professor is simply a duck. His moustache would give you kerwollops of the heart.[6] Have you anything eatable around, Anne? I'm literally starving. Ah, I guessed likely Marilla'd load you up with cake. That's why I called round. Otherwise I'd have gone to the park to hear the band play with Frank Stockley. He boards the same place I do and he's a sport. He noticed you in class today, and asked me who the red-headed girl was. I told him you were an orphan the Cuthberts had adopted, and nobody knew very much about what you'd been before that."

Anne was wondering if, after all, solitude and tears were not more satisfactory than Josie Pye's companionship when Jane and Ruby appeared, each with an inch of Queen's

6. *Ker-* is the first element in numerous onomatopoeic or echoic formations intended to imitate the sound or the effect of the fall of some heavy object. Josie Pye here seems to be saying that her French professor's mustache makes her heart thump hard.

7. Presumably the *Aeneid* of Publius Vergilius Maro, or Virgil (70–19 B.C.), or selected books of that epic poem.

8. Cf. Sir Walter Scott's *Rob Roy* (1817; Chapter 34): "My foot is on my native heath, and my name is MacGregor."

colour ribbon—purple and scarlet—pinned proudly to her coat. As Josie was not "speaking" to Jane just then she had to subside into comparative harmlessness.

"Well," said Jane with a sigh, "I feel as if I'd lived many moons since the morning. I ought to be home studying my Virgil[7]—that horrid old professor gave us twenty lines to start in on to-morrow. But I simply couldn't settle down to study to-night. Anne, methinks I see the traces of tears. If you've been crying *do* own up. It will restore my self-respect, for I was shedding tears freely before Ruby came along. I don't mind being a goose so much if somebody else is goosey, too. Cake? You'll give me a teeny piece, won't you? Thank you. It has the real Avonlea flavour."

Ruby, perceiving the Queen's calendar lying on the table, wanted to know if Anne meant to try for the gold medal.

Anne blushed and admitted she was thinking of it.

"Oh, that reminds me," said Josie, "Queen's is to get one of the Avery Scholarships after all. The word came to-day. Frank Stockley told me—his uncle is one of the board of governors, you know. It will be announced in the Academy to-morrow."

An Avery Scholarship! Anne felt her heart beat more quickly, and the horizons of her ambition shifted and broadened as if by magic. Before Josie had told the news Anne's highest pinnacle of aspiration had been a teacher's provincial license, Class First, at the end of the year and perhaps the medal. But now in one moment Anne saw herself winning the Avery Scholarship, taking an Arts course at Redmond College, and graduating in a gown and mortar board, all before the echo of Josie's words had died away. For the Avery Scholarship was in English, and Anne felt that here her foot was on her native heath.[8]

A wealthy manufacturer of New Brunswick had died and left part of his fortune to endow a large number of scholarships to be distributed among the various high schools and academies of the Maritime Provinces, according to their re-spective standings. There had been much doubt whether one would be allotted to Queen's, but the matter was settled at last, and at the end of the year the graduate who made the highest mark in English and English Literature would win the scholarship—two hundred and fifty dollars a year for four years at Redmond College.[9] No wonder that Anne went to bed that night with tingling cheeks!

"I'll win that scholarship if hard work can do it," she resolved. "Wouldn't Matthew be proud if I got to be a B.A.? Oh, it's delightful to have ambitions. I'm so glad I have such a lot. And there never seems to be any end to them—that's the best of it. Just as soon as you attain to one ambition you see another one glittering higher up still. It does make life so interesting."

9. A made-up name. Montgomery attended the original prototype of Redmond, Dalhousie College in Halifax, Nova Scotia, in 1895.

PRINCE OF WALES COLLEGE, CHARLOTTETOWN, P.E.I.

Top: Old Prince of Wales College, Charlottetown, P.E.I., 1894.

Bottom: First-class students at P.W.C., 1893–94. Lucy Maud Montgomery is seated in the second row, wearing white.

CHAPTER XXXV

THE WINTER AT QUEEN'S

ANNE'S HOMESICKNESS wore off, greatly helped in the wearing by her week-end visits home. As long as the open weather lasted the Avonlea students went out to Carmody on the new branch railway every Friday night. Diana and several other Avonlea young folks were generally on hand to meet them and they all walked over to Avonlea in a merry party. Anne thought those Friday evening gipsyings over the autumnal hills in the crisp golden air, with the homelights of Avonlea twinkling beyond, were the best and dearest hours in the whole week.

Gilbert Blythe nearly always walked with Ruby Gillis and carried her satchel for her. Ruby was a very handsome young lady now, thinking herself quite as grown up as she really was; she wore her skirts as long as her mother would let her and did her hair up in town, though she had to take it down when she went home. She had large, bright-blue eyes, a brilliant complexion and a plump showy figure. She laughed a great deal, was cheerful and good-tempered, and enjoyed the pleasant things of life frankly.

"But I shouldn't think she was the sort of girl Gilbert would like," whispered Jane to Anne. Anne did not think so either, but she would not have said so for the Avery

Scholarship. She could not help thinking, too, that it would be very pleasant to have such a friend as Gilbert to jest and chatter with and exchange ideas about books and studies and ambitions. Gilbert had ambitions, she knew, and Ruby Gillis did not seem the sort of person with whom such could be profitably discussed.

There was no silly sentiment in Anne's ideas concerning Gilbert. Boys were to her, when she thought about them at all, merely possible good comrades. If she and Gilbert had been friends she would not have cared how many other friends he had nor with whom he walked. She had a genius for friendship; girl friends she had in plenty; but she had a vague consciousness that masculine friendship might also be a good thing to round out one's conceptions of companionship and furnish broader standpoints of judgment and comparison. Not that Anne could have put her feelings on the matter into just such clear definition. But she thought that if Gilbert had ever walked home with her from the train, over the crisp fields and along the ferny byways, they might have had many and merry and interesting conversations about the new world that was opening around them and their hopes and ambitions therein. Gilbert was a clever young fellow, with his own thoughts about things and a determination to get the best out of life and put the best into it. Ruby Gillis told Jane Andrews that she didn't understand half the things Gilbert Blythe said; he talked just like Anne Shirley did when she had a thoughtful fit on and for her part she didn't think it any fun to be bothering about books and that sort of thing when you didn't have to. Frank Stockley had lots more dash and go, but then he wasn't half as good-looking as Gilbert and she really couldn't decide which she liked best!

In the Academy Anne gradually drew a little circle of friends about her, thoughtful, imaginative ambitious students like herself. With the "rose-red" girl, Stella Maynard, and the "dream girl," Priscilla Grant, she soon became intimate, finding the latter pale, spiritual-looking maiden to be full to the brim of mischief and pranks and fun, while the vivid, black-eyed Stella had a heartful of wistful dreams and fancies, as aerial and rainbow like as Anne's own.

After the Christmas holidays the Avonlea students gave up going home on Fridays and settled down to hard work. By this time all the Queen's scholars had gravitated into their own places in the ranks and the various classes had assumed distinct and settled shadings of individuality. Certain facts had become generally accepted. It was admitted that the medal contestants had practically narrowed down to three — Gilbert Blythe, Anne Shirley, and Lewis Wilson; the Avery Scholarship was more doubtful, anyone of a certain six being a possible winner. The bronze medal for mathematics was considered as good as won by a fat, funny little up-country boy with a bumpy forehead and a patched coat.

Ruby Gillis was the handsomest girl of the year at the Academy; in the Second Year classes Stella Maynard carried off the palm for beauty, with a small but critical minority in favour of Anne Shirley. Ethel Marr was admitted by all competent judges to have the most stylish modes of hair-dressing, and Jane Andrews — plain, plodding, conscientious Jane — carried off the honours in the domestic science course. Even Josie Pye attained a certain pre-eminence as the sharpest-tongued young lady in attendance at Queen's. So it may be fairly stated that Miss Stacy's old pupils held their own in the wider arena of the academical course.

Anne worked hard and steadily. Her rivalry with Gilbert was as intense as it had ever been in Avonlea school, although it was not known in the class at large, but somehow the bitterness had gone out of it. Anne no longer wished to win for the sake of defeating Gilbert; rather, for the proud consciousness of a well-won victory over a worthy foeman.[1] It would

1. An echo of Scott's *The Lady of the Lake*. See n. 13, ch. 30.

2. From Tennyson's "The Brook": "On such a time as goes before the leaf / When all the wood stands in a mist of green" (ll. 13–14). See n. 1, ch. 31; n. 4, ch. 1; and Appendix, "Literary Allusion."

be worth while to win, but she no longer thought life would be insupportable if she did not.

In spite of lessons the students found opportunities for pleasant times. Anne spent many of her spare hours at Beechwood and generally ate her Sunday dinners there and went to church with Miss Barry. The latter was, as she admitted, growing old, but her black eyes were not dim nor the vigour of her tongue in the least abated. But she never sharpened the latter on Anne, who continued to be a prime favourite with the critical old lady.

"That Anne-girl improves all the time," she said. "I get tired of other girls—there is such a provoking and eternal sameness about them. Anne has as many shades as a rainbow and every shade is the prettiest while it lasts. I don't know that she is as amusing as she was when she was a child but she makes me love her and I like people who make me love them! It saves me so much trouble in making myself love them."

Then, almost before anybody realized it, spring had come; out in Avonlea the Mayflowers were peeping pinkly out on the sere barrens where snow-wreaths lingered; and the "mist of green"[2] was on the woods and in the valleys. But in Charlottetown harassed Queen's students thought and talked only of examinations.

"It doesn't seem possible that the term is nearly over," said Anne. "Why, last fall it seemed so long to look forward to— a whole winter of studies and classes. And here we are, with the exams looming up next week. Girls, sometimes I feel as if those exams meant everything, but when I look at the big buds swelling on those chestnut-trees and the misty blue air at the end of the streets they don't seem half so important."

Jane and Ruby and Josie, who had dropped in, did not take this view of it. To them the coming examinations were constantly very important indeed—far more important than chestnut buds or May-time hazes. It was all very well for Anne, who was sure of passing at least, to have her moments of belittling them, but when your whole future depended on them—as the girls truly thought theirs did—you could not regard them philosophically.

"I've lost seven pounds in the last two weeks," sighed Jane. "It's no use to say don't worry. I *will* worry. Worrying helps you some—it seems as if you were doing something when you're worrying. It would be dreadful if I failed to get my license after going to Queen's all winter and spending so much money."

"*I* don't care," said Josie Pye. "If I don't pass this year I'm coming back next. My father can afford to send me. Anne, Frank Stockley says that Professor Tremaine said Gilbert Blythe was sure to get the medal and that Emily Clay would likely win the Avery Scholarship."

"That may make me feel badly to-morrow, Josie," laughed Anne, "but just now I honestly feel that as long as I know the violets are coming out all purple down in the hollow below Green Gables and that little ferns are poking their heads up in Lover's Lane, it's not a great deal of difference whether I win the Avery or not. I've done my best and I begin to understand what is meant by the 'joy of the strife.'[3] Next to trying and winning, the best thing is trying and failing. Girls, don't talk about exams! Look at that arch of pale green sky over those houses and picture to yourselves what it must look like over the purply-dark beech-woods back of Avonlea."

"What are you going to wear for commencement, Jane?" asked Ruby practically.

Jane and Josie both answered at once and the chatter drifted into a side-eddy of fashions. But Anne, with her elbows on the window sill, her soft cheek laid against her clasped hands, and her eyes filled with visions, looked out unheedingly

3. From Felicia Dorothea Browne Hemans's "The Woman on the Field of Battle": "Some for the stormy play / And joy of strife;– / And some, to fling away / A weary life:–" (Stanza 12). In her journals Montgomery quotes Byron's "Ode to Napoleon Buonoparte," including the phrase: "The rapture of the strife" (*SJ* II [Nov. 12, 1918]: 277).

4. An echo of Milton's *Aeropagitica* (1644): "I cannot praise a fugitive and cloistered virtue, unexercised and unbreathed, that never sallies out and sees her adversary, but slinks out of the race, where that immortal garland is to be run for, not without dust and heat."

across city roof and spire to that glorious dome of sunset sky and wove her dreams of a possible future from the golden tissue of youth's own optimism. All the Beyond was hers with its possibilities lurking rosily in the oncoming years—each year a rose of promise to be woven into an immortal chaplet.[4]

CHAPTER XXXVI

THE GLORY
AND THE DREAM[1]

ON THE MORNING when the final results of all the examinations were to be posted on the bulletin board at Queen's, Anne and Jane walked down the street together. Jane was smiling and happy; examinations were over and she was comfortably sure she had made a pass at least; further considerations troubled Jane not at all; she had no soaring ambitions and consequently was not affected with the unrest attendant thereon. For we pay a price for everything we get or take in this world; and although ambitions are well worth having, they are not to be cheaply won, but exact their dues of work and self-denial, anxiety and discouragement. Anne was pale and quiet; in ten more minutes she would know who had won the medal and who the Avery. Beyond those ten minutes there did not seem, just then, to be anything worth being called Time.

"Of course you'll win one of them anyhow," said Jane, who couldn't understand how the faculty could be so unfair as to order it otherwise.

"I have no hope of the Avery," said Anne. "Everybody says Emily Clay will win it. And I'm not going to march up to that bulletin board and look at it before everybody. I haven't

1. From William Wordsworth's "Ode: Intimations of Immortality from Recollections of Early Childhood" (1807; Stanza 1):

> There was a time when
>   meadow, grove and stream,
> The earth, and every common
>   sight,
> To me did seem
> Appareled in celestial light,
> The glory and the freshness of a
>   dream
> It is not now as it hath been of
>   yore—
> Turn wheresoe'er I may.
> By night or day.
> The things which I have seen I
>   now can see no more.

See also "Whither is fled the visionary gleam? / Where is it now, the glory and the dream?" (Stanza 4).

the moral courage. I'm going straight to the girls' dressing room. You must read the announcements and then come and tell me, Jane. And I implore you in the name of our old friendship to do it as quickly as possible. If I have failed just say so, without trying to break it gently; and whatever you do *don't* sympathize with me. Promise me this, Jane."

Jane promised solemnly; but, as it happened, there was no necessity for such a promise. When they went up the entrance steps of Queen's they found the hall full of boys who were carrying Gilbert Blythe around on their shoulders and yelling at the tops of their voices, "Hurrah for Blythe, Medallist!"

For a moment Anne felt one sickening pang of defeat and disappointment. So she had failed and Gilbert had won! Well, Matthew would be sorry—he had been so sure she would win.

And then!

Somebody called out:

"Three cheers for Miss Shirley, winner of the Avery!"

"Oh, Anne," gasped Jane, as they fled to the girls' dressing room amid hearty cheers. "Oh, Anne, I'm so proud! Isn't it splendid?"

And then the girls were around them and Anne was the centre of a laughing congratulating group. Her shoulders were thumped and her hands shaken vigorously. She was pushed and pulled and hugged and among it all she managed to whisper to Jane:

"Oh, won't Matthew and Marilla be pleased! I must write the news home right away."

Commencement was the next important happening. The exercises were held in the big assembly hall of the Academy. Addresses were given, essays read, songs sung, the public award of diplomas, prizes and medals made.

Matthew and Marilla were there, with eyes and ears for only one student on the platform—a tall girl in pale green, with faintly flushed cheeks and starry eyes, who read the best essay and was pointed out and whispered about as the Avery Winner.

"Reckon you're glad we kept her, Marilla?" whispered Matthew, speaking for the first time since he had entered the hall, when Anne had finished her essay.

"It's not the first time I've been glad," retorted Marilla. "You do like to rub things in, Matthew Cuthbert."

Miss Barry, who was sitting behind them, leaned forward and poked Marilla in the back with her parasol.

"Aren't you proud of that Anne-girl? I am," she said.

Anne went home to Avonlea with Matthew and Marilla that evening. She had not been home since April and she felt that she could not wait another day. The apple-blossoms were out and the world was fresh and young. Diana was at Green Gables to meet her. In her own white room, where Marilla had set a flowering house-rose on the window sill, Anne looked about her and drew a long breath of happiness.

"Oh, Diana, it's so good to be back again. It's so good to see those pointed firs[2] coming out against the pink sky— and that white orchard and the old Snow Queen. Isn't the breath of the mint delicious? And that tea-rose—why, it's a song and a hope and a prayer all in one. And it's *good* to see you again, Diana!"

"I thought you liked that Stella Maynard better than me," said Diana reproachfully. "Josie Pye told me you did. Josie said you were *infatuated* with her."

Anne laughed and pelted Diana with the faded "June lilies" of her bouquet.

"Stella Maynard is the dearest girl in the world except one and you are that one, Diana," she said. "I love you more than ever—and I've so many things to tell you. But just now I feel as if it were joy enough to sit here and look at you. I'm tired, I think—tired of being studious and ambitious. I mean to spend at least two hours to-morrow lying out in the orchard grass, thinking of absolutely nothing."

2. A phrase probably derived from Sarah Orne Jewett's *The Country of the Pointed Firs* (1896).

"You've done splendidly, Anne. I suppose you won't be teaching now that you've won the Avery?"

"No. I'm going to Redmond in September. Doesn't it seem wonderful? I'll have a brand-new stock of ambition laid in by that time after three glorious, golden months of vacation. Jane and Ruby are going to teach. Isn't it splendid to think we all got through, even to Moody Spurgeon and Josie Pye?"

"The Newbridge trustees have offered Jane their school already," said Diana. "Gilbert Blythe is going to teach, too. He has to. His father can't afford to send him to college next year, after all, so he means to earn his own way through. I expect he'll get the school here if Miss Ames decides to leave."

Anne felt a queer little sensation of dismayed surprise. She had not known this; she had expected that Gilbert would be going to Redmond also. What would she do without their inspiring rivalry? Would not work, even at a co-educational college with a real degree in prospect, be rather flat without her friend the enemy?

The next morning at breakfast it suddenly struck Anne that Matthew was not looking well. Surely he was much grayer than he had been a year before.

"Marilla," she said hesitatingly when he had gone out, "is Matthew quite well?"

"No, he isn't," said Marilla in a troubled tone. "He's had some real bad spells with his heart this spring and he won't spare himself a mite. I've been real worried about him, but he's some better this while back and we've got a good hired man, so I'm hoping he'll kind of rest and pick up. Maybe he will now you're home. You always cheer him up."

Anne leaned across the table and took Marilla's face in her hands.

"You are not looking as well yourself as I'd like to see you, Marilla. You look tired. I'm afraid you've been working too hard. You must take a rest, now that I'm home. I'm just going to take this one day off to visit all the dear old spots and hunt up my old dreams, and then it will be your turn to be lazy while I do the work."

Marilla smiled affectionately at her girl.

"It's not the work—it's my head. I've a pain so often now —behind my eyes. Doctor Spencer's been fussing with glasses but they don't do me any good. There is a distinguished oculist[3] coming to the Island the last of June and the doctor says I must see him. I guess I'll have to. I can't read or sew with any comfort now. Well, Anne, you've done real well at Queen's I must say. To take First Class License in one year and win the Avery Scholarship—well, well, Mrs. Lynde says pride goes before a fall[4] and she doesn't believe in the higher education of women at all; she says it unfits them for women's true sphere. I don't believe a word of it. Speaking of Rachel reminds me—did you hear anything about the Abbey Bank[5] lately, Anne?"

"I heard that it was shaky," answered Anne. "Why?"

"That is what Rachel said. She was up here one day last week and said there was some talk about it. Matthew felt real worried. All we have saved is in that bank—every penny. I wanted Matthew to put it in the Savings Bank in the first place, but old Mr. Abbey was a great friend of father's and he'd always banked with him. Matthew said any bank with him at the head of it was good enough for anybody."

"I think he has only been its nominal head for many years," said Anne. "He is a very old man; his nephews are really at the head of the institution."

"Well, when Rachel told us that, I wanted Matthew to draw our money right out and he said he'd think of it. But Mr. Russell told him yesterday the bank was all right."

Anne had her good day in the companionship of the outdoor world. She never forgot that day; it was so bright and golden and fair, so free from shadow and so lavish of blossom. Anne spent some of its rich hours in the orchard; she went to the Dryad's Bubble and Willowmere and Violet Vale; she called

3. A famous eye doctor. The page of the Charlottetown *Daily Patriot* of 15 July 1893 bearing the names of Montgomery and all others who had passed the Entrance also contains a large advertisement for a visiting oculist from Boston.

4. From the biblical "pride goeth before destruction, and an haughty spirit before a fall" (Proverbs 16:18).

5. A made-up name with Roman Catholic associations. According to Virginia Careless, a collapse of the Bank of P. E. I. took place in 1882 ("The Highjacking of 'Anne'").

6. Behind this sentence are recollections of Tennyson's so-called "Bugle Song" in *The Princess* (1847), which was added, like the other songs, in the 1853 edition: "The splendour falls on castle walls / And snowy summits old in story: / The long light shakes across the lakes, / And the wild cataracts leaps in glory" (Section IV, ll. 1–4). "The Bugle Song" appears in the *Sixth Royal Reader* (362). In *Emily of New Moon,* Miss Brownell slaps Emily Starr for her enthusiasm over this poem (ch. 9).

at the manse and had a satisfying talk with Mrs. Allan; and finally in the evening she went with Matthew for the cows, through Lover's Lane to the back pasture. The woods were all gloried through with sunset and the warm splendour of it streamed down through the hill gaps in the west.[6] Matthew walked slowly with bent head; Anne, tall and erect, suited her springing step to his.

"You've been working too hard to-day, Matthew," she said reproachfully, "Why won't you take things easier?"

"Well now, I can't seem to," said Matthew, as he opened the yard gate to let the cows through. "It's only that I'm getting old, Anne, and keep forgetting it. Well, well, I've always worked pretty hard and I'd rather drop in harness."

"If I had been the boy you sent for," said Anne wistfully, "I'd be able to help you so much now and spare you in a hundred ways. I could find it in my heart to wish I had been, just for that."

"Well now, I'd rather have you than a dozen boys, Anne," said Matthew patting her hand. "Just mind you that—rather than a dozen boys. Well now, I guess it wasn't a boy that took the Avery Scholarship, was it? It was a girl—my girl—my girl that I'm proud of."

He smiled his shy smile at her as he went into the yard. Anne took the memory of it with her when she went to her room that night and sat for a long while at her open window, thinking of the past and dreaming of the future. Outside the Snow Queen was mistily white in the moonshine; the frogs were singing in the marsh beyond Orchard Slope. Anne always remembered the silvery peaceful beauty and fragrant calm of that night. It was the last night before sorrow touched her life; and no life is ever quite the same again when once that cold, sanctifying touch has been laid upon it.

CHAPTER XXXVII

THE REAPER WHOSE NAME IS DEATH[1]

"MATTHEW — Matthew — what is the matter? Matthew, are you sick?"

It was Marilla who spoke, alarm in every jerky word. Anne came through the hall, her hands full of white narcissus — it was long before Anne could love the sight or odour of white narcissus again — in time to hear her and to see Matthew standing in the porch doorway, a folded paper in his hand, and his face strangely drawn and gray. Anne dropped her flowers and sprang across the kitchen to him at the same moment as Marilla. They were both too late; before they could reach him Matthew had fallen across the threshold.

"He's fainted," gasped Marilla. "Anne, run for Martin — quick, quick! He's at the barn."

Martin, the hired man, who had just driven home from the post office, started at once for the doctor, calling at Orchard Slope on his way to send Mr. and Mrs. Barry over. Mrs. Lynde, who was there on an errand, came too. They found Anne and Marilla distractedly trying to restore Matthew to consciousness.

Mrs. Lynde pushed them gently aside, tried his pulse and then laid her ear over his heart. She looked at their anxious faces sorrowfully and the tears came into her eyes.

1. From Henry Wadsworth Longfellow's "The Reaper and the Flowers" (1839, Stanza 1): "There is a Reaper whose name is Death, / And with his sickle keen, / He reaps the bearded grain at a breath, / And the flowers that grown between."

"Oh, Marilla," she said gravely. "I don't think—we can do anything for him."

"Mrs. Lynde, you don't think—you can't think Matthew is —is—" Anne could not say the dreadful word; she turned sick and pallid.

"Child, yes, I'm afraid of it. Look at his face. When you've seen that look as often as I have you'll know what it means."

Anne looked at the still face and there beheld the seal of the Great Presence.

When the doctor came he said that death had been instantaneous and probably painless, caused in all likelihood by some sudden shock. The secret of the shock was discovered to be in the paper Matthew had held and which Martin had brought from the office that morning. It contained an account of the failure of the Abbey Bank.

The news spread quickly through Avonlea, and all day friends and neighbours thronged Green Gables and came and went on errands of kindness for the dead and living. For the first time shy quiet Matthew Cuthbert was a person of central importance; the white majesty of death had fallen on him and set him apart as one crowned.

When the calm night came softly down over Green Gables the old house was hushed and tranquil. In the parlour lay Matthew Cuthbert in his coffin, his long gray hair framing his placid face on which there was a little kindly smile as if he but slept, dreaming pleasant dreams. There were flowers about him—sweet old-fashioned flowers which his mother had planted in the homestead garden in her bridal days and for which Matthew had always had a secret, wordless love. Anne had gathered them and brought them to him, her anguished, tearless eyes burning in her white face. It was the last thing she could do for him.

The Barrys and Mrs. Lynde stayed with them that night. Diana, going to the east gable, where Anne was standing at her window, said gently:

"Anne dear, would you like to have me sleep with you to-night?"

"Thank you, Diana." Anne looked earnestly into her friend's face. "I think you won't misunderstand me when I say that I want to be alone. I'm not afraid. I haven't been alone one minute since it happened—and I want to be. I want to be quite silent and quiet and try to realize it. I *can't* realize it. Half the time it seems to me that Matthew can't be dead; and the other half it seems as if he must have been dead for a long time and I've had this horrible dull ache ever since."

Diana did not quite understand. Marilla's impassioned grief, breaking all the bounds of natural reserve and lifelong habit in its stormy rush, she could comprehend better than Anne's tearless agony. But she went away kindly, leaving Anne alone keep her first vigil with sorrow.

Anne hoped that tears would come in solitude. It seemed to her a terrible thing that she could not shed a tear for Matthew, whom she had loved so much and who had been so kind to her, Matthew, who had walked with her last evening at sunset and was now lying in the dim room below with that awful peace on his brow. But no tears came at first, even when she knelt by her window in the darkness and prayed, looking up to the stars beyond the hills—no tears, only the same horrible dull ache of misery that kept on aching until she fell asleep, worn out with the day's pain and excitement.

In the night she awakened, with the stillness and the darkness about her, and the recollection of the day came over her like a wave of sorrow. She could see Matthew's face smiling at her as he had smiled when they parted at the gate that last evening—she could hear his voice saying, "My girl—my girl that I'm proud of." Then the tears came and Anne wept her heart out. Marilla heard her and crept in to comfort her.

"There—there—don't cry so, dearie. It can't bring him back. It—it—isn't right to cry so. I knew that to-day, but I

2. From *Snow-bound: A Winter Idyll*
(1866) by John Greenleaf Whittier.
The subject of the particular
stanza of the poem (ll. 409–22) in
which this line appears is the
recent death of Whittier's beloved
younger sister, Elizabeth Hussey
Whittier:

> I tread the pleasant paths we
>   trod,
> I see the violet-sprinkled sod
> Whereon she leaned, too frail
>   and weak
> The hillside flowers she loved to
>   seek,
> Yet following me where'er I
>   went
> With dark eyes full of love's
>   content.
> The birds are glad; the brier-
>   rose fills
> The air with sweetness; all the
>   hills
> Stretch green to June's
>   unclouded sky
> But still I wait with ear and eye
> For something gone which
>   should be nigh,
> A loss in all familiar things,
> In flower that blooms, and bird
>   that sings.

See Appendix, "Literary Allusion."

couldn't help it then. He's always been such a good, kind brother to me—but God knows best."

"Oh, just let me cry, Marilla," sobbed Anne. "The tears don't hurt me like that ache did. Stay here for a little while with me and keep your arm round me—so. I couldn't have Diana stay, she's good and kind and sweet—but it's not her sorrow—she's outside of it and she couldn't come close enough to my heart to help me. It's our sorrow—yours and mine. Oh, Marilla, what will we do without him?"

"We've got each other, Anne. I don't know what I'd do if you weren't here—if you'd never come. Oh, Anne, I know I've been kind of strict and harsh with you maybe—but you mustn't think I didn't love you as well as Matthew did, for all that. I want to tell you now when I can. It's never been easy for me to say things out of my heart, but at times like this it's easier. I love you as dear as if you were my own flesh and blood and you've been my joy and comfort ever since you came to Green Gables."

Two days afterwards they carried Matthew Cuthbert over his homestead threshold and away from the fields he had tilled and the orchards he had loved and the trees he had planted; and then Avonlea settled back to its usual placidity and even at Green Gables affairs slipped into their old groove and work was done and duties fulfilled with regularity as before, although always with the aching sense of "loss in all familiar things."[2] Anne, new to grief, thought it almost sad that it could be so—that they *could* go on in the old way without Matthew. She felt something like shame and remorse when she discovered that the sunrises behind the firs and the pale pink buds opening in the garden gave her the old inrush of gladness when she saw them—that Diana's visits were pleasant to her and that Diana's merry words and ways moved her to laughter and smiles—that, in brief, the beautiful world of blossom and love and friendship had lost none of its power to please her fancy and thrill her heart, that life still called to her with many insistent voices.

"It seems like disloyalty to Matthew, somehow, to find pleasure in these things now that he has gone," she said wistfully to Mrs. Allan one evening when they were together in the manse garden. "I miss him so much—all the time—and yet, Mrs. Allan, the world and life seem very beautiful and interesting to me for all. To-day Diana said something funny and I found myself laughing. I thought when it happened I could never laugh again. And it somehow seems as if I oughtn't to."

"When Matthew was here he liked to hear you laugh and he liked to know that you found pleasure in the pleasant things around you," said Mrs. Allan gently. "He is just away now[3]; and he likes to know it just the same. I am sure we should not shut our hearts against the healing influences that nature offers us. But I understand your feeling. I think we all experience the same thing. We resent the thought that anything can please us when some one we love is no longer here to share the pleasure with us, and we almost feel as if we were unfaithful to our sorrow when we find our interest in life returning to us."

"I was down to the graveyard to plant a rose-bush on Matthew's grave this afternoon," said Anne dreamily. "I took a slip of the little white Scotch rose-bush his mother brought out from Scotland long ago;[4] Matthew always liked those roses the best—they were so small and sweet on their thorny stems. It made me feel glad that I could plant it by his grave—as if I were doing something that must please him in taking it there to be near him. I hope he has roses like them in heaven. Perhaps the souls of all those little white roses that he has loved so many summers were all there to meet him. I must go home now. Marilla is all alone and she gets lonely at twilight."

"She will be lonelier still, I fear, when you go away again to college," said Mrs. Allan.

3. A soothing thought found in James Whitcomb Riley's poem "Away" (1884):

I can not say, I will not say
    That he is dead.—He is just
    away!
With a cheery smile, and a wave
    of the hand,
He has wandered into an
    unknown land,
And left us dreaming how very
    fair
It needs must be since he lingers
    there.
And you—O you who the
    wildest yearn
For the old-time step and the
    glad return,—
Think of him faring on, as dear
In the Love of There as the love
    of Here.

4. Another reminder of the Cuthberts' Scottish ancestry. Montgomery recounts (in *AP*) the story of her own great-grand-mother's arrival on P. E. I. from Scotland. See Appendix, "The Settlers of P. E. I."; see also n. 6, ch. 12 and illustration.

5. A large spiral univalve marine shell. The best quality of conch shells would be brought back by sailors from the Caribbean.

6. "The common name of *Lonicera Periclymenum*, also called Woodbine, a climbing shrub with fragrant yellowish trumpet-shaped flowers." See illustration. Long associated with fairies and elves, honeysuckle is an erotic flower. In *A Midsummer Night's Dream*, the bank where Titania sleeps is "Quite over-canopied with luscious woodbine, / With sweet musk roses and with eglantine" (II.i.,ll. 251–252).

Anne did not reply; she said good night and went slowly back to Green Gables. Marilla was sitting on the front door-steps and Anne sat down beside her. The door was open behind them, held back by a big pink conch-shell[5] with hints of sea sunsets in its smooth inner convolutions.

Anne gathered some sprays of pale yellow honeysuckle[6] and put them in her hair. She liked the delicious hint of fragrance, as of some aerial benediction, above her every time she moved.

"Doctor Spencer was here while you were away," Marilla said. "He says that the specialist will be in town to-morrow and he insists that I must go in and have my eyes examined. I suppose I'd better go and have it over. I'll be more than thankful if the man can give me the right kind of glasses to suit my eyes. You won't mind staying here alone while I'm away, will you? Martin will have to drive me in and there's ironing and baking to do."

"I shall be all right. Diana will come over for company for me. I shall attend to the ironing and baking beautifully—you needn't fear that I'll starch the handkerchiefs or flavour the cake with liniment."

Marilla laughed.

"What a girl you were for making mistakes in them days, Anne. You were always getting into scrapes. I did use to think you were possessed. Do you mind the time you dyed your hair?"

"Yes, indeed. I shall never forget it," smiled Anne, touching the heavy braid of hair that was wound about her shapely head. "I laugh a little now sometimes when I think what a worry my hair used to be to me—but I don't laugh *much*, because it was a very real trouble then. I did suffer terribly over my hair and my freckles. My freckles are really gone; and people are nice enough to tell me my hair is auburn now—all but Josie Pye. She informed me yesterday that she really thought it was redder than ever, or at least my black dress made it look redder, and she asked me if people who had red hair ever got used to having it. Marilla, I've almost decided to give up trying to like Josie Pye. I've made what I would once have called a heroic effort to like her, but Josie Pye won't *be* liked."

"Josie is a Pye," said Marilla sharply, "so she can't help being disagreeable. I suppose people of that kind serve some useful purpose in society, but I must say I don't know what it is any more than I know the use of thistles.[7] Is Josie going to teach?"

"No, she is going back to Queen's next year. So are Moody Spurgeon and Charlie Sloane. Jane and Ruby are going to teach and they have both got schools—Jane at Newbridge and Ruby at some place up west."

"Gilbert Blythe is going to teach too, isn't he?"

"Yes"—briefly.

"What a nice-looking young fellow he is," said Marilla absently. "I saw him in church last Sunday and he seemed so tall and manly. He looks a lot like his father did at the same age. John Blythe was a nice boy. We used to be real good friends, he and I. People called him my beau."

Anne looked up with swift interest. "Oh Marilla—and what happened?—why didn't you—"

"We had a quarrel. I wouldn't forgive him when he asked me to. I meant to, after awhile—but I was sulky and angry and I wanted to punish him first. He never came back—the Blythes were all mighty independent. But I always felt—rather sorry. I've always kind of wished I'd forgiven him when I had the chance."

"So you've had a bit of romance in your life, too," said Anne softly.

"Yes, I suppose you might call it that. You wouldn't think so to look at me, would you? But you can never tell about people from their outsides. Everybody has forgot about me and John. I'd forgotten myself. But it all came back to me when I saw Gilbert last Sunday."

7. The author is making a pun on her character's name. "Josie Pye" is the feminine form of "Joe-Pye weed," the name of several different weeds of the genus *Eupatorium* of the daisy or *Compositae* family. Spotted, hollow, and sweet joe-pye weed are all found in eastern North America. The flowers are tiny, purple, and fuzzy, growing in flattish clusters. The eponymous Joe Pye, or Jopi, a traveling Indian medicine man or "yarb man," was supposed to have used the weed that now bears his name to treat typhoid fever. See Jack Sanders, *Hedgemaids and Fairy Candles;* see also illustration.

"She found Anne and Marilla sitting at the front door in the warm, scented summer dusk." Illustration by Sybil Tawse, from the 1933 edition.

CHAPTER XXXVIII

THE BEND IN THE ROAD

MARILLA WENT to town the next day and returned in the evening. Anne had gone over to Orchard Slope with Diana and came back to find Marilla in the kitchen, sitting by the table with her head leaning on her hand. Something in her dejected attitude struck a chill to Anne's heart. She had never seen Marilla sit limply inert like that.

"Are you very tired, Marilla?"

"Yes—no—I don't know," said Marilla wearily, looking up. "I suppose I am tired but I haven't thought about it. It's not that."

"Did you see the oculist? What did he say?" asked Anne anxiously.

"Yes, I saw him. He examined my eyes. He says that if I give up all reading and sewing entirely and any kind of work that strains the eyes, and if I'm careful not to cry, and if I wear the glasses he's given me he thinks my eyes may not get any worse and my headaches will be cured. But if I don't he says I'll certainly be stone blind in six months. Blind! Anne, just think of it!"

For a minute Anne, after her first quick exclamation of dis-

1. Any small meal that is not a main one; not one necessarily served at midday.

may, was silent. It seemed to her that she could *not* speak. Then she said bravely, but with a catch in her voice:

"Marilla, *don't* think of it. You know he has given you hope. If you are careful you won't lose your sight altogether; and if his glasses cure your headaches it will be a great thing."

"I don't call it much hope," said Marilla bitterly. "What am I to live for if I can't read or sew or do anything like that? I might as well be blind — or dead. And as for crying, I can't help that when I get lonesome. But there, it's no good talking about it. If you'll get me a cup of tea I'll be thankful. I'm about done out. Don't say anything about this to any one for a spell yet, anyway. I can't bear that folks should come here to question and sympathize and talk about it."

When Marilla had eaten her lunch[1] Anne persuaded her to go to bed. Then Anne went herself to the east gable and sat down by her window in the darkness alone with her tears and her heaviness of heart. How sadly things had changed since she had sat there the night after coming home! Then she had been full of hope and joy and the future had looked rosy with promise. Anne felt as if she had lived years since then, but before she went to bed there was a smile on her lips and peace in her heart. She had looked her duty courageously in the face and found it a friend — as duty ever is when we meet it frankly.

One afternoon a few days later Marilla came slowly in from the yard where she had been talking to a caller — a man whom Anne knew by sight as John Sadler from Carmody. Anne wondered what he could have been saying to bring that look to Marilla's face.

"What did Mr. Sadler want, Marilla?"

Marilla sat down by the window and looked at Anne. There were tears in her eyes in defiance of the oculist's prohibition and her voice broke as she said:

"He heard that I was going to sell Green Gables and he wants to buy it."

"Buy it! Buy Green Gables?" Anne wondered if she had heard aright. "Oh, Marilla, you don't mean to sell Green Gables!"

"Anne, I don't know what else is to be done. I've thought it all over. If my eyes were strong I could stay here and make out to look after things and manage, with a good hired man. But as it is I can't. I may lose my sight altogether; and anyway I'll not be fit to run things. Oh, I never thought I'd live to see the day when I'd have to sell my home. But things would only go behind worse and worse all the time, till nobody would want to buy it. Every cent of our money went in that bank; and there's some notes[2] Matthew gave last fall to pay. Mrs. Lynde advises me to sell the farm and board somewhere—with her I suppose. It won't bring much—it's small and the buildings are old. But it'll be enough for me to live on I reckon. I'm thankful you're provided for with that scholarship, Anne. I'm sorry you won't have a home to come to in your vacations, that's all, but I suppose you'll manage somehow."

Marilla broke down and wept bitterly.

"You mustn't sell Green Gables," said Anne resolutely.

"Oh, Anne, I wish I didn't have to. But you can see for yourself. I can't stay here alone. I'd go crazy with trouble and loneliness. And my sight would go—I know it would."

"You won't have to stay here alone, Marilla. I'll be with you. I'm not going to Redmond."

"Not going to Redmond!" Marilla lifted her worn face from her hands and looked at Anne. "Why, what do you mean?"

"Just what I say. I'm not going to take the scholarship. I decided so the night after you came home from town. You surely don't think I could leave you alone in your trouble, Marilla, after all you've done for me. I've been thinking and planning. Let me tell you my plans. Mr. Barry wants to rent the farm for next year. So you won't have any bother over

2. Matthew borrowed money the previous autumn, perhaps to help put Anne through Queen's, and payment is now due. "Notes" (from "note of hand") implies that these are unsecured loans. There is no mortgage, or lien, attached to the property, or Anne and Marilla would have no choice but to sell Green Gables.

that. And I'm going to teach. I've applied for the school here —but I don't expect to get it for I understand the trustees have promised it to Gilbert Blythe. But I can have the Carmody school—Mr. Blair told me so last night at the store. Of course that won't be quite as nice or convenient as if I had the Avonlea school. But I can board home and drive myself over to Carmody and back, in the warm weather at least. And even in winter I can come home on Fridays. We'll keep a horse for that. Oh, I have it all planned out, Marilla. And I'll read to you and keep you cheered up. You sha'n't be dull or lonesome. And we'll be real cosy and happy here together, you and I."

Marilla had listened like a woman in a dream.

"Oh, Anne, I could get on real well if you were here, I know. But I can't let you sacrifice yourself so for me. It would be terrible."

"Nonsense!" Anne laughed merrily. "There is no sacrifice. Nothing could be worse than giving up Green Gables— nothing could hurt me more. We must keep the dear old place. My mind is quite made up, Marilla. I'm *not* going to Redmond; and I *am* going to stay here and teach. Don't you worry about me a bit."

"But your ambitions—and—"

"I'm just as ambitious as ever. Only, I've changed the object of my ambitions. I'm going to be a good teacher—and I'm going to save your eyesight. Besides, I mean to study at home here and take a little college course all by myself. Oh, I've dozens of plans, Marilla. I've been thinking them out for a week. I shall give life here my best, and I believe it will give its best to me in return. When I left Queen's my future seemed to stretch out before me like a straight road. I thought I could see along it for many a milestone. Now there is a bend in it. I don't know what lies around the bend, but I'm going to believe that the best does. It has a fascination of its own, that bend, Marilla. I wonder how the road beyond it goes—what there is of green glory and soft, checkered lights and shadows—what new landscapes—what new beauties— what curves and hills and valleys further on."

"I don't feel as if I ought to let you give it up," said Marilla, referring to the scholarship.

"But you can't prevent me. I'm sixteen and a half, 'obstinate as a mule,'[3] as Mrs. Lynde once told me," laughed Anne. "Oh, Marilla, don't you go pitying me. I don't like to be pitied, and there is no need for it. I'm heart glad over the very thought of staying at dear Green Gables. Nobody could love it as you and I do—so we must keep it."

"You blessed girl!" said Marilla, yielding. "I feel as if you'd given me new life. I guess I ought to stick out and make you go to college—but I know I can't, so I ain't going to try. I'll make it up to you though, Anne."

When it became noised abroad in Avonlea that Anne Shirley had given up the idea of going to college and intended to stay home and teach there was a good deal of discussion over it. Most of the good folks, not knowing about Marilla's eyes, thought she was foolish. Mrs. Allan did not. She told Anne so in approving words that brought tears of pleasure to the girl's eyes. Neither did good Mrs. Lynde. She came up one evening and found Anne and Marilla sitting at the front door in the warm, scented summer dusk. They liked to sit there when the twilight came down and the white moths flew about in the garden and the odour of mint filled the dewy air.

Mrs. Rachel deposited her substantial person upon the stone bench by the door, behind which grew a row of tall pink and yellow hollyhocks,[4] with a long breath of mingled weariness and relief.

"I declare I'm glad to sit down. I've been on my feet all day, and two hundred pounds is a good bit for two feet to carry round. It's a great blessing not to be fat, Marilla. I hope you appreciate it. Well, Anne, I hear you've given up your notion

3. Proverbial. In America the politer-sounding *mule* is substituted for the traditional English *ass.* Compare Pope: "Look on Simo's Mate / No Ass so meek, no Ass so obstinate" (*Epistle to a Lady,* ll. 101–102).

4. The plant *Althaea rosea,* of the genus Malvaceae, a native of China and southern Europe, having a very tall, stout stem bearing numerous large flowers on very short stalks. Many varieties, with flowers of different tints of red, purple, yellow, and white, are cultivated. See illustration.

5. The pseudonym of Marietta Holley (1836–1926), the author of a series of comic dialect books featuring the homely philoso-phizing of Josiah Allen's wife Samantha. Holley, once called the female Mark Twain, was one of America's most popular writers between 1873 and 1914. Mont-gomery writes in her journal in 1902, "I really didn't know there were so many different ways peo-ple could make fools of them-selves. But as Josiah Allen's wife says, 'I must not anticipate.' *Is* it Josiah Allen's wife? Well, if not she some other celebrity" (*SJ* I: 282). See Appendix, "Music and Elocution."

of going to college. I was real glad to hear it. You've got as much education now as a woman can be comfortable with. I don't believe in girls going to college with the men and cramming their heads full of Latin and Greek and all that nonsense."

"But I'm going to study Latin and Greek just the same, Mrs. Lynde," said Anne laughing. "I'm going to take my Arts course right here at Green Gables, and study everything that I would at college."

Mrs. Lynde lifted her hands in holy horror.

"Anne Shirley, you'll kill yourself."

"Not a bit of it. I shall thrive on it. Oh, I'm not going to overdo things. As 'Josiah Allen's Wife'[5] says, I shall be 'mejum.' But I'll have lots of spare time in the long winter evenings and I've no vocation for fancy work. I'm going to teach over at Carmody, you know."

"I don't know it. I guess you're going to teach right here in Avonlea. The trustees have decided to give you the school."

"Mrs. Lynde!" cried Anne, springing to her feet in her surprise. "Why, I thought they had promised it to Gilbert Blythe!"

"So they did. But as soon as Gilbert heard that you had applied for it he went to them—they had a business meeting at the school last night, you know—and told them that he withdrew his application, and suggested that they accept yours. He said he was going to teach at White Sands. Of course he gave up the school just to oblige you, because he knew how much you wanted to stay with Marilla, and I must say I think it was real kind and thoughtful in him, that's what. Real self-sacrificing, too, for he'll have his board to pay at White Sands, and everybody knows he's got to earn his own way through college. So the trustees decided to take you. I was tickled to death when Thomas came home and told me."

"I don't feel that I ought to take it," murmured Anne. "I

mean—I don't think I ought to let Gilbert make such a sacrifice for—for me."

"I guess you can't prevent him now. He's signed papers with the White Sands trustees. So it wouldn't do him any good now if you were to refuse. Of course you'll take the school. You'll get along all right, now that there are no Pyes going. Josie was the last of them, and a good thing she was, that's what. There's been some Pye or other going to Avonlea school for the last twenty years, and I guess their mission in life was to keep school-teachers reminded that earth isn't their home. Bless my heart! What does all that winking and blinking at the Barry gable mean?"

"Diana is signalling for me to go over," laughed Anne. "You know we keep up the old custom. Excuse me while I run over and see what she wants."

Anne ran down the clover slope like a deer, and disappeared in the firry shadows of the Haunted Wood. Mrs. Lynde looked after her indulgently.

"There's a good deal of the child about her yet in some ways."

"There's a good deal more of the woman about her in others," retorted Marilla, with a momentary return of her old crispness.

But crispness was no longer Marilla's distinguishing characteristic. As Mrs. Lynde told her Thomas that night:

"Marilla Cuthbert has got *mellow*. That's what."

Anne went to the little Avonlea graveyard the next evening to put fresh flowers on Matthew's grave and water the Scotch rose-bush. She lingered there until dusk, liking the peace and calm of the little place, with its poplars whose rustle was like low, friendly speech, and its whispering grasses growing at will among the graves. When she finally left it and walked down the long hill that sloped to the Lake of Shining Waters it was past sunset and all Avonlea lay before her in a

6. From Tennyson's "The Palace of Art" (1832): "And one, an English home—gray twilight pour'd / On dewy pastures, dewy trees, / Softer than sleep—all things in order stored, / A haunt of ancient peace." See Introduction. In *Kilmeny of the Orchard* (ch. 5) the orchard is referred to by the hero as "a veritable haunt of ancient peace." See Appendix, "Literary Allusion."

dream-like afterlight—"a haunt of ancient peace."[6] There was a freshness in the air as of a wind that had blown over honey-sweet fields of clover. Home lights twinkled out here and there among the homestead trees. Beyond lay the sea, misty and purple, with its haunting, unceasing murmur. The west was a glory of soft mingled hues, and the pond reflected them all in still softer shadings. The beauty of it all thrilled Anne's heart and she gratefully opened the gates of her soul to it.

"Dear old world," she murmured, "you are very lovely and I am glad to be alive in you."

Half-way down the hill a tall lad came whistling out of a gate before the Blythe homestead. It was Gilbert, and the whistle died on his lips as he recognized Anne. He lifted his cap courteously but he would have passed on in silence if Anne had not stopped and held out her hand.

"Gilbert," she said, with scarlet cheeks, "I want to thank you for giving up the school for me. It was very good of you—and I want you to know that I appreciate it."

Gilbert took the offered hand eagerly.

"It wasn't particularly good of me at all, Anne. I was pleased to be able to do you some small service. Are we going to be friends after this? Have you really forgiven me my old fault?"

Anne laughed and tried unsuccessfully to withdraw her hand.

"I forgave you that day by the pond landing, although I didn't know it. What a stubborn little goose I was. I've been —I may as well make a complete confession—I've been sorry ever since."

"We are going to be the best of friends," said Gilbert, jubilantly. "We were born to be good friends, Anne. You've thwarted destiny long enough. I know we can help each other in many ways. You are going to keep up your studies, aren't you? So am I. Come, I'm going to walk home with you."

Marilla looked curiously at Anne when the latter entered the kitchen.

"Who was that came up the lane with you, Anne?"

"Gilbert Blythe," answered Anne, vexed to find herself blushing. "I met him on Barry's hill."

"I didn't think you and Gilbert Blythe were such good

"'Come, I'm going to walk home with you.'" Illustration by Elizabeth R. Withington, from the 1931 edition.

7. From Robert Browning's *Pippa Passes* (1841, Pt. 1, "Morning," ll. 221–28):

The Year's at the spring
And day's at the morn;
Morning's at seven;
The hillside's dewpearled;
The lark's on the wing;
The snail's on the thorn:
God's in his heaven—
All's right with the world.

See Appendix, "Literary Allusion."

friends that you'd stand for half an hour at the gate talking to him," said Marilla, with a dry smile.

"We haven't been—we've been good enemies. But we have decided that it will be much more sensible to be good friends in future. Were we really there half an hour? It seemed just a few minutes. But, you see, we have five years' lost conversations to catch up with, Marilla."

Anne sat long at her window that night companioned by a glad content. The wind purred softly in the cherry boughs, and the mint breaths came up to her. The stars twinkled over the pointed firs in the hollow and Diana's light gleamed through the old gap.

Anne's horizons had closed in since the night she had sat there after coming home from Queen's; but if the path set before her feet was to be narrow she knew that flowers of quiet happiness would bloom along it. The joys of sincere work and worthy aspiration and congenial friendship were to be hers; nothing could rob her of her birthright of fancy or her ideal world of dreams. And there was always the bend in the road!

"'God's in his heaven, all's right with the world,'"[7] whispered Anne softly.

THE END

Campbell's and Macneill's farms.

VARIANTS BETWEEN EDITIONS

There are a few substantial variants between editions of *Anne of Green Gables*. Two main families of editions exist, one springing from the 1908 first edition, published by L. C. Page Co., the other stemming from the first true British edition, published by Harrap's in 1925. The very first British edition of *Anne*, published by Sir Isaac Pitman Co. in 1908, was really just a reprint of the Page edition. The first Canadian edition of 1942 (Ryerson Press) has some readings from both the 1908 and the 1925 editions. In the main, all current publications of *Anne* repeat one or the other of these three versions, including misprints and errors belonging to the original printing. Although some recent editions have regularized spelling and punctuation, substantive variants tend to remain. The list that follows should help readers to recognize from which branch any version of the novel that they may read really stems. The biggest difference is probably found in Marilla's sentence about the preserves in Chapter 16 (p. 178 of this edition); versions of the novel could be divided into "work" editions and "go" editions. In the following list, page numbers refer to the present edition.

45   a Barnado boy (1908); a Home boy (1925, 1942); a Barnardo boy (MS). Some versions of 1925: a Barnardo boy

51   yellowish gray wincey (1908, 1942, MS [?]); yellowish white wincey (1925)

92   dreadful sorry (1908); dreadfully sorry (1925, 1942, MS)

132   practise (1908, 1942); practice (1925) Third Royal Reader (1908, 1942); *Third Royal Reader* (1925)

177   Title to Chapter XVI: Diana is Invited to Tea with Tragic Results (1908, MS); Diana is Invited to Tea, with Tragic Results (1925)

178   it's beginning to work (1908, 1942); it's beginning to go (1925, MS)

182   pathetic tale (1908, 1942); pathetic little tale (1925, MS)

184   frost fairy (1908, 1942); frost-fairy (1925, MS)

186   face downward . . . in an agony (1908); face downward . . . in agony (1942); face downwards . . . in an agony (1925)

192   forevermore (1908, 1942); for evermore (1925)

194   TO ANNE (1908, 1942); To ANNE (1925)

195   Dear Anne, ran the former, Mother says (1908, 1942); DEAR ANNE [ran the former], Mother says (1925); Dear Anne (ran the former), Mother says (MS)

226   silverly sweet (1908, 1942); silvery-sweet (1925, MS)

235   small, red-haired girl (1908, 1942); small-red-headed girl (1925, MS)

237   He'd got so used to (1908, 1942); He's got so used to (1925, MS)

238   Tuesday night (1908, 1942); on Tuesday night (1925, MS)

255   Don't be very frightened, Marilla (1908, 1942); Don't be frightened, Marilla (1925, MS)

260   recite Mary, Queen of Scots (1908, 1942); recite Mary Queen of Scots (1925, MS)

262   Titles are in italics in MS and in 1925 edition, in quotation marks elsewhere. See also p. 265: *The Fairy Queen*

266   a solution of his problem (1908, 1942); the solution of his problem (1925, MS)

270   so fashion (1908, 1942); so-fashion (1925, MS)

283   has to read it out loud (1908, 1942); has to read it out aloud (1925, MS)

303   Marmion (1908, 1942); *Marmion* (1925, MS)

307   found their way to "Beechwood" (1908); found their way to Beechwood (1925, MS)

317   "Ben Hur" (1908); *Ben Hur* (1925, MS)

317- The Lurid Mystery of the Haunted Hall
318   (1908); *The Lurid Mystery of the Haunted Hall* (1925, MS)

324   bad spell with his heart Thursday (1908); bad spell with his heart on Thursday (1925, MS)

336   haunting the post office Wednesday (1908); haunting the post office on Wednesday (1925 and MS)

337   "Dearest Diana," wrote Anne, "here it is Tuesday night and" (1908, 1942); DEAREST DIANA [wrote Anne], Here it is Tuesday night and (1925)

349   There was just one on my bush, and I saved it for you. (1908, 1942); There was just one on my bush, and I saved it, for you. (1925); There was just one on my bush and I saved it for you. (MS)

349   look at our elocutionist, Marilla. Doesn't she look lovely? (1908, MS); look at our elocutionist, Marilla; Doesn't she look lovely? (1925)

356   all silver and shadow and vision of things not seen (1908, 1942, MS); all silver and shallow and vision of things not seen (1925) [This seems merely a typographical error in Harrap's edition.]

360   out-of-doors (1908); out of doors (1925, MS)

360   to take on so about (1908); to "take on" so about (1925, MS)

367   large, bright-blue eyes (1908, MS); large, bright blue eyes (1925)

370   chestnut trees (1908, MS); chestnut-trees (1925)

371   license (1908, MS); licence (1925)

375   tea rose (1908, 1942); tea-rose (1925)

377   First Class License (1908, 1942); First Class Licence (1925)

378   Lovers' Lane (1908, 1925); Lover's Lane (MS)

390   come home Fridays (1908, 1942); come home on Fridays (1925, MS)

TEXTUAL NOTES

The fact that in many cases of the variants the 1925 edition agrees with the MS leads us to believe that LMM had some input into the English edition and that the readings of 1925 are sometimes superior to those of 1908. Therefore, when the MS and 1925 agree, we have regarded that as a sure sign of the desirability of keeping that version in our own text. But we have also gone back to the manuscript for many versions of phrases that seemed more rhythmical or more colloquial than those in printed versions. The editor of 1908 seems, as Matthew might have said, to have "put his oar in," probably in changing "go" to "work" in the sentence about the preserves; almost certainly in taking out the word "on" in phrases like "on Tuesday," perhaps because that seemed too English. Oddly enough, however, the Page editor not only let stand but was consistent about the use of English spelling in words like "parlour" and "flavour," even though LMM herself is not consistent and often spells such words in the American manner. We have kept the first edition's consistent English spelling in all such words. It seems safe to assume that it is the Page editor who insists on inserting the word "that" before all clauses in objective position in a sentence; LMM's usage in the *Anne* MS and elsewhere shows her inclined to dispense with the "that," and we have followed her usage.

In our edition, punctuation has been regularized to a degree, as LMM was not consistent in, for instance, matters of hyphenation. We have universally hyphenated phrases like "cherry-tree," "chestnut-tree," "red-headed," "sitting-room," although LMM does not always do so. We have let stand Page Co.'s consistent use of "to-day," "to-morrow"; although LMM is not consistent about hyphenating these, she does so slightly more often than not. We have, however, followed LMM in not separating into two parts words like "uphill" and "downstairs" as was done in the Page edition. On many occasions we have silently corrected the 1908 edition in favor of LMM's parsimony in the matter of commas, but we have sometimes added punctuation marks, particularly commas, which appear in the MS but are absent from the 1908 text. The Textual Notes will record changes of punctuation in detail only when these seem to affect the sense.

The first and later editions of *Anne of Green Gables* and other of her novels caught LMM's inconsistencies in the formation of phrases such as "post office," which are sometimes hyphenated and sometimes not, sometimes capitalized and sometimes not. LMM punctuates lightly; in a sequence of descriptive words or phrases she may have only one comma, and we have tried to follow her unless it seemed impracticable (because misleading) to do so. The phrase "Lover's Lane" has caused particular headaches. The 1925 edition (which we respect) has rationalized the phrase to "Lovers' Lane," getting rid of the inconsistency found in 1908, which has both "Lover's" and "Lovers'"—as does the manuscript. The English edition's solution is rational and proper; the normal name of such a place would be "Lovers' Lane." It seems, however, that LMM was thinking of the lane as a place in which a single lover could think about love, rather than as the (more prosaic) place for courting couples. Certainly, in the first part of her novel, as we can see in the manuscript, the Lover is singular. We have decided on "Lover's Lane" as the dominant reading. In the following list, page numbers refer to the present edition, and words and phrases italicized in the text appear in roman type.

For Montgomery's system of MS revision, see Introduction, pp. 21–22, and Epperly article in *Harvesting Thistles,* 74–75.

39 *ladies' eardrops*: MS originally "jewelweed"; changed in MS Note A.

39 *cascade. But*: restores MS punctuation.

39 *quiet well-conducted*: MS punctuation; 1908 has comma after "quiet."

39 *people in Avonlea and out of it who*: restores MS punctuation; 1908 has comma after "people" and "it."

39 *Sunday School*: here and elsewhere restores MS version; 1908, 1925, etc., have "Sunday-school."

40 *strongest prop*: MS originally "great prop."

40 *Church Aid Society*: MS originally "Ladies Aid"; "Ladies" crossed out, "Church" inserted.

40 *knitted sixteen*: MS (added in Note) originally "knitted twenty"; "twenty" crossed out.

40 *warm and bright*: MS has "bright and warm."

41 *guess as to*: "as" not in MS.

41 *to have to go among strangers*: the second "to" not in MS.

41 *a good deal further*: as in 1908 and MS; "farther" in English editions.

43 *parlour*: MS has "parlor," one of many instances where LMM in MS spells in American fashion; corrected to English spelling in 1908 U.S. edition.

43 *bloom-white*: hyphenated in MS, not in 1908.

45 *a Barnardo boy*: MS has "a Barnardo boy"; 1908, "a Barnado boy"; some English versions have a "Home" boy (perhaps because Dr. Barnardo's Home as a society objected to this specific and uncomplimentary use of their name). See *Variants*.

46 *disposition is nor*: MS restored; 1908, 1925 have "disposition is like nor."

46 *set fire to it on purpose, Marilla*: MS restored; 1908, etc., have "set it on purpose, Marilla."

46 *feel it my duty*: MS restored; 1908, etc., have "feel it's my duty."

46 *as for the risks*: MS restored; 1908, etc., have "as for the risk."

46 *there's risk in people having*: MS restored; 1908, etc., have "there's risks in people's having."

47 *that poor young one*: MS originally "child"; crossed out, "young one" substituted.

47 *if so be's as he ever had*: MS restored; 1908, etc., have "if so be's he ever had."

49 *The one day of summer in all the year*: in MS "The one day of summer of all the year"; not corrected in MS.

51 *wishing that Marilla were*: MS restored; 1908, etc., have "wishing that Marilla was."

51 *yellowish-gray wincey*: See *Variants*. Later, p. 358, all editions and the MS have "yellowish-brown wincey," an inconsistency never corrected.

52 *to prevent you*: corrected from a slip in the MS which has "to prevent me."

53 *scope for imagination*: MS restored; 1908, etc., have "scope for the imagination."

53 *dreadfully thin*: MS restored as in 1925; 1908 etc., have "dreadful thin."

54 *I'm so homely*: MS originally "I'm so ugly"; "ugly" crossed out, "homely" substituted.

54 *in Hopetown*: MS restored; 1908 and some other editions have "in Hopeton."

54 *I'm glad I'm going to live here*: MS restored; 1908, etc., have "I'm so glad I'm going to live here."

54 *that Prince Edward Island is the prettiest*: MS restored; 1908, etc., have "that Prince Edward Island was the prettiest."

56 *Mrs. Spencer said my tongue*: MS restored; 1908, etc., have "Mrs. Spencer said that my tongue."

56 *one just below*: MS restored; 1908, etc., have "one right below."

56 *feel perfectly happy*: MS restored: 1908, etc., have "feel exactly perfectly happy."

58 *arched over by*: MS restored; 1908, etc., have "arched over with."

59 *It is kind of a pretty place*: MS restored; 1908, etc., have "It is a kind of pretty place."

60- *shut it from the dark-blue gulf*: MS restored;
61 1908, 1925, etc. have "shut it in from the dark blue gulf."

61 *call it Barry's Pond*: restored from MS; 1908, etc., have "call it Barry's pond."

61 *Diana*: MS originally "Laura"; crossed out, above that "Gertrude" crossed out, "Diana" substituted.

62 *when I was born*: 1908 version with italic "I"; MS has no underlining of "I."

62 *marigold sky*: MS originally "saffron"; crossed out, "marigold" substituted.

63 *Oh, it seems as if I must be in a dream . . . we're nearly home.*: Added in MS Note B2

66 *I might have expected it!*: exclamation point restored as in MS; period in 1908.

67 *name. "But—oh, please*: MS restored; "name, 'but oh, please" in 1908, 1925.

67 *I have of late years*: MS restored; 1908, etc., have "I always have of late years."

69 *said* distinctly *you wanted*: MS restored; 1908, etc., have "said *distinctly* that you wanted."

69 *She brought Lily Jones for herself*: MS has "bought" instead of "brought."

69 *she is very beautiful*: MS originally "pretty"; crossed out, "beautiful" substituted.

70 *little scallopped dish*: MS restored, including spelling. 1908, etc., have "little scalloped glass dish."

70 *eyeing her*: MS spelling restored, also in 1925; 1908 has "eying."

71 *bed-clothes*: MS restored; "bedclothes" in 1908, 1925.

71 *that is one consolation*: MS restored; 1908 has "that's one consolation."

72 *four dark, low, turned posts*: MS punctuation restored; "four dark low-turned posts" in 1908, 1925.

75 *First came a*: There may be a dash after "First" in MS, or mark may only represent the crossbar of the "t."

75 *Wasn't it beautiful! . . . a lovely place!*: exclamation points restored from MS; question marks in 1908, 1925.

76 *yes, it's* radiantly *lovely—it blooms as if it meant it*: in MS, added above the line, word "radiantly" not underlined.

79 *of all unaccountable things!*: No exclamation point in MS, but found in all editions; MS has period.

80 *When the meal ended*: MS restored; 1908, etc., have "When the meal was ended."

80 *You're*: italic as indicated in MS; 1908, etc., have "*You're*."

80 *learned the art of wrestling*: MS originally "knack"; crossed out, "art" substituted.

83 *make your mind up firmly*: MS restored; 1908, etc., have "make up your mind firmly."

83 *likely to happen*: MS originally "liable"; crossed out, "likely" substituted.

84 *as if I was a heroine*: MS restored; 1908, etc., have "as if I were a heroine."

84 *I'm rather glad I have one*: First instance of a statement not in the MS.

84 *Barry's Pond*: MS restored; 1908, etc., have "Barry's pond."

84 *Shore Road*: MS restored; words definitely are capitalized in this instance and on most occasions during this chapter; "shore road" in 1908, 1925. We have used capitals in this phrase throughout, although LMM has not always done so.

85 *a husband was enough responsibility*: MS originally "enough of a responsibility"; 1908, etc., have "enough responsibility."

86 *satisfied with me anyhow.*: punctuation as in MS; editions have semicolon after "anyhow."

87   *if I hadn't an imagination*: in MS and 1925; "hadn't had an imagination" in 1908, 1942.

87   *Hopetown*: In MS "Hopeton," an error that survives into 1908, 1925, etc. Corrected in accordance with use on p. 54. The place is always "Hopetown" in other references, including later *Anne* books, e.g., "The evening Mrs. Spencer brought me over from Hopetown," *Anne of the Island* (ch. 3).

88   *Not a great deal*: MS originally "Not much"; "much" crossed out, "a great deal" substituted.

88   *James Thomson*: Our correction. Incorrectly "James Thompson" in MS, 1908, 1925, etc.

89   *express-wagon*: Not hyphenated in MS.

89   *to one's nest.* Period as in MS instead of question mark

92   *dreadfully sorry*: MS and 1925, 1942. See *Variants*.

92   *positively Providential*: MS restored. LMM seems at times to capitalize the important word "Providential"; this is one of the instances. The "p" is invariably lower case in printed editions.

93   *closely-drawn*: hyphen restored from MS.

93   *arm-chair*: hyphen restored from MS.

93   *So, if you're*: comma restored from MS.

94   *"high-strung"*: no hyphen in MS.

99   *just feel a prayer*: "feel" not italicized in MS; italic in 1908, etc.,

99   *about God's love since*: MS punctuation restored; 1908, 1925 have comma after "love."

99   *Gracious Heavenly Father*: MS restored; 1908, 1925, etc., have "Gracious heavenly Father."

99   *ANNE SHIRLEY*: Not in capitals in MS.

100   *luxuriously cuddling down*: MS restored; 1908, etc., have "cuddling luxuriously down."

100   *on the table and*: as in MS; 1908, etc., have "table, and."

100   *until to-night*: MS restored; 1908, etc., have "till to-night."

104   *nobody would notice her except—Him*: MS restored; 1908, etc., have "nobody would notice her—except Him."

107   *long green valley*: MS restored; 1908, etc., have "long green little valley."

107   *any scope for imagination.*: As in MS; 1908, etc., have "any scope for imagination there."

108   *rocking it!*: exclamation point restored from MS; 1908, 1925, 1942 have period.

109   *No it isn't—I can't make that seem real*: The second instance of a sentence that does not appear in MS and must have been added at a later stage, either in the typescript or in copy-editing—a rare example of a truly substantial difference between MS and the printed version.

114   *"I hate you—I hate you—I hate you!"—a*: Exclamation point as in MS; MS originally "I hate you—I hate you—I hate you—! How dare"; "a louder stamp . . . hatred" is added to MS in Note 24.

115   *And you were too hard . . . for doing it*: Added to MS in Note C5.

117   *every day of forty*: MS restored; 1908, etc., have "every day of fifty."

118   *dark, damp dungeons*: MS has "damp, dark dungeons."

118   *dumbfounded*: as in MS and 1925; 1908, 1942 have "dumfounded."

120   *anything at all?*: Punctuation from 1908, etc.; MS has period at end of this sentence.

120   *without loss of time lest*: Punctuation as in MS; 1908 has comma after "time."

122   *"Well?" she said*: Punctuation as in 1908; MS has "'Well,' she said."

122   *as it behoved her*: MS spelling; 1908 has "as it behooved her."

123 *darkened to a real handsome auburn*: MS originally "changed"; crossed out and "darkened" substituted.

126 *gipsy wind*: MS restored; 1908 has "gypsy wind."

126 *at the touch*: changed from all versions' "at touch."

128 *frills and furbelows*: MS restored; 1908, etc., have "frills or furbelows."

128 *and not tear them*: MS restored; 1908, etc., have "and not to tear them."

129 *a golden frenzy of wind-stirred buttercups*: MS shows "golden" added above line. "The glory of wild roses" is also an afterthought, added above line, as is "pink and."

131 *I sat in the corner*: MS version is "sat in a corner"; not changed in MS.

131 *looked right out on the Lake of Shining Waters*: MS has as its first version (more realistically) "looked right out on the graveyard." But "graveyard" is crossed out and "Lake of Shining Waters" substituted.

132 *The Dog at his Master's Grave*: 1908 has "The Dog at His Master's Grave."

132 *That's in the Third Royal Reader*. Another instance of a sentence not found in MS. See *Variants*.

132 *sounds so tragical*: "so" is not underlined in MS, although italicized in printed editions.

136 *skirt-pattern*: hyphenated as in MS; no hyphen in 1908.

138 *over a gorgeous clump of tiger lilies*: MS restored; 1908, 1925, etc., have "over a clump of gorgeous tiger lilies."

138 *scarlet-lightning*: hyphenated as in MS.

141 *sewing-machine agent*: no hyphen in MS.

141 *You're not going to play all your time*: MS restored; 1908, etc., have "You're not going to play all the time."

143 *unbraided hair . . . torrent of brightness*: Added in MS Note Y6.

144 *the reason she said*: MS restored; 1908, etc., have "the reason why she said."

145 *see it, Marilla, won't you?*: Punctuation as in MS; 1908, etc., have "see it, Marilla—won't you?"

146 *behind their chicken house*: MS originally "behind their chicken coop"; "coop" crossed out in MS and changed to "house."

149 *to that small personage . . . Diana's teaching*: Added in MS Note I.

151 *And the brooch is gone, there's nothing surer.*: A sentence not found in the MS.

151 *worse about that than the brooch*: MS restored; 1908, etc., have "worse about that than about the brooch."

152 *That is the plain, ugly truth*: MS restored; 1908, etc., have "That's the plain, ugly truth."

153 *succeeded, but her success*: MS punctuation restored; 1908, etc., have semicolon after "succeeded."

154 *Picnic, indeed!*: Punctuation as in 1908; MS has period after "indeed."

154 *Think of the ice-cream! . . . again!*: Added in MS Note T7.

155 *you're making excuses all the time for her to yourself*: MS restored; 1908, etc., have "you're making excuses for her all the time to yourself." The less coherent sequence in MS sentence seems colloquial and suited to Marilla's mood.

155 *as a personal insult*: MS Note X7, which gives us this statement about Jerry Buote, has the phrase "as a personal interest"—probably a mental slip of the moment.

156 *by its catch.*: Punctuation as in MS, which has period, whereas 1908, etc., have exclamation point.

157 *tired-out*: hyphen as in MS and 1925; not in 1908.

157 *It would be such a romantic experience*: MS (Note E8) restored; 1908, etc., have "It would have been such a romantic experience."

157 *And we had ice-cream.*: MS restored; 1908, etc., have "And we had the ice-cream."

160 *Lover's Lane*: In its first introduction in MS, Note G8 on MS p. 228, spelled as "Lover's Lane." Later (in MS) LMM also spells it "Lovers' Lane," but we sustain 1908's apparent decision to keep phrase "Lover's Lane" throughout, although 1908 also is inconsistent. See *Variants* and Textual Note to p. 247.

160 *Violet Vale*: In MS at first "Violet's Vale."

161 *along it. And*: MS restored; 1908, etc., have "along it; and."

161 *white-washed building low . . . with comfortable, substantial, old-fashioned desks*: MS punctuation restored. 1908 makes "whitewashed" one word, inserts comma after "low," and has no commas after "comfortable" and "substantial."

161 *such an odd*: MS originally "such a queer"; "queer" crossed out, "odd" substituted.

162 dead gone *on her*: MS originally "sweet on her"; "sweet" crossed out, "*dead gone*" substituted.

162 *Our seat . . . Waters*: Added in MS Note N8.

162 *it's a kind of a disgrace*: MS restored; 1908, etc., have "it's kind of a disgrace."

163 *marked all over*: MS restored; 1908, etc., have "all marked over."

163 *And oh, Marilla,*: Commas as in MS and 1925; no comma after "oh" in 1908. See *Variants*.

163 *Gilbert Blythe will be in school to-day*: in this first reference to Gilbert, MS has his name as "Gilbert Blithe"; changed in MS to "Gilbert Blythe."

165 *and driving crickets . . . up and down the aisle*: Added in MS Note J8.

167 *Then Anne looked at him with a vengeance.*: MS punctuation restored; period in place of an

exclamation point after "vengeance" supplied in 1908 and other printed editions, which also make this one sentence into a separate paragraph, as not in MS or present text.

167 *she had been called Carrots.*: Capital "C" restored as in MS; 1908, 1925, etc., have "carrots."

169 *announced before going home to dinner that*: Commas in 1908 deleted to reflect MS.

169 *and, as usual, the*: Commas restored from MS.

170 *with a wreath . . . shadowy places,*: Added in MS Note B9.

171 *ackshually never . . . spots on it*: MS restored; 1908, etc., have "acksually never . . . spots in it."

171 *To Anne, this was the end of all things.*: MS restored; 1908, etc., have "To Anne, this was as the end of all things."

171 *verses, "To Priscilla," before*: MS punctuation restored.

171 *Once when nobody was looking, Gilbert*: MS punctuation restored; 1908, etc., have commas after "once" and after "looking."

171 *"You are Sweet"*: MS restored; 1908, 1925, etc., have "You are sweet."

172 *playing ball next week, and*: MS punctuation restored; 1908, etc., don't have comma.

172 *And we're going . . . reading out loud, Anne.*: Added in MS Note F9.

173 *stubborn when she takes the notion*: MS restored; 1908, etc., have "if she takes the notion."

173 *ten children to school so she*: MS restored; 1908, etc., have "ten children to school and she."

173 *dearly loved*: MS has "dearly liked."

174 *Diana's efforts as peacemaker*: MS restored; 1908, etc., have "Diana's efforts as a peacemaker."

177 *Diana is Invited to Tea with Tragic Results*: See *Variants*.

177 *clutter your room up*: MS restored; 1908, etc., have "clutter up your room."

178 *can I use the rosebud tea-set?*: MS restored; 1908, etc., have "can I use the rosebud spray tea-set?"

178 *I believe it's beginning to go.*: See *Variants*.

178 *I can just imagine sitting down*: MS restored; 1908, etc., have "I can just imagine myself sitting down."

179 *to eat along with it in the afternoon*: MS restored; 1908, etc., have "to eat with it along in the afternoon."

181 *she hated it. Gertie*: Punctuation with period as in MS; 1908, etc., have semicolon before "Gertie."

181 *sitting-room pantry*: Editors' correction; MS and 1908, 1925, 1942 all have "room pantry" here, but that is clearly an error, if an error stemming from LMM's own omission. Marilla told Anne the cordial was "on the second shelf of the sitting-room closet" (p. 179).

181 *bright-red*: Hyphen as in MS; not in 1908.

182 *pathetic little tale*: See *Variants*.

182– *She was terribly mortified . . . scolding*: The tale of
183 the mouse and the pudding sauce was added in MS Note A9.

184 *frost-fairy*: hyphen in MS and 1925; no hyphen in 1908, 1942.

184 *Mr. and Mrs. Chester Ross*: MS originally "Spencer"; crossed out, "Chester" substituted.

186 *face downwards on the sofa in an agony*: As in MS and 1925. See *Variants*.

186 *home-made currant-wine*: Both words hyphenated in our text, though not always in MS, which at this point has "home made currant-wine"; 1908 has "homemade currant wine." MS has "home-made" with hyphen in ch. 19.

188 *Mrs. Barry was a woman*: MS originally "was a lady"; "lady" crossed out and "woman" substituted.

188 *prejudices and dislikes and her anger was of the cold sullen sort*: Punctuation as in MS; 1908, etc., have commas after "dislikes" and "cold."

189 *said coldly*: Punctuation as in MS; 1908, etc., have comma after "said."

189 *such an obstinate woman as Mrs. Barry*: MS restored; 1908, etc., have "such an obstinate person as Mrs. Barry."

192 *Nobody ever loved me*: MS restored; 1908, etc., have "Nobody has ever loved me."

192 *forever more*: MS restored; 1908 has "forever-more"; 1925 has "for evermore."

194 *slate-water*: MS has no hyphen.

195 *Diana might have smiled at me just once*: MS restored; 1908, etc., have "Diana might just have smiled at me once."

195 *(ran the former)*: Punctuation with parentheses as in MS; commas only in 1908, brackets in 1925. See *Variants*.

195 *DIANA BARRY*: Not in caps in MS.

195 *kissed the bookmark*: Not found in MS.

196 *improoved*: MS shows LMM first wrote "improved," then crossed it out and substituted misspelled version.

196 *ANNE or CORDELIA SHIRLEY*: Names not in caps in MS.

197 *algebra*: Appears as "Algebra" in MS.

200 *Gilbert Blythe's triumph*: MS originally "Gilbert Blythe's victory"; "victory" crossed out and "triumph" substituted.

201 *To vote . . . religion*: Added in MS Note B10.

201 *I'm glad . . . Grits*: Added in MS Note B11.

202 *I dunno as*: MS originally "I dunno's"; the "s" is crossed out and "as" follows. Evidently LMM doesn't want to make Matthew sound *too* much of a country bumpkin by having him say "I dunno's I comprehend."

203   *white-faced*: In MS written as one word.

203   *Doctor Spencer would go too. Young*: Punctuation as in MS with period after "too"; 1908, etc., have comma after "too."

206   *that baby's life, for*: MS has no comma.

206   *The trees look as if*: MS restored; 1908, etc., have "Those trees."

207   *blue-plum preserve*: Hyphenated as in MS and 1925; 1908, 1942 have "blue plum preserve."

208   *the great shimmering*: MS has "a great shimmering."

209   *Diana gave me a beautiful card*: MS originally "gave me a lovely"; "lovely" crossed out and "beautiful" substituted.

209   *The taffy wasn't very good . . . thrown away . . . splendid fun*: Added in MS Note V10.

211   *trapesing*: MS spelling; 1908 has "traipsing."

212   *Club concert*: "Club" is "club" in MS.

215   *a "perfectly elegant" tea; and*: MS restored; 1908, etc., have "a 'perfectly elegant tea'; and"

216   *over satin-smooth roads*: MS restored: 1908, etc., have "over the satin-smooth roads."

216   *distant laughter that*: MS punctuation; 1908 has comma after "laughter."

217   *Far above the Gentle Daisies*: MS and 1925; 1908, 1942 have "Far Above the Gentle Daisies."

218   *Do you suppose we will ever be asked . . . of that person*: All added in MS Note I11.

220   *to-morrow, Sunday and all as it is*: MS originally "Saturday"; crossed out and "Sunday" substituted. Sunday would be the correct to-morrow if the concert and the jumping incident took place on Friday night and Aunt Josephine's displeasure was registered on Saturday. Sunday travelling was frowned on.

221   *tell-tale*: Hyphenated as in MS and in 1925; 1908 has "telltale."

222   *Diana did her share in the jumping*: MS restored; 1908, etc., have "Diana did her share of the jumping."

223   *It was simply awful, the way we felt*: Punctuation as in MS; 1908, 1925, 1942 have no comma.

226   *book, I know*: No comma in MS; comma in 1908, 1925, etc.

226   *silvery-sweet*: MS version. See *Variants*.

228   *round it*: MS restored; 1908, 1942 have "around it."

228   *I'm sorry about that pie*: MS restored; 1908, etc., have "I'm very sorry about that pie."

229   *catch you.*: MS punctuation; 1908, etc., have exclamation point after "you."

231   *license*: As in MS and 1908; 1925 has "licence."

231   *cold fleshless hands*: MS punctuation; 1908, etc., have comma after "cold."

231   *long drawn*: As in MS; 1908, etc., have "long-drawn."

235   *quilting frames*: Not hyphenated, as in MS; with hyphen in 1908.

235   *small red-headed girl*: MS restored; 1908 has "small, red-haired girl." See *Variants*.

236   *I thought Mr. Marshall decidedly attractive*: MS restored; 1908, etc., have "was" after "Marshall."

236   *seven hundred and fifty dollars a year and*: MS has "$750 a year and."

236   *life work*: MS version; 1908, etc., have "life-work."

236   *With Mrs. Allan Anne fell*: MS and 1908 punctuation; 1925 puts comma after "Mrs. Allan."

237   *Sunday-school picnic*: With hyphen as in MS and 1908, and with lower case "s" in "school" in adjectival phrase.

237   *He's got so used*: MS restored; see *Variants*

238   *assured Anne . . . promised Marilla*: MS shows both verbs originally "said"; changed in MS.

238   *She talked it all over with Diana on Tuesday night*: MS version. See *Variants*.

238 *baking-powder biscuits*: No hyphen in MS.

238 *having the minister's wife to tea*: MS version, and a striking example of a major difference from published texts, which all have "having a minister's family to tea." We restore the MS version (found in Note U12), as it seems more likely that the responsibility of making a good culinary showing in front of a minister's *wife*, who would be thought of as a leading housekeeper in the community, was on the women's minds. Mr. and Mrs. Allan, newly married and childless, hardly constitute a "family" in common P.E.I. usage, and we suspect Page's editorial intervention at this point. An editor might think the real challenge lay in entertaining a minister—but the minister might often take a cup of tea while on a professional visit to a family in bereavement, etc. The *formality* of the occasion is marked by the wife's accompanying him.

238 *chased all round*: MS restored; 1908 has "chased all around."

240 *sitting here combing*: Punctuation as in MS; 1908 has comma after "here."

240 *what if that cake doesn't rise?*: Not found in MS.

242 *ate steadily away at it*: MS restored; 1908, etc., have "steadily ate away at it."

242 *Oh, Marilla, it must have been the baking-powder*: Added in MS Note B13; no hyphen in MS.

243 *Mrs. Lynde . . . poison her benefactor*: Added in MS Note D13.

243 *taken internally—but not in cakes*: MS (in Note E13) restored; 1908, etc., have "taken internally—although not in cakes."

243 *Providential*: In MS, looks rather like a capital "P." Cf. p. 297.

246 *Marilla had almost begun to despair of*: MS originally "Marilla had almost given up"; "given up" crossed out, "begun to despair of" substituted.

246 *raindrops*: One word as in MS and 1925; 1908, 1942 have "rain-drops."

247 *door, with*: Punctuation as in MS; 1908, etc., have no comma.

247 *over in Lover's Lane*: MS "over in Lovers' Lane" in this instance.

248 *heart-to-heart*: Hyphenated as in MS; not in 1908.

251 *liniment-cake episode*: Hyphenated as in MS; in MS originally "accident"; crossed out and "episode" substituted.

251 *little mistakes . . . worth counting*: All added in MS Note T13.

252 *discomfiture*: As in MS and 1908; 1925 has "discomforture."

252 *tried it. Josie Pye, if*: MS restored; 1908, etc., have "But" before "Josie Pye" here.

252 *You couldn't anyhow*: Punctuation as in MS; in 1908, etc., there is a comma after "couldn't."

253 *said "Oh!" partly*: MS version has no exclamation point; we have removed the comma that 1908 has after "said."

253 *pearl-bead*: Hyphenated as in MS; 1908 has no hyphen. The legacy of the bead ring is added in MS Note W13.

253 *Diana . . . pearl-bead ring then and there*: Added in MS Note X13. Originally, sentence ended "it would probably have been the end of her career."

254 *And I'm sure . . . around the garden*: Added in MS Note Z13.

255 *Don't be frightened, Marilla*: As in MS. See *Variants*.

255 *gone and fainted!*: MS has period; exclamation point supplied in 1908.

255 *white-faced*: hyphenated here as in MS, but one word in MS chapter "Anne to the Rescue."

255 *could blame it on anybody else I would*: MS restored; 1908, etc., have "could blame it on anybody I would."

256   *to bring her flowers and books*: Phrase "and books" not in MS.

256   *sighed Anne*: MS shows "sighed" substituted for "said."

256   *Not a kindred spirit . . . private prayers interesting*: Added in MS Note D14.

257   *and she said it . . . believe I would*: Added in MS Note F14.

257   *physical culture exercises morning and evening*: MS version, also 1925. 1908, 1942 have "physical culture exercises every morning and evening. See *Variants*.

260   *Mary Queen of Scots*: Without comma after "Mary" as in MS. See *Variants*.

261   *brought forward in November*: MS originally "September"; crossed out and "November" substituted.

261   *performers-elect*: The word "elect" not in MS: "of all the excited performers none."

262   The Society for the Suppression of Gossip . . . The Fairy Queen: MS Note N14 shows titles underlined. We have chosen italics for these titles here and elsewhere, as in 1925. See *Variants*.

262   Faith, Hope *and* Charity: Italic as in MS where words are underlined except for "and."

265   *boot-jack*: Hyphenated as in MS; 1908 has as one word.

266   *at the solution of his problem*: MS restored, also as 1925. 1908, 1942 have "a solution of his problem."

266   *soberly gowned*: MS originally "dressed"; crossed out and "gowned" substituted.

266   *Probably some wise*: MS originally "Likely"; changed to "Probably" in MS.

267   *shop-keepers*: Hyphenated as in MS; 1908 has as one word.

268   *with a huge, drooping pompadour . . . smile*: Added in MS Note V14.

268   *She now concluded he was*: MS restored; 1908, etc., have "She now concluded that he was."

269   *I made my cake*: MS restored; 1908 has "I've made my cake."

269   *Have you anything in particular*: MS restored; 1908, etc., have "Have you something particular."

270   *I'd like them made the new way*: MS restored; 1908, etc., have "I'd like them made in the new way."

270   *To herself she added . . . over sixty years*: All added in MS Note Y14

270   *The way Marilla dresses her is positively ridiculous*: As in 1908 and all printed editions; MS has "The way Marilla dresses her is positively absurd." Either a copy editor or LMM herself when typing the story out thought "absurd" too educated a term for Mrs. Lynde to use.

270   *plain and easy as Rule of Three*: MS originally "plain and easy as ABC"; changed in MS.

270   *so-fashion*: See *Variants*.

270   *I'm sure the child*: MS originally "I'm sure Anne"; changed in MS.

275   *a brilliant evening*: MS originally "wonderful"; crossed out and "brilliant" substituted.

275   *looking at me and through me*: "and through me" is not in MS.

276   *what that person does*: MS originally "Gilbert Blythe"; crossed out and "that person" substituted.

276   *And she looked real nice too.*: This sentence not in MS.

277   *spoil people for every-day life*: MS originally "life"; crossed out, "existence" substituted, then crossed out and "life" restored.

279   *behoved*: Spelling as in MS; 1908 has "behooved."

279   *I had such an interesting talk . . . get on better*: Added in MS Note P15.

280 *The Jealous Rival, or In Death Not Divided*: As in MS, except that MS has quotation marks around "The Jealous Rival" and "In Death Not Divided," separated by the word "or," not in quotation marks. It is evident that the second part of the title was to some extent an afterthought, as "In Death Not Divided" is written above the line. 1908 has "The Jealous Rival; or, in Death Not Divided."

281 *to Europe for a wedding tour*: MS shows that LMM seems to have written "trip" or at least "tri-" before crossing it out and substituting the grander "tour."

282 *especially . . . diamond ring*: Added in MS Note Q15.

283 *nom-de-plume*: As in MS and 1908, with hyphens, not italicized; 1925 has italic but no hyphens.

283 *read it out aloud*: MS restored; 1908 has "read it out loud."

283 *the pathetic parts*: MS originally "sad"; crossed out and "pathetic" substituted.

284 *silly forgetful little*: Punctuation as in MS; 1908, 1925 insert comma after "silly."

284 *Is it very wicked of me*: MS originally "bad"; crossed out and "wicked" substituted.

286 *old Aid meetings*: MS restored; 1908, etc., have "Old Aid meeting evenings."

287 *Lover's Lane*: In MS and 1908 at this point it is written "Lovers' Lane."

289 *pedlar*: Spelling as in MS and 1908.

289 *in the house!*: MS has period, no exclamation point.

291 *practise to deceive!* : Punctuation as in MS, with exclamation point; 1908 etc., have period.

291 *dismal sigh*: MS originally "tearful"; crossed out and "dismal" substituted.

291 *never, never look*: MS has no comma.

293 *a red-headed Elaine*: MS originally "red-haired"; "haired" crossed out and "headed" substituted.

294 *short silky curls*: MS punctuation; 1908, etc., have comma after "short."

295 *the previous winter*: MS restored; 1908, etc., have "the preceding winter."

295 *analyzed it and parsed it*: MS restored; 1908 has "analyzed and parsed it."

295 *Anne was devoured*: MS has "Anne was regretfully" crossed out, "secretly" substituted and crossed out before "devoured."

295 *landing-place*: MS has no hyphen.

295 *We can't have the old dumb . . . lying down*: Added in MS Note F16.

295 *crape*: MS spelling; 1908, etc., have "crepe"; same change made on p. 298.

297 *Providential*: MS seems to indicate capital "P" on "Providential" at this point.

298 *in the barge*: MS originally "in the flat"; "flat" crossed out, "barge" substituted—hesitation enters the text itself in next phrase: "I mean the flat."

300 *newly-awakened*: Hyphenated as in MS.

300 *"Carrots"*: Capital "C" as in MS; 1908 has "carrots."

300 *never forgive him.*: Punctuation as in MS with period; 1908, etc., have exclamation point.

302 *shyly. "A little*: Punctuation as in MS; 1908 has comma between "shyly," and "'a little."

303 *It was a September . . . at evening*: Added in MS Note M16.

303 Marmion: Italic as underlined in MS; 1908 has quotation marks only.

305–
306 *She said my old one . . . naturally good people*: Added in MS Note P16.

306 *must have a new coat*: MS originally "must have one"; changed in MS, probably after long addition in Note P16.

306 *My cap is so pretty*: In MS originally followed by "It is one" crossed out.

307 *Beechwood*: No quote marks around this in MS though there are in 1908. See *Variants*.

308 *I just wish Julia . . . parlour*: Added in MS Note S16.

309 *and she, being a church member, thought*: Punctuation as in MS; 1908 has "and she being a church-member, thought."

310 *but oh, they*: Punctuation as in MS; 1908 has "but, oh, they."

311 *Shore Road*: Capitalized to agree with earlier practice in MS. See note to p. 84.

313 *looked at her with a tenderness*: MS originally "looked at her affect"; "affect" crossed out. Presumably LMM is not yet prepared to say that Marilla demonstrated her feelings sufficiently to look "affectionately" at Anne; even though we are told here that Marilla feels affection, a softening is the only change her aspect registers.

316 Ben Hur: Italic, as in 1925; underlined in MS. 1908, 1942 put title in quotation marks.

317 *it was only a story-book*: MS restored; 1908, etc., have "it was a story-book."

317- The Lurid Mystery of the Haunted Hall: In
318 MS originally, more realistically, "*The Mystery of the Haunted Hall.*" Revision (made in MS) makes it clear that this is not a real title— publishers are not likely to allow the word "lurid"; the adjective is frequently used in disapproving criticism of mysteries or thrillers.

318 *silly unwholesome*: Punctuation as in MS, with no comma after "silly."

319 *I'm extremely grateful*: MS shows "so" before "grateful"; "so" crossed out and "extremely" substituted.

321 *wayward feminine little heart*: In MS, "feminine" added above the line.

323 *I don't believe I could have the heart*: MS originally "I don't believe I could have gone on"; "gone on" crossed out, "the heart" substituted.

323 *school-book*: Hyphenated as in MS; not in 1908

324 *They have dinner there . . . her dying day*: Added in MS Note O17.

324 *a bad spell with his heart on Thursday*: MS version. See *Variants*.

325 *trust her in anything now*: MS originally "trust her in anything else"; "else" crossed out.

325 *mistaken and I'm real*: MS originally "mistaken and I'm not one"; "not one" crossed out.

325 LMM twice tries to end this chapter without succeeding, first with "got to be," after which the rule is drawn—then new material is added and another rule is drawn after "like Diana Barry has." But Mrs. Lynde seems to go on beyond her author's original design. The inversion in "She's a real pretty girl got to be" is unusual, perhaps ultimately in the Irish style, instead of "She's got to be [i.e., she has become] a real pretty girl."

327 *out of doors*: MS version, also 1925; in 1908, "outdoors."

327 *gipsyings*: MS has "gypsyings" here; we keep spelling used earlier.

328 *If I was a man*: MS version; 1908, etc., have "If I were a man."

328 *influence for good if*: Punctuation as in MS; 1908, etc., have comma after "good."

328 *to turn to and do the work*: MS has "to turn in and do the work"; present version found in 1908, 1925, etc.

329 *I feel it's a great . . . about that flounce.*: Added in MS Note R17.

330 *dimly foreshadowing*: MS restored, though form arguably less correct than 1908's "dimly shadowing."

330 *pass lists of the Entrance exams*: We keep capital "E" on "Entrance," although at this point MS shows lower case "e."

330 *Hills peeped o'er hills*: Correction in accordance with MS, which has plural form of both nouns; 1908 misprints in dropping "s" in second instance: "Hills peeped o'er hill." Error is repeated in 1925, etc.

331 *queer, sorrowful sense of loss*: Punctuation as in MS; 1908, etc., have no comma.

331 *little eager girl*: Punctuation as in MS; 1908 has comma after "little."

332 *the lure of spring sunshine*: MS restored; 1908, etc., have "the lure of the spring sunshine."

333 *all our essays*: MS originally "all our compositions"; "compositions" crossed out, "essays" substituted.

333 *What has become of your story club? . . . trying to*: All added in MS Note T17.

333 *And so I'm trying to*: As in MS; 1908, etc., have "And so I am trying to."

333 *stumbling block*: No hyphen in MS; hyphenated in 1908.

333 *feels it in his bones*: MS originally "is sure"; crossed out and "feels it in his bones" substituted.

334 *passing the Entrance*: Capital letter sustained on what is in MS "entrance" at this point to accord with usage elsewhere, e.g, three paragraphs above: "we'll have at the Entrance," where MS shows capital "E."

336 *can't be cheerful be as cheerful*: Punctuation as in MS; 1908, etc., have comma after first "cheerful."

336 *you came out splendidly*: MS originally "you came out great"; changed in MS.

336 *horrid, cold fluttery*: Punctuation as in MS; 1908 has no commas. MS shows word originally "awful"; "horrid" substituted.

336 *I'm not superstitious*: MS restored; 1908 etc., have "I am not superstitious"; not changed in MS.

337 Letter taken out of quotation marks that appear in 1908 and elsewhere (but not in MS). 1925 setting out seems closest practicable to MS, so we have copied it.

337 *I couldn't cram*: No quotation marks around "cram" in MS or in 1925, although there are in 1908.

337 *everything he ever knew but*: Punctuation as in MS; comma after "knew" in 1908, etc.

337 *firmly in their proper places*: MS restored; 1908, etc., have "proper place."

338 *when we were assigned*: MS originally "When we went."

338 *good steady sensible*: Punctuation as in MS; 1908 has commas after "good" and "steady."

338 *my heart began beating*: MS originally "My heart began to beat."

338 *If I thought the multiplication table . . . morning*: Added in MS Note Y17.

339 *a minister anyhow*: Punctuation as in MS; comma after "minister" in 1908.

339 *Sometimes I've wished*: MS restored; 1908, etc., have "Sometimes I have wished."

340 *would "beat the whole Island"*: MS restored; 1908, etc., put quotation marks around "would beat the whole Island."

341 *cold, sinkaway feelings, as*: Punctuation as in MS; 1908, etc., have no commas after "cold" and after "feelings."

341 *Mrs. Lynde wanted . . . vote Grit at the next election*: All added in MS Note A18.

343 *That night . . . maidenhood might desire*: Added in Note B18.

346 *no "mahogany furniture" but*: Punctuation as in MS; 1908, etc., have comma before "but."

346 *white painted bookcase*: As in MS; 1908, etc., have "white-painted bookcase."

347   *on his Anne and*: Punctuation as in MS, without comma after "Anne" supplied in 1908.

347   *sought-after*: Hyphenated as in MS; no hyphen in 1908, etc.

349   *half way*: As in MS; hyphenated in 1908

349   *house-rose*: Hyphenated as in MS and 1925; no hyphen in 1908.

349   *There was just one on my bush and I saved it for you*: MS punctuation restored; 1908, 1925 have commas after "bush," and 1908 has another comma after "it." See *Variants*.

349   *always been afraid*: MS originally "always been scared"; "scared" crossed out and "afraid" substituted.

350   *fashionable, and*: No comma after "fashionable" in MS.

351   *big fat stolid*: Punctuation as in MS; 1908 supplies commas after "big" and "fat."

351   *silver clear*: As in MS; hyphenated in 1908, etc.,

352   *her dress which, in the east gable, had*: Punctuation as in MS; 1908, etc., put comma after "dress."

352   *jacket away and*: Punctuation as in MS; comma after "away" supplied in 1908.

352   *scornful-looking*: Hyphenated as in MS and 1925; no hyphen in 1908.

352   *turned her head squarely round*: As in MS and 1925; 1908 has "around."

352   *white-lace girl*: Hyphenated as in MS and in 1925; no hyphen in 1908.

353   *Often as she had recited in public she*: Punctuation as in MS; 1908 supplies comma after "public."

353   *paralyzed*: Spelling as in MS and 1908; 1925 has "paralysed."

354   *certainly was triumphant and taunting*: MS restored; 1908, etc., have "certainly was both triumphant and taunting."

354   *stout pink lady*: Punctuation as in MS; 1908 has comma after "stout."

354   *under her wing and introduced her to everybody, and*: Punctuation as in MS; 1908 has comma after "wing" and semicolon after "everybody."

354   *dining-room*: No hyphen in MS; hyphenated in 1908 and 1925.

355   *partake of this also*: Punctuation as in MS; 1908 has comma after "this."

355   *calm white moonshine*: Punctuation as in MS; 1908 has comma after "calm."

355   *Oh, it was good . . . enchanted coasts*: Added in MS Note J18.

355   *like grim giants guarding*: MS has "like grim guardians guarding."

355   *distinguished artist and*: Punctuation as in MS; 1908 supplies comma after "artist."

356   *imaginations more or less*: Punctuation as in MS; 1908 inserts comma after "imaginations."

356   *all silver and shadow and*: See *Variants*.

356   *so short and stout*: MS restored; 1908, etc., have "so stout and short."

356   *diamonds would comfort a person for*: MS originally "diamonds would make up for"; "make up" crossed out and "comfort a person" substituted.

357   *got "evening dresses" as they call them*: Punctuation as in MS; 1908 has comma after "dresses."

357   *in town last week and*: Punctuation as in MS; 1908 supplies semicolon after "week."

358   *yellowish-brown wincey dress*: So here in all versions. This description of the bad dress's color is not the same as that in ch. 1, where it is "yellowish-gray" in MS and 1908, "yellowish-white" in 1925. See *Variants*.

358   *your little Anne who*: Punctuation as in MS; 1908 supplies comma after "Anne."

360   *—if it was luck . . . I reckon*: Added in MS Note M18.

360   *untearful practical*: Punctuation as in MS; 1908 supplies comma after "untearful."

360   *heart-ache*: Hyphenated in MS; no hyphen in 1908.

360   *acutely miserably conscious*: MS version; 1908, etc., have "acutely and miserably conscious."

360   *to "take on" so*: Quotation marks as in MS. See *Variants*.

361   *but it also meant much more and harder work*: This clause not in MS.

361   *tall brown-haired boy*: Punctuation as in MS; 1908 supplies comma after "tall."

361   *What a splendid chin . . . before*: Added in MS Note N18.

361   *I won't feel so much like a cat in a strange garret*: MS originally "I won't feel so lost and lonely"; "lost and lonely" crossed out.

361   *then there's that pale fair one*: MS and 1925; 1908 has "and there's that pale, fair one."

362   *boarding house*: As in MS; hyphenated in 1908.

362   *table is good and*: Punctuation as in MS; 1908 supplies comma after "good."

362   *All this might be true and*: MS restored; 1908, etc., have "All this might be quite true, and."

362   *great, green, still*: Punctuation as in MS.

362   *sweet-peas*: Hyphenated as in MS; no hyphen in 1908.

362   *Here there was nothing of this. Anne*: Punctuation as in MS, with period after "this"; 1908 has semicolon.

362   *the tramp of alien feet*: Added above the line in MS.

363   *what is connected with*: MS originally "what belongs to"; "belongs to" crossed out.

363   *it isn't becoming for*: Punctuation as in MS; 1908 supplies comma after "becoming."

363   *He boards the same place I do and he's a sport*: MS restored; 1908, 1925 have "He boards the same place as I do, and he's a sport."

363   *you were an orphan the Cuthberts had adopted*: MS restored; 1908, etc., have "you were an orphan that the Cuthberts had adopted."

363–   *Queen's colour ribbon*: Capital "C" on "colour"
364   in MS.

364   *An Avery Scholarship!*: As LMM appears to capitalize in this first instance, we have capitalized "Avery Scholarship" throughout.

364   *at the end of the year and perhaps the medal.*: Punctuation as in MS; 1908 has comma after "year," and all printed editions end this sentence with an exclamation point.

364   *mortar board*: As in MS; hyphenated in 1908.

367   *gipsyings*: LMM has "gypsyings" in MS here.

367   *handsome young lady*: MS originally "handsome girl"; "girl" crossed out, "young lady" substituted.

367   *young lady now, thinking*: Punctuation as in MS; 1908 has comma after "lady," no comma after "now."

367   *bright-blue*: Hyphenated as in MS and 1908. See *Variants* .

367   *complexion and*: Punctuation as in MS; 1908 supplies comma after "complexion."

368   *put her feelings on the matter*: Phrase "on the matter" not in MS.

368   *imaginative ambitious*: Punctuation as in MS; 1908 supplies comma between adjectives.

369   *rainbow-like*: As in MS; 1908 supplies hyphen.

370   *when she was a child but*: Punctuation as in MS, with no comma after "child."

370   *who make me love them!*: Punctuation as in MS; 1908, etc., have period here.

371   *side-eddy*: Hyphenated as in MS; no hyphen in printed editions.

372   *— each year a rose . . . chaplet*: Added in MS Note X18.

374   *laughing congratulating group*: Punctuation as in MS; 1908 supplies comma after "laughing."

375   *Avery Winner*: MS restored; 1908, etc., have "Avery winner."

375   *tea-rose*: Hyphenated as in MS. See *Variants*.

375   *a song and a hope*: MS originally adds "in one" after "hope"; phrase crossed out in favor of longer phrase.

376   *got through, even*: Punctuation as in MS; 1908 has no comma.

377   *with glasses but*: Punctuation as in MS; 1908, etc., have comma after "glasses."

377   *unfits them for women's true sphere*: MS restored; 1908, etc., have "unfits them for woman's true sphere."

377   *Mr. Russell told him yesterday the bank*: MS restored; 1908, etc., have "Mr. Russell told him yesterday that the bank."

378   *The woods were all gloried . . . in the west*: Added in MS Note A19.

378   *silvery peaceful*: Punctuation as in MS; 1908 supplies comma between adjectives.

379   *pulse and*: Punctuation as in MS; 1908 has comma before after "pulse."

380   *shy quiet*: Punctuation as in MS; 1908 has comma between adjectives.

382   *He's always been*: MS a bit uncertain, but it looks like "He's." 1908, etc., have "He'd."

382   *sobbed Anne*: MS originally "implored"; crossed out, "sobbed" substituted.

382   *its usual placidity*: MS originally "its usual calm"; "calm" crossed out, "placidity" substituted.

384   *conch-shell*: Hyphenated as in MS; no hyphen in 1908.

385   *Anne looked up . . . why didn't you—*: One paragraph as in MS, not two as in all printed editions.

385   *you can never tell*: MS restored; 1908, etc., have "you never can tell."

385   *about people from their outsides*: Unmistakable example of real correction of MS error in or by 1908 printing; MS has "about people from their insides."

387   *my eyes may*: MS originally "my eyes will"; "will" crossed out, "may" substituted.

388   *Don't say anything . . . talk about it*: Added in MS Note L19.

390   *come home on Fridays*: MS and 1925; 1908 has "come home Fridays."

391   *checkered lights and shadows*: MS restored; 1908, etc., have "checkered light and shadows."

391   *further on*: MS restored; 1908 has "farther on."

391   *When it became noised abroad*: MS originally "When it was rumoured"; "rumoured" crossed out, "noised abroad" substituted.

391   *I hope you appreciate it*: In MS added above the line.

392   *Josiah Allen's Wife*: MS restored; 1908, etc., have "Josiah Allen's wife." LMM's usage is a correct allusion to the character and pseudo-author created by Marietta Holley.

392   *evenings and*: Punctuation as in MS; 1908, etc., have comma after "evenings."

393   *You'll get along . . . no Pyes . . . isn't their home.* Added in MS Note Q19.

394   *dream-like*: Hyphenated as in MS; 1908 has "dreamlike."

394   *There was a freshness . . . clover.* Added in MS Note S19. This is the last of the Notes.

394   *heart and*: Punctuation as in MS; 1908 supplies comma after "heart."

394   *lovely and*: Punctuation as in MS; 1908 supplies comma after "lovely."

394   *He lifted his cap courteously but he would have passed on in silence if Anne had not*: No commas as in MS; 1908, 1925, etc., have two, one after "courteously" and one after "silence."

394   *by the pond landing, although*: Punctuation as in MS; 1908, etc., have no comma here.

APPENDICES

THE GEOGRAPHY OF *ANNE OF GREEN GABLES*

Prince Edward Island and Cavendish, Lucy Maud Montgomery's childhood home, upon which she based the fictional Avonlea, are both very real places. Prince Edward Island, or P.E.I., is a small, crescent-shaped island off the eastern coast of mainland Canada. It lies north of Nova Scotia in the Gulf of Saint Lawrence. Only 2,000 square miles in size, it is Canada's smallest province. The major industries of P.E.I. today are agriculture, tourism, and fishing. Like the island that Montgomery describes in *Anne*, the real P.E.I. is beautifully green and abounding in natural wonders. As Anne notices upon her arrival there, the soil of P.E.I. is very red, due to high concentrations of iron oxide, which "rusts" upon exposure to air. More than three hundred different kinds of birds, including bald eagles, owls, osprey, Canada geese, black ducks, and teal, make P.E.I. their home. The wildflowers the author describes in her novel are plentiful on the island. Junebells, starflowers, ladies' slippers, and mayflowers still grow as they did in Anne and Maud's childhood, though not as profusely now.

Montgomery's ability to evoke the landscape, flora, and fauna of her beloved home is one of the greatest strengths of her novels. All but one of her many works are set on P.E.I. In *Anne*, as in the other novels, Montgomery uses the raw material of her own childhood to create a landscape that has enchanted readers for generations. Cavendish, the original source for the fictional Avonlea, is located on the north shore of the island at almost the midpoint of

its crescent. The Gulf of Saint Lawrence, which is visible to Mrs. Lynde at the opening of the novel, is a deep fissure in the Atlantic Ocean between the island of Newfoundland and the east coast of Canada. The St. Lawrence River discharges into the Gulf at its northwest end. Avonlea is thus clearly on the north shore of P.E.I. Although it is not particularly emphasized in *Anne*, Cavendish is known for its miles of sandy beaches. Its Micmac name in fact means "sandy beach." And on their ride to Mrs. Spencer's, Marilla points out to Anne the White Sands Hotel, where "heaps of Americans come . . . for the summer. They think this shore is just about right" (p. 90).

Montgomery grew up in the "Old Macneill Homestead" in Cavendish, with her grandparents Lucy Woolner Macneill and Alexander Macneill. There they kept the Cavendish post office and she wrote *Anne of Green Gables*. The homestead, an old-fashioned farmhouse, was surrounded by apple orchards. The house itself has been torn down, but visitors can see the site of the old homestead, which remains in the Macneill family.

Green Gables itself was drawn not from her grandparents' home but from that of David and Margaret Macneill, cousins of the author's grandfather, where Montgomery visited often as a child. Montgomery wrote in her journals that "*Green Gables* was drawn from David Macneill's house now Mr. Webb's—though not the house so much as the situation and scenery, and the truth of my description of it is attested by the fact that everybody has recognized it" (*SJ* II [Jan. 27, 1911]: 41). As Virginia Careless points out, "Montgomery was not necessarily true to that building," in that the interior of the Macneill house had a different floor plan and a fireplace in the sitting room instead of a stove ("The Highjacking of 'Anne,'" *CCL* 67 [1992]: 49). The author has left us a

commentary on the differences in detail between the house of David and Margaret Macneill, the model for the fictional house, and the Green Gables we know from the story: "I did not confine myself to the facts at all. There are, I think, willows in the yard but there are no 'Lombardies' (*SJ* II [Jan. 27, 1911]: 39). The real Macneill place was "by no means as tidy as I pictured *Green Gables*. . . . Quite the reverse, in fact, David's yard was notoriously *untidy*. It was a local saying that if you wanted to see what the world looked like on the morning after the flood you should go into David's barnyard on a rainy day!" (*SJ* II: 39). This homestead, now called *Green Gables House*, has been preserved by the Canadian government since 1937. The house has been restored and visitors can now see how the rooms, including Anne's, would have been furnished, according to the period and the description in the novel.

The Lover's Lane of the novel is based on a real one near this house, which was one of Montgom-

---

Above: The Ernest Webb homestead, pictured here in the 1890s, was restored as the "Anne of Green Gables House," and the surrounding land became a national park in 1937.

Opposite: Webb's field, Cavendish, 1890s.

ery's favorite haunts. Later in life, when she lived in Ontario, far from P.E.I., she would long for the opportunity to walk down Lover's Lane. "I *would* like an old-time walk in Lover's Lane at sunset—or along the old haunted sandshore in the twilight!" (*SJ* II: 212).

Much of the memorable scenery in *Anne of Green Gables* is based on real places on P.E.I. For instance, Mrs. Lynde's home in Lynde's Hollow and the brook that runs through the hollow were taken from the home of Pierce Macneill, another cousin of the author's grandfather. "The brook that runs below the *Cuthbert* place and through *Lynde's Hollow* is, of course, my own dear brook of the woods which runs below Webb's and through 'Pierce's Hollow'" (*SJ* II [Jan. 27, 1911]: 39). (Montgomery also assigned to Rachel Lynde Mrs. Pierce Macneill's name, although she says there was no other connection between them.) Hunter River, a very small place, was the site of the railway station nearest Cavendish. The fictional Bright River and its train station at which Anne first arrives is based on Hunter River and its station, though trains no longer run on P.E.I. Nowadays a sign points out that this is the Bright River of the novel.

If we imagine Matthew and Anne following the present-day Route 13 from Hunter River to Cavendish, Newbridge in the novel would correspond to New Glasgow, not to be confused with the larger town of the same name in Nova Scotia. Montgomery also seems to have created the drive from Kensington to Cavendish along the current Route 6 through Stanley Bridge; *New* Glasgow and Stanley *Bridge* combined into "Newbridge." The town of Carmody, where Matthew goes to buy Anne a dress with puffed sleeves, is based on Stanley, "a pretty village" three miles from Cavendish. As the author recalled, "There are two or three stores in Stanley and we have always gone there to buy household supplies. Stanley used to seem quite a town in my childish eyes." Montgomery once thought it "the hub of the universe . . . or of our solar system at the very least" (*SJ* I [Dec. 31, 1898]: 230). Anne's "Shore Road" is part of what is now known as Blue Heron Drive. White Sands, the scene of Anne's recitation of "The Maiden's Vow," was inspired by the nearby town of Rustico. Montgomery wrote in her journals that "*The White Way of Delight* is practically pure imagination. Yet the idea was suggested to me by a short stretch of road between Kensington and Clinton, which I always thought very beautiful" (*SJ* II [Jan. 27, 1911]: 40).

There was a real Victoria Island in Montgomery's childhood, as her journal reveals: "I went down this morning and took a photo of 'Victoria Island' — that dear old spot down in the school brook, with the old firs on it, and the water laughing about it, just as it glimmered and rippled and laughed in dear days gone by when we schoolgirls and boys played there" (*SJ* I [July 24, 1899]: 238). The Haunted Wood is also based on an actual spot. While a child, Montgomery and her friends Dave and Well Nelson, like Anne and Diana, invented a Haunted Wood for their own

amusement, then found themselves unable to resist the power of their own imaginations. "None of us really believed at first, that the grove was haunted, or that the mysterious 'white things' which we pretended to see flitting through it at dismal hours were aught but the creations of our own fancy. . . . We soon came to believe implicitly in our myths, and not one of us would have gone near that grove after sunset on pain of death. Death! What was death compared to the unearthly horror of falling into the clutches of a 'white thing'?" (*AP*, 30).

Thirteen miles from Montgomery's Macneill grandparents' home lived her grandfather Montgomery and the family of her Uncle John Campbell, at Park Corner. The author notes in her journals that the pond there was her inspiration for the Lake of Shining Waters. "*Anne's* habit of naming places was an old one of my own. The *Lake of Shining Waters* is generally supposed to be the Cavendish Pond. This is not so. The pond at Park Corner is the one I had in mind. But I suppose that a good many of the effects of light and shadow I have seen on the Cavendish pond figured unconsciously in my descriptions; and certainly the hill from which *Anne* caught her first glimpse of it was 'Laird's Hill,' where I have often stood at sunset, enraptured with the beautiful view of shining pond and crimson-brimmed harbor and dark blue sea" (*SJ* II [Jan. 27, 1911]: 40). Montgomery spent many of the happiest moments of her childhood at Park Corner and came back to it later with her sons, Chester and Stuart, when they were children. It is now the site of "Silver Bush," an Anne of Green Gables Museum. Also located on the grounds is the Shining Waters Craft Shop and Tea Room.

Visitors to the P.E.I. can still see all these spots as well as the little house in Clifton where Montgomery was born, which was the inspiration for the house Anne describes as her birthplace. They can picnic on the site of the old schoolhouse where both Anne and her author attended school. And they can visit the Methodist manse on Route 166 where Mrs. Estey put anodyne liniment in the cake, as well as many other spots of interest to both Anne's history and that of her author.

It should be recognized, however, that not every place in *Anne of Green Gables* is based on real sites on P.E.I. The Birch Path, for instance, was not part of the landscape of Cavendish: "But the Birch Path exists somewhere, I know not where. I have a picture of it—the reproduction of a photo which was published in the *Outing* magazine one year. Somewhere in America that lane of birches is" (*SJ* II [Jan. 27, 1911]: 42). Montgomery put the photograph in her journals as an illustration (see *SJ* II: 43). "Willowmere" and "Violet Vale" are also, as she wrote in her journals, "compact of imagination." But although their prototypes exist only in the author's and readers' imaginations, through *Anne* we can feel with Montgomery that "some old gladness always waits there for me and leaps into my heart as soon as I return" (letter to G. B. Macmillan, Sept. 3, 1924).

FURTHER READING

Douglas Baldwin. *Land of the Red Soil: A Popular History of Prince Edward Island*. Charlottetown: Ragweed Press, 1990.

Francis W. P. Bolger, Wayne Barrett and Anne MacKay. *Spirit of Place: Lucy Maud Montgomery and Prince Edward Island*. Toronto: Oxford Univ. Press, 1982.

Andrew Hill Clark. *Three Centuries and The Island: A Historical Geography of Settlement and Agriculture in Prince Edward Island, Canada*. Toronto: Univ. of Toronto Press, 1959.

Department of Tourism and Parks. *Visitor's Guide: Prince Edward Island, Canada*. 1992.

Kathleen Hamilton and Sybil Frei, eds. *Finding "Anne" on Prince Edward Island: Island Pathways*. Charlottetown: Ragweed Press, 1991.

THE SETTLERS OF P.E.I.

THE CELTIC INFLUENCE IN *ANNE*

Anne's beloved Prince Edward Island was once called "Abegweit," or "land cradled on the waves," by the Micmac people who lived there. They told stories of how after creating the universe and the Micmac people the Great Spirit had a large amount of dark red clay left over. The Great Spirit then fashioned that clay into a crescent shape that became the most beautiful jewel in the universe. Then, as in most of North America, the arrival of European explorers and settlers had an adverse affect on the native population. Many First Canadians, including a large percentage of the Micmacs, died of exposure to new diseases such as influenza, smallpox, and measles. Alcoholism became a problem among these people as among many other First Canadian peoples. Moreover, the Micmacs were a migratory hunting and fishing people who moved back and forth between the mainland and the island seasonally. The settlement of P.E.I. by a more agriculturally oriented population, and the fencing and partitioning of land that followed, made maintaining the Micmac culture and way of life extremely difficult. Despite the many changes that have occurred since the days when the Micmacs were the only people on the island, and though their numbers have greatly decreased—today they comprise less than 1 percent of its present population—they have remained on P.E.I.

The first European to "discover" the island was French explorer Jacques Cartier in 1534. In 1603 Samuel de Champlain named it Île St. Jean. Then in 1719 a permanent settlement of some 100 French settlers was established near Porte La Joye, but during the next fifty years dominion over the island changed several times. Under the Treaty of Aix-la-

Chapelle, the British took control of the island in 1745. Then in 1758 it reverted to the French until in 1763 the Treaty of Paris made British control permanent. From 1763 to 1768 thousands of "Acadians," or French settlers, were deported or fled, bringing the population of P.E.I. down from 5,000 to 300. Many of these Acadians eventually ended up in Louisiana, where they became known as "Cajuns" and where their descendants live today. Those that remained on P.E.I. could do so only by hiding in the woods. Although many Acadians eventually returned to P.E.I., Marilla's disparaging comments about "French boys" are indicative of the minority status of the French population.

In February 1799, Île St. Jean officially became Prince Edward Island, named for the son of George III, later the Duke of Kent. This designation was a compromise between the governor's suggestion of "New Ireland" and the British government's countersuggestions of "New Guernsey" and "Anglesey."

According to one historian, "A small German settlement apparently existed briefly on the Island in the Acadian period, but it was not until the Loyalists arrived following the American Revolution that P.E.I. had a permanent German population" (Baldwin, 164). Baldwin also mentions that Lebanese Christians fleeing persecution from the Turks settled on P.E.I. beginning in the 1880s, many of whom became "pack peddlers." Marilla, who is never too discriminating in her prejudices, might well refer to all immigrants from the Mediterranean as Italians (p. 289).

The majority of the settlers who came to P.E.I. once it was under British dominion were not English but Scottish. Many factors contributed to the Scots' departure from their homeland. In the late eighteenth century, systematic efforts known as the Highland Clearances to rid Scotland of Highlanders resulted in mass emigration. The 1745 Jacobite uprising had resulted in defeat at Culloden for the Scottish and eventually led to repression, starvation, and disease. Peasants suffering malnutrition, cholera, and dysentery were expelled from their land to make room for the more profitable sheep farming. Crops failed for several years in a row, and the clan system of the Highlanders was falling apart. They emigrated by the thousands to the New World, which seemed to promise opportunity. Wealthy patrons sometimes subsidized this emigration, as when in 1803 the fifth earl of Selkirk, Thomas Douglas, brought 800 Scottish peasants to P.E.I. to settle. Many other Scots were summarily shipped off by their lairds, or clan chieftains. Many others came to join friends and family already settled on P.E.I. By 1798, 50 percent of the island's population was Scottish. In *Anne's* Avonlea, a Scottish outpost, Scottish names and ancestry prevail.

In 1764–1765 a British surveyor divided the island into sixty-seven lots, or townships, of twenty thousand acres each. Then in 1767 these lots were raffled off to absentee British landlords, creating conflict that lasted for more than a century. In 1875 the government passed a law by which it bought out the proprietors, until by 1895 most of the former tenants owned their land. This long period of strife had enduring repercussions: "Islanders and thus Island politicians remain surprisingly prickly when it comes to issues of land ownership and land use. Provincial legislation still restricts the amount of land any one individual or company can own, and controls sales to non-residents" (MacDonald, 35).

Prince Edward Island came to be known as the "Cradle of Confederation" because of events that took place there in 1864. That September, national leaders met in Charlottetown to discuss prospects for a united Canada. The twenty-three delegates reached agreement on the desirability of unification and even drafted a basic outline for a constitution. As a result, in 1867 the Dominion of Canada was formed. The islanders were not very interested, however; not until 1873 did Prince Edward Island join the Confederation, and even then largely due to economic pressures.

In the first half of the nineteenth century the

steady stream of Scottish immigrants had been joined by Irish men and women leaving an equally troubled and oppressed homeland. By 1861 more than a third of Charlottetown's residents were of Irish ancestry. The ethnicity of P.E.I. was predominantly Celtic. In the second half of the century the Highland Scots' original tongue, Gaelic, was still spoken by many residents of P.E.I. and Nova Scotia. At the end of the twentieth century Nova Scotia still has enough Gaelic speakers to support one Gaelic-speaking institution of higher learning. Unlike some of Montgomery's works, (e.g., *Emily Climbs*), there are no references to Gaelic speaking in *Anne*, but traces of Scottish forms of speech can be found. Phrases like "high dudgeon," which originated in the Highland Scots' clannish and sometimes contentious culture, are still being used by Montgomery after the turn of the century to describe Marilla's feelings.

The importance placed on education on the island in relation to the Scottish heritage of its inhabitants is described by Rubio and Waterston in their introduction to *The Selected Journals of L. M. Montgomery*. They point out that the Scots were teaching British literature as a subject at their universities at a time when Oxford and Cambridge still considered such a subject vulgar. The emphasis on education in Montgomery's books is part of her Scottish heritage, and the curriculum that Anne and her friends are taught has a decidedly Scottish slant as well. The poets and novelists Anne loves are Scottish: Thomas Campbell, James Thomson, William Glassford Bell, Sir Walter Scott. And many of the poems and recitation pieces

From the Charlottetown Patriot, July 19, 1893.

that Anne refers to, such as "Edinburgh After Flodden" and "Hohenlinden," refer to Scottish history, particularly in relation to England. Other pieces in the *Royal Readers*, the primers both Anne and Maud used in school, like the "Story of Bruce and the Spider" and "The Battle of Bannockburn" in the *Fourth Royal Reader*, are further reminders of the islanders' Scottish heritage. Mary, Queen of Scots, is as important an historical figure to the schoolchildren of Avonlea as her cousin Elizabeth, Robert the Bruce as important a legendary figure as Robin Hood. (For further related information, see Appendix, "Education on P.E.I.")

Montgomery's ancestry, like that of her fictional family the Cuthberts, was primarily Scottish, "with a dash of English from several 'grands' and 'greats'" (*AP*, 12). Anne plants on Matthew's grave a cutting from the "little white Scotch rose-bush his mother brought out from Scotland long ago" (p. 383). An attachment to the land of their forebears was still strong in Montgomery's lifetime. "There were many traditions and tales on both sides of the family, to which, as a child, I listened with delight while my elders talked them over around winter firesides. The performance of them was in my blood; I thrilled to the lure of adventure which had led my forefathers westward from the Old Land—a land which I always heard referred to as 'Home,' by men and women whose parents were Canadian born and bred" (*AP*, 12). In this author's novels, English or Welsh names are most often given to unlikable or flawed characters. Emily's teacher Mr. Carpenter is the most salient exception, but even he is called a drunkard.

In *The Alpine Path*, Montgomery tells the family

stories of two of her female ancestors and their arrival in P.E.I. Her great-great-grandmother Montgomery was so seasick on the voyage to North America that when they stopped at P.E.I. for water she got off and refused to set foot on the boat again. As Montgomery describes it, "Expostulation, entreaty, argument, all availed nothing. There the poor lady was resolved to stay, and there, perforce, her husband had to stay with her. So the Montgomerys came to Prince Edward Island" (*AP*, 12). On her mother's side, her great-grandmother was so homesick that "for weeks after her arrival she would not take off her bonnet, but walked the floor in it, imperiously demanding to be taken home. We children who heard the tale never wearied of speculating as to whether she took off her bonnet at night and put it back on again in the morning, or whether she slept in it. But back home she could not go, so eventually she took off her bonnet and resigned herself to her fate" (*AP*, 12).

That Montgomery begins the story of her own life with the history of her ancestors is an indication of the degree to which place and family permeate her books, including *Anne of Green Gables*. The stories likewise emphasize a sense of tradition, history, and familial characteristics. At times this sense of tradition reveals itself as a resistance to change. For instance, Marilla keeps her household the way her mother and her mother before her kept it. Anne's outlandish behavior, like putting flowers on her Sunday hat, upsets the order of Marilla's life and world: the things that Anne does just aren't done.

But Anne is a Celt too, perhaps even more so than Matthew and Marilla. Anne's red hair serves as a cultural reminder that she is a vessel of the true heritage of the Scots-Irish, the so-called English settlers of Nova Scotia and Prince Edward Island. Anne's red hair shows that she is not really English, just as the principal settlers of Anglo-Canada are not really English. Indeed, not only is Anne decidedly redheaded but, if Matthew and Marilla represent the hardheaded practicality and clannishness that are arguably part of the Scottish national character, Anne

represents its other face. Although she is not gifted with second sight like the equally Scottish (if dark-haired) Emily of *New Moon*, she, like Jane Eyre, seems almost "fairy born and human bred." She retains, throughout the novel, an aura of otherworldliness that is almost frightening to the practical residents of Avonlea. A belief in the supernatural brought over from the Old World survived on P.E.I. into the twentieth century. Anne comes "from away" and is an unwelcome replacement to the expected child, like the changelings of Celtic lore. She is fascinated with the folklore of her ancestry, populating the landscape around her with dryads and ghosts, banshees and other eerie folk. The magical and supernatural, along with a close, loving relationship to the natural world, are all part of Anne's character, as of the mythical Celtic landscape itself.

FURTHER READING

Douglas Baldwin. *Land of the Red Soil: A Popular History of Prince Edward Island.* Charlottetown: Ragweed Press, 1990.

A. P. Campbell. "The Heritage of the Highland Scot in Prince Edward Island," *The Island Magazine* 15 (Spring–Summer 1984): 3–8.

Andrew Hill Clark. *Three Centuries and The Island: A Historical Geography of Settlement and Agriculture in Prince Edward Island, Canada.* Toronto: Univ. of Toronto Press, 1959.

Department of Tourism and Parks. *Visitor's Guide: Prince Edward Island, Canada.* 1992.

Edward MacDonald. "The Scots, The Irish, and The British," in *Prince Edward Island.* Halifax, N.S.: Formac Publishing, 1995.

John Prebble. *The Highland Clearances.* London and Harmondsworth: Penguin, 1963.

David Weale. "The Emigrant: Beginnings in Scotland," *The Island Magazine* 16 (Fall–Winter 1984): 15–22.

———. "The Emigrant: Life in the New Land," *The Island Magazine* 17 (Spring–Summer 1985): 3–11.

THE EXCEPTIONAL ORPHAN ANNE

CHILD CARE, ORPHAN ASYLUMS, FARMING OUT, INDENTURING, AND ADOPTION

R.M.D., Route 3
Scotsburn Sta.,
Pictou Co.,
N.S.
Aug. 21st/17 [1917]

To Mayor Martin
Halifax City
Halifax Co., N.S.

Dear Sir,—

Kindly tell me the names of the Homes for boys in your city. I am desirous in getting a good boy (with decent parents) from ages 8–11 yrs inclusive, to bring up and of protestant religion preferably [sic] methodist. Let me know please by return mail. Find enclosed postage stamp for letter.

Also tell me the name of Homes for girls to bring up whether Catholic or Protestant, with address for each home. I mean for both boys and girls.

Answer please by return mail as I wish to inform my mother, who lives in Guysboro, of same. In fact I'm writing this letter for her, that is by her permission.

Wishing to hear from you by return mail
I close and remain
Truly yours
Mrs Ruth Sutherland.

(Courtesy of PANS: 113. 21 RG–35–102 5A.4)

Lucy Maud Montgomery wrote many stories about "lost children"; *Anne* is described in Rea Wilmshurst's introduction to *Akin to Anne* (p. 7) as the "culmination" of the author's wish to provide happy endings. In all her novels at least one orphan is near at hand, from Anne in 1908 to passive Jody, the heroine's neighbour in *Jane of Lantern Hill* (1937). *Anne* was based on a true incident: Montgomery's relative Pierce Macneill adopted a girl, Ellen, who though "one of the most hopelessly commonplace and uninteresting girls imaginable," had a profile strongly resembling the 1908 cover illustration of *Anne* (*SJ* II [Jan. 27, 1911] 40).

Two facts emerge clearly from the historical background: The author tends to understate situations, resulting in subtle nuances that could easily be lost; and Anne is an exceptional, one-in-a-million orphan. She is, in Peter Rider's words (Conversation of Aug. 9, 1995), "articulate, optimistic, intelligent, well behaved, assertive"; in short, not the kind of person likely to come from the system. Over time, Montgomery became more realistic in her writings. In *Rainbow Valley* and *Rilla of Ingleside,* brash and bruised Mary Vance appears as Anne's rough, aggressive double, a kind of shadow side.

Questions about orphans arise from a reading of Anne. Why did orphans come from the Nova Scotia asylum, not from one in P.E.I.? Would anybody check on vulnerable children? Could Anne be transferred so easily to Mrs. Blewett? Answers to these and other questions can be found in a consideration of the historical context.

HISTORICAL BACKGROUND

One aim of Montgomery's stories about children, including *Anne,* was to change attitudes toward the vulnerable young, as valuable simply for themselves. She attempted to dispel attitudes, set in the eighteenth century and continued into her time, holding orphans and poor children as cheap labor.

Children had received little special care in the

chaotic social systems of the eighteenth century and early nineteenth century. Poverty-stricken people went to the workhouse if they were capable of working; if not, they were put in a primitive poorhouse. In the eighteenth century, children were to be found anywhere adults were. A century later, writer-reformer Charles Dickens describes children in poorhouses, workhouses, and jails. Eighteenth-century orphans had caretakers or fended for themselves. Orphanages did not exist in the eighteenth century, with two early, outstanding exceptions: the London Foundling Hospital for Infants, started by retired sea captain Thomas Coram in 1739; and in Halifax, Nova Scotia, an orphanage that existed from 1752 to 1785, apparently failing for lack of financial support.

In the eighteenth century, poor children (whether orphans or not) generally received no formal training, since education was provided only by paying for private instruction or by the various churches. The Roman Catholics took care of their own through the work of nuns and priests. The Anglican and Protestant denominations began the English Charity

Schools to teach the hordes on the streets; destined for hard work, these children learned only the basics. Religious people used Old Testament references to servants as "hewers of wood and drawers of water" (Deut. 29: 11) to justify keeping the poor in the lower classes.

Concern for animal welfare came earlier than concern for children's welfare, as shown through existing organizations and laws. Regulations protecting animals were in effect in Great Britain and Nova Scotia by 1822; the Nova Scotia Royal Society for Prevention of Cruelty to Animals (SPCA) was founded in 1824. Concern for neglected children became general only in the 1850s and after. By 1880 a Nova Scotia provincial act dealt with abused and neglected children. There were no groups concerned with children generally. The SPCA, with its long experience in dealing with abuse, took on the task of rescuing children under sixteen. By 1888 two-thirds of cases concerned children and families. The SPCA

The "dining-room" of Protestant Orphanage in Halifax, August 15, 1918.

secretary and solicitor, Judge R. H. Murray, led the group's efforts toward creating improved facilities, laws, and a separate branch of the society for children. A knowledge of animals' relative importance gives new meaning to Matthew's comment "I wouldn't give a dog I liked to that Blewett woman" (p. 95) and Mary Vance's complaint in *Rainbow Valley*, "I hain't had the life of a dog for these four years" (ch. 5).

In the literature of the late nineteenth century, "orphan" tales and, following a tradition as old as writing, animal stories were popular. Anna Sewell's *Black Beauty* (1877), a horse story, and Canadian writer Marshall Saunders's *Beautiful Joe*, considered its dog sequel, became international best-sellers. In 1893 Saunders's book won a two-hundred-dollar prize from the American Humane Education Society. Writers like Saunders combined a caring for animals and children.

Montgomery wrote at a time when the horse was an important aspect of the culture, especially in rural places like Prince Edward Island. Horses, having genealogies and special sets of names, were considered more a part of the family than other animals, and sometimes these animals were more valued than some family members. In dangerous work situations, P.E.I. inhabitants of Highland descent had more concern for horses' lives than for the safety of women and children. Horses' names were important. The lack of a name for Matthew's prized driving "sorrel mare" is an added, subtle signal, in the exposition of the first chapter (p. 40), to readers of the day that the child was to hold major interest. In *Anne*, unlike other writings of Montgomery, cats and dogs are not present. The orphan heroine, central to the book, goes around naming plants, trees, and places, but not animals.

In Canada, women's and church groups led the needed reform movement for the treatment of children. In the Halifax Poor House of 1832 seventy-four children slept with male or female adults. After 1900, children remained there, without locks or han-

dles on the doors, among fifty-seven mentally unstable inmates roaming at large. The lines became blurred between the P.E.I. mental asylum and its poorhouse and jail. Space available was often the main determinant for where people were sent. Children could be found in the poorhouse.

Male occupations like sailing and mining were dangerous, and fatalities left orphans. Major epidemics also frequently left widows and orphans. By the 1850s, organizations of middle and upper-class women, under male boards, made their first attempts at social reform in setting up orphan asylums. Asylums were supposed to have the characteristics of a home and to provide maternal love for children in an institution. The Canadian Protestant Orphan Homes (POHs) were much better than the larger and more impersonal ones in the United States or England.

Anne's "Hopetown" orphanage refers to the Halifax asylum founded in 1857 by the Reverend Mr. Uniake and a Miss Cogswell. Children taken in between the ages of three and eleven wore uniforms. All the children worked at housekeeping jobs in the asylum. This orphanage depended upon gifts, many in the form of direct donations of goods and services. In 1874 a large brick house at Veith Street, on the waterfront, was acquired. It was destroyed and three staff members and twenty-four children died in the Halifax Explosion of 1917. Other specialized institutions opened, such as the Halifax Industrial School (1865) for boys who did not fit into regular schools, and the St. Paul's Almshouse for Girls (1867).

Supervision for orphans away from the asylum was not the norm. It is noteworthy that a Mr. Bayers, running the Halifax POH, traveled to visit children in 1869 and 1872. There was a real risk of losing track of children who moved to new places. Sending a yearly form out to ministers in the area of the children was one method of checking, but, of course, the form and follow-up had to be sent. Asylums usually depended on hearing complaints from those unwilling to meddle.

The rates of infant mortality were high, even among much-loved children living at home. Margaret Gray Lord's journal for 1876 mentions the deaths of five children aged three years and under. Babies in institutions were even more at risk. To combat high death rates among babies the Halifax Infants' Home was founded, although this institution's mortality rates were high: 35 percent in the first year (1875) and 26 percent in an average year in the 1890s. In Montgomery's *Rilla of Ingleside*, set in the time of World War I, Rilla's doctor-father Gilbert thinks the "war baby" will not survive at "Hopetown," since "delicate babies" do not thrive in institutional care (ch. 8). His reference would be to the Halifax Infants' Home.

Prince Edward Island, a rural province always in need of farm workers, took orphans from other places and had no orphanage of its own until 1907. The expectation was that relatives or friends would make their own arrangements for destitute children, if not always appropriately or happily. In *Emily of New Moon* the orphaned heroine has the most grudging protection of her mother's relatives. The Murrays, however unwilling to take over the care of a child, are too proud to send relatives, even unwanted ones, to orphan asylums (ch. 6). But for the child with no such protectors there was no automatic response from social service agencies. When the woman who worked as the charlady to the educated Shirleys steps in and takes the baby, nobody registers this fact or makes any inquiries.

Such an informal arrangement was perfectly possible, even though there were some rough formal considerations of what was to be done for children without caregivers. A P.E.I. legislative act of 1845 states that an abandoned child between the ages of two and twelve was to be signed up formally as a working apprentice until the age of twenty-one. There was some effort to provide education for destitute children, including orphans. An Education Act of 1861, noting the number of orphans and children of destitute parents, set up a special school for

children ages four to eleven in Charlottetown; this school was commended in an 1869 report. The first Protestant orphanage was founded in 1907. Roman Catholics were usually quick to provide service, but their asylum, St. Vincent's, did not begin until 1910.

The situation in the British colonies was complicated by the added factor of truly "imported" orphans, to adapt Mrs. Lynde's phrase (p. 47). These were considered the lowest of the low, "London street-Arabs," in Marilla's slighting reference (p. 45). Dr. Barnardo's Home took in homeless children from the London streets and raised them in a practical orphanage environment; the objective was to have them earning their own livings as soon as possible. They were considered to be "reformed" and respectable, but their "street Arab" reputations clung to them. The British orphanage movement considered the colonies more "wholesome" than England's own cities and began the mass deportation of children to North America and Australia. Some of these children still had British relatives and ties to England, but they had no choice. Siblings, even twins, were separated, and once the children were placed there was a total lack of supervision. Girls, who were especially vulnerable, could readily be taken advantage of by employers or "hired men." These children, sent out from the great slum-ridden metropolis to rural areas, were considered primarily as farm workers. From 1868 on, the movement of such children, exported, as it were, chiefly by Barnardo's Homes, continued despite protests as early as 1874. The last boatload left in 1939, just before World War II. The war and its shortage of manpower kept England's orphans in England.

Ideas about children and child care changed slowly throughout the nineteenth century. The Enlightenment of Locke and Rousseau had seen the child as highly responsive to education and to stimuli. Aristocratic rule had emphasized heredity, but the new republican and more egalitarian movements saw the child as the product rather of environment. The ideal citizen, who was going to participate in making his world, could be created through an education much pleasanter than the old birch-rod method. Such citizen-oriented ideas of education had less place for little women (who were not thought of as citizens) than for little men. The beginning of the nineteenth century saw a Romantic idealization of the child. Montgomery certainly inherited the Romantic Wordsworthian tradition, which views the child as a "seer blest," gifted with spiritual knowledge lost in the bustle of socialization. But in general, and particularly in rural areas, before 1880 neither the Enlightenment nor Romantic ideas had penetrated. The old idea that the child was a repository of original sin, possessed of an "old Adam" to be beaten out of it, had a persistent hold. When not thought of as a limb of Satan, the child was to be a miniature adult and do its share of the work.

New ideas about the world had an impact on the treatment of children. Even before it was accepted, the theory of evolution had an impact. Ideas of adaptation and continuous modification affected psychology, and organic images abound. Frederick Froebel and his disciples represented the child as a seed or plant for nurturing. Anne's reassuring metaphor to Marilla, "I'm only just pruned down and branched out," fits this principle (p. 358). Tensions between old and new thought in the community create interest. Matthew's quiet, prophetic statements are consistently Froebelian, while Marilla represents old thought to be converted.

One implication of this change is the perception that children needed settings suited to their educational and moral growth. The dangers menacing neglected children seemed more apparent. There was a more active response to taking care of and guarding neglected or destitute children. Reformers under J. J. Kelso founded the Children's Aid Society (CAS), the first such organization in Canada, in Toronto in 1891. In literature a new, sympathetic, burst of "orphan novels" at the turn of the century is symptomatic of new ideas about children and their relation to society.

By the 1890s orphan asylums were seen, in Patricia Rooke's term, as a "necessary evil" (*Discarding the Asylum*, 30). The Protestant Orphan Home directors were suspicious of the new CAS movement which, with professional social workers, tried to keep families together and used foster care. In Halifax, a short-lived CAS formed in 1905 lasted only until 1914, when the SPCA officially took over its powers. The first Children's Protection Act passed the Nova Scotia legislature in 1906. In 1909, a year after *Anne*, the P.E.I. CAS was founded, though it mostly dealt with delinquents. "An Act for the Protection of Neglected and Dependent Children" was passed in 1910.

EXCEPTIONAL ANNE FROM THE ORPHANAGE: APPARENT PROBLEMS

Anne's exceptional qualities of optimism, intellectual development, and "ladylike" behavior could have been crushed under the wrong circumstances. Her very survival would have been chancy. Conditions as a household drudge would not be good for the health, and modern readers might also wonder about the effects of neglect and malnutrition on intelligence. Anne at three months, in that era of high infant death, is in the care of Mrs. Thomas, a charwoman with a drunken husband. Later the girl looks after Mrs. Hammond's many twins, either a double blessing or burden, depending on the circumstances. Although overworked, Anne mentions no illnesses, in contrast to Mary Vance in *Rainbow Valley*, who gives blood-curdling accounts of serious illnesses and near death (chs. 3 and 5). Orphanages were particularly vulnerable to epidemics, so Anne would not have been entirely safe there.

Anne stands out as the kind of orphan the Protestant asylums preferred to have. The Roman Catholic asylums, run by nuns, had to take all the needy and were often overcrowded, but the Protestant Orphan Homes could be selective. They picked the best, that is to say, the "worthy" as opposed to the "unworthy" poor, the unemployed, the drunkard or the lazy. True orphans were preferred over children of a poor parent who might later challenge the institution's powers. The Protestant institutions had regulations specifying that relatives could not interfere with the home's arrangements. Legitimacy, meaning to have married parents, was an important qualification for admittance. (P.E.I. descendants of Highlanders considered unmarried mothers and their children to be servants for life.) Anne meets all three requirements, with very respectable parents, high school teachers who died of "fever" (p. 86). (Later, visiting the house where she was born in *Anne of the Island*, she learns that her parents loved each other and her, also an exceptional fact (ch. 21). Anne contrasts with the more realistic Mary Vance in *Rainbow Valley*: "'My ma had hung herself and my pa cut his throat.' 'Holy cats! Why?' said Jerry. 'Booze,' said Mary laconically" (ch. 5).

The prevalent attitude of looking down on orphans would make self-development difficult. Having no control of circumstances would promote either passivity or anger. In *Jane of Lantern Hill*, Jody's general passivity is more realistic than Anne's creativity. Jody plaintively writes, "Oh Jane, it isn't fair. I don't mean Miss West [sending her to an orphanage] isn't fair, but something isn't" (ch. 38). Rooke's description of the "taint" of public charity clinging "like mildew" to orphans (*Discarding the Asylum*, 163) applies to Marilla's first long speech (p. 45). Josie Pye at Queen's crushes a young man's interest in Anne: "I told him you were an orphan the Cuthberts had adopted, and nobody knew very much about what you'd been before that" (p. 363). More subtle remarks than these pass quickly and may escape an inattentive reader. Matthew's quiet comment "We might be some good to her" (p. 73) is revolutionary, an example of true Christian charity.

Marilla shows herself as decent by giving Anne an upstairs bedroom, although a kitchen chamber couch would have been good enough for the wanted boy. (Matthew also sleeps in the kitchen chamber, to be nearer his workplace in the barn.) Boys were generally more respected and could learn a trade. In the 1917 letter that opens this appendix, the reader will notice that a boy is preferred, who must be Protestant. A girl is clearly second choice, but her religion is not an issue.

Orphans' education was limited. Anne Shirley's experience was truly extraordinary. The reviewer for the *New York Times* in 1908 complained correctly that, with illiterate keepers and four months of school, Anne had "borrowed Bernard Shaw's vocabulary!" (see Reviews, p. 487). Marilla's statement in the first chapter (p. 46) that "We mean to give him a good home and schooling" signals that she is not going to hold the orphan back from school for the sake of work. (The author herself was held back by having to look after her half-brother during her year in Saskatchewan.) Orphans and the poor had to be kept in their class. When a shoemaker applied for an orphan boy in Hamilton in 1854 he was refused, on the basis that orphans were fit only for farm and domestic work. Anne comes in first in the province in her examinations, goes to Queen's for teacher training, and wins a scholarship. Even Montgomery admitted early (Sept. 10, 1908) to her pen friend Mr. Weber that Anne's success at school is "too good for literary art." Anne, like Nellie McClung's Pearl, becomes a teacher and reaches the social heights in marrying a doctor (*Purple Springs*; *Anne's House of Dreams*). Lower-class Mary Vance does well to become a storekeeper's wife (*Rilla of Ingleside*, ch. 35).

There was little distinction between adoption, "farming out" (described below), and indenturing, which all meant hard work and sometimes abuse. Anne, however, does not have to work any more than her friends do in Avonlea. Without machines, the work of ordinary life was hard for everyone. Children in their homes had to work, sometimes beyond their strength. Despite New Thought, obedience and service were still important. Marilla approves Anne's competence as a housekeeper at age fourteen: "she's real steady and reliable now" (p. 325).

For the unprotected, however, abuse and overwork were not uncommon. Orphans rescued from bad circumstances could be sent out again.

"Farming out," as in Anne's history, differed little from adoption, under the system described by Vicki Williams "where no legal definition of the rights and responsibilities of the guardians existed." Williams quotes a young girl, "'doption, sir, is when folks gets a girl to work without wages" (p. 127). Adoption did not necessarily mean a name change or becoming an heir. Indenturing provided a little more protection, due to having a contract. One of the problems of farming out was that the children's work remained unpaid until adolescence. Then the caretakers might simply return the children, so as not to pay them; or a relative who had thus far taken little interest might suddenly lay claim to this economically productive child. Anne could have gone to the "gimlet" Mrs. Blewett (p. 95), a fate more typical than coming under Marilla's care. Anne, however, had experienced only neglect and overwork. In *Rainbow Valley*, Mary Vance, showing bruises and telling of her guardian Mrs. Wiley's abuse, ran away before being sent to an even worse cousin: "I'd rather live with the devil himself" (ch. 5). (One may well wonder what the resentful orphans who set the house on fire and poisoned the well in Mrs. Lynde's accounts (p. 46) had endured!)

The orphan's option of running away was risky. Montgomery's "The Running Away of Chester" (1903) is a moral examination of the right to flee. Chester's neighbors are afraid to interfere and rouse the temper of the nasty Mrs. Elwell. His new, compassionate shelterers come close to admitting that he was right to leave. The 1845 P.E.I. act on apprentices (children working by contracts) includes in its provisions a punishment for anyone harboring a runaway apprentice. Protesting to a magistrate about bad treatment would depend on having witnesses with the courage to back up the complaints.

The prevention of cruelty is helped by supervision of the orphan's placement. Marilla made an extremely casual application. She had only "sent her [Mrs. Alexander Spencer] word by Richard Spencer's folks at Carmody," upon which Anne was sent to an unseen caretaker (p. 45). At least in theory, Marilla could not have done this any later than 1882, when the Halifax orphanage rules included the obligation for applicants to have a certificate from a minister. By 1886 the application had to be in writing. However, unlike today's system using legal papers, social workers, and trial periods for adoption, there was then still little official process.

Attitudes toward orphans were changing from 1914, when children were still found in several Nova Scotia poorhouses. (That province's law supporting the poorhouse for two hundred years was rescinded only in 1958.) It was not until the 1920s that CAS became permanently effective there. World War I increased social change. How could one despise the children of heroes who had died for their country? In *Rilla of Ingleside* the heroine's determination to keep the boy if his father did not return hints at the need for looking after war orphans. Boatloads of Barnardo children came over after 1918.

Orphanages closed only in the 1960s, the Halifax one not until 1969. Recently, Republicans have suggested orphanages for "unwanted" children. We still need an exceptional Orphan Anne to remind us of the value of home and the need to care for the young and vulnerable.

FURTHER READING
LEGISLATIVE ACTS

[Nova Scotia.] "The Twenty-fifth Annual Report of the Ladies' Committee of the Halifax Protestant Orphans' Home" (1882). Halifax: Wm. Macnab & Son, 1883.

"The Twenty-ninth Annual Report of the Ladies' Committee of the Halifax Protestant Orphans Home" (1886). Halifax: Wm. Macnab & Son, 1886.

[P.E.I.] "An Act to repeal the several Acts now in force regarding apprentices, and to substitute other provisions in lieu thereof." 8 Victoria C.14 (1845).

"An Act to consolidate and amend the several laws relating to education." 24 Victoria C.36 (1861).

"An Act for the protection of neglected and dependent children." C.15 (1910).

CRITICAL STUDIES

Gail H. Corbett. *Barnardo Children in Canada*. Peterborough, N.H.: Woodland Publishing, 1981.

John Robert Cousins. "Horses in the Folklife of Western Prince Edward Island: Custom, Belief and Oral Tradition." Unpublished M.A. thesis. St. John's, NF.: Memorial University, 1990.

GENERAL BIBLIOGRAPHIES

Stan Fitzner. *The Development of Social Welfare in Nova Scotia: A History*. Halifax: Dept. of Public Welfare, 1967.

Michael Hennessey. *The Catholic Church in Prince Edward Island 1720–1979*. Charlottetown: Roman Catholic Episcopal Corp., 1979.

M[argaret] G. Jones. *The Charity School Movement: A Study of Eighteenth Century Puritanism in Action*. Cambridge: Cambridge Univ. Press, 1938; London: Cass, 1964.

Heather Laskey. "A Victorian Orphanage." *The Atlantic Advocate*. Nov. 1979: 26–29.

Margaret Pennefather Stukeley Gray Lord. *One Woman's Charlottetown: Diaries of Margaret Gray Lord, 1863, 1876, 1890*. Ed. Evelyn J. MacLeod. Hull, P.Q.: Canadian Museum of Civilization, 1988.

Andrew Macphail. *The Master's Wife*. New Canadian Library No. 138. Intro. Ian Robertson, general ed. Malcolm Ross. Toronto: McClelland & Stewart, 1939; repr. 1977.

Nellie L. McClung. *Purple Springs*. Toronto: Ryerson Press, 1921.

Dorothy Marshall. *Dr. Johnson's London. New Dimensions in History: Historical Cities*. Series ed. Norman F. Cantor. New York: Wiley, 1968.

Claudia Mills. "Children in Search of a Family: Orphan Novels Through the Century." *Children's Lit-erature in Education: An International Quarterly*. 18:4 (1987): 227–39.

Mary Margaret Robb. *Oral Interpretation of Literature in American Colleges and Universities: A Historical Study of Teaching Methods*. N.p. H.W. Wilson, 1941. Rev. ed. New York: Johnson Reprint Corp., 1968.

Patricia T. Rooke and R. L. Schnell. "Childhood and Charity in Nineteenth-Century British North America." *Histoire Sociale/Social History* 15:29 (1982): 157–80.

———. *Discarding the Asylum: From Child Rescue to the Welfare State in English Canada (1800–1950)*. Lanham, Md.: Univ. Press of America, 1983.

———, gen. eds. "Guttersnipes and Charity Children: Nineteenth Century Child Rescue in the Atlantic Provinces." *Studies in Childhood History: A Canadian Perspective*. Calgary: Detselig, 1982, pp. 82–104.

———. "The Rise and Decline of British North American Protestant Orphans' Homes as Woman's Domain, 1850 1930." *Atlantis: A Women's Studies Journal* 7:2 (1982): 21–35.

"Welfare Reform: The Race to Look Tougher." *Newsweek* (Nov. 21, 1994): 46.

Vicki L. Williams. "Home training and the socialization of youth in the sentimental novels of Marshall Saunders, Nellie McClung and L. M. Montgomery." Unpublished M.A. thesis. Ottawa: Carleton University, 1982.

PERSONAL COMMUNICATIONS

Peter Rider, Ph.D., Atlantic Provinces Historian. Canadian Museum of Civilization, Ottawa. Interview Aug. 9, 1995; written communication Aug. 10, 1995.

EDUCATION ON P.E.I.

Concern for education was evident from the beginnings of British settlement in Prince Edward Island. Legislation of 1835 provided for lands to be reserved in each of the original sixty-seven townships: one hundred acres for church use, thirty for schools. The "Free School Act" of 1852 offered the first free public education for children in the whole British Empire (England was not to have its first truly free public school system until 1870). Most P.E.I. schools were one-room establishments, offering grades one through ten. Legislation to establish a Normal School for training teachers was passed in 1855, and a school was set up that year.

Lucy Maud Montgomery and her character Anne both benefited from the "Public Schools' Act, 1877" (one that was not passed without controversy), which put nonsectarian government in charge of public education and thus removed public education from church control. There were still multiple school boards, however, and later, in the twentieth century, this Act was modified to allow regional boards and to phase out one-room schools. The 1877 act included provisions for free schooling for children from five to sixteen years of age and mandatory attendance of children eight to thirteen years old for at least twelve weeks of the year, six weeks of which had to be consecutive. This notion of a limited school year was designed to accommodate parents and employers who needed children's labor on farms. Teachers in one-room schools could have a total of up to forty children. The schools were to be regularly inspected, there were to be public examinations, and school districts shared costs of libraries with the Board of Education.

Each school board had three trustees, commonly men of local importance who did not wish to tax local resources but who might use their influence to benefit a member of their own family or friends' rel-

atives. Mrs. Lynde, for example, claims that Mr. Phillips would never have been given the Avonlea school for another year "if his uncle hadn't been a trustee — *the* trustee, for he just leads the other two around by the nose" (p. 174).

The training of teachers offered new educational opportunities for women, who could then be employed in the newly expanding school system. This meant they needed some education beyond grade-school level. Central Academy had been founded in 1835; in 1860 its name was changed to Prince of Wales College. The Roman Catholic St. Dunstan's University had opened in 1855. The existence of Prince of Wales College for English-speaking Protestants means that the young did not have to go to England or another Canadian city for higher education. Witness the mandate in "An Act to Establish a College in Prince Edward Island . . ." (1860):

> Whereas our education institutions are not complete without a high Seminary or College in which a first class mathematical, classical and philosophical education may be obtained: and it is not desirable that the natives of this colony should have to seek in other lands the attainment of a collegiate education (preamble and clause 1).

This "high Seminary" at first offered its traditional education only to boys.

In 1879, the provincial normal school that had been established in 1855 amalgamated with Prince of Wales College, and the institution was opened to women. This development marked a decided advance in women's general prospects for education. The "Public Schools' Act" ensured that all girls, as well as boys, could get some education. After 1879 they could also go on to "college" to complete what was really a high school equivalency program. For a university degree a student would still have to leave the province. But with the Normal School qualification combined with high school completion, a girl could teach at age sixteen. A boy was supposed to be

eighteen, although exceptions did occur. Because Gilbert is two years older than Anne, they are able to become teachers at the same time. Their setting out to teach school at such a young age is not unrealistic for their era. According to Vicki Williams ("Home Training and Socializing of Youth," 134), it was determined in 1889 that the "great majority of rural teachers were between 17 and 23 years of age." Anne is only seventeen when she becomes a schoolteacher, although her author was twenty when she took her first job teaching, at Bideford, in 1894–1895.

Men and women in Anne's day were on a different pay scale for the same work. Gilbert could therefore better afford to pay board than Anne.

Teaching Salaries (1877)

	Male	Female
First Class	$300	$230
Second Class	$225	$180
Third Class	$180	$130

Women thus became attractive to employers as they would take less pay. Schoolteachers, especially "lady teachers," were expected to behave impeccably in public and in private life. Yet the school was a community center, and the teacher had a status in society. A new "schoolmarm" coming into a district need not lack social life or beaus (see Bliss, "Party Time in Malpeque"). Women were not supposed to continue teaching after marriage, but men could use a schoolteaching job as a stepping stone to other professions by earning enough money to go on for a university education. Gilbert becomes a doctor; Moody Spurgeon Macpherson is expected to become a minister (p. 320). In *Emily of New Moon*, Emily's beloved teacher Mr. Carpenter, "a country schoolteacher at forty-five with no prospects of ever being anything else," is considered a failure and has become an alcoholic (ch. 28). Men were not really expected to stay in schoolteaching as a lifelong career unless they had a distinguished position in a city school or one of the private schools.

Interior of Lower Bedeque School, where Lucy Maud Montgomery taught.

Yet schoolteaching had its own challenges and rewards in the new era, and many were aroused by the promises of new views of child nurture. Frederick Froebel, founder of the kindergarten movement in Germany, followed the philosophical lead of Jean-Jacques Rousseau in emphasizing the value of the child as a living being to be nurtured. This theory had its place in urging educators to make schools more humane and more responsive to children's development. The older schools had been modeled on the English private schools with their emphasis on corporal punishment. The advent of girls in large numbers in public schools made certain forms of corporal punishment less desirable or permissible, and the new theories of education argued against it. Anne herself, as a teacher, resolves not to use corporal punishment but finds herself breaking her resolution (*Anne of Avonlea,* ch. 12).

New theories of education also urged preparing children better for their working lives. The old emphasis on traditional education had met the older standards for the qualifications of a "gentleman"; the new scholars crowding the schools needed, authorities felt, training that would stand them in good stead in farming, seagoing pursuits, or housekeeping. Domestic science, nature study, and physical education emerged as school subjects before and after the turn of the century.

Anne's school at Avonlea undergoes a shift between old and new educational emphases during the course of the novel. Perhaps only a writer who, like Montgomery, had been a teacher herself could give such acute attention to school and its importance. She gives a lively description of the students doing "pretty much as they pleased" before the famous slate incident (p. 165). Mr. Phillips, Anne's first teacher, is a transitional figure. Without much interest, he goes through the old syllabus and offends against both Old and New Thought by his careless-

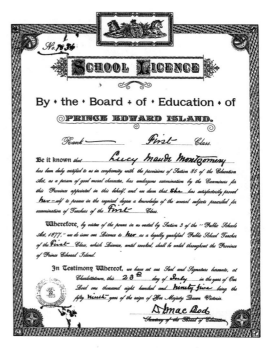

Montgomery's teaching certificate, presented to her on July 23, 1895.

ness and inconsistency. The ever-knowledgeable Mrs. Lynde condemns his lack of order, the result not of kindness but laziness. He certainly has not heard of Johann Heinrich Pestalozzi, who adapted psychology to curriculum and pedagogy. Mr. Phillips punishes Anne by humiliating her; she would "infinitely have preferred a whipping" (p. 168). He discourages her: "Mr. Phillips says I am the worst dunce he ever saw at it [geometry]" (p. 197). He also seems cowardly. He whips Sam Boulter for "sassing" him but is evidently unable to reply to Sam's father, who comes to the school in a rage and "dared Mr. Phillips to lay a hand on one of his children again" (p. 181).

Mr. Phillips, who would be a bad teacher under any system, is replaced by a spectacularly good one, Miss Stacy, who is also a good representative of the best of the new wave. She introduces physical exercises that "make you graceful and promote digestion," according to Anne, although Marilla "honestly thought it was all nonsense" (p. 261). Miss Stacy also begins nature study, attracting criticism when the boys climb trees to look for crows' nests (p. 260). Yet Miss Stacy meets the traditional standards, for she is well qualified to prepare her students for the examination they need to pass in order to matriculate at the college in Charlottetown. She is sufficiently able to teach Latin, Canadian history, French, English literature, and mathematics. She is thus what Avonlea needs to prepare for the future without making too big a break with the past. Anne learns from her the new idea that positive enjoyment contributes to growth.

Undoubtedly, Miss Stacy has to deal with certain tensions in the community. Other schoolteachers often had to plead their causes before unsympathetic bosses in the form of old-fashioned school trustees. This situation is well caught in Robert Harris's famous painting *A Meeting of the School Trustees,* in which the anxious and refined-looking teacher awaits the dictates of the stolid, middle-aged men. Miss Stacy is good at disarming Avonlea. She holds a school concert (an innovation) and allows—indeed urges—the students to learn self-expression. She makes the event palatable because it is for a patriotic purpose—to raise funds for a flag. Anne's defense of the event, evidently taken from Miss Stacy, is, "Well, when you can combine patriotism and fun, isn't it all right?" (p. 262). This has a flavor of Froebel, who believed that recreation and moral purpose could and should be mingled with educational activities.

Anne at age thirteen is already inspired by Miss Stacy to want to be a schoolteacher. "I would call it a worthy purpose to want to be a teacher like Miss Stacy, wouldn't you, Marilla?" (p. 319). In order to reach this goal, Anne must attend the college that Montgomery calls "Queen's College" in Charlotte-town, based on Prince of Wales College. Academic preparation for the entrance examination included the study of arithmetic, geometry, geography, Latin, French, and English literature. The author studied Greek for a year also, but she does not offer this knowledge to Anne, who is, however, able to read Latin. *Anne of Avonlea* opens with the heroine "resolved to construe so many lines of Virgil" (ch. 1). For author and heroine alike, access to the traditionally masculine bastions of knowledge is important.

Anne is an ardent scholar, with a love of knowledge for its own sake and a strong competitive streak. She competes successfully against Gilbert. Patricia K. Santelmann (*Harvesting Thistles,* 69) comments on Anne's "determination to excel" as a marked contrast to the sensibility expressed in John Greenleaf Whittier's poem "In School Days" where the little girl apologizes to the boy she loves for having been a better speller in a class competition. As Santelmann says, Gilbert "admires her intelligence and competitive spirit," and his question at the novel's end, "You are going to keep up your studies, aren't you?" (p. 394), marks him as worthy of her.

Montgomery passed on to her heroine her own dislike of geometry, her remarkable knowledge of English literature, and her enthusiasm for poetry. We may note, however, that the *Royal Readers,* compiled for schools after the British Education Act of 1870, gave all children access to poetry (something we may not be able to count on today). The works presented were by a variety of poets, including women. Teaching elementary students to recite and to participate in public speaking helped them overcome bashfulness and become capable citizens. Once the orphan Anne is settled in Avonlea and is given the opportunity a public school offers, she quickly makes up for earlier school time lost. Unlike her author— or Gilbert—Anne does not have a break in her education (caused in Montgomery's case by a visit to Saskatchewan), and she achieves everything a shade earlier in life than her author did. Montgomery did extremely well in her entrance examination, coming "fifth in a list of 264 candidates" (*SJ* I: 91), but Anne comes in first (p. 342).

At college, Anne concentrates on the traditional classical syllabus. Montgomery is evidently suspicious of education that tries to divide knowledge according to class and gender, in which she parts from some of the new thinking. It is no wonder that "plain, plodding, conscientious Jane," not Anne, should take domestic science and carry it off with "honours" (p. 369). Domestic science came into the curriculum after 1900. Anne's education cannot be dated, since her courses are not consistent with one period. Anne also does not appear to take chemistry, which Montgomery had studied at Prince of Wales College. Anne and Gilbert, like their creator, go through their college work as fast as they can, taking second-year work from the beginning, which meant "getting a First Class Teacher's license in one year instead of two, if they were successful; but it also meant much more and harder work" (p. 361).

After she has put so much effort into getting her high school education and her teacher's license, it is not a sad thing that Anne is to become a teacher. The Education Acts of 1852 and 1877 opened schools to all children and created a demand for teachers that led to the opening of the college to women. Anne has been a model to several generations of women because she expresses the twentieth-century woman's desire for education, for a fair salary, and for professional status. Anne expressed these wishes simply to Marilla: "I think it's a very noble profession" (p. 319).

FURTHER READING

Michael Bliss. "Party Time in Malpeque: The Social Life of Lucy Palmer, School Teacher 1887–1890," *The Island Magazine* 36 (Fall–Winter 1994): 13–19.

A. G. Hunter, "The Old Royal Readers: Another View," *Newfoundland Quarterly*, 75th Anniversary Special Edition (1976): 232.

Patricia Kelly Santelmann. "Written as Women Write: *Anne of Green Gables* within the Female Tradition." *Harvesting Thistles*, 64–73.

Vicki Williams. "Home Training and Socialization of Youth in the Sentimental Novels of Marshall Saunders, Nellie McClung and L. M. Montgomery." Master's thesis, Carleton College (Ottawa, Ont.), 1982.

GARDENS AND PLANTS

Lucy Maud Montgomery passed on her love of gardens to all her heroines. The description of every important house in Montgomery's novels, and in many of her short stories, requires a description of a garden. Anne Shirley is less interested in actually working in a garden than are Emily Byrd Starr or Jane Stuart, but she yields to none in her love of the flowers with which she is constantly associated.

The gardens of farmhouses on Prince Edward Island customarily included a kitchen garden, with vegetables in neat rows, and sometimes flowers mixed in to fight off insects. The flower garden itself would usually be contiguous, a sheltered grass plot with beds and walkways. Part of the art of such a garden entails making some flowers grow in the grass to look like a natural part of the landscape. In some of her later books (see *Anne of Ingleside, Jane of Lantern Hill*) Montgomery describes the practicalities of gardening, such as the use of seaweed and cow manure as fertilizer. The gardens Montgomery writes of are typical of her Maritime region, with nothing that does not grow in her P.E.I. of real life. The basic model for such a garden is ultimately the manorial garden of the late Middle Ages and Renaissance, before curious knots and elaborate beds became the custom. Such farmhouse gardens had also been influenced by the Romantic vogue for what was perceived as the "wild" and the "natural." Each of Montgomery's gardens is to some extent a "wild" garden, however carefully cultivated, resembling the related descendant of the manorial style of horticulture known as the English cottage garden. The effects striven for in late Victorian and Edwardian cottage gardens, as described in 1900 by W. R. Robinson in *The English Flower Garden and Home Grounds*, are the ones Montgomery most admires.

English cottage gardens ... often teach lessons that "great" gardeners should learn, and are pretty from Snowdrop time till the Fuchsia bushes bloom nearly into winter.... Cottage gardeners are good to their plots.... But there is something more and it is the absence of any pretentious "plan" which lets the flowers tell their story to the heart. The walks are only what are needed, and so we see only the earth and its blossoms (32–33).

The eighteenth century had created a taste for large sweeps of restful green space, with artful arrangements of shrubbery. Montgomery is not at all interested in this "park" look and is not concerned with shrubs unless, like the spirea, they distinguish themselves by bearing flowers. Her ideal garden includes an orchard of fruit-bearing trees in the background, with bloom that can be as important as flowers. Orchards yield the fruit enjoyed by children and adults, as when Anne and Diana go into the orchard in the October sunshine (pp. 180–81). The Barrys and the Blythes have good orchards, with the Blythes growing the "strawberry apple" that almost tempts Anne (see p. 194 and n. 5).

The author loves trees, which have a definite place in the garden, not least because P.E.I.'s flower gardens and orchards alike need the shelter of certain strong trees like fir or spruce or mature maples to protect more delicate plants from the sea wind. But in Montgomery's gardens, these trees must have been planted long ago. Nobody in her works plants trees, though good people become upset when trees are cut down or even just threatened with the axe, even as people of sensibility did in Cowper's and Jane Austen's time at the turn of the nineteenth century. Cowper's often-anthologized poem of lament for felled poplars may have influenced Montgomery's love for that tree. The Lombardy poplar is insistently introduced in her novels, including *Anne* (p. 42 and n. 12).

The late nineteenth century and early twentieth saw a growing taste for garden ornament, including

fountains, pergolas or arbors, and neoclassical statuary, not to mention more aggressive ornaments like a cast-iron deer on lawns or among shrubs. Montgomery successfully resists such furniture and adornment for her gardens, although by 1925 she relented sufficiently to allow the garden at New Moon a stone bench, a sundial, and even a summer-house. But the latter is an "old summer-house, covered in vines," and the sundial was brought by a great-great grandfather—no modern gimcracks here (*Emily of New Moon*, ch. 7).

Other changes in gardening in Montgomery's era are largely passed over, if not treated with scorn: "By the early twentieth century, Americans had felt the influence of the work and writings of Gertrude Jekyll, famous for her designed borders in which great attention was paid to color, texture, and the combination of forms and mass" (Favretti, *Landscape Gardens for Historic Buildings*, 56). Montgomery does indeed pay attention to color, texture, and mass, but the prevailing taste for elaborate borders is one she steadily resisted. Indeed, Montgomery pokes fun at it, making the disagreeable sister-in-law in *Mistress Pat* (1935) the champion of a "herbaceous border." And May Binnie is evidently too crass to understand the beauty of Silver Bush's old garden. What's more, new flowers that have no fragrance are repudiated or attached to stupid characters: "'Can you tell me,' said

"Green Gables House" at *P.E.I. National Park.*

Cousin Ernestine . . . 'if a calceolaria is a flower or a disease?'" (*Anne of Windy Poplars*, ch. 8).

Green Gables is unusual among the central houses in Montgomery's works in being too prim and well kept to have a flower garden. Marilla has simply a grassy yard, kept with such regimented neatness that even Mrs. Lynde is unfavorably impressed. It would be out of keeping with the novel's motifs to have Marilla represented as an energetic grower of flowers before Anne arrives. Marilla has only one flower within her purview, the brightly blooming geranium, which Anne declares "Bonny" and Marilla calls "the apple-scented geranium" (p. 81). This plant can be used for flavoring in cookery, thus passing Marilla's test of utility. Otherwise, the unregenerate Marilla has little use for flowers, which are, for her, messy things. We know she is softening, however, when she permits Anne to bring the apple-blossoms indoors (p. 105).

Anne herself tries to unite the domestic and the wild, admiring both cultivated and wild flowers and laying hands upon the blossom of cherries and apples as well as flowers of the hedgerow and wild thicket. When she first goes to Sunday school, Anne wreathes her hat with buttercups and wild roses (p. 129). Elizabeth Waterston points out rightly that Anne appreciates the natural, whereas other little girls are already wearing artificial flowers. More dubiously, Waterston proposes that the combination of pink and yellow "carries a suggestion of distaste" wherever it is found in the novel (*Kindling Spirit*, 51). Pink and yellow are in fact found throughout the novel, in things both artificial and natural, but the colors seem associated with the feminine and the floral, as in the honeysuckle that Anne puts in her hair at the end of the novel.

Anne the flower-crowned is like a Greek maiden (or at least the Victorian idea of a Greek maiden), a kind of pastoral Chloe. Her desire to wear flowers in her hair is a touch of the "paganism" she represents, in conflict with Avonlea and its ways. Anne is late for school because she spends recess like a dryad or

nymph, singing to herself in shadowy places and wreathing wildflowers in her hair (p. 170). Anne is generally considered "crazy" because she talks to the trees and flowers, but if we read more closely we find that she is not the first character in this novel to talk to flowers. Mrs. Lynde in her private remarks after hearing Marilla's news is represented as addressing plants: "So said Mrs. Lynde to the wild rose bushes out of the fullness of her heart" (p. 48). This is one of many little touches uniting the seeming opposites, Rachel Lynde and Anne Shirley.

It is in the Barry garden that Anne, like the reader, finds her *locus amoenus*, or place of pleasure. This garden epitomizes all the qualities approved of by the author. It is an old and "wild" garden, a "bowery wilderness of flowers" (p. 138). It has old trees, and the primness of its little paths is more than balanced by the freedom of its plants: "old-fashioned flowers ran riot." We realize from personal comments by the author in her journals (*SJ* I: 263–64) the extent to which the Barry garden represents Montgomery's ideal:

There is nothing in the world so sweet as a real, "old timey" garden. . . . There are certain essentials to an old-fashioned garden. Without them it would not be itself. Like the poet it must be born not made—the outgrowth and flowering of long years of dedication and care. The least flavor of newness or modernity spoils it.

For one thing, it *must* be secluded and shut away from the world—a "garden enclosed"— preferably by willows—or apple trees—or firs. It must have some trim walks bordered by clamshells, or edged with "ribbon grass," and there must be in it the flowers that belong to old-fashioned gardens and are seldom found in the catalogues of to-day—perennials planted there by grandmotherly hands when the century was young. There should be poppies, like fine ladies in full-skirted silken gowns, "cabbage" roses, heavy and pink and luscious, tiger-lilies like gorgeously bedight sentinels, "Sweet-William" in striped attire, bleeding-heart, that favorite of my childhood, southernwood, feathery and pungent, butter-and-eggs—that is now known as "narcissus"—"bride's bouquet," as white as a bride's bouquet should be, holly hocks like flaunting overbold maidens, purple spikes of "Adam and Eve," pink and white "musk," "Sweet Balm" and "Sweet May," "Bouncing Bess" in her ruffled, lilac-tinted skirts, pure white "June lilies," crimson peonies—"pinies" —velvety-eyed "Irish Primroses," which were neither primroses nor Irish, scarlet lightning and Prince's feather—all growing in orderly confusion.

Most items on this special list of favorites appear in *Anne*, if not in the detailed description of the Barry garden then elsewhere. Even the "flaunting" hollyhocks appear toward the end of the novel. Only a few make no appearance, like prince's-feather (*Amaranthus hybridus erythrostachys*). What was "Bouncing Bess" in the journal entry becomes in *Anne* "Bouncing Bets," the more usual name for *Saponaria officinalis Caryphyllacae*, or soapwort. Both the list in the journal and the catalog of flowers in the Barrys garden refer to flowers that have long been cultivated, as well as to a number that can still be found wild, like mallow, the "wild musk-flower." When in 1914 Montgomery answered a magazine questionnaire and recorded the results in her journal (*SJ* II: 145), her answer to the question "What is your favorite flower?" included a similar mixture of wild and cultivated plants:

> Well, I love all flowers so much it is hard to choose. But of wild flowers I love best the shy sweet wild "June Bell"—the *Linnea Borealis*—of Prince Edward Island spruce woods; and of garden flowers the white narcissus—the old "June lilies" of girlhood days. We did not have them but they grew in the grassy nooks of many old Cavendish gardens.

The "June Bell" figures in Anne (p. 56), and the narcissus is used as a recurrent motif. At the end of the story this flower becomes associated with Matthew's death, so that Anne cannot bear her favorite flower for a long time afterward. Anne's letting the narcissus fall (p. 379) may have a symbolic resonance, as she puts away forever the innocent narcissism, the self-involvement of childhood.

All of Montgomery's writing about trees, plants, and flowers, whether in her published fiction or journals, maintains a balance between art and nature, the wild and the civilized. In the important description of the Barry garden we see how a balance is kept between wild and tame. The clover, a wildflower, is fragrant, while the little Scots roses have thorns. We do not focus on this garden as the work of Mrs. Barry or of anyone else; it is a magical garden, a garden of poetry, a garden of the heart. The journal quotes the phrase "garden enclosed," an English version of the old *hortus conclusus*, long a metaphor for females both sacred and profane, for the Virgin Mary, and for the site of female sexuality. The Barry garden is just such a *hortus conclusus*, a garden enclosed, a haven of femininity and peace.

Elizabeth Waterston has dealt with this garden in relation to the image patterns of the novel (*Kindling Spirit*, 53). This soft, fragrant garden belongs to the two girls. Their friendship begins here, in a sacred moment and sacred space, among the rosy bleeding-

Garden of Alma Macneill, Cavendish, 1897.
Montgomery liked this sort of old-fashioned garden.

hearts and crimson peonies suggesting passion and fulfillment. The bleeding-heart carries an appropriate reminder of Anne's former loneliness and misery. We see this garden in late spring and early summer. It seems somewhat unlikely that one would see all of these flowers blooming heartily at the same time, narcissus and daffodils generally being finished before the roses and the scarlet lightning come on.

In the description of Diana's garden, the garden of a rich maidenhood, there are two touches suggesting that the girls' important "bosom" friendship will have to accommodate the advent of male lovers, first in the reference to Adam and Eve and then in a hidden reference within the allusion to southernwood, which has another common name: "They called it 'lad's love'" (*Pat of Silver Bush*, ch. 3). The flowers found in the Barry garden recur, and embrace both passion and death. The crimson peonies, the scarlet lightning harmonize with Anne's hair, temper, and ardent emotions.

The white flowers in *Anne* become associated with the novel's theme of death and the acceptance of death. The little white Scotch rose (an emblem of the tie with the Old Country) recurs as the white rose of heaven. Anne knows that Matthew treasured his mother's white rosebush, so she plants a slip of it on his grave (p. 383). White flowers are associated too with Anne's virginal state. In Chapter 33 she has a "spike of white lilies" perfuming her room, and she wears in her hair the "little white house-rose" that Diana gives her (pp. 349, 352). In short, the floral detail and emblematic use of flowers in *Anne* recall the work of Montgomery's contemporaries, the Pre-Raphaelite painters.

Anne, however, sees trees and flowers not as emblems but as friends. Her desire to give names to growing things was shared by her author. When a girl in Malpeque gave the girl Maud "a little geranium slip in a can," she called it "Bonny": As she says, "I like things to have handles even if they are only geraniums. . . . And it blooms as if it *meant* it." Young Maud recorded this in her girlhood journal

(*SJ* I: 1), a passage that Montgomery picked up in describing Anne's response to plants (pp. 76, 81).

In today's Prince Edward Island, the Malpeque Gardens on Route 20 feature the Anne of Green Gables Gardens, where a special point is made of including Montgomery's favorite flowers.

FURTHER READING

Rudy J. Favretti and Joy Putnam Favretti. *Landscape Gardens for Historic Buildings*. Nashville: American Association for State and Local History, 1991.

W. R. Robinson. *The English Flower Garden and Home Grounds*. London: John Murray, 1900.

HOMEMADE ARTIFACTS AND HOME LIFE

The women of rural Prince Edward Island carried on the Anglo-Saxon, Scottish, and Irish traditions of home crafts in Anne's time and, like women in the United States, worked to very practical purposes. Rural crafts flourished in a frugal context. Patchwork quilts made use of extraneous pieces of material after other articles had been made, or were created from outworn garments. Hooked mats and braided rugs were made of rags collected from articles no longer of household use. Anne's bedroom has a "round braided mat . . . such as Anne had never seen before" (p. 72), but it is odd that Anne has never seen one, for such articles were common in the Maritime Provinces. Montgomery may by this intend to indicate the extreme poverty and listlessness of Anne's former employers.

Nineteenth-century countrywomen were still, like their forebears in the Middle Ages and the Renaissance, producers rather than merely consumers of clothing and household goods. At the very opening of *Anne* we encounter Mrs. Rachel Lynde, who has knitted sixteen "cotton warp" quilts (see p. 40 and n. 7). These spreads Mrs. Lynde makes are knitted replacements for older woven bedspreads, which were famous for their designs. Anne is taught to make, but does not like, patchwork, in which she resembles George Eliot's Maggie Tulliver: "It's foolish work . . . tearing things to pieces to sew 'em together again" (*The Mill on the Floss*, ch. 2). For a number of women in the later nineteenth century, such chores as patchwork seemed to reflect the abject, futile, repetitive nature of female work. As Cheryl Torsney and Judy Elsley have shown, some feminists of the time hoped that such work would soon be abolished, to become only a curiosity of the happily bygone past (*Quilt Culture*, 2). Montgomery refuses to make a simple polarized judgment, neither rejecting such crafts nor upholding them in the name of heritage or duty. She allows instead for questioning the role of such crafts while still delineating their importance. Her novel interweaves this theme of handicrafts either in harmony with or in opposition to the arts. In fact, crafts in general are an ongoing theme. Anne herself, like the traditional wise woman, is a mistress of craft in knowing what to do with a sick baby (ch. 18). Here she reveals her capacity to live and work in the world outside herself, where her capacity for observation is useful to others and binds her to the community. As a healer she proves so valuable that Mrs. Barry must restore the connection with her.

Anne sees the point of learning the craft of cookery, for she likes being able to feed people and, despite some misadventures, she succeeds. Marilla for her part is a better cook than a needlewoman (albeit with a limited repertoire); her skill in winemaking, however unappreciated by her neighbors, is not only valuable and shows her artistic and even hedonistic aspects. Marilla produces a cordial and a currant

A "quilting bee" (quilt-making party), P.E.I., c. 1910.

wine that is a true cordial (good for the heart, or *cor*, according to old medical theories). She and the cordial Anne Cordelia are good at healing and at sustaining the heart in people.

Anne does not care for sewing, however, and asserts that "there's no scope for imagination in patchwork" (p. 145). But women's imagination had found scope in patchwork design throughout the nineteenth century. Mrs. Lynde's skill in creating both colorful patchwork quilts and patterned knit spreads shows that in a way she shares Anne's appreciation of the color and vitality of the natural world. Her "apple-leaf" pattern shows that on some level she has an appreciation like Anne's of the beauty of the spring. It might be said that Mrs. Lynde's imagination flows through her needle, which is not what Anne expects of an imagination.

Women in the nineteenth century had to sew in order to keep the family clothed and provided with necessities like sheets. Even during their "leisure" moments, women were expected to have a needle in hand, as in the eighteenth century, and not only the sturdy pioneers but the elegant ladies of the English manor houses. In Charlottetown, Prince Edward Island's first and only approach to a city, the wives and daughters of the leading citizens were constantly to be found with needle in hand. For example, Margaret Pennefather Stukely Gray, granddaughter of a famous general and daughter of an important statesman, notes in her diary for March 28, 1863, that

"we have got through a lot of work this winter—8 pairs of Drawers for Mama and her bl[ac]k dress" (*One Woman's Charlottetown*, 5). After her marriage in 1869, Margaret, then Mrs. Artemas Lord, had even more work to do, such as making a topcoat for her little son and beautifying the home; as she typically notes in her diary (April 22, 1890), "Busy making a cake and dying [*sic*] rugs for the mat" (*ibid.*, 123). Here is a woman who belonged to the very top echelon of Prince Edward Island society and could even afford some servants. She could thus occasionally indulge in some recreational needlework, at least in her youth: "A long lonely day but I did a yard of tatting" (Feb. 20, 1863).

The basic skill of sewing a good seam was essential, hence Marilla's anxiety that Anne learn to sew. The poorer the woman, the more basic and less ornamental her sewing. Marilla has evidently not gone in for fancywork. (She apparently had trouble with her eyes long before she admitted it, so perhaps

A Victorian lady at her needlework in her parlor.

she should not have bothered with sewing at all.) One of the novel's little ironies is that sewing is no more a pleasure for Marilla than for Anne. As a childless woman, Marilla had time in which to engage in fine needlework had she wished. Even Rachel Lynde, with her numerous offspring, always found time for needlework.

The Cuthberts, the Sloanes, the Pyes, the Lyndes, the Barrys: whatever their minor social and economic differences, all rely on their women's capacity to sew. If the girls and women want their own clothes ornamented in any way, they must acquire an interest in their production. At one point Mrs. Lynde sews Anne's dress with remarkable skill, adorning it with "frills and shirrings," "pin tucks," and lace (p. 272). Diana, who shares Rachel's ability, is interested in patterns and designs. Women and girls in the novel as well as real life shared the patterns of clothing and ornament that by this time had become big business for companies that published paper patterns for garments according to size. Such firms offered their own catalogs, and magazines published patterns for fancy needlework that were passed around in the cooperative female community. Sophia Sloane offers to teach Anne "a perfectly elegant new pattern of knit lace, *so* nice for trimming aprons" (p. 194). Edgings of knit lace were used on pillows and other household furnishings as well as on garments. Actual lace, the product of a complex process, was imported from Europe and very expensive. With the possible exception of convents in Quebec, there were no sources for real lace in Canada, and women with little spare time were unlikely to turn regularly to making needle lace or "pillow lace" for recreation, because it takes a long while to produce enough even for a simple edging.

Machines had been producing lace from the early nineteenth century, when looms in Nottingham first made open network lace that could be embroidered on, as in Limerick lace. By the Victorian era a number of lace patterns were being machine produced, but such lace was considered inferior.

A more modest but still admired kind of lace could be produced quickly by the art of crocheting. It is generally agreed that this process of making ornamental patterns with linen or cotton thread by means of a hook first took hold in Ireland as part of an endeavor to provide a money-making manufacture for Irish peasant women. Mary Sharp, in *Point and Pillow Lace* (p. 181), says that efforts to interest Irish women in lacemaking go back to at least 1743, when a prize was offered for the craft. It was not first introduced at the time of the Great Famine but was reintroduced to Ireland in 1847 in the urgent effort (made largely by women, especially nuns) to provide Irish women with a means of raising money to feed their families: "It was then that crochet-work was introduced; very good patterns of old Lace were procured. . . . The work was vitiated by the use of cotton instead of linen thread, a mistake so generally made in recent Lace revivals." Cathy Grin, in *Heritage Crochet* (7), argues that "not for another twenty years [i.e., after the Great Famine] did crochet become popular among upper-class women," but books like *A Winter Gift for Ladies* (1845) show that the art of crocheting had spread by then to the middle-class morning room.

Knitting permits an even faster production of mock lace than crochet. Lace or a lacy garment could be made by using knitting wool, crochet cotton, or the traditional and more costly linen thread. In general, women in England, the United States, and Canada used the cheaper and more readily available cotton for all their "lace." Pattern books offered many examples and instructions. *Weldon's Practical Knitting*, for example, touted its own company's thread while offering numerous exciting new patterns for knitters of "lace." In 1889, for instance, this source offered patterns for Spanish Point Lace, Willow Leaf Edging, and Harebell Lace, among others. "Willow Leaf Edging" was recommended for trimming children's clothes and may well have appeared on Anne's aprons.

Anne of Green Gables carefully registers a world in

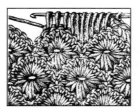

transition from a largely self-dependent pioneering rural style of living to a new economic system characterized by an increasing use of urban manufacture, by the employment of machines within the home, and by a new reliance on information exchange, including that which was spread through advertisements. The same magazines that carried Montgomery's stories and poems (and Anne's and Emily's) existed largely as means of getting advertising into the homes of rural people all over North America. Matthew, for instance, reads the *Farmers' Advocate* and the ever-popular *Family Herald* (pp. 200, 247). In *Anne of the Island*, Diana sends in Anne's short story to a baking-powder company, which runs it as an advertisement in newspapers that carry serial stories. And in *Anne of Green Gables*, Diana possesses a valued advertisement from "a sewing-machine agent" (p. 141 and n. 17 with illustration).

The sewing machine, a new invention to relieve women of the time-consuming drudgery of sewing seams by hand, stirred the ambitious production of more elaborate garments while at the same time connecting women to the mechanized world and having them enter into a larger sphere as consumers. By the time *Anne* was written, folk arts such as hooked rugs had already become "a cottage industry" (*Hooked Rugs*, 13). In all her novels, Montgomery registers a consciousness of both the economic change and the change in sensibility that was giving a new aesthetic and monetary value (partly based on nostalgia) to the old homely female arts and crafts. There is thus a certain irony in her dealings with

The beehive pattern (left) and the rice stitch (right), two common crocheting patterns.

them. On the one hand, she understood well the delightful effect that descriptions of the simple life might have on readers. Yet even though she was truly recording the life that she herself knew at the time of writing and had known in girlhood, that life was already partaking of the appeal of the pastoral. Anne's room near the end of the novel exhibits many more objects of urban and machine-made production than that same room described earlier. The curtains, for instance, must be imported (p. 346). If Anne is to progress, it is away from the world of simplicity and homely craft toward imported fabrics and a mirror with Cupids on it in imitation of the high Rococo style.

In *Anne of the Island*, a millionaire wants to buy Mrs. Lynde's patchwork quilts when he sees them on the line, somewhat incongruously, in Halifax. By the time *Anne* was written, the arts and crafts movement of the 1880s had given a new value to the traditional homely crafts of rural people in the English-speaking world. At the same time, constant local, national, and international exhibitions were changing ideas of design. "The Centennial Exposition of 1876 [in Philadelphia] was important to the evolution of American crazy quilting because the Japanese pavilion there was highly successful," notes Patricia Wilens in *America's Heritage Quilts* (131). By the turn of the century, the taste for things Japanese has come to Avonlea. The girls use a Japanese scarf, which customarily draped the piano, among the accoutrements of Arthurian Elaine (p. 296). Even rural exhibitions, like the one at Charlottetown that the girls attend (ch. 29), spread a taste for novelty. Montgomery herself took part in such exhibitions at Charlottetown, entering her own needlework. She was in fact much more interested than Anne in such things, having picked up some of the tastes as Mrs. Lynde, as she records (*SJ* II [Jan. 27, 1914]: 142):

To-day *I began to knit a quilt*. . . . There have been so many days lately that I could do absolutely nothing. . . . Now, *knitting* has always

had a good effect on me when I am nervous. . . . So I began the quilt. It doesn't matter if I never finish it.

Quilt knitting, in this particular pattern especially always makes me think of Malpeque. I spent a winter there once with Aunt Emily. Every girl and woman in Malpeque had knitted, was knitting or intended to knit a quilt— some of them several quilts. They possessed many patterns and considerable rivalry went on. Lace knitting was very popular also. I caught the fever and began a quilt. I think I was three years knitting it. It was very pretty but was worn out long ago. Ten years ago I knitted a second which I still have.

This quilt fever must have possessed the women of Malpeque at the end of the 1880s and the beginning of the 1890s. Montgomery would have started her first quilt when she was around thirteen years old and, if she had started another in 1904, would have been working on it about the the time she began writing *Anne*. An interesting connection exists here between the author, her authorial craft, and the fateful fabrication of her emblematic (if ostensibly naturalistic) Mrs. Lynde.

Unlike certain other novels and stories by Montgomery, *Anne of Green Gables* pays no attention to specifically masculine arts and handicrafts. Matthew, for example, carries out the basic work of the little farm but does no wood carving or decorating. In Montgomery's stories it is the seagoing men who tend to be the male artists with their hands. In *Anne of Green Gables* the focus is on the women and their creative lives. The value Montgomery places on the work of material creativity can be seen in her late novel *Jane of Lantern Hill* (1937), in which the young heroine, stifled and restricted by privilege and emotional deprivation in her urban life, is empowered by recapturing a rural existence where she has the freedom to do and to make, to work in the material world. Away from unhealthful Toronto, on Prince

Edward Island, Jane learns cooking and sewing, gardening and fishing—even how to shingle a roof or, when needed, to drive a load of hay. Learning the old female skills, and some skills formerly considered masculine, Jane frees her mind and personality to become a modern, fearless woman. *Jane* is consistent with the author's earlier novels, for Montgomery sees in the work that women do—including needlework—an opportunity to make an impact on one's environment instead of being the victim of an environment wholly imposed from without. In *Anne of Green Gables*, the author is more cautious in her approach to the female crafts, for Avonlea is only too convinced of the value of its material culture; it needs to appreciate the work of the mind and its words.

FURTHER READING

Anon. *A Winter Gift for Ladies: Being Instructions in Knitting, Knotting and Crochet Work: Containing the newest and most fashionable patterns.* From the latest London edition. Revised and enlarged by an American Lady. Philadelphia: G. B. Zieber, 1845.

Cathy Grin. *Heritage Crochet for Your Home.* Kenthurst, NSW, Australia: Kangaroo Press, 1995.

Leslie Linsley. *Hooked Rugs: An American Folk Art.* Photography by John Aron. New York: Potter, 1992.

Margaret Pennefather Stukely Gray Lord. *One Woman's Charlottetown: Diaries of Margaret Gray Lord 1863, 1876, 1890.* Ed. Evelyn J. MacLeod. Hull, P.Q.: Canadian Museum of Civilization, 1988.

Mary Sharp. *Point and Pillow Lace: A Short Account of Various Kinds Ancient and Modern, and How to Recognize Them.* London: John Murray, 1905; Detroit: Tower, 1971.

Cheryl B. Torsney and Judy Elsley. *Quilt Culture: Tracing a Pattern.* Columbia, Mo.: Univ. of Missouri Press, 1994.

Marie D. Webster. *Quilts: Their Story and How to Make Them.* New York: Doubleday, Page, 1915.

Patricia Wilens, ed. *America's Heritage Quilts.* Des Moines: Meredith, 1991.

FOOD PREPARATION, COOKERY, AND HOME DECORATION

In the rural world described by Lucy Maud Montgomery, small landowners were expected to be largely self-sufficient. Even on a very small piece of land, a family would keep pigs, chickens, and at least one cow. Gardens and small fields of vegetables supplied much of the produce for home use. Housewives in North America were more involved in basic food production than they are now. In her married life Montgomery performed processes in the kitchen that today we expect to be done in the factory: "with due housewifely care I took a batch of hams out of my pickle barrel and put a fresh batch in. . . . I am fond of ham and one cannot live on tragedy and romance so somebody must do the pickling" (*SJ* II: 396–97).

Marilla is involved in food raising, not just food preparation, raising pigs and poultry. Anne is expected to help with such chores, as a daughter of the house would do. From her bringing the cows back from pasture to the barn for milking in the evening (p. 303) we discover that the Cuthberts are well enough off to have more than one cow. Because cows supply the family with milk and butter, they are too valuable to be killed off for veal or beef. Pigs are a readier supply of meat. In *Anne of Green Gables* the killing of animals is referred to only indirectly and as a sorrowful necessity, but we do recognize that Matthew sometimes has to kill "an innocent little creature" (pp. 63–64). Elsewhere in Montgomery's works are references to the ritual of pig killing in the autumn, followed by the salting down and boiling or smoking of meat for winter and spring use.

Even in mid-summer, the Cuthberts are to be found eating the "unromantic" boiled pork and greens (p. 155). This is winter fare, even the greens—

Swiss chard or turnip leaves or beet tops—being capable of being preserved through the cold months, although perhaps by now the greens are in fact fresh. In contrast, on that same day Anne goes to the Sunday-school picnic, with its rapturous treat of ice-cream. Cookbooks of the period offer detailed advice on how to make ice-cream, including many delicious flavors: strawberry, "tutti-frutti" (with strawberries, raspberries, cherries, and many other fruits), pistachio, coconut, almond, peach, and orange, as well as vanilla and chocolate. (See Maude Cooke, *Breakfast, Dinner, and Supper,* 507–15). Such home-made ice-cream was based on real cream, as few commercial products of that name are in our own day. For Avonlea's Sunday-School treat somebody, presumably the Bells and the Lyndes, generously contributed cream from their best cow or cows. Jerseys and Guernseys supplied the best milk, and the better-off families kept one "cream cow"—a term found in *Pat of Silver Bush.*

The ice for the ice-cream would have come from an icehouse, where ice from winter streams was kept packed deep in a cold part of the earth. (Cookbooks of the day offered advice as to the best way of smashing large blocks of ice into pieces small enough to serve in making ice-cream.) In June, with a supply of fresh grass, the cows would be producing lavish supplies of rich milk, so that families could spare enough cream to make the cold treat traditionally thought suited best to hot weather. Later, however, when Anne is treated by Josephine Barry to ice-cream served in an electrically lighted restaurant in Charlottetown (p. 310), we get a glimpse of the other more affluent world in which the time of the day and the season can both be ignored; ice-cream can be served at any time of year if it can be purchased rather than having to be produced. Anne's original contact with the sublimity of ice-cream involves a pastoral pleasure the author knows will become increasingly rare, because ice-cream will become more common.

The novel follows the seasons in its references to food. Anne's arrival in Avonlea in the early spring means that she is soon enjoying high summer, the time of ice-cream and the period when fresh vegetables grow. She is soon shelling peas while singing "Nelly of the Hazel Dell" (p. 149). Nowadays most people's contact with peas is with the frozen variety, available—perhaps tiresomely so—in any season of the year, but in Anne's day peas were strictly a summer pleasure. They were not a convenience food, as preparing them meant picking the long pods from the vines, then opening the pods to extract the four or five plump, round green peas within each.

Marilla is a good cook, according to the standards and knowledge of her time and place and her opportunities to expand her skills. Like other cooks of her class and period, she exhibits her abilities chiefly in the variety of the sweet foods she can produce. Good, inexpensive flour sent by railroad from the western plains; a constant supply of refined sugar, which was relatively cheap (the Cuthberts disdain brown sugar, except for use on the hired man's porridge; p. 269); and the ready availability of what had been previously somewhat exotic and expensive sources of flavor such as vanilla, lemons, and oranges had started North Americans on the dessert path.

Marilla enjoys setting a good table for company; her sense of appropriateness is demonstrated when

Rachel guesses that a coming guest is not important by noting that there is to be only one kind of cake served for tea, and the preserves are merely crabapple (p. 43). Preserving was in fact an important skill in the farm kitchen. Montgomery herself put up not only tomatoes but "canned chicken," as well as making strawberry and other "preserves." Strictly speaking, canning, jam-making, jelly-making, and pickling are all modes of preserving food, but the word *preserves* by itself refers to sweetened fruit kept more or less whole, as is not the case with jam or jelly. Basically, preserves are made by sorting and carefully washing whole fruit in good condition, then pouring a sweet syrup over it. The resulting combination of fruit and syrup is then packed tightly into carefully sterilized jars and kept from the air by some form of seal. This method is also known as "canning," though no tin cans are used in it. In Marilla's day the jars would be of stone, or crockery pots, rather than the glass jars then coming increasingly into use. (Pressure cooking was not yet a function of the home kitchen.) This traditional mode of preserving saved some soft fruit for winter eating and maintained balance in the diet.

Marilla has a variety of preserves on hand. The crabapple is a sour fruit, reflecting her grudging view of the promised orphan, but later we hear of strawberry preserves and cherry preserves. Marilla lets Anne treat Diana to cherry preserves in a crock that is "beginning to go"—either developing mold or starting to ferment, thus being strangely like the cordial that turns into wine. Marilla, like Anne, has a taste for fruit and sweet things that belies her apparently stern outlook. Diana goes off to school with "toothsome" raspberry tarts (p. 159) made of preserved raspberries or, more probably, raspberries of the late summer crop. Marilla's, and Anne's, and Diana's taste for fruit-derived sweets links them with other females in the story, such as the friend who offers Anne "blue plums" as an early autumn treat in school (p. 193). Apples and root vegetables can be kept whole through the winter by storage in a

cool, dry place, as potatoes and apples are kept in the Green Gables cellar (pp. 81, 202). Any rotten fruit or vegetables or other spoiled foods could be fed to the pigs. So nothing goes entirely to waste—even Anne's liniment cake is fed to the pigs in the end (p. 243).

Anne herself learns to cook during the course of the story, though her efforts are somewhat halting. She is definitely not a superbly good cook by nature, unlike the later heroines Pat Gardiner and Jane Stuart. At the end of the nineteenth century it had become a kind of fashion in literature to depict the trials of young people engaged in cookery. In the very popular *Five Little Peppers and How They Grew* (1880), the author known as Margaret Sidney (Harriet Mulford Lothrop) depicted the trials of twelve-year-old Polly Pepper, who valiantly endeavors to make a birthday cake for her mother, coopting the dubious aid of the younger children in her effort. Her problems arise not from her own insufficiency but from the family's dire poverty, which means that the stove is full of holes and the only flour available is a coarse brown type. And in the comic tale "An Old-Fashioned Thanksgiving" (1881), Louisa May Alcott plays with incompetent child cookery when some New England children of the 1820s try to cook Thanksgiving dinner, making many mistakes:

> Meantime Tilly attacked the plum pudding. She felt pretty sure of coming out right.... So in went suet and fruit, all sorts of spice, to be sure she got the right ones, and brandy instead of wine. But she forgot both sugar and salt, and tied it in the cloth so tightly that it had no room to swell, so it would [have] come out as heavy as lead and as hard as a cannonball, if the bag did not burst and spoil it all. Happily unconscious of these mistakes, Tilly popped it into the pot....

The popular English writer for girls L. T. Meade picks up the motif in *Polly: A New-Fashioned Girl*

(1889). In this story, Doctor Maybright, widowed with nine children, allows his fourteen-year-old daughter to take up housekeeping and cooking for the family. At first everything goes wrong, though this is largely owing not just to a lack of advance planning but even more to the actions of hostile or careless servants. For of course Polly's family is respectable enough to have servants, and Meade is very conscious of the class barriers surrounding the practice of cooking. Thus, abandoned by her servant maid, Polly has to do some very basic work:

> She must not wait any longer for that naughty Maggie; she must put coals on the fire herself, and wash the potatoes, and set them on the boil.
>
> This was scarcely the work of an ordinary lady-like housekeeper, but Polly tried to fancy she was in Canada, or in even one of the less civilized settlements, where ladies put their hands to anything, and were all the better for it. (81)

L. T. Meade was widely read in both the United States and Canada as well as in Australia, where readers must have been chagrined to see their country counted among one of the "less civilized settlements." The snobbery and anxiety of the English about what was considered ladylike affected their depiction of cooking, even in fiction set in North America. It is notable that Montgomery makes no pretense that her characters are in a higher condition of life than that which Montgomery herself knew, and she treats the labor of her women respectfully and as a normal aspect of existence.

Earlier, women writers had largely avoided cookery and housework as subjects in fiction. Women who participated in the suffragette movement and promoted the advancement of women's education were often reluctant to talk too much or too em-

phatically about women's traditional work in the house. Yet in real life in modern North America, women did need to know how to cook. The use of fictional child characters as a device to discuss the difficulties and hazards of cookery offered a certain insulation for the subject. Within *Anne of Green Gables*, as in the world around the novel, a debate is taking place about the "old-fashioned" and "new-fashioned" ways. Fannie Merritt Farmer, in her preface to the *Boston Cooking School Cook Book* (1896), says she hopes the work "may not only be looked upon as a compilation of tried and tested recipes, but that it may awaken an interest through its condensed scientific knowledge which will lead to deeper thought and broader study of what to eat." Farmer includes a discussion of the principles involved in the various processes of cooking and gives the chemical formulas of basic foodstuffs like sugar. Throughout, she says that if the New Woman is a true cook, she will not only master the skills of her ancestresses but will outdo them in making many more dishes and more elaborate ones than her foremothers did, and will surpass them utterly in understanding the subject and its principles scientifically.

In the nineteenth century, women had taken the lead in creating a new scientific approach to the work of the kitchen. Isabella Beaton was a pioneer with her *Book of Household Management* (1861), a work that influenced and was copied by many other writers. Beaton herself succeeded Eliza Acton, who

Illustrations ("The Old Way" [left], "The New Way") from Breakfast, Dinner, and Supper *by Maude C. Cooke.*

wrote books on cookery carefully considering ingredients, economics, and the like. In America at the turn of the twentieth century there was much earnest talk about what constituted scientific nutrition and an appropriate understanding of chemical and other processes at work in home cookery. *The Boston Cooking School Cook Book* successfully presented a system of rational, nutritious recipes that also helped to familiarize users with standardized American measurements, as this was the first important cookbook to use them throughout. The measuring cup and measuring spoons were already familiar—Farmer says they "may be bought at any store where kitchen furnishings are sold"—but they still required explanation and illustration, with a warning not to confuse the measuring tablespoon with other spoons. From the end of the nineteenth century onward, cooks in the United States and Canada used the standard measuring cup, teaspoon, tablespoon, and so forth, thereafter parting ways with their British sisters, who continued to rely on the older imperial system of weights standardized in 1826.

An important innovation was commercial baking powder, which became a feature of modern North American life in the last two decades of the nineteenth century. Before that time, women had had to make their own mixes, blending soda with cream of tartar, to ensure the rising of baked goods. The commercial product combined and standardized everything that was needed, so that the ability to make cakes and other baked goods rise was to be bought in one easily obtainable, reliable ingredient. Not all baking powders were in fact reliable, however, for it required some commercial research to create powders that did not deteriorate almost immediately. Some low-grade powders turned out to be cut with ammonia or alum. Rival companies

—often local pharmacies—boasted of their own product and spread alarm about those of others. In short, housewives at the end of the century tended to talk a lot about baking powders. Hence, we can understand Anne's seemingly ridiculous remark when confronted with the horrible taste of her cake: "It must have been the baking powder" (p. 241).

Women were accustomed to blaming a bad baking powder for a failure in their cookery, but in this instance the baking powder has visibly done all that it could be asked to do and the cake has risen beautifully; it is indeed "light and feathery as golden foam" (p. 280)—a phrase that could have come out of an advertisement and certainly describes the North American ideal cake.

Baking-powder companies promoted their wares by offering cookbooks using them, and women collected recipes for dishes that required the new kinds of kitchen products. The fine, tall cakes that North Americans are so fond of date from this moment in time. English women (and for that matter Australians and New Zealanders) on the whole continued to use traditional methods of making a cake rise, which depend largely on eggs and egg-white, and the English cake, a modest "sponge," risen largely because of the eggs used in it, came to seem very flat and dull to the North American eye. Only after World War II did English cooks catch on to tall cakes. Marilla offers the Allans both the old and the new, "pound cake and layer cake" (p. 238). Her pound cake is the traditional English kind, strong in butter and eggs, while the layer cake is suited to displaying the North American talent for making tall cakes with elaborate icing or filling.

Avonlea certainly sustains its British tradition in

ROYAL
BAKING
POWDER
Absolutely Pure.

An advertisement for Royal Baking Powder.

cookery. At one point Marilla sets a "plum pudding" before one set of guests as an autumn dessert (p. 184). This very traditional English sweet is made as Alcott's story suggests, by mixing flour with suet and sugar and then adding "plums"—actually raisins or currants, often with other winter fruits such as candied or dried citrus of various kinds. Recipes for "plum pudding" can be found in Acton and Beaton and in all the standard Canadian cookery books (see "Recipes," below). Plum pudding is quite old, probably the first pudding dessert known to ordinary people in England. In the Renaissance it was a great delicacy, associated with Christmas; in the Commonwealth era the Calvinists forbade it to be served at Christmas.

The Puritan invention of Thanksgiving allowed a festive meal to be served in the winter at a date other than Christmas; traditional Thanksgiving fare included plum pudding. Canadians do not celebrate the American Thanksgiving, but Marilla does serve plum pudding in the fall. Her festive dish turns out not to be consumable, however, because of the party's perhaps understandable sensibilities. We don't know what kind of sauce the mouse fell into, save that it was a liquid one, not the hard sauce often used in England with plum pudding. It might have been a lemon-flavored sauce or some form of custard sauce (see "Recipes"). We know, though, that Marilla would not have used sherry or wine for flavoring her sauce, as many cookbooks, including Canadian ones, suggest doing. Other steamed puddings, such as ginger pudding, could be made by the same method as required for the plum pudding. Such "puddings" are in fact boiled puddings based on fat, sugar, and flour, and are not the kind of liquid puddings of butterscotch, chocolate, or jelly that many associate with the word *pudding* nowadays.

In *Anne* the Allans are to be regaled with a choice of many sweets, including lemon pie, which need not have been a lemon meringue pie, although this kind was then known. However, it requires a perfect oven and great attention at nearly the last minute. It is more likely instead that the Allans were served a pie with a filling of lemon custard, such as had been popular from much earlier in the century (see "Recipes"). Montgomery always won compliments for her lemon pies (*SJ* II: 18–19). The Allans are also to be offered "two kinds of jelly, red and yellow" (p. 238); we may assume that one was strawberry-flavored and the other flavored with lemon, but some sort of dye (no doubt cochineal in the case of the red) may have been used. This kind of stock-based sweetened "jelly" is different from the jelly made by simmering fruit and sugar together and then straining and refining the result.

The gelatin for making jellies (both savory and sweet) was another new commercial standardized product that made it much easier for the ordinary family to produce what had hitherto been a delicacy. Jelly, once chiefly valued as a food for invalids, had formerly required the boiling of a part of an animal (usually a calf's or cow's foot) in order to create the gelatine. The new clean commercial product removed this ugly phase of activity from the kitchen and offered a reliable mode of ensuring that the jelly would set properly.

Home refrigerators were unknown in Anne's world, and the rural folk in it do not use iceboxes. The children use the brook (p. 161), while at home the pantry has to do for storage; recipes call only for "a cool place" (see "Recipes"). Jellies were poured into attractive molds so that the jelly would come out in a pretty shape, but once taken out of the mold they would need to be eaten fairly soon. In the height of summer a jelly would melt away.

Traditionally, recipes for making good dishes for the home were passed down from mother to daughter and traded with relatives and friends. Many families valued a handwritten cookbook composed of its members' contributions. Montgomery herself owned a handwritten recipe book and collected recipes from the compilations of female friends and relatives. After her Aunt Annie's death she records, "I copied some recipes from Aunt Annie's old cook-

book. It spoke very eloquently of her. Never was such a cook as Aunt Annie" (*SJ* III: 193). A cookbook that had simply been owned but not written or compiled by another woman would not "speak eloquently" of her. But recipes, like needlework patterns, were becoming part of the commercial world, detached—though never utterly so—from the emotional moorings of female affectional traditions. Newspapers and magazines attracted female readers by offering recipes. Even *Godey's Lady's Book* (which changed its title in the 1890s to *Godey's Magazine*) published recipes. (It may seem surprising to us that such an up-market magazine should have dealt with a number of recipes based on the use of stale bread, but such recipes proved more practical than the fashion pictures for which the magazine was famous.)

In both Canada and the United States, church groups published their own cookbooks in order to raise money. It is interesting that "The Ladies of Grace Church Sewing Circle," in Brantford, Ontario, did not disdain the inclusion of brandy in the plum-pudding recipe published in their 1900 cookbook (see "Recipes"). Church groups and other amateur organizations give us some insight into the contents of the home cookery books of the time, including the old-fashioned use of weights and measures and a certain vagueness as to directions, indicating that only experienced cooks are being addressed. Publishers also found that cookery books and works on home management generally made money, so cookbooks poured off the presses, customarily with more systematic measurements and instructions than the

church ladies' cookbooks, still in the older style, were likely to offer.

As with sewing and handicrafts, women at the turn of the century were performing both within the old home-centered traditional world where female skills were passed on personally, and in the commercially based world of quick exchanges and rapid developments.

Contemporary books on cooking and home management also included advice about the beautification of the home. Anne is truly up to date in her tastes in home decoration, whereas Marilla represents old-fashioned views. Marilla's older, simpler view of what the interior of a house should look like has not caught up with the 1890s. Her mother's taste in furnishing has been left unaltered in the parlor, the shrine of the home. Furniture, for example, is meant to be sturdy and lasting. The only additions on Marilla's part would seem to be copies of a picture of Christ and Queen Victoria's jubilee picture. Both of these products are cheap commercial items in general circulation and belong to the ephemeral world of periodicals, but they are each treated as solid and serious representations, icons of church and state. Within Marilla's parlor, they express her vision of enduring value.

Anne, on the other hand, prefers what is temporary, less fixed. She wishes to fill the house with plants, with blossoms that will be present only briefly. The late nineteenth century favored a domestic style that was more fleeting and subject to rearrangement: knickknacks, throws, cushions, conversation pieces were supposed to be changed or moved about, flowers and plants to be introduced into unexpected places in living quarters. Harriet Beecher Stowe in *We and Our Neighbors* (1875) approved the new fashion for including growing things and making them blend in with the furniture. When the Stowe heroine is giving a party, she is able to make her little rooms into "bowers of beauty" for the occasion:

A nineteenth-century potato masher.

The pictures were overshadowed with nodding wreaths of pressed ferns and bright bitter-sweet berries ... the statuettes had backgrounds of ivy.... The little dining-room was also thrown open, and dressed, and adorned with flowers, pressed ferns, berries and autumn leaves.... (179)

Stowe is here describing a New York party, but what was fashionable in New York in the mid-1870s had reached to almost everywhere else by the 1890s. Even Mrs. Barry knows about making a dinner table a feast for the eye as well as the palate (p. 240).

Anne's love of wildflowers and plants is not uncommon — is indeed fashionable — in the 1890s. Readers of *Godey's* were advised on how to transplant wildflowers to the domestic garden and how to search out and transplant wild ferns. Anne's penchant for picking not only flowers and ferns but also branches of trees and bringing them inside the home is in the very latest style. However, when she picks apple-blossom boughs for home decoration in her very first day at home at Green Gables (p. 105) Marilla can see in Anne's floral arrangements only "messy things" (pp. 105, 177). But Anne has not gone nearly as far as she might have, considering the rhapsodies of the author of *Canada's Favourite Cookbook* (18):

Ferns of all varieties are very handsome and appropriate, for either special occasions or for ordinary use. Similax deeply festooned round the chandelier and suspended from the ceiling ... is ever appropriate....

Asparagus in its fragility ... is a sweet bit of luxury. The same is true of autumn leaves strung on a thread lengthwise, and hung fringe-like all around the sides of the room, not forgetting the table....

I can conceive how beautiful the country dining-room may be made to appear in spring with a generous use of apple-blossoms, loosely twined and festooned, also made into garlands for the wall, reserving ever a generous supply of the latter, to crown the heads of the guests.

It is hard to believe that any hostess in Montreal or Toronto — let alone Charlottetown — ever made apple-blossom garlands to crown the heads of her embarrassed guests. Anne at least does not twine or festoon. But in her insistence to Marilla that the dinner table set in honor of the Allans be decorated she is (as adolescents so often are) in tune with the newest fashions and cultural desires.

In everything Marilla prefers solidity; her taste is really the earlier Victorian taste of the 1850s. There is a certain charm about that, too, however, as Montgomery said of the Macneills' room that she remembered from her childhood, that it was "prim" and "quaint" but had a certain charm, like the "tea" they served: "raspberry preserves, cheese, small squares of fruit cake and the invariable round thin cookies which completed the unchanging menu of a supper there" (*SJ* III: 46). There is an undeniable attraction in solidity and dependability. The late-Victorian and Edwardian taste runs to that which is movable, fragile, expressive, bright, and transient. We can also see in reading *Anne* that developments making for more ease in housework than had been possible earlier in the century were balanced by new attentions to the home and new demands on the housewife's time and ingenuity.

RECIPES

Filling for Lemon Pie

Take 1/2 pound rolled loaf sugar, the juice and grated peel of 2 large lemons, the yolks of eight, or four whole eggs, well beaten, 3 ounces butter melted alone, mix all well together, adding butter last. Put in a shallow dish with paste under.

—from *Two Hundred and Fifty Recipes. Specially Selected and Recommended by the Ladies of Grace Church Sewing Circle* (30)

Plum Pudding

One and one half pound raisins, 1/2 pound currants, 1/2 pound mixed peel, 3/4 pound bread crumbs, 3/4 pound suet, 8 eggs, salt, dark sugar, spices to taste, 1/2 pound almonds, 1 wineglass brandy; stone and cut raisins in two, but do not chop them. Boil five or six hours the first time and two hours the day it is served.

—from *Two Hundred and Fifty Recipes* (31)

Pudding Sauce

One tablespoon flour, butter size of an egg, one-half pint sugar, grated peel and juice of one or two lemons, to suit taste; mix flour and butter together, then add sugar and lemon; then put into one-half pint boiling water, boil until it thickens, cool a little, then add well beaten egg.

—*Mother Hubbard's Cupboard, Or, Canadian Cook Book* (35)

A nineteenth-century flour sifter.

Foam Sauce

One cup pulverized sugar, two eggs; beat sugar and yolks together in a bowl; set in boiling water; stir until hot; then add whites beaten stiff. Put a small piece of butter and tablespoon of brandy in a dish; pour over them the sugar and eggs just before serving.

—*Mother Hubbard's Cupboard* (35)

Lemon Jelly

One-half box Cox's gelatine, soaked in one-half pint cold water one hour; add one pint boiling water, and one and one-half cups sugar, three lemons, grated. Stand on stove until boiling. Strain into a mould and set in a cool place.

—*Mother Hubbard's Cupboard* (37)

Canned Fruits

Berries and all ripe, mellow fruit require but little cooking, only long enough for the sugar to penetrate. Strew sugar over them, allow them to stand a few hours, then merely scald with the sugar; half to three-quarters of a pound is considered sufficient. Harder fruits, like pears, quinces, etc., require longer boiling.

The great secret of canning is to make the fruit or vegetable perfectly air-tight. It must be put up boiling hot, and the vessel filled to the brim. . . .

Use glass jars for fruit always, and the fruit should be cooked in a porcelain or granite-iron kettle. If you are obliged to use common large-mouthed bottles with corks, steam the corks and pare them to a close fit, driving them in with a mallet. Use the following wax for sealing: one pound of resin, three ounces of beeswax, one and one-half ounces of tallow. Use a brush in covering the corks, and as they cool, dip the mouth into the melted wax. Place in a basin of cold water. Pack in a cool, dark and dry cellar. After one week examine for flaws, cracks or signs of ferment.

—*The New Cook Book*, ed. Grace E. Denison (318–19).

FURTHER READING

Anon. *Mother Hubbard's Cupboard, Or, Canadian Cook Book.* Hamilton, Ont.: G. C. Briggs & Sons, 1881.

Maude C. Cooke. *Breakfast, Dinner and Supper Or What to Eat and How to Prepare It.* St. John, N.B.: R. A. H. Morrow, 1897.

Grace E. Denison, ed. *The New Cook Book. A Volume of Tried, Tested and Proven Recipes by The Ladies of Toronto and Other Cities and Towns.* Toronto, Ont.: E. W. Gillett Co. Ltd., 1906.

Fannie Merritt Farmer. *The Boston Cooking School Cook Book.* Facsimile ed. of 1896 original *Boston Cooking School Cook Book.* New York: Hugh Lauter Levin Associates, 1996.

Annie R. Gregory. *Canada's Favorite Cook Book.* N.p., 1907.

The Ladies of Grace Church Sewing Circle. *Two Hundred and Fifty Recipes.* Brantford, Ont.: Donovan & Henwood, 1900.

L. T. Meade. *Polly: A New-Fashioned Girl.* New York: A. L. Burt Company, 1889.

Harriet Beecher Stowe. *We and Our Neighbors.* New York: J. B. Ford & Co., 1875.

BREAKING THE SILENCE

MUSIC AND ELOCUTION

Cavendish in Montgomery's time was "no cultural backwater," as Mary Rubio points out in her introduction to the first volume of the author's *Selected Journals* (xv). It had its own organizations and musical traditions, such as brass bands, orchestras, step-dancing competitions, French ballads (*complaintes*), and a long history of toe-tapping fiddle playing. Charlottetown in 1895 had an opera house, which became the Prince Edward Street Movie House by 1915. Montgomery, however, left out most of these traditions to present a strict, dour, and somewhat silent community, making passing references to the local debating club and the Charlottetown Symphony Club (pp. 212, 351).

Besides homegrown entertainment, "the Island" was visited by speakers, evangelists, politicians (like John A. Macdonald, pp. 199, 207), elocutionists (p. 352), singers, and musicians. In her Charlottetown diary for 1890, between May 20 and August 15 Margaret Gray Lord records the concert given by the Jubilee Singers, a Negro group from Nashville raising funds to establish Fisk College; two speeches on temperance; and a performance by the local St. Peter's Boys' Band. Concerts, which often had a public-spirited aim and were a means of fundraising, offered a mixture of forms, like the Promenade Concert for the City Mission with its songs, readings, and a formal walk to music.

Whether or not children should attend concerts was a source of controversy. Marilla, representing traditional values, denies Anne her first concert: "You're not going to begin gadding about to concerts and staying out all hours of the night. Pretty doings for children." Anne pleads her case by describing the debating club as a worthy cause, the moral pieces and songs as "pretty near as good as hymns," and the minister's address as "about the same thing as a sermon." But Marilla reasons: "She'll go there and catch cold like as not and have her head filled up with nonsense and excitement. It would unsettle her for a week" (pp. 213–14). In *Anne of Windy Poplars*, Mrs. Campbell, a strict grandmother, has another reason: "I do not approve of children of Elizabeth's age singing in public. It tends to make them bold and forward" (pt. II, ch. 7). Even nurturing and reform-minded parents were still worried about the effect that attending entertainment might have on young minds.

Marilla still believes that "gadding" and "racing about" are sinful (p. 261). She tells Anne: "You are simply good for nothing just now with your head stuffed full of dialogues and groans and tableaus" (p. 262). (Montgomery's own grandmother had kept her from meetings of the local literary society (*SJ* 1 [Jan. 7, 196]: 386). Later, however, Anne's recitation at the hotel concert makes Marilla proud (ch.33).

Montgomery's statement that the school concert has "the laudable purpose of helping to pay for a schoolhouse flag" (p. 261) is ironic. Her comment underlines the wisdom of Miss Stacy, who has chosen the safe cause of patriotism to counter objections to the concert from both the traditionalists and the reformers. Montgomery's choice of references follows a Maritime tradition of underlying, and underlining, irony. Montgomery's use of music and literary references in *Anne* have striking similarities in style with that of New Brunswicker May Agnes Fleming (1840–1880). Stories and novels of Fleming, the first internationally known Canadian writer, were reprinted until 1915. A favorite theme of Montgomery's is the contrast between Victorian sentimentality and the hard reality of Anne's situation.

Ronald Pearsall in *Victorian Popular Music* describes the times as the age of "the large choir and the small piano" (12). Montgomery was a piano teacher and—not happily—a church organist (*SJ* 1 [Jan. 25, 1909]: 357; [Jan. 7, 1910]: 387). In the novel, Diana is in danger of losing her music lessons. Her Aunt Josephine had been going to pay for them until the two girls jumped on her in the spare bedroom. Anne, who never has music lessons, pleads Diana's case successfully (p. 222).

Montgomery uses music from the "parlour," that is, songs in fashion, usually sung in formal settings. One of the most popular musical forms was the ballad, melancholy but rarely tragic, which dealt superficially with issues of romance and death. Heaven, or the Hereafter, as the Victorians termed it, was a hoped-for place of meeting. "Far above the Daisies" and "The Hazel Dell," both mentioned in *Anne*, belong to this category as well as to popular culture imported from the United States. The solemn song, a kind of secular hymn on noble themes, also appears in *Anne*. (Montgomery herself patriotically wrote "The Island Hymn," performed at the Charlottetown Opera House in 1909.)

Each of the three songs in the book adds its own twist to Anne's situation; to understand their impact, it is important to play or hear them as they were intended. "The Hazel Dell" is a key contrast with the pieces that follow. Anne sings it with a "vigour and expression that did credit to Diana's teaching" (p. 149). Since this tearful song, popular for over fifty years, was meant to be sung plaintively, readers of Montgomery's day would have found Anne's vigorous rendition humorously inappropriate. "Vigour" and "expression" are contradictory in reference to this song. Additionally, Anne sings this drawing-room song while shelling peas. (She has no Walkman radio or "boombox" for entertainment.) Below the humor, the song's sentimentality contrasts with Anne's very real loss. The pathos increases, since she has never even had the comfort of seeing her parents' distant graves, contrasting with Nelly's grave nearby in the dell. (Visiting cemeteries regularly was a Victorian custom.) Anne sings this just before her protector, Marilla, comes to accuse her of stealing, an operatic situation. Easy tears are associated with the less profound emotions. After Matthew's death, Anne has "no tears, only the same horrible dull ache of misery that kept on aching until she fell asleep, worn out with the day's pain and excitement" (p. 381).

"Far above the Daisies" is also humorous in that the school choir would look bright and lively singing about hopeful reunion after death (p. 217). Anne, however, had parents to meet in the Hereafter. Also, the danger of an early death due to epidemic infection was ever present, as in the 1885 Charlottetown smallpox epidemic.

"My Home on the Hill," a variation on the immensely popular 1823 song "Home, Sweet Home," contains sentiments that do not apply to Anne's past: "The vines and the trees that have grown up with me/ The paths 'mid the flow'rs I have sown/ The scenes that are bright and the hearts that are light/ And fondly I call them my own." Anne, seeking "new roots," names plants, trees, and places as a method of making them her own.

Intelligence, education, and the power of speech are all important themes that merge in the subject of elocution. The ancient Greeks and Romans stressed the art of public speaking, and the eighteenth century revived this art. Classical rhetoric consisted of five aspects: the *inventio* (discovery of material), the *disparitio* (organization), *elocutio* (style), *memoria* (store of illustrative material), and *pronuntiatio* (delivery). The revived emphasis fell on one aspect, delivery, though taking its name from style, or *elocutio*. Conflict existed between two schools, one naturalistic and the other mechanical in method, with many rules. One leading scholar, John Walker, outlined a mechanical model—with sixteen rules for pauses alone! Dr. James Rush provided the scientific background to elocution in his 1827 *The Philosophy of the Human Voice*. The "golden age of oratory," from 1827 to 1870, bore witness to much public debate on contentious questions, from slavery to evolution. On "the Island," men engaged in public debate on subjects such as free trade versus protectionism.

From 1870 to 1915, however, elocution based on classical methods declined under pressure to adapt it to practical needs. Alexander Melville Bell, father of Alexander Graham Bell and professor of elocution at London, was an important influence; beginning in 1849 with *Principles of Elocution*, he wrote forty-eight books. The first to insist upon the importance of ear training and to identify the hearing mechanisms in speech, he influenced North American thinking on the subject through his books and visits.

David Charles Bell, uncle of the telephone's inventor, an author and a professor of elocution at Dublin, made a tour of Ontario and New York around 1878. The "elocutionary evening" he presented in Toronto included comic segments, excerpts from Dickens and Shakespeare, and recitation pieces such as "The Battle of Flodden," "The Death of

Marmion" and "Edinburgh after Flodden." These three works are typically found in school readers; Anne mentions memorizing "Edinburgh after Flodden" (p. 88). Rote memorization was important and considered essential for mental discipline. An important aim of the *McGuffey's Readers* in the United States and the British *Royal Readers* used in Canada was training students not only in reading but also in elocutionary practice. By Montgomery's era, effective silent reading, leading to the *Dick and Jane* series, was beginning to replace the long-dominant oral tradition.

The third aim, distinguishing the *Royal Readers* from later replacement series, was their reputed ability to stir "noble" emotions, often sorrow. In real life, Nellie Mooney burst into tears reading the selection "The Faithful Dog" in the Manitoba *Second Reader*, a piece of verse obviously similar to "The Dog at his Master's Grave," which Anne encountered in the *Third Royal Reader* (p. 132). Nellie McClung's teacher pronounced, "Here is a pupil who has both feeling and imagination; she will get a lot out of life." (The pupil did, by becoming a prominent suffragette and author whose novel *Sowing Seeds in Danny* outsold *Anne* in 1908.)

The Scots placed emphasis on developing confidence and eloquence in public speaking. Skills in various speech situations were valuable enough to contribute to social status. Friday afternoons, when children tend to be restless, were often used for recitation. In 1879, T. S. Denison published *The Friday Afternoon Series of Dialogues*, from which come several titles in *Anne*. Anne's Miss Stacy and *Emily of New Moon*'s Mr. Carpenter both use Fridays for recitation and plays. Mr. Carpenter, a university-trained teacher, coaches "without mercy" Ilse, the future elocutionist, in recitations and trains Perry, the future politician, in speeches (ch. 28).

A difficult, if popular, form of piece for public recitation was the prose or verse work written in dialect. From the 1830s on there was a burst of humorous works in dialect. During the latter part of the nineteenth century, North American writers produced a number of stories and novels in dialect, of which Mark Twain's *Huckleberry Finn* (1885) is the most famous. (Mark Twain, like the British Dickens, used localisms to display social reality.) An early, well-known Canadian writer, Judge Thomas Chandler Halliburton, created the shrewd and unscrupulous Yankee character "Sam Slick." Slick, who first appeared in *The Clockmaker; or, the Sayings and Doings of Samuel Slick of Slickville* (1837), narrates his exploits in a New England dialect. The modern reader may feel frustrated by deliberate misspellings and unfamiliar phrases encountered in such works, but reading them aloud makes them much more comprehensible.

The comic dialect recitation pieces so popular in the later nineteenth century helped give readers and hearers a feeling of solidarity and a sense of superiority perhaps morally questionable. Such works were a subtle compliment to readers who, through attending public school, had learned to spell even difficult or unusual words like *ebullition* (p. 164). Citizens having contact with standardized pronunciation could look down on old-fashioned, provincial, or immigrant speakers. Willard Thorp in *American Humorists* claims that "verbal humor" was to give the effect of "shrewd illiteracy" (19). This is certainly true of Marietta Holley, one of Montgomery's favorite authors, whose comic term *mejum* (for *medium, moderate*) is quoted by Anne (p. 392). (Careless compares these terms with the present "Yabba-dabba-doo" from *The Flintstones*.) But the timeworn piece about an immigrant's farm misadventures, "How Sockery Set a Hen," applauded by Anne at her first concert, shows the newcomers as nearly imbecilic (pp. 217; 477–78). (The words "Sam Sloane proceeded to explain and illustrate 'How Sockery Set a Hen'" have S's and soft C's, difficult for those who stutter. Historian Michael Halleran wonders if Montgomery is implying that the speaker had this problem?)

The comic dialect piece in the nineteenth and early twentieth century served as a way of coping with groups perceived as a threat or as different. Nowadays it is embarrassing to Canadian readers to find that Jane of Lantern Hill shares with her father a talent for reciting "habitant" poetry. Such pieces were first written by William Henry Drummond, whose *The Habitant and Other French Canadian Poems* was a great success in Canada, the United States, and England in 1897. Drummond and his successors among Anglo-Canadian writers produced verses rendered in English but spoken supposedly in a broken French-Canadian accent by one of the *habitants*, or rural settlers in French Canada.

All the recitation pieces mentioned in *Anne* fit in thematically with the motifs of the novel. The play *The Society for the Suppression of Gossip* alludes to the theme of gossip as a controlling, community power. "The Maiden's Vow" (ch. 33) foretells the promise that Anne will make to Marilla after Matthew's death (ch. 38). A woman giving a vow would bring to the minds of readers of Montgomery's day the most famous vow of love in literature: "Whither thou goest, I will go; and where thou lodgest, I will lodge; thy people shall be my people, and thy God, my God: Where thou diest, I will die" (Ruth 1: 16–17). Like the biblical Ruth to her mother-in-law, without blood relationship, Anne will vow, despite sacrifice, to stay with the older woman.

Furthermore, Anne chose this piece carefully: "It's so pathetic. Laura Spencer is going to give a comic recitation, but I'd rather make people cry than laugh" (p. 351). Victorians generally liked to inspire tears, but Anne might have a more personal reason. She had never cried seriously about her real losses and by choice remained optimistic. Now older, she perhaps likes having other people do her crying for her. No more cheerful singing of "The Hazel Dell"! Whittier's simple phrase "loss in all familiar things" showing daily grief for Matthew also contrasts with the "parlour" melancholy of "The Hazel Dell" (pp. 149, 382).

Quotations take on an ironic twist. For example, "One moonbeam from the forehead to the crown" comes from *Aurora Leigh* (see p. 350 and n. 9). In context, it is the kind of compliment a young man like Romney would say to gain a girl's attention. Marilla, when she "stalked downstairs" after a humorous plain-speaking speech to an angelic Anne dressed in white organdy, is thinking in terms expressed by Barrett Browning's line. Marilla the Puritan cannot say aloud what she deeply feels. Compliments seem like falsehoods; her inbred Scots reserve stands out clearly.

Modern readers cannot understand the importance of music and elocution in Anne unless they imagine a world of fields and farms without the noises and entertainments to which we have become so accustomed: compact disks, video games, VCRs, cassette recorders and audio tapes, television, radio, movies, and phonograph records. Take away the constant accompaniment of Muzak, indoor and outdoor machinery like vacuums and dishwashers, lawnmowers and jackhammers (although telephones were coming into general use by 1908). Substitute a horse's neigh and clip-clop and the gentle calls of farm animals for the metallic noise of engine-run transportation. Only then can we enter the turn-of-the-century countryside's silence, free of mechanical distraction and electric entertainment.

Even with the inventions of the new century, Montgomery preferred "the old 90s with the feeling that they were a nice, unhurried, leisurely time." On September 3, 1924, after hearing the radio, she wrote prophetically to her friend Mr. MacMillan:

> It was all very wonderful—but do you know, I found it a little *depressing*. Is it because I'm getting on in life that these wonderful inventions and discoveries, treading on each other's heels, give me a sense of *weariness* and a longing to go back to the slower years of old? . . . But I really do think we are rushing on rather fast. It keeps humanity on tip-toe. But I think this will go on for two or three hundred years more —I mean the flood of great discoveries and

inventions. . . . And none of these things really "save time." They only fill it more breathlessly full.

FURTHER READING

Georges Arsenault. "Venez Ecouter La Complainte." *The Island Magazine* 37 (1995): 3–12.

Douglas Baldwin. *Land of Red Soil: A Popular History of Prince Edward Island*. Charlottetown: Ragweed Press, 1990.

———— and Thomas Spira. *Gaslights, Epidemics and Vagabond Cows: Charlottetown in the Victorian Era.* Charlottetown: Ragweed Press, 1988.

Margaret Pennefather Stukeley Gray Lord. *One Woman's Charlottetown: Diaries of Margaret Gray Lord, 1863, 1876, 1890.* Ed. Evelyn J. MacLeod. Hull, P.Q.: Canadian Museum of Civilization, 1988.

Lorraine McMullen, ed. *Re(Dis)covering Our Foremothers: Nineteenth-Century Women Writers.* Ottawa: University of Ottawa Press, 1990.

———— and Sandra Campbell, eds. "May Agnes Fleming." *Pioneering Women: Short Stories by Canadian Women: Beginnings to 1880.* Canadian Short Story Library, Series 2, No. 17. Ottawa: University of Ottawa Press, 1993, pp. 109–38.

Ronald Pearsall. "Music by Proxy: The Invention Revolution of Mechanical Music." *Impact of Science on Society* 37 (1987): 261–67.

————. *Victorian Popular Music.* Newton Abbot, England: David & Charles, 1973.

Mary Margaret Robb. *Oral Interpretation of Literature in American Colleges and Universities: A Historical Study of Teaching Methods.* N.p. H. W. Wilson, 1941. Rev. ed. New York: Johnson Reprint Corp., 1968.

Patricia Kelly Santelmann. "Written as Women Write: *Anne of Green Gables* within the Female Tradition." In *Harvesting Thistles,* 64–73.

Willard Thorp. *American Humorists.* University of Minnesota Pamphlets on American Writers, No. 42. St. Paul: Univ. of Minnesota, 1964.

Vicki L. Williams. "Home training and the socialization of youth in the sentimental novels of Marshall Saunders, Nellie McClung and L. M. Montgomery." Unpublished M.A. thesis, Carleton University, Ottawa, 1982.

PERSONAL COMMUNICATIONS

Virginia Careless, Curator of History, Royal British Columbian Museum, Victoria, B.C., July 5, 1995.

Michael F. H. Halleran, Historian [of the Victorian Period], Victoria, B.C., July 23, 1995.

MICROFORM

"Professor Bell's elocutionary evenings: Mr. D. C. Bell of Dublin ... will deliver the following selection of readings and recitations from the works of Shakespeare, modern poets and humorists, commencing at 8.o'clock precisely ... Toronto, fl. 1878." Ottawa: Canadian Institute for Historical Microreproductions, Canadian History Dept., 1987.

LITERARY ALLUSION AND QUOTATION IN *ANNE OF GREEN GABLES*

Lucy Maud Montgomery's knowledge of English literature and love of it as a girl were, like Anne's, remarkable, despite the fact that the Macneills frowned on novels and novel reading (Maud later remembered that there were only three novels in the house: Scott's *Rob Roy*, Dickens's *Pickwick Papers*, and Bulwer-Lytton's *Zanoni*). "Fortunately, poetry did not share the ban of novels. I could revel at will in Longfellow, Tennyson, Whittier, Scott, Byron, Milton, Burns" (*Alpine Path*, 49). Later generations have given quite different values to these poets and would not arrange them thus in this promiscuous list, but Montgomery gives the impression that her girlhood reading ranged through volumes of nineteenth-century poets, both British and American, that were traditional and almost contemporary. The language of these poets in various ways influenced her style, but by the time Montgomery wrote *Anne* she was exercising discriminating control of her poetic resources. The pattern of allusions woven into *Anne* seems quite deliberate. Because many of the original sources have sunk into relative obscurity, identifying allusions to them uncovers a palimpsest of meaning and a map of sorts to other imaginary lands in the world of literature.

Many of the poems referred to in *Anne* reflect the situations of the Scottish immigrants to Canada. The first poems that Anne mentions—"The Battle of Hohenlinden," "Edinburgh after Flodden," and others in the personal history she gives to Marilla—reflect the unhappy state of a homeless expatriate. It seems almost subversive, or at least pleasantly defiant, for these emigrants to teach these poems and legends to their children in a country within the British Commonwealth. Like the thousands of emigrants expelled from their native country, when we first see her Anne is a homeless waif. Unwelcome and unwanted, she must make a new home for herself in a strange new place, much as Montgomery's ancestors had. "The Battle of Hohenlinden" and "Edinburgh after Flodden" are reminders to the schoolchildren who learned them in their *Royal Readers* of the defeat and oppression the Scots suffered at the hands of the English. Later in the novel Anne is identified with Mary, Queen of Scots, when she recites the poem of that name by Henry Glassford Bell. Ruby Gillis reports feeling her blood run cold upon hearing Anne speak as Mary (p. 260). It is natural, however, for red-haired Anne to be identified with the queen of Scotland, for she does, in a sense, become queen of this island of expatriated Scots. Before the end of the novel, Anne can say with Scott's Rob

Roy that "her foot is on her native heath" not only in the subject of English but on P.E.I. as well.

Anne's fascination with "The Dog at His Master's Grave" also reveals something about the state of mind of the orphaned, and in this sense masterless, Anne. One of her favorite phrases, "kindred spirit," is also a subtle reminder of Anne's orphanhood. This term comes originally from Thomas Gray's "Elegy in a Country Churchyard": "For thee, who mindful of the unhonored dead / Dost in these lines their artless tale relate; / If chance, by lonely contemplation led, / Some kindred spirit shall inquire thy fate." A kindred spirit is thus one who can share mindfulness of the dead or show sympathy for one's loss, as Matthew and Marilla do.

Montgomery calls upon Sir Walter Scott often, not only as a reminder of the national heritage he represents but frequently to make a subtle, comic point, as for instance when she notes in an echo of *Marmion* that for Matthew, walking up to Anne and speaking to her is "harder for him than bearding a lion in its den" (p. 51). Montgomery in fact alludes to *Marmion* several times throughout the novel. When Anne dyes her hair, for instance, she exclaims to Marilla in the bitterness of regret, "Oh, Marilla, 'what a tangled web we weave when first we practise to deceive.' That is poetry, but it is true" (p. 291). The reader is again struck by the comic contrast between the dramatic tone of Scott's historical poem and Anne's unfortunate experience with the hair dye. And in Chapter 29 Anne brings the cows home as she recites the battle canto from *Marmion*, "exulting in its rushing lines and

Illustration to accompany the poem "The Lake of Geneva," by Lord Byron (artist unknown).

the clash of spears in its imagery" (p. 303). Clearly, Scott must be seen as a major source for Anne's sense of the dramatic and for her sometimes incongruously elevated language.

Scott became a writer of public proverbs, statements of moral or historical fact, which links him with the authors of the recitation pieces. The selections in the school readers that are used as concert performance pieces, like "Curfew Must Not Ring Tonight" and "Bingen on the Rhine," belong to a world of public poetry, although it is an odd world of public statement, too, full of aggressiveness, martyrdom, violence, and complaint. The language of the narrative plays off the set "recitation pieces" against the less obtrusive pattern of literary allusion, reference, and embedded quotation that serves the novel by supplying important aspects of its thoughtful idiom and varied verbal texture.

The American poets quoted within the narrative web seem all to serve a positive function. They are as a group associated with statements about growth and possibility, helpers in dealing with change and development. Longfellow is invoked for his "standing with reluctant feet / Where the brook and river meet" as a description of adolescence. Anne's life is indeed like the brook and the river; from the first page to the last, her life is represented as a widening and deepening flow. The American poets cited here—Lowell, Whittier, Longfellow—seem to record the inward and tender, combined with a poignant need for experience, acceptance, and growth. Lowell's "The Vision of Sir Launfal" (p. 49) offers the mood appropriate for the June day of Anne's arrival, a day not just of spring but of spiritual challenge and renewal. Sir Launfal sets out to search for the Grail and encounters a begging leper, to whom he bestows a piece of gold out of a sense of duty. Returning many years later to his castle, he meets the same leper again but now sees in him the image of Christ, and shares with him his crust of bread for Christ's sake. The leper is then revealed as Christ himself, who tells Sir Launfal that the grail is the wooden cup of charity they have drunk from and that "Who bestows himself with alms feeds three, / Himself, his hungering neighbor, and Me." This reference turns Matthew into a humble knight on a quest whose action of generosity toward a person apparently commonplace is foreshadowed by the active event of charity in Lowell's poem. John Greenleaf Whittier, America's "fireside poet" par excellence, supplies the phrase "loss in all familiar things" from *Snow-Bound, A Winter Idyll* (p. 382). Whittier's expression of recollection, of the pain of memory experienced by a speaker recollecting a sister and her loss, is drawn in to express the important intimacy of the loss of Matthew. And James Whitcomb Riley's poem "Away" fulfills a similar function (see p. 383).

The English poets perform a function somewhat different from the American ones in *Anne*. If allusions to American poets evoke moral sympathy and quiet effort, allusions to the English poets draw on vivid representations of triumph and disaster. Byron, along with Scott cited in Montgomery's journals as one of her favorite poets (*SJ* II: 146), is not left out of *Anne*. When Anne becomes separated from Diana (p. 195), Montgomery quotes *Childe Harold's Pilgrimage*, which runs thus in the original: "The Caesar's pageant, shorn of Brutus' bust, / Did but of Rome's best Son remind her more" (Canto IV, Stanza 59).

An embedded quotation is sometimes also used with humorous effect. When the Allans dine at Green Gables, the dinner is successful until culinary disaster strikes in disguise: "All went merry as a marriage bell until Anne's layer cake was passed" (p. 241). This reference constitutes an allusion to Byron's description of the great party in Brussels that comes to a sinister end (Canto III, Stanza 21):

There was a sound of revelry by night,
And Belgium's capital had gather'd then
Her Beauty and her Chivalry, and bright
The lamps shone o'er fair women and brave
    men;
And all went merry as a marriage bell;
But hush! hark! a deep sound strikes like a ris-
    ing knell!

Anne's terrible cake is thus equated hyperbolically with the giant upheaval and disaster of the Battle of Waterloo.

Neither Wordsworth nor the Brownings figure in the account of the holdings in the Macneills' library, yet they are important in *Anne*. Montgomery takes from Wordsworth the title of her Chapter 36, "The Glory and the Dream," from "Ode: Intimations of Immortality from Recollections of Early Childhood." This phrase from Wordsworth summons up the theme of the entire poem, that one's childhood harmony with the cosmos and transcendental vision of the world are lost with the advent of adulthood, which provokes a sober recognition of mortality. The child loses the "vision splendid" in becoming an adult, seeing then by "the light of common day." In the chapter for which the quotation serves as title, Anne is on the threshold of gaining her adult consciousness. Her bright dreams are on the verge of being realized, but this chapter just before Matthew's death puts an end to her childhood, and her young womanhood begins. Her subsequent gain in moral strength is, in Wordsworth's poignant verse, paid for by the loss of vision. It seems no accident that in this same chapter Marilla is to visit a "distinguished oculist" about her own failing vision. The first strophe of Wordsworth's ode ends with the line "The things which I have seen I now can see no more," and the middle of the poem strikes us with the anguished questions "Whither is fled the visionary gleam? / Where is it now, the glory and the dream?" The very idea of "the glory and the dream" is itself a conceptualizing of loss.

The vivid Brownings supply material directly to aid in the description of Montgomery's heroine. Anne in her late girlhood is described in a phrase drawn from Elizabeth Barrett Browning's *Aurora Leigh*: that Anne is a moonbeam illustrates not only her beauty but her virginity, her unripened quality, her spiritual power. The heroine of Barrett Browning's long poem is a woman writer. Both Aurora Leigh and Barrett Browning were doubtless significant to Montgomery, as to other women writers. In her fantasy story about Geraldine, Cordelia, and Bertram (pp. 280–82), Anne is presumably influenced by Barrett Browning's "Lady Geraldine's Courtship," in which Geraldine's lover is also named Bertram. Anne supplies her own alter-ego, Cordelia, in her story, thus making it one of friendship and jealousy, a subject more interesting to Anne than a simple heterosexual romance, for she weeps at the very thought of Diana as a bride.

Robert Browning's "Evelyn Hope" supplies the epigraph to the entire novel. The chosen couplet gives an impression of the divinely appointed power of personality, of a female persona that can act also as an agent of fate and is acted on by fate. If Anne has "good stars," we know that she too has reason to feel hope, and not only she but we will catch hope from her stars.

The images from the Brownings—fire, dew, moonbeams—suggest a combination of the spiritual with the energetic. The Brownings belong to the most positive end of the poetic spectrum of Montgomery's prose. Tennyson, however, is the English poet drawn upon most freely and fully, and it is he who supplies the darker registers.

Tennyson might be called the prevailing poet of *Anne of Green Gables*. His influence is to be found not merely in obvious quotations but in the very language and idiom of the novel. Tennyson's "The Brook" stands behind the very first paragraph of the novel. The same poem is echoed, as well as Longfellow's, in the aforementioned title of Chapter 21, "Where the Brook and River Meet," and "The Brook" is resorted to again near the very end of the novel, where its phrase "mist of green" is picked up as a quotation (p. 370). The reference here to the mist created by spring buds returns us to the tone of the spring opening of the novel. Secret shades of Tennyson's brook harmonize with the personality of Anne and the hopeful progress of her life.

But if Tennyson is the dominant poet in *Anne,* he is also the one who is most argued with. Anne undertakes to identify herself with Tennyson and his unfortunate Elaine in her dramatic version of a section of *Idylls of the King* (ch. 28). The mistaken self-dramatization of herself as "the Unfortunate Lily Maid" puts her in the thraldom of imitation death; threatened with permanent silencing by the insistent water, she rapidly scrambles to safety, not at all in love with death. The images of Tennyson's Elaine suggest a purity of feminine silence, reflected in the "dumb servitor" who rows the romantic barge containing the corpse of the sad Elaine. The association here with the lily ties Anne-as-Elaine to the less fortunate Montgomery heroine in *Kilmeny of the Orchard,* who first appears surrounded by "Mary-lilies." This distressing heroine of an earlier work (revised, expanded, and republished by Montgomery after the success of *Anne*) is literally what contemporaries called "dumb." Kilmeny (how unlike Hawthorne's little Pearl) literally cannot speak, because her proud mother has been effectually silenced through the cruelty of the community. Anne's "chatter," in which she resembles Tennyson's living brook, shows her refusal to accept the roles of silence, reclusiveness, and self-repression that Tennyson seems to value in Elaine. The comic anticlimax of the catastrophe of Anne's venture into Tennysonian story is an implicit critique of Tennyson. Anne's romantic conception of death by drowning, the attempted rescue by a hero in her story "The Jealous Rival" in the preceding chapter, is also undercut by Anne's discovery that such a scenario may in fact be totally unromantic. She thus finds it more humiliating than gratifying to be rescued by Gilbert as she clings to a bridge pile.

The end of the novel employs the language of Tennyson's "The Palace of Art." In the novel's last scene, Avonlea at sunset is spread before the heroine: "all Avonlea lay before her in a dream-like afterlight 'a haunt of ancient peace'" (p. 394). This initially seems a satisfactory description of Avonlea, but if the original context of these lines is understood the matter becomes more troubling. The narrator of the poem has built himself his palace of art as a refuge from the pain of human life and decorated it with brilliant scenes of landscapes and human life. One of these representations (ll. 85–88) embodies the impressions of Englishness, safety, home:

> And one, an English home gray twilight pour'd
> On dewy pastures, dewy trees.
> Softer than sleep all things in order stores,
> A haunt of ancient peace.

What is wrong with this picture is that it is merely a picture, a pallid image promising escape from flesh-and-blood pain and struggle. Like other images in the "Palace of Art," it leads to stagnation. In this closing scene Anne, who has been mourning Matthew, turns from the retreating mood and quiescent desires invoked in the Tennyson quotation when she meets Gilbert and then blushes, proving herself of blood and desire. She meets him "half-way down the hill" (p. 394) and continues her walk into human life, ridding herself of the loftiness of the cemetery hill and the yearning for too much of "peace."

Montgomery takes the first and last words of *Anne* from Browning, who supplies not only the epigraph but the last sentence: "'God's in his heaven, all's right with the world,' whispered Anne softly" (p. 396). This is a well-known quotation from a poem not so well known, Browning's long narrative work *Pippa Passes* (1841), a species of poetic drama with some scenes in prose. Pippa, the heroine, is apparently an orphan girl of the people (actually one cheated of her inheritance) who works in the silk mills. On her one day's holiday she determines to enjoy herself by

going out and seeing God's world. As she wanders through the countryside singing she profoundly affects the feelings and actions of others whom she unknowingly encounters as she passes by, affecting them at crises in their lives, inspiring one young man to take revolutionary action. At the end of Part I she unwittingly brings an end to a murderous and adulterous love affair when the lover overhears her singing this song (ll. 222–29):

> The year's at the spring
> And day's at the morn;
> Morning's at seven;
> The hill-side's dew-pearled;
> The lark's on the wing;
> The snail's on the thorn:
> God's in his heaven—
> All's right with the world!

Illustration by Gustave Doré for the poem "Lancelot and Elaine," by Alfred, Lord Tennyson.

Pippa cannot know the influence she has on others, and part of what she does is unconscious. She is a conduit of grace and an inspirer of spiritual energy, as is Anne. Like Anne, Pippa is a democratic heroine and her last song (repeating the first lines of her first song) speaks against hierarchy and for the holiness of all people, especially laborers (Part IV, ll. 113–15):

All service ranks the same with God—
With God, whose puppets, best and worst,
Are we: there is no last nor first.

Anne, who is taking up her service at Green Gables and having to forego for the present the higher and more glamorous path of a university career, is here also reassuring herself of this truth in her closing allusion to Pippa.

SONGS

Sheet music covers from "My Home on the Hill" by W. C. Baker (1866) and "Far above the Daisies," by George Cooper and Harrison Millard (1869).

"[Nelly of] The Hazel Dell" by George Frederick Root (1852), as found in the collection Heart Songs Dear to the American People *(1909).*

LITERARY WORKS AND RECITATION PIECES

THE BATTLE OF HOHENLINDEN

"The Battle of Hohenlinden," or "Hohenlinden," is a poem by Scottish poet and journalist Thomas Campbell (1777–1844). He was born on July 27, 1777, in Glasgow. In 1803 he moved to London and remained there until shortly before his death. During his long period of absence from Scotland he maintained links with his homeland through a friendship with Sir Walter Scott. He was also three times Lord Rector of the University of Glasgow. Although Campbell's literary interests led to the publication of long poems like *Gertrude of Wyoming* (1808) and *Theodoric* (1824), he is best remembered for his composition of such stirring ballads as "Hohenlinden" and "Lord Ullin's Daughter," both popular recitation pieces.

> On Linden, when the sun was low,
> All bloodless lay the untrodden snow,
> And dark as winter was the flow
> Of Iser, rolling rapidly.

> But Linden saw another sight,
> When the drum beat at dead of night,
> Commanding fires of death to light
> The darkness of her scenery.

> By torch and trumpet fast arrayed,
> Each horseman drew his battle-blade,
> And furious every charger neighed
> To join the dreadful revelry.

> Then shook the hills with thunder riven,
> Then the steed to battle driven,

> And louder than the bolts of heaven
> Far flashed the red artillery.

> But redder yet that light shall glow
> On Linden's hills of stained snow
> And bloodier yet the torrent flow
> Of Iser, rolling rapidly.

> 'Tis morn; but scarce yon level sun
> Can pierce the war-clouds, rolling dun,
> Where furious Frank and fiery Hun
> Shout in their sulphurous canopy.

> The combat deepens. On, ye brave,
> Who rush to glory, or the grave!
> Wave, Munich! all thy banners wave,
> And charge with all thy chivalry!

> Few, few shall part, where many meet;
> The snow shall be their winding-sheet;
> And every turf beneath their feet
> Shall be a soldier's sepulchre.

EDINBURGH AFTER FLODDEN

This poetic narrative of the Battle of Flodden is by William Edmonstoune Aytoun (1813–1865), a poet, humorist, and lawyer. It appeared in *Lays of the Scottish Cavaliers and Other Poems* (1849), for which he is best remembered. The Battle of Flodden was fought on September 9, 1513, between the armies of James IV of Scotland and the Earl of Surrey on behalf of Henry VIII of England. James had been drawn into the war through the "Auld Alliance" with France. The Scottish army, consisting of Highland

and Lowland troops, surrendered their superior tacti-
cal position and were defeated by the larger English
force. King James was killed in the battle, along with
several nobles and members of the royal household
and, according to English sources, 12,000 Scots sol-
diers. This version from the *Sixth Royal Reader*
(59–62) teaches the vocabulary words *lamentation,
mischance, overthrow, piteous,* and *shrieking,* among others. This battle is also described in Canto 6 of Sir
Walter Scott's *Marmion: A Tale of Flodden Field.* See
also n. 4, ch. 2.

News of battle! news of battle!—
 Hark! 'tis ringing down the street:
And the archways and the pavement
 Bear the clang of hurrying feet.
News of battle? who hath brought it?
 News of triumph? who should bring
Tidings from our noble army,
 Greetings from our gallant King?
All last night we watched the beacons
 Blazing on the hills afar,
Each one bearing, as it kindled,
 Message of the opened war.
All night long the northern streamers
 Shot across the trembling sky:
Fearful lights, that never beacon
 Save when kings or heroes die.

News of battle! who hath brought it?
 All are thronging to the gate;—
"Warder—warder! open quickly!
 Man—is this a time to wait?"
And the heavy gates are opened:
 Then a murmur long and loud,
And a cry of fear and wonder
 Bursts from out the bending crowd.
For they see in battered harness
 Only one hard-stricken man;
And his weary steed is wounded,
 And his cheek is pale and wan:

Spearless hangs a bloody banner
 In his weak and drooping hand—
What! can that be Randolph Murray,
 Captain of the city band?

Round him crush the people, crying,
 "Tell us all—oh, tell us true!
Where are they who went to battle,
 Randolph Murray, sworn to you?
Where are they, our brothers—children?
 Have they met the English foe?
Why art thou alone, unfollowed?—
 Is it weal, or is it woe?"
Like a corpse the grisly warrior
 Looks from out his helm of steel;
But no word he speaks in answer,
 Only with his armed heel
Chides his weary steed, and onward
 Up the city streets they ride;
Fathers, sisters, mothers, children,
 Shrieking, praying by his side.
"By the God that made thee, Randolph!
 Tell us what mischance hath come."
Then he lifts his riven banner,
 And the asker's voice is dumb.

The elders of the city
 Have met within their hall—
The men whom good King James had charged
 To watch the tower and wall.
"Your hands are weak with age," he said,
 "Your hearts are stout and true:
So bide ye in the Maiden Town,
 While others fight for you.
And if, instead of Scottish shouts,
 Ye hear the English drum, . . .
Then let the warning bells ring out,
 Then gird you to the fray,
Then man the walls like burghers stout,
 And fight while fight you may.
'Twere better that in fiery flame

The roofs should thunder down,
Than that the foot of foreign foe
Should trample in the town!"

Then in came Randolph Murray,—
    His step was slow and weak;
And, as he doffed his dinted helm,
    The tears ran down his cheek:
They fell upon his corselet,
    And on his mailed hand,
As he gazed round him wistfully,
    Leaning sorely on his brand.
And none who then beheld him
    But straight were smote with fear,
For a bolder and a sterner man
    Had never couched a spear.
They knew so sad a messenger
    Some ghastly news must bring:
And all of them were fathers,
    And their sons were with the King.

And up then rose the Provost—
    A brave old man was he,
Of ancient name, and knightly fame,
    And chivalrous degree....
Oh, woful now was the old man's look,
    And he spake right heavily—
"Now, Randolph, tell thy tidings,
    However sharp they be!
Woe is written on thy visage,
    Death is looking from thy face:
Speak!—though it be of overthrow,
    It cannot be disgrace!"

Right bitter was the agony
    That wrung that soldier proud:
Thrice did he strive to answer,
    And thrice he groaned aloud.
Then he gave the riven banner
    To the old man's shaking hand,
Saying—"That is all I bring ye

From the bravest of the land!
Ay! ye may look upon it—
    It was guarded well and long,
By your brothers and your children,
    By the valiant and the strong.
One by one they fell around it,
    As the archers laid them low,
Grimly dying, still unconquered,
    With their faces to the foe.
Ay! well ye may look upon it—
    There is more than honour there,
Else, be sure, I had not brought it
    From the field of dark despair.
Never yet was royal banner
    Steeped in such a costly dye;—
It hath lain upon a bosom
    Where no other shroud shall lie.
Sirs! I charge you, keep it holy,
    Keep it as a sacred thing,
For the stain ye see upon it
    Was—the life-blood of your King!"

Woe, woe and lamentation!
    What a piteous cry was there!
Widows, maidens, mothers, children,
    Shrieking, sobbing in despair! ...
"O the blackest day for Scotland
    That she ever knew before!
O our King! the good, the noble,
    Shall we see him never more?
Woe to us, and woe to Scotland!—
    O our sons, our sons and men!
Surely some have 'scaped the Southron,
    Surely some will come again!"—
Till the oak that fell last winter
    Shall uprear its shattered stem,
Wives and mothers of Dunedin,
    Ye maye look in vain for them!

BINGEN ON THE RHINE

This popular poem is by Caroline Sheridan Norton (1808–1877), the third child of Thomas Sheridan and Henrietta Callander of Craigforth, Scotland, and the granddaughter of dramatist Richard Brinsley Sheridan. "Bingen on the Rhine" appears in the *Sixth Royal Reader* (26–27) where the note informs us that "the spirit of the poem is independent of place or time. It gives expression, in a very touching way, to the dying thoughts of a soldier stricken down in a foreign land, far away from friends and home." "Bingen" teaches the words *faltered, foreign,* and *mournful.*

A soldier of the Legion lay dying in Algiers;
There was lack of woman's nursing, there was
    dearth of woman's tears;
But a comrade stood beside him, while his life-
    blood ebbed away,
And bent, with pitying glances, to hear what he
    might say.
The dying soldier faltered, as he took that com-
    rade's hand,
And he said: "I never more shall see my own, my
    native land:
Take a message and a token to some distant
    friends of mine;
For I was born at Bingen — at Bingen on the
    Rhine.

"Tell my brothers and companions, when they
    meet and crowd around,
To hear my mournful story, in the pleasant vine-
    yard ground,
That we fought the battle bravely; and when the
    day was done,
Full many a corpse lay ghastly pale beneath the
    setting sun.
And amidst the dead and dying were some grown
    old in wars —
The death-wound on the gallant breasts, the last
    of many scars;

But some were young, and suddenly beheld life's
    morn decline;
And one had come from Bingen — fair Bingen
    on the Rhine.

"Tell my mother that her other sons shall comfort
    her old age,
And I was aye a truant bird, that thought his
    home a cage;
For my father was a soldier, and, even as a child,
My heart leaped forth to hear him tell of strug-
    gles fierce and wild;
And when he died, and left us to divide his scanty
    hoard,
I let them take whate'er they would, but kept my
    father's sword;
And with boyish love I hung it where the bright
    light used to shine,
On the cottage-wall at Bingen — calm Bingen on
    the Rhine!

"Tell my sister not to weep for me, and sob with
    drooping head,
When the troops are marching home again, with
    glad and gallant tread;
But to look upon them proudly, with a calm and
    steadfast eye,
For her brother was a soldier too, and not afraid
    to die.
And if a comrade seek her love, then ask her in
    my name
To listen to him kindly, without regret or shame;
And to hang the old sword in its place (my
    father's sword and mine),
For the honour of old Bingen — dear Bingen on
    the Rhine!

"There's *another* — not a sister: in the happy days
    gone by,
You'd have known her by the merriment that
    sparkled in her eye;

Too innocent for coquetry—too fond for idle
    scorning!—
O friend, I fear the lightest heart makes some-
    times heaviest mourning!
Tell her the last night of my life (for ere this
    moon be risen
My body will be out of pain—my soul be out of
    prison)
I dreamed I stood with *her*, and saw the yellow
    sunlight shine
On the vine-clad hills of Bingen—fair Bingen
    on the Rhine.

"I saw the blue Rhine sweep along; I heard, or
    seemed to hear,
The German songs we used to sing in chorus
    sweet and clear;
And down the pleasant river, and up the slanting
    hill,
That echoing chorus sounded, through the
    evening calm and still;
And her glad blue eyes were on me, as we passed
    with friendly talk
Down many a path beloved of yore, and well-
    remembered walk;
And her little hand lay lightly, confidingly in
    mine;—
But we'll meet no more at Bingen—loved
    Bingen on the Rhine!"

His voice grew faint and hoarser; his grasp was
    childish weak;
His eyes put on a dying look; he sighed, and
    ceased to speak:
His comrade bent to lift him, but the spark of life
    had fled;
The soldier of the Legion in a foreign land—was
    dead!
And the soft moon rose up slowly, and calmly she
    looked down
On the red sand of the battle-field, with bloody
    corpses strown;

Yea, calmly on that dreadful scene her pale light
    seemed to shine,
As it shone on distant Bingen—fair Bingen on
    the Rhine!

ON THE DOWNFALL OF POLAND

This is an excerpt from Thomas Campbell's first, and
some think his best, poem "The Pleasures of Hope"
(1799), which contains the often-quoted line "'Tis
distance lends enchantment to the view." The subject
of this segment is the fall of General Kosciusko in
1793 and the loss of Poland's independence. The
poem appears in the *Fifth Royal Reader* (254–55).

Oh, sacred Truth! thy triumph ceased awhile,
And Hope, thy sister, ceased with thee to smile,
When leagued oppression poured to Northern
    wars
Her whiskered pandoors and her fierce hussars;
Waved her dread standard to the breeze of morn;
Pealed her loud drum, and twanged her trumpet-
    horn:
Tumultuous Horror brooded o'er her van;
Presaging wrath to Poland—and to man!

Warsaw's last champion from her height surveyed
Wide o'er the fields a waste of ruin laid:
"O Heaven!" he cried, "my bleeding country
    save!
Is there no hand on high to shield the brave?
Yet, though Destruction sweep those lovely plains,
Rise, fellow-men! Our country yet remains!
By that dread name we wave the sword on high!
And swear for her to live!—with her to die!"

He said; and on the rampart-heights arrayed
His trusty warriors,—few, but undismayed;
Firm-paced and slow, a horrid front they form,
Still as the breeze, but dreadful as the storm;

Low, murmuring sounds along their banners fly,
"Revenge or death!"—the watchword and reply;
Then pealed the notes, omnipotent to charm,
And the loud tocsin tolled their last alarm!

In vain, alas!—in vain, ye gallant few!
From rank to rank your volleyed thunder flew:—
Oh, bloodiest picture in the book of Time!
Poor Poland fell, unwept, without a crime!
Found not a generous friend, a pitying foe,
Strength in her arms, nor mercy in her woe!
Dropped from her nerveless grasp the shattered
    spear,
Closed her bright age, and curbed her high
    career:
Hope, for a season, bade the world farewell,
And Freedom shrieked—as KOSCIUSKO fell!

The sun went down, nor ceased the carnage
    there,—
Tumultuous Murder shook the midnight air;
On Prague's proud arch the fires of Ruin glow,
His blood-dyed waters murmuring below;
The storm prevails—the rampart yields a way—
Bursts the wild cry of horror and dismay!
Hark! As the smouldering piles with thunder fall,
A thousand shrieks for hopeless mercy call!—
Earth shook! red meteors flashed along the sky!
And conscious Nature shuddered at the cry!

Departed spirits of the mighty dead!
Ye that at Marathon and Leuctra bled!
Friends of the world! restore your swords to man,
Fight in his sacred cause, and lead the van!
Yet for poor Poland's tears of blood atone,
And make her arm puissant as your own!
Oh! once again to Freedom's cause return
The patriot Tell—the Bruce of Bannockburn!

"The Dog at his Master's Grave" is from the **Third Royal Reader** *(first series).*

THE DOG AT HIS MASTER'S GRAVE.

An'guish, very great grief.
Ca-ressed', made much of ; fondled.
Con-trolled', kept in check ; ruled
Fleet, flying very quickly.
Gaunt, wasted away ; thin.
Grate'ful, full of thanks

Guard'ed, kept watch over.
Heed'ed, minded ; noticed.
Mor'tal, causing death ; deadly.
Pleas'ant-ly, in a kind way.
Quiv'er-ing, shaking from strong feeling ; trembling.

" HE will not come," said the gentle child ;
    And she patted the poor dog's head,
And she pleasantly* called him, and fondly smiled :
But he heeded* her not in his anguish* wild,
    Nor arose from his lowly bed.

'Twas his master's grave where he chose to rest—
    He guarded* it night and day ;
The love that glowed in his grateful* breast,
For the friend who had fed, controlled,* caressed,*
    Might never fade away.

And when the long grass rustled near,
    Beneath some hastening tread,

He started up with a quivering* ear,
For he thought 'twas the step of his master dear,
    Returning from the dead.

But sometimes, when a storm drew nigh,
    And the clouds were dark and fleet,*
He tore the turf with a mournful cry,
As if he would force his way, or die,
    To his much-loved master's feet.

So there, through the summer's heat, he lay,
    Till autumn nights grew bleak,
Till his eye grew dim with his hope's decay,
And he pined, and pined, and wasted away,
    A skeleton gaunt* and weak.

And oft the pitying children brought
    Their offerings of meat and bread,
And to coax him away to their homes they sought ;
But his buried master he ne'er forgot,
    Nor strayed from his lonely bed.

Cold winter came, with an angry sway,
    And the snow lay deep and sore ;
Then his moaning grew fainter day by day,
Till, close where the broken tomb-stone lay,
    He fell, to rise no more.

And when he struggled with mortal* pain,
    And Death was by his side,
With one loud cry, that shook the plain,
He called for his master—but called in vain ;
    Then stretched himself, and died.

                                        MRS. SIGOURNEY.

CURFEW MUST NOT RING TONIGHT

by Rose Hartwick Thorpe (1850–1939)

Slowly England's sun was setting o'er the hilltops
    far away,
Filling all the land with beauty at the close of one
    sad day;
And the last rays kissed the forehead of a man
    and maiden fair,
He with footsteps slow and weary, she with sunny
    floating hair;
He with bowed head, sad and thoughtful, she
    with lips all cold and white,
Struggling to keep back the murmur, "Curfew
    must not ring tonight!"

"Sexton," Bessie's white lips faltered, pointing to
    the prison old,
With its turrets tall and gloomy, with its walls,
    dark, damp and cold—
"I've a lover in the prison, doomed this very
    night to die
At the ringing of the curfew, and no earthly help
    is nigh.
Cromwell will not come till sunset"; and her face
    grew strangely white
As she breathed the husky whisper, "Curfew must
    not ring tonight!"

"Bessie," calmly spoke the sexton—and his
    accents pierced her heart
Like the piercing of an arrow, like a deadly poi-
    soned dart—
"Long, long years I've rung the curfew from that
    gloomy, shadowed tower;
Every evening, just at sunset, it has told the twi-
    light hour;
I have done my duty ever, tried to do it just and
    right—
Now I'm old I still must do it: Curfew, girl, must
    ring tonight!"

Wild her eyes and pale her features, stern and
    white her thoughtful brow,
And within her secret bosom Bessie made a
    solemn vow.
She had listened while the judges read, without a
    tear or sigh,
"At the ringing of the curfew, Basil Underwood
    must die."
And her breath came fast and faster, and her eyes
    grew large and bright,
As in undertone she murmured, "Curfew must
    not ring tonight!"

With quick step she bounded forward, sprang
    within the old church door,
Left the old man threading slowly paths he'd
    often trod before;
Not one moment paused the maiden, but with
    eye and cheek aglow
Mounted up the gloomy tower, where the bell
    swung to and fro
As she climbed the dusty ladder, on which fell no
    ray of light,
Up and up, her white lips saying, "Curfew shall
    not ring tonight!"

She has reached the topmost ladder, o'er her
    hangs the great dark bell;
Awful is the gloom beneath her like the pathway
    down to hell;
Lo, the ponderous tongue is swinging. 'Tis the
    hour of curfew now,
And the sight has chilled her bosom, stopped her
    breath and paled her brow;
Shall she let it ring? No, never! Flash her eyes
    with sudden light,
And she springs and grasps it firmly: "Curfew
    shall not ring tonight!"

Out she swung, far out; the city seemed a speck
    of light below;
She 'twixt heaven and earth suspended as the bell
    swung to and fro;

And the sexton at the bell rope, old and deaf,
    heard not the bell,
But he thought it still was ringing fair young
    Basil's funeral knell.
Still the maiden clung more firmly, and with
    trembling lips and white,
Said, to hush her heart's wild beating, "Curfew
    shall not ring tonight!"

It was o'er; the bell ceased swaying, and the
    maiden stepped once more
Firmly on the dark old ladder, where for hundred
    years before
Human foot had not been planted; but the brave
    deed she had done
Should be told long ages after—often as the set-
    ting sun
Should illume the sky with beauty, aged sires with
    heads of white,
Long should tell the little children, "Curfew did
    not ring that night."

O'er the distant hills came Cromwell; Bessie sees
    him, and her brow,
Full of hope and full of gladness, has no anxious
    traces now.
At his feet she tells her story, shows her hands all
    bruised and torn;
And her face so sweet and pleading, yet with sor-
    row pale and worn,
Touched his heart with sudden pity lit his eye
    with misty light;
"Go, your lover lives!" said Cromwell; "Curfew
    shall not ring tonight!"

HOW SOCKERY SET A HEN

Under the title "Setting a Hen," this piece was popular from the 1870s to the turn of the century and
was anthologized in *Shoemaker's Best Selections* and in
Best Things From Best Authors (Philadelphia: The Penn
Publishing Co., 1900). See also n. 11, ch. 19.

Meester Verris—I see dot mosd efferpoty wrides
someding for de shicken bapers nowtays, and I
tought praps meppe I can do dot too, as I wride
all apout vat dook blace mit me lasht summer;
you know—odor of you dond know, den I dells
you—dot Katrina (dot is mine vrow) und me, ve
keep some shickens for a long dime ago, und von
tay she sait to me, "Sockery" (dot is mein name),
"vy dond you put some of de aigs under dot olt
plue hen shickens, I dinks she vants to sate."
"Vell," I sait, "meppe I guess I vill"; so I bicked
out some uf de best aigs und dook um oud do de
parn fere de olt hen make her nesht in de side of
de haymow, poud five six veet up; now, you see, I
nefer vas ferry big up und town, but I vos putty
pig all de vay around in de mittle, so I koodn't
reach up dill I vent and get a parrel do stant on;
vell, I klimet on de parrel, und ven my hed rise
up by de nesht—dot olt hen gif me such a bick
dot my nose runs all ofer my face mit plood, und
ven I todge pack dot plasted olt parrel he preak,
und I vent town kershlam; I didn't tink I kood go
insite a parrel before, put dere I vos, und I fit so
dite dot I koodn't get me oud efferway, my fest
vas bushed vay up unter my armholes. Ven I fount
I vos dite shtuck, I holler "Katrina! Katrina!" und
ven she koom and see me shtuck in de parrel up
to my armholes, mit my face all plood and aigs,
she shust lait town on de hay und laft and laft, till
I got so mat I sait, "Vot you lay dere und laf like a
olt vool, eh? vy dond you koom bull me out?"
und she set up und sait, "Oh, vipe off your chin,
und bull your fest town"; den she lait back und
laft like she vood shblit herself more as ever. Mat

as I vas I tought to myself, Katrina, she sbeak English pooty goot, but I only sait, mit my greatest dignitude, "Katrina, vill you bull me oud dis parrel?" und she see dot I look booty red, so she said, "Of course I vill, Sockery"; den she lait me und de parrel town on our site, and I dook holt de door sill, und Katrina she bull on de parrel, but de first bull she mate I yellet "Donner und blitzen, shtop dat; dere is nails in de parrel!" you see de nails bent town ven I vent in, but ven I koom oud dey schticks in me all de vay round; vell, to make a short shtory long, I told Katrina to go und dell naypor Hausman to pring a saw und saw me dis parrel off; vell, he koom, und he like to shblit himself mit laf too, but he roll me ofer und saw de parrel all de va around off, und I get up mit half a parrel around my vaist; den Katrina she say, "Sockery, vait a little till I get a battern of dot new oferskirt you haf on," but I didn't sait a vort. I shust got a nife oud und vittle de hoops off und shling dot confountet olt parrel in de vootpile.

Pimeby ven I koom in de house Katrina she sait, so soft like, "Sockery, dond you goin' to but some aigs under dot olt blue hen?" Den I sait, in my deepest woice, "Katrina, uf you effer say dot to me again, I'll get a pill of wriding from de lawyer from you," und I dell you, she didn't say dot any more. Vell, Mr. Verris, ven I step on a parrel now, I dond step on it, I git a pox.

MARY, QUEEN OF SCOTS

This poem is by Henry Glassford Bell (1803–1874), a Scottish lawyer, poet, founder of the *Edinburgh Literary Journal*, and an ardent defendant of the reputation of Mary, Queen of Scots. Mary Stuart (1542–1587) was Queen of Scotland from infancy and maintained a claim on the crown on England also. She resided in Scotland from 1561 to 1567, when she fled to England. Mary was taken captive by her cousin Queen Elizabeth I, held a prisoner for twenty years, and finally beheaded upon Elizabeth's order at Fotheringay Castle. In her journal (*SJ* III [Jan. 27, 1922]: 38), Montgomery comments: "I've always been on Elizabeth's side in that famous struggle. . . . Mary Stuart has intrigued the world's fancy by her charm, her passion, her tragedies, her misfortunes. Elizabeth, by contrast, seems sordid and shrewish. Yet in spite of all this I am glad she won. I think, though, she made a mistake in executing Mary." Yet Montgomery's heroines are sometimes identified with Mary (see *Emily of New Moon*, ch. 28, and *Anne of Windy Poplars*, ch. 5). The poem appears in the *Fifth Royal Reader* (38–39).

I looked far back into other years, and lo, in
    bright array
I saw, as in a dream, the form of ages passed away.
It was a stately convent with its old and lofty
    walls,
And gardens with their broad green walks, where
    soft the footstep falls;
And o'er the antique dial stones the creeping
    shadows passed,
And all around the noonday sun a drowsy radi-
    ance cast.
No sound of busy life was heard, save from the
    cloisters dim
The tinkling of the silver bell, or the sisters' holy
    hymn.
And there five noble maidens sat beneath the
    orchard trees,
In that first budding spring of youth, when all its
    prospects please;
And little recked they, when they sang, or knelt at
    vesper prayers,
That Scotland knew no prouder names — held
    none more dear than theirs;
And little even the loveliest thought, before the
    Virgin's shrine,
Of royal blood and high descent from the ancient
    Stuart line;

Calmly her happy days flew on, uncounted in
   their flight,
And as they flew they left behind a long-continu-
   ing light. . . .

The scene was changed: it was an eve of raw and
   surly mood,
And in a turret chamber high of ancient
   Holyrood
Sat Mary, listening to the rain and sighing with
   the winds
That seemed to suit the stormy state of men's
   uncertain minds.
The touch of care had blanched her cheek, her
   smile was sadder now,
The weight of royalty had pressed too heavy on
   her brow;
And traitors to her councils came, and rebels to
   the field;
The Stuart sceptre well she swayed, but the sword
   she could not wield.
She thought of all her blighted hopes, the dreams
   of youth's brief day,
And summoned Rizzio with his lute, and bade
   the minstrel play
The songs she loved in early years—the songs of
   gay Navarre,
The songs perchance that erst were sung by gal-
   lant Chattilor.
They half beguiled her of her cares, they soothed
   her into smiles,
They won her thoughts from bigot zeal and fierce
   domestic broils;
But hark, the tramp of armed men, the Douglas'
   battle cry!
They come! they come! and lo, the scowl of
   Ruthven's hollow eye!
The swords are drawn, the daggers gleam, the
   tears and words are vain—
The ruffian steel is in his heart, the faithful
   Rizzio's slain!

Then Mary Stuart dashed aside the tears that
   trickling fell:
"Now for my father's arm!" she cried; "my
   woman's heart farewell!" . . .

The scene was changed: it was a lake, with one
   small lonely isle,
And there, within the prison walls of its baronial
   pile,
Stern men stood menacing their queen, till she
   should stoop to sign
The traitorous scroll that snatched the crown
   from her ancestral line;
"My lords, my lords," the captive said, "were I but
   once more free,
With ten good knights on yonder shore to aid my
   cause and me,
This parchment would I scatter wide to every
   breeze that blows,
And once more reign a Stuart queen o'er my
   remorseless foes!"
A red spot burned upon her cheek, streamed her
   rich tresses down,
She wrote the words, she stood erect, a queen
   without a crown!

The scene was changed: beside the block a sullen
   headsman stood,
And gleamed the broad axe in his hand, that soon
   must drip with blood.
With slow and steady step there came a Lady
   through the hall,
And breathless silence chained the lips and
   touched the hearts of all.
I knew that queenly form again, though blighted
   was its bloom;
I saw that grief and decked it out—an offering
   for the tomb!
I knew that eye, though faint its light, that once
   so brightly shone;

I knew the voice, though feeble now, that thrilled
    with every tone;
I knew the ringlets almost grey, once threads of
    living gold;
I knew that bounding grace of step, that symme-
    try of mould!

Even now I see her far away in that calm convent
    aisle,
I hear her chant her vesper hymn, I mark her
    holy smile;
Even now I see her bursting forth upon the bridal
    morn,
A new star in the firmament, to light and glory
    born!
Alas, the change! she placed her foot upon a triple
    throne,
And on the scaffold now she stands—beside the
    block—alone!
The little dog that licks her hand the last of all
    the crowd
Who sunned themselves beneath her glance, and
    round her footsteps bowed.
Her neck is bared—the blow is struck—the soul
    is passed away!
The bright—the beautiful—is now a bleeding
    piece of clay.
The dog is moaning piteously; and, as it gurgles
    o'er,
Laps the warm blood that trickling runs
    unheeded to the floor.
The blood of beauty, wealth and power, the
    heart-blood of a queen,
The noblest of the Stuart race, the fairest earth
    has seen,
Lapped by a dog! Go think of it, in silence and
    alone;
Then weigh against a grain of sand the glories of
    a throne.

THE SOCIETY FOR THE SUPPRESSION OF GOSSIP

From T. S. Denison, *Friday Afternoon Series of Dialogues: A Collection of Original Dialogues Suitable for Boys and Girls in School Entertainments* (1879). Freeport, N.Y.: Books for Libraries Press; Granger Index Reprint Series, 1970.

Characters (in order of appearance):

MRS. HARTWELL, Chairman
MISS BETSEY PRUDENCE, Secretary, with a
    squeaky voice
MISS WISE, with glasses
MRS. MAJOR WARNER, with a military disposi-
    tion
MRS. STARCH
MISS NUTT
MRS. FILBERT
MRS. RIPPLE

All busy talking as the curtain rises.

MRS. HARTWELL (*raps on the table*): The society
will please come to order. (All quiet.) Sisters, you
all know what we have met for, so let us proceed
at once to business. Miss Prudence, is there any
unfinished business before the society?
MISS PRUDENCE: Mrs. President, I think the
business is about all unfinished. All we did at the
last meeting was to organize.
MRS. H: To be sure, we all know that. But was
there not some particular matter left over?
MISS P: Oh, certainly. This society agreed at the
last meeting to call itself the "Society for the
Suppression of Gossip," and furthermore formerly
voted to discuss methods of suppression the first
thing at this meeting.
MISS WISE: And I think we had better begin at
once. What is the use of delay, when we agreed to
take that up the first thing?

MRS. STARCH (*with show of dignity*): Miss Wise, you forget that certain formalities must always be gone through with in parliamentary bodies.

MISS W: Indeed! This is a parliamentary body is it? Well, I should not have known it if you hadn't told me. I'm not in favor of making a body of any kind out of this society, and wasting the time in reading minutes and voting and discussing. That is what the men do.

MRS. S: I don't care a hair-pin what the men do, but I want things done properly.

MRS. FILBERT: And so do I. But what is the sense of so much ceremony?

MISS NUTT: That is just what I want to know.

MRS. MAJOR WARNER: It is fitting that our society should do everything with due deliberation, and keep a proper record. The eyes of the world are on us.

MISS W: If we don't do less talking, the *ears* of the world will be on us.

MISS MAJ: Who is talking, I should like to know? For my part the voice of Mrs. Major Warner shall always be for *deliberation*.

MISS W: *Deliberation!* That is just what the men do. They meet and deliberate. And what does it all amount to?

MRS. RIPPLE: Mrs. Chairman, call this house to order. Here we have been talking for half an hour about nothing. I am in a great hurry to get home. Why can't we begin?

MRS. H (*raps*): Order! The next thing before the house is to suggest the best methods for the prevention and suppression of gossip.

MRS. MAJ: Is this discussion to be carried on in a dignified manner and proper record made in the journal, or is to be an undignified jumble of remarks.

MRS. S: I think the lady's language reflects.

MRS. MAJ (*snappishly*): On whom?

MRS. H: What is the pleasure of the society?

MISS W: My pleasure is that we don't want any *discussion*. Discussion is what the men like, and I don't want to be like a horrid man.

MRS. MAJ. Miss Wise, if you had married a horrid man long ago, you might have a different opinion of them.

MISS W: Oh I dare say it wouldn't improve my opinion of them.

MRS. STARCH: For my part I have never regretted that I became Mrs. Starch.

MRS. MAJ: Nor do I regret that I became Mrs. Major Warner. Men are not so bad after all, if you know how to manage them. *I* never feared matrimony.

MISS W: Nor would I, but men aren't worth the managing. I have a higher mission than to manage an insignificant man.

MRS. FILBERT (*aside*): Good reason! You can't get a man to manage.

MISS NUTT: Mrs. President, if we are not going to talk about anything but matrimony, how are we going to suppress gossip?

MISS P: We are wasting our valuable time. If we have a mission, we had better begin; if we have not, we had better go home.

MRS R: So say I.

MISS N: And I

MRS. F: And I.

MRS. H: I suppose the members of the society all have their views upon the subject of the suppression of gossip, and are ready to state them.

MISS W: I have mine, and am prepared to state them to the point.

MRS. MAJ (*with dignity*): I have mine, and am prepared to state them becomingly.

MISS W (*aside*): And tediously.

MRS. H: I shall by virtue of my position, state my views first.

MISS P (*aside to another*): It would 'a looked better if she had called on somebody else first.

MRS. H: I think the best way to stop gossip is, to have people stop talking about one another. When that is done, gossip will die of itself. I have resolved that I will not say anything at all when people come to me with stories, and some of them do come pretty often. They are near neighbors, too.

MRS. S: Whom do you mean, I'd like to know.

MRS. H: Oh, I shan't mention any names. Come to think of it, that is a good idea too. If you must talk, don't mention any names.

MRS. F: But what are you going to do for news? A body must have news.

MISS N: And how are you to avoid mentioning names if people ask you?

MRS H: Don't tell 'em. Let 'em guess. They will guess near enough. If you want news, my plan don't prevent *listening* when people talk to you, only do not, for the life of you, mention any names.

MISS W: That plan won't work.

MRS. H (*with dignity*): Perhaps some member will present a better one.

MRS. MAJ: It has no method to it.

MISS W: It has too much method.

MRS. S: The method seems to be to hear all you can, and say all you can, but don't mention any names.

MRS. R: It won't work.

MRS. H (*spiteful*): Tried it, have you? Now, Mrs. Starch, will you present a *better* plan?

MRS S: I will try. The late lamented Mr. Starch always used to say, my dear, be careful how you speak. It is not so much what you say, as how you say it. Now, there is the secret of the whole process in a nutshell. Be careful *how* you say things.

MISS W: That is a very good *family* regulation, but it would not effect much in public. Doubtless the late lamented Mr. Starch intended that excellent maxim strictly for domestic use.

MRS. S: I *will not* have the memory of the late Mr. Starch insulted. I shall not proceed further if I can not be protected from unbecoming interruptions. (*Seats herself with stately disdain.*)

MISS W: My idea in regard to suppressing gossip is to suppress it. What is the use of talking about it. Let everybody stop gossiping and the thing is done. When people talk to you don't encourage them. Tell them you do not wish to hear it. When a horrid man elopes with some other horrid man's wife, pay no attention to it. You can read it all up in the papers, and get it all at once. Woman must have the news. She has a mission, and should store her mind. But let her store it from the papers.

MISS P: I declare! That is worse than talking.

MISS W: If you please, Miss Betsey Prudence, I will state my opinions first.

MRS. F: How about that trouble with the Smiths?

MISS W (*sarcastically*): Oh, I am glad you mentioned that. I can tell you all about it. Everybody believes that Smith beats his wife. I happened to say so. I mentioned it to but five or six people. They went and told it and that is where the trouble comes in. If people did not tell what you told them, there would be no need of suppressing gossip.

MRS. MAJ: Better not tell them anything.

MISS N: Just what I think.

MRS. MAJ: Major Warner, my husband, says, always to move on the enemy in proper military order. That is the motto of his wife, Mrs. Major Warner. Take the enemy in detail, and compel him to surrender. I would have a pledge circulated for ladies to sign by which they would pledge themselves to abstain from gossip all the rest of their lives.

SEVERAL: Oh, no! No! Dreadful!

MRS. H: Every lady who signs such a pledge would admit herself to be a gossip. It would never work.

MRS. S: I should consider it the the very worst thing we could do for our noble cause.

MISS P: Such a measure would be a little too strong.

MRS. R: You don't catch me signing such a

paper. When I want to talk I'll talk. Oh, I nearly
forgot. Mr. Ripple is conducting that divorce case
in the county court. He says the developments are
startling, and from what he told me at noon, I
should say they were.

MISS W (*running to Mrs. R.*): Do tell us.

MRS. MAJ: Wait till I finish my speech.

MRS. S: Oh, bother your speech.

MISS N: Go on, Mrs. Ripple.

MRS. F: Please do.

MRS. MAJ: As I said, I would have a pledge
drawn up in due form—

MISS P: Oh, Mrs. Ripple, do not keep us in suspense.

MRS. R: Well, you all know that Mr. Henry
Dellmont overheard—

MRS. MAJ (*rushing up*): What was that about Mr.
Dellmont? (*All rush up around Mrs. R. crying,* "Go
on, go on!" *Curtain falls.*)

THE FAIRY QUEEN

This poem by Bishop Thomas Percy (1729–1811)
could be found in recitation and poetry books from
1878 until well past the turn of the century.

Come, follow, follow me,
You, fairy elves that be:
Which circle on the greene,
Come follow Mab your queene.
Hand in hand let's dance around,
For this place is fairye ground.

When mortals are at rest,
And snoring in their nest;
Unheard, and unespy'd,
Through key-holes we do glide;
Over tables, stools, and shelves,
We trip it with our fairy elves.

And, if the house be foul
With platter, dish, or bowl,

Up stairs we nimbly creep,
And find the sluts asleep:
There we pinch their armes and thighes;
None escapes, nor none espies.

But if the house be swept,
And from uncleaness kept,
We praise the houshold maid,
And duely she is paid:
For we use before we goe
To drop a tester in her shoe.

Upon a mushroomes head
Our table-cloth we spread;
A grain of rye, or wheat,
Is manchet, which we eat;
Pearly drops of dew we drink
In acorn cups fill'd to the brink.

The brains of nightingales,
With unctuous fat of snailes,
Between two cockles stew'd,
Is meat that's easily chew'd;
Tailes of wormes, and marrow of mice
Do make a dish, that's wonderous nice.

The grasshopper, gnat, and fly,
Serve for our minstrelsie;
Grace said, we dance a while,
And so the time beguile:
And if the moon doth hide her head,
The gloe-worm lights us home to bed.

On tops of dewie grasse
So nimbly do we passe,
The young and tender stalk
Ne'er bends when we do walk:
Yet in the morning may be seen
Where we the night before have been.

MARS LA TOUR, OR, THE MAIDEN'S VOW

A LEGEND OF 1870-1871

by Stafford MacGregor, late British Vice-Consul, late German Vice-Consul. Privately printed, Southampton, 1883. Courtesy of the English Language Collection, The British Library.

In the valley of Avranches, the vespers were ring-
    ing,
A lullaby soft at the close of the day,
The white fleecy clouds the sunset was tinging
With many hued lights fading swiftly away,
Oft darkening to purple, now brightening to
    crimson,
Here braiding the edges with bands of bright
    gold,
As though the Aurora would win from the ocean,
Once more the avow that at daylight was told,
And increase the deep love that was whispered at
    dawn,
By enriching in splendor her robe of the morn.

As peaceful and bright in the year's opening days,
As that sunset, O France! Was thy future por-
    trayed,
Though dark as the thunder-fraught cloud of the
    night,
Was that future when rolled page by page to the
    light.
O! where are the legions that bled for thy fame,
In the glory of victory on Austerlitz plain?
'Tis Valhubert of Avranches who heads the death
    roll,
"Died as general for France," so reads the scroll
On the statue in marble which Avranches has
    reared,
And which from his boyhood a grandson revered.

Not the fairest of maidens was Reinette de Veer,
Graceful in form, but of features severe,

Though equal in gifts always nature had blent,
And wreathed round her lips the smile of a saint,
And now as she hastens last adieux to hear
From that Valhubert's grandson, a young
    grenadier,
And nears the old abbey's ruined ivy clad aisle,
Her face wears in sadness that saintlike smile,
As kneeling she prays to our lady above
To shield from war's dangers her country and love.

As the white maid of Avenel, who of yore would
    appear
When a breast free of guile to her shrine should
    draw near
So a mystic white vision in the moonlight did
    gleam,
And in accents melodious as murmuring stream
To Reinette gave response, "thou art not alone,
At the altars of Munich, of Dresden, of Cologne,
Are Germany's daughters now breathing like
    prayer
For those who must shortly for battle prepare,
Imploring at foot of the glory girt throne
Protection for loved ones, for country, for home.

Alas! gentle maiden, as ten moons shall wane,
Each moon by ten thousand shall number the
    slain,
As the billows that surge in yon bay's wide
    expanse,
Their green graves shall rise o'er their birthland
    of France.
And the blood of her sons by their kindred shall
    flow,
And your Paris be wrapped in a mantle of woe,
Domremy shall mourn, Vancouleurs hear the wail
That is born on the wings of the death-laden
    gale,
And the ramparts of Orleans all powerless shall be
To arrest the inroad of that wide spreading sea.

To far Northern Cambray the war note soon
  speeds,
And Laon and proud Lille hear the clattering
  steeds,
Whose riders bear message of bloody fields lost,
And foretell the advance of that merciless host.
The echoes of Tinchebray ten leagues from your
  town
Shall fling back the notes of the conqueror's
  drum,
From the passes of Vosges to the channel's far
  shore
From the forest of Ardennes to the vine-bordered
  Loire,
Exulting and proud with victorious glance,
Black eagles shall wave o'er one-fifth of fair
  France.

The shrine of St. Genevieve desecrated shall be,
And palaces flame to the roofs topmost tree,
The Seine shall run red to Mante's ancient town,
Whose hamlets shall blaze and rafters crash down,
As in ages of yore when Duke William's bold
  band
Brought sword, flame and famine to ravage the
  land,
And whose wraith might well rise to see Calais in
  flames,
Rouen surrendered, Paris enchained,
And Normandy's sons, forgetting their line,
Marched by thousands as captives away to the
  Rhine.

Ah! Maurice, Reine faltered as forward he sped,
Methought that a vision appeared from the dead,
And grimly foreshadowed destruction and shame
To the sons of our country, but if with the slain
'Tis thy fate to be numbered, hear but my vow,
Ne'er at the high altar the knee I will bow,
As bride to another, but weep thee till death,
Encircle my brow with a funereal wreath,

And to another my troth I will plight,
Or cease to forget the adieu of to-night.

The forest of Scissy shall start from their bed,
Those forests that now deep in ocean are hid,
And the floods that surge hoarse in yonder broad
  bay,
Shall cease to spread shoreward their murmuring
  lay,
And St. Michael's weird towers that loom through
  the mist
Shall quake to their basement and crumble to
  dust,
And—but derisive and sharp o'er the deep shad-
  owed glade
The notes of departure a bugle now played,
Proclaiming the hour of their parting was near,
To young Maurice Valhubert and Reinette de
  Veer.

On Mars la Tour high shone the sun and flashed
  again the Prussian Guns,
That swiftly wheel across the plain to wake the
  echoes of Lorraine,
And when towards the waning light had ceased
  their vengeful roar,
The Prussian sentries pace the heights of con-
  quered Mars la Tour,
And as the roll was called that night by Metz's
  watch fires glare,
No answer to the name was heard of Maurice
  Valhubert
For why? the grandsire's scroll so terse, spoke not
  of when to fly,
But only taught to Valhubert, the lesson how to
  die,
And though no tablet marks the Grave of that
  young Grenadier,
To love and country true, he died for France and
  Reine de Veer.

BOOK REVIEWS

"It could only have been written by a woman of deep and wide sympathy.... Throughout this delightful story reminds one of the captivating humor of 'Mrs. Wiggs of the Cabbage Patch.'"

The Boston Herald

"A farmer in Prince Edward's Island ordered a boy from a Nova Scotia asylum, but the order got twisted and the result was that a girl was sent the farmer instead of a boy. That girl is the heroine of L. M. Montgomery's story, "Anne of Green Gables," ... and it is no exaggeration to say that she is one of the most extraordinary girls that ever came out of an ink pot.

"The author undoubtedly meant her to be queer, but she is altogether too queer. She was only 11 years old when she reached the house in Prince Edward's Island that was to be her home, but, in spite of her tender years, and in spite of the fact that, excepting for four months spent in the asylum, she had passed all her life with illiterate folks, and had had almost no schooling, she talked to the farmer and his sister as though she had borrowed Bernard Shaw's vocabulary, Alfred Austin's sentimentality, and the reasoning powers of a Justice of the Supreme Court. She knew so much that she spoiled the author's plan at the very outset and greatly marred a story that had in it quaint and charming possibilities.

"The author's probable intention was to exhibit a unique development in this little asylum waif, but there is no real difference between the girl at the end of the story and the one at the beginning of it. All the other characters in the book are human enough."

"A Heroine from an Asylum," *New York Times Saturday Review of Books,* July 18, 1908

"Anne should be a permanent figure in fiction, for she is one of the most delightful girls that has appeared for many a day. She is a whirlwind talker, a trenchant debater never satisfied to let an argument rest, a quaint philosopher, and, in spite of the red hair which is ever a great trial to her, she is a charming girl. She is restrained by no social laws or conventions, and she insists upon 'scope for her imagination,' which is her strongest characteristic. Withal, she is a good girl, who never does anything she cannot tell the minister's wife about. Thus, says she, a minister's wife is as good as a second conscience. She comes from a 'home,' a great disappointment to the good Matthew and Marilla of Green Gables, who had sent for a boy, but she talks her way into the heart of the innocent old farmer at one sitting, and even the narrow and prim Marilla surrenders after twenty-four hours deliberation. So she stays at Green Gables, the happiest child in Prince Edward Island.

"In the same way she talks her way into the affections of readers of her adventures, for she is positively irresistible, and no one who has a sense of humor or appreciates genuine originality can fail to enjoy the story of her experiences in school and at home in the little village of Avonlea. She is surprised to find so many 'kindred spirits' in the world, but this is due, in many cases, rather to her own disposition and imagination than to good fellowship on the part of those of whom she makes friends, and there is inspiration as well as unbounded amusement in her example. She is generally good natured, but reference to her hair is the unpardonable insult, and this, in one instance at least, results in almost endless enmity against one of her schoolmates, over whose head she smashes a slate early in her school days. The tale takes a romantic turn as it nears the end and the disappearance of her last enemy is in sight. Her vivid imagination helps her through many trials, for she can imagine that even her severely plain dresses are attractive, that stumps are dryads and that bushes are fairies. Only her red hair is impervious to imagination, she tries dye on it. But, alas! the dye is green, and even red hair is better than green. This exploit, however, cures her imagination, and a new Anne emerges with short hair, which seems to be turning 'auburn' a long felt hope realized. Other personages in the story are also attractive and well drawn, especially so is good Matthew Cuthbert, who admits everything with a 'Well, now, perhaps it is so.' Everyone will join him in his fondness for Anne of Green Gables."

"Books of the Day," *Boston Evening Transcript*
July 22, 1908

"Whether Miss L. M. Montgomery is a Canadian or not, we know not, but if she isn't she has taken a Canadian countryside, and peopled it, in a manner marvelously natural, and if she is a Canadian she has succeeded in writing one of the few Canadian stories that can appeal to the whole English-speaking world. 'Anne of Green Gables,' is a charmingly-told story of life on the north shore of Prince Edward Island, but the local coloring is most delicately placed on the canvas and in no respect weakens the impression created by the central figure, Anne. This waif from an orphan asylum in Nova Scotia, adopted by an old farmer and his maiden sister, is covered with a sensitive and imaginative mind and the story of her hopes, struggles and ambitions, will appeal to every reader, old and young. She is certainly one of the

An ad for Anne *appearing in* The Nation, *July 16, 1908.*

most attractive figure[s] Canadian fiction has yet produced, while the characters of the farmer and his sister are drawn with a delicacy of touch that is most refreshing and charming. The book is an ideal volume for growing girls, being as pure and sweet as the wild flowers of the Island which Miss Montgomery describes so lovingly. In fact, one of the great attractions of the story is the author's love of nature which finds expression everywhere, without once appearing exaggerated or forced. The story is one which will give profit and pleasure to all its readers."

Montreal Daily Herald
July 21, 1908

"We have much pleasure in drawing attention to this novel, not only because it is in our opinion the most fascinating book of the season, but because its author, Miss Montgomery, is a resident of Prince Edward Island where the scene of the story is laid, and is evidently a keen student of both nature and human nature. The fact that the volume was published quite recently and is now in its second large edition is a sufficient guarantee of its unusual merit, but it is almost impossible for readers to guess even vaguely the treat that awaits them in its perusal.

"It was a happy thought that suggested to Miss Montgomery's fancy the main incident, without which the book would not have existed for our delight. Matthew Cuthbert, a farmer sixty years old and his sister, Marilla, both unmarried live together comfortably and happily at "Green Gables" in Alvonlea [sic] on a peninsula of Prince Edward Island that juts out into the Gulf of Saint Lawrence. The farm is in the midst of woods and is very productive, but proves too much for the old man, who requires some constant assistance in managing his property. He accordingly determines to adopt a boy, and hears that he can attain suitable aid by applying to the Hopeton [*sic*] Asylum for Orphans situated a great distance from 'Green Gables.' As he is a modest, silent man, he entrusts his application to a neighbor, Mrs. Spencer, who through her brother, has promised to supply his want. She soon acquaints him that she has been successful, and that on a certain day she will leave the orphan at a railway station a few miles distant from the farm. To this station, in full dress for the occasion, he drives at the appointed time to meet the boy whom he has agreed to adopt, but learns from the station master that no boy has arrived, and that the only passenger dropped by the train was a little girl of about eleven years of age. He sees her sitting alone, as if waiting for somebody, and in a pleasant manner she at one [*sic*] addresses him, and informs him that she is Anne Shirley, an orphan from the Hopeton Asylum, and that she is bound for 'Green Gables' where she is going to live as the adopted child of Matthew Cuthbert. This, of course, is astonishing news to him, but he refrains from telling the child that some mistake has evidently been made in the matter, and leaves the explanation to the quicker intelligence of his sister. Anne is by no means a rustic beauty, having flaming red hair and a profusion of freckles, in addition to being thin and tall for her age, but, as Shakespeare says of 'the lunatic, the lover and the poet' she is all 'of imagination all compact' and amuses and interests Cuthbert immensely by her quaint and fanciful remarks during the drive homeward. The astonishment of his sister, Marilla, when the elfish waif arrives may be imagined. She at once attributes the mistake about the sex of the required orphan to Mrs. Spencer's niece, a flighty, thoughtless girl. Marilla verifies the fact and determines to send back Anne Shirley. This determination nearly breaks the girl's heart, as she is charmed with the beauty of 'Green Gables,' and Marilla, following the evident wish of her brother, finally decides to keep the heroine of the story. Her subsequent career is described

in the book in a manner which, by its humor and pathos, will inevitably draw laughter and tears from every reader of the gentler sex."
Reviewed by George Murray,
Montreal Daily Star
August 8, 1908

"Not since Kate Douglas Wiggin's 'Rebecca' has so engaging a miss appeared in the fiction written for the consumption of older folks, as 'Anne of Green Gables,' the heroine of L. M. Montgomery's first book. This little, slim, red-haired, freckled face girl was an inmate of an orphan asylum across the Canadian border when the story opens. There lived on Prince Edward Island an elderly brother and sister, sole occupants of the old Cuthbert place, and both long past the marrying age. Matthew felt a growing need of a lad's help about the place, and a neighbor was commissioned to secure an orphan boy. Through an error a girl was sent to the Cuthberts, and the plodding Matthew was greatly dismayed when he discovered the undesirable Anne at the railroad station. She was certainly not prepossessing to look upon, but she proved to be an extraordinarily bright miss who had long since tired of life at the orphan's home for the reason that it 'did not give any scope for the imagination.' Indeed this imagination with which eleven year old Anne Shirley was endowed was her most valuable asset, but her tongue, according to one of the women of the island, was hung in the middle and was ever active except when silenced with a reprimand. First it was proposed to send Anne back and demand a boy but Matthew and Marilla became so attached to the miss that neither had the heart to deprive her of their home to which she at once became attached. The book is devoted entirely to her exploits, for with her temperament and her curiosity she was continually in the proverbial hot water. Although born of educated parents Anne had apparently not been taught to say her prayers; when Marilla attempted to teach her the first night she ended her petition to the

Deity with these words: 'Please let me stay at Green Gables, and please let me be good looking when I grow up. I remain, Yours respectfully, Anne Shirley.' When the prim and orthodox Marilla recovered from the shock she taught Anne better. There is an escapade in every chapter, ranging from smashing her slate over the head of a boy who teased her at school to attempting to walk the ridge-pole of a house with disastrous results. She is accused of attempting to intoxicate her girl playmate, she dyes her red hair green, and uses anodyne liniment for flavoring extract when making cake. Through it all her imagination is given free scope and eventually she becomes the best scholar at school, and a little romance with a young man of the town is suggested. The conventional ending to a fresh and entertaining book was to have been expected. Of course, Anne is altogether too precocious a youngster to find in real life, but she is a most diverting book heroine. The author might have made more of her background, for Prince Edward Island has not figured in fiction; she is congratulated on her maiden effort."

"New Books," by Anne Benszen Bradfird,
Boston Budget and Beacon
August 8, 1908

"Anne is a truly delightful little girl who goes from an orphan asylum in Nova Scotia to a home on Prince Edward Island. The people to whom she was to go had written for a boy, and when, with her undeniable freckles, her tawny head, and lively little tongue, appeared, she was so far from the original idea of some one to 'save steps now and lean upon later,' that was in the good people's mind when they had decided upon the adoption of a child, that it was felt wiser to return her to the asylum. However, Anne's ready acceptance of her fate, her willingness to make the best of whatever came to her and the pathetic revelations she unconsciously made of the bareness of her life win over the friends and she finds with them a home, 'a really truly home,' where she is wanted and where later, she makes her-

self a necessity. Her career in the village among her friends, and with her school mates, the development under kindly influence of a generous impulsive nature, form the background of a pretty story that by its naturalness will charm its readers. 'Green Gables' is the name of the home to which Anne comes and where she finds a happiness that even in her wildest flight of imagination she had never compassed. She is not by any means an unusual girl, but falls into all sorts of mischief, her impulsiveness carrying her far into the world of mistakes, but having to depend on her own resources through eleven dreary years of 'living out,' she has a well developed mind and on more than one occasion comes to a timely rescue. She is lovable, naughty, bright and stubborn, but under kindly influences develops into a fine young woman, and one leaves her reluctantly on the threshold of a romance, feeling that he would like to hear more of her. Like Miss Alcott's girls, she has become in this story of her life at Green Gables a friend."

St. John's Globe
August 8, 1908

"The craze for problem novels has at present seized a large section of the reading public, and it must be confessed that several recent stories have not been healthy reading, and can serve no useful purpose that we can see. In these days of unhealthy literature it is, however, a real pleasure to come across a story so pure and sweet as 'Anne of Green Gables,' by L. M. Montgomery, from the press of Messrs. L. C. Page & Co., of Boston, Mass. There are no pretensions to a great plot in the story, but from the first line to the last the reader is fascinated by the sayings and doings of the girl child taken from a Nova Scotia home, adopted by the old Scotch maid and bachelor, brother and sister, who owned Green Gables, a Prince Edward Island farm, situated in one of the garden spots of the beautiful Island Province in the St. Lawrence Gulf.

"The quaintness of the child, the funny scene when the old bachelor brother finds a girl waiting at the station for him, and not a boy, as ordered from the home, are pictured in irresistible drollery. Then the reader's interest is evoked as the author pictures how the poorly trained and often hitherto harshly-treated little maiden develops into womanhood, under the strict yet kindly training of the strange couple who loved her so dearly, and who, Scotch like, could not find words to give utterance to that love. Every Canadian boy and girl who has had the happy chance of going to a rural school, and who has had ambitions to be something different to the ordinary individual, will take 'Anne of Green Gables' to heart, and will laugh and cry with her in her school and home troubles, and many will easily call to mind people who are the very doubles of the tart, the gossipy yet always lovable characters sketched so faithfully by Miss Montgomery in her story; and those who have had the privilege to visit the Island Province will revel in the simple, yet splendid de-scriptions of the people and scenery of the Island which are to be found on almost every page of this excellent story. 'Anne of Green Gables' is worth a thousand of the problem stories with which the bookshelves are crowded today, and we venture the opinion that this simple story of rural life in Canada will be read and re-read when many of the more pretentious stories are all forgotten. There is not a dull page in the whole volume, and the comedy and tragedy are so deftly woven together that it is at times difficult to divide them. The story is told by an author who knows the Island of Prince Edward thoroughly, and who has carefully observed the human tide which flows through that Island, as it does over all places where human beings live. With the pen of an artiste she has painted that tide so that its deep tragedies are just lightly revealed for she evi-dently prefers to show us the placid flow, with its steadiness, its sweetness, and witchery, until the read-er stands still to watch the play of sunshine and shadow as it is deftly pictured by the hand of the author of 'Anne of Green Gables.'"

The Globe, Toronto
August 19, 1908

"'*Anne of Green Gables*' is one of the best books for girls we have seen for a long time. It is cheerful, amusing, and happy. Anne is a sort of Canadian 'Re-becca of Sunnybrook Farm' in her imaginativeness, love of high flown language and propensity to get into scrapes. But the book is by no means an imita-tion; it has plenty of originality and character. More-over, it will please grown-up people quite or nearly as well as the school-girls for whom it is primarily designed. It ought to have a wide reading."

"Comment on Current Books," *Outlook*
August 22, 1908

Mary Miles Minter as Anne in the 1919 film.

"Lively story of an orphan girl, sent from an asylum by mistake to an elderly brother and sister, who wanted a boy to assist them on the farm. Anne is a lovable, impulsive, imaginative but obedient child who gets all there is out of her narrow life, receives a good education and becomes a great source of pride and comfort in the Green Gables home. A story that all girls from 12 to 15 and many grown-ups will enjoy."

American Library Association Booklist
November 1908

"In the whole range of Canadian fiction one might search a long time for a character study of equal charm with 'Anne of Green Gables,' a novel that easily places the author, Miss L. M. Montgomery, in the first rank of our native writers. The story of Anne, of her 'ups and downs' in life is excellent in technique, development and consistency. It contains much genuine, quaint and wholesome humour, and it also appeals in a very intense way to the best human sympathies. Anne is indeed a most interesting and entertaining person and she might well be placed with the best character creations in recent fiction. Her environment, a picturesque section of Prince Edward Island, is thoroughly Canadian, and Miss Montgomery presents it in piquant literary style, full of grace and whole-heartedness.

"Anne is an orphan who, owing to an error, is sent instead of a boy from an orphanage to live at 'Green Gables' with Marilla Cuthbert, a spinster, and her brother Matthew, a bachelor, both persons of rather set and precise notions of propriety. Anne is an extremely impetuous girl and early in life she is bowed down in sorrow with red hair and freckles and an angular form, almost as angular as Marilla's. But she has a very accommodating imagination, a faculty that relieves her of many a heartache. She is continuously seeking 'scope for imagination.' On her first morning at 'Green Gables' she looked out from her bedroom window and saw an apple tree in full bloom. Her delight was unbounded, and she expressed it generously to Marilla whose appreciation of picturesqueness and romance is not very keen.

"It's a big tree," said Marilla, "and it blooms great, but the fruit don't amount to much never—small and wormy."

"Oh, I don't mean just the tree of course it's lovely—yes, it's radiantly lovely—it blooms as if it meant it—but I mean everything—the garden and the orchard and the brook and the woods, the whole big dear world. Don't you feel as if you just loved the world on a morning like this? And I can hear the brook laughing all the way up here. Have you ever noticed what cheerful things brooks are? They're always laughing. Even in wintertime I've heard them under the ice. I'm so glad there's a brook near 'Green Gables.' Perhaps you think it does not make any difference to me when you're not going to keep me, but it does. I shall always like to remember that there is a brook here, even if I never see it again. If there was not a brook I'd be haunted by the uncomfortable feeling that there ought to be one. I'm not in the depths of despair this morning. I never can be in the morning. Isn't it a splendid thing that there are mornings? But I feel very sad. I've just been imagining that it was really me you wanted after all and that I was to remain here for ever-and-ever. It was a great comfort while it lasted. But the worst of imagining things is that the time comes when you have to stop and that hurts. . . . The world doesn't seem such a howling wilderness as it did last night. I'm so glad it's a sunshiny morning. But I like rainy mornings real well too. All sorts of mornings are interesting, don't you think? You don't know what's going to happen through the day, and there's so much scope for imagination. But I'm glad it's not rainy to-day because it's easier to be cheerful and bear up under affliction on a sunshiny day. I feel that I have a good deal to bear up under. It's all very well to read about sorrows and imagine yourself living through them heroically, but it's not so nice when you come to have them, is it?'"

"The author is a resident of Cavendish, P.E.I. and is a young woman of unusual ability as a writer."

"The Way of Letters," *The Canadian Magazine* November 1908

"We can pay the author of *Anne of Green Gables* no higher compliment than to say that she has given us a perfect Canadian companion picture to *Rebecca of Sunnybrook Farm*. There is no question of imitation or borrowing; it is merely that the scheme is similar and the spirit akin. To all novel-readers weary of problems, the duel of sex, broken Commandments, and gratuitous suicides, Miss Montgomery provides an alternative entertainment, all the more welcome because what we get in place of those hackneyed features is at once wholesome and attractive. As for Prince Edward Island, in which the scene is laid, no better advertisement of the charm of its landscape could be devised than the admirable descriptions of its sylvan glories which lend decorative relief to the narrative. Miss Montgomery has not merely succeeded in winning our sympathies for her *dramatis personae*; she makes us fall in love with their surroundings, and long to visit the Lake of Shining Waters, the White Way of Delight, Idlewild, and other favourite resorts of 'the Anne-girl.'

"The mechanism of the plot is simple enough. An elderly farmer and his unmarried sister decide to adopt an orphan boy and bring him up to assist them on the farm; but owing to a blunder on the part of an intermediary, a girl, and not a boy, is sent from the asylum in Nova Scotia. Anne Shirley, an 'outspoken morsel of neglected humanity,' with a riotous imagination, a genius for 'pretending,' a passionate love of beauty, and a boundless flow of words, bursts like a bombshell on the inarticulate farmer and his dour, honest, undemonstrative sister. But the law of extremes prevails. Matthew succumbs on the spot, and after a short space Anne casts her spell over Marilla as well, for in three weeks that excellent dragon admitted to her brother that it seemed as if Anne had been always with them:—

'I can't imagine the place without her. Now, don't be looking I-told-you-so, Matthew. That's bad enough in a woman, but it isn't to be endured in a man. I'm perfectly willing to own up that I'm glad I consented to keep the child, and that I'm getting fond of her, but don't you rub it in, Matthew Cuthbert.'

"The process of Anne's education both at home and at school is chequered and dramatic, and the way in which this little lump of human quicksilver and her grim but just mistress act and react on each other is brought out by scores of happy touches and diverting incidents. Anne is a creature of irresistible loquacity when we first meet her, and meeting with kindness and consideration for the first time after years of poverty and neglect, she expands in a way that is at once ludicrous and touching. Perhaps her literary instinct is a little overdone, but otherwise Miss Montgomery shows no disposition to idealise her child heroine, and one can readily forgive exaggeration when it leads to such pleasing conceits as the child's suggestion that amethysts were the souls of good violets, or her precocious appreciation of the 'tragical' sound of the lines:—

'Quick as the slaughtered squadrons fell
In Midian's evil day.'

"Miss Montgomery has given us a most enjoyable and delightful book, which, when allowance is made for altered conditions, is in direct lineal descent from the works of Miss Alcott. It needed considerable restraint on her part to leave off where she did without developing the romantic interest hinted at in the last chapter, but the result is so excellent that we trust she will refrain from running the greater risk of writing a sequel. Having sown her wild oats, 'the Anne-girl' could never be so attractive as the little witch, half imp, half angel, whose mental and spiritual growth is vividly set forth in these genial pages."

The Spectator, London
March 13, 1909

BIBLIOGRAPHY

THE WORKS OF LUCY MAUD MONTGOMERY

FICTION

Anne of Green Gables (1908)
Anne of Avonlea (1909)
Kilmeny of the Orchard (1910)
The Story Girl (1911)
The Golden Road (1913)
Anne of the Island (1915)
Anne's House of Dreams (1917)
Rainbow Valley (1919)
Rilla of Ingleside (1920)
Emily of New Moon (1923)
Emily Climbs (1925)
Blue Castle (1926)
Emily's Quest (1927)
Magic for Marigold (1929)
A Tangled Web (in England, *Aunt Becky Began It;* 1931)
Pat of Silver Bush (1933)
Mistress Pat (1935)
Anne of Windy Poplars (in England, *Anne of Windy Willows;* 1936)
Jane of Lantern Hill (1937)
Anne of Ingleside (1939)

COLLECTED SHORT STORIES

Collected and published in Montgomery's lifetime
Chronicles of Avonlea (1912)
Further Chronicles of Avonlea (1920)

Collected and published posthumously
The Road to Yesterday, ed. Dr. Stuart Macdonald. Toronto: McGraw-Hill Ryerson, 1974.
The Doctor's Sweetheart and Other Stories, ed. Catherine McLay. Toronto: McGraw-Hill Ryerson, 1979.

Akin to Anne: Tales of Other Orphans, ed. Rea Wilmshurst. Toronto: McClelland & Stewart, 1987.
Along the Shore: Tales by the Sea, ed. Rea Wilmshurst. Toronto: McClelland & Stewart, 1989.
After Many Days: Tales of Time Passed, ed. Rea Wilmshurst. Toronto: McClelland & Stewart, 1990.
Among the Shadows: Tales from the Darker Side, ed. Rea Wilmshurst. Toronto: McClelland and Stewart, 1990.
Against the Odds: Tales of Achievement, ed. Rea Wilmshurst. Toronto: McClelland & Stewart, 1993.

POEMS

The Watchman and Other Poems. Toronto: McClelland, Goodchild, and Stewart, 1916.
The Poetry of Lucy Maud Montgomery, John Ferns and Kevin McCabe, eds. Don Mills, Ont.: Fitzhenry & Whiteside, 1987.

AUTOBIOGRAPHICAL AND BIOGRAPHICAL WORKS

Francis W. P. Bolger. *The Years Before "Anne."* Halifax: Nimbus Publishing, 1991.
———— and Elizabeth Epperly, eds. *My Dear Mr. M.: Letters to G. B. MacMillan.* Toronto: McGraw-Hill Ryerson, 1980.
Wilfrid Eggleston, ed. *The Green Gables Letters from L. M. Montgomery to Ephraim Weber 1905–1909.* Toronto: Ryerson, 1960.
Mollie Gillen. *The Wheel of Things: A Biography of L. M. Montgomery, Author of Anne of Green Gables.* Don Mills, Ont.: Fitzhenry & Whiteside Ltd., 1975.
L. M. Montgomery. *The Alpine Path: The Story of My Career.* Don Mills, Ont.: Fitzhenry & Whiteside, 1975. (First published in *Everywoman's World,* June–Nov. 1917.)

Mary Rubio and Elizabeth Waterston. *Writing a Life: L. M. Montgomery*. Canadian Biography Series. Toronto: ECW, 1995.

———, eds. *The Selected Journals of L. M. Montgomery*. Vol. 1 (1889–1910), Vol. 2 (1910–1921); Vol. 3 (1921–1929). Don Mills, Ont.: Oxford Univ. Press, 1985, 1987, 1992.

FULL-LENGTH CRITICAL STUDIES

Gabriella Ahmannson. *A Life and Its Mirrors: A Feminist Reading of L. M. Montgomery's Fiction*. Vol. 1. Uppsala, Sweden: Univ. of Uppsala, 1991.

Sylvia DuVernet. *Theosophic Thoughts Concerning L. M. Montgomery*. Toronto: Univ. of Toronto Press, 1988.

Elizabeth R. Epperly. *The Fragrance of Sweet-Grass: L. M. Montgomery's Heroines and the Pursuit of Romance*. Toronto: Univ. of Toronto Press, 1992.

Mavis Reimer, ed. *Such a Simple Little Tale: Critical Responses to L. M. Montgomery's Anne of Green Gables*. Metuchen, N.J.: Scarecrow Press, 1992.

Mary Henley Rubio, ed. *Harvesting Thistles: The Textual Garden of L. M. Montgomery. Essays on Her Novels and Journals*. Guelph, Ont.: Canadian Children's Press, 1994.

John Robert Sorfleet, ed. *L. M. Montgomery: An Assessment*. Guelph, Ont.: Canadian Children's Press, 1976.

Elizabeth Waterston. *Kindling Spirit: L. M. Montgomery's "Anne of Green Gables."* ECW Press, 1993.

PERIODICAL STUDIES

Rosamond Bailey. "Little Orphan Mary: Anne's hoydenish double," *Canadian Children's Literature: A Journal of Criticism and Review* [*CCL*] 55 (1989): 8–17.

Temma F. Berg. "'Anne of Green Gables': A Girl's Reading," *Children's Literature Association Quarterly* [*CLAQ*] 13: 3 (Fall 1988): 124–28.

Jacqueline Berke. "Mother I can do it myself: The self-sufficient heroine in popular girl's fiction," *Women's Studies* 6:1 (1978): 187–203.

Jane Burns. "Anne and Emily: L. M. Montgomery's Children," *Room of One's Own* 3:3 (Dec. 1977): 37–48.

Virginia Careless. "The Highjacking of 'Anne'" (review of *The Anne of Green Gables Treasury*), *CCL* 67 (1992): 48–55.

Constance Classen. "Is 'Anne of Green Gables' an American Import?" *CCL* 55 (1989): 42–50.

Susan Drain. "Feminine convention and female identity: The persistent challenge of 'Anne of Green Gables,'" *CCL* 65 (1992): 40–47.

———. "Community and the Individual in Anne of Green Gables: The Meaning of Belonging," *CLAQ* 11:1 (Spring 1986): 15–19.

Frances M. Frazer. "Island Writers," *Canadian Literature* 68 69 (Spring Summer 1976): 76–87.

Barbara Carman Garner, and Mary Harker. "Anne of Green Gables: An Annotated Bibliography," *CCL* 55 (1989): 18–41.

Carol Gay. "'Kindred Spirits' All: Green Gables Revisited," *CLAQ* 11:1 (Spring 1986): 9–12.

Nancy Huse. "Journeys of the Mother in the World of Green Gables," *Proceedings of the Thirteenth Annual Conference of the Children's Literature Association,* Univ. of Missouri Kansas City, May 16–18, 1986. West Lafayette, Ind.: Purdue Univ., 1988.

Yuko Katsuro. "Red-haired Anne in Japan," *CCL* 34 (1984): 57–60.

Eve Kornfield and Susan Jackson. "The Female Bildungsroman in Nineteenth-Century America: Parameters of a Vision," *Journal of American Culture* 10:4 (Winter 1987): 69–75.

Anne Scott MacLeod. "The Caddie Woodlawn Syndrome: American Girlhood in the Nineteenth Century," *A Century of Childhood, 1820–1920*. Rochester, N.Y.: Margaret Woodbury Strong Museum, 1984.

T. D. MacLulich. "L. M. Montgomery and the literary heroine: Jo, Rebecca, Anne and Emily," *CCL* 37 (1985): 5–17.

———. "L. M. Montgomery's Portraits of the Artist: Realism, Idealism, and the Domestic Imagination," *English Studies in Canada* 11:4 (1985): 459–73.

Perry Nodelman. "Progressive Utopia: Or, How to Grow Up without Growing Up," *Proceedings of the Sixth Annual Conference of the Children's Literature Association.* Univ. of Toronto, March 1979. Villanova, Pa.: Villanova Univ., 1980.

Mary Rubio. "Anne of Green Gables: The Architect of Adolescence," *Touchstones: Reflections on the Best in Children's Literature,* Vol. 1. West Lafayette, Ind.: Children's Literature Association, 1985.

———. "Subverting the trite: L. M. Montgomery's 'room of her own,'" *CCL* 65 (1992): 6–39.

———. "L. M. Montgomery: Where Does the Voice Come From?" *Canadiana: Studies in Canadian Literature (Proceedings of the Canadian Studies Conference).* Jorn Carlsen and Knud Larsen, eds. Aarhus, Denmark: 1984, 109–19.

Marilyn Solt. "The Uses of Setting in 'Anne of Green Gables,'" *CLAQ* 9:4 (Winter 1984–1985): 179–80.

Barbara Wachowicz. "L. M. Montgomery: at home in Poland," *CCL* 46 (1987): 7–36.

E. Weber. "L. M. Montgomery as a letter-writer," *Dalhousie Review [DR]* 22 (1942): 300–10.

———. "L. M. Montgomery's 'Anne,'" *DR* 24 (1944): 64–73.

Janet Weiss-Town. "Sexism Down on the Farm? Anne of Green Gables," *CLAQ* 11:1 (Spring 1986): 12–15.

Muriel A. Whitaker. " 'Queer Children,' L. M. Montgomery's Heroines," *CCL* 3 (1975): 50–59.

Lesley Willis. "The Bogus Ugly Duckling: Anne Shirley Unmasked," *DR* 56:2 (1976): 247–51.

Rea Wilmshurst. "L. M. Montgomery's Use of Quotations and Allusions in the 'Anne' Books," *CCL* 56 (1989): 15–45.

ADDITIONAL SOURCES

A. Kenneth Bell. *Getting the Lights,* ed. David Kellum. Charlottetown: P.E.I. Museum and Heritage Foundation, 1989.

Virginia Blair, Patricia Clements, Isobel Grundy, eds. *A Feminist Companion to Literature in English: Women Writers from the Middle Ages to the Present.* New Haven: Yale Univ. Press, 1990.

Ruth Brandon. *A Capitalist Romance: Singer and the Sewing Machine.* Philadelphia: Lippincott, 1977.

The Canadian Encyclopedia. 2nd Ed. 4 vols. Edmonton: Hurtig Publisher, 1988.

John Robert Cousins. "Horses in the Folklife of Western Prince Edward Island: Custom, Belief and Oral Tradition." Master's thesis, Memorial University, 1990.

Margaret Drabble, ed. *The Oxford Companion to English Literature.* 5th ed. Oxford: Oxford Univ. Press, 1985.

Hubbard Freeman. *Encyclopedia of North American Railroading: 150 Years of Railroading in the United States and Canada.* New York: McGraw-Hill, 1981.

James D. Hart, ed. *The Oxford Companion to American Literature.* 5th ed. New York: Oxford Univ. Press, 1983.

New Grove Dictionary of Music. 20 vols. London: Macmillan, 1980.

T. V. Pratt, ed. *Dictionary of Prince Edward Island.* Toronto: Univ. of Toronto Press, 1988.

Rosemary Radford Ruether and Rosemary Skinner Keller, eds. *Women and Religion in America.* Vol. 1, *The Nineteenth Century: A Documentary History.* San Francisco: Harper and Row, 1981.

Jack Sanders. *Hedgemaids and Fairy Candles: The Lives and Lore of North American Wildflowers.* Camden, Maine: Ragged Mountain Press, 1993.

ACKNOWLEDGMENTS

The Annotated Anne of Green Gables inspired wonderful good will from experts in varied fields from different countries, many of whom shared with the editors the privilege of contributing to the book. We would like to thank those people and institutions for making *The Annotated Anne* possible.

First of all, we acknowledge the assistance of the Estate of L. M. Montgomery for giving us permission to publish and for making suggestions about photographs.

We owe special thanks to institutions with particular connections to *Anne*. We must give our sincere thanks to Kevin Rice and to all the staff of the archives at the Confederation Centre of the Arts, Charlottetown, P.E.I., for their kind assistance to Margaret Doody during two separate visits to go over LMM's manuscript and for answering questions about it. Because of the Centre's careful stewardship we are able to present a new text of this novel. We also have reason to be grateful to Richard Landon, Chief Librarian of the Thomas Fisher Rare Book Library, University of Toronto, for permitting Margaret Doody to inspect first editions and other works and also for giving us access to a special collection of nineteenth-century cookery books. Katharine Martyn, Assistant Director of the Fisher Library, also provided information as to various editions of *Anne*. Caroline Pawley and Ellen Morrison of the Archives and Special Collections of the McLaughlin Library at the University of Guelph, Ontario, were most helpful to Margaret Doody during a personal visit in 1996.

We have corresponded with and talked to staff at the Green Gables Museum and at Park Corner, P.E.I. We have received help from Mary Barnett, Curator (retired) at the P.E.I. Museum and Heritage Foundation, Charlottetown; Frank Piggot, Reference Librarian (retired), University of Prince Edward Island; Barbara MacDonald, Canadian Heritage Parks, P.E.I. Elsewhere in the Maritime Provinces, we are indebted to Scott Robson, Curator of Collections, Nova Scotia Museum, Halifax, N.S.; Dr. Gerald L. Pocius, Professor of Folklore, and Phillip Hiscock, Folklore Archivist, Memorial University, St. John's, Newfoundland; Charlotte Stewart, Archivist, Public Archives and Records Office of P.E.I. Mary Flagg, University Archivist, Harriet Irving Library, University of New Brunswick, Fredericton, N.B., helped us to find and reproduce selections from the *Royal Readers*.

Other institutions and individuals in Canada, the United States, and England have helped us on our way. They include: Anita Campbell, Curator, Professional and Technical Services, Canadian Heritage Parks, Halifax, N.S.; Andrew Rodger, Visual and Sound Department, National Archives of Canada, Ottawa; Mary Bond, Senior Reference Librarian, and Frances Gaudet, Head of Research and Systems Support, National Library of Canada; Jennifer Iredale, Curator, and Theresa Molinaro, Curatorial Assistant, British Columbia Heritage Properties.

At the Library of Congress, Washington, D.C., we received important assistance from Geraldine Ostrove, Senior Policy Specialist, Cataloguing; Betty Culpepper and Evelyn Timberlake, Humanities and Social Sciences Department. Roberta Zhongi, Rare Book Room, Boston Public Library, and Dr. Richard Price, English Language Collection, British Library, London, helped us in locating material.

As the reader will notice, we had need of help in very specialized matters in preparing background material. So, in addition to those already mentioned, we want to give particular thanks to those who have helped us in specific areas:

TECHNICAL ASPECTS, WRITING, FINDING EDITIONS, AND RESEARCH: At Vanderbilt University: Bill Longwell; University of Toronto: Anne Dondertman; Virginia Clark and Freda Bradley (Halifax); Victoria: Gerry Howell Jones (Victoria); Kevin Bell (Boston); Lysanne Fox (Vancouver); Elizabeth Ilg, Jeff Bollier

APPLES AND PLANTS: Richard Eldridge (B.C.); Bob Osborne (N.B.); Fred Janson (Ontario); Joanne Gardiner (N.S.); Wendell Boyle, Kate MacQuarrie (P.E.I.)

POPULAR SONGS: At the University of Victoria: Sandra Acker and Dale McIntosh; University of Chicago: Dena J. Epstein (retired); National Library of Canada: Marcia Calderisi (retired) and Marlene Wehrle; University of British Columbia: Kirsten Walsh; College of William and Mary: Dale Cockrell; Library of Congress: Wayne Shirley; British Library: V. H. Cummings; Vanderbilt University: Cecelia Tichi; Megan Howell Jones (Victoria)

POPULAR, SOCIAL, AND MATERIAL CULTURE: At the Royal British Columbia Museum: Shirley Cuthbertson, Tina Strange, Frederica Verspor; P.E.I. Museum: Boyde Beck, Marilyn Thomsen, Rosemary Driscoll, Scott Bateman; B.C. Information Management Services: Brent McBride, James Cline; University of P.E.I.: Leo Cheveries, Sherri McBride; National Parks, Canada: Ruth Mills; Government House, Ottawa: Auguste Vachon, Saint-Laurent Herald; Canadian Red Cross Society: Ann Butryn; International Committee of the Red Cross: M.-B. Meriboute; National Archives of Canada: Andrew Rodger, Roanne Mockhtar; National Gallery of Canada: Susan Campbell; Vancouver Public Library: Terry Dobroslavic, Jeannie Cockcroft; Vancouver City Archives: Carol Haber; Confederation Centre Art Gallery: Terry Graff; Academy of Motion Picture Arts and Sciences: Janet Lorenz; Hofstra University: Paula Uruburu; University of Victoria: Joan Fraser, John Davis; in Victoria: Michael F. H. Halleran, John Hall, Monica Oldham. Also: quilting expert Sherry Davidson (P.E.I.); 96-year-old P.E.I. artist Eleanor Wheeler

LITERARY SOURCES AND BACKGROUND: University of Toronto: the late Rea Wilmshurst; University of Guelph: Mary Rubio and Elizabeth Waterson; National Library of Canada: Mary Bond, Franceen Gaudet, Anne Pichora; Canadian Stage Company: Candace Burley; The Bookmark Store (P.E.I.)

We are especially grateful to Dr. Barbara Garner, Carleton University, Ottawa, who let us see her work *The Vertical File on Lucy Maud Montgomery: A Companion to Anne of Green Gables: An Annotated Bibliography* and gave us permission to reproduce from it eight early reviews of *Anne*.

For generous imparting of information and advice, we are grateful to Virginia Careless, former Curator of Modern History, Royal British Columbia Musem, Victoria, and David Leach, English Department, University of Victoria. We regret that our expression of gratitude to Professor Patricia Koester, Victoria University, must be a posthumous recognition.

We especially appreciate those who, repeatedly, quickly, and often on short notice, provided important materials: Maureen McKnight, researcher, University of British Columbia; Ellen Morrison, McLaughlin Library, University of Guelph, Ontario; Edward MacDonald, Curator of History, P.E.I. Museum and Heritage Foundation; Mary Collis, Children's Literature Services, National Library of Canada, Ottawa; Peter Rider, Canadian Museum of Civilization; Betty Howatt, Heritage Orchardist, P.E.I.

The editors owe a debt to their mothers. For wonderful help in understanding the world that L. M. Montgomery describes, we must record our gratitude to Anne Ruth Doody (b. 1905), who drew on her own recollections and the lives of her parents in rural Nova Scotia to give us a real feeling for the Maritime Provinces as Montgomery knew them. To Barbara Barry, quilter extraordinary and source of detailed help on needlework, our deepest thanks.

Finally, we wish to express our gratitude to all who have been involved in typing or otherwise preparing the manuscript: Carolyn Levinson and Angela Saylor, Vanderbilt University; Andrew Tate, Victoria, B.C.

CREDITS

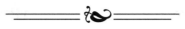

ILLUSTRATIONS

The editors and publisher wish to thank those who have kindly given permission to reproduce the illustrations on the following pages:

University of Guelph Special Collections, L. M. Montgomery Collection, Guelph, Ontario: 4, 9, 10 (top left), 13, 14, 15, 18, 19, 22, 24, 29, 42, 60, 77, 84, 86, 113, 131, 160, 162, 183, 204, 229, 264, 294, 304, 332, 346, 361, 366 (bottom), 396, 416, 417, 437, 444

Confederation Centre Art Gallery and Museum, Charlottetown, Prince Edward Island: 10 (bottom right), 432

Courtesy of Island Nature Trust, Prince Edward Island, from Dr. Hal Hinds, *Flora of New Brunswick*: 39, 153

Green Gables, Prince Edward Island National Park, Parks Canada: 41, 71, 72 (bottom), 79, 201 (used by permission of the artist, Goldie Freeman, and the Department of Canadian Heritage, Parks Canada), 435

Public Archives of Nova Scotia: 44 (neg. 1987–265#5), 423 (neg. #N–4840)

Courtesy of the Library of Congress, Washington, D.C., from *Godey's Magazine*: 46 (vol. CXXXIII); 54, 128 (vol. CXXII); 216 (vol. CXXXV); 247, 310 (vol. CXXXII, 1896); songs: "Far Above the Daisies" (M1621.M0), 217, 463 (right), 465; "The Hazel Dell," from *Heart Songs Dear to the American People*, Boston: Chappell, 1909 (M1619.H51), 464

Smithsonian Institution, Washington, D.C.: 52

Courtesy of Houghton Mifflin, Boston, from Mrs. William Starr Dana, *How to Know the Wildflowers* (1989): 56, 112, 139 (top, center), 161, 225, 385

(illustrations by Marion Satterlee)

Prince Edward Island Archives and Public Records Office: 57 (Acc. 3466 [HF.72.66.16.5]); 179, 212 (Acc. 2767/79); 267 (Acc. 4275/8); 305 (Acc. 3218/173); 309 (Acc. 3218/172); 366 (top [Acc. 3218/86]); 377 (Acc. 2755/216); 420 (Acc. 2755/217), from the Charlottetown *Patriot* (19 July 1893); 439 (Acc. 3281/20); 440 (Acc. 3109/224)

Prince Edward Island Museum and Heritage Foundation: 72 (top, HF 70.1248.1 [photo by Barbara Morgan]) (donated)

The Metropolitan Museum of Art, Rogers Fund, New York: 62

Courtesy of Universe Books, New York, from *The Compleat Farmer*, compiled by the Main Street Press (1975): 81, 125, 143, 235, 265, 384, 447

The National Library of Canada, Ottawa, Ontario: 89, 172, 458

The New-York Historical Society, New York: 99

The New York Public Library, Astor, Lenox, and Tilden Foundations, New York: 100, 141, 278, 290, 461, 488

Alinari/Art Resource, New York: 104

Courtesy of John Murray, London, from W. Robinson, *The English Flower Garden* (1900): 107, 124, 139 (bottom), 152, 391

Courtesy of Margaret Anne Doody: 147

Courtesy of Oxford University Press, Toronto, from Kate Macdonald, *The Anne of Green Gables Cookbook* (1985): 176, 229 (illustrations by Barbara Di Lella)

Courtesy of Department of Canadian Heritage, Parks Canada: from *Weldon's Practical Knitting* (Vol. 5),

194; from *Weldon's Practical Shilling Guide to Fancy-work*, 441 (photos by R. Chan)

Archive Photos, New York: 210

Archive Photos/Popperfoto, New York: 228

Art Resource, New York: 260

International Committee of the Red Cross, Geneva: 261 (donated)

Canadian Museum of Civilization, Ottawa, Ontario: 263 (donated)

Art Gallery of Nova Scotia: 289 (30.2/photo by George Georgakakos)

Oberlin College Archives, Oberlin, Ohio: 328

Courtesy of John Sylvester (photographer), Prince Edward Island: 431

University of Toronto, Thomas Fisher Rare Book Library, Ontario, from Maude C. Cooke, *Breakfast, Dinner, and Supper* (1897): 446, 449, 451

Courtesy of the Library for the Performing Arts, Lincoln Center, New York: "My Home on the Hill," 463 (left), 466

Courtesy of the University of New Brunswick, Harriet Irving Library, Archives and Special Collections, Fredericton, New Brunswick: "The Dog at his Master's Grave" from *Third Royal Reader* (first series), 475

Courtesy of the Boston Public Library, film still from the Mary Miles Minter edition of *Anne of Green Gables* (Boston: Page, 1920), 487

TEXT

Quotations from *The Selected Journals of L. M. Montgomery*, Volumes I, II, and III, © 1985, 1987, 1992 University of Guelph, edited by Mary Rubio and Elizabeth Waterston, and published by Oxford University Press Canada, are reproduced with the permission of Mary Rubio, Elizabeth Waterston, and the University of Guelph, courtesy of the L. M. Montgomery Collection, Archives and Special Collections, University of Guelph Library.

Quotations from the unpublished journals of L. M. Montgomery © University of Guelph are reproduced with the permission of Mary Rubio and the University of Guelph, courtesy of the L. M. Montgomery Eollection, Archives and Special Collections, University of Guelph Library.